AMERICAN DREAMS

Also by John Jakes
in Large Print:

North and South
Heaven and Hell

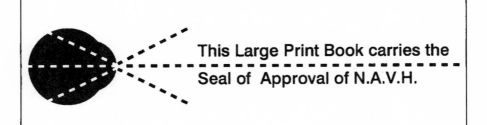

AMERICAN DREAMS

JOHN JAKES

G.K. Hall & Co. • Thorndike, Maine

LP

Published in 1998 by arrangement with Dutton Plume, a division of Penguin Putnam Inc.

G.K. Hall Large Print Core Series.

The text of this Large Print edition is unabridged. Other aspects of the book may vary from the original edition.

Set in 16 pt. Plantin by Al Chase.

Printed in the United States on permanent paper.

Library of Congress Cataloging in Publication Data

Jakes, John, 1932–
    American dreams / John Jakes.
      p. (large print) cm.
    ISBN 0-7838-0379-6 (lg. print : hc : alk. paper)
    1. Large type books. I. Title.
    [PS3560.A37A77 1998b]
    813'.54—dc21   98-39744

The man who worked with me on *California Gold* was one of the great editors of recent times. I wanted to thank him publicly for his help but could not; he didn't like to have his name used in that way. He said a book, not its editor, should receive credit.

Though I was disappointed I honored his wish. You won't find his name in *California Gold*, which he improved vastly with his advice and editorial pencil.

Now, with sadness, but a sense of closure too, I can finish what was left undone in 1989. Gratefully, I dedicate this book to the memory of the late Joe Fox.

America has been a land of dreams. A land where the aspirations of people from countries cluttered with rich, cumbersome, aristocratic, ideological pasts can reach for what once seemed unattainable. Here they have tried to make dreams come true.
— DANIEL BOORSTIN

"Eddie," Papa said, "you're a lucky boy to be born when you were. There are a lot of new things in the making, and you ought to have a hand in them." Those were the last words Papa said to me. . . . It was August, 1904.
— EDWARD V. RICKENBACKER

CONTENTS

Part One DREAMERS

Part Two STRIVING

Part Three PICTURES

Part Four CALIFORNIA

PART ONE

DREAMERS

Blow the Domestic Hearth! I should like to be going all over the kingdom . . . and acting everywhere. There's nothing in the world equal to seeing the house rise at you, one sea of delighted faces, one hurrah of applause!

> — CHARLES DICKENS, on tour with his company of amateur actors, 1848

Tell all the gang at Forty-second Street that I will soon be there.

> — GEORGE M. COHAN, written for the musical *Little Johnny Jones*, 1904

1. Actress

Fritzi Crown flung her bike on the grass and ran down to the water's edge. She skipped across wet boulders strewn along the shore until she stood where the waves broke and showered her with bracing spray. It was first light, the dawn of a chill morning in early December 1906. Along the horizon the sky was orange as the maw of a steel furnace, metal gray above.

Remembering a recurring dream that had held her in the moments before she woke — a dream in which she stood on a Broadway stage while thunderous applause rolled over her — Fritzi threw her arms out, threw her head back like some pagan worshiper of the dawn. The wind streamed off Lake Michigan, out of the east, where lay the mysterious and alluring place that occupied her thoughts in most of her waking moments.

The waves crashed. The wind sang in her ears, a repeating litany that had grown more and more insistent in past weeks. *Time to go. Time to go!*

Red faced, windblown but exhilarated, she stepped down from the rocks and turned toward the bike lying on the grass shriveled and browned by the autumn frost. The bike was a beautiful Fleetwing with a carmine enamel frame, gleaming silver rims and spokes. It was a "safety" — wheels of equal size — now the standard after years of high-wheel models, the kind on which she'd learned.

Fritzi was a long-legged young woman with an oval face, a nose she considered too big, legs she considered too skinny, a bosom she considered flat. She was dressed for cold weather. On top of a suit of misses' long underwear she wore her bathing costume of heavy alpaca cloth — a separate skirt, a top with attached bloomers, both navy blue. Her cycling shoes were tan covert-cloth oxfords with corrugated rubber soles. For added warmth she'd put on wool mittens and her younger brother's football sweater, a black cardigan with an orange letter P. He had bequeathed it to her after he was thrown out of Princeton. A knitted tam barely contained her long, unruly blond hair. Altogether it was the kind of costume that her father, General Joseph Crown, the millionaire brewer, disapproved of — vocally, and often.

"Ta-ta, Papa, you must remember I'm a grown girl and can pick out my own clothes," she would say in an effort to tease him out of it.

He disapproved of that, too.

The spectacular sunrise burst over the lake and burnished a row of trees near the footpath. Wind tore the last withered leaves off the branches and flung them into fanciful whirlwinds. The leaf clouds spiraled up and up, like her buoyant spirits. There were great risks in the decision she must make. They started right here in Chicago, in her own family.

Returning to her bike, Fritzi stopped abruptly. In thick evergreens planted behind the trees, a pair of eyes gleamed like a rodent's. But they

14

didn't belong to a rodent, they belonged to a man — a filthy, ragged tramp who'd been spying on her. He lurched out of the shrubbery, coming toward her. Fritzi was sharply aware of how early it was, how isolated she was here.

The tramp planted his feet a yard in front of her. The sleeves of his coat shone like a greasy skillet. "Hello, girlie." Fritzi swallowed, thinking desperately. Even upwind of the man she caught his stupefying stench — mostly liquor and dirt. He was burly, obviously much stronger.

He winked at her.

"Girls out wanderin' by theyselves this time of morning, they're either runaways or little Levee whores." His baritone voice was thickened by hoarseness and phlegm. He stuck out his arms, wiggled his fingers with an oafish leer. His nails were broken and black with dirt.

"Come give us a kiss." He dropped his left hand to his pants. "Anywhere you please."

For want of her usual weapon of defense, a long hat pin, Fritzi called on her primary talent. She replied in a loud and almost perfect imitation of his wheezy baritone: "Don't let this long hair fool you, bub. You've got the wrong fellow."

The tramp's eyes bugged. He was confounded by the male bellow issuing from Fritzi's chapped lips. She'd always been a keen mimic, sometimes getting into a pickle because of her rash choice of subject, especially schoolteachers. The tramp's confusion gave her the extra seconds she needed. She sprang to her bike, wheeled it onto

15

the path, ran and threw a long leg over the saddle. She took off in a flying start, pedaling madly.

Flashing a look back, she saw the tramp thumb his nose, heard him shout something nasty. She sped around a curve, snatched her tam off and let her curly blond hair stream out. She laughed with relief, pumping harder.

At least her talent proved to be worth something this morning. It could be worth a lot more in New York City.

Time to go . . .

Of that she was certain. And never mind the trouble it was likely to cause.

As Fritzi pedaled away from the lake shore, she reflected on all the things that had driven her to the emotional epiphany this morning.

Shapeless things, like the growing malaise of living day after day under the roof where she'd been raised but definitely no longer belonged.

Silly things, like a little easel card noticed on a cosmetic counter at The Fair Store.

OVER TWENTY-FIVE?
LUXOR CREME PREVENTS AGEING!

Ironic things, the most recent being a well-meant remark by her father only last night. The family had been seated at *Abendbrot* — literally, evening bread, the light supper traditional in German households. Ilsa, Fritzi's mother, remarked that she was still receiving compliments on the lavish anniversary party which the

16

Crowns gave annually for close friends, Joe Crown's business associates, and others they knew from their years in German-American society in Chicago. The party in early October had celebrated thirty-seven years of marriage.

The General agreed that it was indeed a fine party, the best ever. He then turned to his daughter with a thoughtful expression:

"Fritzi, my dear, your birthday will be on us in another month. We must plan. What do you want most?"

Fritzi sat to her father's right, on the long side of the dining table. Her older brother Joey — Joe Crown, Junior — sat opposite, sunk in his chair and his customary, vaguely sullen silence. Poor Joey was a permanent boarder. In 1901 he'd dragged himself home from the West Coast, crippled for life in a labor union brawl. Under a tense truce with his father, Joey worked at *Brauerei Crown*, doing the most menial jobs. He and his father traveled to and from work separately, the General in his expensive Cadillac motor car — he had become an avid automobilist — and Joey on the trolleys.

Fritzi thought about asking for motoring lessons, then reconsidered. The General believed women had no place at the wheel of an auto. She said, "I haven't an idea, Papa. I'll try to think of something."

"Please do. How old will you be?" It was a sincere question. Her elegant silver-haired father was in his sixty-fourth year, occasionally forgetful. He had never lost the accent he'd brought with him as the immigrant boy Josef Kroner

17

from Aalen, a little town in Württemberg that had been the home of the Kroner family for generations.

"Twenty-six." Somehow it sounded like a sentence from a judge.

With this latest realization of her age thrust on her, Fritzi spent a restless night in her old room on the second floor — the room she'd occupied since she had returned to Chicago almost a year ago.

In 1905, during a late summer heat wave, the General had suffered a fainting spell only later diagnosed as a mild heart attack. He collapsed on a platform from which he was quietly and reasonably defending the brewers of beer, attempting to separate them in the collective mind of his audience from distillers of hard spirits. The audience wanted none of it, because he was presenting his message to a temperance society.

Ilsa Crown had called her husband foolish for agreeing to appear. None of his colleagues who ran breweries in Chicago had the nerve to speak to a cold-water crowd. The General insisted he'd faced worse in the Civil War and Cuba in '98 (this Ilsa reported to Fritzi later). Besides, he might do some good.

Twenty minutes into the speech, he clutched the podium, his knees gave way, and he fell sideways.

Ilsa's telegram reached Fritzi in that mecca of culture, Palatka, Florida. She was appearing with the Mortmain Royal Shakespeare Combination, a seedy professional company with which she'd apprenticed in 1901. The Mortmain Combination brought the Bard and other classic dramatists to the border and cotton South — what Ian Mortmain's collection of washed-up *artistes* called "the kerosene circuit" because Southern theater owners apparently had never heard of electric footlights, or were too cheap to cast technical pearls before swinish audiences.

Moments after reading the telegram, Fritzi gave her notice to Ian Mortmain. That night she caught a train for Chicago, to help take care of her father. Never entirely smooth tempered, the General would not be an ideal patient for Fritzi's mother. His recuperation in bed would tax Ilsa; she, too, lacked the patience and energy of her younger years.

Though Ilsa didn't ask her daughter to come home, Fritzi believed she could help, and thought it her duty. Besides, after four years of midnight train rides, bug-ridden hotel rooms, gallons of greasy white chicken gravy and biscuits hard as stove bolts — after repetitive visits to dreary mill and cotton and tobacco towns, each with its enclave of Negro shanties — after sloppy rehearsals with the male actors hung over, sleazy productions with the flats threatening to totter, not to mention audiences that wouldn't know fine acting from hog calling — after all that Fritzi felt she'd learned as much as she could from her four-year apprenticeship.

The General left his sickbed far too soon for Ilsa or his physician. He went back to driving himself off to the brewery at six every morning, to put in his usual ten- to twelve-hour day. Fritzi had planned on staying only a short time, and her father never invoked his illness to induce her to prolong her visit. Somehow it just happened.

To fill her time she kept as busy as possible. She was faithful about daily exercise — morning set-ups in her room, tennis, cycling, swimming in season. She joined a local amateur dramatic society, playing everything from a heroine in a Clyde Fitch melodrama to Mrs. Alving in a private reading of *Ghosts* — private because Mr. Ibsen's play was still too controversial for the group to perform publicly.

When she wasn't rehearsing, she painted scenery, sewed costumes, distributed leaflets to drum up trade. She soon realized her ambition went beyond that of her fellow players, who wanted little more than praise from Aunt Bea or Cousin Elwood, whether merited or not. A few who were married sought furtive liaisons. Fritzi had rebuffed one such masher with her trusty hat pin.

The wind raked her face and hummed in her ears as she pedaled into the downtown, where sleepy citizens were dragging to work and even the dray horses seemed to move with an early morning lethargy. The wind's murmur couldn't hide a faintly taunting inner voice.

You'd better get on, my girl.

The voice belonged to an imaginary companion who'd been with Fritzi for years. She was the magnificent and regal Ellen Terry, goddess of the international stage. Fritzi had seen Miss Terry as Ophelia opposite Henry Irving's Hamlet when the couple toured America in the

1890s. The great lady was pictured in a colored lithograph hanging on the wall above Fritzi's bed. The litho reproduced John Singer Sargent's famous full-figure portrait of Terry as Lady Macbeth. Fritzi had stood endlessly before the painting when it was exhibited at the 1892 Columbian Exposition. Ellen Terry had not been her initial inspiration for an acting career; that was a magical production of *A Midsummer Night's Dream* she had attended with Mama and Papa when she was seven. As Fritzi walked out of that matinee into the glare of the day, her course was set forever. Miss Terry later became her favorite star, the supreme emblem of her ambition.

That Fritzi held silent dialogues with a nonexistent person didn't strike her as bizarre, though she didn't make a habit of telling others. She considered the conversations a natural part of the life of the imagination, and she had a very vivid one. Typically, Ellen Terry offered comments about Fritzi's shortcomings, something like a personified conscience.

Remember how old you'll be next month.

She was annoyed; she needed no further reminders that, come January, she would be but a scant four years from thirty, the threshold of "spinsterhood," a state devoutly to be avoided by proper young women.

Of course, proper young women didn't mount their bikes before daylight and go scorching off to greet the sunrise. Fritzi had long ago realized that she wasn't cut out to be proper, physically or temperamentally. Her Fleetwing, for example, was always her bike, never her "cycle" or, God forbid, her "velocipede." No matter that she might have wished to be proper (never!) — no matter how greatly her father and mother wished for it, too — she was stuck with being something else entirely. Herself.

And how to define that? So far as she knew, she fit only one recognizable pigeonhole — "actress."

The cold yellow morning light fell on the city's busy commercial heart as she headed south along Michigan Boulevard. It fell on telephone and telegraph wires, hack and wagon horses, here and there a humming electric or a puffing steam auto. It fell on the growing crowds of people hurrying along the sidewalks or charging across the manure-littered streets ahead of wheeled vehicles. Fritzi wove in and out of traffic, pedaling hard and swerving often to avoid collisions.

Near an intersection, a dairy wagon had somehow overturned, spilling metal cans and a flood of milk and blocking all of Michigan Boulevard. Fritzi quickly rode up over the curb at the corner and shot west on Jackson two blocks to State, where she went south again. The sun was higher, splashing a storefront near Van Buren that had been converted into a five-cent theater showing pictures that moved. The place was exotically named the Bijou Dream. Display windows were heavily draped, concealing, the public supposed, illicit behavior within. Tastelessly crude signboards on the sidewalk pleaded for patrons.

NEW PROGRAMS DAILY!
WHOLESOME ENTERTAINMENT FOR
GENTLEMEN, LADIES, AND CHILDREN!

Fritzi sniffed in disdain. A boy in the play group worked at the theater, turning the crank of the projector. He gave his fellow actors free tickets; Fritzi always threw hers in the nearest trash barrel, because respectable people never set foot in such low-class places. As for appearing in one of the crude little story pictures — she'd sooner die. She was, after all, a *legitimate* actress from the *professional* theater.

Or would be, again, if she could summon the nerve to get out of town and follow her dream to New York.

2. Drifter

About the same hour, hundreds of miles to the east in Riverdale, a hamlet on the northern edge of New York City, Carl Crown was knocking on doors in search of work and food.

Fritzi's younger brother had turned twenty-four in November. He'd been wandering without direction ever since Princeton cast him out at the end of his junior year. "Bull" Crown had been a star on the Princeton football line, but a failure in the classroom. He was smart enough, but not diligent, or interested.

For a change Carl was shaved and barbered. In Poughkeepsie he'd swept out a barber shop in exchange for the barber's services. His oddly assorted clothes were reasonably clean — faded jeans pants, a blue flannel work shirt, a plaid winter coat with a corduroy collar, and high-topped hunter's boots, laced on the side. He did his best to keep clean, first because he had been brought up that way, and also because it made a better impression at a stranger's door. Most tramps looked like they'd crawled out of a weed patch, bringing the weeds with them.

All morning doors had slammed in his face. The afternoon was no different. As the wintry sun dropped near the western palisades on the great river, he was discouraged, and famished. He knocked at the kitchen door of a neat cottage with a white picket fence and a small garden plot lying fallow for the season.

A woman in her early thirties, plain and pale, opened the door. She stepped back a pace, wary. "Yes?" Carl tried not to look at two golden pies cooling on a kitchen table.

"Any work, ma'am? My name's Carl. I'm just passing through. I'm good with my hands."

He showed them, clean, the nails kept short by a little file that folded out of his clasp knife. For someone as stocky as Carl, the hands were surprisingly slender and delicate.

The woman looked him up and down in the fading light. "Well, my daughter Hettie wrecked her cycle last Saturday. If you can repair it, I'll pay you thirty cents. I'm a widow, not mechanical at all."

From another room a girl called out, "Ma? I need the pot."

"Hettie," the widow said. "Broken ankle. Tools are in the shed."

"Yes, ma'am, I'll get right to it while it's still light." Carl gave her one of the warm smiles that came naturally to him. He was good looking in an unobtrusive way. He had his father's short legs, his mother's long upper body; he resembled Ilsa rather than the General. His hair was thick like hers before it grayed. His brown eyes shone bright like his sister's.

No longer suspicious, the woman with the lined face smiled back. "Knock when you're done." She closed the door as her daughter bleated again.

Carl crossed the yard. The cottage was set on a little rise, with a spectacular view of the graying

25

valley over intervening rooftops. The sky was clear and filled with flawless colors — dark blue shading down to lavender, then vivid red along the palisades. The air was cold and bracing to breathe.

He found the damaged two-wheeler in the shed. It was a black Wright Safety Cycle, manufactured in Dayton by the brothers who'd started in that business while they pursued their studies of aeronautics. Now the Wrights enjoyed worldwide fame and prosperity as a result of their flights at Kitty Hawk and elsewhere; they no longer needed to make or repair bicycles. Aeroplanes and all the mechanical wonders of the age fascinated Carl. He just didn't have the opportunity, or the wherewithal, to learn about them.

He crouched with one hand resting on the bicycle's triangular frame. After a minute of study he searched in the shed, found a shelf of old tools. He shoved aside a pile of hacksaw blades and files, picked up a wrench and pliers brown with rust. The pliers slipped from his fingers. As he stepped sideways to catch them, his shoulder hit another shelf, tilting it off its brackets and throwing half a dozen empty fruit jars to the dirt floor. Two broke.

He looked around for a broom. He couldn't find one. He picked up the largest pieces of glass and after a moment's consideration dropped them into an empty nail keg. He was annoyed with himself because he'd never licked an unconscious clumsiness born of great strength, high energy, and an urge to get things done fast.

26

All through his childhood and adolescence, his mother had feared for her fine furniture and dishes. He never meant to damage things, but it happened. Sometimes it left a mess that he didn't know how to clean up. This time it wasn't so hard, a matter of minutes to put the other large pieces in the keg and with his heel grind the smaller ones to gleaming dust.

A dog barked in the distance. Someone played "My Gal Sal" on a parlor reed organ. For a moment he felt lonely and lost, drifting through life without a plan, a destination, or two nickels to rub together most of the time. He tried not to think about it as he set to work.

He demounted the front wheel and patched the flat balloon tire, punctured in the mishap. He straightened the bent fork with his bare hands. He finished the job in twenty minutes. He didn't want to tell the widow how easy it was, so he wiped his greasy fingers on a rag and walked to the picket fence, gazing at the enormous western sky. The vista brought memories of the years spent in New Jersey during his disastrous college career.

He still remembered vividly the day it had ended. On a Friday in May 1904, Carl's father arrived in Princeton in response to a letter from the university president. The General stepped off the local from New York at two in the morning, grimy, tired, and in short temper. "I do not like to be taken away from business because of your scholastic failings," he said as Carl conducted him to the Nassau Inn for what remained of the night.

The General was calmer, refreshed with a shave and talc on his cheeks, when he preceded a nervous Carl into the president's office at nine the next morning. Dr. Woodrow Wilson, a lawyer and the son of a Presbyterian cleric, was a prim and austere man whose smile always had a forced quality. Pince-nez on a ribbon only heightened his severity. The General took the visitor's chair. Carl stood behind him, praying this would go the way he hoped.

Dr. Wilson reviewed Carl's record at the university. He had attended for four academic years and still had the status of a junior. Wilson made only passing reference to the accomplishments of the Princeton eleven's star lineman. The president's conclusion was dry and devoid of sympathy:

"Facts are facts, General. I am afraid we have no choice but to suspend Carl until such time as remedial work elsewhere merits his reinstatement."

Carl wanted to jump up and shout hurrah. He loved the sociability of college, the hard knocks of football, the thrill when Princeton scored on a bright autumn afternoon. But he didn't love academics.

The General placed both hands on the silver head of his cane. "I do want to observe that I've made substantial contributions to this school, Dr. Wilson."

"I am certainly aware of it, sir. Princeton is grateful. But we can't afford to mar our reputation with any taint of special privilege. Failing grades are failing grades." He removed his eyeglasses. "I'm sorry."

At the depot afterward, as the New York local clanged and steamed in, the General said, "Many fathers would disown a son who behaved so recklessly. I did that to your brother Joe and regretted it later. I won't repeat my mistake. But neither will I support a son who has failed to repay my investment in his education. You may have a job at the brewery, and earn your keep henceforth."

It took all of Carl's nerve to say, "I'm sorry, Pop, I don't want to work in the brewery the rest of my life."

Carl could see that the words hurt his father, but the General's response was tightly reined anger. "Where, then, may I ask?"

"I don't know."

"Well, until you decide, you're on your own. Just don't look to me for help. Is that understood?"

"Yes, sir."

"You're a grown man, Carl. Matured physically if not in character as yet." That stung. "Look out for yourself. Avoid bad companions. Maybe this spell will pass in a few weeks. If so, we have a place for you at home. You mean a great deal to your mother and me, never forget that."

Father embraced son, the General boarded the car, and the train pulled out. . . .

At the picket fence Carl shook himself out of the reverie. He still believed in all the possibilities represented by the new century and its wonderful new machines. But where in that great landscape of adventure and opportunity did he belong? He hadn't found the place — maybe never would.

His cousin Paul had faced the same grim possibility for years; he'd confessed it once in a long talk with Carl. Paul found his place, behind a camera. "You'll find yours unless you give up too soon. But you won't, Carl. You're not that kind."

He knocked at the kitchen door to tell the widow he'd finished the job. She paid him, then fed him supper and handed him two blankets.

"You can sleep in the shed if you want. I should tell you that the sheriff and his men are hard on tramps. In the morning I'd advise you to move on."

"Sure," Carl said, smiling in a wry way. "I'm used to that."

3. Paul and His Wife

A day later, across the Atlantic in crowded and clamorous London, Carl and Fritzi's cousin Paul was anxiously pacing on the north side of Derby Gate where it intersected Victoria Embankment by the river. It was Friday; Parliament was not sitting. Most MP's would be found in their offices in the building across the way.

"See them?" Paul asked his friend Michael, a reporter for the *London Light*.

"Not yet," Michael called from the corner. He was looking south toward the Underground entrance near Bridge Road, with Big Ben and the Gothic splendor of Westminster Palace just beyond.

Paul Crown was twenty-nine. He was a professional cameraman who filmed "actualities" — dramatic events and rare sights from all over the globe. He'd learned his trade in Chicago, working for a profane genius named Colonel R. Sidney Shadow. Before the colonel died he sold the assets of the American Luxograph Company to a British press baron who kept the company name and its star camera operator; Paul had moved his family to London three years ago.

Paul's camera stood on the curbstone, amid a cluster of reporters and still photographers. There were three other cameras similar to his, belonging to competitors. The WSPU march had been planned for some time, though not

31

publicized. Somehow word of it had reached the authorities and the press.

The man from Pathé said, "Hey, Dutch, what happens if they toss your missus in the clink?" In America, all Germans were "Dutch." The nickname had stuck.

"Then I guess I'll feed the kiddies for a while," Paul said with a forced grin. He worried about Julie taking part in marches, but he knew better than to ask her to stay home. Paul's wife was an ardent "New Woman." Perhaps it was a reaction to her girlhood in Chicago, when her nervously sick mother had repressed Julie's every impulse toward independence and forced her into a short-lived and loveless marriage.

Michael hurried back from his outpost. "They just came up from the tube. Oh, what a bloody menace to society," he said with his usual sarcasm.

Paul sprinted to the corner, heedless of an aggravating pain in his lower back. Some weeks ago, in French Morocco, he'd lifted a crate the wrong way and wrenched something. Though the pain woke him at night, he never complained.

He saw the women marching north in the middle of the road, twelve or fifteen of them in two ranks. They walked like soldiers in long skirts and plumed hats. Each woman carried a rolled-up paper. The driver of a hansom blocked by the marchers demonstrated his disgust by whipping his horse. Paul spied his beautiful wife in the second row, her face a porcelain white oval beneath her hat brim. Julie and the others belonged to

Mrs. Emmeline Pankhurst's Women's Social and Political Union. Their militant middle-aged leader marched in the front rank, flanked by her daughters Sylvia and Christabel. Mrs. Pankhurst, child of a free-thinking Manchester industrialist, was the widow of a barrister of even more liberal bent.

Tying up more traffic, the marchers were smiling, chatting among themselves. Though the day was raw, with a sooty sky, they might have been enjoying a picnic outing in May.

Paul strode back to Michael, shaking his head. "Seems like there are more damn demonstrations all the time. Shorter workdays, temperance, disarmament, votes — everyone wants something. The world's going crazy."

"That's your profession speaking. Disturbances and disasters are your livelihood. You see little else." It was true enough; earlier in the year Paul had rushed from Manila to San Francisco after the devastating earthquake and fire. His pictures had caused a sensation, and copious weeping, wherever they were shown.

"Besides, these little set-to's are nothing compared to what's coming," Michael said.

Michael Radcliffe was a tall, cadaverous man ten years older than Paul. His paper, the *London Light*, was owned by his father-in-law, Lord Yorke, who was Paul's boss as well. Born Mikhail Rhukov, and existing for years as a stateless and starving freelance, he had turned up in Paul's life with mysterious suddenness several times. After an affair with Cecily Hartstein, the press lord's daughter, he'd undergone a remarkable conversion: cut his hair, Anglicized his name, muffled his nihilism, and married Cecily, who loved him without regard to his gigantic deficiencies of character.

The two men presented a sharp physical contrast: from his gleaming shoe tips to his bowler hat, Michael was smartly turned out, while Paul's clothes might have come from a church rummage sale. His shoes were scuffed, his corduroy trousers wrinkled. His single-breasted khaki coat had a black stain on the sleeve. His plaid golf cap had traveled around the world and looked it. Few would take him for what he was — a star of his profession.

"You never stop beating the war drums," he said with a sigh. Michael shrugged and tossed his half-smoked cigarette into the street.

"Merely describing the inevitable, old chum." Paul remembered his friend talking drunkenly in a cantina in Cuba in 1898: *I have seen the great ships building. I have seen the rifled cannon. Armageddon in our lifetime . . .* " He'd pounded the table, quoting Revelations. " *'And there were lightnings, and thunderings — and the cities of the nations fell . . .'* " Michael mocked Paul's dreams of a contented life in a peaceful world. He said they'd turn to nightmares sooner than anyone imagined.

Paul stuffed his unlit cigar in a pocket and checked his tripod for steadiness. He sighted over the camera to the office building. A dozen policemen from the station in Richmond Terrace guarded the doors, the picture of authority with their tall hats and truncheons. Some of

34

Mrs. Pankhurst's women — the *Daily Mail* had christened them suffragettes — had already been arrested and forced to serve short terms in Holloway Prison for attempting to question speakers at Liberal Party meetings, the self-promoting Winston Churchill among them. Women weren't permitted to speak out, or have any role, in politics. Mrs. Pankhurst vowed to change that.

The marchers swung around the corner into Derby Gate. Paul began cranking the camera with a practiced, steady rhythm — *one,* two, three; *one,* two, three. Julie saw him and waved. Paul waved back with his free hand.

On the Embankment, auto drivers sounded klaxons in derision. Men leaned from their cabs to swear and jeer at the suffragettes forming a semicircle in front of the constables. The policeman in charge, a slightly built fellow with a gray mustache and a tough demeanor, strode forward to confront Mrs. Pankhurst.

"Good day, madam. May I ask why you're interfering with traffic?"

Emmeline Pankhurst held up her rolled paper. "We are here with resolutions to be presented to members of Parliament. Please step aside so that we may speak to them." Others, including Julie, echoed the demand. The constable shook his head.

"Can't be done, madam, and well you know it. You're not allowed to enter the building, or speak with any of the members. It's best you turn right around and cease this disruption of the public order."

"We are going in," Mrs. Pankhurst announced. "Ladies? Forward."

She walked past the dumbfounded constable, who was unprepared for disobedience. No doubt he expected the women to trot off like dutiful pets. Mrs. Pankhurst bore down on the cordon of policemen blocking the doors. Two of the officers had no choice but to push her back, then grapple with her.

The women broke ranks. Paul cranked steadily but kept a wary eye on his wife. The women feinted this way and that, trying to dodge between the constables, open the doors. The horns, jeering, and cursing had risen to a bedlam.

The police fended the suffragettes with their hands and jabs of their truncheons. It was evident to Paul that the officers, well trained and physically stronger, would overwhelm the women. Antagonized by rough handling, some of the suffragettes punched and kicked. Paul saw rage in the eyes of several beleaguered bobbies. A truncheon opened a bloody gash in one lady's cheek. Another whacked Sylvia Pankhurst's ankle, tripping her and sending her sprawling.

The exchange of blows went on for another minute or so. Then Mrs. Pankhurst took stock and rallied her troops with a cry. "All right, all right! Retreat! We shall try another time, I want no serious injuries."

Just that quickly the assault fell apart. But the women didn't seem disheartened; they'd given the coppers a lively run. Shouting and catcalling, they promised to return.

Paul kept cranking, thankful Julie hadn't been hurt. He watched her lean over with a piece of chalk. The WSPU often left messages for all to see. VOTES FOR WOMEN. END MALE DOMINANCE. WE SHALL BE HEARD.

Julie bent forward from the waist to write. The chief constable, short of breath and angry, took note, ran at her, and delivered a hard, vicious kick to her backside. Paul heard the sickening sound of Julie's head hitting the pavement.

He yelled her name, abandoned the camera, charged across the street, ignoring a hot iron of pain that seared his back. Julie lifted her head groggily, supporting herself on her hands a moment before she collapsed again.

"Stand back, bucko," a bobby said, hanging onto Paul's lapels. "You've no call to —"

"Get out of my way, that's my wife." Paul punched the copper in the stomach, bruising his knuckles as he sent the man reeling. He dodged another truncheon, shot his hands out to seize the officer who'd kicked Julie; the man was turned away from him, issuing orders.

A policeman behind Paul grabbed him, smashed the small of his back with a truncheon, and sent him flying forward. Paul's temple hit the curb, jarring and dazing him. He rolled over. His assailant crouched down to club him again. Paul drove a heavy shoe into the man's groin. The man reeled away.

On hands and knees, Paul crawled to Julie. He pressed his mouth to hers frantically; felt the warmth of her breathing. He groaned with relief. When he raised his head he saw that bright blood from a cut on his cheek smeared her pale chin.

Rough hands fastened on his neck and arms. He was dragged up, spun around. The policeman in charge fairly spat at him:

"That's all, laddie-buck. I saw you assault an officer. You're for the clink, sure."

Struggling futilely — there were three holding him now — Paul looked across the street and felt his stomach churn. Michael Radcliffe was gone.

So was the camera.

But he didn't go to jail. Instead, mysteriously, he was released after three hours. He went home from magistrate's court to the flat overlooking the Thames on Cheyne Walk, Chelsea. Julie was resting comfortably in bed. Philippa, the housemaid, was looking after the children, Joseph Shad Crown, called Shad, who was six, and Elizabeth Juliette, called Betsy, two.

Paul sat beside the bed while Julie drowsed. Presently she opened her eyes; recognized him. "You must think I'm a dreadful fool."

He bent to kiss her cheek, scrubbed clean of blood. "I think you're a remarkably brave woman mixed up with other women who tend to do foolish things for a noble cause." He kissed her mouth, long and sweetly; squeezed her hand. "Sleep now."

She murmured assent and turned her cheek into the pillow.

Next morning, still baffled by the abrupt way he'd been set free, Paul was summoned from his office in Cecil Court to the owner's suite on the highest floor of the *Light*, in Fleet Street. A male secretary with an embalmed look ushered him into the opulent grotto in which Lord Yorke conducted his affairs.

The proprietor was a short, round man, bald as an egg. Michael Radcliffe, married to his lordship's only child, had described him as having the eyes of a startled frog and the disposition of a cornered cobra. His lordship wasn't a likable man, but he paid well and looked after his employees with the fervor of a reformed Scrooge. Born Otto Hartstein, child of a Dublin rag-and-bone merchant, he'd bought his first provincial newspaper when he was twenty-two, and built it into a publishing empire.

"Well, sir?" he said, dwarfed by the great padded throne seat behind his desk. "What do you have to say for yourself?"

"I did what any husband would do if his wife was brutally attacked."

"But her assailant was a police officer in pursuit of his duty."

"I come from America, your lordship. No one's above the law. Is it different here?"

With a raucous snort that substituted for a laugh, Lord Yorke slapped the chair arm. "Cecily's husband saved you." Michael was always "Cecily's husband," and it was always said with distaste, as someone might refer to a troll under a bridge.

"Before the film ran out, you caught that bobby kicking your wife in a most barbarous way. How is she, by the by?"

"Doing well. She was more bruised and frightened than anything."

"Pleased to hear it. As I was saying, Cecily's husband hauled your cinematograph to safety before the coppers could smash it. Then he rang me. I in turn called two persons in Whitehall who would not wish to have that kind of police behavior shown to the public. Of course, we've already destroyed the offending section" — in light of his good fortune, Paul restrained a protest — "but that shall be our secret. Count yourself lucky."

"I do, sir. And I thank you."

"Give your lovely wife my warm regards, and urge her to be more careful. I urge you to do the same. You are a valuable employee, Paul. Try to stay out of trouble. Don't antagonize persons in authority, here or elsewhere."

"If I do that, I won't get good pictures."

Crankily, Lord Yorke said, "The newsman's dilemma. Damned annoying sometimes. Good day."

4. Ilsa's Worry

Cold December rain created a virtual lake in Wells Street. Nicky Speers carefully poked the long maroon Benz touring car through the water, fearful of stalling the engine. He parked successfully at the curb outside Restaurant Heidelberg and climbed out with arthritic slowness. Nicky was the family's English chauffeur, loyal but elderly. He hobbled around to the passenger door with the umbrella to shepherd Fritzi, then Ilsa to the ornate entrance. "I'll be standing here in an hour and fifteen minutes exactly, mum."

"Thank you, Nicky," Ilsa said.

The first person she saw in the foyer was Rudolf, the maître d'. He was one of the few human beings Ilsa actively disliked. It stemmed from the man's haughtiness and bad manners, more appropriate, in her opinion, to the worst sort of Prussian colonel. Speaking on the podium telephone, Rudolf didn't deign to notice them.

"We shall expect you, Herr Klosters, *vielen Dank*." Rudolf banged the earpiece on the hook and immediately bent his shaved head over a reservation book big as an altar Bible. As he wrote away, Ilsa tapped her shoe. General Crown's wife was not a woman to be trifled with.

"Rudolf. May we have a table for two, please? I didn't have time to telephone ahead."

"Out of the question, we are completely —"

41

He looked up. "Oh. *Gnädige Frau!* Humblest apologies! Of course we have room for you. Who is this young lady?"

"Our daughter, Fritzi."

"Ah, certainly. Grown so big! Follow me, please."

He jammed two enormous menus under his arm, pivoted, and marched off with a stride suspiciously like a military goose step. Fritzi lifted her skirts and started to mimic it, but Ilsa whispered, "Don't be naughty." Fritzi clasped her hands with a penitent's long face. Ilsa couldn't help smiling.

Rudolf seated them, unaware of the byplay. "Boris will attend you momentarily, *meine liebe Damen.*" After an unctuous bow he marched away. Fritzi removed her hat, the ribbon damp from the rain.

Ilsa Crown had matured into a stout, commanding woman with the kind of strong yet feminine features magazine writers loved to call "handsome." Ilsa was fifty-nine. Her silvery-gray hair, worn in a high pompadour, showed no trace of its original reddish brown color. She always dressed smartly and expensively, today in a white blouse with a large bow under a dark green tailored suit with a shoe-top hemline. Though long skirts with dust ruffles were still common, they were in her opinion dirt- and mud-catchers. She couldn't tolerate men who sneered at shorter skirts, and the women who wore them, as "rainy-daisies." On a nasty day like this, how could they be such idiots?

She drew off her long mauve gloves, still

42

amused. "You are a wicked child sometimes, *liebchen.* Several other people enjoyed your little impersonation. They must know Rudolf."

"Well," Fritzi said with an airy shrug, "bullies deserve whatever they get. Rudolf thumped me on the head once."

"Is that so? When?"

"When I was little. I was here with you and Papa. You were both talking with the Leiter family. Rudolf came by and hissed like a snake — I mustn't fold my leg under me and sit on it! I don't remember what I said, but he thumped me, like this." She flicked her middle finger off her thumb.

Ilsa laughed in spite of her tense state. She'd brought her daughter to the restaurant with serious intent. She knew Fritzi was unhappy. It was no sudden flash of insight; she'd known for months. She remembered her daughter in better times. When Fritzi was content, she wasn't restless. She seldom frowned, and her brown eyes glowed; everyone succumbed to her lighthearted charm. Fritzi wasn't a conventional beauty, to be sure, but she had a shining prettiness born of good humor, keen wits, and an inner niceness that people quickly sensed. To Ilsa's regret, no suitable young man had discovered those good qualities. At least she knew of none.

"I confessed I was feeling like a caged tiger all morning," Fritzi said as she opened her menu. "I was ever so glad you thought of coming downtown for luncheon."

"Piffle, not *luncheon,* that's for little birds. We'll have a proper *Mittagessen.* This is a German establishment, after all."

German to a fault, with a strolling accordion player in lederhosen and a green Tyrolean hat, fresh flowers on spotless white tablecloths, massive shelf displays of foot-high beer steins, and an overabundance of cuckoo clocks that tweeted and bonged with annoying regularity.

Ilsa regarded the menu through rimless bifocals connected by a chain to a matching gold case pinned to her formidable bosom. "Many fine specialities here, *liebchen*. I really hope you will eat something substantial. If you don't mind my saying so, you are too thin."

Fritzi pulled a face. "You mean not enough chest."

"*Ach.* Such bold language everyone uses these days."

"It's a new age, Mama. It's all right to say words like *leg* and *bosom*."

"Well, I don't agree, and I for one understand too little of this so-called new age. Now, what shall we eat? The liver and dumplings are good." Ilsa nodded toward some fish mournfully awaiting their fate in a lighted tank. "Also the carp."

"Believe me, Mama, I do eat properly. I stuff like a horse sometimes. It never seems to put on weight where I need it."

Ilsa leaned forward to pat Fritzi's hand. "I recently saw something at Field's that might be helpful. Christmas is coming."

It pleased Ilsa when Fritzi ordered a decent meal of beefsteak, potatoes, and string beans. Ilsa chose carp, preceded by noodle soup. She asked for a bottle of Liebfraumilch. She raised

44

her first glass of the sweet wine, clinked it with Fritzi's. *"Prosit."* The wine slid down golden-warm, buffing a little of the edge off her nerves. She was worried about Fritzi's future in a profession that was not secure, or even respectable. Unlike German parents of long ago, Ilsa and her husband couldn't direct or influence Fritzi's life, though Ilsa was concerned enough to make an attempt.

Before she could, Fritzi asked, "Have you heard from cousin Paul?"

"No, only from Julie. You know Pauli, always dashing somewhere with his camera. Julie said she is marching and demonstrating with Mrs. Pankhurst's organization." Ilsa's expression suggested a lack of enthusiasm for the militant British suffragists. "She prides herself on being one of the New Women, as they're called. I hope she is not endangering herself. I admire her idealism, but she has responsibilities to her husband and children."

"Julie's a lovely, courageous person. I'm awfully glad Paul is so happy with her. I just adore him."

There was a wistful quality in Fritzi's remark. After Paul had come from Berlin to live with the family, Fritzi, age thirteen, had confessed to Ilsa that she desperately wanted to marry him. It fell to Ilsa to say that in proper and upright families, marriage between first cousins was not permitted.

Fritzi lapsed into silence. Ilsa reached across to clasp her hand again. "How I wish you felt better."

"Mama, I'm fine."

"No, no, I see the signs. A generous heart brought you home when your papa was ill, and you've stayed. But I know you're all at sea. Do the amateur dramatics no longer interest you?"

"Truthfully, no."

"Social work isn't your cup of tea."

"It was kind of you to introduce me to Jane Addams again. I know she's a great friend, and Hull House helps ever so many poor people. But all the women I met there — your friends who volunteer with you — they're not my age. They're settled, with different interests."

"They are old, like me," Ilsa said crisply, without self-pity. "I understand."

The waiter brought Ilsa's soup and a basket of rye and black bread. While Fritzi buttered a thick piece of pumpernickel, her mother said, "I've thought of ever so many things to suggest to you, some quite outlandish. Cooking lessons from a French chef, for instance."

Fritzi giggled. "You know I'm a failure at the domestic arts. I couldn't cook a missionary if I were a cannibal."

Ilsa took another sip of wine, and a deep breath, and leaped. "There is something your papa would like, you know. For you to settle down. He longs for a son-in-law, grandchildren."

Silence again. Fritzi remained motionless with both hands on the stem of her glass. Ilsa had never pried into her daughter's romantic affairs. From scattered hints in letters she knew Fritzi had fallen madly for a young Georgia boy when

46

Mortmain's company played two weeks in Savannah. The boy apparently liked her, but only that. No doubt he thought her fast, a judgment made of all actresses. The boy was from an old family — an aristocrat, which in Ilsa's view often equated with snob. The tone of Fritzi's letters had been sad for months.

A not unfamiliar story, Ilsa thought. Sometimes after a particular boy was lost, a girl never recovered. Never found another to match the first love, and so withered into spinsterhood. Ilsa knew at least four middle-aged women who'd had that misfortune. People said they were "disappointed in love." One was Ilsa's dear friend Jane Addams who ran the settlement house.

Ilsa would die a mother's living death of sorrow if Fritzi spent her life alone. Yet she knew of no way to save her daughter. Only Fritzi could do it — Fritzi and some man who had no name, no identity, nor any real existence except as a shadow in a mother's hopeful imagination.

At last Fritzi spoke. "Mama, I don't think it will ever happen."

"Why not? *Liebchen,* you're a treasure. Is your mind made up against marriage?"

"No, but I know what I am. I'm an actress. I'm cut out for that and very little else. I love acting. That's why —" Sudden spots of color in Fritzi's cheeks prepared Ilsa for something dire.

"I've decided to go to New York after the first of the year."

"I don't believe it. You would move to that awful place?"

Fritzi took her mother's hand, speaking ear-

47

nestly. "You're a smart, cultured woman, Mama. You know perfectly well that theater, *real* theater, only happens in New York. I refuse to spend my life playing tank towns from Florida to Texas — or a church hall in Chicago. If I try and fail, so be it. But I have to try."

Now it was Ilsa's turn to be silent, while her mind raced. She didn't doubt her daughter's ability to look out for herself, even in such a sinful and crime-ridden place as New York. What alarmed her was the thought of another person in the equation:

"Have you told Papa of this decision?"

"Not yet, but I will soon."

"You know he may react badly."

"Dictatorially, you mean? Mama, I can't alter my life for fear of an argument."

"I don't ask that. Please think it over, that's all. Think it over very carefully." The catch in Ilsa's voice made Fritzi blink; Ilsa's panic had shown itself. "Who knows, perhaps you'll change your mind."

Fritzi didn't reply, concentrating on her food. The renewed silence left Ilsa hanging in a state of uncertainty and despair.

5. A Dream of Speed

At a coal stop in Maryland, some miles above Baltimore, a railroad man rousted Carl from the southbound freight train. He'd headed south after the first snow whitened the Hudson Valley. In Maryland he found the milder weather he was seeking, though the sun was setting early, casting long, sad shadows.

He walked along dirt roads for a few miles, working up a ravenous appetite. He stopped at a country tavern, a rambling frame building with a dirt yard where stagecoaches must have parked years ago. By the door he noticed buckets of cinders and a heavy shovel, reminders that it might snow in Maryland too.

The tavern was smoky and warm. At the bar he ordered pork roast and a stein of beer, paying with his last forty cents. Two men in double-breasted suits leaned on the bar rail, speculating on the outcome of the forthcoming Harry Thaw murder trial in New York. Thaw, a well-connected socialite, had murdered architect Stanford White in the rooftop theater at Madison Square Garden. White had dallied with Thaw's wife, a former showgirl. At a table in the corner, four other men played cards.

Carl wandered to a smaller table, pulled out the chair, sat down heavily without judging the chair's fragility. The old dry wood protested noisily. Behind the bar, the whale-sized propri-

49

etor gave Carl a look. Carl jumped up and examined the chair.

"Nothing broken."

"Lucky for you. Furniture ain't cheap."

Presently he had his food and drink. The loudest of the card players, a lanky man with a blotched nose, kept hectoring the others. Finally an older man folded his hand and threw it down.

"I'm tired of your lip, Innis. We'll play again when you're sober."

Innis staggered up, overturning his chair. "Hey, you bastard, you can't quit. You're winning."

"I'm quitting, Innis. Right now." The older man gave Innis a hard stare. Carl sopped up gravy with a piece of oatmeal bread, noting that the older man was a head taller than Innis. Innis didn't challenge him. The older man left.

Carl didn't put his head down in time. Innis caught his eye. "You a card man, mister?"

Carl didn't like Innis's looks and perhaps showed it when he said, "No."

"Come on, sit in for a few hands. Straight draw poker."

"I haven't got any money. I'd like to finish my supper."

Innis blinked, mean-eyed. "Ain't got any manners, either."

One of the other card players tugged Innis's arm. "For Christ's sake, sit down, you've got to get over it sometime."

Innis flung off the man's hand. "I don't know this bozo, and I don't like his lip." Innis lurched

50

forward, punched Carl's shoulder. "What you got to say to that?"

Carl was no dime-novel hero like Nick Carter or Frank Merriwell, but his father had taught him to stand up to bullies because they usually went to pieces if you did.

"I say you better not hit me again."

Innis snickered. Slapped Carl's face lightly. "Like that?"

Stomach knotting up, Carl pushed his chair back. The proprietor rushed from behind the bar. "Outside, outside. I don't want no damage."

Carl spread his hands in a final peace gesture. "There's no reason we have to —" Innis slammed his fist into Carl's jaw.

Carl windmilled backward, bounced off the wall. Damn stupid bully, he thought as Innis shambled toward him. Before Innis could punch him again, Carl caught his shirt in both hands. He yanked Innis sideways. The tavern owner leaped to the door and held it open so Innis could sail through backward, landing on his rear in the dirt.

Carl walked out after him. "Let's forget it. I've no quarrel with you. Go someplace and dry out."

Innis crawled up on his knees, wiping his mouth with his cuff. For a moment Carl thought everything was settled; Innis's sickly, dung-eating smile deceived him.

"Well, now," Innis began, hitching forward on his knees. Too late Carl realized what he intended. Innis's right hand clamped on Carl's ankle and spilled him. Innis jumped up, kicked Carl's ribs twice, grabbed the shovel by the handle.

"Now," he panted as Carl wobbled to his feet, head buzzing. "Now, you smart-mouth son of a bitch."

Carl chopped down with the edge of his right hand, into the V of Innis's left elbow. It loosened his grip. Carl wrested the shovel away. From his side pocket Innis pulled a clasp knife like Carl's, snapped it open. Carl retreated a step. Innis turned sideways and stabbed. Carl swung the shovel like a baseball bat.

At the last second he pulled the swing so he wouldn't kill the man. Even so, the shovel gave off a metallic ring. Innis dropped, his left ear bleeding. He flopped on his stomach, sighed, and passed out.

The owner and the card players stood in a half circle around Innis while Carl caught his breath and rubbed what felt like a pulled shoulder muscle. The owner emptied a water bucket on the fallen man. Innis licked water from his lips and kept on sleeping.

"He's been mad as hornets for a week," the owner observed. "First they fired him at the track, then his old woman locked him out. He's been on a rip ever since. Wouldn't stay around to see him wake up, I was you. I'd move on."

"Sure, I'm used to that," Carl said with an odd smile. "I need work, maybe I could take his place. Where's this track?"

"Baltimore Downs. North edge of the city."

"Thanks kindly." Carl turned and limped out

of the tavern yard.

He slept that night underneath a bench in a park in a small village, half awake with his teeth chattering. The wind blew out of the northwest, smelling of winter.

In the morning he found the Baltimore Downs racetrack. It was a splendid one-mile layout with a big flag-bedecked grandstand, a two-story clubhouse, extensive stables and paddock. A groom exercising a filly pointed the way to the office. There a man named Reeves made short work of the interview:

"You want Innis's job? He mucked out the stables, helped the grooms, did whatever else needed doing. You game for that?"

"I'm game for eating once in a while," Carl said.

Reeves liked that. "Met Innis, did you?"

Carl touched a purpling bruise on his jaw. "Unfortunately, yes."

"Who won?"

"I did."

Reeves liked that even better. "Well, the stables are clean and warm. You can sleep in an empty stall till you find a boardinghouse. Start tomorrow morning, six sharp." As Carl thanked Reeves, he heard the deep growl of a motor.

"Sounds like a gasoline car."

"Yep. When the ponies aren't running, I've found there's a sporting crowd that will turn out for automobile races. Our track's popular with the drivers, too. Ever seen a race?"

"I saw the first one run in this country. Thanksgiving day, 1895, in Chicago."

53

"The famous race in the snow," Reeves said with a nod.

"Fifty-four and three-tenths miles. The Duryea brothers won it with their Number 5 in ten hours, twenty-three minutes. Frank Duryea drove the car, only they called them motor wagons then."

Since that wintry day when a wide-eyed boy had watched horseless carriages slipping and sliding along Michigan Avenue, Carl had carried on a constant if unfulfilled romance with autos. He had seen scores of autos in New York City. Whether they had hissing boilers, buzzing batteries, or sputtering gas engines didn't matter. They all excited him. They were machines, and he loved machinery. Autos were no longer jokes, as they had been at first; now they were symbols of power and wealth — rolling, snorting, smoking marvels of the new century.

Still, not everyone liked them. Dr. Wilson of Princeton had stated publicly that they were frivolous and ostentatious toys only the rich could afford. Thus they promoted unrest, socialism, and anarchy among the poor. Didn't that just prove Wilson was a stuffy old bore?

Of course, autos were as yet far from reliable. Likely as not, you'd see one sitting broken down instead of moving. Wandering a country road in Ohio, he'd come on a butter yellow Stanley mired in a muddy ditch. A farmer with his mule team hitched to the frame struggled to haul it out. Carl volunteered to push on a rear wheel. The farmer prodded his reluctant mules; brown ooze flew out behind the tires. The Stanley regained the road, and Carl's grin shone in his mask of mud.

He often dreamed of sitting behind the wheel of an auto, driving fast. Back in Indianapolis, where he'd worked for three months earlier this year, the dream had become feverish. He hadn't stepped inside a legitimate theater since he was a boy, but he bought a gallery seat for a musical play called *The Vanderbilt Cup*. It celebrated the great Long Island road race started in 1904 by the socialite William K. Vanderbilt. The show was touring with its original Broadway star, race driver Barney Oldfield.

Oldfield was a former Ohio bike racer who had taken the wheel of an auto for the first time in 1903. He drove Henry Ford's big "999" against the favorite, the "Bullet," owned by Cleveland auto maker Alexander Winton. "999" won.

Barney Oldfield wasn't much of an actor, but he gave a convincing performance in the climactic scene in the second act. Two racecars, the Peerless Blue Streak and Barney's Peerless Green Dragon, raced side by side on treadmills while painted scenery flew by behind them. The cars spewed smoke and sparks and blue exhaust flame in a frighteningly realistic way. Barney wore his familiar forest green driving suit, green leather helmet, and goggles. The cast cheered him on. Naturally he won. He was the uncrowned king of fast driving, and he wasn't being paid two thousand a month to lose.

It was the first time Carl had seen Barney Oldfield, who was at the height of his fame. It was also the first and only time he saw what his sister meant about the magic of theater. The stage spectacle thrilled him.

Carl's fever heated up again when Reeves said, "Two fellows in a Fiat are running practice laps for a hundred-mile race the end of the week. Go have a look."

He ran out into the pale winter sunshine, wove between stable buildings to the track, where an engine roared in a cloud of tan dust. He stepped on the lower rail, dust settling in his hair and on his shoulders as the racecar sped toward the turn. It resembled half a tin can set forward on a chassis with unprotected wheels. The Fiat was right-hand drive, like all cars on the road. The driver and his riding mechanic perched in bucket seats, eating dust and wind. Each wore goggles and fancy gauntlets. Carl dreamed of being the man gripping the wheel.

On the back stretch the Fiat gathered speed. Carl's jaw dropped. "My Lord, they must be doing forty or fifty."

He hung on the rail as the Fiat slewed through the turns, leaving a great rooster tail of dust behind. He watched it for nearly an hour. To Reeves, afterward, he said, "I've got to learn to drive. I don't know where, or how, but I'm going to do it, you can count on that."

6. Paul's Pictures

Nicky the chauffeur was waiting with the umbrella when Fritzi and her mother left Restaurant Heidelberg. On the drive home Fritzi said little. Obviously her mother was upset about her decision.

The Crown mansion on South Michigan was an enormous Victorian castle, twenty-six rooms, twice remodeled and forever symbolic of its owner's success in the brewery trade. Joe Crown owned the entire block from Twentieth to Nineteenth; the half lot nearer Nineteenth was given over to a well-kept garden with a reflecting pool, empty now; neat beds for rose bushes; a marble statue of an angel symbolizing peace, all screened from the traffic by high shrubbery. Ten minutes after Fritzi reached her room, Ilsa rushed in with a letter.

"*Liebchen,* your prayers are answered! See what came in the afternoon mail delivery? Pauli posted it in Gibraltar six weeks ago. He even sent a snapshot."

Ilsa gave her the Kodak print. A smile spread on Fritzi's face as she gazed at her sturdy cousin, photographed with his motion picture camera and tripod on a hotel veranda. Paul had his usual cigar clenched in his teeth. One arm was hooked around his tripod; with his other hand he lifted his Panama hat to greet the lens.

Paul's vest was unbuttoned. His cravat hung askew. The knees of his white suit showed smudges. He was his old self, forever careless about his appearance though he was never careless about his work. Paul occasionally sent photos to his loved ones because of a lifelong habit of gathering, and distributing, souvenirs and keepsakes.

Quickly Fritzi read through the letter. Paul had visited North Africa, photographing nomads and exotic locales in Morocco and the Sahara, then Gibraltar to film the new British warship HMS *Dreadnought* steaming into the Mediterranean.

> She is the first of her kind — 17,000 tons, faster than anything afloat. Her big guns can throw a shell for miles. My friend Michael says she has already touched off a naval arms race. Alas, the blasted British would not permit me to photograph her. N. African pictures will be edited and in theaters by December. Am planning another trip to the States next year, will surely see you. Till then much love to all.

"We must find out who shows the American Luxograph pictures," Ilsa said with great excitement. "I know you'll want to see them. We'll go together, have another outing."

In one of those awful nickel theaters? Ye gods. But Fritzi couldn't deny the stout, graying woman she loved dearly. She sighed a small inner sigh and said, "That would be lovely."

The General made some inquiries at Ilsa's request. A foreman at the brewery happened to know an enterprising German Jew from Oshkosh who had jumped into the picture business that year. Carl Laemmle was his name. He distributed films and operated a nickel theater on North Milwaukee Avenue. Laemmle said a good downtown theater showing American Luxograph "actualities" was the Bijou Dream on State near Van Buren, the very place Fritzi had noticed on her bicycle ride.

Fritzi and her mother bought their tickets at ten past two on a dismal afternoon. Looking around, she had to admit the Bijou Dream was better than the few other theaters she'd visited in occasional pursuit of her cousin's films. The windows of the converted store were hung with green velvet drapes. The projector was shielded in a curtained booth at the rear of the long, rectangular room. Fritzi didn't recognize the operator tinkering with the machine; the young man from the play group wasn't on duty. Thank heaven for that. She'd never bothered to hide her feelings about the moving pictures.

Instead of wooden benches there were chairs, a hundred or more, not an assortment from drugstores, ice cream parlors, and secondhand shops, but all alike. The Bijou Dream employed a piano player whose upright sat next to the canvas screen, and a lecturer, a gentleman in a midnight blue tuxedo who introduced and explained each batch of footage from a podium on the opposite side. Pictures shown in five-cent theaters typically carried no explanatory legends. Many didn't even have an opening title.

About twenty people attended the two-fifteen

show. Fritzi and her mother were by far the best dressed. Some of the spectators reeked of garlic, wine, or a lack of bathing facilities. It wasn't snobbish, merely truthful, for Fritzi to observe that the pictures served primarily an audience of disfranchised immigrants. Pictures depended for success on a universal language of panto-mime, and on accessibility. Slum dwellers could often walk to a theater, saving carfare.

In a roped area at the front, children were seg-regated. Half a dozen noisy boys in patched knickers and cloth caps joked and punched each other. Ilsa whispered, "Truants?"

"Or artful dodgers," Fritzi said. She and Ilsa responded to a lantern slide requesting ladies to remove their hats. The grand dame in the illus-tration wore a wide-brimmed number carrying enough fruit and wild fowl to serve a banquet.

The professor left the piano to separate two of the boys rolling in the aisle and pummeling each other. When they were back in their seats, the operator switched off the tin-shaded ceiling lights and a new lantern slide appeared.

The Latest
T. B. HARMS
SONG HIT!

— Words and Music By —
HARRY POLAND

As Featured By
FLAVIA FARREL
"The Irish Songbird"

"Oh, it's Pauli's friend," Ilsa said, meaning the composer.

Two faces filled oval frames on either side of the slide copy. The Irish Songbird was a pouchy-eyed woman who must have been pretty before middle age and sagging flesh caught up with her. The man in the other frame, Harry Poland, had crossed the Atlantic in steerage with Paul in 1891. A Polish immigrant boy, he'd adopted a new name, found his way into the music business, and now wrote popular songs successfully. Harry was a long-jawed young man with a broad smile and lively eyes. The photographer caught him lifting a summer straw hat off his dark curly hair; the pose reminded Fritzi of Paul's snapshot. Paul was lighthearted much of the time, and the composer looked like that, too. Maybe that's why they had become friends, and saw each other in New York whenever they could.

The first song slide appeared, illustrated by a photo of a man in goggles and a young woman in a big hat and dust veil seated in an auto. Song lyrics were superimposed on the machine's long hood. The professor played the catchy tune.

THAT AUTO-MO-BILING FEEL-ING
IS STEAL-ING O-VER ME

Next slide: stuffed doves hovering above the couple, who were hugging. The rowdy boys jeered and made farting noises.

IT'S AN AP-PEAL-ING FEEL-ING,
RO-MAN-TIC AS CAN BE

61

"Get the hook," cried one of the boys. The lecturer stepped from the podium and thwacked the offender by flicking his index finger off his thumb, a painful reminder of Rudolf.

Ilsa sang along in her heavily accented voice. Fritzi found herself singing too. Paul's friend wrote infectious melodies.

When the song slides ended, a clackety noise in the booth said the operator was turning the crank of the projector. A beam of light shot over the audience. The boys clapped and whistled as a young woman with a leashed terrier paraded in a sunlit park. The picture was dim, the image scratched and filled with annoying bubble-like eruptions of light. The lecturer announced, "Mary's Mutt, a comic novelty."

The three-minute sequence started with Mary accidentally letting go of the leash, then reacting with outrageous mugging as her dog dashed off. Chasing him, she enlisted a policeman, then a young gent eating a sandwich on a park bench. The crude film was no more than an excuse for the three actors to run around wildly, bumping into trees and each other.

"The Gigolo, a spicy import from Paris."

This picture involved a dandy with a pointed mustache, an older woman, and a young waitress he attempted to pinch. The set consisted of table, chairs, and a canvas backdrop painted as a restaurant. Halfway through the silly story someone behind the canvas bumped it and made it ripple. The actors went right on. How could anyone be a steady patron of such stuff?

"The latest from the American Luxograph."

"Oh, here it is," Ilsa said, grabbing Fritzi's hand.

"Teddy in Panama." Paul's first actuality showed President Roosevelt inspecting canal construction.

"Exotic sights of Morocco. Fierce Berber tribesmen." Men in sheet-like garments and burnouses stalked past the camera, glowering and waving scimitars. This was followed by a camel race in the desert.

"The bazaar at Marrakech." Though dimly lit because of heavy shadows, Paul's scenes of awning-covered stalls and veiled women examining merchandise caught the essence of the place. The bored urchins stomped and whistled.

The clicking projector filled the screen with an image of a hotel veranda, the same on which Paul had been photographed. British naval officers in white paraded in and out, many quite fat and most looking self-important. An occasional gowned lady relieved the tedium.

With an unexplained jerk — perhaps a repaired break in the film? — the scene changed. The audience had a glimpse of an immense battleship steaming past far below the camera, which was evidently positioned high up on the Rock. HMS *Dreadnought*? The image stayed only a few seconds; a hand swooped over the lens and the screen went black. One of the urchins booed. A new scene appeared: the Union Jack snapping on a flagstaff.

Another repetitive chase picture ended the fifteen-minute show. "That was thrilling, wasn't it?" Ilsa said as they left their seats. Fritzi agreed that Paul's pictures were special, and worth-while, in contrast to the cheap little dramas and comedies.

Outside, she turned up her coat collar. The weather had worsened. Heavy gray skies pressed down on the city. A bitter wind blew off the lake. The air smelled of snow and was full of soot, the stink of horse dung, the rattle and roar of El trains tying their iron loop around the downtown.

"Pauli has seen so much of the world. What an exciting life he leads," Ilsa said.

"He should write a book about it," Fritzi said. The thought had just occurred to her. Paul wasn't a writer, like his friend the journalist and novelist Richard Harding Davis, but he was smart, and she was certain he could do it.

Ilsa and Fritzi bent into the wind, heading for the trolley stop. Ilsa had relieved Nicky of the duty of picking them up. On the corner she bought two roasted sweet potatoes from a vendor, to warm them up while they waited.

"Fritzi, those people in the little stories — are they actors?"

"They may think so. What they're doing isn't real acting, it's old-fashioned scenery chewing. The style of fifty years ago. Modern acting is — well, smaller. Intense but restrained. Edwin Booth pioneered it in this country."

"I suppose picture people have to play broadly to convey an idea. Would there be acting opportunities for you?"

Fritzi reacted emphatically. "Not me, Mama. I'll never have anything to do with that kind of entertainment. I'd rather not act at all."

"I thought acting was acting," Ilsa said with a little shrug of puzzlement. "Life was so much simpler in the old days."

7. The General and His Children

His Cadillac started on the second spin of the crank. It was a dependable four-cylinder 1906 model that developed 40 hp. Black with matching leather seats, it had its winter hardtop latched in place. The machine had cost a little more than $3,700 new, which put it in the luxury class. It wasn't the General's most expensive auto, though. That was the glittering $5,700 Welch touring car he kept garaged in bad weather.

He slid under the wheel on the right side. He put on his expensive driving goggles, resembling a domino mask made of leather inset with two front lenses and a side lens at each temple. He drove out the east gate into Larrabee Street, passing a line of delivery wagons piled high with kegs of the dark and hearty beer they brewed especially for Christmas.

Creeping along congested streets of the Near North Side, Joe honked at a Simplex that almost ran into him at an intersection. He cursed when horse dung splattered his fenders. He shook his fist at a Reo that swerved too close. In the east, clouds like gray granite slabs layered the sky. Sleet began to tick against the windshield. Fortunately, his velvet-collared motor coat had a warm leather lining. His mood matched the bleakness of the day.

The sleet had turned to snow by the time he drove into the big four-bay garage at the rear of his property. He parked the Cadillac next to his prize vehicle, the beautiful cream-colored seven-passenger Welch touring car. Its four cylinders developed 50 hp. Brilliant brass coachwork and leather upholstery, fire-engine red with a diamond pleat, dazzled the eye. Made in Pontiac, Michigan, the Welch was a top-of-the-market vehicle for rich men. Joe had long coveted a chain-driven Mercedes, but they cost more than twice as much. He thought $12,000 for a motor car excessive.

In the house he handed his automobiling clothes to Leopold, the steward. Leopold was middle-aged, phlegmatic, less of a trial than his martinet predecessor, Manfred. Leopold hailed from Bavaria, but Joe saw none of the lazy traits he associated with Germans from that region.

In the kitchen, Ilsa and the cook, Trudi, were mixing batter for *stollen,* the traditional raisin-and-sugar-dusted cakes of the season. Joe kissed his wife, who laughed when she saw she'd transferred flour to his chin. He said he'd be ready for *Abendessen,* the evening meal, by eight o'clock.

"I'll be in the office going over sales reports. Sound the buzzer." Joe operated the house with an elaborate system of bells and buzzers that suited his orderly nature, while annoying others. Ilsa buzzed at five past eight, and Joe proceeded to the dining room.

The Crown mansion reflected the season. A nine-foot fir tree stood beneath the huge electric chandelier in the two-story foyer. A marvelously detailed wooden crèche was arranged beneath. The tree wore a festive cloak of glass balls, enameled ornaments, gold chains, and silver tinfoil. Scores of white candles were clipped to the branches. They wouldn't be lighted until Christmas Eve; that was the German way.

In the dining room, two candles in the Advent wreath in the center of the long table were already lit. On the sideboard stood a carved St. Nicholas, two feet high with his long beard, miter, and bishop's crozier appropriately painted.

Joe sat at the head of the table. He heard his older son coming, announced by the scrape of his artificial foot and a hacking, phlegmy cough. Joe Junior smoked too much; nothing his parents said would make him stop. The General bridled his annoyance and unconsciously brushed nonexistent specks from his immaculate vest.

Joe Junior created fierce pity and anger in his father. The boy was a tragic misfit. Mired in socialist dogma — he was friendly with the very red Gene Debs — he'd taken part in a strike at a shingle factory out in Everett, Washington, where he worked for a time. The strikers fought a bloody brawl with hired goons. Two of the goons threw Joe Junior onto one of the buzz saws that split cedar blocks into shingles; the saw tore off his right foot.

Only the quick action of a Norwegian woman, Anna Sieberson, kept him from bleeding to death. He later married Anna, and was planning to adopt her son when influenza carried her off suddenly. The boy went to live with relatives, and Joe Junior slunk home to Chicago, a bitter and defeated man.

"Good evening, Joe," the General said as his son limped in.

"Hello, Pop." Joe Junior sat — no, that wasn't quite right, he took his seat and slouched, his right shoe stuck out as if to defiantly remind everyone of the cork foot it covered. Look at him, Joe thought. Dirt under his nails. Sweat rings on his shirt. Joe Junior was always demonstrating that he was one of the "common people," although he lived under Joe Crown's roof at no cost, and ate Ilsa's food, and enjoyed a life monumentally better than any other man who did low work at the brewery. Joe Junior was thirty. The same height as his father, he'd resembled Joe Senior until beer and overeating ballooned his stomach and dissipation put gray rings around his blue eyes.

Ilsa and Fritzi came in. Ilsa sat at the far end of the table. Fritzi kissed her father's forehead, murmured, "Papa," and took her place opposite Joe Junior on the side. The two serving girls set platters on the long table, a family heirloom of dark walnut with fat carved legs. Ilsa kept it covered with a lace tablecloth of intricate design.

Joe said to Fritzi, "Did you and your mother see Paul's pictures this afternoon?"

"We did."

"How was the theater?"

"Dark, but clean. Mr. Laemmle's recommendation was all right."

"You know he named his own theater the White Front, hoping it would suggest cleanliness and respectability, and attract a better crowd. A vain hope, in my opinion. Thank you, Bess." Joe nodded to the girl who set his stein of Crown lager by his right hand.

Ilsa said, "Pastor Wulf claims picture theaters are spawning grounds for vice, but we saw nothing immoral. Just some loud boys wasting their afternoon."

"Paul's films are really remarkable," Fritzi said. "They show places and events that people would never see otherwise. We saw Morocco, and watched the president operate a big steam shovel."

Joe helped himself to a large slab of Ilsa's dry pot roast and passed the platter. Careless, Joe Junior almost dropped it. Joe shot him a look, then said, "Theodore's energy and curiosity are boundless."

"It's a shame Paul's work is exhibited only in five-cent theaters," Fritzi said. "The other pictures, the ones that try to tell stories, are trash."

"We agree on that," her father said with an amiable nod. Joe Junior looked bored, sitting head down, devouring mashed potatoes. He continued, "I saw a few story pictures a year ago. What a mistake. They offer nothing but low comedians chasing girls in scanty outfits or running around smashing down picket fences and trampling flower beds. Total disregard for property."

Joe Junior snickered. "Property. Of course."

"We all know what you and your friend Debs think of the idea of property," his father shot back. "I need no commentary from —"

Loud knocking at the front door interrupted. Ilsa looked toward the foyer as Leopold rushed to answer. The front door opened; Joe heard the wind. Ilsa said, "Who on earth can be calling at this hour?"

Leopold rushed in. "Sir — madam — it's your son."

"Carl? *Mein Gott.*" Ilsa leaped up, ran past Leopold exclaiming, "Where did he come from?"

"Pittsburgh, Mama," Carl's voice boomed. "Pittsburgh and South Bend, on the boxcar Pullmans."

Elated but baffled, Joe followed his wife into the foyer. Snow was melting on Carl's hair and the shoulders of his patched overcoat. A long red scarf wrapped round and round his neck trailed to the floor. Carl hadn't shaved in several days. His boots dripped water on the marble.

Carl rushed to hug his mother, swinging her off her feet and whirling her. Ilsa's flying heels nearly knocked over a tall Chinese jar. When Carl's clumsiness combined with his boisterous energy, there often was damage. Tonight no one cared.

Carl released his mother and shook his father's hand. "Greetings, Papa. Hello, Joey. Fritzi, let me hug you." She received a three-hundred-sixty-degree whirl like Ilsa's. She was breathless when he put her down.

"No one expected you, Carl," she said.

"I'm on my way to Detroit."

"Detroit?" Joe Crown said in a baffled way.

"To look for a job. I've been studying fast cars lately. I want to find out how they're built. I want to drive one."

Joe said, "You looking for employment? In an auto factory?" He was almost afraid that asking would hex the whole thing. Carl grinned, threw an arm over his father's shoulder, and leaned down to him.

"Yes, Papa, your wayward boy has found something he wants to do. It happened back East — Baltimore. Tell you all about it later."

"You'll be here for Christmas, won't you?" Fritzi asked with a curious look of expectancy.

"Through the holidays, but that's all," Carl said.

"This is wonderful news," Ilsa exclaimed. Only Joey, leaning against the door jamb at the dining room entrance, looked indifferent. It maddened Joe.

"Come in, come in, there's plenty of food left," Ilsa said, fairly bubbling.

"Could use some," Carl said. "No dining-car service on the boxcars."

"You could be killed riding that way without paying," Ilsa said.

"Oh, no, I had an expert teacher. Paul. He learned to do it in Berlin."

"Glad you're home, Carl," Joe Junior said as the others trooped back to the dining room. "But I'm bushed, we'll talk tomorrow." He limped to the staircase with his crippled right foot scraping, scraping — Joe clenched his teeth as he watched his son drag himself up the long staircase.

He called for a bottle of schnapps and another place setting. Ilsa and Fritzi and Carl chattered away while he alternated sips of coffee and schnapps. Soon he felt much better. Carl had given them a grand Christmas present.

Joe observed Fritzi from the corner of his eye. With Carl's life unexpectedly going in a new and more positive direction, it was time to concentrate on her. He needn't leave matchmaking entirely to Ilsa. He would start looking among his well-to-do friends for eligible bachelor sons who might be interested in a fine match with a millionaire's daughter. Fritzi needed a proper husband and a good home right here in Chicago. He wouldn't permit her to follow any other course.

What a happy holiday season this was turning out to be!

8. Courage from Carl

Next morning everyone rose early. After eating *Frühstuck* — breakfast — big enough for two, Carl took himself out of the house to shop for Christmas presents, extracting a promise from Fritzi that they'd play some ball later. It was a pastime they'd enjoyed together when they were children.

The morning's burst of sunshine and warmth quickly melted an inch or two of snow from last night. Nicky drove Ilsa to a board meeting of the Orchestra League. Left alone, Fritzi drew up her own Christmas list, then leafed through the mail that Leopold brought to the music room. Eagerly she opened a letter to the family from Julie.

She caught her breath when she read Julie's description of her treatment at the hands of London policemen in the Whitehall demonstration. Fritzi admired Julie's devotion to the cause of woman suffrage. She shared Julie's enthusiasm for it, though so far she'd never taken part in any marches.

Julie's letter concluded with a paragraph about cousin Paul.

For years, since that evil Jimmy Daws went to prison, he has carried and handled all his heavy equipment by himself. On his African trip he severely strained his back and suffered for weeks. Lord Yorke has offered to hire an assistant, but Paul refuses. When I tell him a helper would be no reflection on his manhood, he turns a deaf ear. Germans can be maddeningly stubborn — and none more so than my dear husband!

Sending you all much love . . .

Fritzi left the letter on a silver tray for her mother and, as the winter morning wore on, sat down to write a reply of her own. She asked Julie to use wifely persuasion in another area: Paul must write a book.

Why not? He's intelligent. His letters are lively and literate (when he takes time to put pen to paper!) — I should think many people would like to read about all the fascinating sights and events he's photographed — the difficulties and dangers he's faced and overcome. His friend Richard Harding Davis does very well with such books. Won't you convince him to make an effort? Say that if he doesn't, he will sadly disappoint his favorite cousin!

Carl smacked his fist into his fielder's glove. "All right, Fritz, let's see if you have anything left in old age."

Fritzi squinted against the afternoon sun. Across Nineteenth, a curtain moved in an upstairs window. Fritzi waved her calfskin fielder's glove, a simpering smile on her face. "Hello, Mrs. Baum, you old biddy."

She wound up and delivered the hardball with a wild curve that took it over Carl's head. He stabbed his mitt up and neatly caught it. For someone bulky and clumsy, he could be surprisingly agile. "Hey, you're not so creaky," he said, grinning.

The sun felt wonderful on Fritzi's face. The thawing earth of the side yard smelled rich and warm. They fired the ball back and forth, developing a rhythm that echoed moments in their childhood.

The ball smacked into the gloves with a clean, hard sound. Carl threw one wild pitch; Fritzi went after it in a dive and slide that dirtied her skirt. Brushing herself off, she bowed toward Mrs. Baum's window. If they arrested girls for unladylike behavior, their neighbor would be calling for the Black Maria this minute. Fritzi's dinner-table impersonations of the nosy widow made even her father laugh.

"I'm thrilled you're going to Detroit, Carl."

"Pop made a point of congratulating me last night. He's happy too." That unnerved her. Would the General feel the same about her decision to leave? Doubtful; she was female.

"I made up my mind in Baltimore, where I watched that Fiat," he went on. "I hung out with the driver and his riding mechanic for three days. I paid for so much beer I thought I'd wind up in debtor's prison. Learned a lot, though. Decided I had to drive one of those cars. Then I decided I should know how to build them too." The smack of the ball hitting leather came at shorter intervals. "I'll get a job in an auto plant, or one of the machine shops like Dodge Brothers that supply parts. There are dozens, I've studied up at librar-

76

ies. Detroit's a boomtown. What about you? Haven't given up acting, have you?"

"Never."

"I didn't expect to find you in Chicago now that Pop's back in harness."

"I've overstayed. I'm planning to do something about that."

"Tell me."

Fritzi smacked the ball into her mitt, took a deep breath and threw.

"I'm going to try Broadway."

Carl thought about that a moment, then broke into a smile. "Sure, it's the obvious place for someone as talented as you."

"It's a secret until I tell Papa."

"That won't be so easy, sis."

"Tell me something I don't know," she said with a rueful pucker of her mouth. "But I have to go, Carl. If I don't, I'll regret it always."

He kept tapping the ball into his glove as he asked, "How do you feel about it? Are you scared?"

"Terrified. All the actors I've met say New York's a cold, heartless city. But I'm unbelievably eager at the same time."

"When are you leaving?"

Fritzi felt a chill that had nothing to do with the temperature. "Right after Christmas. I've told Mama. She doesn't like it, but she won't stand in the way. Papa's the obstacle. I've promised myself I'd tell him before the holiday. I dread it."

Carl shot the ball over his shoulder onto the grass, put his brawny arm around her. "I'm not too qualified to give advice, but I will anyway. You know Pop will probably rant. He's stuck in the past in some ways. Every woman needs a wedding ring and children, that kind of thing. Well, sure — if it suits you. But I think you're kind of like me, Fritzi. A maverick — that's what they call wild steers in Texas, I read it in the *Police Gazette*. We both have different dreams. They're not like Pop's when he came to this country a poor boy eager to make a fortune. We're living in an incredible new century. All the rules have changed. Did you see that little black car that putted by a while ago? Henry Ford introduced them this year, and he's already sold more than a thousand. I pity the fellow with a buggy whip factory, because all the rules have changed. Including Pop's. So don't be talked or bullied out of your dream." He pointed at the pale sky in the east. "If your dream's there, sail out and find it."

He planted a chaste kiss on her cheek.

"Promise me you will."

"I do, Carl, I do — bless you! You give me the extra courage I need. It won't be easy facing him."

Carl ambled over to pick up the ball. He tossed it to her underhand. "Just remember, Pop respects strength. If your knees quake, don't let him see. You can do it. Hell, sis, you're an actress, aren't you? Act!"

She ran to him. "Oh, Carl. 'What impossible matter will he make easy next?' "

"Huh? What's that?"

"A line spoken by a character named Antonio,

in *The Tempest*. Act two, scene one. Fits you perfectly," she exclaimed, throwing her arms around him. With thoughtless enthusiasm Carl wrapped her in a huge hug that left her breathless and gasping, but braver and more confident than she'd felt for days.

9. Obligatory Scene

The season's frenzy consumed the household. Fritzi plunged into Christmas shopping, dashing through Marshall Field's and the Fair and Carson's in search of presents. She spent carefully from her savings, holding back forty dollars for a ticket to New York and subsistence until she found work.

Every morning Ilsa dashed off to shop, or help with children's parties at Hull House, or socialize with her wealthy friends. Nearly every night she and the General went out to a party or banquet. Joe Junior either disappeared after supper or didn't come home from work at all, leaving Carl and Fritzi to play checkers and talk for hours. Joe Junior came home long after everyone was in bed.

The Crowns attended Sunday services at St. Paul's Lutheran together, again without Joey. Nor did he join them in the music room when Fritzi played carols and the General sang in his strong baritone voice and Carl bellowed like an enthusiastic but tone-deaf steer.

Wednesday of the week before Christmas — all four Advent candles glowed on the dining table now — Fritzi went to the depot to buy a ticket on the New York Central's Empire State Express. "One way, day coach, please." She would not spend money for a berth. The Mortmain company had given her a great deal of experience with sitting up all night; she knew how to race for a seat nearest the stove, and use available newspapers for covers.

She constantly rehearsed what she wanted to say to her father, but put off the actual encounter. Joe Crown did have a temper. That fact tempted her to flee without facing him. Couldn't she resort to a letter?

No, said Ellen Terry, most emphatically:

You know that in any well-wrought drama, certain obligatory scenes must be played because everything previous leads up to them. To omit them is a cheat. It's the same in a family. Your father is not some minor character to be dismissed offstage with a few lines in a scented envelope.

The other reason you must speak to him is personal. Cowardice doesn't become members of your family, including you.

All right, she would do it Saturday, before the family left to attend the annual party for employees of the brewery. The General paid for the event every year.

She was up early that day, her stomach on fire, her palms already damp. She began to dress about four. It was a clear, cold afternoon, with a few winter stars already showing beyond her bedroom window. She struggled into her gown, red satin with a deep lace bertha. Ilsa had bought her the dress for last year's party.

Groping at the nape of her neck, she closed the clasp on the pearl dog-collar choker borrowed from her mother. Then she yanked a comb through her tangled hair. Her hair reminded her of frayed yellow rope. She threw the comb at the glass and stuck out her tongue.

A clock on the mantel of the small fireplace showed half past four. Her father had announced their departure time as six o'clock. Fritzi supposed the General would drive them to Swabian Hall in the Welch; the streets were dry.

She heard a heavy tread in the upstairs hall, ran to the door.

"Papa! You're home early."

"Yes, I managed to get away."

"Could I speak to you a moment?" Her heartbeat was thunder in her ears.

"Why, of course," he said with a benign smile. "Shall I come in?"

"It might be better if we go down to your office."

"Whatever you prefer." He offered his arm at the head of the stairs. "You look very fetching. You'll be the belle of the party."

"Hardly." Nervous, she almost stumbled twice on the long descent past the stunning Christmas tree.

In the office, Joe Crown drew the visitor's chair away from the wall. Outside, the deep blue shadows of Illinois winter shrouded the grounds. Bare tree limbs shook in a lake wind.

Fritzi sat on the forward edge of the chair, clasped her hands in her lap to keep them still. Stage fright! She couldn't remember Carl's words of encouragement.

"Now, my girl. What's on your mind?"

"Plans, Papa. I want to tell you my plans."

"Please do," he said, smiling again. He crossed his legs, folded his hands over the little paunch developing at his middle. She smelled beer along with his hair lotion. Perhaps he'd celebrated a bit at the brewery. He seemed in a fine mood.

"I'm going to New York," she said.

His forehead wrinkled. "How interesting. You're going to shop?"

"To live. To look for work in the theater."

Somewhere in the west, dying daylight broke out beneath clouds, striking the office window and painting it red. Joe Crown never changed his posture or expression. Yet Fritzi fancied the blood left his cheeks.

"I see. Well. It's good you told me."

He crossed to the door, which stood open a few inches. He closed it with a dungeon-like bang. He stood with his back to the window and his feet wide apart, like a military officer. She could see nothing but a black silhouette against a rectangle of red.

"When did you decide this, may I ask?"

"Some time ago. I bought my railway ticket Wednesday."

"Let's discuss this reasonably." He still sounded calm and, if not exactly friendly, then not antagonistic either. She was emboldened.

"With all respect, Papa, discussion isn't necessary."

"Permit me to disagree. It isn't healthy for a girl your age to venture to New York for a career in a dubious and risky profession. A career that might not exist at all."

"Carl's going to Detroit without the promise of a job. You approve of that."

"Carl is a man. It makes a difference."

"Oh, Papa. That's so old-fashioned." The challenge to his authority was blurted without thought; she was angry.

His voice remained steady, controlled: "New York's a filthy, wretched city, I've seen it many times. It's dangerous for a single woman. Go to a public theater" — he gestured energetically, warming to his case — "as innocent people went to the rooftop theater at Madison Square Garden last summer, and it's you and not Stanford White who might be shot down by a jealous madman. It simply isn't safe, Fritzi. Please reconsider."

He was adamant. Well, so was she:

"I've considered it carefully, Papa. I'm just informing you as a courtesy."

"How thoughtful," he replied, with real rancor.

"You know Broadway is the only theater that matters. If I don't find out whether I can succeed there, I'll hate myself the rest of my life."

Joe Crown peered out the window, his profile etched by red light. "Please understand, Fritzi, I'm not arguing to be difficult, or have my own way." *Oh, no?*

He held out his small, well-manicured hands, pleading. "I want the best for you. A husband. A home. Children."

"I'm hardly the kind of raving beauty a man's going to marry."

"You underrate yourself, terribly. You'll find someone. Perhaps you mustn't set your sights so high. In any case, a young woman of good character belongs —"

She jumped up. "*Kirche, Küche, Kinder?* Papa, that was your century. This is mine. My life."

"Your life! You must regard it very cheaply if you insist on consorting with low theatrical people."

His voice had risen. Fritzi clenched her hands. The scene was veering out of control. "How can you say that? You're the one who gave me permission to join the Mortmain company."

"Touring the South — a section of the country far safer than New York." He hooked a finger in his collar and jerked, a sign of his agitation. "I thought a year or two on the road would cure your ambition. You'd see the sordid lives of actors, most of whom fail to achieve anything significant. You'd endure wretched conditions for a while, and then your eyes would open and you'd give it up."

"You really thought that when you let me go?"

"Yes."

"You didn't support me? You deliberately sent me out to fail?"

He took hold of her red satin sleeves. "Please calm down."

She wrenched free. "I'm not a child, to be patronized and pacified. You keep making that mistake." Her color was high, her forehead hot, her stomach unbearably painful.

"No, you misunderstand. I repeat, I want nothing but the best for you. When you left, I thought you were foolish, misguided. But I felt that trying to reason with you was futile. I did *not* send you out to fail, only to get the theater out of your system. It appears I'm the one who failed. I must try again. I beg you not to go. New York is a cesspool of criminals, radicals, pseudo-intellectuals with their Ivy League noses in the air. And those damned new women with their short hair! I've seen photos of them strutting in trousers and neckties and derby hats. Some of them even flaunt cigars and pipes. In public! I don't want you going that way."

"Papa, that's ridiculous. I won't."

"You're a lovely girl" — she avoided his eyes — "but emotional. At this moment I would say slightly hysterical. Let me be plain. If you persist with this mad idea, you'll incur my deep displeasure."

But she already had, it was evident in the set of his mouth, the crow's feet around his eyes. She marched to him in two quick strides, confronted him without blinking.

"Then what, Papa? You'll disown me?"

"I dislike your tone of voice."

"I'm sorry, I'm a grown woman. I'll always be your daughter, but I'm not your slave."

"I forbid you to go. I forbid it!"

The office had grown dark as a cave; the last red light was gone, and the stars were strewn high on the other side of the glass, which vibrated in the lake wind.

"You have nothing to say about it, Papa. Goodbye."

Fritzi was almost in tears. She dashed out, giving the office door a mighty slam. It was a splendid curtain cue, for a play. The difference was, when a play ended, there were no consequences.

10. Eastbound

"*Liebchen,* don't do this," Ilsa said. Fritzi threw stockings and underwear into the muslin-covered tray of her steamer trunk. It was a fine old trunk, basswood covered in canvas and reinforced with top, bottom, and side slats. It bore the scars of her years of one-night engagements: grease marks that wouldn't surrender to repeated scrubbing, deep dents in the brass corner bumpers.

"I'm going, Mama. He despises me."

"You're wrong, it's only the acting. And the thought of you alone in New York."

"What's the difference? That's what I am, an actress. Actresses belong in New York." She stuffed a pair of shoes into her brown leather bag on the bed. A slot under the handle held a wrinkled card she'd inscribed with care, in ink, in 1901:

Miss Frederica CROWN

❧

MORTMAIN'S
Royal Shakespeare Combination

Birmingham ALABAMA

Ilsa wrung her hands, clearly desperate for a new avenue of argument. Outside Fritzi's window the sunless sky had a murky, menacing look. "Papa hasn't said three words to me since the party night before last. He's avoided me around the house. I never spent a worse Sunday. I'll be on the four o'clock train."

"Fritzi, it's *Heiligabend*. Christmas Eve. We gather together, Papa lights the candles on the tree —"

"I'll celebrate by myself. He can't change, Mama. Or grant me the right to live my own life — to fail, if that's the outcome. Which it will not be, I promise. Papa's reverting to his old self. He orders everyone about according to what he thinks is right, and when they don't obey like dutiful little soldiers he rejects them, freezes them out with his glaring and huffing."

"I'll admit your papa is a complicated man. Difficult to live with sometimes."

"Difficult? The word is *impossible*. I should have left months ago, as soon as he recovered."

"Is there nothing I can do to change your mind?"

"Nothing. Carl's taking me to the depot, you won't have to bother."

"Bother? You are my child, my only girl."

"Well, don't worry, your only girl will be fine in New York City." Fritzi said it with much more confidence than she felt. She yanked the leather bag open and folded a skirt into the bottom, lined with buff-colored leather.

Ilsa dabbed her eyes with her handkerchief. "I have gifts for you."

"Mine are under the tree. There's a plaid muffler for Papa, I'm sure he'll burn it or throw it in the trash."

"You judge him too severely."

"I don't think so."

"You must take your presents. Wait."

Fritzi went on packing. Moments later Ilsa returned with two white boxes, a large one imprinted with the name of the Fair Store and a smaller one, about six inches square, from Field's.

"Here, open them. Please."

Giving her mother a look that mingled affection and melancholy, Fritzi pulled the red ribbon off the larger box, unfolded the tissue paper.

"Oh, Mama, how handsome."

"A winter coat. You need a new heavy coat whether you're here or in that terrible city."

Fritzi lifted it by the shoulders, admiring it. The coat was dark brown cheviot, with a small black and brown plaid. The body of the coat buttoned all the way down the front with pearl buttons. The lining was bright yellow silk. A velvet collar ornamented the double-breasted cape.

"I guessed at the length, sixty inches," Ilsa said.

Fritzi held it against herself, secretly pleased. If her father had given it to her she'd have refused it, but she could compromise herself because it was from her mother. She was sensible enough not to want to freeze all winter; her old coat had been bought for the milder South.

"Perhaps the other gift will be useful as well."

Fritzi opened the Field's box, discovered two white pads nested there. She poked one; it was stuffed with a spongy material. Ilsa said, "They call them gay deceivers. You pin them inside your —"

"Yes, Mama, I get the idea."

"You really don't need them, of course."

Fritzi dropped the pads into the trunk tray and hugged her mother. "You're terrible with fibs. Of course I need them. Thank you."

Holding the embrace, she felt tears welling, forced them back. When sentimentality, or the uncertainty of her future, prompted her to start unpacking again, she only needed to imagine the face of Joe Crown as he turned away from her at the brewery party. It put iron back into her spine.

At the depot, amid travelers setting out on holiday journeys, Fritzi said goodbye to Carl and her mother. She was wearing her new brown coat and a scarf tied over her hat to protect her ears. Under one arm she had a round tin of Ilsa's *Pfefferkuchen,* ginger-flavored Christmas cookies in the shape of stars and hearts and rings.

A freezing wind blew through the train shed, dispersing the steam billowing from under the cars. Carl walked up the platform to deliver her trunk and leather bag to the freight car. Ilsa said, "You must let me know at once that you are safe and settled. Telegraph collect."

"I will if you insist, Mama."

"Yes, otherwise I won't sleep for weeks. Oh! Hat pins! Do you have enough hat pins? In case you're molested on the street?"

Fritzi laughed. "Yes, I have a supply."

"Then I have one more thing to give you." From Ilsa's handbag came a sealed white envelope. Fritzi turned the envelope in her gloved hand.

"What's this?"

"One hundred dollars."

Fritzi shook her head. "No, I can't. I am going to succeed in New York without taking one cent of Papa's money."

"This comes from me," Ilsa protested.

"Take it back, Mama." Fritzi held out the envelope. "If you don't, I'll put it in Carl's pocket when he isn't looking. Or I'll give it to a stranger."

"Oh, please, *liebchen* — don't hate your papa so much."

"I don't hate him. But I'm going to prove I'm old enough, and brave enough, to take the worst New York has to offer, and succeed." What she said was impulsive bravado. Another hundred dollars would sustain her for a long time. Her anger and resentment just wouldn't permit her to take it.

Carl returned. They all hugged and kissed and said their farewells. Inside the day coach, Fritzi pressed her forehead against the cold glass and waved a handkerchief as the Empire State Express pulled out.

Ilsa disappeared in the steam. Burly Carl ran beside the moving train, waving his cap until he was left behind. The Express headed south to go around the bottom of Lake Michigan. Winter darkness was already settling on the land.

Fritzi had never been by herself on Christmas. Even touring, she'd had the boozy companionship of other actors. She tried not to think about it.

But it was hard. Village depots and main streets passed by, warmly lit like toy towns. At a level crossing, three farm children dragging a fresh-cut Christmas tree waved at the train. Later, Fritzi glimpsed a family through a window, gathered around a pump organ. She averted her head.

The conductor stopped by her seat. "Ticket, ma'am." He was a round, avuncular man, no happier to be working on Christmas Eve than she was to be traveling. "New York City," he said, clicking his punch to perforate the ticket. "Live there?"

"I will when I arrive," Fritzi said with a smile.

"Dining car's forward. Roast turkey and roast goose tonight."

"Thank you." She had no intention of paying for an expensive meal. She'd dine from the tin of *Pfefferkuchen* on the seat beside her.

The vast winter dark swallowed the train. Its whistle trailed across bleak fields like a mourner's cry. She tried to read a pro-suffrage article in a *Ladies' Home Journal* but couldn't concentrate. She speculated about the other eight passengers scattered throughout the car. That red-faced man, was he a tinware or button salesman hurrying home to his family? The woman with her two noisy boys, was she a young widow? And the swarthy gentleman in the green plaid suit across the aisle? He had large, powerful hands; could he be a circus aerialist? Perhaps an unemployed musician? She noticed a mouth organ in his breast pocket.

East of Toledo, snow began to fall. Wind rose to storm strength, and before long the Express reduced its speed. Evidently it had been snowing heavily up ahead. As the engine swung around a curve Fritzi saw its headlight stabbing through the raging storm. Drifts were building.

Half an hour later, with the drifts growing higher, the train chugged onto a siding and stopped. The conductor came through.

"Track's blocked. Have to wait here for a work engine to plow us out. By the way, folks, it was midnight five minutes ago. Merry Christmas."

He sneezed into a handkerchief and shuffled on. Dread and loneliness crushed Fritzi.

Ellen Terry reprimanded her:

Come, girl. Cowardice doesn't become you. This is a great adventure — of your own devising, may I remind you.

Across the aisle, the swarthy man rattled the pages of a *Chicago American.* "I beg your pardon," Fritzi said. "Do you play that harmonica?"

"Some," he said in a strange accent.

"Do you know 'One-Horse Open Sleigh'?"

He played the first twelve notes. " 'Jingle Bells.' "

"Well, I grew up calling it 'One-Horse Open Sleigh.' It's terrible sitting here on Christmas like mourners at a funeral. Will you play it?"

"Okay," he said with a cheerful display of white teeth. He tipped his soft hat. "Aristopoulous my name. Christos Aristopoulous. New to this country five years ago."

"Like it?"

"Just fine."

"Good."

"I am going to New York to meet my sweetheart, Athena, she come from Piraeus on big boat. We marry."

"Congratulations. I hope you'll both be very happy. Will you play?"

She sang with him. The rowdy little boys ran back and joined in. Soon the whole car was singing.

They sang "God Rest Ye Merry, Gentlemen." They sang carols for half an hour, all except the button salesman, who folded his arms, Scrooge-like in his scorn. The dining car opened and dispensed free coffee and cocoa. Fritzi slept a little, thankful for the new coat. Around five A.M. a work train with a plow on the engine rumbled past from the west, opening the right-of-way.

The sun came up cold and dazzling over the white fields. Looking out the window at the horizon, she could see for miles. She'd survived the night, thrown off her gloom. She could take the worst that New York had to offer and defeat it. So she thought early on Christmas morning, 1906, without the benefit of experience.

PART TWO

STRIVING

And do not say 'tis superstition . . .
      — SHAKESPEARE, *The Winter's Tale*

We're going to expand this company, and you will see that it will grow by leaps and bounds. The proper system, as I have it in mind, is to get the car to the multitude.

      — HENRY FORD

11. Adrift in New York

In the spring of 1908, the New York papers announced a return engagement of one of the great ladies of the stage, Mrs. Patrick Campbell. She had launched her American tour at the Lyric Theater the preceding fall, then toured coast to coast for twenty-six weeks, traveling with her company in a private train. "The immortal Stella" would conclude the tour with a farewell week at the Lyric, again playing Hedda Gabler, the Electra of Sophocles, and the title role in Pinero's *The Second Mrs. Tanqueray*, the play that had scandalized the West End and propelled her to stardom in 1893.

Fritzi had seen most of the great women of the stage, from the young and beautiful Ethel Barrymore to the old and wooden-legged Sarah Bernhardt, and of course her idol, Ellen Terry. Last November she'd gotten to the box office too late; the run was sold out. She vowed to see the great lady this time, even if she went hungry to buy the ticket.

Which, as a matter of fact, she did.

At ten A.M. on a Monday morning in May, in response to an audition notice in the *Dramatic Mirror*, Fritzi climbed the stair of a building on Sixteenth Street a few doors from Union Square West. Her destination was the office of one of the casting agents scattered throughout the neighborhood. She didn't like casting agents;

most were venal, and tended to take liberties with women. They shoved the same question-naire into her hand time after time. *Parts played? Wardrobe owned? Sing or dance? Learn lines fast?* If a producer cast you, the agent took a third to a half of the first week's salary and thought he was doing you a great favor.

So far agents had done her no favors; she'd au-ditioned for scores of parts without landing a role. At the Mehlman agency this morning she read for a new drama by Edward Sheldon called *Salvation Nell*, soon to open. Eleven other ac-tresses read for the same small part, eighteen lines. Mehlman didn't even bother with the courtesy of taking each into a room by herself; they all huddled together in his rehearsal studio. The most brazen performance was given by a redhead with breasts the size of cantaloupes. Mehlman beamed as the redhead emoted two feet from his chair, leaning forward to be sure he noticed her assets. At the end of an hour and a half — surprise! — Mehlman asked the redhead to stay and told the others to go.

She had another reading scheduled in the af-ternoon; perhaps that one would be better. At least the agent had telephoned to ask that she ap-pear.

But she couldn't help feeling discouraged. All she had to show for more than a year of effort was a walk-on as a supernumerary, fifty cents a night, in a flop called *The Mongol's Bride*. It had lasted one week. She hadn't even reached the lowest rung of the acting ladder, utility player. For that you had to speak a few lines.

During much of her sixteen months in New York, Fritzi had supported herself as a waitress at a cheery restaurant called the Dutch Mill. She liked the owner, who permitted her time off to audition. She was strong enough to handle the long hours and heavy trays. She objected only to the silly starched Dutch girl hat with wings that she had to wear, along with wooden shoes that caused corns.

Unfortunately, the Dutch Mill's owner was elderly. Just in March he'd decided to retire and move in with his daughter in Virginia. The new owner immediately converted the restaurant to a five-cent theater, or nickelodeon as the contemptible places were being called. Fritzi was thrown back on the streets she'd tramped for weeks before finding the waitress job.

She'd recently gotten a new position, night chambermaid at the Bleecker House, a seedy hotel in the theater district. The hotel manager, Mr. Oliver Merkle, was no gentleman. He was in fact a slimy specimen, representing to Fritzi all that was repulsive and frightening about New York. The female staff referred to him as Ollie the Octopus or, alternatively, Oh-Oh — the cry of alarm when they saw him coming.

At two o'clock she sat on a bench in the waiting room belonging to Shorty Lorenz, a little blond wart of a man who'd been married seven times. Crowded on the benches or standing nervously were six other young women, all strangers but one; Fritzi recognized a tiny, pale girl with black bangs whom she'd seen at other readings. Pauline Something. Pauline gave her a glance without recognition.

Shorty Lorenz breezed into the room at two-fifteen clutching a batch of sides which he handed out. "Okey-dokey, girls, this here's a society drama called *Shall We Divorce?* The producer is Brutus Brown." There were a few gasps, and a provocative sigh from the tiny girl. Brown was a noted philanderer.

"His stage manager's inside," Lorenz said. "He'll hear you one at a time. The part's Allyson, the sister of the divorcing husband. She's kinda high-strung, has one pretty good scene, four pages. Take five minutes, look it over, we'll start with Miss Abrams."

Fritzi was third to read for the paunchy stage manager, who had a face like granite. He sat in the middle of the audition room in a straight chair. Shorty Lorenz read the male part, Allyson's brother. Fritzi stumbled over words — the playwright's diction was clumsy — and pitched her voice too high; she made a mess of the reading. At the end, however, the granite face cracked and the stage manager shook her hand with a fatherly smile.

"What's your name again?"

"Fritzi Crown."

"Nice reading, Fritzi. We'll phone you tonight if we want you to come back."

"Thank you, sir."

Lorenz called Pauline next. She breezed past Fritzi as if Fritzi were invisible, and of no consequence in the competition.

That evening Fritzi sat in the second-to-last

row of the Lyric Theater's upper balcony. Her ticket had cost sixty-five cents, fifteen cents more than usual. Orchestra seats were five dollars; not one was empty. Only stars of the magnitude of Mrs. Patrick Campbell could inflate prices and fill a house.

The Second Mrs. Tanqueray was hurtling toward its conclusion. Mrs. Pat had made her tragic fourth-act exit moments ago. Paula Tanqueray had been undone by her past — a revelation that she'd once "kept house" with an army officer who later formed a romantic attachment with Tanqueray's daughter from a first marriage. The daughter rushed on stage and cried, *"I've seen her! It's horrible!"*

Tanqueray's bachelor friend recoiled. *"She — she has — ?"*

"Killed herself? Yes — yes! — so everybody will say."

Fritzi felt faint, whether from excitement or starvation, she didn't know. Since Sunday midnight she'd had only weak tea and some stale kaiser rolls thrown out by the dining room of the hotel where she worked. She preferred not to eat before readings. Hunger sharpened a performance, while too much food made an actor sluggish. She hadn't eaten after the Lorenz reading because she couldn't afford it.

Tanqueray's daughter wrung her hands. *"But — I know I helped to kill her —"*

Fritzi strained forward. There wasn't a sound, a stir, anywhere but the lighted drawing room far below.

"— if only I'd been more merciful!"

The daughter fainted gracefully onto the ottoman. The audience gasped.

The bachelor friend hesitated, then strode to the open door and gazed out, his face and stance perfectly conveying consternation, and horror. . . .

A red velvet curtain flew across, ending the play.

Fritzi's pulse raced; her temples throbbed. She'd seen great ladies of the stage but never a more sensitive or commanding performance than Mrs. Pat's.

The electric foots brightened on the curtain. The orchestra, the boxes, the whole theater, exuded a sense of pressure mounting like steam in a cooker. The curtain flew open again. One by one the actors ran down to the footlights as the pressure erupted in thundering applause.

Lined up on the apron, the supporting cast parted in the middle. A blazing circle of blue-white light struck between them. The star entered through the veranda doors upstage. Everyone was up, yelling and applauding.

When Mrs. Pat reached the blue-white circle and stepped in, waves of sound beat on the walls and frescoed ceiling. The galleryites around Fritzi whistled and stomped and threw empty sandwich wrappers over the rail; no one up there could afford the calla lilies or glads or orchids flying over the footlights from the orchestra.

"Bravo, bravo!"

Mrs. Pat was a tall, pale, long-necked woman of forty-two, with cascades of dark hair and big glowing eyes inherited from her Italian mother. She was literally dazzling in a red-orange gown covered with gold sequins. She had the star quality that riveted every eye to her smallest move; in scenes with other actors she simply made them vanish.

A man rushed from the wings with a dozen red roses. Mrs. Pat took them, smiled, and bowed again. The entire cast bowed together and left the stage. Of course Mrs. Pat had to return, hand in hand with her co-star. She and Mr. Webster bowed. Then he retired, giving the stage to her with a wave and a smile. Mrs. Pat stayed in the circle of the carbon arc, calmly gazing around the theater, graciously smiling to acknowledge the love she heard in the ovation. Fritzi clapped so enthusiastically, her palms hurt.

As the applause diminished, Mrs. Pat raised her hand in farewell, stepped back. The scarlet curtain closed. The carbon-arc spotlight burned a moment longer, as if in tribute. Then it blinked out and the house came up full.

The gallery crowd began a stampede to the exits. A precious program in her hand, Fritzi shoved and elbowed like an experienced New Yorker. Broken peanut shells crackled under her shoes. Her left foot hurt because of a pea-sized darn in her stocking. She still couldn't sew.

She descended the steep staircase to the beautiful marble lobby, crowded with men in evening clothes, women in furs or gold cloaks with linings of colored satin. It was impossible to tell whether the people were genuinely rich or just

"Astorbilts" — gauche pretenders. Either way, they pointed up the poverty of her own appearance. Her high-top button shoes were cheap. So was her gray melton walking skirt and her percale shirtwaist, the white and blue stripes laundered into a gray sameness. Her straw sailor hat was out of season and out of style. Her only decent article of clothing was the brown winter coat from her mother.

Outside, rain pelted Forty-second Street. She'd have to trudge home in that, all the way down to First Avenue near Eighth Street. Paying for public transportation was out of the question.

Under the marquee, whose hundreds of electric bulbs contributed to the dazzle of the white-light district, she secured her hat with a pin and opened her umbrella. Walking east, she passed the Belasco, then Hammerstein's Victoria at the corner of Times Square. It had been Longacre Square until the newspaper moved uptown and built its pink granite tower over the new subway station. Gaudy electric signs hawked SAPOLIO SOAP, KELLOGG'S CORN FLAKES, ARROW COLLARS.

Horse-drawn cabs and chugging autos with flickering kerosene headlamps filled the night with noise and a miasma of manure and gasoline. White plumes spouted from steam cars. Obnoxious klaxons sounded on little black autos that sped among the others like aggressive bugs — "taxi-meter" cabs, the latest import from Paris.

After a long walk to lower First Avenue, she

saw light under her landlady's door, knocked softly.

"I'm sorry to disturb you this late, Mrs. Perella."

"Not to worry, was just reading the paper." Mrs. Perella was a Neapolitan woman of fierce visage but good heart. She liked Fritzi, was tolerant about late rent payments, and took messages on the downstairs hall telephone without complaint.

Hesitant, Fritzi asked, "Did I have any messages this evening?"

Mrs. Perella shook her head, saw Fritzi's disappointment, and gently squeezed her hand. Fritzi thanked her and trudged upstairs.

Her room at the third-floor front was large, but that was about all you could say for it. Even with the jets unlit it smelled of gas; the building hadn't been modernized.

Weary and damp, she hung her sailor hat and coat in the wardrobe. Leaning in the back corner was her tennis racket, a 1905 birthday gift from her parents. The ash frame was beveled, the cedar handle finely scored for a good grip; it must have cost ten dollars at least. Carefully brought to New York in her steamer trunk, it had stood untouched since she unpacked. Lawn tennis was a game for those who didn't have to count pennies.

An elevated train rumbled, approaching from the south. Fritzi pulled the blind. The train went by in a roar and rush of sound; lighted car windows threw patterns across the blind, black-yellow, black-yellow. The floor shook. The pitcher on the washstand danced. She was used to it.

She lit the gas mantle near a crazed mirror and with much reaching and wiggling unfastened the buttons at the back of her shirtwaist. To dress and undress, a single woman needed a maid, a lover, or the talents of a contortionist.

She pulled the waist off sleeve by sleeve. She laid her skirt on top of it on the bed. Underneath her chemise she wore a one-piece undergarment combining drawers and a brassiere top with fancy lace around neck and armholes. Looking at the ceiling, she reached under and unpinned her gay deceivers.

She put on a cotton robe and stretched on the bed, reliving the evening. Mrs. Pat's performance had produced great excitement while Fritzi was in the theater, but in retrospect it was disheartening. She brooded about her gallery seat and the magic circle of the arc light. The physical distance between them was not great, but for an aspiring actress the gulf was very nearly infinite.

What did it take to leap from one place to the other? She was still searching for the secret. What if she never discovered it? What if she woke up to find her dream nothing more than an adolescent delusion she should have abandoned long ago?

She hardly dared think about that.

12. Fritzi and Oh-Oh

"Try one," Maisie whispered.

Fritzi said, "I've only smoked cigarettes a few times. I don't like them much."

"Don't be a stick. These are special." She showed the colorful packet. "Parfum de Paree. That means scent of Paris."

It was fifteen minutes until midnight, a day after Mrs. Pat's performance. The Bleecker House on West Forty-seventh was quiet — nothing to be heard but the distant creak of the old elevator cage. The dingy hall smelled of dust, cigar butts in sand urns, the washing solution the Bleecker seemed to use by the tanker load. Fritzi was used to more frenetic evenings: doors banging, couples checking out at two A.M., whimpers and moans and strident oaths from the closed bedchambers. During a typical night she not only did routine dusting of the hall furniture and fixtures, she jumped from room to room cleaning up washstands and commodes, righting overturned chairs, whipping on fresh bed linen to replace that bearing evidence of recent carnality. She was never bothered by these signs of passion, only bemused and, sometimes, a little envious.

Maisie Budwigg had come down to the third floor from her station on four. It was against the rules, but the maids often ignored that. Fritzi was grateful for a respite.

"Well, come on," Maisie urged.

"Mrs. Patrick Campbell smokes perfumed cigarettes. They're very stylish," Fritzi mused, weakening. "Aren't they expensive?"

"I'll say. A guest gave me these. A little reward for a special service." Maisie winked. Poor Maisie — so hefty and homely, she had to give her favors away.

"All right, I'll try one."

"We better go in here. I saw the boss prowling a while ago."

They hid in a roomy linen closet, the door shut, the bare bulb flickering. Taking matches from her apron pocket, Maisie lit two cigarettes. The closet was quickly filled with smoke and an indefinable floral odor. Fritzi took a puff. She didn't draw the smoke past her mouth, but it was enough to start her hacking and wheezing.

"These things can't be good for your voice —" she began.

The door opened, startling her. The cigarette hanging on Maisie's lower lip fell to the floor as she looked over Fritzi's shoulder.

"Oh-oh."

"I thought I smelled smoke," Oliver Merkle cried. He jumped into the closet and did a wild Spanish dance on Maisie's cigarette. "For God's sake, what's wrong with you? We'll have a holocaust." Since the floor was linoleum, that was unlikely, but Fritzi quickly scuffed her own Parfum de Paree under her heel. A new aroma now dominated — the whiskey the hotel manager consumed in quantity.

Merkle thrust his head forward and dry-washed his hands. "I won't stand for malingering." He grabbed Fritzi's arm. "You come along to my office. I'll deal with you later, Miss Budwigg."

Fritzi said, "I'd prefer to discuss it here, sir."

"You'll discuss it where I say."

Maisie gave Fritzi a look; both knew she was in for more than a reprimand. "I'm the one who lured Fritzi in here to smoke," Maisie began. But Merkle had already about-faced, gesturing like a general. His pop eyes roved over Fritzi as she passed on her way to the stairs.

On the ground floor, Merkle strutted into his office ahead of her. After Fritzi entered, he slammed the door with a flourish. She listened for the click of the key. Hearing it, she steeled herself.

Merkle casually touched her, gave her a smarmy smile as he walked to his desk, perching on a corner. "Miss Crown — Fritzi. You realize we have rules in this hostelry, don't you? Without rules we'd have disorder." Fritzi thought of certain nights when the slamming doors sounded like a gun battle in progress. She deemed it wiser not to remind him.

"I'm very sorry. Please don't lay the blame on Maisie. I consented to join her in the closet."

"Blame? Who's talking about blame? We can work this out. You're an intelligent girl, not like that cow."

"Sir, Maisie is a decent, hardworking —"

"Nuts. She gives it away to any two-bit drummer or washed-up actor who asks." On a sideboard under a stern lithograph of William

Jennings Bryan, the perennial Democratic candidate for president, Merkle kept liquor decanters and glasses. He poured two whiskeys, offered her one.

"No, thank you, I can't."

"Why not?"

Quickly she said, "I'm reading for an agent in the morning." It was a convenient fib to shorten the encounter.

"Oh, right, I forgot, you're a famous star in disguise." He set both glasses on the desk and moved close. "You've committed a serious offense, Fritzi. We have to work things out." He stroked the sleeve of her black bombazine dress. "Are you willing to work things out?"

"Mr. Merkle, please take your hand away."

Blowing his boozy breath in her face, he closed his fingers on her sleeve; the pain almost buckled her knees.

"Mr. Merkle, let go."

"I'm giving you a chance. You'd better take it." Holding her forearms, he thrust against her. His pop eyes fluttered shut. Fritzi felt something stiff poking her apron.

She had no hat pin for defense, only her athletic strength. She yanked her arms down and lunged backward. When her right hand came free, she swung her open palm into his face. It rocked him, giving her time to speed to the door, unlock it with a twist of the key.

"Goddamn you, change your clothes and get out. You're fired! You take so much as a rag out of this hotel, I'll have you arrested."

White and shaking, she wanted to run. Something compelled her to face him and say, "Mr. Merkle, do you know your nickname in the hotel?"

His pop eyes appeared to vibrate in his head. "Do I want to hear this?"

"Everyone calls you Ollie the Octopus. I'd say that's an insult to octopuses. Octopi."

"Get out of my sight!" he screamed. "Try to find another job good as this one. You won't. You'll be humping for pennies like your fat friend."

She couldn't think of another retort, so she shot her head forward and dry-washed her hands in a perfect imitation of him. Merkle turned red and made gobbling sounds. *"You — you —"*

Fritzi fled, caroming off the night clerk rushing down the hall in response to the noise. *Lord, what have I done?*

She left the Bleecker House bedeviled by thoughts of a small rectangular box, tin, hidden in a drawer in her room. Originally the box had contained lemon drops. Now it held all the money she had left — four dollars and change.

In the morning, as she went out to buy a newspaper, Mrs. Perella was waiting by the newel post. The landlady murmured softly about *"la pigione."* The rent. Fritzi promised a partial payment, two dollars, by nightfall. Mrs. Perella murmured, *"Bèllo, bravo."* Beautiful, excellent. "All my tenants should be as good as you."

Fritzi searched the columns and that day answered ads for three positions. Dishwasher — she was too well educated. Typewriter in an

111

insurance office — her typing speed was too slow. "Artist's model." The grubby room overlooking the Bowery was obviously a front for something else, probably unsavory. The "agent" had pimples and the eyes of a ferret. Merkle and now this; she fled.

That night she paid Mrs. Perella, reducing the content of the tin box by half. Next day she walked to a shop on Second Avenue to pawn her tennis racket. She had surrendered it to the gnomish owner once before.

"One dollar," the pawnbroker said, starting to write her ticket.

"Mr. Isidor, it was a dollar-fifty last time."

"I know, Fritzi, but that was a year ago. Things depreciate."

"I surely hope you won't sell it. I intend to redeem it as soon as I can."

He patted her hand. "I believe you. One dollar."

"I'll take it."

She went up to Forty-seventh and peered through the lobby window of the Bleecker House. The dreaded Merkle being nowhere visible, she went in. The day clerk, a friend, told her that within an hour of Fritzi's dismissal Maisie had likewise gotten sacked. She hadn't taken it well, had in fact bashed Merkle with an iron skillet from the kitchen.

"The night cook was cleaning up when she asked for it. Soon as he found out why she wanted it, he took it back and gave her a heavier one. Coppers from the precinct came around, but Maisie had already left town to visit relatives in Wyoming." He winked. "That's what we told 'em, anyway. Merkle can't help them. He's in a Yonkers hospital for an indefinite stay."

So she wouldn't be seeing Maisie again. Fritzi was sorry; she liked the fat girl.

She sat in Union Square in the pleasant afternoon sunshine. The dying day washed the square in pale yellows and umbers. Paper trash and pigeon droppings and peanut hulls collected at her feet. The air rang with the curses of cabmen, the clatter of buried traction chains, the neighing of horses, the chanting of newsboys, the violins and squeeze boxes of corner musicians, the horns of taxis, the popping of gasoline engines, clamorous voices speaking foreign tongues — all the music of New York that she loved. Today she didn't hear it. She was busy marking ads.

On a nearby path a man shouted, "I need four supers." He held up four fingers. "Pay is sixty cents." Fritzi guessed the stranger was one of the freelances called super captains. They worked the square around this time every day, rounding up supernumeraries for evening performances.

Fritzi had disliked her work as a super in *The Mongol's Bride*. It wasn't acting; supers never rehearsed. They showed up for costumes and minimal instructions thirty-five minutes before curtain. Most didn't know or care what play they were in. Many were lowlifes who needed drinking money, and the super captains weren't much better.

It was no time to be choosy, though. She raised her hand.

The man came to her bench. He wore an old but clean corduroy jacket and pants, a blue railroad bandanna knotted in the open throat of a work shirt. In his thirties, he had a pleasant face, deeply lined. He tipped his cap.

"Hello, dear. Earl's my name." His eyes were oddly unsettling, a strange light brown, gold-speckled.

"Are you hiring for a performance tonight?"

"Yes, but I can only use gents. Sorry." He smiled. He had a wide mouth, allowing a display of large teeth of spectacular perfection and whiteness. Though his smile made him attractive in a rough way, somehow he scared her.

Looking Fritzi up and down, he said, "I haven't seen you before. Been missing something. I don't do this work regularly, you understand."

"I don't do it at all if I can help it." She started to edge away.

He followed. "Actress, are you?" She nodded, kept moving. "Care to join me for a beer after I round up my four?"

"No, thank you." She spun and hurried off.

When she glanced back, he was coming after her, scowling — offended by her refusal. Others were looking at him; he stopped, yelled after her:

"Go walk the streets, slut, I don't give a damn." He pivoted and went off the other way. "Four here, I need four tonight."

She ran for two blocks before slowing and

looking back. Why had the man upset her so? Something about his eyes, his angry insistence —

Or was she reacting too strongly, unnerved by her encounters with Oh-Oh and the Bowery "agent"? Without knowing the answer, she was thankful to escape the stranger and have New York's teeming crowds around her, hiding her.

13. Smash-up

In the twenty-second lap, Artie Flugel in the little Mason deliberately whipped into a skid ahead of Carl, spewing dust over Carl's windscreen and blinding him. It was a dangerous trick of experienced drivers. Artie wanted to win not only the purse but a five-dollar side bet with Carl.

Coming out of the turn in a thick tan cloud, Carl took the middle of the straightaway by instinct alone. The dust blew away; the grandstand and pits loomed in the sunshine. Three more laps to catch Artie, who was already sprinting into the next turn, toward the backstretch. Through the oil-specked lenses of his second-hand Zeiss goggles, Carl saw spectators sitting on the white rail fence at the turn beyond the stands. Damn fools.

The track was in a northern suburb of Detroit. The race was the closing event of the day, a hot, dry Sunday in early summer. Carl worked six days a week at Henry Ford's auto plant, and on the seventh day he raced.

Today, four earlier races had rutted the track and torn out chunks of the hard soil the drivers called gumbo. A piece of it flew up over the radiator and hit the windscreen, cracking it. Above the engine roar Carl heard his riding mechanic yell. It might have been, "Lord Jesus," or "Oh, God," because a chunk of flying gumbo could smash goggles and put out a driver's eye. This piece luckily glanced away to the right, gone.

Four cars remained in the race, a Peugeot, a National, Artie's Mason, and Carl's Edmunds Special with lightning bolts painted on the cowl. The Peugeot and National were a lap and a half behind; they had no chance. Carl was on Artie's tail, battling for the lead.

By now the race was taking its toll. His rear end hurt, and his legs were killing him, not only cramped but aching from working the accelerator and clutch pedal up and down, up and down, every few seconds. Carl looked like a mummy: long-sleeved shirt, leather gauntlets, leather helmet, goggles, chamois face mask. Underneath his shirt hot, itchy burlap wrapped his chest and belly to help absorb the severe vibration of the frame. It came through the wheel to his gloved hands, his arms, and his shoulders.

The first sections of the crowded grandstand flashed by on his right. Seated to his left, Jesse, his mechanic, was constantly in motion, peering at the gas and oil gauges, pumping up the gas pressure to spurt gas to the front carburetor from the rear tank, watching the four smooth rubber tires, especially the rear ones. They'd already changed two tires in the pit halfway through the race. Jesse also kept a lookout behind, signaling Carl if someone wanted to pass. The signal was one tap on Carl's left knee. With all the noise, shouting and being understood was impossible.

Halfway past the grandstand now, clocking something like fifty mph. On the fence rail at the turn coming up, amid people wearing drab clothes, something bright white shone. Artie

Flugel roared out of sight into the far back turn. Carl shoved the accelerator pedal down. Jesse tapped his knee frantically, twice. *Tire going.*

Carl looked at Jesse for a second. Jesse stabbed a finger over his right shoulder. Right rear. It always took the worst beating.

He knew he should slow down for the turn, but Artie was already showing him too much dust, and driving was more than a friendly sport, it was a game of high risks. Carl roared into the turn high up on the track near the fence where all those people roosted like crows on a wire. Jesse shouted another warning an instant before the rear tire blew like a Fourth of July torpedo.

Carl pushed his cars, took chances. This time, as the Special began to slew and slide, he knew he'd guessed wrong. The Special headed straight for the fence sitters, who were screaming and scrambling and trying to get down, get away, but couldn't, not fast enough.

As the Special hurtled toward the fence through the sun-bright dust, Carl experienced a strange, suspended moment, the kind of moment that had come to him in tight places before. He was scared, terrified, but it was an exhilarating kind of fright — nearly unendurable, but if you survived it, if you tricked fate one more time, the fear would be followed by a giddy pride — fast breathing, laughter at nothing — when you walked away from the car. This time, unless he did something fast, he and Jesse wouldn't walk away.

If he drove into the fence, a lot of people would die. At the fence's far end, hay bales were banked in the turn. Carl yanked the wheel over left, stood on the brake. The rear end juddered and slid. The Special just cleared the end of the fence, where all the spectators were diving for their lives. Carl shouted a pointless "Hang on, Jess" as the Special hit the hay bales, burst through, slammed down into a ditch, and threw them both out of the car like rag dolls.

A tree limb raked the top of Carl's head. He landed violently on his back in long grass, wind knocked out, ready to wet his pants because he reckoned that if he'd sailed an inch or two higher, the tree limb would have decapitated him, *chop.*

He clawed his way out of the grass, ripped his goggles and helmet and mask off, sucking air. The Special lay nose down in the ditch, its front end crumpled like a tin can someone had stomped on. Oil smoke leaked out. The smell of gas was raw in the Sunday air. People were running from the fence, from the grandstand — the racetrack vultures who'd loot any available souvenir from a smashed-up car.

Carl didn't see his riding mechanic. He had a queasy feeling that his friend lay in the ditch with a broken neck.

"Jesse?"

Nothing — silence, broken only by the greedy cries of the vultures around the Special and the faraway snarling of the cars finishing the race. The Special's owner, Hoot Edmunds, walked slowly toward the looters. Hoot's straw hat was tilted at its usual rakish angle. His striped seersucker blazer was properly buttoned, and he twirled his Malacca cane. Carl had just thrown away Hoot's latest investment of several thousand dollars.

Then Carl saw the bright white person from the fence. The white was a shirtwaist, and the person was a girl with blond hair.

Curly black hair, a long-jawed head, coffee-and-cream skin poked up from the ditch. Blood ran from a gash over the man's left eye, dripping on his coverall.

Jesse climbed out of the ditch with a dolorous expression. He was taller than Carl, starvation thin. He was colored, though clearly one or more ancestors had mixed a lot of white blood with his blackness. Jesse Shiner was ten years older than Carl, and lucky to be riding as a mechanician. He had the job because Carl had insisted Jess's color didn't matter, only his skill as a self-taught mechanic.

Jesse and Carl stood a foot apart, staring at each other. As if by thought transmission, they came to the same realization at the same moment: they were miraculously whole. Both started to laugh wildly.

"Jess, you crazy high-yellow bastard, are you all right?"

"Tell you later, when all my bones knit up again." Giddy in the wake of fear, they threw their arms around each other and slapped each other on the back. Both men stank of sweat, and oil, and neither gave a damn. Hoot Edmunds strolled up, twirling his cane.

"Boys, are you in one piece?" Hoot liked to call them boys even though he was three years younger than Carl, twenty-two. Hoot was the only son of Magnus Edmunds, a man who'd made a fortune, as some other Detroiters had, manufacturing marine engines for Great Lakes steamers and freighters. The heir to Magnus Marine Motors ("Triple M") hated his baptismal name, Elwood, so he'd looked around for something sportier.

"Think so, Hoot," Carl said. "Those goddamn tires don't last long enough. Firestone and his pals should be hung out to dry till they come up with better ones."

Hoot took off his straw hat, revealing a head of brown ringlets above a bland pink face. He wiped his perspiring brow and agreed.

"That was a fine bit of driving at the last moment," he said.

"Only thing to do." Carl's legs shook from the up-and-down pedal pressure. He waved toward the great sycamore that had nearly guillotined him. "Need to sit down."

He sat with his spine against the bark. The vultures were all over the Special, cutting away, carving out pieces of the tires with pocket knives, working the windscreen back and forth to free it. *My God, that man even brought his own tin snips.*

"I'm sorry I wrecked the car, Hoot."

"Don't worry, there's plenty of money to manufacture another." Like a lot of young heirs to Detroit's factories and machine shops, Hoot Edmunds had little to occupy his time, and had adopted autos because of their speed, and sportiness, and aura of luxury.

"Why were those fools squatting on the rail?"

Jesse complained. "Why didn't the stewards drive 'em off?"

"They tried," someone standing behind Hoot said in a sweet, light voice. "We refused to leave. It's such an excellent vantage point." The speech was overlapped by a man in the ditch who said loudly, "Say, look at that, Jack, his mechanic's a *nigger*."

Jesse rolled his eyes and turned away with a weary expression. Carl shot a look at the loud-mouthed man. The person behind Hoot stepped to one side, so as to be visible. Sycamore leaves threw a lovely shadow pattern onto the full bosom of her bright white shirtwaist.

"But you really did save lives. It was a very brave thing to do," she said. Carl found himself looking at — drowning in — the loveliest dark blue eyes he'd ever seen.

Ever the prescient young gentleman, Hoot saw Carl's interest and excused himself. He strolled back to the crumpled Special. His presence did nothing to discourage the scavengers ripping and bending and cutting with abandon. Hoot put his cane over his shoulder and looked on with mingled wonder and dismay.

Jesse went the other way, off from the white people, to roll himself a smoke with Bull Durham from his pocket sack.

The girl said, "You're a very accomplished driver." Carl wondered where she got the experience that let her judge. "Have you been doing it long?"

"Started last summer. It isn't that hard. You

need strong arms and shoulders, and you have to be willing to be killed before you're thirty." He said it smiling. She laughed.

"You need a lot more than that, sir. There's skill. In my estimation you possess a great deal of it."

Carl had never met a young woman quite so forward. She wasn't fresh in a sexual sense, just plain-spoken, direct. She was about his age, about his height, with a pleasing roundness to all her parts. Her hips were broad, her breasts big and full. She had a pretty, round face, blond curls, full lips that would be tasty to kiss. And those vivid eyes — dark blue as he imagined the South Seas to be. He planned to see the South Seas one day. Meantime, her eyes would do fine. She was nicely though not expensively dressed, with a ribboned straw hat and striped summer parasol.

He grabbed the sycamore trunk and stood, despite her protest that he needn't. As he walked to her, he noticed Hoot watching them in a funny, speculative way.

"Well, I do thank you for the compliment, miss —"

"My name's Teresa. I prefer Tess."

"Carl. Carl Crown." He put out his hand, still encased in a greasy leather glove, which he peeled off with embarrassed haste. Her fingers were cool and firm. He felt his body react; he hadn't been with a woman in months.

"The kind of selflessness you exhibited should be rewarded in some way," the girl said. "So many people think only of themselves. Might I invite you to supper at our house? I'm sure my father would enjoy meeting you."

Surprised, Carl took a moment to react. "Sure, of course. But it isn't necessary."

"I know that. I would like it. I'm afraid I have to ask you to come a rather long way. Our residence is Woodward Avenue, but during the summer we live at Grosse Pointe."

"The electric cars run out there, don't they?"

"Indeed," she said, dropping her parasol in the grass and opening her reticule. "Would Saturday evening be convenient?"

"Yes, fine, perfect," he exclaimed. Then he grinned. "I don't think I've ever met a pretty young woman who likes racing."

"My father has a small connection with the auto business. That's how I got interested. Father doesn't like me to attend the races alone, though. He tries to forbid it, and I have to remind him I'm of legal age. He finds it very annoying. I seem to annoy a lot of men that way. That's why I'm still single, don't you suppose?" She said it teasingly, though he detected a certain hint of sadness. "May I borrow your shoulder?"

She put a slip of paper against it and wrote with a pencil. "This is the address. Is six o'clock convenient?"

"I don't get off work until six."

"Half past seven, then?"

"That should do fine, Miss — um, Tess."

"I'll see you then." Solemnly, she shook his hand a second time, then walked away, opening her parasol as she crossed the ditch into the sunshine by the white fence. Carl watched the movement of her hips under her skirt. He was hard as a stick.

Panicked, he realized he hadn't asked her about the proper attire. For Grosse Pointe, where the rich of Woodward and Jefferson Avenues had their second homes, he'd probably need a necktie. He didn't own any. If he couldn't borrow one from Jess, he'd have to buy one at Mabley's or Rothman's.

Tess disappeared behind the grandstand, taking Carl down from the heights abruptly. He noticed Artie Flugel talking to Hoot. He walked over to them, legs and shoulders aching. He kept a bottle of Mustang Liniment in his room at all times. Tonight he wouldn't be able to get to it fast enough.

"Tough luck, kid." Artie shook Carl's hand. Artie was forty or so, stumpy, with a lined, windburned face.

"I'll give you some dust next time." Carl dug in his pocket and paid off the bet. Artie went away chuckling.

Hoot regarded him in a quizzical way. Carl said, "Something funny?"

"That girl. You were quite friendly."

"Why not? She's pretty. She invited me to supper on Saturday."

"Really. I assume you know who she is?"

"Her name's Teresa. Should I know more than that?"

"I suppose not, you don't hang out with the Detroit elite. Especially the ones who build automobiles. Teresa Clymer is Lorenzo Clymer's daughter."

Jesse strolled up in time to hear. "You mean Clymer as in Clymer, the Quality Car for Quality People?"

"That's the one."

"He owns foundries," Jesse said to Carl. "Owns the one I work at." Doing the miserable, dangerous work with molten metal that white men wouldn't touch. Jesse didn't say that to Hoot, but he and Carl were friends, and he'd said it to him. Jesse called it "the nigger work."

"Clymer doesn't actually run an auto plant," Hoot explained. "He merely lends his name to the company. That's common, J. L. Hudson does the same thing. Clymer's put money into auto ventures for some years now. I suggest you develop a sudden bellyache Saturday night. Clymer and the rest of his friends who make autos costing $2,000 think your employer is a man with stupid ideas. Clymer owned shares in Henry's second company, the one Henry walked away from — it's Cadillac now. I'd say most of the Grosse Pointe crowd hates Henry's guts, and to my knowledge it's mutual."

Carl stood speechless. The Henry referred to was Ford, proprietor and resident genius of the Ford Motor Company.

14. Paul's Anchor

The flat on Cheyne Walk was quiet. Betsy, three, still took an afternoon nap. Seven-year-old Shad sat next to his father in the bay window seat, examining a book with a look of wonderment. Paul and Julie called the boy Shad because too many Joes in the family created confusion.

It was June, Sunday, warm and drowsy. The casements were cranked open. Against the lush green background of Battersea Park on the far riverbank, barges and slow sightseeing boats moved along the Thames between the bridges. The boy traced a finger across his father's name under the book's title, *I Witness History.*

"You really wrote this, Papa?"

Paul smiled, stuck a match to his cigar. Vest unbuttoned, sleeves rolled up, he rested one arm companionably on his son's shoulders.

"Every word, good or bad."

"Oh, it's all good, Papa, isn't it?" Shad was a bright-faced, sturdy boy whose dark brown eyes, from Paul, complemented the thick ink-black hair inherited from Julie.

"Well, people seem to think so. It's only been in the stalls since March, and they're printing a second edition." He'd called at the publisher's offices in Bridewell Place, Blackfriars. Everyone including the proprietor, Collins, had congratulated Paul on the book's success.

Success had certainly surprised the first-time

author. Paul had hooted when Julie first showed him Fritzi's letter suggesting he write about his experiences. Julie was the one who'd encouraged him whenever he could find a week or two at home to write in the midnight hours. She was the one who'd hired a female typewriter to prepare the manuscript, which she'd carried personally to several publishers. The fourth she called on took it immediately. Paul had just signed a contract with a New York firm, Century, for an American edition.

Shad turned pages. "I can't read a lot of these big words."

Paul ruffled the boy's hair. The children, Julie, the two-story flat on the upper floors of the Cheyne Walk town house were anchors that held him secure when he ventured to remote parts of the world where life was cheap and survival uncertain.

"You'll understand them when you're a little older."

Like all youngsters, Shad kept his attention focused on one subject only for a few minutes. He gripped his father's knee to show his earnestness. "Can we go to the zoo next week?"

"Saturday. My ship sails from Liverpool on Sunday."

"You're going back to America?"

"To make more pictures, and to give a few lectures. I've never done that before."

"What's a lecture?"

"A talk to an audience. Mine's all about some of the places I've been, things I've seen. I've fixed up two reels of film to show during the talk." A man in New York, one William Schwimmer at a company called American Platform Artists, had gotten a copy of his book and written to say he could arrange some lucrative auditorium appearances on Paul's next trip. Nervously, Paul agreed to try it. Lord Yorke didn't object, in fact thought the exposure might help open doors for his star cameraman.

"I'll see the family in Chicago, I hope," Paul went on. "Aunt Fritzi in New York, perhaps, but Uncle Carl definitely. I'm going to Detroit."

"Where's that?"

"In the state of Michigan. A man named Henry Ford is going to introduce an automobile that's said to be remarkable, because it's both strong and cheap." He shifted the position of the pillow at the small of his back. *Thirty years old and aching like Methuselah,* he thought with considerable disgust. Julie was continually urging him to hire an assistant. Even Michael said he was an idiot to operate without one. Julie teased Paul about wanting to do everything himself — which wasn't far from the truth.

Paul's study had been converted from a front bedroom. There was not much to be done with the rather feminine stained-glass flowers in the upper sections of the bay windows, but Julie had decorated the room itself to suit a man's taste: striped wallpaper, dark furniture, two Chippendale-style bookcases, electric table and floor lamps with fringed shades of vivid red silk, a rolltop desk opposite the small fireplace. Edwardian fashion dictated less clutter than in the pre-

129

ceding age, but Paul remained an unconscious Victorian: he filled up every inch of space with books, papers, metal cans holding film reels, or souvenirs of his travels: beer coasters; matchboxes; picture postcards; a tin-plate Eiffel Tower; a Malay kriss with cruelly serrated blade; a Japanese folding screen; a spiked helmet from Germany that Shad loved to wear with a wooden rifle on his shoulder; a small Chinese gong struck at mealtime and, occasionally, to annoy parents; a raffish Indian floor mat that covered a fine Persian carpet. Paul sorely missed the room when he was away.

Shad started to ask another question, but the door opened. Julie peeked in from the hall. "Oh, my. Smoky as a cave in here." Shad sprang up to throw his arms around his mother and bury his head against her skirt. A moment later, he slid out the door, grinning.

Julie — Juliette Vanderhoff when Paul first knew her in Chicago — was a slightly built woman with delicate fair skin and large, luminous gray eyes. His heart leaped when he saw how fetching she looked in her afternoon dress, silk chiffon with pleated sleeves, in a becoming shade of dusty rose. Over the wide neckline she wore the pearls he'd given her last Christmas, and matching earrings.

Julie was almost completely free of the terrible depressive spells she'd suffered as a young woman, when her crazed and possessive mother hounded her, constantly told her that sickness, weakness, nervous disorders were a woman's lot. She had been forced into an arranged marriage with an abusive man, a playboy eventually shot to death by his mistress while she looked on, helpless to stop it. It had left scars: a marked fragility, a certain shadow in the eyes at times. Her children, her marriage to a husband who adored her had made the difference between surrender to the darkness and victory over it.

She was still soldiering for Mrs. Pankhurst, whom they'd come upon a week ago in Jean Tussaud's museum, immortalized in a new wax statue. Julie's dressing closet was piled high with packets of WSPU literature. She worked regularly at a desk in a corner of the sewing room, writing letters, petitions, and, just lately, a speech for a rally that was expected to attract thousands to Hyde Park in a few weeks.

Violence on behalf of the cause was escalating. Two women, unauthorized, had thrown rocks through windows at 10 Downing Street. There was talk of a mass invasion of Parliament and of hunger strikes. Prime Minister Asquith insisted the suffrage issue lacked sufficient support to merit legal reform. Every time that was mentioned, Julie fumed.

"What would you like Barbara to prepare for supper?" she asked now.

Paul slipped his arms around her. "Should be a fine warm evening. Why don't we walk with the children for fish and chips?"

"I'd love that." Julie spied the book in the window seat. "I'm so proud of you, Paul."

"Without you, I wouldn't have had the nerve to try the first paragraph."

She slipped her arms around his neck. "Just

don't get so famous that hordes of women chase you."

"I only care for one," he said, drawing her into an ardent kiss. Julie's lips tasted sweet and warm. Her body strained into his. She rested her chin on his shoulder, sighing. "I'm losing you to the world again."

"Only for a few months."

She kissed his ear, fondled the back of his neck. "An eternity. At least there's no danger this time."

A swift ironic smile passed over Paul's face, unseen by his wife as they stood embracing. In seconds a reel of past events played on the screen of memory:

A crazed Bengal tiger charging while he filmed from an elephant howdah. Down on the ground, the mahout stumbled on a vine, and before the tiger was driven off, the little brown man was fatally clawed. . . .

The rain-soaked soil of an earthen terrace gave way in the Culebra Cut, and a giant Bucyrus steam shovel tilted, then fell with a terrible slow majesty, crushing two workers to death on a lower terrace, where Paul had been filming; he ran with his tripod on his shoulder at the last moment. President Teddy Roosevelt, white suit and flashing smile, had come to inspect the great Panama canal project; not an hour before, he'd boisterously pulled control levers on the very same machine. . . .

A tribesman in Morocco's Atlas Mountains, seeing the camera and fearing it would magically steal his soul, tried to prevent it by firing at Paul with an ancient long-barreled fusil. . . .

No danger? There was always danger if you did the job right. He'd narrowly escaped death in Cuba in '98, in the Boer War, in the Philippine insurrection put down by the U.S. army. He always minimized such incidents to Julie.

"Don't worry, I always look after myself," he said as he kissed the warm curve of her throat. "I want to be sure I come home to you and the children."

"I've been thinking, Paul. Betsy's at the age when she might like a brother or sister. I spoke to Shad, and he agrees."

Paul laughed and grabbed a fresh cigar from the cluttered desk.

"Capital! Shall we see about that tonight, in private?"

15. Three Witches and Four Actresses

Days went by — no jobs. She reduced her expenses to starvation level. For breakfast she ate two-day-old bakery bread and hot tea. Her main meal was another slice of stale bread and, once a week, oyster stew made on the gas ring in her room. She bought a single oyster from a delicatessen and warmed it in a pan of broth. She veiled her situation in every letter to her mother. "Everything fine! Prospects good!"

In all the months since she'd left Chicago, she hadn't heard from the General or written to him. She foresaw no change in the situation. Some of the pain of their estrangement had worn off, leaving a resigned numbness that flared up severely only once in a while.

By late August she had descended to a nadir of discouragement. One particularly difficult Tuesday — four ads answered, no job — she presented herself at a wicket at the Grand Central Terminal.

"Schedule of passenger trains to Chicago, please."

Five minutes later she threw the schedule in a street corner rubbish barrel. Ellen Terry scolded her for even thinking of running home.

Footsore and depressed, she trudged downtown as a sultry rain began to fall. She was soaked when she climbed the stairs at Mrs. Perella's. Wasn't two years in New York enough? She set a deadline. If she couldn't find at least one good part by her birthday, next January 5, she would pack up, go home, admit defeat to her father, and look for something else to do with her life. Perhaps she'd work for a teaching certificate. She could always instruct in German and run a school drama club.

With the thought of this kind of retreat depressing her spirits, Fritzi stoically washed her face and put on her thin robe. Fitful air drove rain and the stinks of the city into her room, which she had begun to hate. She pulled her chair under the gas mantle and opened the *New York Clipper*, one of the publications that regularly carried theatrical notices. In the midst of ads for trained dogs and tots who could turn cartwheels, she found a notice that made her breathe faster.

CASTING IMMEDIATELY.

WITCHES, for new production of "THE SCOTTISH TRAGEDY" starring and personally presented by famed English tragedian HOBART MANCHESTER. Distinguished international company includes MRS. VAN SANT as Lady M. All ages considered. Readings 2:30–5 Weds., Novelty Theater, 48th St. Kindly use artists' entrance immed. West of Cort Theater.

She experienced a delirious rush of excitement. She had played all three of the Weird Sisters in wretched Mortmain productions of "the Scottish Tragedy." That and "the Scottish Play" were theatrical euphemisms for the name of the Shakespearean drama actors regarded as a bad-luck vehicle. A whole web of superstitions surrounded the play — things you couldn't do or say in rehearsal or performance. Horrible accidents happened to actors who played in *Macbeth*, it was said.

Fritzi laughed at such drivel. Even the presence of Beelzebub himself, brandishing an invitation to Hell, wouldn't keep her from showing up at the Novelty.

Next day she dressed neatly in her dark blue and tried to defeat most of the tangles in her blond hair. Her stomach ached as she rode the Broadway cable car, choosing to spend the fare so as not to dirty her clothes before reaching her destination. She was almost flung through the window when the grip man swung the car around Dead Man's Curve at Union Square. She hoped nothing worse happened.

She stepped off at Forty-eighth, her shoulder throbbing. Walking east, she approached a garish marquee whose electric bulbs illuminated the name 5¢ VARIETY. The show was just letting out. She was buffeted by chattering men, women, and youngsters. In New York it seemed as though nickelodeons were opening in every other block. Fritzi sniffed and hurried on to the alley between the Novelty and the Cort.

"Sign the sheet and take a seat in the auditorium," said the old man who kept watch on the stage door. He was busy feeding scraps to the theater cat, an overweight calico. Fritzi picked up the pen, inked it from an open bottle. She blanched. She was looking at a sheet already filled with names.

Horrified, she discovered a second full page underneath. Her elation about this audition, her feeling that her luck was changing, broke like a Christmas ornament in the fist of Sandow the Strongman. By her rough count, forty actresses had already put their names down.

Ye gods, she thought, not the *Macbeth* curse already?

Her rivals were scattered throughout the orchestra. They eyed Fritzi as if she carried the plague. She took a seat on the aisle near the back, tried to compose herself.

She noticed a hole in the aisle carpet. Paint was peeling from the navel of a cherub in the ceiling fresco. On stage, a work light on an upright pole lit a small table and chair. Sandbagged fly ropes hung down in front of the masonry wall at the rear. Though the Novelty had a reputation as a second-rate house, like all theaters it promised illusions and delights. Aromas of paint, mold, and dust were still sweet perfumes.

Three more hopefuls came in. A minute later a flurry of conversation in the wings preceded the appearance of a fat middle-aged man wearing an English walking suit, long opera cape, and wide-brimmed soft hat of the kind affected by bohemians. He carried a book and papers which he put on the work table. He flung his hat away and came down to the footlights, fists on his hips. He shouted at the gallery:

"Is anyone awake up there? Let's have more

light, sir, and right away." The man's voice surprised Fritzi with its baritone richness. From the high darkness a curse floated down. Instruments hanging on the front of the balcony blazed on. The fat man was fully lighted.

"Good afternoon, ladies." He made a leg, a courtier's bow. His accent was upper-class, his words perfectly enunciated. He unfastened the tie strings of his cape and whirled it away like a bullfighter. "I am Manchester." He beamed, as though expecting applause. One or two sycophantic applicants obliged.

Fritzi didn't know what to make of the "famed English tragedian." She guessed his height at five feet six, his weight two hundred or more; he was round as one of Count von Zeppelin's airships. He was decidedly bow-legged, and she could clearly see the height-enhancing heels of his shoes. His face was red as a beef roast. Bovine brown eyes slanted downward from the center of his forehead, a reverse Oriental effect. His shoulder-length hair reminded her of pictures of Oscar Wilde.

"I see no red-haired gentlemen in the house," Manchester said cheerily. "Upon entering the theater I tripped on the alley step. These are sure signs no ill fortune will attend our proceedings." *Oh, he's one of those.* Fritzi had encountered a few other actors who believed every superstition in the book.

Manchester strode to the table, picked up the signature sheets. Though he radiated self-importance, she liked his panache and his wonderful resonant voice.

Manchester was a traditional actor-manager, a combination of producer and star. The great actor-managers had dominated the nineteenth-century stage, but their day was passing. New forces drove the modern theater. The director, a relatively new position in stagecraft. The producer, the powerful money man who controlled everything from some hidden cubby upstairs. The star, an actor people came to see even if he or she did no more than juggle apples for three hours. Mrs. Van Sant, Manchester's Lady Macbeth, was that sort of star.

At the footlights again, the great man addressed them.

"We all know why we have gathered here, do we not, ladies? The call of Thespis. The lure of the lights, the claques, the crowd! That literary giant, Mr. Charles Dickens, understood the lure full well. He was an outstanding actor. Organized amateur theatricals, gave platform readings of his own works which fairly tore the heart from your bosom. I was privileged to witness those as a youth, sometimes performing the most undignified menial labor round about the theater to garner admission."

An older actress in front of Fritzi half turned and whispered, "Full of himself, ain't he?"

Manchester touched the book on the table. "I trust I needn't explicate or even summarize the famous work we are casting. We never speak the name of the play within a theater, unless we utter it as it occurs in the text. Today we want three witches. First witch will also play Lady Macduff in act four. Second Witch doubles as the Gentle-

139

woman in act five. Third witch has only that role in which to shine, but it's she who utters the fateful prediction that the title character shall be king over all. Each witch shall understudy all others. We shall conduct the tryout here on the stage, since we have no smaller space available. Kindly be courteous to your fellow professionals. Come up as I call your name." He consulted the sign-up sheets. "Miss Dorcas, Geraldine."

So began Fritzi's ordeal of waiting through readings by actresses of every shape and disposition, actresses lamentably bad, competent, or dangerously good. Manchester chose the scene for each candidate. When Fritzi's turn came, ten minutes past five, he gave her a side and said, "This is act four. Kindly begin with the speech at line twenty-two. I shall throw you the cue."

His magnificent voice rolled out. *"Double, double, toil and trouble — fire burn and cauldron bubble."*

"Scale of dragon, tooth of wolf, witch's mummy, maw and gulf," Fritzi read. *"Add thereto a tiger's chaudron —"* She hesitated; the word always threw her.

"Entrails," Manchester exclaimed. "Guts! Pray continue."

"Thank you, um, *tiger's chaudron, for th' ingredients of our caldron.*"

"Excellent, please be seated. Who is next? Miss Levi."

They finished at a quarter of six. Manchester studied comments he'd penciled on a separate sheet. "Permit me to thank you all most sincerely for participating. I regret I am not able to use each and every one. Will the following four ladies kindly report back to this stage tomorrow morning, ten sharp? The Misses Sally Murphy, Cynthia Vole, Elspeth Ida Whittemeyer, and Frederica Crown."

Fritzi let out a little squeal, then blushed. The actresses not chosen, angry or wearily resigned, gathered their things and left. She heard one snap, "Hell with him, I hear he can't pay his bills anyway."

Four actresses for three roles. Miss Murphy was a soft-cheeked young woman with perfect features and startling blue eyes. Miss Whittemeyer was older, with wild, spiky gray hair and a wall eye; she was sure to be cast.

The third rival, Miss Cynthia Vole, appeared the most formidable. She had a dark, almost demonic beauty, a bosom like the Matterhorn, and a husky voice that had frankly thrilled Fritzi almost as much as Manchester's. With a glacial smile Miss Vole strode up the aisle. She happened to glance over at Fritzi. That glance said she would if necessary kill someone to get a part.

All she had for breakfast was a glass of water and two stale crackers. At that, she was afraid she'd heave it all up.

She tore her comb through her frizzy hair and donned her best suit, dark red silk. When she walked into the Novelty, Miss Vole was signing in.

"Oh, good morning, dear. That is the loveliest outfit. Let's wish each other well, shall we?"

During this gush of goodwill Miss Vole continued to poke the nib of the pen at the open ink bottle. Somehow the nib tipped it. She cried, "Oh, dear," as the bottle rolled over, splashing ink on Fritzi's skirt.

"Oh, horrors. I'm so sorry. Whatever can we do?"

Speechless, Fritzi stared at the stain on her gored skirt. The old doorkeeper said, "Try washing it out before it dries. C'mon, there's a dressing room with hot and cold taps."

"My dear, I am so terribly sorry," Miss Vole said as they left. She had laid out the rules for the contest: there weren't any.

In the dingy dressing room the doorkeeper tested the sink taps, found an old towel. "Damnation," Fritzi said, scrubbing the stain. "It's ruined."

"I'll tell Manchester you'll be a minute late."

"Will he be mad?"

"No. He's a gas bag, but decent enough when you let the hot air out."

Fritzi worked valiantly but could wash away only some of the ink, leaving a large wet place over her thighs, with a black bull's-eye. "Sorry about the mishap," Manchester said when she walked on stage. "Don't let it throw you, my girl."

It already had, though Fritzi fought to hide it. Miss Vole hovered. "Whatever will you do if the stain won't come out?"

Fritzi smiled sweetly. "Oh, just put the suit in the ashcan, I have many more." She wanted to break something. Like Miss Vole's neck. Seated in the front row, Miss Murphy gave her a solicitous smile.

The doorkeeper appeared between dusty tormentor curtains. "Sir? It's Mrs. Van Sant. On the telephone. She don't like her room at the Astor."

"For God's sake — she demanded to be put there."

"She says the room's smaller'n a loo. What's that?"

"I shall not answer that question in the presence of ladies."

"Well, she wants to talk to you."

"Impossible. Inform the lady she may contact me later this afternoon at the Players Club."

"She won't like that," the old man muttered as he shuffled away.

Manchester passed out sides to the other three actresses. He pointed at the orchestra and said to Fritzi, "You may wait down there."

He auditioned the first three hopefuls using the third scene of act one — the witches meeting Macbeth on the blasted heath. Manchester read both the title role and Banquo, pitching his voice differently for each. He really was remarkable when he projected. Composed and confident, Miss Vole nearly matched him with her memorable huskiness.

Manchester sent Miss Whittemeyer down and called Fritzi. The stout lady gave her a good-natured pat as they passed on the steps, but Fritzi was confused about looking at the right eye or the left. She couldn't remember being so nervous.

143

Manchester gave her a side. "Second witch."

They read the scene, then did it a second time with Fritzi as first witch, Miss Murphy as second, Miss Vole as third. Miss Vole had a little trick of retiring a few steps upstage, forcing the other two actresses to turn awkwardly. Positioned down right of them, Manchester noticed but said nothing. The upstaging made Fritzi read more passionately.

After ten minutes Manchester called a halt and produced new sides.

"Now for something completely different. This is act five. I would like each of you to read Lady Macbeth, as the doctor of physic discovers her madness. Miss Murphy? If you would join me. You ladies kindly take seats and await your turn."

Fritzi was all nerves again, hot one moment, chilled the next. She'd never played Lady Macbeth. She knew the part, though not well.

Miss Murphy read competently, Miss Whittemeyer too. Manchester played the Gentlewoman as well as the doctor.

"Miss Crown, please."

She nearly tripped as she started up the steps. Behind her in the auditorium, someone laughed. If she had Macbeth's dagger, she'd know what to do with it.

As the doctor, Manchester read, *"Hark! She speaks. I will set down what comes from her, to satisfy my remembrance the more strongly."*

"Out, damned spot!" Fritzi read. "Out, I say! One, two: why, then —"

"Pardon me, excuse me." The unmistakable

voice came out of the dark. "I'm terribly sorry to interrupt, but I'm seated way back here and I can't hear Miss — what is her name? I want to hear her, she's excellent."

"Thank you, Miss Vole," Manchester said. "We appreciate your constructive interest, but kindly don't speak again. It tends to unnerve the artists." He whispered, "A little louder, can you?"

Completely thrown by the interruption, she struggled to the end. *"What's done cannot be undone. To bed, to bed, to bed . . ."*

And to hell with it. Disgusted with herself, she flung the side on the table. Manchester patted her arm and thanked her.

Of course, Miss Vole read magnificently, with volume that probably rattled the doors all the way up in the gallery. Manchester took the stage for a final word.

"As you leave, please write down your correct address. I will send a note to the three chosen, in tomorrow afternoon's mail. To one and all, however, my sincerest thanks."

He made a point of intercepting Fritzi in the wings. "I do hope the damage to your dress can be remedied." He gave her a little bow and crinkled his eyes. She felt he liked her. In the end, though, that would count for nothing.

Back in her room, she shed a few tears. Then she wiped her eyes and worked on the ink stain. She couldn't remove it. And she couldn't afford a new suit. The more she thought of Cynthia Vole's sneaky tactics, the angrier she became.

"I'm not going to be beaten by that witch." When she realized what she'd said, she laughed. Just like that, a beautiful idea popped into her head.

For a long time she paced the room. One moment she told herself the scheme was too wicked. The next moment she started for the door, only to stop. She had been raised to play fair. Must she therefore lose to someone who didn't?

No!

She rehearsed aloud for half an hour, saying lines over and over to get the huskiness just right. She'd always thought it a silly talent, useful only to amuse.

Maybe not this time . . .

Downstairs, she knocked on Mrs. Perella's door to make sure the landlady was out for her regular late-afternoon pushcart shopping. At the wall telephone, she called the Novelty and asked for Manchester.

"His lordship's gone. Try the Players down in Gramercy Park," the doorkeeper said.

"Thank you, I shall, it's urgent."

"Is that Miss Vole?"

Fritzi clicked the receiver on the hook and sank against the wall, eyes shut, hands trembling. Any minute a copper would march in and arrest her.

Another tenant came off the street and tipped his derby. Fritzi gave him a wiggly little wave and a queasy grin. As soon as he went upstairs she telephoned the actors' club. She was in luck:

"Manchester here."

"It's Miss Vole, sir" — every syllable of the impersonation was a fight for control. "I regret to tell you I've been offered another role, which I've accepted."

"Oh, I'm so sorry. For the sake of my production, I mean to say. To you I offer congratulations. May I ask the vehicle in which you'll be appearing?"

Oh, my God, she hadn't thought of that.

"Sir, I'm sorry, I didn't hear you, it's a bad hookup."

"Who is the producer? What is the play?"

Fritzi turned away from the brass carbon-cup receiver, covered her mouth, and said, "I can't hear you, Mr. Manchester, I'm very sorry, goodbye."

She rang off. Suddenly her eyes focused on a figure in the street doorway. Mrs. Perella, a string bag full of onions in hand.

"Why you talk in that crazy voice, Fritzi? You sick?"

"No, no, I feel wonderful," Fritzi cried. She seized Mrs. Perella by the shoulders and danced her around, onions and all.

Next afternoon's delivery brought a note on stationery of the Novelty Theater. Mr. Hobart Manchester begged to inform Miss Crown that he desired her to play Second Witch in his forthcoming production, and would she please arrange to be at the theater at ten tomorrow morning to discuss salary?

16. Grosse Pointe Games

The Rapid Interurban carried Carl and a box of chocolates out to Grosse Pointe, a journey of almost ten miles. He got off by a two-story brick waiting room across the street from one of the most photographed landmarks in Wayne County, the large and brightly lit Country Club of Detroit. Music and laughter drifted from Dobson's Road House opposite.

Nearly every big, imposing house that he passed was brightly lit. Windows were open, sending animated voices, the cries of children, the music of a piano roll, into the soft darkness. The village of Grosse Pointe was essentially still a summer resort, and the season was in full swing.

As he turned the corner from Grosse Pointe Drive onto Lakeland, he smelled a warm wind redolent of fish blowing off Lake St. Clair. At the end of the street, by the water, the windows of a two-story house laid yellow rectangles on the manicured lawn. The house was done in the rustic shingle style. A pier extended from the side yard into the lake. A small lacquered sign on the fence said this was VILLA CLYMER. If a place this fancy served as a summer cottage, what must their home be like? he wondered.

A long black Clymer touring car parked in front reflected the lights in the curved brass of its enormous headlights. The top was folded down, showing off the gray leather seats. Perhaps the most telling sign of the car's cost was the hand-painted decorative pinstripe on each wheel spoke. Who owned the car? Wouldn't Lorenzo Clymer park his in a garage?

He'd taken great care to be presentable. Taken a bath after work, even washed his hair. He wore a new fifty-cent necktie and his coat sweater, black ribbed wool — a bit too warm for the evening. He wished he hadn't given his Princeton sweater to Fritzi.

A voice from the porch startled him. "Carl? Is that you? Do come in."

The sweet sound of it banished his anxiety. He charged up the walk, swept off his cap. Tess stepped into the light from the open front door.

"You found us with no trouble?"

"Oh, yes, easy. Here, these are for you."

"Why, thank you. Chocolate creams are my favorite."

They gazed at each other in awkward silence. Maybe other men wouldn't find Tess Clymer beautiful, but he did; a certain chemistry had started bubbling the moment she spoke to him at the racetrack.

She knew how to show herself to advantage. She wore a short fitted jacket, navy blue, with a matching skirt, and a filmy blouse that enhanced the billowy curve of her breasts. She'd fixed her hair in a chignon, fastening it with three tortoise-shell combs inset with rubies.

"Would you care to sit, or look at the lake? Supper won't be served until half past eight."

"I thought I saw a yacht tied at the end of your pier."

"You did. It's my father's. He commutes to his office in Detroit when we're living out here. The captain sleeps aboard."

They strolled down the gently sloping lawn to a concrete sea wall. A bright yellow half-moon the color of butter hung above the lake, tinting the wavelets. The long white yacht bobbed gently. A half mile offshore Carl saw the running lights of another.

"People claim to have seen sea serpents in the lake," Tess said.

"Drunk or sober?"

"The people, or the sea serpents?" It made him laugh. She said, "We could play croquet if you like."

"Croquet? It's dark."

He felt like a dunce when she said, "Oh, Father's taken care of that. He installed brand-new lights for the tennis court and the back lawn. Come." She took his hand.

She stepped inside the four-bay garage behind the house. Bright lights on poles suddenly bathed the croquet court. Handsome pear trees grew in neat rows behind it.

"I should caution you," Tess said as they walked to the mallet rack. "You mustn't be upset by Father's manner. He's rather blunt with everyone, me especially. He's ruled me with a strict hand ever since my mother died when I was fifteen. At twenty-one I'm still trying to break him of that. Which color would you like?"

"Do you have a favorite?"

"Green."

He handed her a ball and mallet, took red for

himself. They walked to the starting stake. "Is your father in the house?"

"Yes, he's meeting with his advertising agent, Wayne Sykes. Wayne's an old friend of the family. A Detroit boy. He handles the Clymer auto account. He's been waiting since three o'clock, poor man. Father was detained in the city at an emergency board meeting. He's on the board of two banks. My father works seven days a week and expects everyone else to do the same."

"Do you have any brothers or sisters?" He regretted the question when her face clouded.

"I did have. Roger, my older brother, died of influenza when I was thirteen. My younger sister, Winona, was killed in a cycling accident a year later. Mother passed away the year after that."

"I'm really sorry. I didn't mean to bring up —"

"We live through these things," she said with a smile meant to reassure him. "It's been lonely without them, that's all. You go first."

The mallet felt small as a toothpick in his big hands. His stroke caromed the ball off the first of the two wickets, shooting it to one side. "Hell," he said without thinking. "Oh, sorry. I haven't played for a while."

"Just take your time. We're not competing for a prize," Tess said gently.

Still, she was adept at the game, and competitive — no posturing as the winsome girl outmatched by the big man. She made clean, confident strokes that went where she aimed. Behind from the start, Carl stayed behind, missing wickets and steadily losing ground. He was approaching the stake at the far end when she intercepted him, hit his ball, and whacked him away. As he chased the ball, his shoe caught a wicket and he fell. He jumped up, brushed himself off. *Dumb ox. Keep it up, she'll never want to see you again.*

"Are you hurt?" She was solicitous, not scornful. She stood barely two feet away, her dark blue eyes reflecting the moon. He wanted to grab her and kiss her, devil take the consequences.

"No, fine." He picked up his ball. He returned to the end wickets and went through on his next turn. He missed the stake on both follow-up shots. "Blast."

By the time he hit the stake and started back, she was already at the other end of the court, in front of the starting wickets, although a foot and a half to one side. She bent over the ball, studied the path, hit. The ball rolled through the first wicket, struck the second, miraculously slid through. She tapped it against the stake.

"Good game. You beat me."

"Unfair advantage. I play golf. There's Father, with Wayne." She turned off the lights. On the porch Carl saw two men, one with a lighted cigar; his voice carried.

"I'm just not sure of the advisability of featuring my portrait as the main illustration."

"Lorenzo, take my word. It's the right approach. Everyone knows you or has heard of you. The ad speaks not only through the copy but more subtly. It says the Clymer must be a quality car if a man of your stature and reputation puts his name on it. The picture drives the nail in solidly." The speaker had an unctuous voice Carl disliked at once.

"All right, but I definitely don't care for that fancy border on the ad."

"We'll change it. Whatever you want. What would you like?"

"I don't know. Show me a few other ideas."

"Certainly. You're the client."

"Tess, hello. I've asked Wayne to stay for supper since I kept him late. This is your guest? Good evening, young man, I'm Lorenzo Clymer."

Clymer shook Carl's hand with a firm grip. Wayne Sykes merely nodded. They went inside to a huge dining room, where two serving girls were placing platters of veal and side dishes and pouring water and wine. Clymer's fine white suit and the trim blazer and gray trousers worn by Wayne Sykes made Carl feel shabby. He stepped toward Tess's chair to hold it for her, but Sykes was quicker.

Under the glittering electric chandelier he could see the two men clearly. Lorenzo Clymer's features were unremarkable. He was short and slightly built, with small hands and sleek dark hair. Evidently Tess got her height from her mother. Carl had learned a few things about his host. A self-made millionaire, Clymer had established a successful iron foundry, bought another, plus a heat-treating plant, then expanded into casting wheels for locomotives and railway cars. This business made him rich, then rich a second time when he sold it to the giant Michigan Car Company. He kept his other operations;

Jesse worked at Clymer's first foundry.

Clymer said, "Tell us about yourself, Carl. Where do you hail from?"

"Chicago. My father owns the Crown brewery."

"Crown Lager? Never tried it," Sykes said as he helped himself to rice and passed the bowl. "Personally I'm a whiskey man. If not Kentucky bourbon, then French champagne. Eh, Tess?"

He said it as though they shared a secret Carl couldn't possibly appreciate. Sykes was a few years older than Carl, auburn-haired, slender, and tan. He had a look of supple strength, as though he rowed or played a lot of tennis. His nose was long, his mouth mobile, his eyes black, with a mean light in them. *Or am I just jealous?*

"What college did you attend, old man?" Sykes asked.

"Princeton."

"Graduated when?"

"I didn't."

"Really? Um. I'm Harvard '98 myself."

"And a bit uppity about it," Tess teased. "Just like all Harvard men."

Lorenzo Clymer waved at the serving girl by the sideboard. "Don't stand there sleeping, Greta. Fill up the water glasses."

"Sorry, sir."

"Where do you work, Carl? What's your profession?"

He was prepared for the question. He'd discussed it with Jesse, who counseled him to be truthful, regardless of Clymer's feelings about Henry Ford. "You got to tell him sometime if

154

you're as crazy about this girl as you act like" was Jesse's languid comment.

"I don't exactly have a profession, sir. I'm a driver for the Ford Motor company."

"Well." Sykes tossed his napkin aside and sat back, folding his arms. The single word conveyed a clear meaning: Carl had done himself in. To judge from the look on Lorenzo Clymer's face, he agreed.

"I don't expect you to condemn an employer, Carl. In fact, to do so would be base disloyalty. But neither will I hide my personal feelings about Henry Ford. The man's a bumpkin, with an ego big as a barn."

"A clown," Sykes said. "His people were shanty Irish from Cork."

"Seven years ago, right here in Grosse Pointe, Henry's 999 race car beat Alex Winton's Bullet," Clymer said.

"Yes, I know about that," Carl said.

"On the strength of that victory," Clymer said, "the Henry Ford Company was organized. I put a considerable sum of money into it. In six months Henry damned near wrecked the company with his dilatory tinkering. The board got rid of him and put a good old Detroit name on the door, Cadillac. I made money when I sold out my interest, but I'll tell you, son, Henry's ideas are all wet. This new Model T won't amount to a thing after the first flurry of interest. Personally I wouldn't be seen in the kind of car he wants to build. The top of the market is where a smart auto man aims his product."

Defensive, Carl said, "Excuse me, Mr. Clymer,

155

but aren't there a lot more ordinary people than rich ones?"

"Well, yes," Sykes laughed, "but who'd want to associate with them?"

Lorenzo Clymer wanted to be sure he made his point. "Henry Ford is a renegade in the auto business. A man of no education or breeding — a stubborn farmer with the wrong market orientation. He'll be gone in five years, if not sooner."

These men are damn snobs, Carl thought. No wonder Ford hates the Grosse Pointe crowd.

Tess looked uncomfortable. Clymer noticed and tried to lower the temperature of the discussion. "Nothing at all wrong with your drawing a salary from him till that happens. Do you like working there?"

"I like being around automobiles, but I'm not one for fixed hours or time clocks."

"Tess tells me you race."

"I drive for Hoot Edmunds."

"I wouldn't suppose there's a great future in that."

"Not unless you're Barney Oldfield," Sykes said. "And he's throwing his money away on drink and cards and cheap women. Got a wife, too. His second." He sniffed.

Carl said to Clymer, "I never worry too much about a future as long as I'm doing something I like."

"Crown's is a large brewery, isn't it?"

"Eighth or ninth in the country. And growing steadily."

"Does your father have plans for you to join the firm?"

156

"I suppose he does. But I don't."

"I see." Lorenzo Clymer looked at his daughter in what Carl took to be a pointed way.

The supper limped on. Clymer discussed the arrival of America's Great White Fleet in Yokohama. Carl apologized for not knowing about it; he seldom read a newspaper. After a nervous cough or two, Sykes said, "Say, Lorenzo. On the way out here I got a speeding ticket. I didn't want to be late for our appointment."

"How fast were you going?"

"The officer said seven miles over the fifteen-mile limit."

"Send me the ticket, I'll fix it. I'm a village trustee."

"That's why I mentioned it. Thanks ever so much."

Sykes brought up a forthcoming banquet of the Employers' Association, leaving Carl to his food and awkward attempts to chat with Tess. The conversation shifted to the presidential election. Theodore Roosevelt had personally chosen the Republican candidate, his successor; both Clymer and Sykes were Bill Taft stalwarts, predicting a sure defeat for "that liberal radical Bryan," in Clymer's words. He said that the perennial Socialist candidate, Debs, was an even worse menace, and should be brought to heel, "preferably with tar and feathers."

"No, shoot him," Sykes said. Carl said he didn't know much about politics, but his older brother knew Gene Debs and considered him an honorable man devoted to change by nonviolent methods. Sykes looked at Carl as though he

157

came from the moon.

Carl had had enough. He excused himself from coffee in the front parlor and rose to leave. Lorenzo Clymer shook his hand, thanked him for coming, said he'd be happy to see Carl anytime, which was an obvious lie. Clymer was already absorbed in the *Detroit Evening News* by the time Carl walked out of the parlor with Tess.

Wayne Sykes followed them. Carl's present lay on a marble-topped table in the hall. "Where'd this come from?" Sykes said.

"Carl brought it," Tess said. Sykes wasn't a complete dolt; he saw the lightning flash in her eye and responded with an insincere smile.

"Very thoughtful. May I try one?" He opened the box, popped a chocolate into his mouth. "Tasty. Never had drugstore candy before."

Carl's neck turned red above his collar. Tess took his arm, steered him to the door. "Try several, Wayne. Meanwhile, excuse us."

They hurried down the walk to the gate. "Oh, Carl, I do apologize. Neither of them was at all nice to you."

"Guess I'm not too good at any of the games they play out here."

"Wayne was awful. I expect he thinks you're competition."

"For what?"

"Me," Tess said, linking her arm with his. "Keep walking. He's on the porch, watching us."

They turned right toward the main avenue. Darkness closed around them, relieved by patchy moonlight falling through trees all but bare. Tess's round bosom pressed gently against Carl's sleeve, arousing him.

"Did Wayne make you angry?"

"I wanted to pick up a chair and knock his brains out."

"Well, you're a true gentleman to hold back. You hide your temper well."

"It cuts loose when I'm really and truly provoked."

"Does that happen often?"

"Every five years maybe."

At the corner of Grosse Pointe Drive he said, "I'll go on from here." He faced her in the leafy shadow of a moonlit tree. He felt the warmth of her breath, savored the faint scent of orange blossom on her skin. He wanted to gather her in his arms, kiss her, but he dared not be too forward. The evening was already somewhat of a disaster.

"Look, Tess. Your father doesn't think I'm worth a nickel — no, let me finish. I'm just not his kind of person. If I'm going to see you again, we should meet somewhere else. Anywhere but here or your house in town."

She reached for his hand. "I think so too. I know a dozen places in Detroit where we can be out in the open, but by ourselves."

"Would you like that?"

She lifted her beautiful face in the moonlight.

"I would, very much."

"How can I get in touch without causing trouble?"

"You can write notes. No one looks at my mail. Do you have a telephone?"

159

"Not where I live. The landlady has an arrangement with the widow next door, for emergencies. I can go to the public exchange, though."

"Call during the day, when Father's downtown."

"One way or another, I'll be in touch."

"Soon, I hope. Good night, Carl." On tiptoe, she brushed her lips against his cheek, then turned and hurried away toward home.

Carl fairly danced all the way to the Interurban. He thought no more about Sykes the boot licker, or of the possible consequences of the good-night kiss, except for the joy it promised.

17. Bad Omens

In a Ninth Avenue saloon, at a table overlooked by framed chromos of a prizefighter and a race-horse, the man baptized Cuthbert Mole ate stew and drank pale ale. "Cuthbert Mole" was the ugly egg from which the bird of plumage Hobart Manchester had hatched himself at eighteen. It was either change the name or be laughed at forever.

Hobart was an only child. His parents were shareholders in a seedy stock company based in Warwick, Oxfordshire. Mowbray Mole died of drink when Cuthbert was fifteen, his mother, Eurydice, three years later. Young Cuthbert buried her and fled Oxfordshire for London, having awarded himself a new name.

After a rugged apprenticeship he achieved a measure of success and bought a heavily mortgaged theater in St. Martin's Lane. A year ago, a series of disastrous productions had forced him to put the theater on the block. He sold everything, including a cottage hidden in a wood in Kent where he entertained privately. With a portmanteau and a treasured makeup box inherited from his father, he crossed the ocean in steerage, to the land in which so many millions of others had found opportunity.

Every farthing he'd salvaged after his string of West End flops was sunk in this production of the Scottish play. Expenses were strapping him, particularly the salary and housing demands of

Mrs. Van Sant. He had reluctantly telephoned, pleading delays caused by conferences with the scene designer (a fiction — scenery was coming out of a rental warehouse). After enduring several paragraphs of abuse, he agreed to move his leading lady to a suite at the Hotel Astor.

He tried to convince himself that it was a sound investment. Mrs. Van Sant wasn't an especially good actress. Nor was she one of those players such as Mrs. Patrick Campbell — able to save even the most dismal vehicle. But she had a following, on both sides of the Atlantic. She would draw.

She could be a terror in rehearsal — as if he hadn't terror enough producing a play cursed from the night it opened at Hampton Court in 1606. Unfortunately, "that play" was eternally popular. Even those who believed in its evil aura were induced to stage it. If this production flopped, however, he was bankrupt, finished.

He sopped up stew with stale bread and comforted himself with one fact. He had his cast. The last person, Miss Crown, had signed this morning. He had praised her audition lavishly, concealing the real reason he was delighted to have her. She came cheap, a mere thirteen dollars a week. Miss Murphy was engaged for fifteen, the experienced Miss Whittemeyer for seventeen-fifty.

Charming child, Miss Crown. Not beautiful in the conventional sense, yet there was something damnably attractive about her. A warmth, a winning sprightliness. Lovely eyes too.

The piano player came out of the gents'. After

a few warm-up runs, twangy because of the piano's mandolin attachment, he played "The Mansion of an Aching Heart." The waitress stopped. "Another ale, dearie?"

"Indeed, yes."

"Anything else you'd like, later on, when we close?"

"Oh, no! Thank you very much."

He kept thinking of Miss Crown, and smiling. It had taken colossal nerve to mimic Miss Vole on the telephone. Miss Vole knew all the tricks for upsetting and upstaging her competition. No crime there, but she used those tricks viciously, he'd quickly observed that.

Miss Crown's impersonation had actually fooled him for a moment. He only hoped she'd be competent on stage, and his other actors too. He'd have trouble enough with his leading lady, and the dark demons that had haunted the Scottish play since Shakespeare's day.

What to do for the rest of the evening? Perhaps a nickelodeon — the little pictures amused him. Two slices of bread remained on his plate. Glancing around, he slipped them under his cape and left.

Fritzi arrived at the Novelty at nine A.M. the following Monday, the first day of rehearsal. The doorkeeper looked out of the cubby, where he sat scratching the neck of the overweight calico. Fritzi introduced herself.

"Oh, I remember you, miss. Foy's the name. Most call me Pop. You're a whole hour early."

"I've learned it's a good idea to get the feel of a theater. That's a handsome cat. What's her name?"

"Queen Gertrude. I wanted another black one when Cyrano died, for black's the luckiest color for a theater cat. Just didn't have the heart to turn this one away when she wandered down the alley." Queen Gertrude miaowed and arched against his hand. "Go on in, you're not the first."

In the dark auditorium, Fritzi spied someone under the balcony. She stepped through a semi-circle of chairs on stage. "Hello?"

"Hello, yourself. Who's that?"

"Fritzi Crown."

"Are you one of the three ladies in our coven?"

"Yes."

The spiky-haired actress with the wall eye came down the aisle. "Ida Whittemeyer, welcome."

"Thank you. You came in to study the theater too?"

"I did. It's useful to get a fix on the size, how voices carry. And it's good luck." Miss Whittemeyer trooped up the steps to the stage. "For this little adventure we need it. They say the first time they gave the Scottish play, the boy actor playing Lady M fell ill and the Bard himself had to read the part. It's been an accursed script ever since. Actors have gotten hurt, maimed, even killed doing this play."

"But you took the risk."

"I need the work."

"So do I, Miss Whittemeyer."

"You must call me Ida. My right eye's the good one."

By ten the full company had assembled — thirty-one adult actors and two boys with loud, obnoxious mothers. The stage manager, a stringbean named Simkins, called them to order. As if on cue, Manchester bounded on stage.

"Good morning, good morning. All present, are we?"

"All but Mrs. Van Sant," Simkins said.

"We shall begin without her." He strode to the apron, hands clasped behind his back. "Members of the ensemble. We are met in a great endeavor, about to labor together on one of the supreme works of stage literature. I have every confidence that our efforts will be rewarded critically and at the box office. To ensure an auspicious start, this morning I donned the very tie I wore on the occasion of my professional debut in London. Notices were extremely favorable, and the tie has brought me good fortune ever since."

He touched his outdated teck cravat, two crossed tabs of dingy brown fabric with a greasy sheen. Fritzi noticed a rabbit's foot hanging on a chain stretched across Manchester's considerable paunch. It seemed she was swimming in a sea of superstition.

"I wish to say a word about the text, which I have personally adapted and condensed. You will discover that I have eliminated the character of Hecate. Shakespeare's authorship of the Hecate material is suspect. So are the scenes with the weird sisters, but the public expects those."

A noise at the back of the hall interrupted him. Manchester peered. "Who is there?"

A galleon of a woman sailed down the aisle. Halfway to the stage she stopped and planted a tall ebony walking stick surmounted by a large gold knob.

"You have two eyes, Hobart. Use 'em."

"Mrs. Van Sant. You are late."

"We were detained outside," the woman said in a foghorn voice. She pointed her stick at a young man following her. "This is Charlie, he's a bellhop at the Astor. Take a seat, Charlie. Don't speak. Mr. Manchester can get quite cross in rehearsal."

Charlie waved and did as he was told. Handsome and muscular, he wore a cheap green suit and derby. Sally Murphy tweaked Fritzi's arm. "One of her lovers, don't you suppose? They say she has dozens."

Eustacia Van Sant was about Manchester's age but a head taller. She had an enviable hourglass shape, and a squarish face softened by wide lips and brilliant dark eyes. Vivid hair of the shade Fritzi called Irish red contrasted dramatically with her black velvet cape and dress. A scarlet dust ruffle flashed under the billowing skirt. Her hat was a large black velvet Gainsborough, ornamented with ostrich plumes. Altogether, it was a dated look, but it flattered her figure, especially her spectacular bosom.

Manchester said, "Permit me to make something clear, madam. We have a mere five weeks until opening night. I expect all players to be present at the hour specified for rehearsal."

166

"Oh, stuff that, Hobart. I told you, we were detained."

"By what, may I ask?"

"The hearse."

Manchester gaped. "Hearse, did you say?"

"Just outside. There was a copper with the undertaker's men. He refused to let us enter until they carried out the corpse."

Gasps and exclamations. Fritzi felt her pulse speed up. Manchester squeaked, *"Corpse?"*

"Some bookkeeper chap in the front office. Keeled over on top of his ledgers, dead as Jacob Marley."

A chill seemed to invade the theater. Manchester threw a look at Pop Foy, who was standing stage left. Foy nodded. "It's true. Poor fella was only forty."

Manchester pulled out a big kerchief and swabbed his cheeks. "Tragic. But it has nothing to do with us."

"It may," Ida Whittemeyer whispered. "It's the Scottish play."

Manchester moved the actors to the semicircle of chairs on stage. They read the play from sides. Hobart and Mrs. Van Sant knew long passages from memory.

Fritzi was fascinated by Manchester's leading lady. She had great energy. Coupled with her deep voice, it achieved a powerful effect. Not on a dark, suave-looking man named Mr. Scarboro, however. He was their Banquo. Fritzi caught him wrinkling his nose. She assumed it was professional jealousy. On the theater's ladder of status, he was only a featured actor, not a leading man or star.

During the lunch break she wandered into the theater's green room, where she found Mrs. Van Sant examining photographs of scenery.

"Will you look at these?" the older actress exclaimed. "I thought we were to have original designs. No! He's hauling this rubbish out of some warehouse." She thrust a photo at Fritzi. "I ask you, darling. Is that a blasted heath? It's a garden drop left over from some silly operetta. The shrubs are trimmed. On a Scottish moor we have trimmed shrubs, for God's sake! I was a fool to agree to this engagement."

Fritzi examined the photo, then another of a unit set which included high rostrums stage right and left, and an even higher one center. Ramps zigzagged up the side of each; from the top, ladders and steps went up to notched battlements. In the lower face of each rostrum was a curtained arch. Mrs. Van Sant led the witness:

"Horrible, isn't it?"

"All those levels and ladders look dangerous."

"Of course it's dangerous. This is the most dangerous play Shakespeare ever wrote. Twenty-six short scenes, one change after another. Nearly everything happens at night, so the lighting's always wretched. Thirty actors in armor rush about with swords, dodging scenery movers, marching and counter-marching with prop trees and hacking at each other — how could there not be accidents?" From her silver handbag she took a cheroot and matchbox.

"Care for a smoke?"

"No, thank you."

Mrs. Van Sant lit up. "What's your name again, dear?"

"Frederica Crown, but I'm called Fritzi."

"Frankly, Fritzi, I don't believe a lot of the superstition attached to *Mac* — our play. But I don't tempt Old Nick, either. I observe the rules as a courtesy. One never knows. Very nice to make your acquaintance, dear. We'll chat again."

She sailed out, cheroot in her teeth, leaving a wake of blue smoke.

Very quickly the actors began to gossip.

"Doesn't Mrs. Van Sant have the most fantastic wardrobe?" Sally Murphy gushed to Fritzi and Ida. "I suppose her lovers provide most of it. She's had three or four husbands, including Brutus Brown."

Mr. Scarboro became a target of backbiting. He had an ego as big as Mrs. Van Sant's, without her credentials. He treated everyone but the two stars haughtily. Fritzi thought his English accent peculiar.

"Because it's phony," said Mr. Allardyce, an elderly red-nosed actor playing the Porter. He sucked mints to mask a constant aura of gin. "Name's Louie Scalisi. Bridgeport, Connecticut."

Late on Thursday, Manchester rushed off to the costumer's, leaving the actors at liberty for a half hour. Fritzi again went to the green room. She was pouring coffee from a pot on the gas ring when Daniel Jervis, a fair-haired young man playing Malcolm, walked in whistling "Hello, My Baby."

Scarboro flung down his copy of a new trade paper called *Variety*. "You stupid little bastard, don't you know better than to whistle in a theater?"

That outraged Fritzi's sense of fair play. "Oh, come on, Mr. Scarboro. I know he shouldn't do it, but that's no way to talk to a fellow actor."

"Who asked you, Miss Nobody?" Scarboro was flushed, sweating — terrified. "When you whistle up the Devil, he comes. Especially in this play. Someone will pay for your mistake, Jervis."

Mrs. Van Sant had just arrived, and Scarboro bumped her as he rushed out. Daniel Jervis withdrew to a corner, mortified.

Mr. O'Moore, a grizzled actor playing the thankless part of Ross, lit his pipe and said, "So. In addition to our peerless star, we have a second believer in the dark powers."

"Lot of rubbish," said Mr. Denham, Macduff. He rattled his *London Times* to emphasize his opinion. Fortyish, Mr. Denham had served in the British army in India. He resumed his reading.

Mrs. Van Sant drew Fritzi aside. "Decent of you to stand up for the lad."

"Mr. Scarboro's a boor."

"We agree on that. I wonder, would you care to join me for tea on Sunday?"

"At the Astor?"

"I wasn't thinking of the middle of the Brooklyn Bridge, dear. Shall we say four o'clock?

When I'm at leisure, I never rise before two."

Manchester returned a few minutes later. Fritzi was standing with Mr. O'Moore behind a stage left tormentor, waiting for the rehearsal to resume. A faint sound made O'Moore look up. "Get out of the way!"

He rolled his shoulder into her and knocked her off her feet. She landed painfully on her spine and rear. Dazed, she sat up. The stage manager, Simkins, ran to her. "What happened?"

A few feet away, visible to Fritzi between the toes of her shoes, was a large sandbag counterweight tied to a length of frayed rope. What had happened was clear. Up in the fly gallery the rope had snapped. Simkins lifted the bag. "Blasted thing must weigh fifty pounds."

O'Moore clasped Fritzi's hand to help her stand. "Anything broken?"

"Don't think so."

Simkins said, "I'll speak to the cheapskates who own this theater. Get 'em to inspect every rope and piece of machinery."

"Scarboro predicted something like this, didn't he?" O'Moore said.

18. Confessions

When Mrs. Van Sant woke, she felt low. Last night that bastard Charlie had deserted her. Quit his bellhop job and left without notice with a kitchen girl. Hadn't even written a note. She'd heard about it from the staff.

She poured the remainder of a bottle of Mumm's into her bath water, reclined, and idly read a few pages of Freud's book on the interpretation of dreams. She liked to delve into unusual or advanced ideas, but this afternoon the Viennese doctor couldn't seduce her. She looked forward to four, when the frizzy-haired Miss Crown, an undernourished but likable young person, would take tea with her.

Like Hobart Manchester, Eustacia Van Sant was self-created. She'd been born Sophie Zalinsky, in Liverpool. Her father, a woolens draper, never made much money and died when Sophie was ten. At fifteen she went to London, soon after being deflowered by her mother's landlord.

Battling through a succession of tiny roles, she purged her vocabulary of Scouse, the Liverpool argot, and her voice of the Merseyside accent. She learned to speak like an Oxford don's wife. Success came slowly, but it came, because she would have it no other way.

Fritzi was waiting downstairs at the correct hour. Eustacia led them into the opulent Astor restaurant done, and overdone, in Beaux Arts style. It was spacious, with a high ceiling, many potted palms and ferns, and a live peacock in a gilded cage. A string quartet murdered "The Merry Widow Waltz."

The head waiter ushered them to a remote table. "Are you going to smoke, madam?"

"Yes, Viktor, I am going to smoke."

"I do apologize," he said as he set up a three-panel screen. To Fritzi he explained, "We simply can't allow a woman to be seen using tobacco."

"You colonials are so bloody puritanical." Eustacia settled herself. "Well, dear, how nice to see you."

"Thank you, Mrs. Van Sant, I'm delighted you asked me. Sundays are always quiet."

"Please, dear. Call me Eustacia. It's a privilege I reserve for those I like." She poured tea from a china pot painted with small blue flowers.

"All right," Fritzi said, "thank you."

"You're doing well in your part. Need a little more authority, though."

"So Mr. Manchester advised me yesterday."

"Trust him. The old gas bag knows his craft, even if he can't keep books or stay within a budget. Are you getting on well with the company?"

"With most of them, yes. Do you know that Mr. Scarboro apologized for calling me Miss Nobody?"

Eustacia beamed. "Indeed. Give me every detail."

She did, concluding, "I can't imagine what brought him to it."

"Oh, I can, dear. I took the preening ass aside and told him that unless he did, I'd speak to Manchester and arrange for him to be cast at once in another play we're all familiar with. It's called 'At Liberty.' " She guffawed, poured a second spoonful of sugar into her tea, and lit a cheroot with a flourish.

A miasmic blue cloud soon hung about the table. Tendrils trailed over the screen. A gentleman invisible to them coughed violently.

Fritzi said, "May I ask where Mr. Van Sant lives?"

"There isn't any Mr. Van Sant. He exists solely in programs, and the imagination of my audiences. I have been married thrice, but Mr. Van Sant is an invention. Ever so helpful in discouraging undesirables at the stage door."

"That's delicious."

"It's necessary because I have a following. I'm not being conceited, it's true. I am what is called a personality actor. Audiences do not come to see a fine talent personating Lady You-know; they come to see Eustacia pretending to be her. Sometimes they come merely to see Eustacia's frocks. For this engagement I brought thirty-five ensembles from England."

She quizzed the young lady about her background. Fritzi described her family, and the General's anger when she left Chicago.

"You'll show him, won't you, dear?" She swigged more champagne. "I say, this is jolly. Help me finish the cucumber sandwiches, and we'll continue in my suite. Viktor? There you are, dear. Please send a cold bottle of Mumm's upstairs, that's a love."

A few minutes later, they sat with glasses in hand, a silver champagne bucket between them on the suite's Oriental carpet. Eustacia knocked back two glasses in the time it took Fritzi to enjoy three sips.

"You gave my spirits a much needed boost this afternoon," she said to the younger actress. "Charlie, the chap I brought to rehearsal, left me. I don't choose liaisons wisely. I grew up with nothing, and tend to live thoughtlessly. That's particularly true as regards men. Bernard Shaw, nasty fellow, once told me I take men the way ordinary mortals take headache powders. Frequently, for immediate relief."

Fritzi laughed and nearly spilled her champagne.

"What about you? Have you a lover?"

Looking at her lap, Fritzi said, "Not just now."

"Surely there have been some, you're very personable."

"I'm afraid personable isn't enough." A bronze boy on the mantel clock struck a bronze gong with a bronze hammer: half past five. The suite faced east on Broadway, and Fritzi noticed it had grown dark as the sun sank beyond the Hudson.

"I'm homely, Eustacia."

"Nonsense, you're quite attractive."

"I'm homely and I know it. Too skinny."

"Then eat more."

"Oh, I've tried. I stuff myself and put on a few pounds, but then I get busy, or run out of

175

money, or I'm in some greasy hotel serving vile food and I can't stand to do it." Fritzi touched her bosom. "Anyway, food doesn't help here. Too flat."

"From the vantage point of someone overburdened in that department, it looks fine to me, dear."

"Gay deceivers." Fritzi covered her mouth. "I can't believe I'm saying these things."

"It's the champagne. Have some more. And don't be misled. Bosoms are overrated. A big prow cannot guarantee happiness. Remember Charlie, that ungrateful little sod." She heaved a long, maudlin sigh. "People think it's such a bloody glamorous life, the theater. Really it's lonely."

Fritzi said, "I've found it so. In the theater you make a thousand acquaintances but very few lasting friends."

"Well, you have one now. Yes, indeed." She reached over to pat Fritzi's hand, pleased and warmed by the surprise and delight on the young woman's face. She reeled up from her chair. "I'll ring down for another bottle. Where's the telephone?"

"Oh, thank you, I don't think I can —"

"Some light supper, too. It goes on Hobart's bill. If he objects I'll sit on him. He won't soon get over *that*," Eustacia bellowed, slapping her rump. She and Fritzi laughed like schoolgirl chums — naughty ones.

19. Reunions

Cunard's *Lusitania*, the world's largest ship, brought Paul into New York harbor. He thrilled again to the statue he'd seen for the first time in 1892.

At the Hudson pier he supervised the unloading of trunks holding camera equipment, raw stock, and a dozen copies of the British edition of *I Witness History*. Cleared through customs, he hired an electric taxi to haul everything to the New York Central terminal, then telephoned Fritzi at the theater number. She came on the line against a background of yelling and banging she assured him was just a sword fight in rehearsal.

"Is that really you, Pauli, you're here?"

"Yes, but I have to catch a train tonight. Could we have a quick supper beforehand?"

They met in a restaurant at Times Square, hugging joyously before they settled down at the table. Paul apologized for leaving so quickly; he would be traveling when *Macbeth* opened. "I'll be sure to see it when I come back to New York to sail home."

A chunky, well-set-up man about Paul's age hailed him and approached the table. Paul stood. "Fritzi, let me present an old friend of mine, Bill Bitzer. We met in Cuba. Billy's a cameraman too."

"The Biograph studio," Bitzer said, shaking Fritzi's hand.

"Fritzi's in a play at the moment," Paul said.

"Shakespeare," she pointed out.

"That's swell," Bitzer said. "If you ever need some extra work, drop down to Fourteenth Street, I'll introduce you. It's great pay. Five dollars for a day's work. You're mostly out in the open, we shoot a lot on the roof."

"Thank you, Mr. Bitzer, but I'm afraid stage actors don't have time for the moving pictures."

Amiably he said, "Oh, we know all about that. The flickers are beneath you Broadway folks. You'll get over it as soon as we turn a few actors into stars. Offer's open anytime. Call me when you're back in town, Paul," he said with a tip of his hat.

After Bitzer walked away Paul said, "You were pretty hard on him."

Fritzi looked rueful. "I suppose I was, I'm sorry. It's the way I feel. I should have kept it to myself."

In Buffalo, after a day spent filming Niagara Falls, he delivered his first lecture, nervously, but with good response from the audience. Bill Schwimmer, the lecture agent, had taken a sleeper from New York to catch the performance. A quiet, scholarly man who made occasional unsmiling references to his wife, he called Paul a "natural" — said he could book him for an extended tour whenever he returned. On this trip Paul had only two more speaking engagements, Cincinnati and Louisville. By the time he left Louisville to photograph the splendid horse farms near Lexington, he felt like a seasoned trouper.

In Indianapolis he filmed a spectacular flagpole sitter, then arranged to look at the real object of his trip, the site of a proposed new motor speedway. One of the developers, James Allison, picked him up at his hotel and drove him out, talking the whole way about his company, Prest-O-Lite, makers of running-board gas tanks for headlights.

Allison and his three partners believed Indianapolis had a great future in racing. He proudly showed off raw land west of the city, but that's all it was at the moment, raw. Paul thanked him, tipped his cap, and said he'd return when the track opened. At four A.M., he climbed aboard a train for Detroit, the new auto capital.

Americans hadn't invented the horseless carriage, as it was called at first. A couple of Germans, Gottlieb Daimler and Karl Benz, took those honors. But America seemed to be developing the motor car faster and more aggressively than Europe. Companies sprang up like mushrooms, produced a few vehicles, or none, then sold out, merged or just disappeared. There were presently over a thousand different auto makers. Most assembled their cars from components bought outside.

Paul had read an article in *Harper's* that enumerated the trades in which auto makers got their start. Colonel A. A. Pope had manufactured bicycles, confidently declaring, "You can't get people to sit over an explosion." Ransom Olds originally made stationary gas engines,

179

White made sewing machines, David Buick plumbing fixtures. Studebaker was formerly the world's largest producer of horse-drawn vehicles.

Of the many companies, the one bearing the name of Henry Ford seemed to emerge in the press oftener than others. Paul had read about Ford in the *London Light*, the flagship paper of the press lord who employed him.

Sometimes called a self-taught genius, Ford had been in the auto trade about ten years, starting companies, then dissolving or walking away from them in the wake of disputes with partners, which had included bankers, a coal merchant, and a bike racer. It was Ford's latest model that Paul meant to photograph. The car had been designed and worked on in secret for two years.

The trip to Detroit in an old wooden day coach wasn't exactly Paul's idea of a high time, though this observation was tempered with an admission that success was probably spoiling him. The air blowing through the car reeked of coal smoke and toilets. Sandwich wrappers and broken peanut shells littered the floor. The water tank on the wall at one end was empty, the dipper missing. After the sun came up the car felt like a fiery furnace. Some god of discomfort had further decreed that all the windows would remain stuck in the closed position. Though Paul wasn't the neatest of men, or much concerned with externals, he spent a lot of time on the open platform between cars, puffing a cigar.

The train arrived at the Michigan Central Depot on the shore of the Detroit River. Paul claimed his lacquered case from the baggage car, checked to be sure his camera had arrived unbroken, and hailed a hissing steam taxi. He consulted a tobacco-flecked card from his vest pocket.

"Hotel Ponchartrain."

His first impression of Detroit improved his mood. It seemed a modern, bustling city. Its population of nearly four hundred thousand included Poles and Finns, French and Sicilians, Rumanians, Armenians, and Chinese. And of course plenty of German-Americans, in a section called Little Berlin.

Some streets were old-fashioned cedar blocks sealed together with pitch; even on this cool, crisp day he could smell the tar. But the buildings were tall, the monuments imposing, and all the streetcars electric, a hallmark of progress.

He had an address for Carl, had telegraphed asking his cousin to meet him in the Ponchartrain bar when he got off work. Paul unpacked, soaked in a hot bath to relieve his back ache, then rested a while with his hands laced under his head, daydreaming of Julie. He strolled around Cadillac Square and the town's central plaza, Campus Martius, for a half hour. At six-thirty he put his foot on the brass bar rail and ordered a Crown lager. They had it. Good for Uncle Joe.

A large and lively bar crowd, mostly well-dressed gentlemen, kept up a loud chatter. Eavesdropping, Paul found that much of the conversation had something to do with the auto trade. He heard the words "damnable unions."

Someone else said, "Don't worry, the E.A. has four men undercover in that plant."

One section of the back bar held an amazing array of auto parts, everything from a cast-iron engine block to fenders, brass coach lamps, dashboards, and radiators. A man set a coat tree near the engine block, hung a linen driving coat on it, and began to extol the coat's virtues to a couple of prospects.

"Paul!" Carl waved a cloth cap as he charged across the barroom. His shoes were scuffed and his brown suit looked secondhand — too short in the jacket and trousers. But his smile was as broad and bright as Paul remembered. The cousins hugged each other.

Paul ordered schooners of beer. Carl asked questions about Julie and the children. After Paul answered them, he said, "What about you? How are you doing at Ford's?"

"I love it, it's an exciting place." Carl planted his elbows on the bar with his palms cupping the frosted schooner. "Oh, I don't love everything about it. I hate the time clock. Job's taught me plenty about automobiles, though, and gotten me in with the racing crowd. Lots of automakers race to show off their cars." He reached for a bowl of peanuts, clumsily let it slide out of his fingers, spilling some.

"What do you do exactly?"

"I don't stay inside, thank God, I couldn't stand that. Henry Ford can't stand it either. He comes and goes at all hours. 'Course, he's the boss. I'm a lowly utility driver. Pay's not bad for unskilled work — twenty-eight cents an hour for a nine-hour day. Mostly I drive Model T's down to the freight yards for shipment. Sometimes I deliver a special-order car to a sales agent in Ohio or Michigan or northern Indiana. Occasionally I take a car on a test run."

"Ford has its own test track?"

Carl laughed. "Right outside. Cadillac Square, Woodward Avenue — the streets."

"I've an appointment to film the new Model T in the morning. A man named Couzens arranged it."

"James Couzens. Money man. Kind of a sour apple. Smiles maybe once a year. God, it's good to see you. Let me tell you about this gorgeous girl I met."

In the Ponchartrain dining room, they ate a huge meal of pot roast, potatoes, corn on the cob, cauliflower and summer squash, hard rolls and pumpernickel, with a constant flow of beer. Paul asked how it happened that Detroit was becoming the auto center. The earliest manufacturing had been widely scattered from the Midwest to Massachusetts.

"They say it's because a lot of local people had experience in building marine engines for the lake boats. Nobody had to start machine shops or foundries, because they were already here. And there's money all over the place. Millionaires whose fathers got rich building carriages or railroad cars are looking for another plunge. There's a good spirit in Detroit. People are willing to take risks. Mr. Olds, the Dodge brothers — they're born gamblers."

183

How had Carl learned to drive? He grinned. "In secret. Six inches at a time."

He explained that he'd formerly worked at a bicycle repair shop in Columbus, Ohio. A few wealthy men stored their autos at the shop, taking them out only in good weather. Carl observed the drivers carefully for a few weeks. Then late one night he took his first untutored "drive" in a one-cylinder Packard runabout, going forward six inches, then back inside the storage barn, with only a few light bumps against the walls.

Two nights later the shop owner walked in unexpectedly and caught him at it. The owner admired his cheek and his eagerness to learn, told him to take the Packard around the block the next day. He'd be liable if he banged it up or put a single scratch on the paint.

"I told him I wouldn't, and I didn't."

"And you got on with Henry Ford with no trouble?"

"I wouldn't say that. I was nervous as hell when he interviewed me."

Paul took his cigar out of his mouth. "The head of the company talked to you personally?"

"Well, it doesn't usually work that way, but when I came here from Columbus, I wrote a letter to Mr. Ford. Pretty crude stuff, I'm an awful writer. I couldn't believe it when he wrote back. He invited me to his house. Said he hardly ever did the hiring, except at the top level, but there was something in my letter that he liked."

"What was it?"

With an ingenuous smile Carl said, "I was

kicked out of Princeton." Then he described his memorable first meeting with his employer.

On the night of the interview, Carl had stood beneath one of the verdant old elm trees on Harper Avenue for a long time, feet fidgeting, stomach flip-flopping. He couldn't remember being in such a state of nerves, probably because no other moment that he could recall, not even stealing a first kiss from Hilde Retz on a chaperoned sleigh ride in seventh grade, was so charged with tension and anticipation.

Harper Avenue was far from a poor street, but neither was it upper crust. The object of Carl's attention was a large but plain frame house, not at all what you'd expect of a man supposedly on his way to riches. Henry Ford had grown up in the country out by Dearborn, and he'd grown up poor, that much Carl knew. Maybe he didn't like to associate with the Woodward Avenue crowd, most of whom had inherited their wealth.

Finally, with an exertion of will Carl overcame his anxiety and stepped off the curb. In the shrubs around the wide porch, birds twittered in the twilight. A plain-faced woman answered his knock.

"You must be the young man Henry's expecting. I'm Mrs. Ford, won't you come in?"

The principal shareholder of the Ford Motor Company bounded into the hall to greet him. Ford's celluloid collar hung by one button; he'd discarded his tie. He was a tall, skinny man with big ears, piercing deep-set eyes and a craggy face that reminded Carl of Civil War photos of Lin-

185

coln, only less wrinkled. Mid-forties, Carl judged.

"Come in, Carl, have a seat. Care for a cup of coffee, or Malto Grape? That's a fruit drink. We serve nothing stronger."

The front parlor was furnished with a lot of old, dark, unpretentious furniture. The major pieces were surrounded by a Victorian clutter of fern pots, footstools, taborets, and curio cabinets. As Carl sat down, awaiting a grilling, an adolescent boy ran down the stairs into the front hall. Ford hailed him and introduced his son, Edsel. "What do you want, son?"

"Can I take the car out, Pa?"

"Sure, but be back before dark." The front door banged. Ford said, "Fine lad. Our only child. Named him for my best friend. Started him driving at age eight." Thumbs stretching and unstretching his suspenders, Ford regarded Carl soberly. "So you want a job at our factory. Tell me why."

Carl drew a long breath and delivered a halting but fervent statement about his fascination with machinery, autos in particular. He said that driving, even on the roughest roads in the foulest weather, thrilled him.

Ford asked whether he was a native Detroiter. No, Chicago. What was his father's trade? *Oh-oh.*

"He's a brewer, sir. Crown's beer."

Ford gave him another long, searching stare. "Heard of it. I won't hold it against you."

Mrs. Ford brought a tray with glasses of Malto Grape. Ford settled back and cracked a couple of jokes while they sipped their drinks. Then he pulled a letter from his shirt pocket and examined it. Carl recognized the note paper. Ford folded the letter and complimented Carl on being dismissed from Princeton. "I left school at fifteen and I've done all right. Far as I'm concerned, college is mostly bunk. Emerson said, 'A man contains all that is needful to his government within himself.' Have you ever read Emerson?"

"No, sir, I'm afraid not." A lit professor had assigned it, but Carl had been too busy playing football.

"You should." Ford sprang out of his chair. "Let's sit on the porch while it's still light. I like to watch the birds." He led Carl out a side door. The wide porch bent around the corner of the house. Ford took the swing, Carl one of the white wicker chairs. The evening was fragrant with the smell of mown grass.

"You have any questions, Carl?"

"Well, sir, could you tell me what kind of work I might do if — ?"

"By jiminy!" Ford leaped off the swing, pulled a brass telescope from a wicker basket. Whatever he saw made him exclaim, "Have a look, have a look. Baltimore oriole. I love birds."

Carl screwed his eye to the eyepiece. In the fading light he saw a flash of orange in a spirea bush, but that was all. He murmured something he hoped sounded appreciative.

"Since you like to drive, we'll try to find a driving job. I must warn you of one thing. I insist that men who work for me conduct themselves in a moral way at all times. No cursing, no carousing or brawling, nothing to bring shame on the organization or themselves. I have a saying: At Ford's we want to build men along with automobiles. Clear about that?"

Carl said he was. "Good." Ford launched into a monologue to which he clearly expected his visitor to pay heed. "There's a future at Ford. We're a dynamic company in a dynamic industry. Of course, my ideas are different from most of the other fellows turning out cars. They all want to cater to the well-to-do. Fancy touring models with high price tags. Not my way, not my notion. The cars we've marketed up to now, they're all right, but they still cost too much. I want to deliver a simple car, soundly made, speedy, dependable, but priced low enough for millions to afford it. That's where I see the big profits — getting the car not to the elite but to the multitudes."

He stroked a finger along his lower lip and smiled. It was a curious smile, cold and cynical.

"They think I'm crazy, the rich boys from Grosse Pointe. I know what they call me. Henry the Shiftless. Always tinkering. Never had a good idea in his life. We'll see. To be great is to be misunderstood, that's what Emerson said. I was put into this life for a purpose. I've lived before, you know. We've all lived before, many times." As the night fell and cicadas began to whir, Carl's hair almost stood up. Ford was saying mad things in a perfectly sane voice.

"I believe in my last life I was a soldier, killed at Gettysburg the first or second of July, eighteen

188

hundred and sixty-three. I was born into this present life at the end of that very same month, July 30. One life slipping into another, easy as the seasons changing." Carl sat in stupefied silence, having no idea of how to reply. He was reprieved by the clatter of a telephone bell. Ford's wife called him through the screen. "Take the number, Clara. I'll call back."

He shook Carl's hand again. "Report to the personnel department on Monday, seven A.M."

"Mr. Ford, thank you. Thanks very much."

"Don't be late. Personnel will sign you up, settle what we're going to pay you. Frankly speaking, I like the cut of your sails. Just remember what I said about the behavior we expect. There are no exceptions. Say, care for a cigar before you go?"

"No, thanks, I don't usually — well, sure."

Ford handed him a cigar as they strolled into the hall, held a match for him. Carl puffed. The cigar had a strange flavor, like tobacco adulterated with some chemical. He felt he should say something complimentary anyway. He was about to do so when the cigar exploded.

Ford slapped his thighs, convulsed. His wife rushed into the hall. "Oh, no, Henry. Not this nice young man. My husband is an awful practical joker," she said in an apologetic tone.

In a hall mirror Carl saw his singed eyebrows and the burst cigar growing out of his mouth like a weird flower. He plucked out the cigar and said, "Yes, ma'am, I see."

"Sense of humor's important to a man," Ford

said. "Sign of a good character. No hard feelings, right?"

"Oh, no, sir." He wondered how long it would take his eyebrows to grow out.

"Well, then, thanks for coming over. Oh, and don't forget. Go to the public library. Read some Emerson. Good night."

In the lobby of the Ponchartrain, Carl said good night. The food and beer had left Paul logy, craving fresh air. "I'll walk you to your place if it isn't in the next county."

"Only about a mile. North of Gratiot. What they used to call the Kentucky district. It's nothing to see. A lodging house for single men. The neighborhood's run down."

"Hell, I was raised in a rundown neighborhood. Lead on."

They strolled up Woodward past dark office blocks and lighted saloons. Carl said, "When will your book be published here?"

"You know about that?"

"Mama wrote me."

"It'll be next winter." Paul hadn't mentioned the book. Carl was leading a fairly aimless life, self-indulgent, without a clear future. Talk of the book could be construed as Paul bragging about his success. He loved his cousin too much to risk making him feel bad.

He needn't have worried.

"That's wonderful. I can't wait to read it. I'm proud of you. The whole family's proud."

Carl spoke truthfully about his neighborhood. Antoine Street was trash-strewn, lined with ugly

190

two-family houses, most with weedy yards, peeling paint, broken stoops or porch railings, the whole feebly lit by corner street lamps a block apart. Somewhere a baby squalled. Someone picked at a banjo. In the shadows a gaunt hound snarled at them. The dog's eyes glittered like yellow stones.

Looking between the houses toward the service alleys, Paul saw shacks that were evidently lived in; lanterns shone in several of them. The surroundings depressed him.

A white woman in a squeaky porch rocker watched them pass. In the next yard two black children played jacks in the dirt. Carl said, "The street's what they called mixed. It's cheap to live here. Jesse, my riding mechanic, is a Negro. He has a little bachelor house two streets over. He keeps it tidier than most of these."

"Do the colored and the white get along?"

"Pretty well. Most of the trouble comes from outside. Irish gangs run through and beat up people for sport. There's my place." He pointed to a frame house at the end of the block. A man lay prone on the porch. A woman stood over him, weeping. "Hey, that's my landlady."

Carl dashed ahead. Paul followed quickly, through a gate in a low white fence with many pickets missing. The man on the porch raised his head, tried to raise himself. Blood dripped from his mouth. A couple of upper teeth hung by red threads. One slitted eye was puffed up big as a hen's egg. The man sprawled flat again. "Oh, God, it hurts. I think they broke a rib."

Carl said, "Mrs. Gibbs, what happened to Ned?"

Mrs. Gibbs sobbed. "He came home from the shop real late. He said they jumped him at the corner and dragged him in the alley. I'd already locked the back door. He had to crawl all the way around the house. He called me, but not loud enough. I didn't find him laying here till five minutes ago."

"Who did it? One of the gangs?"

After a struggle to raise his head again, the injured man tried to curse. He only managed to spit more blood.

"Oh, sure, the gangs," the woman said with a bitter toss of her head. "A gang sent by the E.A., that's who. The foreman's threatened to fire Ned for being what they call quarrelsome, a troublemaker. You know my Ned, strong for a union shop. He speaks out."

"Detroit's an open-shop town," Carl said to Paul. "The E.A. can be pretty nasty about enforcing it."

"What's the E.A.?"

"Employers' Association of Detroit."

"Do you have trouble like this?"

"Not at Ford's. My mechanic's had a brush or two at his foundry. Listen, Paul, I have to lend a hand here. It was a swell evening."

"I'll help you carry him inside."

They lifted the moaning man carefully. Mrs. Gibbs held the screen door. They laid Gibbs in a mussed bed in a fetid bedroom. Mrs. Gibbs asked Carl to fetch Dr. Stein. "I'll see you in the morning," Paul said as they left. He turned toward the river. Carl trotted the other way.

Paul walked back to the Ponchartrain in the stillness of the night. In the distance an auto backfired. Or was it a pistol going off? A couple of minutes later a wailing siren suggested the answer.

A gaudy whore accosted him. Deep in thought, he waved her off with his cigar. On a picture screen in his head he saw the landlady crying, the blood running from her husband's mouth. Detroit, the booming auto capital, wasn't as peaceful as it seemed on the surface.

20. Model T

Friday morning, a taxi brought Paul to the Ford plant on Piquette Avenue, about three miles north of the city center. Tall white letters painted on the cornice of the brick building proclaimed the HOME OF THE CELEBRATED FORD AUTOMOBILE.

The plant was some four hundred feet long and sixty or seventy wide, as dull and dreary as any manufactory anywhere in the world. Through the open windows came the sound of mallets pounding metal, the hum and whine of machine tools and motorized belts, a cacophony that made him crave earplugs. The air was a miasma of motor oil, gasoline, paint, and God knew what else. In a holding yard to his left, several boxy black autos were lined up. Another drove from behind the building, through the gate and parked. The driver ran back in the building. It wasn't Carl, he noticed.

Paul straightened his tie and lugged his case toward the factory entrance. A truck carrying axle assemblies rolled up behind him. Lettering on the cab said DODGE BROS.

Entering, he turned left, past a bullpen of stenos and clerks and into a small reception lobby at the end of the corridor. He asked for James Couzens, the man in charge of finance, bookkeeping, shipping, advertising, and sales for the company. Carl had warned Paul about

194

Couzens, said that while virtually everyone at Ford liked Henry, most feared and despised Couzens, whose mistress was a balance sheet and whose temper could be volcanic.

Paul sat on a bench and read through two issues of *Motor Age* before Couzens came out of his corner office. He was a pudgy man with pince-nez and a cold, patrician manner. He shook Paul's hand without smiling.

"This going to take long?"

"It shouldn't. The light's fine this morning."

"You can't do any filming inside, we have secrets to protect."

"You covered that in your letter."

Couzens acted as though he hadn't heard. "This is a busy plant. We roll out twenty-five cars a day."

Bristling, Paul said, "Mr. Couzens, my pictures are shown in hundreds of theaters in the U.S. and Europe. I thought the company wanted publicity for the Model T."

"Henry's the one who wants publicity. He arranged this. I just did the paperwork."

"Maybe I'd better talk to him."

"I'll take you up. He went to body painting and trimming a while ago. Leave that case here. Follow me."

Couzens led him down the hall past the main entrance. Not completely boorish, he pointed out things as they went along. "Employment office. Our machine shop. Bar stock storage. In there we keep cushions, running boards, tops, steering columns. This is shipping. This is the electrical department — magneto assembly."

He rang a bell to bring down a freight elevator. Paul said, "My cousin works here. Carl Crown. He's a driver."

"I recognize the name."

"Would you happen to know where he is?"

"We have three hundred and forty-six employees. I don't keep track of all of them."

The rattling elevator dropped into sight. Behind the gate was a shiny black Model T with its motor ticking. Couzens opened the gate, and they stood aside as the auto rolled across the wide aisle and out the door. "Where did that come from?" Paul asked.

"Manufacturing. Top floor." Couzens slammed the gate and punched the button. Paul was getting angry. He figured Couzens for some kind of idiot bookkeeper who knew nothing about the power and reach of moving pictures.

Henry Ford couldn't be found at the noxious paint booths on the second floor. They backtracked through another large machine shop, a storage area for frames and axles, a chassis-assembly room. Finally they were back at the north end of the building above Couzens's office. "Design and experimental tool room," he said, leading Paul through a closed door into a combined office and drafting room crowded with drawing tables and blackboards chalked with diagrams and sketches of parts.

"Well, well. There's Henry where you least expect to find him."

Ford's corner office consisted of a plain desk and a few utilitarian furnishings. Ford saw them outside his door, jumped up, came out with a quick, energetic step. Men in the room worked in shirtsleeves, but Ford wore his coat and vest.

"You must be Crown. Henry Ford. Very happy you're here." They shook. "I'll take over, Jim."

"Good. I have work to do." Couzens pivoted like a soldier and marched off without saying goodbye.

Paul said, "I saw a Model T in the elevator, Mr. Ford. How's the reception been so far?"

"Call me Henry. Or Hank. The reception couldn't get much better. We ran our first ad a week ago today. In the Saturday mail we had over a thousand inquiries. Envelopes full of cash have come in all week. It's price, don't you see? Our Model F touring car sold for a thousand dollars. The Model K, six cylinders with a torque drive, that was twenty-eight hundred. I designed those cars for the shareholders because they pounded the table and insisted. This one I designed for myself. The price is low, but we'll drive it down even more. Let me show you around."

"If it isn't too much trouble." The remark came out unexpectedly sour.

"Too much trouble to show off our prize offspring? Not on your life." Ford laid an arm on Paul's shoulder as if they were old friends. Put the lanky man in overalls and plow shoes, you'd take him for a hick. But he had charm. It worked on Paul like a drugstore nostrum. His anger popped like a boil, gone.

On the third floor, small areas were devoted to

wood-pattern making and storage of frames and axles. The rest of the floor was final assembly. Chassis with wheels and motors in place stood in a row on either side, facing inward. A long line of these stretched away down a wide center aisle. The cars nearest Paul and Ford were the least complete.

The assembly floor was noisy, everyone running about like mad worker bees. Gangs of men pushed rolling carts along the line, stopping to lift a fender or dashboard out of the cart and mount it before moving to the next car. At the head of the line a finished Model T with everything in place and connected drove into the elevator. Ford kept up a running commentary:

"We have a new plant on the drawing board. Sixty acres. Everything on one floor. Much more daylight in the work areas. Architect's name is Kahn. I don't generally like Jew boys, but Kahn's an honest one. Say, are you a Jew? You've got a little bit of the look."

"I'm German originally, but not Jewish. If it matters."

Ford missed or overlooked the sarcasm. "In the new factory we'll do something about this system of bringing the parts to the car. It doesn't work anymore, we can't produce enough. Took me years to grasp that manufacturing is the key to this game. To build a lot of cars you need a different set of skills than you do to build one prototype. We're in this for volume. My philosophy is, build a lot of cars for a lot of people and you'll make a lot of money. Some in this town think I'm stupid. I'll show them."

They passed more gangs mounting brass-framed windshields, headlights, side lamps. Paul noted the litter-free floor, the aisle painted with hard enamel, the clean windows. He commented on it. "Can't stand dirt," Ford said. "Got that from my dear mother. Let's go down, there's a car ready to photograph."

Paul retrieved his camera case, and they left the building by a rear door. He set up the camera in a large open area while Ford pointed out the power plant and paint barn. A fitful roar issued from a third building, little more than a shanty. As Paul adjusted his tripod, a man staggered out and collapsed on the grass, gasping. Paul's inquisitive stare required an explanation. For the first time Ford was hesitant.

"That's the motor test room. We set the carburetor, see that she's running on all four cylinders. We don't have machinery for taking out monoxide gas yet. Every so often we have to pull men out, sit them down and let them breathe."

A finished auto, gleaming black, waited in a service bay of the factory. Paul reversed his cap. "All set." He started cranking. "Bring it out."

A driver pulled the Model T into the sunshine and swung it around in front of the lens. Paul photographed the same sequence twice more. Then he had the driver demonstrate start-up using the radiator choke wire and crank. Meanwhile Ford went on with his encyclopedic recitation of the car's virtues: a cylinder block from a single casting; tough vanadium steel; a unique flywheel magneto. Since Paul couldn't show any of that, they dramatized the price by having Ford carry a large show card into the frame. He set it down against the radiator. Below the company's blue oval medallion with the word *Ford* in graceful script, bold lettering said

FORD MODEL "T"
ONLY $825!

Ford played to the camera as though born to it. He gestured to the card dramatically. Paul waved. "Good." Before he could suggest something else, Ford ran back a few steps, then turned a perfect cartwheel in front of the Model T. He struck a heel-and-toe pose and grinned. Paul laughed. "Wonderful." The man certainly had a knack for dramatizing himself.

The morning had grown hot, and Paul wiped his forehead with his sleeve. "I'd like some panoramic shots from the roof. I don't need to bother you, I can do that by myself."

"Let me give you a little souvenir of your visit." Ford handed him a small paper-covered book titled *Nuggets of Inspiration from R. W. Emerson.* Ford's signature slanted across the cover.

"Good things in here, Paul. High-minded moral things. I print these at my own expense." He tapped the signed cover. "So you won't forget me, or my cars."

"Impossible, Henry. You strike me as a born promoter."

"Why, so they tell me. I confess I like talking to the press."

"You're fast on your feet too."

"Do you square dance? No? That's a pity, it's

nice clean entertainment. Well, Paul, goodbye, and thanks for coming. Can't wait to see those pictures."

"In theaters in two to three weeks," Paul said. As they walked back toward the service bay, he mentioned Carl in passing.

"That's your cousin? I hired him personally. Fine sense of humor, I like that in a man. His boss says he doesn't have pals in the factory, he's more of a lone wolf. Handy new expression. Heard it the first time day before yesterday. Your cousin's a hard worker. 'Course, no interesting work's ever truly hard, don't you know? I'll send someone to find him." Ford hurried into the building. His gait made Paul think of an overwrought stork. He was a dynamic man, though peculiar in some of his opinions; Carl had described Ford's reincarnation beliefs. As for his dislike of Jews — where did that come from? You found the same thing in a lot of rural people, Paul had discovered. Middle Westerners were suspicious not merely of Jews but of Wall Street financiers, journalists, painters and poets — all things "Eastern."

Carl came out of the building as Paul was packing up. "I just got back from delivering a car to Dearborn. I'm off to Flint at noon with another one."

"I'm catching a train to Chicago."

"Will you see the folks?"

"Absolutely."

"Give Mama a kiss and hug for me. Tell the General I'm doing fine."

"I see that you are. Going to settle down in

Detroit, do you think?"

Surprised by the question, Carl cocked his head and pondered it. "I've never thought of settling down anyplace. I don't think it's in my blood. That girl I met — Tess — she might change my mind, though."

21. Jinxed?

On Monday in the third week of rehearsal, Manchester stopped the seventh scene of act one, Macbeth's castle, to speak to Eustacia Van Sant.

"Madam, your delivery is too slow. The wife of the Thane of Cawdor is the driving engine of this act. She pushes her husband forward relentlessly. He is the one who hesitates."

Eustacia was in no mood for a reprimand in front of the company. "I have my interpretation of the role."

"That may be, madam. But I remind you that I have the pen which signs the salary vouchers."

"See if I care, you dictatorial little bastard." She stormed off.

Fritzi hurried to her friend's dressing room and talked to her for ten minutes. "He's excitable. The whole weight of this production's on his shoulders, not just the leading role." Eustacia returned to the stage in a half hour, without apologizing. Manchester shot an appreciative look at Fritzi, and the rehearsal went forward under a fragile truce. Fritzi wasn't comforted. Nerves were raw, tempers shorter and shorter as they careened toward opening night.

Manchester insisted on a short break at tea time every afternoon, and that Monday, Fritzi took her coffee in the green room. She was visiting with cast members when a shout startled them. "Get out of this dressing room, you fucking idiot."

They crowded into the hall to find a furious Scarboro confronting Mr. Allardyce. Scarboro had previously expressed displeasure about sharing a dressing room with the old actor, on grounds that the part of the Porter was inferior to Banquo.

Allardyce was blinking and weaving on his feet. Fritzi smelled gin. "Listen, Scarboro, I'm right sorry —"

Ida Whittemeyer interrupted. "Just a moment. Mr. Scarboro, your language is offensive."

"I don't give a damn. This old sot walked into the dressing room saying his lines. *You do not say lines from this play aloud anywhere but on stage.*"

Mr. O'Moore snorted. "What's he supposed to do for punishment, open his veins?"

"He knows what to do. One of the exorcisms. Quote the line from *The Merchant of Venice*, Allardyce."

Befuddled, the old actor said, "I don't remember it."

"Then stand outside the dressing room, turn around three times, spit, knock on the door three times, and beg for readmission."

"What humbug," O'Moore said. "Mr. Denham's right. Tell you something, Scarboro. I'll say lines aloud anytime I please. *Is this a dagger which I see before me, the handle toward my hand?*"

"Don't!" Scarboro cried.

"Come, let me clutch thee. I have thee not, and yet I see thee still —"

Scarboro's lunge threw Sally Murphy against the wall. With a looping sideways punch he knocked Mr. O'Moore to the floor. Fritzi heard an awful snap.

Writhing, Mr. O'Moore clutched his thigh. "I can't get up. Oh, God, I think something's broken."

By five o'clock Mr. O'Moore was in traction at a hospital, Manchester had fired Scarboro, and the demoralized company lacked a Ross and Banquo. As Fritzi and Mrs. Van Sant left the theater, the older actress said, "Perhaps I should buy a new pair of shoes."

"Shoes? You showed me at least twenty pair at the hotel."

"Cheap shoes, dear. Shoes that squeak. Squeaky shoes on stage are supposed to ward off trouble. I am beginning to share the dreadful feeling that we're jinxed."

Wednesday brought Mr. Charles Seldon, a new Ross. Their Banquo, Mr. Bruno Gertz, showed up on Friday. He was a disappointing little blob of a man with a thin voice. It didn't matter that he knew the part perfectly; his poor appearance was discouraging.

Things were no better the following week. Bad feeling had developed between Ida Whittemeyer, playing a somewhat overage Lady Macduff, and her son, personated by one of the child actors, an obnoxious boy named Launcelot Buford. In rehearsal he accused Ida of upstaging him. When she laughed, he kicked her shins. She boxed his ears. Manchester frantically canceled rehearsal of the scene.

Next day when the scene rehearsed again, Miss Whittemeyer introduced a new bit of business. She grasped the boy's hand to demonstrate affection. Launcelot looked down and shrieked. A large brown toad jumped out of his fingers and went hopping frantically toward a flat.

The murderers were convulsed. The boy actor had hysterics. Mrs. Buford charged up from the auditorium to confront Ida. She threatened her with her umbrella. It took Manchester an hour to negotiate peace terms.

How he managed to rehearse his own role amidst these alarms, Fritzi couldn't imagine. She supposed it was experience combined with desperation. She watched admiringly from the wings as he spoke the beautifully tragic speech from act five. *"Tomorrow and tomorrow and tomorrow creeps in this petty pace. . . . Out, out, brief candle! . . . A poor player that struts and frets his hour upon the stage. . . . A tale told by an idiot, full of sound and fury signifying nothing."*

Macbeth was a complex part, physically demanding. Manchester not only carried it off but held his own in the duels. When he was acting you forgot his age, his paunch, his bowed legs. He was the doomed king. When he died, Fritzi had goose bumps.

"So thanks to all at once and to each one," Daniel Jervis said at the end. He didn't speak Malcolm's final line; another superstition said the dark powers were provoked by the human

conceit of perfection, so it was better to leave the play unfinished, the last line unspoken, until performance.

Perspiring in his rehearsal doublet, Manchester struggled to his feet. Fritzi and her fellow actors broke into spontaneous applause.

On Monday of the last week of rehearsal, a crew of four scene shifters reported. They were unremarkable except for one, introduced as Mutt. Whether Mutt was a first or last name, no one said.

Mutt tended to swagger and boss his three colleagues. He obeyed orders from Simkins or Manchester with a great deal of muttering and complaining. Mutt's handsome profile caused a flutter among the ladies of the company. By the end of Monday's rehearsal he was chatting up Sally Murphy. He and Sally left the theater together.

Next day Sally appeared in the dressing room all pink-cheeked and sleepy. She didn't mention Mutt, who quickly proved fickle, spending the lunch hour in a back row, forehead to forehead with Launcelot Buford's mother. Sally Murphy crossed the stage several times, shooting looks at them. That night Mutt left with Mrs. Buford.

Wednesday the weather turned warm. The run-through was a sweaty torment. Manchester complained about slow clearance of the banquet furniture in act three. Mutt blamed one of the other scene shifters, who told him to go to hell. Mutt grabbed the man, lifted and flung him. The man fell, and Mutt started to kick him.

Simkins dashed between them. "We'll have none of that." He pushed Mutt away. Mutt glared and did his own push.

The stage manager went to Manchester. Keeping his back turned and his voice low, Simkins was clearly arguing for some action. Fritzi heard Manchester say, "I will speak to him."

He approached the younger man; laid his hand on Mutt's wrist, giving Mutt a look Fritzi found puzzling. Manchester said something, and the two walked off stage.

Afterward, Manchester astonished Fritzi by asking her to supper. This set her to worrying. Would he fire her this close to the opening? And would he spend supper money to do it?

They went directly from the Novelty to Shanley's, a Times Square café popular with theatricals. It was a noisy, cheerful place; Manchester seemed to know a lot of people. He introduced Fritzi as "My friend and fellow player, Miss Crown."

Over lobster tails, she wondered again why he was squandering money when he had so little. Yet, made comfortable by the fine food and two glasses of Crown lager, which induced sentimental thoughts of her father, she didn't ask.

"It was a lovely meal, Mr. Manchester, thank you."

"Away with formality. Henceforth Hobart. Now and always, Hobart." He patted her hand. "Best we go now. Another intense day with the Bard awaits us."

He greeted more acquaintances on the way

out, effusively. He saw her to a taxicab, but she refused the fare money he offered. She leaned from the window, waving goodbye to the odd but oddly likable man as the taxi swung into the traffic of Broadway.

Several in the company including Ida had seen Fritzi and Manchester go off together. She was teased about it, and saw no reason to deny it. Mutt stopped her backstage, carrying a gory wax head which resembled Manchester — Macduff's trophy at the end of the play.

"Have a nice evening with himself, did you? I guess he needs 'em to keep people fooled."

"Fooled? How?"

"He doesn't go with women. He's queer as they come."

"What do you mean?"

Mutt folded his arms. "You're not that naive, are you? Manchester's a sissy. Probably wears pink underwear with ribbons. One of the other boys warned me about him."

She stammered. "I've heard of that, but I never met — I've never believed —" She couldn't find words; she didn't know what she was talking about. Vague references to men who loved men, heard in oblique conversations as far back as her Mortmain days, had largely passed over her because she didn't understand the basic premise.

Mutt enjoyed her shock and confusion. "Now you know, sis. He'd only squire a girl like you for a beard. A cover." He walked off laughing.

Fritzi rushed to Eustacia's dressing room, shut

the door, blurted out what Mutt had told her. "Is it true?"

Mrs. Van Sant sighed. "Yes." Day by day her hair had changed color, from the Irish red of her first appearance to a more suitable dark henna. She'd taken off the gown Manchester had allowed her to wear for the early part of the play, royal blue velvet with white ermine trim. In her black stockings and black satin corset with pendant garters she was, to say the least, an astonishing sight.

Fritzi slumped against the door. "Then he used me, just the way Mutt said?"

"It's necessary, dear. Men of his persuasion live in constant fear of discovery. People in the theater genuinely like Hobart, so no one's eager to unmask him. In the outside world people aren't so charitable. They crucified poor Oscar Wilde. Hobart and I had a long talk about it years ago, when I appeared with him in the West End. A wardrobe girl pointed out a young railroad navvy who showed up after curtain every night. That's how I found out. Hobart discovered his nature when he was nineteen. For years he believed he was one of the very few men, if not the only one, whose temperament led him down a different path. He's met others since, but it doesn't make him any less terrified of being found out, or caught in an open scandal. If he was caught that way, even the most tolerant managers would ostracize him. It may be unjust, but that's how things are. So you mustn't be too hard on him. Under his bombast he's a kind and decent person."

"I still can't believe there is — sexual activity between men. I never heard a whisper of it as a girl."

"There was no mention of it in my household either. It's old as the Greeks, but it's largely a forbidden subject."

"When two men — you know, when they're together —" Fritzi was red. "What do they do?"

Mrs. Van Sant reached into a wooden box with a feathered Indian chief decorating the lid. "Oh, I expect you'll catch on if you think about it. Live and let live's a trite motto, but useful. In the theater it's an absolute necessity."

Fritzi did think about it overnight. Next morning she asked Manchester to step down the street with her, to a coffee shop, at noon.

"I can't, I've no time."

She looked at him squarely. "I know why you took me to supper. It wasn't Fritzi Crown you wanted for company, it was a woman. Any woman."

"Oh, dear heaven." Pale and trembling, he said, "In front of the theater. Twelve sharp."

At the coffee house, she chose a rear table with no customers near. "I feel used," she said when the waiter left.

"I am deeply ashamed. Who gossiped? Was it that harpy Van Sant?"

"Oh, no. How I heard isn't important. I can't tell you how angry I felt. I did discuss it with Eustacia later. I wanted us to have this minute away from the others so I could tell you I'm not angry any longer. You've been kind to me. I want to return that kindness. Your private life doesn't matter."

He collected himself, took a deep breath. "Fritzi, to cleanse my soul I must reveal another act of duplicity. I hired you not solely for your talent but because I could pay you less than I am paying the other witches. If you throw that coffee in my face I'll not blame you. But if you can possibly forgive me I'll raise you at once to sixt— fifteen dollars. I have used you ill, but I'll never do it again if you'll remain my friend. God knows I have few enough."

She squeezed his hand. "Forgiven on all counts. I meant what I said."

He gulped and blew on his cooling coffee. "Well. I feel ever so much better. I hated to deceive you. Poverty and necessity are cruel masters. But the masks are off. It's your turn to answer a question candidly. How do you feel about the play?"

"I'm feeling fine about it. I believe we'll have a great success on Monday night."

Which was an outright lie.

"You're sincere?"

"Oh, a hundred percent."

Which was another. By now Fritzi had almost been seduced by the spell of the Scottish play. Bright as any display in the white-light district, an electric sign in her imagination kept flashing a single word.

Disaster.

22. Tess

The weekend forecast promised unusually fine weather. Carl got the information from Jesse, who read one or more papers every day. He picked them up after white workers had discarded them at the foundry.

During his Saturday lunch period Carl telephoned the Clymer residence on Piety Hill, a stretch of Woodward Avenue noted for churches and posh mansions. He waited nervously while a servant summoned Tess to the phone.

"I thought you'd gone to China, or forgotten me."

He laughed. "I'm a working man. Last Sunday I had a race down in Monroe, which I lost. It'll be a fine day tomorrow. Would you like to go out to Belle Isle?"

"Yes."

She met him at the Third Street docks. He bought two round trips, a total of twenty cents. It was a spectacular late summer afternoon, windless and fair. The one-fifteen ferry was packed with families carrying picnic hampers to the city's favorite playground.

Though it was Sunday, traffic on the Detroit River was heavy. Paddle-wheel ferries plowed back and forth between Windsor and Detroit. Great iron-hulled lake boats loaded with ore or wheat passed steamers inbound from Cleveland, outbound to Buffalo. A freighter named *Alpena*

213

Beauty maneuvered toward the piers with huge stacks of cordwood on fore and aft decks. Carl and Tess leaned on the railing, Tess clutching her flat-crowned straw hat.

Instead of the lush green of May and June, Belle Isle wore a patchwork coat of parched yellow and dull brown, the mark of a scorching summer. The family groups dispersed to picnic tables. Carl and Tess followed the path to the canoe concession. He rented a canoe and handed her into it, grinning like a fool when she squeezed his hand and gave him a deep look with her beautiful blue eyes. He was so flustered he nearly missed the canoe as he stepped in.

Pushing off, he noticed a sudden pallor on her cheeks. She put a hand to her lips.

"What's wrong?"

"Nothing, nothing. Just a little dizzy spell. My, isn't it a gorgeous day?"

He paddled from one lagoon into another. Bare willow branches touched the water beside the banks. In an open area high school boys played a rowdy game of baseball. Carl said, "Seen anything of Wayne lately?"

"No. Why should you care about him?"

"You said he's keen on you."

"Oh well, yes, but it's hopeless. Unfortunately, he and my father don't know it."

"What's hopeless?"

"The prospect of my marrying Wayne. Father brings it up often. Wayne proposed last year. He nearly burst a blood vessel when I turned him down. I wouldn't marry him if we were the only two people on earth."

"You're an independent sort. Where did that come from?"

"Not Piety Hill or Grosse Pointe, I assure you." She unpinned her hat, laid it in her lap, drew the combs out of her hair, and shook it free in the sunshine, a glittering golden fall. "It was my mother. She taught fourth grade in the public schools. When Father began to make money, climb up the social ladder as he'd always wanted, he asked her to stop teaching. She wouldn't. She said she still had important missionary work among the heathen."

"Heathen? In the schools?"

"It was just her expression. She meant young children who would be condemned to lowly jobs and sordid lives if they didn't finish a basic education — assuming they had the opportunity. She taught in a white school, where there's a twelve-year program. She wanted the colored schools to offer just as much. Black children got only six years of schooling — still do. Mama made herself unpopular over that, but she never gave up the fight. She believed that whoever you were, you couldn't be strong in this world, couldn't survive, if you were stupid. She said it took brains to defy conformity and find your own path. I took it to heart long before she died."

Carl beached the canoe. They strolled along a secluded path to the island's Canadian side, isolated from the picnic crowds and baseball games. In a patch of shade, Carl took her hands in his. "I've got to tell you something. Like your friend Wayne, I'm keen for you."

215

She looked at him steadily. "I like you too, Carl. A lot. But you don't strike me as a man who'd want a permanent attachment with a girl. Any girl."

"I would —" He swallowed to clear a great lump in his windpipe. "I would if I fell in love with her."

A sudden joy sprang into her eyes, and perhaps a tear; in the muted shade it was hard to be sure. She gripped his hand fiercely, then kissed him, a long, ardent kiss.

He threw his arm around her, plunged his face into her sun-warmed hair. He felt her whole body, her billowy breasts, her hips and legs, tight against him. "Oh, God," he whispered. "I'm shaky."

"Me too."

"How did this happen?"

"I don't know, it just did."

"What do we do?" What he wanted to do was carry her into some hidden glade and make love. His body was reacting to hers; surely she felt it.

"For now, nothing. Just let it take its course."

He held her tightly, bringing his right hand up to caress her hair. They heard voices coming near — broke apart, saw two youngsters, a boy and a girl, playing tag. They stepped away from each other. Both were red-faced.

For the rest of the afternoon they avoided the subject of their newly confessed feelings. Each seemed to understand that there was a degree of impossibility, impracticality, in a permanent relationship. Yet Carl had a strange conviction that he was already in the middle of one, excitingly but perhaps dangerously entrapped.

On the ferry back to the city, Tess grew faint again. She had to sit down in the main cabin. Carl sat beside her, anxious.

"Tess, tell me, what is it?"

"Something we can't talk about."

"I never heard of an ache or a fever people couldn't talk about."

"This is neither. It's a female matter. One that even women don't discuss, unless they use code words. It isn't serious, just maddening because it comes regularly." She took out a handkerchief, wiped her eyes, gave him a regretful look. "What must you think of me? I almost wrote you a treatise, didn't I?"

"I apologize for asking. I embarrassed you."

She squeezed his hand again, managed to laugh. "If it was anyone but you I wouldn't stand for it. Now you know for certain that I'm not a proper girl, don't you?"

"That's what I like. That's why I took to you. How many young ladies would sit on a fence to watch a bunch of idiots kill themselves in automobiles?"

23. Jesse and Carl

Smiles were plentiful on Piquette Avenue. Orders were pouring in for the new little car that was noisy, and homely, but pleased people with its price, especially farmers who'd never had such a cheap and comfortable way to get to town. A pattern of strong orders from Ford agencies in rural areas quickly developed. So did jokes about the Model T. Employees passed them around like medals of heroism. If Mr. Ford hadn't won the class war in the auto business, he'd won a major engagement. Carl discussed it with Tess when he next saw her. Tess said the instantaneous acceptance of the Model T made her father "livid."

Success created problems at Ford, the biggest being the company's inability to produce cars in greater volume. Late one Saturday Carl rode up to the third floor to bring down the last car of the day, and came upon a curious scene. A chassis without axles, wheels, or an engine stood on a large wooden pallet in the main aisle. A young fellow named Charlie Sorensen was talking earnestly to Mr. Ford, Jim Couzens, and a few other bosses. Sorensen came from the department that made wooden patterns. He was a Dane, blond and handsome as a matinee idol. A tow rope tied to the pallet hung over his right shoulder.

"It's a pretty simple idea, Henry. We do most if not all of the assembly in a single pass. We speed up the work by assembling the car while

218

it's moving. No more stopping to attach parts. We do everything on one floor."

One of the bosses, a perennial skeptic, said, "And where we do put everything, Charlie? If we stockpile engines and axles up here, what happens to the smaller parts? We don't have room."

"We move the smaller parts out of here. We build things like the radiator and hose assembly elsewhere, and store them. We figure out how many subassemblies we need on a given day and have those brought up exactly on schedule. Every hour, every two hours — we'll figure it out. But the line never stops. Watch."

Ford stood with arms folded as Sorensen and a foreman named Ed Martin picked up the rope and pulled, slowly moving the pallet while gangs of men rushed in to lift the chassis and mount front and rear axles, then wheels.

"Hank, it'll never work," the skeptic said to the boss.

Ford ran a finger up and down his chin. "I don't know, boys. In the new plant it might. Let me think about it a while. I appreciate your worrying about this, Charlie. We're already backlogged till next January. If we add a shift, our unit cost goes up. But if we don't go faster, we'll have to cut off dealer orders."

"You'll have to fire me first," Couzens snorted. "Cash flow's thin enough now."

"I'll think on it," Ford promised. Carl thought the idea of a moving line was interesting, but he too doubted its workability.

Jesse Shiner worked at Clymer Foundry No. 1

on Detroit's east side. The foundry cast engine blocks for Maxwell, Reo, and some other local car manufacturers. It was nasty, dangerous work. Clouds of soot filled the air. The melting furnaces were so hot, five minutes into his shift Jesse's clothes were glued to him and stayed that way all day. If a ladle tipped at the wrong moment, he could be roasted alive.

A few white men, Polish immigrants with little or no English, worked alongside the blacks. It amused Jesse to see soot and grease darken them till they were all but indistinguishable from those of his race. The white men had one advantage, though. If they could find better jobs, they wouldn't be turned down because of color. Jesse and the other blacks had no place to go, unless it was into the poisonous atmosphere of an auto paint shop. Or you could always be a janitor.

Jesse Shiner was the son of a South Carolina slave who had worked cotton and tobacco fields until he jumped on the Underground Railroad before the Civil War and took the long, perilous journey to Canada. He settled in Chatham, Ontario, and there married a light-skinned woman who'd traveled the same freedom path from the South. The Shiners had two sons, Jesse and Lester. After their parents died, the brothers split a $300 inheritance, and Jesse emigrated to Detroit, lured by the possibility of a better life in the growing industrial city.

Jesse endured the heat and grime of Clymer No. 1, and the occasional abuse of white foremen who had one name to cover all their black workers — "Hey, nigger" — because his weekly pay envelope let him live his life outside the foundry with some regularity and order. When he was thirty he bought a frame cottage on Columbia, two blocks below the lodging house where Carl settled. He furnished the cottage from secondhand stores, a piece at a time. He whitewashed it and planted flowers. He joined a black Masonic lodge and Ebenezer A.M.E. Church on Calhoun Street. There he met a handsome young black woman named Grace, the only woman he ever truly loved. They courted for a while, but she saw a better future with a young black dentist. She left Detroit as the dentist's bride and broke Jesse's heart.

Jesse stood foursquare for the rights of laboring men of whatever color. In a wave of strikes that swept the Detroit metal industry in 1907, mostly to promote closed union shops, Jesse picketed with his mates outside Clymer No. 1. In return for that show of courage, he got his head beaten and his shoulder dislocated by the clubs of strike breakers sent by the Labor Bureau. The Bureau was a city-wide recruiting station for thugs. Owners of businesses funded it. The Bureau kept records on forty thousand men in the work force, identifying known trouble-makers to prospective employers.

The strike fizzled out; there would be no union shop at Clymer No. 1. The irony was, the bosses had to rehire many of the strikers, including Jesse, because the inexperienced scabs quit after a few days in the hellish heat.

Jesse was self-educated and never stopped learning. A white friend in the scheduling department drew books for him from the public library; it wasn't prudent for a black man to show up there. He'd taught himself about gasoline engines by reading trade magazines and hanging around auto races on Sunday, usually doing some dirty job like sweeping, throwing out oil cans, or lugging tires to the pits in return for the privilege of watching the white mechanics. He met Carl Crown that way.

In a small shed he built on the alley behind his house, he installed an elaborate arrangement of drawers and bins for storing miscellaneous auto parts, everything from bolts and washers to fan blades and patched tires, an inventory that he built up gradually over several years. The shed had a dirt floor but was otherwise a model of cleanliness. Working by the light of several coal oil lanterns, Jesse did repairs for local garages facing an overload. Sometimes he worked until three and four A.M. to make his extra money.

Of an evening Carl helped out. He tended to blunder about clumsily sometimes, spill things or knock them over. Once he dropped a whole drawer of nuts and washers, upsetting Jesse so much he swore at his friend. Oddly, though, when Carl climbed into a race car, he was different. He was alert, careful, precise. When he turned a screwdriver to repair a carburetor or an old chain-drive transmission, he never broke anything, never scratched anything.

One cool Monday night when Carl came over, Jesse noticed a change in his friend. Carl had a distracted, dreamy air. Jesse knew it was the girl, Clymer's daughter, said to be a fine young woman, though highly independent. Because Jesse knew what kind of man his friend was, he wondered if Carl understood the possible consequences of his obsession. If he did, fine. If he didn't — well, maybe someone should set him straight, as an act of friendship.

Carl and Jesse sat in the shed with a single large growler of beer between them and a fire burning in the small wood stove in the corner; the evening was cool. Carl was patching a balloon tire inner tube. Jesse scratched his chin.

"See Miss Tess again yesterday, did you?"

Carl nodded as he roughed the tube surface with a little tin gadget in preparation for applying the cement.

"Pretty serious about her, are you?"

Carl looked up. "I guess I am, yes."

"Speak out plain. You in love with her?"

Carl looked up. "Since you ask, Mrs. Nosy, yes."

"She feel the same way?"

"I think so."

"She want to marry up with you?"

"What the hell is this, a police investigation?" He shook his head. "Someone already called the plant today, asking where I live."

Jesse frowned. "Who was it?"

"Some phantom from the Employers' Association. Wouldn't say why he wanted to know. Ford's doesn't give out that kind of information without a reason. Let's get back to the subject. Why are you asking all these questions?"

"Just having a friendly talk. You listen to me a minute."

Carl's eyes narrowed down. He took up the growler, drank some of the warm beer, passed the can to Jesse, and waited.

"You marry that girl, for the rest of your natural life you'll be marrying one of those time clocks you hate so much. That is, if you want to do right by her."

"Would I do anything else? Don't make me sound like a damn criminal."

"Trying to tell the truth, that's all."

Carl scratched the palms of his hands. Jesse was pushing him to face an issue he'd consciously run away from. His voice dropped. "And?"

"I just want to know, Carl. You got it in you to be a steady husband, with a steady job? I'm not against folks marrying. I wanted to marry Grace Williams like I never wanted anything, but she wouldn't have me. So I'm not against folks marrying, no sir, but I'm against them marrying and then making each other miserable. Life's mean enough the way it is. You're my friend. Maybe the best friend I ever had. White men at the foundry, they don't bother to spit on this nigger 'less they want something. Want me to speed up work, mostly. You've got a lot of good stuff, Carl. So be careful. Don't leap too quick. There's lots of other white girls who —"

Carl's brown eyes flashed. "Shut up. There aren't any like Tess."

Jesse sighed. "Figured you might say something like that. Wasted my breath, did I?"

"Yes."

But he'd planted a seed.

24. Rehearsal for a Tragedy

"Places!" Simkins clapped as he crossed from the prompt side to the o.p., opposite prompt, side like a fussy mother. "Clear the stage, ladies and gentlemen. Places for act one. Dress rehearsal is already an hour behind schedule. Mutt?"

A trap dropped open behind the witches' cauldron set center stage. Above, lights tinted by colored gels dimmed to the proper levels. The prompter, Mr. Entwistle, fussily arranged himself at his table behind the proscenium opening stage right. Hobart marched up to Fritzi. He rubbed his thumb under her right eye.

"You're a highland enchantress, not a red Indian. Try a number four stick, even a three. Let Miss Whittemeyer help you. Please don't come on looking so florid."

Hobart's costume was stained with simulated mud and blood. He sweated fiercely under his powder and grease paint as he inspected one actor after another. In the wings Simkins shouted, "Where's Mutt?"

"Not down here," yelled the scene shifter in the trap. He lit his smoke pots and turned on the electric fan that blew smoke upward behind the cauldron. Fritzi thought the effect cheap and pathetic. She adjusted her straggly wig.

Ida Whittemeyer fanned herself. "Sally had better get up here or Manchester will flay her." Sally had arrived late, puffy-eyed. Fritzi looked stage left, to the stairs leading down to the dressing rooms.

At that moment Sally screamed:

"Stop him, someone, stop him. Thief!"

A man bolted up the stairs, ran toward the artists' entrance. The actors milling on stage were agog. Fritzi gasped. "Mutt!"

Sally kept screaming. Mutt reversed himself suddenly. Pop Foy appeared behind him with a fire ax, blocking Mutt's retreat. Mutt ran on stage. Sally came up the stairs. "He stole my money!"

"Simkins, call the bobbies," Hobart bellowed. He pulled his prop claymore from its scabbard, whirled it over his head with two hands. "Hold right there, sir."

Mutt cursed and charged him. Hobart swung the prop sword sideways and down. Mutt leaped in the air, and the painted blade passed under his boots. The momentum of Hobart's swing, though, whirled him like a top. Mutt slammed both hands into Hobart's back, dashed up the ramp to the stage left rostrum. Mr. Gertz and Mr. Seldon chased him. Mutt jumped from the rostrum, a leap that landed him on stage a foot from Fritzi. He grabbed her, spun her, choked her with his elbow. He pushed her toward Hobart. "Chop her, you fat fraud."

Mutt dodged between the actors like a football runner. He overturned the prompt table, and Mr. Entwistle. He vanished in the wings but reappeared chased by Simkins, now armed with a short two-by-four.

Mutt grabbed the proscenium, pivoted

around it, and jumped into the orchestra pit without looking. He vaulted over the rail and ran up the aisle and disappeared.

Fritzi took deep breaths, rubbing her throat. Eustacia Van Sant pulled Hobart against her bosom. "Bravely done, Manchester."

"Athletic bugger," Hobart panted. "Fritzi my girl? You all right?"

"Yes."

The cast and crew swarmed up both aisles and out the glass doors to Forty-eighth. The street shone with reflections; rain blew under the marquee. The thief was gone.

In the foyer, Sally broke down, huddled in Fritzi's arms. "I walked in on him. He'd pulled my purse out of the drawer and was counting the money. When I told him to stop, he threw a chair at my head. Then he hit me, here." She rubbed her breast. Tears made her eyeliner melt and run.

"How much did he take?" Ida asked.

"All that was left of this week's salary, twelve dollars. I can't believe he'd steal from me. I was with him last night — all night, in his room. The bastard."

It took an hour to calm Sally and get her into her costume, ready for the dress rehearsal. During that time the police arrived. Three officers searched the theater and nearby streets and alleys, without result.

At a quarter of ten in the evening, Simkins again called places. The witches found their marks behind the cauldron. Fritzi straightened her wig again. Mr. Entwistle flipped to the first page of his prompt book.

Simkins called cues into a speaking tube. Red and amber gels went on above the cauldron. The cheap fan whirred in the trap. A flood in the wings spilled green light on the witches. Smoke rose. Fritzi crossed her fingers.

The curtain puller worked his rope, and they began.

Fritzi agreed with Mrs. Van Sant that the rehearsal was draggy, not to say dreadful. Of course, one rather lost one's perspective in a dark theater at half past one in the morning, listening to notes from a director as weary and nervous as his actors. How could one expect better of Hobart, or any of them, after the shattering excitement of a robbery?

Hobart said, "That concludes notes. Let me say in summary, it was a damn poor show. So take heart. We all know that a botched dress rehearsal means a flawless opening night. Please rest yourselves and come in refreshed. You are dismissed."

"Line rehearsal tomorrow at three," Simkins reminded them. "The evening call is thirty-five minutes before curtain. Five before seven."

Conclusion of the ordeal had a remarkable restorative effect on Fritzi and the others. Mrs. Van Sant and the witches agreed that they needed a bowl of oyster stew and a libation. Fritzi fairly flew through the cold-creaming of her face, and the four ladies hurried along largely empty streets to an oyster palace on Forty-third, near the Grand Central terminal. By twos and threes the company drifted in, excepting Manchester, Launcelot Buford, and his repellent mother, and the other boy actor. The oyster house had hours until four, but patrons were scarce in the early morning — just a straggle of drinkers at the long mahogany bar. The manager turned on lights in a private dining room which had a piano. Lethargic waiters served oyster stew with little yellow globules of butter floating in it, bowls of crackers, steins of beer, and cups of coffee. Fritzi ordered coffee. Eustacia drank two gins in short order. "Eases the torture of the corset stays, don't you know?"

Old Mr. Allardyce, wide awake despite his age, rolled up his sleeves and played a succession of popular numbers. Members of the cast, singly or in impromptu pairs and trios, rose to warble the lyrics and receive tipsy applause. Soon everyone was having a fine time, roistering in a way that would hurt damnably in the morning but, for the present, warmed the soul. These little parties in which actors forgot their wounds and fears and inhibitions were among the greatest joys of Fritzi's life in the theater.

At three A.M. Mr. Allardyce showed no sign of flagging. More trays of drinks arrived. The waiters looked slightly more perky, anticipating tips. They didn't know actors, Fritzi thought.

Soon she felt her eyelids drooping. Another half hour had gone by. Eustacia sat with her stocking feet resting on a vacant chair. She held out a full tumbler of gin. "Care for any? I can't swallow another drop."

Fritzi shuddered. "Oh, no, thanks. I must go home. I don't want to be completely exhausted tomorrow night." She gathered up her wrap and purse. "How do you suppose the opening will go?"

Eustacia stifled a huge yawn. "Given a smidgen of luck, we'll get through all five acts with no one dead or maimed. Beyond that, I am not sanguine."

Fritzi wanted to be brave, exuberant — confident. But she wasn't. Murmuring goodbyes, she and Eustacia left the oyster house in search of taxis. Fritzi's wan and weary face perfectly masked the doubt and anxiety churning within her.

25. Tragedy

Fritzi arrived at the Novelty a whole hour before curtain. A drizzly rain dampened the streets. She felt wretched. Not only was she tired from the late night at the oyster house, she had cramps. They were no less painful for being familiar.

Eustacia whispered that she'd seen Hobart. "His eyes are standing out of his head big as eggs. Simkins told me the little worm encountered a funeral procession on his way to the theater. Should have kept to the alleys, the fool. Dear Lord, what next?"

Making up, Fritzi couldn't remember her first line. This had never happened before. She searched among the pots and tubes and sticks until she found her crumpled side for I-i. She folded it and tucked it under the frayed rope that belted her ugly dirt-colored smock. Another cramp attacked her. She hugged herself with her eyes shut until it passed.

Some actors traditionally gave small gifts on opening night. Though she could scarcely afford it, she had nickel cigars for the gentlemen, rose petal sachets for the ladies, and cheap penknives for the two surly boys. Mr. Denham received his cigar while fingering worry beads. Mr. Gertz showed her a Roman Catholic medal with a likeness of St. Genesius, the actor's patron saint reputedly martyred by the emperor Diocletian. She discovered her friend in her dressing room with hands clasped and head bowed in front of an engraving of a person in a periwig.

"Eustacia, who on earth is that?"

"David Garrick. Some say he's lucky. It can't hurt."

A cold sweat of terror bathed Fritzi then.

Pop Foy mournfully told them the rain showers had become a downpour. The audience arrived sodden. People sneezed and complained. Listening behind the curtain — only amateurs peered out to count the house — Fritzi despaired. Some audiences generated an electricity that excited and inspired actors, but others had, as it were, dead batteries. Audiences like that applauded limply, if at all. They always laughed in the wrong places.

At twenty past seven Manchester called the company together on stage. He did indeed look queasy and shaken. "I am delighted to report that the house is more than three quarters subscribed." A few strained expressions lightened briefly. "But with great regret I must announce that earlier today, Mr. Entwistle sprained his back when thrown from his chair by that cur Mutt. The prompt table will be empty this evening. Mr. Simkins will hold the book, but you must remember he will be extremely busy calling cues. I am sure all of you will surmount this small problem with no difficulty."

Fritzi felt bilious, dizzy. Her teeth chattered. She'd experienced symptoms of stage fright many times before, but never so severely. She unfolded the side but couldn't read it under the dim lights.

Simkins called places. Fritzi touched the curtain for luck. Ida Whittemeyer quickly hugged each of her weird sisters. Fritzi held up crossed fingers. Sally Murphy squeezed their hands and said, "Break a leg," which was supposed to insure that you wouldn't, and everything would go swimmingly.

The curtain rose.

The tragedy began.

In the first scene the cheap electric fan in the trap shorted. With a squeal the blades stopped revolving. Smoke immediately thickened behind the cauldron. Ida Whittemeyer was convulsed by coughing. For nearly half a minute she was unable to continue.

Making his first entrance on the blasted heath, Hobart ripped his cloak on a nail. The sound, unfortunately loud, resembled a bodily function. It caused titters throughout the audience.

In Hobart's dagger speech, the follow spot sputtered, sizzled, and expired.

One of the murderers fell off a ramp. It wasn't a graceful tumble but a pratfall. In the wings, Fritzi cringed at the laughter.

By the time the curtain rose on act three, everyone's timing was off. Lines were delivered at locomotive speed, or dragged out unendurably. Mrs. Van Sant went up. She stood slack-jawed, staring at the prompt side of the stage. Simkins lost his place in the book. Mrs. Van Sant snarled, "Line, you blithering ass, *line!*" Those in the front rows heard, and laughed.

Simkins found the line. She recovered and delivered it. The damaged play rolled on like a cart with a wheel missing.

In Launcelot Buford's scene with Miss Whittemeyer, he slipped her a live goldfish. She shrieked and threw it away. Unfortunately, many people saw the fish flopping on the stage, with predictable mirth. One of the murderers broke up in laughter and had to exit.

In any large production there was usually at least one actor drunk, and tonight was no exception. It wasn't Mr. Allardyce, however, but a hired super, a Birnam wood marcher who waved his branch so vigorously that he knocked the helmet off the man next to him. The helmet rolled off the apron and fell in the orchestra pit, onto the snare drum. Hobart had engaged a two-piece orchestra, violin and drum — not an ideal combination for a classical play, but cheap.

The helmet bounced on the drum. After several impromptu taradiddles, it bounced out of the drummer's reach and concluded its performance by striking the floor like a Chinese gong. The entire audience howled, entertained at last.

In the climactic duel Macduff's tin-plate sword nicked the edge of a rostrum and bent like taffy. Completely thrown, Mr. Denham dropped the sword twice as he attempted to straighten it. Hobart tried to cover by staggering about, indicating pain from a wound. Since Macduff hadn't touched him yet, it looked more like an attack of indigestion. The audience hooted and whistled.

Hobart's prop claymore was made of stouter stuff: wood. When he finally struck a defensive blow, the claymore snapped in half at the hilt. In the stunned silence Hobart could be heard to say, *"Oh, my gawd."*

Hilarity reigned everywhere but on stage.

The audience fled the theater after one curtain call, which included a good many boos and catcalls. Fritzi wanted to weep. Their Scottish play was not a tragedy but a farce. The three-wheeled cart was pointed downhill and accelerating madly toward the graveyard of all such misbegotten vehicles, the morning reviews.

The *New York Rocket* was first on the street. Mrs. Van Sant rose and read the notice aloud in a private room on the upstairs level of Charles Rector's swanky Broadway restaurant. The cast had gathered for a party that had the appearance and atmosphere of a wake for victims of an earthquake.

" 'Mr. Hobart Manchester's production at the Novelty suits the venue, as it is so novel, so unique in its particular badness, as to numb even the most insensitive devotee of the Bard, and wring floods of pity from any compassionate Christian who has the misfortune to attend. Ill-conceived and miserably acted by a company of almost amateurish awfulness, it quickly descends into unintentional comedy and never recovers. Further, I have seldom if ever seen a more tawdry' — so on and so forth," she muttered, skipping down the columns. " 'Evidence of penny pinching is everywhere evident. Costumes appear to come from a rag bag, except for those worn by the English actress Mrs. Van Sant, which are more appropriate to the runway of a vaudeville house.' Bastard!" She threw the paper on the floor.

"Can you imagine a human being devoting his life to dispensing such cruelty? He must be sick. If I ever meet this man, he'll be a bloody eunuch before I'm through."

The actors applauded, but Fritzi noted a lack of enthusiasm. Ida Whittemeyer said, "I'm sure our valiant director and star echoes that sentiment. Where are you, Hobart?"

"Hobart! Hobart!" They stomped and clapped and looked around until Simkins said from the back of the room, "He sneaked out five minutes ago."

26. Closed

Simkins posted the closing notice before Thursday night's performance. Late Friday afternoon, Fritzi went uptown to the Novelty. The rain had let up only sporadically since Monday. The streets were dark, rank from garbage rotting in pools of water.

The theater had a sad, empty feeling again. Backstage she met Sally Murphy and Mr. O'Moore and Ida, all as dispirited as she was. They embraced and exchanged addresses and promised to write, fully understanding that they probably never would.

She'd already spoken to Eustacia by telephone. Her friend had booked a cheap cabin on the first available trans-Atlantic ship, a Greek vessel sailing Monday for Cherbourg and Piraeus. Hobart had cut off her Astor subsidy, and she was forced to move at her own expense, to a lesser hotel on Ninth Avenue. "A humiliation not to be endured."

Simkins said pay vouchers for the week would be ready at noon Saturday. Fritzi asked him, "Is Mr. Manchester in the theater?"

"Yes, but he's incommunicado."

"Well then, I'll see you tomorrow."

"No, I'll be in Albany. I signed on with a *Prisoner of Zenda* road company. The house treasurer will hand out the vouchers."

"So it's goodbye, Mr. Simkins. It's been a

pleasure knowing you."

"Oh, yes, very much so, Miss Crown." They shook hands like a couple of mourners.

Outside, she stood under the marquee, pelted by blowing rain. Her hands were cold and raw. Her knit gloves had fallen apart. She could hear her mother say, "*Liebchen,* a young lady doesn't appear in public without gloves." No, but unemployed actresses did.

Water roared off the edges of the marquee and rushed in the gutter behind her. The bitter September air felt more like winter. She stared at the paper strip pasted diagonally on the poster. CLOSED. Her cheeks were wet, but not from rain.

She'd looked on the *Macbeth* engagement as a benchmark, a full and final test of her ability to succeed in New York. She knew she wasn't personally responsible for the fiasco, but the result was the same. "What now?" She didn't realize she'd spoken until a peanut vendor going by with oilcloth covering his tray gave her a queer stare.

A lobby door swung open. Turning up the collar of his cape, Hobart emerged. "Fritzi! Did you come to see if it's true?"

"I suppose so," she said with a rueful smile.

"What have you found? Any suitable auditions on the horizon?"

"Not immediately."

"Too bad. How are you fixed?"

"I won't starve for another two or three weeks."

"Ah, the cruelty of the profession. I am only

slightly more solvent. This afternoon I settled with the scenery and costume houses. I didn't do it until I determined that we had enough to pay everyone in the company full wages."

"I want to tell you again how sorry I am."

"No sorrier than I, dear girl."

"Tuesday and Wednesday's performances were very good. Last night's was thrilling."

"Nevertheless, the curse on the play overtook us. I should have produced *A Midsummer Night's Dream*. Fairies are harmless. I shall miss you, Fritzi. But we needn't say goodbye just yet. I have enough in my pocket for supper at Rector's. If you don't order too much."

He opened his cape, pulled out his pocket watch, disdainful of the rabbit's foot hanging on the chain. "We can't dine respectably for at least an hour. Let's go see some galloping tin-types."

"You mean pictures, at a nickelodeon?"

"Yes. I enjoy them. The Variety's just there. Come." He linked his arm with hers. She didn't have the heart to tell him how much she disliked the cheap entertainment.

As they walked along beneath her umbrella, Fritzi said, "I understand the picture companies hire legitimate actors. I've heard the wages are good, five dollars a day. Would you act in one?"

"I? Certainly not."

"I feel the same way."

Hobart paid for tickets to the 5¢ Variety. Another program was just letting out. They found seats on a hard bench near the back. Soon the nickelodeon was full. The projector clattered, and a light beam pierced the dark. A flickering image appeared — a title card.

"Ah, good, another Biograph," Hobart whispered. "They make rather thrilling little stories."

In the one-reel melodrama, lasting about fifteen minutes, a young society girl was abducted by kidnappers and rescued by the family chauffeur with whom she finally eloped, love and courage having triumphed over social class. Fritzi was a bit embarrassed to find herself caught up in the story. A sequence of actualities, the kind Paul photographed, came next. A strong man lifted a lioness over his head; a Zeppelin floated past the Eiffel Tower; Kaiser Wilhelm's Death's Head hussars galloped through a Berlin parkland; five girls in bathing costumes frolicked in the surf at the Jersey shore. The program concluded with another reel split between a pair of short comedies. Characters stepped in buckets and fell off ladders. Autos came within an ace of crashing into one another. All this the audience, Fritzi excepted, found hilarious. She did observe that no actors were named on the title cards of the pictures, only the studio and, in one case, the director.

Later, seated on the upstairs level of Charles Rector's swanky restaurant, they ordered platters of fried oysters, a house specialty. Fritzi said, "What will you do? Try the West End again?"

He fixed a melancholy eye on the ceiling. "No, I think not. Too many there know me. My professional failures, my — personal life. Furthermore, I admire this country of yours. I'd jolly well like to remain here. I know I can mount another production in a year or two. Then I'll be right back on top."

She recognized the unreality of his optimism. Actors were universally guilty of deluding themselves. It was how they survived in a frequently hopeless profession. She was no exception.

"I've made a few inquiries already," he said. "William Gillette's taking his *Sherlock Holmes* on another extended tour, a year or more. I might do Moriarty. It's that or an outing with James O'Neill's chestnut, *The Count of Monte Cristo*. Whatever happens, I want us to remain friends, and keep in touch."

"We shall do both, Hobart. That's a promise."

Eustacia Van Sant's suite on *Athena* was a luxurious accommodation of rosewood and red plush. She introduced Fritzi to a small, grinning Greek gentleman in a white jacket with shoulder boards. "Mr. Ragoustis is chief purser. The dear man moved me up from a cabin no bigger than a coffin to this suite. We're going to be great friends." She bent to kiss his forehead, giving him a peek into her cleavage. He left wearing an expression of bleary bliss.

"Here's my address in Sloane Square," Eustacia said. "Do not forget me."

"That's impossible, Eustacia."

Eustacia moved in and out of a maze of trunks and grips, counting silently. "What are your plans?"

241

Fritzi sighed as she sat on a green velvet otto-man. "I honestly don't know."

"Don't give up. You have an excellent talent."

"It's hard to keep believing that."

The ship's horn sounded. They hugged, kissed, and Fritzi ran down the gangplank to the pier. Eustacia appeared at the rail of the prome-nade deck. She waved, Fritzi waved, a band played. Passengers threw confetti and colorful paper streamers as *Athena* backed into the Hud-son, swung about, and steamed toward the At-lantic. Fritzi discovered she was crying again.

27. Paul and Harry

In the last bright days of autumn, just before the national election, Paul returned to New York. He'd finished his trip in California, photographing spectacular scenery on the wild coast around Monterey, and then the remarkable rebuilding in San Francisco.

He checked into the small but smart Hotel Algonquin on Forty-fourth and telephoned his cousin. A woman with an accent said, "Just a minute, I go get her."

"Aunt Ilsa told me about the play when I came through Chicago," he said when Fritzi came on the line. "I'm really sorry. Are you in anything now?"

"My waitress oxfords," she replied with a laugh. "I'm back in another hash house. When can I see you?"

"I'm afraid tonight's out. My American publisher and his wife are taking me to dinner at Rector's. What about tomorrow?"

"Sunday's grand, I'm off."

He suggested a picnic in Central Park. He'd make the arrangements. "With your permission I'll invite an old friend. I met him on *Rhineland* when I came over in '92. Herschel Wolinski was his name then. Now he's Harry Poland. He writes music."

"Oh yes, I know his songs. I'd love to meet him."

243

They set the hour, half past twelve. "I'll hire a cab and pick you up."

"No, no, I'm too far downtown, I'll meet you." A sudden suspicion told him she didn't want him to see where she lived.

He waited for her by the great equestrian statue of Sherman on Fifth Avenue. A big wicker hamper packed by the hotel kitchen rested on the pavement beside a lacquered case holding his stereoscopic camera. He had to have photos of the reunion. Even when he was Pauli Kroner, the boy who turned into Paul Crown, people had teased him about being a pack rat. He'd already collected mementoes of this trip — souvenir menus saved from *Lusitania*, picture postcards from cities he'd visited, a small metal Statue of Liberty for Shad, a doll for Betsy. He still needed a present for Julie. He missed her keenly. Today promised a small respite from his homesickness.

He checked his pocket watch. Twelve-fifteen. Just then he heard, "Pauli! Here I am!"

Waving, she bounced on her toes on the opposite side of Fifty-ninth. She darted across in front of a steam car and threw herself into his arms. They whirled around, hugging, while Sunday strollers stared. Fritzi wore a dark blue gored skirt and a long-sleeved shirtwaist, blue and white check with white piping. A navy blue admiral's cap perched on her blond hair.

She kissed his cheek. "Don't you look wonderful."

"You too." Actually, he thought she looked pale and starved.

"Where's your friend?"

"He'll be here presently. He knows where to meet us."

"Tell me about him. How old is he?"

"Younger than I am. Twenty-seven, twenty-eight."

"Married?"

"I'm afraid so."

"Oh, too bad. Lives in Manhattan, I suppose?"

"He has an office in the Tin Pan Alley district on Twenty-ninth Street, but he lives in Port Chester. He's taking a noon train."

"Is he bringing his wife?"

"No, she's in a wheelchair." They walked along a winding footpath. It had turned into a glorious day, clear and bracing. The trees showed vivid fall color; the light through the leaves had a theatrical quality. Leaf smoke from bonfires mixed with the pungent odor of horse droppings on the nearby bridle path.

"Harry's wife suffered a stroke some years ago," Paul continued. "She was a very successful singer, Flavia Farrel, twenty years older than Harry. He was her accompanist and musical conductor." Her lover too. He didn't mention that.

"Flavia helped Harry break in, gave him his first musical job. When the stroke ended her career, he married her. He's cared for her ever since." Harry was that kind — sentimental and loyal. Paul stopped on the path, studying a rise to their left. "There's the place Harry described. Come on."

He carried the hamper, she took the stereo camera, and they climbed to the sunlit summit of the knoll. The next half hour passed in a rush of questions about his trip, his lectures, Julie and Shad and Betsy. There were moments of sadness when they discussed her estrangement from her father.

Paul took off his cap and coat, loosened his cravat, rolled up his sleeves. Fritzi unbuttoned her cuffs and laid her hat aside. He handed her something wrapped in brown paper, which she undid.

"Oh, Paul." She held up the book. "I'm dying to read it."

"It's the London edition. Whatever success I have with it, I owe to you. Dick Davis wrote me to say he liked it tremendously — oh, there's Harry."

On the footpath, a tall, slender man with broad shoulders waved to them as he ran uphill with a canvas satchel. He wore a fine black suit, worsted with a faint gray check. His shoes had fancy kidskin tops and patent leather needle toes shiny as black mirrors. His white linen shirt sported thin vertical red stripes and a detachable white collar. A Windsor tie matched the wine-colored band on his derby.

Fritzi stood smiling while the two men danced around one another, hugging and slapping backs. They'd reached Ellis Island together, but immigration doctors had denied entry to young Herschel Wolinski and his family because the mother had trachoma. Herschel passionately wanted a new life in America, but he wouldn't abandon her and his two sisters. He returned to Poland with them while Paul went on to Chicago.

Determination brought him back to Ellis Island a second time. In 1901 he and Paul met by chance at Woolworth's on Sixth Avenue. Another song plugger was playing a hit of the day, a slow, faintly melancholy piano novelty called "Ragtime Rose" by Harry Poland. The composer was standing there listening when Paul recognized him.

"So this is Fritzi the actress. Charmed." Harry swept off his derby, kissed her hand. Curly black hair gleamed in the sunshine. His blue eyes were infectiously merry. "I've heard so much about you."

"I can say the same, Mr. Poland."

"Please, it's Harry."

"You write very catchy songs."

"And his own words," Paul said. "Good ones too. Pretty remarkable for someone who spoke only Polish ten years ago."

"That's very kind of both of you. I love American music. I write it for ordinary people who like tunes they can remember and hum. Do you mind if I remove my coat?" His suspenders were bright red, with brass buckles. Paul felt like a hobo in comparison.

"How's Flavia?" he asked.

"Alas, no change." He explained to Fritzi. "My wife is paralyzed below the waist. For a year she couldn't speak. Her singing career ended abruptly."

"I'm sorry, that's sad."

"We're doing fine now. We have an excellent nurse-housekeeper who lives in, and I look after Flavia when I'm home. I can't do any less. She did so much for me when I was a greenhorn who didn't know a soul in the music business."

Paul opened the picnic hamper, spread a white cloth. "Started your own publishing company yet?"

Harry was busy with the clasps of his satchel. "I'm still working freelance for other firms. Thinking a lot about it, though."

"Your automobile song's all over England and the Continent."

Harry smiled. "Seven hundred forty thousand copies worldwide — so far. I'm happy for the income, but I don't want to write topical novelties forever." He turned to Fritzi. "My dream is to write for the stage. I'm working like the dev— working hard to get a song or two interpolated in a show."

"I'm sure you will."

Harry's eyes sparkled. "As a matter of fact, so am I. There are no limits in this country. Everything's possible, including Harry Poland on Broadway. And I *will* start my own company one day. Meanwhile —"

He pulled gaudy sheet music from the satchel. "Let me present you with two of my latest." Paul read the titles. "Statue of Liberty Rag." "Sadie Loves to Fox Trot."

Paul exchanged another book for the sheet music, then handed the music to Fritzi. "Oh, no, take it to Julie," she said, and he acquiesced.

Harry brought out a worn concertina. "I

thought we should have music while we dine."

The hotel had packed cold chicken, liver paté, crackers and crudities, potato salad and rye bread and a bottle of claret. At the foot of the knoll a little girl rolled a hoop with a stick. A small boy jumped out of some shrubbery and yanked her braid. She screamed and ran. Seeing them, Paul longed for Julie and his children, and a day like this in Green Park.

Harry began to play "On a Sunday Afternoon." He followed it with "Take Me Out to the Ballgame." He's giving a concert for her, Paul thought with amusement. Fritzi was enchanted.

"The Road to Mandalay" came next, and "Aloha Oe." At Paul's insistence Harry played "That Automobiling Feeling." The music attracted a strolling policeman on the path. He stood listening and tapping his billy against his leg. He saluted Harry before he moved on.

Harry played the first notes of "Meet Me in St. Louis" before he said, "I wish I'd written this, it's truly American."

Fritzi clasped her hands, swaying. Harry laughed and bobbed his head. "Yes, it fairly begs you to dance, doesn't it? Do so!"

Fritzi jumped up, lifted her skirts to show the ankles of her long legs. She began to turn, surrendering to the music. Harry quickened the tempo. As she danced, she sang. She whirled faster, the afternoon sun lighting her blond hair from behind. Nimbly, she danced in the grass while Harry played, never looking at his fingering, only at her.

When the song ended, she sprawled out and

leaned on her elbows, laughing and breathing hard. Paul said it was time for photographs. He took Fritzi with Harry, Fritzi alone, and then, using a clever built-in shutter timer, the three of them together.

Paul rolled his coat up for a pillow and smoked a cigar. Harry asked Fritzi about her career. She described the failed Scottish play, able to laugh about some of the worst mishaps. She did an imitation of a Mr. Scarboro, and although Paul had never met the man, he knew him, and his nasty arrogance, instantly. Harry's applause egged Fritzi on to give them Teddy Roosevelt's grin and high-pitched voice, then the waddling gait of the enormously fat Bill Taft.

Soon it was four o'clock, and Harry announced that he had to catch a train. Clouds blackened the west; a storm was building. Harry took Fritzi's hand in a courtly way.

"It's been a wonderful afternoon. What a pleasure to meet you." He bent slowly and kissed her hand once more.

Fritzi murmured something appropriate and appreciative. Harry picked up his satchel and quickly disappeared in the Fifth Avenue crowds. Thunder boomed over the Hudson.

"I think he's keen for you, Fritz," Paul joked.

"He's charming, but he's married. I don't expect I'll see him again. Too bad. I liked him."

Paul studied his cousin. She meant it.

28. Boom Times

For Christmas Carl spent much more than he could afford — $9 — for Tess's present. He couldn't resist the gold bracelet in the jewelry case at Hudson's. It was a twist design, one of the golden strands smooth, the other embossed with tiny flowers. A $5 gents' vest chain he had his eye on for his father was bypassed in favor of a silk chain costing $1.90. His brother got a large two-blade pocketknife with a staghorn handle. To his mother and sister he sent souvenir plates hand-painted with a picture of the city's Soldiers' and Sailors' Monument. The art of buying appropriate gifts for Ilsa and Fritzi eluded him.

Tess said she loved the bracelet. In return she gave him a fine steel razor with an onyx handle and a wide leather belt in brown alligator finish with a silver eagle buckle.

The gloomy Michigan winter dragged on. Carl was desperate for the March thaw, the drying of the roads and dirt tracks, the chance to climb into the new Edmunds Special under construction in Hoot's five-bay carriage house behind his Jefferson Avenue mansion. Only Tess kept him sane, kept him crawling out of bed on sunless mornings, kept him trudging downstairs to hot gruel and battery-acid coffee with the three other lodgers, kept him trudging to the trolley stop through snow or fog or freezing rain to punch in at Piquette Avenue.

Through the winter their romance ripened, given an urgency by what Carl hoped and believed the eventual climax would be. He thought of that moment every time he took a nickel or a penny from the drawer where he kept miscellaneous articles, including a packet of safeties.

Was Tess a virgin? Given her bold ways, he guessed she wasn't. The question bedeviled him because he'd never deflowered a girl and didn't intend to make Tess the first. Yet he wondered about his own strength of will. Wondered whether he could hold back if she was unsullied but offered herself anyway.

Tess said the secrecy of their relationship was wearing her down. It went against her nature. She finally told her father she was seeing Carl; she didn't inform Carl until afterward.

Carl hid his annoyance. "Does he know we meet once or twice a week?"

"I didn't say so. I'm sure he can guess from all my absences. Besides, he was sufficiently exercised by the first piece of news. I'm afraid I got a little hot myself. I said he really had nothing to say about my beau. He hasn't spoken to me for two days. He'll get over it."

"I'm sorry I cause you trouble."

"Never say that." She laid her fingers on his lips. "Never. I'd walk through fire for you, Carl." She blushed. "One more shameless admission. With you I make a habit of them, don't I?"

On their Sunday outings he and Tess sometimes took trolleys, but if the streets were clear of snow and ice, she drove her runabout. When they could find no other place for intimacy, they hid behind the isinglass side curtains that snapped to the folding top. They kissed passionately in the front seat. As time passed their embraces grew bolder and more heated — lip rouge smeared, cheeks rubbed red, clothing mussed, hair rumpled till both of them resembled vaudeville clowns in fright wigs. Why not? He loved her, and said so. She said she loved him. Each said it often, like a devotion recited in church. Tess never mentioned the future, nor did he, except to say he couldn't wait to take her to a Tigers baseball game at Burns Park in the spring.

The popularity of the Model T created pressures at the factory. Hiring began for a second shift, but Detroit had a labor shortage. The motor car had finally caught on with a vast majority of the public; the auto plants were booming. Couzens complained that Ford had ten thousand orders for Model T's on the books, and a legion of irate dealers who couldn't get cars fast enough. Carl had no fear of losing his job unless it was by his own choice.

One night in April, Carl went to the repair shed to help Jesse but didn't find him. He sat down to wait, puzzling about an auto he'd noticed when he left the Gibbs house. It was a black two-passenger Clymer, parked the wrong way on the other side of the street, the top closed, the motor running. As Carl walked to the front gate, the driver suddenly clashed the gears and shot away. A corner street lamp shone briefly on the driver's face. Carl was almost sure it was Wayne Sykes. Walking to Jesse's, he asked himself whether he should laugh, or worry. He still didn't know. But he was damn sure he didn't like to be spied on.

After forty minutes Jesse walked in. A large gauze patch was taped below his left eye; a wound had bled through, staining the bandage.

"Where the devil did you get that?"

"Foundry," Jesse said. "They had some boys waiting for a few of us when the whistle blew. Boys had lead pipes and brass knuckles. I got in some licks, but they pasted me good anyway."

"Are you stirring up the shop issue again?"

"Not *stirring up* anything," Jesse said with a flash of temper. "Just asking politely for what's fair. We got up a petition for a vote on a union shop. I signed. No demand like last time, no strike, just a democratic vote. You see anything wrong with that?"

"No, but obviously Clymer does. Tear up the damn petition."

"Hell we will."

"Guess you don't plan to live to a ripe old age." He reached for pliers. "You be careful. I don't want to scramble around for a new riding mechanic."

"You one selfish white man. Use the nigger for all he's worth, right?"

"I don't like that word. Let's say the gentle-man — the *gentleman* — happens to be my friend."

The very next week Carl and Jesse picked up a

ride in a fifty-mile race over in Ann Arbor, Washtenaw County. The car was one of two entered by the small Belwin Motor Company of Pontiac. When the regular driver fell ill, Mr. Belwin himself called garages all over Detroit. Someone suggested Carl. Tuesday before the race Belwin left a message at the lodging house. Carl was hired over the telephone.

After work on Saturday, he and Jesse traveled to Ann Arbor in a car sent by Belwin. "Who drives for your team?" Carl asked the man chauffeuring them.

"Fellows from the Michigan zone."

"Salesmen?" It wasn't unheard of, but Carl had no faith in drivers with that background. "Do they have any experience?"

"They've got a hell of a lot of experience selling the cars," the driver said testily. "I'm one of them. Murphy's the name."

Crowded in the rear seat of the Belwin, Carl and Jesse exchanged looks.

The Belwin company didn't pay for lodging, so the two men rolled up in blankets under the grandstand. Luckily it was a mild night, though Carl woke chilly and stiff. Before eight o'clock he and Jesse looked over the Belwin Tiger they would race that afternoon. Following their usual pre-race routine, they gassed it and took it around the half-mile track. Carl braked, accelerated, tested the turns and straightaways until he had a sense of the track surface and how fast he could travel.

Turned out to be hardly worth it. In the lead in the seventh lap, the blustery Murphy broke wheel spokes on his Belwin, lost control, and smashed into a brick retaining wall at the front of the grandstand. Spectators in the first rows screamed and ran. Murphy's car spewed smoke from the cowl, then flames. Murphy jumped out — no racecar had any kind of safety harness — while oil smoke black as midnight stretched a curtain across the track.

A Chalmers-Detroit in front of Carl steered wildly into the infield to avoid the smoke and fire. Jesse pointed straight ahead, Carl nodded, and they drove blindly into the smoke. Coming out, they saw a wheel from the wrecked Belwin lying in their path. Carl couldn't avoid it. The undercarriage of their low-slung racer gave a tremendous crack as it struck the wheel and bounced over. In the next turn Jesse pounded the oil gauge. The line was broken. Coming around to the pit, their car was doing five miles an hour with smoke plumes from the overheated motor streaming out behind.

"God damn it," Carl said, ripping off his helmet as he climbed out.

"My sentiments too," Jesse said. They collected their pay, handed to them reluctantly by a disgusted Mr. Belwin, and asked directions to the Interurban. Both men were in a foul mood when they came upon a gaudy poster at the track entrance.

WAYNE COUNTY FAIR GROUNDS
SUNDAY MAY 9

ONE DAY ONLY!

SPECTACULAR EXHIBITION BY
"The Speed King of the World"
— IN PERSON!! —
BARNEY OLDFIELD
WILL ATTEMPT
NEW MILE RECORD!

Carl rolled a cigarette. "Ever see Oldfield come into a town? I haven't, but I hear it's something. A real carnival."

"How'd you like to drive for that boy?" Jesse said.

"I'd sure as hell like it better than delivering Model T's the rest of my life," Carl said.

When he got back to Detroit after the Ann Arbor fiasco, he met Tess at a chili parlor on Grand Boulevard. He came right out with what was on his mind:

"It was a miserable, rotten race, and yet after I calmed down, I decided that winning or losing didn't matter half so much as driving. I love the speed of a race, the way it challenges you every second, fills you with this rush of excitement — and I'll never get enough of that working a steady job. I just don't know how much longer I can stand that damn factory."

Tess stirred her chili; dropped in some oyster crackers. "You are what you are, Carl. Do what you want. I'll never interfere."

But she looked troubled, and said little the rest of the meal.

257

29. "Speed King of the World"

Berna Eli Oldfield claimed to be the world's fastest driver. He held all kinds of speed records, had in fact broken many that he himself set. If someone thirty-one years old could be a legend, Barney Oldfield was legendary, in Europe as well as in the States.

Automakers offered him fast cars and fat contracts if he'd drive for them. He switched cars and loyalties like a sleight-of-hand magician. The somewhat snooty American Automobile Association had once branded him an outlaw and banned him from its sanctioned events for failing to show up at a starting line. He went on the barnstorming circuit until he recovered his status.

Wherever he appeared he drew crowds. People loved him because he was fearless and colorful. He wore gaudy vests and striped shirts, a thousand-dollar ankle-length sealskin coat, a knockout of a diamond ring. He smoked two-dollar Cuban cigars and passed out five-dollar tips like candy. Many a time on a drinking spree he passed out.

He traveled in a private railway car with his second wife, Bess, and his pet Irish terrier. His barnstorming team included an advance man, two other drivers, and a pit crew. When he raced he chewed on a cigar. He had a reputation as a boozer, woman chaser, a confirmed gambler with bad luck. He made three thousand dollars for an afternoon's exhibition, not bad for an unlettered kid born in a cabin in the woods of northwest Ohio.

Oldfield's advance man arrived in Detroit on Monday before the exhibition. He spoke at the Detroit Athletic Club, the Rotary, and other civic organizations. He drummed up excitement for Oldfield's attempt on his own one-mile speed record, and for the arrival in the Michigan Central yards of the boxcar carrying Oldfield's three racecars. Both sides of the boxcar carried huge bright lettering.

BARNEY OLDFIELD
SPEED KING OF THE WORLD

On Friday Barney and entourage rolled into Detroit in the private rail car. The mayor and several hundred citizens welcomed the Speed King when he stepped to the rear platform, shot his arms over his head, and shouted his favorite greeting, "You know me — Barney Oldfield." The crowd's roar said they certainly did.

Carl could catch up on all this only by doing something rare for him, reading the papers. They printed photos and lengthy copy about the famous driver. Carl thought him a pretty ordinary-looking fellow, round faced and dark haired, though his smile had a certain pixie charm.

Carl invited Tess to the fairgrounds, but she declined, saying she didn't want to hold him back when he tried to meet Oldfield, as he said he wanted. Carl knew Tess well enough to suspect that she looked on the reckless world of auto racing the same way Sykes looked at him — as competition. She wasn't overt about it or the least bitter. But she was firm. It made him uneasy. He didn't want to face a choice between two loves.

Sunday turned out bright and beautiful, with the fairgrounds grandstand packed to capacity. Carl had a cheap seat, high up in the shade under the roof. His heart started beating fast the moment he sat down with his five-cent program in hand.

Trotting races took up the first hour, building the crowd's anticipation. After the last sulky left the track, a water wagon drawn by two heavy Clydesdales circled the dirt oval to wet it down. Barney's advance man stepped in front of the grandstand with a megaphone.

"Ladies and gentlemen, boys and girls, here's the moment you've awaited — the man you came to see. You know him as the Old Master. World's Champion Automobilist. The Speed King of the World. Please give a warm welcome to *Barney Oldfield.*"

From behind the grandstand, pit mechanics pushed Barney's National racecar, painted with red and white stripes and white stars on a blue field. The stripes ran the length of the cowl, the stars decorated the front end. At the wheel, solo, Barney Oldfield waved to the crowd, a familiar figure from scores of news pictures: white coverall, goggles, cotton plugs in his ears, half-smoked cigar between his teeth. He shouted greetings to the stands, unheard because of the cheers and stomping and whistling.

"We are now ready for Barney's attempt on his one-mile speed record. Barney, are you all set?"

"All set, Mr. Pickens."

"Judges in the grandstand ready?" They waved handkerchiefs. "Start your engine."

The crowd roared. One of the pit mechanics spun the crank. And again. With a cough and a mighty backfire explosion, the engine of "Old Glory" started. But something was wrong, and Barney jumped out. A wave of silence swept upward through the stands. In the hush everyone heard the roughness of the motor.

Looking grim, Barney pushed his goggles up on his forehead and unlatched the cowl on the side away from the stands. He lifted the hinged cowl, held it with one hand, and reached into the guts of the car with the other. After a minute or so he suddenly withdrew his hand, grinned, and gave the thumbs-up sign. Carl and several thousand others shouted deliriously when they heard the motor running smoothly.

Barney latched the cowl, jumped in the car, and waited as the advance man lifted his starting pistol. Barney snugged his goggles on his nose; chomped his cigar. The pistol fired. The crowd screamed.

Barney sped away to the first turn, spewing dust behind. The National circled the track and blazed past the grandstand, this time taking the green flag to signal the start of the test lap. Carl was on his feet, yelling. He tried to time Barney by taking his pulse but soon lost the count in the excitement.

Barney took the checkered flag and slowed down. He U-turned at the head of the back-stretch and drove to the stands. Just as he arrived, the advance man rushed down from the judge's booth, where he'd collected timing slips. Barney chugged to a stop in front of the center stand, timing it perfectly to hear the advance man shout through his megaphone:

"Ladies and gentlemen, we have the official results. The Speed King of the World has just set a new record for the measured mile — forty-three and two-tenths seconds, which breaks his previous record by one-tenth of a second!"

Pandemonium. People tossed programs, threw confetti; Carl's head was draped with crepe paper streamers. In his excitement Tess was completely forgotten.

Barney and his team followed the speed run with three five-mile heat races. The competing cars were a Peerless and a Stearns. Barney took the first heat by two car lengths. In the second heat the driver of the Peerless, Red Fletcher, passed him going into the final lap. Barney fought back, gunning it and trying to maneuver around Fletcher. He failed, and the Peerless won by a length.

At the start of the final heat Barney looked grim as a man on death row. The race was a heart-stopping duel between the Peerless and "Old Glory," one nosing ahead, then the other as they ran wheel to wheel, dangerously close.

Going into the last lap, Barney trailing on the outside, it looked like a repeat of the second heat. As the two leaders screamed down the home stretch — the Stearns was still rounding the far back turn — Barney suddenly wheeled over behind the Peerless, accelerating between his rival and the fence.

Too narrow, you'll crash! Carl didn't know whether he shouted it out loud or only in his head. Barney drove relentlessly, never looking to right or left. He roared over the finish line half a length ahead of his rival, who slowed down, shaking his head in despair.

Carl had a brief suspicion about the outcome. Was it rigged? Didn't matter, the spectacle was thrilling. The celebration in the stands was as great or greater than that after the speed run. Barney leaped out of his car, tore off his goggles, made nearly opaque by dust, shot both arms over his head triumphantly. The standing ovation lasted five minutes.

Carl limped down the grandstand stairs, exhausted. As the May twilight settled, he leaned against the stand and rolled a cigarette. He knew what he wanted to do with the rest of his life.

After the crowds dispersed, Carl loitered near the livestock barn being used as a garage. The evening was cool, the red of the western horizon shifting chameleon-like through shades of delicate blue-green, pale blue, dark blue high up where the stars winked. Eventually Barney emerged from the barn with his teammates, pit mechanics, and his wife, a brunette with a lush figure and smoky good looks. Barney wore his long sealskin coat. Laughing and chattering, they all climbed into two Chalmers touring cars provided by the track. Carl heard someone say there was a good roadhouse a half mile up the pike. The open autos drove away. Carl flipped his cigarette into the dust and followed on foot.

At the roadhouse, more hangers-on appeared, including four women with the rouged look of whores. Carl squeezed into a spot at the bar, awaiting his chance. Barney bought drinks for his crowd, polishing off three whiskeys with little apparent effect. The advance man started a stud poker game, and Barney's wife drew up a chair to watch. In another corner the whores clapped and cheered for men shooting dice on their knees. Carl saw his opportunity, walked up to Barney, and offered his hand.

"Can I talk to you a second? My name's Carl Crown."

"Hey there, Carl Crown. You know me — Barney Oldfield." Up close, Barney's eyes had a filmy, not quite focused look. Both men had to speak up because of the noise.

"I sure do," Carl said. "That was a great performance this afternoon."

"Why, thanks. Enjoyed it myself."

"I thought for a minute that the National might not run."

"You kidding? We loosen a spark plug lead ahead of time so these magic fingers can fix it." Barney showed the hand with the glittering rock. "They love it."

"I've driven some races around here," Carl said. "Is there a chance I could get on your team?"

Barney eyed him up and down. "Tell you another little secret. Fellas who drive for me don't win unless I order it."

That answered his question earlier. "Well, I wondered. It would be okay with me. I just want to get out of Detroit and drive full-time."

"Sure you know what you're doing? I can't count the times I've crashed. Anytime you race, you're liable to wind up with a head full of stitches, or a leg sawed off, or a neck broken. Webb Jay wrecked his Whistling Willy steamer last year, twenty-seven fractures and a brain concussion. He may never get out of bed. It isn't a game anymore, it's a blood sport. The crowds want wrecks. They want to see you bleed and die."

"I understand the risks."

"Then if you're not scared out of your drawers, you must be born to do it. Got a job right now?"

"Yes, at Ford."

"Family?"

He didn't answer right away. "No. But there's —"

He stopped, aware of someone shouting Barney's name. At the tables and along the bar, people swiveled to look at a man standing in the middle of the sawdust floor. A haggard man, wearing a suit that would have done credit to an undertaker. He had a hot-eyed look.

"Barney Oldfield," the man said.

Barney leaned back against the bar, resting on his elbows. He gave the stranger a bleary smile. "You have the advantage of me, pal."

"James Marble. South Bend. I accuse you of having an assignation with my wife at the railroad hotel the night after your exhibition."

Barney considered the charge for about two seconds, then waved. "You're all wet, pal. Who told you that fairy story?"

"My wife. After I beat it out of her with my belt."

Softly but audibly, Bess Oldfield said, "Oh, my God."

"Bess honey," Barney said without looking at her, "this bird's loony."

The haggard man trembled and sweated. Men near Carl began to edge away. He heard one of the bartenders moving behind him. James Marble stabbed a hand into his coat, came up with a blued revolver. He aimed to the left of Barney.

"Hands above the bar, you. Reach for anything, I'll blow your head off."

Barney pushed Carl, then the man on his other side. "Get clear, boys. I don't want anyone hurt because of some drunk's half-baked fairy tales." Carl stepped over in front of a threesome at a table. He stood rigid, the backs of his legs against an empty chair. Everyone was motionless except Marble, who shuddered continually. Layers of cigar smoke coiled under the tin-shaded lights.

"Fairy tales?" Marble said. "Everybody knows your reputation. You're a dirty lecher who corrupts other men's wives." He swung the blued revolver suddenly, aiming it at Bess. She covered

266

her ears and ducked.

"You took that tramp to bed before —"

"You shut your fucking mouth. Bess was a respectable widow."

"— before you divorced your first wife. Well, you're all through."

Barney was sweating as heavily as Marble. He rubbed his left hand against his shiny cheek; the knockout diamond flashed.

"Marble, let's cut a deal. Let's you and me step out that door and discuss it. I don't want that gun to go off and hurt any of my friends."

"They get it after you get it," Marble screamed. He clutched the pistol with both hands to steady his aim. At that moment Carl grabbed the empty chair behind him and hurled it. The chair caught Marble at his knees, making him stumble. Barney dove to the floor. Marble's pistol went off, but the bullet clanged on a tin shade and ricocheted harmlessly.

Men from Barney's team swarmed on the floundering man, ripped the gun out of his hand, knocked him down, pummeling and kicking him. Marble stuck his rear in the air and propped himself on his elbows, protecting his head. Barney's advance man kicked him in the side.

"Awright, let the poor slob alone," Barney said, pulling them off. "Someone haul him out of here and tie him up and call the sheriff. Bess, you all right?"

"I'm all right, Barney," she said, shaken. Still, she was looking at him with a strange expression.

"Come on up here, have a drink. Everybody have another drink, the drinks are on Barney.

Sorry for the fracas," he said to the three bartenders. He handed five dollars to each. While the crowd swarmed to the rail, Barney approached Carl.

"You saved my ass, kid. Got a quick head on you. Do you drive the same way?"

"Well, I try."

"Tell you what. I'll be all over the map this summer, but in August I know I'll be in Indianapolis to open the new motor speedway. I think my second driver, Red, may leave me about July. His wife's got a loaf in her oven. If he does leave and I haven't filled the opening, I'll try you out."

"I'll find you. Thanks."

"No guarantees, understood?"

"I'll take my chances."

"Good, that's the game we're in, taking chances. What's your name again?"

"Crown. Carl Crown."

"Carl. Got it." Barney cocked his thumb like a pistol and shot him. "Step up and have a drink on Barney Oldfield."

30. A Desperate Call

Carl leaned in the doorway, in his nightshirt, wakened by loud knocking. Mrs. Gibbs stood there, with a candle set in a dish. It burned so dimly, her head seemed to float bodiless in the dark.

Carl knuckled his eyes. "What time is it?"

"Half past four." Tuesday, two days after he'd met Oldfield. "Not a decent hour for anyone to be calling a respectable household."

"Calling?" His voice was fogged with sleep.

"Some female on the line says it's an emergency. Mrs. Wallauer ran over from next door and woke me up."

"Good God," Carl said, alert suddenly. "I'll go right over."

"Put a coat on, you're not decent," the landlady cried, but he was already thumping down the stairs.

Mrs. Wallauer was a tiny woman with moles. She handed him the earpiece and retired a few steps down the hall. Carl turned his back, wondering. Had his mother or the General died suddenly?

"Hello?"

"Carl, it's me. I can't talk long."

"Tess. What is it?" He heard a tremor in her voice. Something dire had happened.

"I wanted to wait until tomorrow, but I couldn't sleep, I'm too upset."

"Tell me what's wrong."

"I can't go into it now, I'll tell you in the morning. I'll pick you up at half past eight."

"Tess, it's a workday."

"Give them an excuse. Call in sick."

The little boy raised with stern German rectitude kicked and squalled. "I've never lied to get a day off."

"Well, aren't you a saint? Aren't you just wonderful? Do you give a damn about me or not?"

"You know I do."

"Half past eight."

With a click the connection broke.

He hung the earpiece on the hook. A noise behind him reminded him of Mrs. Wallauer. "Something bad?" she said, with an ill-concealed hopefulness.

Bewildered and scared, he looked at her. "Yes. Yes, I think so."

Tess arrived in the red Clymer fifteen minutes early. By the time Carl ran out the gate, cloth cap in hand, she'd moved to the passenger side. He was in such a rush, he'd barely remembered to button his suspenders onto his pants.

He opened the door, stepped on the running board, horrified by the sight of her — cheeks raw from weeping, eyes like blurs of watercolor in larger splotches of shadow. She wore a tan driving duster and a broad-brimmed hat held under her chin with a red silk scarf. She was kneading her hands in her lap. He'd speculated about her monthly female complaint but decided it had to be something far more serious.

"Where do you want to go?"

"Out in the country. Anywhere."

Ducking his head so as not to bang it on the top, he shut the door, grasped the wheel. "Did the woman on the telephone raise the devil about my call?" she said.

"It doesn't matter, she knew it was an emergency. Did someone hurt you?"

"Not physically." She closed her eyes; it squeezed tears onto her cheeks. "Just drive." He'd never seen her this way. She was always so strong and sure.

He negotiated the busy morning traffic, heading west across Woodward and out to the northwest along Grand River. The air in the Clymer was stuffy, and he unsnapped a side curtain. Tess stared ahead through the windscreen.

Two miles past the city limits the brick pavement ended. The Clymer lurched along a more typical road — essentially sand, with deep ruts. Sunburned men worked in bean fields, pea patches, apple orchards. Tess roused a little, opened the curtain on her side. Carl was aware of the bounty of the countryside, maples and sycamores and cherry trees budding, wildflowers blooming, birds warbling, a jackrabbit jumping across the road in front of them chased by another.

He saw a track leading off through the tall grass of a fallow field and wheeled the Clymer into it. He braked and shut off the engine.

"I can't wait any longer, Tess. What's happened?"

"Let's walk." She left the car, blinked in the sunshine. He felt the warmth of the earth around them. She threw her duster on her seat, took her hat off but left the red silk around her neck like a long, bright banner. Hand in hand they walked up the track toward a willow grove. Without looking at him she began to talk.

"It happened last night. After supper. Father asked to speak to me in his study. I thought it was something unimportant, but he shut the doors and I knew it wasn't. He said Wayne had been pressing him about marrying me." The hackles on Carl's neck rose.

"Father said he thought Wayne would be an ideal catch and I should say yes. I told him I couldn't possibly. He said my feelings didn't matter; in this I'd have to bow to his wishes. We argued for ten or fifteen minutes." The strain in her voice, the little stumbles and dead spaces between words, told him she'd found Lorenzo Clymer a determined opponent whose will wouldn't be denied, not even by a modern, free-minded woman.

"I said I didn't love Wayne. He said it didn't matter. It was what he wanted, for my own good, and I'd recognize and appreciate that in a few years. That's when —" Amid the tall grass bending over the track, Tess held his hand tightly. The morning breeze from the north blew her white blouse against her breasts.

"That was when my strength gave out. I was hysterical. I told Father no, I wouldn't ever marry Wayne. I told him I'd marry you and no one else." A spasm twisted Carl's belly.

"Father leaned back in his big chair and just stared at me. You would think I'd said I wanted to marry a leper. He said he couldn't believe that I was so willful and stupid. I said I wouldn't talk about it anymore, he had my answer." She dabbed her eyes with her free hand.

"I'm afraid I was pretty much of a wild creature by then. He was like stone. I knew he and Wayne must have conspired together. He said we'd talk about it when I came to my senses. He ordered me out, just like some clerk. That was about nine o'clock. I couldn't sleep. Once I called you I felt better. I dozed off and woke up around seven. Father had already left the house. That's the whole pathetic tale," she said with a smile that lacked heart. A noisy crow flew over the sunlit track, sailing up into the sky dotted with small white clouds.

"What do we do, Carl?"

"Honestly, I don't know." He'd never been so deeply involved with a woman before, or loved one the way he loved her. Jesse's words about a lifetime of responsibility haunted him.

Tess found his hand again. "Come on, let's sit in the shade and rest. I'm worn out."

"God, I can imagine."

Among the budding willows they came on a slow-moving brook. Carl sat down facing it with his back to a tree trunk. Tess cuddled against him, wrapped in his protecting arm like a child. The rounded ball of his right thumb rested against her warm cheek. Her outstretched legs lay touching his. The bow of her blouse had come undone; the ends lay between her round breasts. He held her and hoped he was comforting her with his presence; he wasn't a sophisticated person, didn't know the right words. The creek flowed over rocks, making a faint sound like paper rustling.

"Carl, do you love me?"

"More than anything."

"Make love to me."

"Tess —"

She struggled to her knees, her skirt riding up her legs; he could see her black stockings. She put her palms against his face and brought her mouth near his.

"There's no one to see, no one for miles. Please." She kissed him, her lips open, her tongue finding his. He grew stiff tasting her mouth, smelling the sweet warmth of her hair, her skin.

He slid his hand under her arm, touched her breast. Through her blouse and whatever under-garments she wore he felt her nipple. She leaned back, pulled the blouse buttons with her right hand. He took her wrist.

"I ran out of the house fast, like it was burning down. I didn't bring any safes."

"I don't care. I love you. We might never get another chance. *Please.*"

They looked into each other's eyes. Feeling like a diver stepping off a cliff above a deep, dark ocean, he reached under her skirt and fumbled with her stockings.

They made love twice more before noon. Then Tess looked at her small gold wristwatch. She said perhaps they'd better return to the city. Carl said she could drop him near the factory if she didn't mind; he'd tell them he felt better, work a half day. He didn't know what this latest turn in their relationship signified. Didn't know what she'd want because of it.

A part of him had no regret about what had happened in the willow grove. The lovemaking had been consuming, shattering — wonderful. At the moment he'd readied himself to thrust in the first time, he asked the essential question. No, she said, she'd had one lover before him, when she was eighteen. The affair had lasted an entire summer. He needn't fear causing her pain.

She let him out in front of a small cigar store a block from the Ford plant. She seemed herself again, seated at the wheel, her hair more or less arranged, her clothing too. The sun in her dark blue eyes made them sparkle.

"Carl, believe me, I didn't set out to seduce you."

"Let's have none of that. My God, I've wanted it ever since I met you. I just don't know what we're going to do. I have to think."

"Plenty of time for that." She caressed his face. "I won't marry Wayne, but I'd never force marriage on you."

With a smile that reminded him of their first meeting, she drew the red silk motoring scarf from her neck, reached above him, and draped it over his shoulders.

"My shining knight on a gasoline charger. There's a token so you don't forget me."

"Forget you? I love you, Tess."

"Shall we plan on Sunday?"

"What about a picnic on Bois Blanc island? I'll telephone."

"No, all the servants recognize your voice now. They might tell Father and I'd rather avoid another scene. I'll meet you at the Wayne Hotel, outside the roller-skating pavilion. I'll bring the lunch basket. Eleven o'clock?"

"Perfect," he said. "I love you."

She kissed her fingertips and touched his cheek. She worked the clutch and drove away, passing an oncoming truck laden with barrels that bore a familiar crown emblem. Carl stared at the delivery truck as it crossed the intersection within six feet of him. It was like the hand of God, or the hand of Joe Crown, reaching down at that fated moment to remind him of things like duty, decency, the honor of womanhood. He didn't know what to do, except talk to Jesse. Ask his advice. Right away.

A black boy sweeping out the cigar store watched Carl curiously. The boy saw a stocky white man with a troubled look and a red scarf blowing in the spring air as he trudged away toward Piquette Avenue.

31. Savagery

"If you're this shining knight like she told you, don't you suppose you got to rescue her?" Sitting on a keg, an oily rag in his hand, Jesse watched Carl. A coal oil lantern lit the shed. Cigarette in hand, Carl paced back and forth, back and forth, laying heel prints one over another.

Carl hadn't found Jesse until this evening, Wednesday. The night before he'd waited two hours on Jesse's front porch, but Jesse never came home. Turned out he was meeting with other men from the foundry, pondering how to force an answer to the petition for a vote on a closed shop.

Carl dragged on the hand-made cigarette. "Yes, it's up to me," he agreed. He'd told his friend about Clymer's ultimatum to Tess and her reaction. He said they'd discussed it on a drive in the country, but he said nothing else.

"You got any ideas about that?"

"Barney Oldfield said he might have an opening on his team later this summer. If he'd hire me, and Tess would marry me, we could leave Detroit."

Jesse puckered his mouth. "To travel with that race crowd? You told me they're a pretty low bunch, drinking and whoring all the time. Think she'd be happy? Might last — what? Six months? Maybe a year if she loves you as much as you say."

"She said she'd walk through fire for me, Jess. Her exact words."

"People in love say lots of things. Then years go by, and the chore of living comes down hard day after day and they wonder how those words ever came to pass their lips. I'd think real hard before dragging a high-class young lady away from all she's used to, into a lot of barrooms and low-down hotels."

Carl dropped the cigarette and stepped on it. Jesse was right; to be convinced of that he only had to remember the road house where he'd cornered Barney. He wondered whether this concern for Tess wasn't also a handy way to hide something he feared. The duty that went with marriage.

He started to speak, but a noise outside forestalled it. He heard footsteps in the backyard. Reflections of the lamp wick glittered in Jesse's eyes as he turned his head. He'd heard it too.

"Somebody out there, Jess."

"Isn't your fight," Jesse said hoarsely. "Get into the alley." He bobbed his head toward a second door behind him.

"What fight? With who?" A man in the yard gave a gruff order, and the footsteps quickened. Jesse grabbed a hammer from the tool bench.

"The damn E.A. The petition. Bosses must have sent somebody to —"

The door facing the yard flew open, the peg latch splintering. Carl found himself staring at a hobnailed boot.

Then the man was inside the shed, followed by another. Both had coarse faces, shabby clothes.

The first man carried a fish gaff, the second an iron pipe. Just as Carl stepped in front of them, the door behind Jess burst open. A man wearing a dirty driving coat and pea cap came in swinging a ball bat.

Carl shouted at the first two, "What the hell are you doing here? Turn around and get —" A blow to his skull set lights dancing behind his eyes. The man with the ball bat had struck from behind.

Carl fell forward, crashed head first into the shed wall. His flailing hands pulled down parts cabinets, spilled hundreds of sheet metal screws of all sizes.

The man with the gaff dodged in beneath Jesse's swinging hammer. The gaff hook whirled and sank three inches into Jesse's left thigh. Pain glazed Jesse's face; the hammer flew out of his fingers. The man tore the hook out with a vicious motion of his wrist. Clenching his teeth, Jesse sank to one knee. The second man raised the iron pipe to brain him, but the man in the driving coat screamed, "Elroy, you fucking idiot, it isn't the spade, it's the other one."

Carl was clawing the shanty wall, pulling himself up when he heard that. Lorenzo Clymer had told someone about Tess's refusal, and Carl knew who it was.

The ball bat smashed his legs. He fell on his face. As the man with the gaff made to step on his head, Carl rolled over, kicked the shins of the man with the bat. The man danced back, snickering. He took a firm two-handed grip, lifted the bat over his head. Helplessly, Carl rolled to the right. But the bat never came down. Just then Jesse broke the lamp over the man's head.

Coal oil soaked the man's neck and collar. The wick touched it off. The man's hair and cap burst into flames. He screamed, dropped the bat. More coal oil splattered a work table and ignited. Fire ran up the flimsy wooden wall. In their haste to escape into the alley, the man with the gaff and the man with the iron pipe bumped each other like circus clowns.

Screaming, the other man pulled his long coat over his head. Somehow he snuffed out the flames. Dragging to his feet, Carl had a last look at him as he ran after the others and disappeared, leaving a stench of burned hair.

The wooden walls burned fast, popping like oily fatwood. "Jesse, get up." Jesse couldn't get up, or hear; he'd passed out. His trouser leg was blood-soaked from thigh to shoe top.

Carl dragged him outside, laid him in the yard a safe distance from the fire. As a white man from next door rushed through a gate in the board fence, Carl yelled, "Call the fire station, for God's sake."

"Already sent my boy Tolliver. What happened to Mr. Shiner?"

"Man sunk a gaff hook in his leg."

"Oh, Lord. Looks awful."

The neat backyard with its carefully tended flower beds tilted under Carl. He stumbled to the fence, swallowing sour vomit. He hung on the fence till the spell passed.

A dozen terrified neighbors gathered. Several threw buckets of water on the fire, to little avail.

The clanging bell of a fire wagon reached them. A woman said, "Merciful God, hurry up before all the houses burn."

Carl reeled back to his fallen friend. "Someone help me lift him. He needs a hospital."

The neighbor ran to hitch up his horse and buggy. Carl ripped a piece off his pants for an improvised tourniquet. He tied it above the mangled mess of flesh and muscle in Jesse's leg. Thank God Jesse was out.

They left in the buggy seconds before the fire horses charged down the alley from the other end of the block. The fire brigade unreeled hoses to soak the glowing ruins of the shed. Only a few sparks floated in the windless air.

Ten minutes later, Carl and the white man carried Jesse through the emergency door of Samaritan Hospital on Jefferson Avenue. A doctor examined him.

"We'll get him to the operating theater right away. Stitch him up. There's muscle damage, I don't know how much."

Attendants covered Jesse with a sheet and rolled him away on a gurney. The hospital was dark, silent, full of the smell of chemicals and disinfectants. Carl sank down on a bench, filthy with sweat and grime. He was still shaking.

The neighbor said, "Why did those men attack him? Mr. Shiner's a gentle soul."

"It was a mistake. They were after me."

"Do you know where they came from?"

"I do. I know exactly where they came from."

Sykes & Looby, Advertising Agents, occupied

281

rooms on two floors of the Penobscot Building on Fort Street West. The hushed reception lobby with its gold and forest green color scheme, its dim wall lamps with tiny shades, had a studied quaintness. Several times Joe Crown had taken young Carl with him to the Chicago agency that prepared and placed the brewery's ads. Crown's advertising agents were plain-spoken men, working from offices that were, like them, unpretentious. Here, by contrast, there was a rotten air of sham. Busts of Shakespeare and Tennyson gazed from marble pedestals, as though to suggest that the commercial work ground out in these rooms had something in common with the creativity of genius.

"Where do I find Sykes?"

Carl's tone made the female typewriter draw back warily at her desk. "His offices are up-stairs." She pointed at an ornate circular stair-case in the corner. "But he never sees visitors without —"

Carl was already halfway to the next floor.

He pushed people aside, not seeing their faces, how they were dressed, how they reacted to the sight of a man in workman's clothes stalking along glaring at the brass nameplate on each door. Carl found the plate that said F. WAYNE SYKES, JR. He twisted the ornate doorknob.

"— and I want this radiator, the whole damn auto, larger. I told you yesterday — larger. Are you stupid? I won't take garbage like this to Mr. Clymer."

Carl pounded the door open with his fist. Wayne Sykes, smartly dressed in a brown three-piece suit, sat at a mammoth desk littered with layouts. Standing at one side, a gray-faced man with chalk smudges on his shirt and hands nervously made notes on a pad.

"Miss Rumford, I've told you expressly, knock before —" Sykes's eyes focused. "Jesus Christ. What are you doing in this office?"

Carl took in the opulent furniture, framed photos of the Clymer factory, Clymer automobiles, Mr. Clymer, an elderly man who resembled Sykes. There were gaudy plaques, award certificates, a Harvard diploma.

"Thought you'd like to know your hoodlums didn't do the job."

"Are you drunk? Are you a madman? I don't know what you mean."

To the flunky Carl said, "You'd better get out." The flunky ran.

"You're the one who'd better get out," Sykes said. "I'll have you put away for ten years."

"I don't think so. One of the men you sent was named Elroy. If the police round up all the Elroys in town and put them through the sweat box, I'll bet one of them will lay out a trail straight to you. If you've bought off the police, then I'll hire a lawyer through my father in Chicago. A lawyer like Darrow who loves to wipe up scum like you." It was an outrageous bluff. He'd given the police Elroy's name and descriptions of all three men. The detectives took down the information as though they intended to forget it in ten minutes. But Sykes didn't know any of that.

Sykes's eye shifted to ivory buttons on a box

beside his upright phone. Carl pulled the box off the desk, broke its wire, threw it on the floor. Then he tore the telephone loose and hurled it against the wall. The glass on Lorenzo Clymer's portrait splintered and rattled down. Sykes screamed, "Someone phone the police! Miss Rumford —" Carl reached across the desk and hauled him up by his necktie.

"So you like rough stuff, do you?"

He broke Sykes's nose with his first blow. The second blow brought a gout of blood from both nostrils. Sykes collapsed on the layouts, bleeding on the sketches of Clymer autos. Carl ran around the desk and dumped him out of his chair.

"Oh please, oh please," Sykes said, on his knees, hands protecting his gory face.

"Shut up, shut the hell up," Carl shouted, slapping Sykes backhand, slicking his knuckles with blood. "Your thugs hurt my friend so bad he may not walk again."

"I'm sorry, I'm sorry." Sykes's tears ran into the blood and mucus dripping from his nose. His crotch was dark; he'd urinated on himself. "I love Tess, I had to do something."

Carl hauled him up and pounded him twice in the gut, then flung him against the wall. The Clymer plant photo fell on his head, sprinkling broken glass in his hair. Carl wanted to hit him again, but he wasn't so possessed by rage that he failed to see Sykes couldn't fight back. Anything further wouldn't be punishment, just brutality.

He heard noises in the corridor. "In there, in there! He's killing Mr. Sykes!" Three policemen with hickory billy clubs piled through the door and beat Carl to the floor.

He spent the night in jail. He ached from the beating, couldn't keep food down, couldn't sleep. He was sure he'd go to prison for what he'd done.

To his astonishment they released him early in the morning. No charges had been filed by Wayne Sykes. Was there a more telling admission of guilt? Carl derived no satisfaction, though, from the obvious answer.

He visited Jesse in the charity ward. His friend was awake, drowsy, and falsely cheerful. As Carl left, a staff doctor confided to Carl that the damage to Jesse's leg was severe. He would be on crutches for a while. He might be on crutches permanently.

"He works in a foundry. You can't work in a foundry on crutches."

"I'm sure that's true. He'll have to do something else."

Carl found the nearest saloon and knocked back two whiskeys at half past ten in the morning. His world was rapidly collapsing.

At noon he punched the clock at Piquette Avenue. The timekeeping clerk looked out of his booth, stared at Carl's bruises. "Boss has been looking for you all over the place."

"You mean Gogarty?"

"The big boss. Henry. You better hightail up to the second floor."

In the main hall and on the staircase he felt everyone was looking at him. Men in the drafting room stopped their work and broke off conversations when he entered. He walked to Ford's open door. Ford looked up from a blueprint.

"About time you showed up, Carl. Step in here. You may sit down."

Ford rolled up the blueprint, snapped an elastic around it. A shaving nick showed on his jaw. Little blue flowers patterned his necktie. He was about as warm and friendly as a piece of iron bar stock.

"Last night I had a telephone call at home from Lorenzo Clymer. He told me something outrageous. He said you beat up a friend of his." Among papers on the desk Ford located a memo slip. "Sykes. Young fellow in advertising. Is that the truth?"

"Yes, sir."

"They hauled you to jail and you spent the night there?"

"Yes, sir. I wasn't charged with anything."

Ford waited a little. "That's all? You have nothing else to say?"

"Sykes deserved it. It's a personal matter."

Ford shook his head. "I don't make a habit of climbing out on a limb to hire somebody at your level. I made an exception because I thought I saw some fine stuff in your attitude and deportment. Good potential. You fooled me. You let me down. You let the whole company down. You violated the rules I described at my house. I did describe them, didn't I?"

"Yes, sir, you specifically said no public brawling to embarrass Ford Motor Company."

"Yes, I certainly did. You broke the rules and tied a ribbon on it." Ford gave him a severe look. "You're discharged. No severance, just your wages for this week. I'll give you a half hour to empty your locker and leave the plant. That's all."

"Mr. Ford, will you allow me to say I'm sorry for — ?"

"No, I will not." He glared like a wrathful preacher. "You keep on, Carl, you'll amount to nothing. I believe every man should get a second chance. When someone gives you yours, I hope you won't be stupid and ruin it."

The telephone rang.

"One more thing. Clymer said that if you set foot on his property, here or in Grosse Pointe, he'd put you away for five years."

Again Carl tried to speak. The phone rang a second time. Angrily, Ford waved him out as he picked up the receiver and said, "Henry. Go ahead."

32. Separation

At Third Street and the river, next to the Michigan Central depot, stood the Wayne Hotel. With its marble floors and fountains, its three bars, five restaurants, and ten-chair tonsorial parlor, it vied with the Ponchartrain for the honor of being "Detroit's finest." Carl had strolled through once under the suspicious eye of front-desk men, but he couldn't have afforded so much as a breakfast at the Wayne, where he arrived Sunday morning at half past ten, wearing his old brown corduroy coat with Tess's scarf wound around his neck. He waited by the closed ticket booth of the hotel's roller-skating pavilion. A sleepy black man was opening the shutters one by one. Out on the sunny river a coal boat sounded its whistle.

Tess appeared breathlessly at fifteen before eleven. She carried a small hamper. She looked rested, refreshed. They walked down to the ferry terminal, where day trippers lined up to board *Pleasure*, the gleaming white boat of the Detroit, Belle Isle & Windsor Ferry Company.

"Father told me what you did to Wayne."

Fishing in his pocket for seventy cents, Carl looked at her for signs of condemnation, saw none.

"I hurt him pretty badly. The men he sent spiked the leg of my riding mechanic with a fish gaff, by mistake. You met Jess. He may never walk without crutches. You can't work in a foundry on crutches."

"Oh, God, that's dreadful."

"Damn right. Jesse's built a fairly good life working in the foundry. It's my fault."

He paid for two round-trip tickets. They boarded *Pleasure* as a brass bell rang, signaling departure.

"Did Wayne admit he sent the men?"

"Yes, but I can't prove it to anyone. It's a terrible mess."

Tess sank down on an outside bench overlooking the starboard rail. "Yes, it is. At the same time, these are the sweetest months I've ever known. Why is life always so mixed up, the good with the bad?"

"Maybe someone brainy like Emerson knows. I sure as hell don't."

The Detroit River ran between the lakes for a distance of about thirty miles. Downstream from the city, opposite Amherstburg, lay Bois Blanc, one of the area's most popular destinations for lovers, Sunday school classes, and all manner of excursionists. It was not yet warm enough for the island bathhouse to be open. The stone dance pavilion was closed on Sundays, but the café was busy, the shady pathways and athletic fields crowded in the early afternoon. Carl and Tess ate their picnic at a rustic table. She'd brought a jar of cold tea, lukewarm by the time they drank it but delicious. No alcohol was allowed on Bois Blanc.

Carl brushed crumbs off the checked cloth; she'd baked a loaf of oat bread for thick liver-wurst sandwiches enhanced with strong Swiss cheese and hot German mustard. Unused to the deep waters he was treading, Carl was awkward in bringing up the subject that was bothering him so deeply.

He held her hand across the table. Sun and shadow from the new leaves above them played on her face. He said, "Do you regret what we — what happened out in the country?"

"Not for a minute. Do you?"

"No. Well, yes if I took advantage of you."

"You didn't." Carl's gaze remained fixed on the table, and she squeezed his hand. "You didn't."

He looked at her. There was no way to make the leap but to do it. "Will you marry me, Tess?"

"No."

Stunned, more than a little hurt, he sat back. "Why not? We could leave Detroit, settle down somewhere else."

"Is this guilt talking?"

"It's *me* talking, damn it. I've told you over and over. I love you."

"And I love you. Which is exactly the reason I wouldn't say yes. You're not a factory man, a time-clock man, how often have you told me? I know some other things you are. Brave, kind — very exciting, because there's a wild streak in you. What's deeper than that, I'm not sure. Maybe you don't know either." Sun glistened in her eyes suddenly. "But you won't discover the answer staying here out of some misguided sense of duty. I release you, Carl. I've never really had any hold on you, or intended one. I want you to leave. Chase down Barney Oldfield. I know it's what you want."

"Tess, please let me —"

She stood up, smoothing her skirt. "Subject closed. Shall we walk? It's a lovely afternoon."

He mentioned marriage twice more during the afternoon, but she refused to discuss it. She was cheerful, spoke rapidly, with a flush on her cheeks as she chatted of other things. At five o'clock she said they should go home.

He left her in Detroit's central square, at the monument to the city's founder, Antoine de la Mothe Cadillac, Knight of St. Louis. Behind the empty granite chair she rearranged the red scarf, smoothing the ends over the lapels of his coat.

"My shining knight. Off to chase the Saracens and dragons."

"The only dragon I know is the green one Oldfield drove. I can't go unless we settle —"

"Carl, we've settled it. Godspeed. Please don't call or try to see me again. My heart's breaking already."

She threw her arms around him, shocking the automobilists and buggy drivers passing in the spring twilight. He felt her tears as they kissed. She struggled to smile as she snatched up the basket and ran for the streetcar.

He withdrew all his savings from the Dime Bank down on Griswold Street, nine dollars. He settled accounts with Mrs. Gibbs, who said he'd been a good boarder, no trouble, he'd be welcome back anytime. He wrapped the red silk scarf around his neck and set off with his grip for Jesse's house. He found his friend in the back-yard, trying to cultivate a flower bed one-handed.

Jesse let the hoe drop and rested on his padded crutch. His left trouser leg looked fatter than the right; it was still bandaged.

"Came to say so long, Jess."

"So long, Carl. I'll miss you, you've been a true friend. When you looked at me, you never saw a colored man, except maybe the first time. Do you figure to hunt up Oldfield like you said?"

Carl nodded. He pointed at the ashy black remains of the shed. "Will you rebuild that?"

"Sure. I can work sitting down. I'll sort out the metal first, then use the ashes. Wood ashes make good cheap mulch."

"What are you going to do for a regular job?"

"Oh, I won't have trouble. There's always some kind of nigger work long as white folks don't want to dirty their hands. Maybe I'll go to barber college. I could buy a stool, tall, so I wouldn't have to stand. Got nice steady hands."

Carl was appalled at the thought of a strong, free spirit like Jess reduced to cutting hair in some colored barber shop. "Hoot Edmunds will always hire you as a riding mechanic."

"I suppose he might. Can't ever drive, though. Can't work those pedals."

"I'm God damned sorry about it, Jess. I caused it."

"Oh, hell, no," Jesse said, waving. "It would have come down on me some other way, because I'm strong for the rights of the laboring man.

That's trouble in this town. You seen Tess?"

"We said goodbye Sunday. She gave me this scarf."

"That's it?"

"That's it." He hugged Jess.

It was right to leave abruptly, make the cut swift and clean, although part of him longed to stay. That night he jumped a Michigan Central freight in the yards, headed south.

33. Postcard from Indianapolis

Fading summer wrapped Grosse Pointe in haze and lassitude. Yet August, no matter how hot, no matter how stale, always brought with it the sense of imminent change. No one felt it more than Tess. With the first lightning storm that swept a wave of cold air from the north woods, with the first brown curl at the edges of the leaves, with her father's impatience to move back to town, she saw a chapter in her life closing.

On a Saturday afternoon in late August, lacking any prospects for the evening, she sat in a canvas sling chair under a beach umbrella on the lawn near the sea wall. A mandolin lay beside the chair. She'd started lessons but couldn't get interested.

She was writing a letter to Carl, never knowing when or whether she'd hear from him with a proper address. She felt that even if he wrote her once or twice, she would certainly never see him again. Ironically, she was at the same time enjoying a new sense of physical health. The headaches were gone; cramps too; her skin glowed. Father had remarked on it.

Emotionally she was far from whole. Often she cried for hours. The trauma of releasing Carl might fade but would never leave. She knew she couldn't have held him with the blackmail of love. To do that she'd have committed herself to years of watching his soul shrivel before her eyes as he tried to live as a conventional husband.

She felt a certain nobility and pride over her gesture. At other times she mocked it, asking how warm her high-minded attitude would keep her on long December nights. When she grew too annoyed at her own inconsistencies, she rallied by saying to herself, *I am not a saint and he wasn't one either.* God, far from it. He was merely the man she would always keep closest to her heart.

She wished she'd understood him more. She yearned for some all-seeing oracle to explain him. Tell her, for example, whether being the last child of dominant parents contributed somehow to his wayward nature.

She interrupted the letter, turned the sheet of the tablet over to reveal a blank one. She drew on it with her pencil, a musing, almost whimsical smile on her face. She wore an old dress this afternoon, white, with puffed sleeves, and smart new gray stockings and her white summer shoes. She was the pretty picture of one of Gibson's girls on an outing.

The hot breeze blew stray strands of her hair. Pensively, she looked at what she'd sketched. Three initials, in fancy script:

$$cTc$$

Ice tinkling in a pitcher broke her reverie. Giselle, from the kitchen.

"I thought you might like more lemonade, ma'am." Giselle set the dewy pitcher on the white iron table beside Tess's tumbler and napkin. Giselle was sixteen; probably thought of Tess as hideously old. Which, in fact, she was getting to be.

"Thank you, Giselle, very thoughtful of you."

"This came in the afternoon post."

She handed Tess a gaudy postcard showing a cigar store Indian and the words SOUVENIR OF INDIANAPOLIS. She turned the card over, caught her breath. The message was one sentence, written in an obviously disguised hand but not signed. *Have a job with "Barney O"!*

She almost cried. For the message that said so little but set so many fears to rest, she was thankful. It made her decision easier to act upon.

"What's that you're drawing, ma'am, if you don't mind me inquiring?" Giselle had Old World courtesy. Her last name was DePere; she was only a couple of generations removed from French farmers who had planted all the gorgeous fruit trees that graced the region.

"Just a monogram, for pillow slips and things."

"It's so pretty. So neat and balanced." Slightly flushed from the heat, or boldness, Giselle then said, "Is it yours?"

Tess looked up, her dark blue eyes unreadable. "Well, it would be if I could find the right man."

Perplexed, Giselle took refuge in gazing at the lake. A long, graceful yacht had appeared. "Look, ma'am, I believe it's your father."

"He's early. He'll want supper by half past seven."

"I'll tell Cook." Giselle tripped off through the sunburnt grass.

Tess stretched, considered again what she'd planned to say to him. She firmed her resolve by gazing at the monogram one last time, then tearing off the sheet and crumpling it in a ball. If only the hurt in a heart could be disposed of so easily.

The yacht's captain docked the *Hiawatha* smartly with the aid of a local boy who crewed for him. Lorenzo Clymer strode up the pier.

His white linen suit and white hat broke the deep blue canvas of the lake. Tess rose, smoothed her skirt, ran her hands over her waist with a pleasurable shiver. How cross he looked. She was about to change that.

"Father," she said, stepping to the head of the pier as he came stomping along.

"What is it?"

"I want to speak to you. I've changed my mind about Wayne. If you'll give your consent, I'll marry him."

PART THREE

PICTURES

The five-cent theaters make schools of crime where murder, robbery, and hold-ups are illustrated. The outlaw life they portray in their cheap plays tends to the encouragement of wickedness. They manufacture criminals to infest the streets of the city. Not a single thing connected with them has influence for good. The proper thing for the city authorities to do is to suppress them at once.
— CHICAGO TRIBUNE, 1907

When Griffith walked, I walked. I fell in, matched strides, asked questions. "I want to put together full-length stories," he would say. "And I don't see any sense in always showing so much. For instance, we have a scene in Room A. We finish with it and the characters go to Room B. Why do we have to photograph the people walking from Room A to Room B? Just cut to Room B."
— MACK SENNETT, *King of Comedy*

34. Ilsa to the Rescue

Since 1902 the Pennsylvania and New York Central railroads had competed for business between Chicago and New York with extra-fare luxury trains, the Broadway Limited on the Pennsy, the Twentieth Century Limited on the Central. The Broadway's route was fifty miles shorter, but the Central claimed an advantage, advertised on a signboard at the depot gate.

THE WATER LEVEL ROUTE
— YOU CAN SLEEP —

When the Limited arrived in the great shed of the Grand Central Station, the porter lifted the drop plate that covered the vestibule steps and Ilsa descended, a regal woman wearing a smart suit and a Merry Widow skimmer, black straw with a wide brim and low crown.

"Your bags will be waiting at the counter inside, ma'am," the porter said.

"Thank you." Ilsa handed him seventy-five cents, a lavish tip.

Ilsa had told Joe that she wanted to shop in the great stores on New York's famed Ladies' Mile — Wanamaker's at Eighth Street, Siegel-Cooper's on Eighteenth, James McCreery's on Twenty-third, R. H. Macy's at its new location on Herald Square. Even this elicited a sharp challenge:

"You don't give a hang about shopping. It's

Fritzi taking you there."

"Is that so terrible, Joe? Am I to feel guilty for wanting to see my only daughter? So far as I know, it isn't against the law. You and Fritzi are the ones estranged. It's your doing, and it's time you got over it."

His answer to that was the same as his answer to similar pleas in the past — a steely look and silence.

At least he didn't retaliate by forbidding her, or seeing to it that she had no funds for the trip. Under existing law even the wealthiest women were almost completely dependent on their husbands. Joe gave Ilsa a monthly allowance, which she kept in a separate bank account. He never questioned her about how she spent it.

Fritzi burst through a cloud of steam, waving. How good it was to see her beautiful brown eyes again. Of course, her blond hair remained a bramble patch. And, Ilsa noted with concern, she was wan and desperately thin.

"Fritzi. *Liebchen.*" They flung their arms around each other.

"I've missed you, Mama. Where shall we go first?"

"My hotel, please. After I collect my bags. I want to hear about this play of yours, *Macbeth*. A friend showed me your name in a New York paper. You were a naughty girl to keep such a thing secret."

"I wanted it to be a good show, then I was going to tell you. It wasn't good, it was awful. We closed in a week."

"I missed my only daughter starring on Broadway. What are you doing now?"

"Nothing to brag on. I am, as they say, between engagements." Ilsa listened with dismay to her daughter's recitation of her work during the spring and summer: waitress at a rundown restaurant destroyed by a mysterious midnight fire that did not seem to upset the owner; four weeks demonstrating a potato peeler at Woolworth's; a just concluded two weeks as a typewriter for an insurance agency.

"They fired me for being slow," Fritzi said with a shrug and a sigh.

Inside the terminal, a porter with a hand truck moved Ilsa's trunk and suitcase to the clamorous curb on Forty-second Street. It was September, a day of bright sunshine and bracing air. On the short taxi ride to the Hotel Astor, Fritzi said, "How is Papa?"

"Constantly angry — with me, his workers, the prohibition people, but most of all with himself, I think. The heart attack damaged him more than I realized at first. Not only the illness itself, but the fact that he had it. The undeniable evidence of weakness made him furious. His physician told me in private that it's a common reaction."

Fritzi shook her head sadly. "And Carl?"

"Carl writes a letter as often as snow falls in August. It's better that way. If I knew exactly what he was doing, I couldn't sleep."

"What about Joey?"

"What can I say? Joey is Joey. No change."

"I saw Paul. He gave me a copy of his book. Have you read it?"

"*Ja, wunderbar.* Who would have dreamed little Pauli would be a writer too?"

At the Astor, an assistant manager showed them up to a one-bedroom suite. Fritzi had offered to share her bed with her mother, but Ilsa politely refused. When the Crowns traveled, they stayed in deluxe hotels. Joe said he'd earned it.

Ilsa unpacked with Fritzi's help. They hung up her dresses and arranged her hats and shoes in the closet. "Are you tired, Mama? Do you want to rest?"

"No. I would like to have a look at your flat. Last year you wouldn't show it to me."

"We never had time. Actually, it's just one room. But very nice," Fritzi added hastily, suggesting an opposite meaning. "We'll take the elevated railroad. It's cheaper than the cars or subway, and everyone rides it."

They walked east, buffeted by morning crowds. Everyone seemed surly and in a hurry. Ilsa was winded by the time they reached a covered wrought iron staircase. Over Fritzi's objections she paid for their tickets. A man with a metal box collected the tickets, and they passed through a ladies' waiting room to the open platform, thronged with ill-clad New Yorkers who rudely walked in front of Ilsa at every opportunity. She was shocked by a man pounding a vending machine with his fists, as though it were a human enemy.

"Where exactly is this railway taking us?"

"Downtown. This is the Second Avenue line, but it runs along First Avenue below Twenty-third. Here comes the train."

Ilsa and Fritzi crowded into a claret-colored car with the company name, MANHATTAN, blazoned in gold along the roof line. A man stepped on Ilsa's foot in his haste to beat her to a seat. She wanted to swat him with her handbag.

Even with the windows open, the car was a stew of smells — onions, sausages, garlic, sweat, cheap perfume, and someone's flatulence. Ilsa sat with her handbag clutched on her knees, half expecting to be robbed at any moment. The train swayed and shook. Fortunately, the ride was short. As they descended the stairs at their destination, Ilsa studied the street, latticed by sunlight and shadow from above.

"What kind of neighborhood is this?"

"A German neighborhood, Mama."

"I don't see any people who look like Germans. I see pawnshops, a tavern — a lot of pushcarts." One cart piled high with sorry-looking cabbages bore down on her, but Ilsa refused to give ground. The pushcart vendor veered and shouted, "Watch out, lady!"

"Actually, it's an *old* German neighborhood," Fritzi said. "Most of the families have moved up to Yorkville. Now it's what we call mixed."

"Mixed what? Drunks and bums?" One was noisily vomiting in the gutter. "Why did you have to rent a room on a street with trains running up and down?" Tiredness edged her voice. She already knew the answer; she didn't need a detective to find out that her daughter was doing poorly.

"Rooms on the El line are much cheaper," Fritzi said.

Ilsa was appalled by the filthy, littered side-walk in front of the building to which Fritzi led her. "Which floor is yours?"

"The third. That window is mine."

"The same as the elevated? They can look right in."

"That's why the third-floor front is always the least expensive."

They ascended three dark flights. The room was worse than she'd imagined. No sofa, not even a nice potted palm, just a bed, a wardrobe, an old dresser, one chair. An elevated train approached. Ilsa had all she could do not to shudder as the entire room and its furnishings shook.

"Is there a private bath?"

"It's private if you lock the door," Fritzi said blithely. "Half a dozen people use it. I keep a chamber pot under the bed."

Down on First Avenue a woman screamed, and Ilsa ran to the window. She saw a fat man pursuing someone into an alley, waving a meat cleaver. She felt profoundly depressed.

Seeing this, Fritzi said, "I have a gas ring. There, in the alcove. Why don't I fix a nice lunch?"

Recalling some of Fritzi's terrifying and inedible fiascos in the kitchen, she said, "No, dear. You need a hearty restaurant meal, you've lost too much weight. We'll dine out while I'm here."

Lüchow's on the south side of Fourteenth Street was the only suitable choice. While a waiter uncorked a bottle of Liebfraumilch, a four-piece band oomphed away with von Tilzer's "Down Where the Wurzburger Flows."

"These days you hear all kinds of songs about brands of beer," Fritzi said. "Has Papa commissioned one yet?"

"No, he thinks they're cheap. I can tell you privately, he isn't sorry that 'Under the Anheuser Bush' is no big hit."

Ilsa studied her daughter. She thought Fritzi too careless about her grooming. Of course, she couldn't afford a fine wardrobe or expensive beauty preparations. Still, she should take better care of herself. Tame her hair, iron her frocks — be a little more feminine. She seemed to have no sense of what an attractive person she was and therefore didn't care much about appearances.

They touched their glasses. *"Prosit."* After they drank Fritzi said, "Have you heard the latest joke about President Taft? On the streetcar he got up and gave his seat to three ladies."

"That's very amusing. But I'd prefer to hear all about this play which I regrettably missed."

Fritzi gave a summary of her *Macbeth* experience. She'd become friendly with the director and leading actor, a Mr. Manchester, and with the leading lady. Ilsa knew Mrs. Van Sant's name, and she was impressed.

Some of Fritzi's colleagues sounded less winning. Fritzi's mimicry of one, a Mr. Scarboro, made Ilsa giggle.

"Your imitations, they're always priceless."

"Carl and Joey and some of my teachers never thought so. Pauli liked them, though. I guess imitating people isn't nice, but sometimes I can't help it. I don't tolerate fools very well."

"Like your papa."

Ilsa's heart was overflowing with motherly concern. Very clearly, Fritzi was struggling. In Ilsa's opinion she had stayed too long in New York already. Ilsa took another sip of Liebfraumilch for courage.

"Let me speak seriously a moment. Haven't you grown discouraged here?"

Soberly, Fritzi said, "I'm discouraged sometimes, yes."

"Then come home. Give it up."

Fritzi looked at her. "To appease Papa?"

"No, no. To free yourself from this awful life."

"I came to New York by choice, Mama. I dreamed of it for years. I'm doing what I want to do."

"How can you say that after so many disappointments? What comes next? What you've done before, carrying dishes, making beds, typing for no-goods who don't appreciate it? None of it's fit work for a young woman of your intelligence."

With an odd, nervous look Fritzi said, "I know where there's an acting job that pays fairly well."

"You hardly sound enthused."

"I'm not. But it's work. I'm thinking seriously about it. I don't want to say more until I've investigated. Shall we order dessert?"

During her four-day visit, Ilsa bought Fritzi three new outfits, a pair of good patent leather pumps, a pair of galoshes, a set of handsome tortoise-shell combs for her unruly hair, a new flat-iron, and a small potted palm to bring a little cheer into the rented room. At the Rogers Peet store she bought a tastefully striped madras four-in-hand for Joe. She couldn't guess whether he'd wear it.

Fritzi accompanied Ilsa to Grand Central. Together they walked down the two-hundred-foot red carpet of the Limited. Fritzi had been with her mother every day. Whatever the nature of this new acting opportunity, it certainly hadn't taken her time. Nor had Fritzi said any more about it.

On the noisy platform, Ilsa harked back to their conversation at Lüchow's. "I wish you would come home."

"To what? Amateur theatricals and charity work? No."

"Why are you so determined? Is it to defy your father?"

Fritzi's brown eyes sparked; Ilsa had touched something. "I want to prove to him that he's wrong. That I can do this."

"What will you do if this next acting job fails like all the others? Just keep marching on forever until you're gray and no longer able?"

"I am going to make this one succeed, Mama."

"Why won't you tell me what you're doing?"

"Plenty of time for that later."

"Fritzi. It isn't something to be ashamed of, is it?"

"No, Mama," she answered, — a little too quickly, Ilsa thought. She did her best to conceal her dismay, her feeling of frustration, personal failure at the end of this rescue mission.

The conductors called final boarding. The huge black locomotive chuffed like an impatient horse. Ilsa threw her arms around Fritzi. As they hugged, she slid her right hand down to Fritzi's left pocket with fifty dollars in folded bills.

The Twentieth Century Limited carried Ilsa north along the Hudson in a spectacular autumn twilight. The palisades were brilliant yellow and scarlet. A little steamer going downstream looked white as wedding-cake icing. She saw none of the beauty, only an imaginary reflection of Fritzi's face in the glass. She sat with her elbow on the sill, her chin in her hand, and a tear shining on her cheek.

35. Biograph

Fritzi discovered Ilsa's fifty dollars at the end of the day. She was touched and overcome. A few dollars put aside would stave off starvation again.

Ilsa's gift didn't remove the need for serious thought about the future, however, or the need of some positive step in that direction. She left messages at the Biograph studio all through the following week. Sunday evening she was in her room, trying to interest herself in copies of the *Times* and *Tribune* thrown away by other tenants. Through the ceiling came the talking-machine voice of Carrie Jacobs Bond singing "The End of a Perfect Day," a sweet song, but not when played twenty times a night. Someone knocked.

"It's Mrs. Perella. There's a gent telephoning."

"Thank you for calling back, Mr. Bitzer," Fritzi said when she answered. "I didn't imagine you worked Sundays."

"We work seven days. Last week was hell. What can I do for you?"

"I'd like to accept your kind offer. When we met, I know I made a rather sharp comment about the pictures —"

"Nothing we haven't heard before. Forget it. I'll be glad to introduce you to our star director, Mr. Griffith. Used to be an actor. A few months back he directed his first picture, and we sold twenty-five prints. The most we ever sold before was fifteen. Now he can't make pictures fast enough."

"When should I be there?"

"Tomorrow morning, six-thirty. Ask for Griffith. I'll set it up. One little tip. No snooty words about pictures to him, or you'll be out the door. Griffith wants people who take the business seriously. He thinks it's a new art form."

Daylight was rising above the East River when Fritzi came rushing along east Fourteenth Street, a cardboard portfolio of programs and reviews clutched tightly in her glove. She'd included a *Macbeth* review with a cast list, hoping the review itself would be overlooked. She'd been up since five, pressing her skirt and scrubbing a soup spot out of her shirtwaist and fretting.

Trash of all sorts sailed along the street. A west wind beating at her back blew ominous clouds. As always before an important interview she was frantically nervous. She almost tripped over a scruffy mutt raising its leg at the wheel of a milk wagon.

At the correct address, number eleven, she stared up at a five-story brownstone. Staring right back at her were four would-be actors shivering on the stoop in the chill morning light. Their expressions ranged from the mild curiosity of a handsome Negro boy in patched pants to the raging hostility of a hard-looking redhead. Fancy gold letters on a plate-glass window to the right of the high stoop said

The redhead snarled at her. "You're supposed to wait out here till someone looks you over, sister."

Not feeling a bit genteel, Fritzi snapped, "Oh, thank you, I mistakenly thought this might be a new trolley stop." The boy laughed.

She stepped aside to make way for men and women arriving with newspapers, lunch pails, makeup boxes. A young fellow who looked like an Irish ironworker said to a companion as they approached, "I don't care what the boss says, I think cops are funny." He winked at Fritzi, tipped his cap, and bounded up the steps.

Two young women, beautiful ash blondes and obviously sisters, followed close behind them. To the gathered hopefuls the pert one said, "Good morning." The ethereal one said, "Good luck."

Just as the crowd cleared and Fritzi prepared to go in, a man in a heavy football sweater came out. He studied a sheet of paper, then the actors. To the redhead he said, "Nothing today." He repeated it to the two men and the boy. He looked Fritzi up and down. "You're new."

"Yes, sir, I —"

"Nothing for you either."

"I have an appointment with Mr. Griffith. Mr. Bitzer arranged it."

Though doubtful, he said, "All right, come on in. The boss is busy, but he does like to see new girls. Follow me."

Allowing herself a little smile of vindication, she started up the steps. It was that moment Ellen Terry chose to hand down one of her opinions.

The galloping tintypes? Shameful. No good can come of this.

It might be true. Head high, she marched up the steps and into the building anyway.

Fritzi quickly decided the Biograph studio was one of the oddest, noisiest, grubbiest places she'd ever seen. The yellow walls were water-stained and peeling. The air reeked of paint and cigars. From upstairs came a din of hammering and sawing.

They climbed two flights to the second floor; there the din was worse. The man pointed at a bench. "Wait here. Don't go in, that's the main stage." When he disappeared through a wide archway, though, Fritzi promptly stepped over to peek.

It might have been the ballroom of the once fashionable town house; certainly it was big enough. High-intensity arc lights hanging from overhead pipe battens lit the room. On the floor, banks of glowing purplish tubes shed a different, more diffuse light on the peculiar scene. A canvas flat rose up before her eyes to establish a wall with patently fake table and chairs painted under an equally fake, in fact, horrible landscape. A second flat appeared beside the first, propelled by invisible hands that butted them together while invisible hammers pounded invisible nails into invisible cleats.

A practical door in the flat opened; a man walked out carrying two potted plants. A scene shifter unrolled a faded Turkey carpet that exhaled clouds of dust. Off to one side a carpenter at a sawhorse sawed a two-by-four at maniacal speed. In another dim corner a wardrobe woman snatched garments out of a trunk, snarling, "Hell's hard-boiled eggs in a basket, where is the goddamn thing?"

A young woman in Oriental pajamas bumped Fritzi from behind. To a stocky man wearing a straw hat she said, "Is the makeup okay, Billy?" The girl's face was plastered with golden greasepaint; she looked like a terminal jaundice case.

"Definitely not. The lip rouge is too heavy. You dames keep forgetting, red photographs black. Hey," he exclaimed, noticing Fritzi. "Good morning. You made it."

"I did, Mr. Bitzer, thank you," she said. "I really do appreciate —"

"Swell. Got to rush. Good luck."

The man in the football sweater returned and crooked a finger. She followed him into the big room. He pointed.

"Someone's with Mr. Griffith. Go in and wait till he speaks to you. Over there, in the corner. Don't step on anything."

Half blinded by the lights, she squinted at a folding screen decorated with golden peacocks. A third flat wobbled into place, creating a crude drawing room. Billy Bitzer left off polishing the lens of his camera and yelled at someone while the carpenter yelled at someone else and the wardrobe woman screamed epithets and yanked

315

more costumes out of the trunk. What kind of crazy place was this? Fritzi had assumed that studios where silent pictures were made would be — well, silent.

Behind the Oriental screen a man held forth in a baritone voice almost as fine as Hobart's. "I'm sick and tired of being hauled to the front office every week to explain how I cut my pictures."

Hovering near the screen, she patted her hair, unbuttoned her jacket, smoothed her shirtwaist. This must be Mr. Griffith.

"If we end a scene in room A, we go right away to room B. It isn't necessary to show the players walking from A to B. The dunderheads don't get it because every other director *does* show the actors walking. Pack of illiterate damn Yankees. Never read Dickens or any other fine writer."

Steeling herself, Fritzi stepped around the screen into an office improvised from a rolltop desk, two swivel chairs, and a gooseneck lamp. A tall, dignified man was speaking to the burly young Irishman who'd tipped his cap outside.

"Maybe I should look for another studio. Oh, good morning, my dear."

"Mr. Griffith?"

"Yes, I am David Griffith. This is Mike Sinnott, one of our actors with ambitions to direct."

"Only my kind of picture, boss." Sinnott gave Fritzi a little salute. "Pleased to meet you."

"Yes, likewise."

Griffith ushered Sinnott to the ornamental screen. "You make your nonsensical comedies and I'll make five-reelers that have room to tell a real story, and we'll see who wins." Over his shoulder he said, "Be back shortly. Please be seated."

She took the guest chair, fidgeting. As a distraction she studied the director's cluttered desk, a mad confusion of letters, memoranda, cost sheets, books — Poe's *Tales of the Grotesque and Arabesque*, several works by Dickens, Thomas Dixon's *The Clansman*, a novel her father despised because it glorified the Ku Klux Klan.

A voice behind her made her jump. "Very sorry, my dear. We're always plagued with last-minute details." Griffith was nearly six feet tall, in his early thirties. His hair was thick and brown, his sideburns long and full, his nose sharp; he reminded her of schoolbook pictures of the Roman Caesars. Unlike most of the raffish inmates of the Biograph, he was smartly turned out in a suit, vest, cravat, high-winged collar.

He sat down, crossed his legs, and regarded her with deeply set blue eyes. "Now, my dear, to business. Billy Bitzer tells me you're an actress."

"Yes. Here are a few things I've done."

He examined the contents of the cardboard portfolio. "I've heard this *Macbeth* was execrable."

"I'm afraid that's too kind."

He smiled. Leaning back, he scrutinized her. His eyes were heavy lidded, with a hypnotic intensity. He seemed oblivious to the shouting, banging, cursing on the other side of the screen.

"Tell me something about your background,

Fritzi. Please don't mind my using your first name. In pictures there's none of the stuffy formality of the stage." Except, of course, everyone so far had referred to him as Mr. Griffith or boss.

She began with her Mortmain days. He drew her out with brief but precise questions. In his speech she heard the South. Not the deep cotton South but the border — Kentucky, Tennessee. He kept twisting a large ornate ring, silver and black enamel decorated with an Egyptian or Oriental character.

"Thank you," he said when she'd finished. "Please don't be offended if I tell you what I tell all applicants who come to us from the rarefied precincts of legitimate theater — in which I apprenticed as an actor, by the way. Motion-picture companies, particularly this one, are not fond of thespians who are merely slumming."

"Mr. Griffith, I'm serious about applying to work in pictures. I have no experience, but I learn quickly."

"Excellent, we've cleared the air. Most who gravitate here find that what we do is pleasant, even exciting. The pay is good, five dollars per day, whether one's a featured player or an extra. There are no lines to memorize, though I insist my actors make up dialogue suitable to the context of a scene. Lip readers have caught us up short a few times. We work outdoors a good deal, so it's healthful. As a matter of fact, certain members of the company will soon enjoy the balmy air of southern California. We'll be filming out there until spring brings sunshine back to the East." She decided that the word suiting him best was *pompous*.

"Please stand up, Fritzi."

Nervously she did. He slid two silver dollars from his pants pocket, began to pass them from hand to hand, *clink, clink.*

"Turn toward me. That's fine. Turn again. Now sit. Stand. Register sadness. Let it become happiness."

She obeyed each instruction, feeling like a mugging chimpanzee.

"Now show elation. That's good. Amusement. Scorn — oh, very nice. Hatred. Excellent." He stood suddenly, slipped his right hand forward to rest lightly just below her padded bosom. "Are you free this evening? We might discuss opportunities over a bite of supper."

Oh, no; he was *that* kind of director.

"Mr. Griffith, if that's the price of employment at the Biograph studio, I refuse to pay it, thank you very much." She pulled away and snatched her portfolio off the desk. He was still holding her; somehow her shirtwaist had come out of her waistband. He cocked his head.

"This is puzzling. You don't strike me as a prude."

"I am not. But the only thing I'm selling is whatever talent I may have."

There was a long, horrible moment of mutual staring. The lamp threw glittering pinpoints in Griffith's eyes. She was sure he was going to curse her. Instead, he tossed his head back and laughed.

"Can't blame a fellow for trying, Fritzi." He

picked up her jacket. "I'm sorry I have nothing suitable for you at the moment. We employ several fine actresses in the company already. However, I do know of one opportunity."

"In a picture?" She was fumbling, put off by his return to courtesy.

"Of course in a picture. From time to time I hear from other directors in need of particular talent. In this case I'm speaking of a young fellow who was assistant camera here for ten months. He's good. When he came to work for me, I threw him in the deep end and he swam immediately. His name is Eddie Hearn. A Yale man, but don't hold that against him. He's working for Pelzer and Kelly, Pal Pictures. It's a blanket company."

"What's that?"

"Oh, just a technical term. Eddie is scheduled to start filming on Tuesday, but he hasn't found a suitable leading lady." *Leading lady?* Could she be hearing correctly? "If the weather's bad, it won't be too comfortable, I'm afraid. Eddie's shooting outdoors."

"I'll wear a warm coat!" Fritzi's cry amused him. "What type does he need?"

"An ingenue who's a bit unusual. Not a jaded city woman, someone earthy. Countrified. Fresh-scrubbed, like you." *Ye gods, what's next? "Wholesome"?*

Griffith clinked the silver dollars. "I'd be happy to recommend you."

Dumbfounded, she said, "May I ask why? I insulted you, didn't I?"

"You spoke frankly. I like actors with backbone. They bring something to a part beyond a slavish desire to please." He scribbled on a memorandum pad. "I'll telephone Eddie this afternoon. You should go see him tomorrow. This is the address. It's an exchange." She didn't understand what he meant. "Eddie rents a desk there."

"Pal Pictures doesn't have a studio?"

"They're a small company. Sometimes they rent a loft on west Twenty-third." Griffith's answer struck her as curiously glib. She didn't want to examine her luck too closely, though. Like a soap bubble, it might vanish.

A young man in knee breeches popped around the screen. "All set, boss. Billy's lit the set. Do we have a scenario?"

Griffith tapped his forehead. "In here. It's all we need." Tall and correct, he took Fritzi's hand between his. This time she didn't resist.

"If Eddie hires you, here's a bit of advice. Make a friend of your cameraman. He'll soon know what lighting and makeup will show you to advantage."

"Yes, sir, thank you, for the opportunity and the advice. I'll remember it."

He patted her hand almost paternally. "I have a feeling you will. Oh, I should ask whether you can ride a horse."

"Why, yes, I rode a lot when I was growing up in Chicago."

"Good. I don't know that the role requires it, but Eddie's picture is a western."

"Western? Heavens, will I have to travel?"

He laughed. "No farther than the other side of

the Hudson. Fort Lee, New Jersey, is the western capital of America these days."

He hurried to the set, where preparations had escalated to a level approaching pandemonium. One of the sisters she'd seen coming to work, the pert one, didn't like her gown and was cursing like a sailor. There was a lot of shouting, but no one appeared to be listening. The only calm individual was Billy Bitzer. Straw hat tilted over his eyes, he examined the lens of his camera. Griffith tapped him on the shoulder and began to speak. Others noticed the director; silence was instantaneous.

Fritzi was almost dizzy with excitement. She put her portfolio on the hall bench and stuffed her shirtwaist back in her skirt. An incredibly pretty young girl, sixteen or seventeen, raced up the stairs, long gold ringlets bouncing. She saw Fritzi straightening her clothes.

"Bet you were with the boss. Did he get fresh?"

"Well . . ." Fritzi's hesitation amounted to a confession.

"Don't think anything of it, it's just his way. He's married, you know."

"Married!"

"One hundred percent. His wife makes pictures for the Biograph. He pretends he hardly knows her. In public he calls her Miss Arvidsen." She giggled. "Is there any work?"

"Not here, but possibly with another company."

"That's grand. It's really a lot of fun making pictures. Mr. Griffith's a regular dictator, but we all think he's a genius."

"Thank you, miss —"

"Smith, Gladys Smith. But they bill me as Mary Pickford. My brother acts too. Jack Pickford."

"Pleased to know you, Mary. I'm Fritzi Crown."

"Hope I see you again, Fritzi." Miss Smith-Pickford rushed off.

Bitter wind assaulted Fritzi the moment she stepped outside. A loose garbage can rolled east, clanging like a cymbal. Westbound pedestrians held their hats and leaned at a forty-five-degree angle. Fritzi clutched her cheap cardboard folder and fairly danced down the steps. Who cared if the picture was a western? It was work, and Ellen Terry would just have to shut up.

36. Westward Ho

David Griffith's bad handwriting directed Fritzi to something called the Klee & Thermal Film Exchange on Fourteenth Street near Third Avenue. Going in, she was buffeted by a rude man with round metal cans under his arm. Five more men clamored for attention at a front office counter staffed by a lone clerk. He was examining a perforated strip of film.

"You damaged it, Cohen. We'll have to cut out the frames with the torn sprocket holes before we rent it again. That'll be an extra dollar."

"Robber," said the indignant customer.

Fritzi waved above Cohen's head. "Excuse me, can you direct me to Mr. Hearn's office?"

The clerk seemed pleased to see a rose among the thorns. "Mr. Hearn's coat closet," he corrected, "is that way, fourth on the left."

She plunged into a musty hall decorated with lurid posters for pictures from Biograph and Vitagraph and other producers. Strong chemicals afloat in the air made her eyes water. Another clerk rushed at her with a stack of cans. She flattened against the wall to avoid being run down, then proceeded to Hearn's open door.

A coat closet, all right. Its poverty was only slightly relieved by some black-and-white magazine advertisements tacked to the wall. All included the words PAL PICTURES and a logo, a racing palomino horse. A slogan appeared at the bottom of every ad. *Follow the Pal Pony to Profitable Programs!!!!* Someone loved exclamation marks.

Eddie Hearn saw neither the posters nor Fritzi. He was absorbed in a sheet of yellow foolscap. Silver wire spectacles were set on the tip of his nose. Unruly black hair over his ears demanded a barber. He wore riding breeches tucked into scuffed brown cavalry boots whose heels rested on the desk.

She knocked on the doorjamb. Hearn glanced up, showing her a long, narrow face, vivid dark eyes behind the spectacles. A holy medal gleamed in the V neck of his loose white shirt, a gold wedding ring on his left hand.

"Golly, I didn't see you. Miss Crown?" He said it while swinging his feet off the desk; he nearly fell out of his chair.

"Yes, sir."

"Please come in." In his haste to stand he dropped the typewritten sheet. When he bent to pick it up, he banged his forehead on the wall. "Sorry to meet you in such surroundings. This office is too small. It's only temporary." For his sake she hoped so.

At his invitation she took the visitor's chair. He looked her over. He seemed friendly as a puppy. "Have you ever visited an exchange?"

"No. I've no idea what goes on here."

"What the name says. Exchange. When the picture business was getting started, producers sold their films directly to people who showed them. But that proved to be cumbersome and wasteful. What do you do with an old, scratched print no one wants to see again? About four years ago someone in San Francisco opened the first exchange and solved the problem. The idea of middlemen caught on. Exchanges buy the pictures, then rent them to owners of nickelodeons who show them, bring them back, and exchange them for a new program. There are lots of exchanges on Fourteenth Street — over a hundred in the U.S. This is one of the busiest. Klee and Thermal run a film-processing laboratory in back." Which explained the chemical smell. "There's also a projection room that can be rented."

"Thank you, Mr. Hearn. That's very interesting."

"So here we are."

"Yes. Here we are."

Hands in her lap, Fritzi waited.

"I'm grateful to David for sending you over. The man's aces with me, though working for him was like serving in the army of Attila. He taught me how to stage a scene, and how to cut it together. Billy Bitzer taught me lenses and lighting. Did David tell you what I'm doing now?"

"A western picture."

"There's a strong market, domestically and in Europe. Look at Broncho Billy Anderson. Essanay can't churn out Broncho Billys fast enough. People are wild about him. And he has a paunch!" Eddie Hearn grinned in an apologetic way. "Excuse me if I get carried away. I love the West. I've seen Buffalo Bill's arena show at least twenty times. When I was little, I hid dime novels under my pillow. They weren't considered proper reading for rich boys in Greenwich."

"Connecticut?"

"Born and bred." He nodded. "Pop's on Wall Street. He expected me to follow him there, but I heard a different call when I played an Indian in a prep school pageant. Pop insisted I follow him to Yale. I did, but in my junior year I switched from business to drama. Pop stopped paying my tuition. I had to wait tables and paint houses to graduate. Doesn't matter, I'm doing what I want. I fell in love with pictures the day I saw Edwin Porter's *Great Train Robbery.*"

He leaned back. He was good looking, with plenty of Irish charm. He spoke beautifully. His smile and his gregarious style made her feel at ease.

"What's your acting experience?" After she summarized it he said, "Made any other pictures?"

"No, this would be my first."

"I like honesty. I know a dozen actresses who'd lie like the very devil to get a part."

"Can you tell me a little about the picture?"

"I grew up on Cooper's Leatherstocking tales. I wondered why an Indian should always be portrayed in pictures as the skulking villain. Why not a noble savage? A true native American hero? So I wrote this scenario." He showed the typed yellow foolscap. "My original title was 'The Lone Indian.' Mr. Pelzer, one of the partners, approves all the scenarios. He wanted money in the title. He said everyone's interested in money."

After his spurt of confidences Eddie Hearn

seemed unable to think of more to say. They stared at each other. He blushed from his throat to his cheekbones. Fritzi smiled sweetly.

"Mr. Hearn, do I dare ask whether you have any interest in hiring me?"

"Yes! Definitely! I like your appearance, I love the way your eyes dance when you smile, and I take David's word that you can act. We'll soon find out, won't we?" She was forced to laugh at his little jest, though its underlying truth was chilling.

"I can offer two, possibly three days of work if we have fine weather. Wages are four dollars per day. Mr. Kelly also pays for trolleys, the ferry, and your lunch over in Jersey."

"Who is Mr. Kelly?"

"The other partner. In charge of the money. You know how they say all the Irish are merry and whimsical as leprechauns? They never met Kelly. He squeezes a dollar ten cents out of every dollar we spend." His cloudy brow suggested it wasn't a well-loved trait.

"Four dollars a day," Fritzi mused.

"Yes, and — what's wrong?"

She was on her feet, acting her heart out to register disdain. "Mr. Hearn, you may be under instructions to buy talent cheaply, but the standard salary at the Biograph and other good studios is five dollars a day, regardless of the role. I won't take less."

"I see." He gnawed on his lip, tried to keep his expression that of the flint-hearted capitalist. He didn't have it in him.

"All right. Five."

From a drawer he pulled another typed sheet, folded it, and handed it across the desk.

"Please study the scenario. Tuesday morning report to the 129th Street ferry terminal at six-thirty sharp. We'll meet our cameraman in Fort Lee, then proceed to Coytesville — that's a little hamlet several miles farther on. Dress warmly. This time of year it may be cold even when the sun's well up."

"Thank you, Mr. Hearn. Thank you very much. I'll do my best to repay your confidence."

"Everyone calls me Eddie. You must too. See you Tuesday."

She floated out of the exchange in a state of bliss. At a shop near Herald Square she treated herself to hot tea and a biscuit. She sat in delicious reverie, imagining how she'd splurge on Christmas presents. Then she pictured all the things she could at last buy for herself. An oval throw rug for the cold, bare floor of her room. A rectangular wall mirror without flaws or cracks.

Underwear.

What contortions and deceptions she'd gone through during Ilsa's visit so Ilsa would never see the sorry state of her undergarments. Because of her inept mending, small rips had become lumps of thread hard as pebbles; they hurt when she sat the wrong way. Lace trim on one pair of drawers resembled a fringe of string, and the fabric was worn so thin, a man could have seen everything, had there been a man in the universe who cared to look. New underwear! She gave the thought a whole string of Pal Pictures exclamation points. New underwear was better than a gold strike.

Oh, the horizons that opened when you had a job *and* the huge sum of fifty dollars hidden in a tin box! The thought of Ilsa's surreptitious gift, the love and generosity it expressed, always turned her teary. The moment in the tea shop was no exception.

She ordered a second pot and unfolded the scenario, noting its wretched typewriting, the many strikeovers.

"THE LONE INDIAN'S GOLD"
(1 REEL)
SCENARIO BY EDW. B. HEARN JR.

The melodrama opened with Chief White Eagle of the Apache riding up to a general store. A "genial old-timer" ran the store, together with his "spunky daughter" (she would have to stand before her new mirror and experiment with various attitudes and faces that might register spunk). An interpolated note said the store interior would be filmed outdoors, using a canvas backdrop supplied by a relative of money man Kelly. This was not going to be high art.

The chief had a sack of gold from the "tribal mine." He'd ridden to town to have it assayed. No expert on Indian affairs, Fritzi nevertheless doubted that a people who had been relentlessly harried and nearly annihilated by the United States cavalry had a tribal gold mine to fall back on.

Three skulking bad men spied on the chief as he showed his sack of gold to the storekeeper's daughter. The head ruffian demonstrated by what the scenario termed "salacious leering" that he coveted the girl along with the gold. The bad men jumped the chief and fired pistols to make him "dance" (Fritzi rolled her eyes and hastily drank some tea).

With the Indian knocked unconscious, girl and gold were abducted. Of course, the chief found and rescued both, in the woods following a "titanic battle." The girl clearly adored White Eagle, but he had other business, possibly further excavations of the tribal gold mine. He rode off with a wave and an "expression of manly stoicism."

Title card
THE LONE INDIAN WILL RETURN!!!

Fritzi sighed. Eddie Hearn of Greenwich and Yale had stuffed one too many dime novels under his pillow. The scenario was hokum, cheap blood-and-thunder. Did it matter? Shamelessly, she felt that it did not. She had a part. She was going to *act* again.

William Gillette fell ill upstate; a week of the *Sherlock Holmes* tour was canceled. Hobart took leave of his role as the Napoleon of Crime and rushed back to the city from Buffalo — "the fundament of the world," as he expressed it to Fritzi. His timing was perfect; she was dying to visit a new-style restaurant said to be popular with the acting crowd. She took him to supper.

The Forty-second Street "Automat" caught their fancy at once. You entered a bright and spotless dining area done in white tile. You laid a tray on a continuous counter and pushed it along in front of little metal-framed windows, each displaying its item of hot or cold food. You paid for each dish separately by putting two pennies or a nickel into a slot. The window sprang open, you placed your purchase on your tray, and a partitioned turntable revolved an identical dish into the window. American ingenuity!

Hobart saw several colleagues dining. He darted off to chat, bow, make a show of confidence while his food got cold. "Yes, *The Tempest* is a definite possibility. Belasco is interested." Fritzi giggled as she broke her kaiser roll. Her friend had never met Belasco.

Finally he came back. He remarked that her decision to investigate the picture studio was wise.

"I'm nervous about next Tuesday, Hobart. Do you think I'll be all right?"

"If you work hard and don't leaven it with contempt, undoubtedly."

Stuffed with good food and affection for her bombastic companion, Fritzi took his arm as they left. The cold night air made Hobart's nose shine like a Christmas tree ornament. A wind blowing along Forty-second Street whirled a few snowflakes around them. Hobart squired her to the elevated stairs where they embraced and wished each other luck. They promised to be reunited soon.

"You are a dear girl, Fritzi. I would propose marriage were I younger and, ah, inclined toward the female of the species."

Fritzi kissed him and ran up the stairs. Hobart walked away jauntily in a cloud of snow swirling under the street light.

37. Blanket Company

Tuesday's dawn was dark and foggy. Fritzi was in a state of nerves the moment she woke up, said state compounded by a bellyache. Last night she'd treated herself to a meal at a neighborhood saloon, entering in by the side door ("Tables for Ladies — Refined Atmosphere"). She'd enjoyed a bowl of navy bean soup followed by liver and onions; she wasn't enjoying the aftermath. Her stomach gurgled like faulty plumbing.

She reached the ferry pier at six-fifteen. Other actors came drifting out of the murk, giving her a close look or casual nod. A pretty black girl in a thin wool coat arrived. She had a friendly face but stood well apart from the others, shivering.

Spears of light pierced the fog: a Stoddard-Dayton with headlamps blazing. Eddie Hearn was at the wheel. Seated next to him, arms folded, was a slight red-faced man in a high celluloid collar and dark gray double-breasted suit with a light gray shadow check. He had beautiful thick white hair and a slit of a mouth. Kelly?

A deck hand waved Eddie across the ferry ramp to a parking place. Eddie jumped out, summoned the others aboard, and performed introductions. The sour man was indeed Alfred A. (for Aloysius) Kelly. He grunted something to Fritzi while he eyed her up and down. It set her on edge, which was probably the effect he wanted.

A young man with blond hair and a bull neck was introduced as Owen Stallings. He was playing the Lone Indian. He looked about as Indian as Lief Eriksson. After shaking Fritzi's hand enthusiastically, he sauntered to the rail and from there continued to smile at her, as though confident it would bowl her over. Handsome men were worse than beautiful women.

Fritzi's father was Noble Royce, a jolly red-nosed old ham wearing a pea coat and watch cap. One sniff and Fritzi decided he'd flavored his morning oatmeal with beer. The leader of the bad men was a wizened, sullen actor, Sam Something.

A Ford F Model touring car chugged out of the fog. The car was several years old and showed it. Doors were dented; one running board sagged. Eddie hailed the stout and homely young man at the wheel. "Bill Nix, our chief carpenter and prop man." On the seat of Nix's car Fritzi noticed three film magazines lashed together. She saw no camera anywhere.

The bell rang, deck hands closed the stern gates, and the ferry churned into the Hudson, sounding its horn. Gulls hunting garbage wheeled over the wake. Half a dozen workmen crossing the river with lunch pails eyed the picture people curiously. Kelly called Eddie to the rail with a brusque wave, hectored him in a low voice. Owen Stallings stepped up to Fritzi and tipped his cap.

"Hello again, little lady."

Stabbed by a cramp at precisely that moment, she retorted, "Would you mind calling me something else? I hate to be patronized."

He blinked his big brown eyes. "Why, sure. Say, are you one of these brassy new women always marching and demanding their rights?"

"You don't approve, Mr. Stallings?"

"No, ma'am, I'm old-fashioned. It's a man's world. What's your name again?"

Fritzi could have rushed to the barricades and fought this fool, but it would get things off to a bad start. She replied calmly. "Fritzi Crown."

"Any relation to Crown's beer? Used to drink that by the gallon back in Ohio."

And his stomach was starting to show it. Big, silly ox — all those good looks and he didn't know how to use them.

"Yes, my father owns the brewery. I'm a little chilly. I think I'll sit in the car if you don't mind."

"Sure, Fritzi, I'll see you later," he said with another tip of his cap.

She climbed into the backseat of the Stoddard-Dayton. She noticed the black girl standing near, smiled at her. "Cold, isn't it?"

"I'll say."

Fritzi patted the seat. "You're welcome here, there's plenty of room."

"I'm not supposed to sit next to white folks."

"Who says?"

"Practically the whole world."

"Doesn't include me." Fritzi pushed the handle to open the door. "Sit."

Gratefully the girl climbed in. She introduced herself as Nell Spooner, in charge of the wardrobe trunk lashed to the back of the Ford. Once she discovered that Fritzi wouldn't bite, she chatted freely. She was a native New Yorker, she said, born on Thompson Street, in a district called Little Africa.

"We live in Harlem now, Lenox and 134th — practically the country. Daddy's pastor of St. Jude's Colored Methodist Episcopal Church. He says this picture business is tainted and godless." Nell frowned. "I tell him work's work."

"Exactly," Fritzi said. She noticed Sam Something giving them disgusted looks, and she stared right back. With a sneer he opened his morning *Post*.

The Jersey palisades loomed. The ferry docked, and the autos drove along a road at the base of spectacular cliffs for a distance of about three miles. Then the road slanted up the face of the palisade to the high bluff. Eddie asked them all to get out and walk. The cars lurched and wheezed and hesitated frequently during the climb. Sam Something complained about walking, and about the temperature, although the morning was beginning to feel more like a chilly October day than early December.

At the summit the actors rode again, bumping through pleasant countryside to Fort Lee. It wasn't much of a place, drab buildings along a dirt street. A trolley track ran down the middle, and telephone and trolley wires crisscrossed above. A few New Jersey rustics idled on the sidewalks.

They turned off on a side street, reached a stable where Eddie jumped out to greet a ruddy middle-aged man with orange hair turning white around his ears. The man had evidently arrived in a closed delivery wagon that once might have carried milk or meat; now its wooden sides were painted over.

"Everybody, this is Jock Ferguson, our cameraman. Anyone follow you, Jock?"

"Don't think so, laddie. Hardly anyone's up at half past four but thieves and inebriates. Forty-second Street ferry's dead too."

"We'll leave the wagon here."

"Aye." Ferguson opened the rear doors. He and Eddie unloaded something bulky wrapped in a bright red blanket with Navaho designs. They lugged their mysterious burden to the Ford. A stable boy with a broom wandered over and craned on tiptoe to look in. Al Kelly stepped between him and the car.

"Get the hell out of here," he roared, and the boy fled.

They left Fort Lee on a dirt road, bound for Coytesville. Fritzi said to Nell, "What are they hiding under the blanket?"

"The camera. Pal is a blanket company."

"So I heard. I thought it was a technical term."

"It's technical, all right. Mr. Kelly's partner, Mr. Pelzer, he designed the camera and sort of accidentally included some features Mr. Edison invented and patented. Mr. Ferguson told me Edison's even got a patent on the sprocket holes in the film. If your camera uses his inventions, you're supposed to pay royalty to something called the Motion Pictures Patents Company, which he helped organize. It's a trust, most of the big studios belong. Kalem, Essanay, Selig,

Pathé — they all pay. So do exhibitors. If they show pictures with a patented projector, they pay the trust two dollars a week."

"You know quite a bit about the business."

"Been working for Pal almost a year. I listen. Plenty of time for that, nobody talks to me except to give orders." She wasn't bitter, only matter-of-fact.

"Does the Biograph belong to the trust?"

"Yes. Blanket companies are independents that don't. They hide their cameras and move around a lot. The Patents Company keeps a whole flock of detectives hunting them to stop production. Worst one used to be a Pinkerton, Pearly Purvis is his name." Nell thought a moment before she added, "They carry guns."

Fritzi shivered. "You don't mean it. Do they actually shoot at actors?"

"No," Nell said, "generally they shoot the camera."

Coytesville had a dusty main street even more primitive than Fort Lee's. There were no emblems of progress — no autos, trolley tracks, or telephone wires. The little place could easily pass for a town out West.

The sun had cleared the trees behind them, burning away the murk. The air was warmer. They parked at a frame building with a wide veranda and steeply pitched roof. A sign above the porch eave identified RAMBO'S HOTEL, offering a choice of ROOMS, BATHS, EATS, and LAGER BEER. An assorted half dozen males jumped up from benches and rockers on the porch and surrounded Eddie. "Any work today?"

"Two outlaws needed," Eddie said. A couple of the men fell into ludicrous poses of savagery. One flexed his biceps. Eddie inspected them while Al Kelly stood by with his arms folded and his face sour.

"You." Eddie pointed. "And you. Two and a half dollars per man for the day. Dressing rooms are inside, upstairs." He glanced at Nell, already untying the knots around the costume trunk. "We'll shoot here all morning and go to the woods right after lunch. Bill?" The carpenter raised his hand. "Jock knows our afternoon location. Go out there, hang up the drop for the store interior, and knock out a couple of counters. Buy the lumber you need."

"Don't spend a lot," Al Kelly said in his sand-paper voice. "We're not shooting the Second Coming here."

Nix walked off grumbling about doing it all himself, in the woods, without company. Owen Stallings sniffed. "I've never heard anyone complain so much."

"Yeah, he makes me tired," Kelly said. "Pretty soon he won't have a job."

Eddie clapped for attention. "Actors! Get inside. Dress quickly, we start in fifteen minutes." Young as he was, he spoke with an authority that made the actors move fast.

A porter dragged the costume trunk upstairs. The men dressed in one room, Fritzi in another. Nell helped her into a cotton dress washed colorless. "Stand still, the hem's got to come up two inches," Nell mumbled, on her knees with a mouthful of pins. "Sleeves fit all right. Your top's fine." Fritzi had of course put in her gay deceivers.

Eddie came in with a wooden makeup box. He put Fritzi in a chair and worked quickly with grease sticks and powder while Nell stayed on her knees, sewing the hem.

"Jock will tell us if we need to adjust the makeup, but I think it'll do." He showed her a small mirror, then ran out again, shouting, "Let's go, everyone, time is money."

Fritzi walked down to the porch. To her discomfort, her stomach was making unholy noises again. Eddie strung sash cord to stakes, forming a rectangle directly in front of the steps. Jock Ferguson was setting up his camera and tripod in the street, covering the rectangle, steps, and porch. A boy led a white horse around the corner of the hotel. Eddie inspected the animal, said, "I can use him."

"How much does the nag cost?" Kelly said.

"Two dollars for the day," Eddie answered.

"Christ. You'd think our name was Midas Pictures."

Eddie looked sore but didn't say anything. He opened his makeup box, quickly mixed water-based black paint in a small pie tin and painted an eagle feather on the horse's rump.

Nervous, the horse relieved himself, and Eddie leaped back just in time. Al Kelly snorted, evidently his version of high mirth. Fritzi absolutely did not like the man. She wondered about the other partner, Mr. Pelzer. He could hardly be worse.

341

Sam Something and the extras came outside wearing fringed shirts and coon-tail caps, suitably grimy. Two minutes later the impossibly handsome Owen appeared in leggings, moccasins, a black wig with a center part and long braids. He'd darkened his face, arms, and brawny chest with reddish paint. He flexed his arms and grinned, looking around for admirers.

Eddie said, "We'll start with the storekeeper being dragged out by the bad men. Noble, they knock you out and you fall down."

"Nothing to it," the old actor wheezed. He was weaving like a sapling in a gale, and Fritzi thought the question might be, Could he stand long enough to fall on cue?

"Sam, hit him with the butt of your pistol. Pull the blow, don't hurt him."

"Yeah, yeah," the sullen actor said, busy spinning the cylinder of his rusty gun.

"All of you remember this. You must stay inside the roped area."

Fritzi's nerves were wound tight as Eddie chalked the name of the picture on a school slate, and a scene number. The porter had come out to gawk, joining a few locals. From his car Eddie fetched a wooden sign lettered GENERAL STORE. He hung this on a nail pounded into a porch post. "Jock, be sure you're tilted down far enough to miss the hotel sign."

"Aye," Ferguson said, unscrewing something on the tripod's pan head.

"Actors inside," Eddie ordered. Fritzi crowded through the door with the others. They hid to either side of grimy windows. "Everyone

342

ready?" Eddie's voice had a queer, hollow sound, and she peeked quickly to see why. He had a small megaphone. Very handy in those noisy studios, she imagined.

"Here we go, people. *Camera.*"

She dabbed her upper lip with a handkerchief. Her stomach growled so loudly, Sam Something looked around. Eddie shouted, "Action. *Outlaws!*"

Giving Noble a shove, Sam Something snarled, "Let's go." It motivated the proper indignation in the old actor. In a moment Noble, Sam, and the two extras were through the door. Fritzi leaned against the wall, closed her eyes, clasped her hands prayerfully.

"Rough him up, that's it, that's it. Sam, bash him. That's it, swell. On your knees, Noble — groggy, groggy! Daughter! *Now!*"

Fritzi ran out the door. She heard the camera grinding away, Eddie calling encouragement.

Then disaster struck. As she rushed down from the porch, she stepped on her hem and went flying.

It would have been a bad fall had she not reacted instantly. She tucked her head, shot her hands out, landed on her palms, and somersaulted forward, springing up disheveled but unhurt. It was so surprising, everyone but Kelly burst out laughing.

Eddie shouted, "Cut. Fritzi, are you all right?"

Slapping dust off her sleeves, Fritzi said, "Oh, yes. When I was nine or ten, my brother and I spent every afternoon pretending we were tumblers in the circus."

Al Kelly's face was wrathful. "This isn't the big top, sister. We aren't making a comedy."

"I apologize for spoiling the shot, Mr. Kelly."

"I thought it was funny," Eddie said. "Especially the expression on your face when you popped up on your feet. You looked as surprised as anyone. Catch your breath and we'll do the scene again."

"I'm truly sorry."

"It was an accident," Eddie said, chuckling.

Kelly said, "Hearn, get this. On the budgets I write, we don't have accidents. Your girlie better do it in one take, every time, or we'll hire someone else. My aunt Flora isn't that clumsy, and she weighs two fifty."

Fritzi wanted to tell him politely that he was a boor, but an interruption forestalled it. They all heard a rattling and chugging from the direction of Fort Lee. She turned around as a black Oldsmobile drove into sight. One driver, one passenger, both male. Jock Ferguson wiped his forehead with his sleeve.

"We're in for it now, laddie."

She didn't need to be told that patent detectives had found them.

38. Our Heroine

As the Oldsmobile chugged toward them, Kelly exploded. "It was that damn kid who brought the horse. I'll bet my hat his old man telephoned the city."

Sam Something said, "Why?"

"Why? You idiot, the Patents Company. Jersey's thick with snitches. The going price is two bucks a tip."

Fritzi was mesmerized by the sinister black auto. The man in the left-hand passenger seat casually draped his arm over the side. Sunshine gleamed on the silver-blue metal of a revolver. Kelly shouted at Eddie, "Did you bring a gun?"

"A gun? I didn't think that was part of a director's equipment."

"Next time you better think again." Eddie flushed. Kelly stabbed a finger at Fritzi. "You. Stand next to the camera. Where's the other one?" He found Nell. "You too, the other side. They won't shoot women."

Eddie said, "Mr. Kelly, I have to protest."

"Protest all you want. I'm the boss." Turning back to Fritzi, he said, "Do it."

She looked at Nell, who gave a little shrug, as if to say, *Who knows? Maybe he's right.*

Closer now, the detectives could be seen wearing proper suits and neckties. Her heart racing, Fritzi walked to the camera quickly, put her back against it. Nell positioned herself on the opposite side. Eddie and Ferguson exchanged angry looks.

Yellowed by road dust, the Oldsmobile kicked up a cloud when the driver braked. He jumped out, strode forward with an air of authority. His helper, a hulk squeezed into a too-tight suit, followed.

The detective wore a black suit with a fine chalk stripe. On his black vest a shiny Masonic emblem dangled from a gold chain. His cream-colored hat resembled a Western sombrero with a narrower brim. There was something familiar about him, she thought.

"Well, look here. Kelly and the forty thieves." The detective showed his teeth in a brilliant smile, and recognition hit like an avalanche. Union Square. *I need four supers.* What had he been wearing that afternoon? *Hello, dear, Earl's my name.* A corduroy coat, a blue railroad bandanna knotted around his neck. *Care to join me after I find my four?* Terrified by something in his strange eyes, light brown with gold speckling, she had refused and fled. He'd come up in the world since his days as a super captain.

He glanced around the group of actors, looking at Fritzi a second longer than the others. His beautiful smile never wavered. Kelly said, "Hello, Pearly."

"Do I get the camera without a fight, Al?"

"When hell freezes."

"Nuts," Pearly sighed. "It's too nice a day for rough stuff." So it was, with sunshine pouring from the clear bright sky to warm Fritzi's face and trembling hands. The detective fanned back

346

his coat to show a silver pistol hanging butt forward in a harness. "Stand by, Buck." The hulk cocked his revolver, an ominous sound in the stillness.

The detective walked over to Fritzi, doffed his sombrero.

"Hello, miss. Earl Purvis is my name. I sure don't want to use force on a woman, but I mean to take possession of that illegal camera."

Let him smile all he wanted, she thought. He was the enemy, trying to throw her out of work.

"Step aside," he said.

She drew herself up like Mrs. Patrick Campbell playing Paula Tanqueray. Her stare registered unmistakable defiance. "No."

He blinked; evidently he hadn't expected resistance from a mere woman. As he scratched his chin, his features softened to something like amusement.

"You're new in this crowd. What's your name?"

"None of your business."

"Well. Sassy. Have we met before?"

"I hardly think so."

Doubtful, he gazed at her a moment longer. "I'll ask one last time. Move away from the camera."

"The devil I will."

He sighed again, heavily burdened. "Buck, take the coon." When Purvis lunged and grabbed her shoulders, Fritzi shrieked. She stamped on his pointed black shoe. Her heel connected solidly.

He swore, hopping backward on the other

foot. Meanwhile, Buck ran around to Nell. Seeing Fritzi's example, she seized Buck's outstretched arm at the elbow and bit his wrist with the force of a snapping bear trap. "Jesus Christ," he screamed, firing his revolver into the dirt with a reflexive jerk of his finger.

Purvis retreated a couple of steps, lowered his head like an annoyed bull. When he charged, Fritzi used a tactic she'd employed twice with Southern yahoos when her hat pin wasn't handy. She stabbed at his eyes with both index fingers.

"Huh?" Purvis reared back in time to avoid contact. Dumbfounded by her move, he hesitated just long enough for her to whip her foot up in a high kick that hit him where it mattered. He cursed, doubled over, clutching himself.

Kelly yelled at Ferguson, "The camera!" Ferguson threw the tripod over his shoulder and dashed to the Ford. He shouted to Eddie to follow and crank the engine.

Eddie whirled the crank so hard, he could have broken his shoulder. Purvis was still lurching around; she'd hit him harder than she knew. Kelly jumped forward and pounded the back of his neck with both fists. Purvis dropped to his knees.

The Ford's engine caught. Eddie leaped back and the car careened down the street. Ferguson skidded left, around the corner of a general store out of sight. A plume of dust slowly settled. A couple of locals drawn by the gunshot gawked from a barn door a block away.

Buck stared at his tooth-marked wrist. "You nigger bitch." He hauled his arm back to smash

348

Nell's face with the gun barrel. From behind, Fritzi grabbed the gun. Eddie ran up, snatched it from her, and bashed Buck on the head twice, then propelled him with a kick in the rear. Buck sprawled against the porch rail and slid off, out of action.

As Kelly ran to the rear of the Oldsmobile, the blade of a big pocket knife flashed.

By this time Purvis was upright again. His eyes were different now, savage as a tiger's as he yanked the silver pistol out of its harness. Eddie stepped up beside Fritzi, pointed Buck's revolver at the detective.

"Throw it down. If you don't I'll shoot."

Fritzi assumed Eddie was as frightened as she was, but he was doing a magnificent job of concealing it. Glaring, Purvis dropped the pistol in the dirt. Kelly shouted, "Everybody in the car."

Owen Stallings and Sam Something and old Noble and the extras bumped each other like a pack of clowns to get to the Stoddard-Dayton. They were so comic, Fritzi thought there should be a camera running. Eddie grasped her elbow to move her along. Passing Purvis, she had a brief terrifying look into his eyes.

"You did this, girlie. You'll pay for it."

"Shut up, you thug," Eddie said as they ran.

Kelly jumped in the car; Eddie spun the crank. Four spins and the engine started. Eddie took the passenger seat with Fritzi on his lap. Sam Something, Owen, and one of the extras jammed the backseat. Nell hung on the left running board, Noble and the other extra on the right one. The Stoddard sagged and responded sluggishly as Kelly wheeled it into a turn. Fritzi heard scraping noises, and hoped they didn't peel the bottom off the car.

They passed Purvis beating his sombrero against his leg and kicking the Oldsmobile's left rear tire, deflated to match the one on the right. Fritzi understood the pocket knife. Through the choking dust Kelly yelled, "Get a horse, Pearly." He whinnied. Purvis fired a shot at them. Sam Something squealed as the bullet pinged off the rear bumper.

Fritzi bounced up and down on Eddie's lap, her heart pounding, her blond hair flying. Suddenly she cried, "The carpenter."

"Oh, God, that's right, Bill's waiting in the woods," Eddie said.

"Forget him," Kelly said. "He'll find his way home."

After a mile Kelly stopped, said to the extras, "You two get out. Take off those clothes and throw them in the car." When they complied Kelly paid them from a wad rolled up in a rubber band. As the Stoddard puttered off, they stood on the shoulder in their underwear, forlorn. Stardom had been snatched from them by fate in the person of Earl Purvis.

39. Onward, If Not Exactly Upward

They finished *The Lone Indian's Gold* in two days in the country near Mamaroneck. No one troubled them. Presumably the Patents Company hadn't yet recruited a snitch corps in Westchester.

Bill Nix, the carpenter-prop man, wasn't with them. The day after Purvis's attack, he had gone to Kelly to protest his abandonment. Words grew hot. Never long on patience, Kelly fired him. "No loss," Eddie said.

After the excitement in Coytesville, filming was uneventful, in fact dull. Eddie, who had praised her profusely for protecting the camera, invited Fritzi to join Owen in the projection room of the K&T exchange to see the results — a thousand feet of film assembled into a coherent fifteen-minute story.

The room was cramped, just a few straight chairs, a screen, and a pervasive smell of overflowing spittoons. Eddie introduced Fritzi to the other partner, B. B. Pelzer. ("People call him Benny, but never to his face," Eddie had warned ahead of time.) B.B. was a short, round man with a lot of curly gray hair and a warm, paternal manner. He grabbed Fritzi's hand between his, like a fish he was buying at market.

"Pleased to meet you, you're working with a fine boy." He gave her hand a vigorous shake before sitting down. He rested his elbow on a small table and put his hand to his head, as though worrying over what he was about to see. Fritzi shared the feeling. To watch herself act would be a new experience.

Kelly slipped into the last row, saying nothing. Eddie said, "Okay, Hap." The operator, as he was called, switched off the lights.

A girl seated next to Eddie said, "I spliced some extra footage on the end. I think you'll enjoy it." Eddie didn't object. The girl seemed extraordinarily young, like the whole industry.

Hap turned on the clattery projector. The moment Fritzi saw herself she let out a nervous giggle. She was mortified by her big feet, her angular elbows, her flying hair. Her movements were jerky, her emoting more like scenery chewing. She could hardly stand it. She covered her face and peeked through her fingers.

Of course, the rest of the cast gave similar exaggerated performances; the style suited the melodramatic plot. Owen seemed taken with his acting, beaming at his image and at one point saying loudly, "Oh, that's rather good."

Eddie watched attentively, making occasional comments to the girl. Fritzi had quickly developed respect for Eddie. He had a clear sense of purpose. He knew he wasn't putting *Hamlet* or *An Enemy of the People* on film, but he'd worked energetically and thoughtfully to make his little picture fast paced and suspenseful.

Fritzi noticed something she'd missed before. On the porch of Rambo's Hotel, someone had placed a wooden plaque bearing the company's racing pony symbol. Very peculiar.

Fifteen minutes seemed like fifteen hours as

she sat squirming in the dark. At the fade-out she risked a quick look at Kelly. He had the same dyspeptic sneer she'd noticed when he came in.

Abruptly, a new scene appeared — the shot in which she had rushed out the door and fallen. Horrified, she watched herself adjust in midair and finish with the somersault. All of them laughed, even Kelly.

As Hap put the lights on, Eddie patted her arm. "You're quite a comedienne."

"Not intentionally."

"Ought to be some way we can use it." *Let's hope not.*

Kelly rose, said, "Okay," and walked out. Why such a sour man was in the entertainment business she couldn't imagine. B. B. Pelzer rushed up to her and again made a sandwich of their hands.

"Say, Eddie's right, you're a sketch. I liked you in the picture. Talented little gel. Like to see more of you at Pal."

She asked Eddie about the partners. He said Pelzer had been an optician in Hoboken before he got interested in pictures. He and his brother-in-law, a salesman in New York's garment district, had started Pal. Within a year Kelly had bought out the brother-in-law's interest. The company was organized with a hundred shares of stock. B.B. and his wife, Sophie, controlled fifty-two percent.

Kelly had once owned livery stables but foresaw dwindling profits and eventual insolvency when autos came in. He switched to manufacturing stereopticons, with a subsidiary to supply the picture cards. That parlor craze waned when nickelodeons proliferated, so Kelly changed trades again.

"Kelly is the cross we bear. Benny's the other way. Generous to a fault. Drives Kelly crazy."

Pal Pictures ground out a minimum of two one-reelers every week, plus an occasional reel split between two playlets, one a comedy, the other a drama; split reels were popular. Pal's production quality was uneven. In moments of gloom Eddie called the pictures sausages. "And not very good sausages, at that."

The board displaying the Pal pony appeared at least once in each picture. "Lot of thievery in this business," Eddie explained. "Crooked nickelodeon owners, sometimes crooks in an exchange. They strike a print and sell the picture as their own. Companies protect themselves by including their identifying marks."

Thanks to B.B.'s enthusiasm and Kelly's endorsement after the Coytesville trouble, Fritzi worked fairly regularly during the following winter and spring. Always wary of the detectives, they filmed in rented lofts in Manhattan and Brooklyn. For exteriors they went back to Mamaroneck, or out to rural Long Island. Some days they didn't start until mid-morning because of the secrecy with which the camera was moved. Fritzi never learned where Ferguson concealed it at night.

After she'd done several small parts, Eddie chose her for the leading role in *Daring Daisy*, in which she played a clever private investigator. In one scene Daisy was supposed to pursue the villain into a restaurant kitchen. Eddie produced a large plaster of Paris ham and improvised a wild chase around a chopping block, action not written in the scenario. When a pistol went off with a puff of smoke, the startled chef swung around suddenly and nearly brained Fritzi with the ham. Following Eddie's direction, she ducked and dropped, doing a full split. The result was approving laughter in the screening room. She understood why he'd insisted she wear riding breeches that day.

Eddie and B.B. were so delighted with the picture, they concocted a flat-out farce called *Something Fishy*. Playing a pet shop clerk, Fritzi was tossed into a tank of water and slapped in the face with a large cod. She worked without complaint but told Eddie afterward that she didn't care to repeat the experience.

Yet there was more to come. *The Lone Indian's Gold* had produced higher than usual rentals across the country, so Eddie concocted more offerings in the series. Late spring saw completion of *The Lone Indian's Courage*. They next returned to Westchester for *The Lone Indian's Battle*, in which Fritzi rode for the first time. The White Plains stable owner who rented horses showed her how to mount bareback by jumping and throwing a leg over, like a Plains Indian. He taught her to vault up over the horse's tail. She fell three times but succeeded on the fourth attempt. Eddie asked her to do it again, but fall off, while a bad man menaced her with twin revolvers. "Land on your derriere, jump up, and cross your eyes. He's stupefied. That gives Owen time to disarm him and punch the stuffing out of him."

"Oh, Eddie, no. It's low comedy."

"Low comedy's very respectable. Shakespeare uses it all the time. Bring on a clown right before the bloody climax, it breaks the tension and the climax hits twice as hard. Trust me."

So the bit went into the picture. Fritzi did it with maximum energy, and sat on a pillow all evening.

Reasonably steady work allowed her to spend $14.95 on something she'd wanted for a long time, a talking machine with a handsome golden oak cabinet and beautifully sculpted flower horn. It played flat discs rather than the older wax cylinders. She splurged for a half dozen twenty-cent records featuring anonymous vocalists performing with tinny orchestras. Her favorite of favorites was "A Girl in Central Park," a new hit composed by Paul's friend Harry Poland. The song came from a Broadway revue called *Girls Galore*. After a long day's work she would slip off her shoes, roll down her stockings, put the disc on the turntable, crank up the machine, lower the needle, and listen to the soulful tenor.

"I met a girl in Central Park,
Fair as the morning's fair —"

The song was beautiful but melancholy; the anonymous gentleman never saw the girl again.

By the second playing her eyes misted. The seventh or eighth time through, tears were streaming down her cheeks.

40. New York Music

Harry Poland loved his adopted language. He knew it wasn't correct to call it American, but he did so anyway. He thought of American speech as a giant tray of luscious appetizers, each with a special flavor suited to a special moment. A smart and tasty word he relished was *spiffy*. He liked to wear spiffy clothes, and was beginning to be able to afford it. If not yet a byword in Muncie or Boise, the hinterlands, the name Harry Poland was well recognized in the tight little community of New York music publishing.

On a day in the spring of 1910 when Fritzi was making one of her first pictures, he took care to look spiffy for an afternoon visit with his wife. He chose a three-piece single-breasted suit of English cut, narrow trousers with a sharp crease, a blue-striped white shirt with wing collar, a blue tie, a rakish bowler hat, gray spats, and a walking cane.

His destination was the suburban village of Rye, in particular one of its shady streets between the Boston Post Road and Long Island Sound. He parked his Model T, black and brand-new, in a gravel area in front of the rest home.

Never did he feel chipper in this sad and sterile place where the old and infirm sat in their chairs and murmured to invisible listeners. But he refused to let it show. As he strode up the walk, a

tall and vibrant man of thirty, he looked successful and happy.

The April afternoon brought a gentle, warm
breeze off the Sound. An attendant wheeled
Flavia outdoors, and Harry sat with her under a
budding sycamore tree, holding her hand while
she stared vacantly into his eyes, groping for his
identity. Flavia's hair was thin, spiky, and white.
At her doctor's urging Harry had moved her to
the home during the winter. He strove to be
chipper, smiling as he related tidbits of news
while gently stroking her hand.

"Shapiro, Bernstein's hoping to reach a million copies with 'A Girl in Central Park' in a few
months. Their band department's marketing a
symphonic arrangement. 'Blue Evening' is doing well, eighty thousand copies. And guess
what? This is exciting. Tomorrow morning I'm
seeing one of the biggest producers in New
York. Ziegfeld. He called *me*. He's doing another *Follies* this year."

Each tidbit was received with the same fey,
slightly bewildered smile that broke his heart. A
little silver line of drool spilled from Flavia's
mouth and spotted her gown. The attendants always reminded Harry that she was increasingly
incontinent and had to receive special, personal
care. He knew they did it to extract tips, but he
paid without complaint.

When the shadows lengthened and the air
turned cool, he signaled a bull-necked man in
white, rose, and kissed Flavia's forehead.
"Goodbye, dear girl. I'll see you next week."
And every week as long as she lived. Flavia had

done so much for him, he could never desert or divorce her, even though he often thought of another woman. She was the one for whom he'd written "A Girl in Central Park."

He didn't know what had become of Paul's cousin. He read the cast list for every Broadway play and never found her name. Perhaps she'd left the city.

He watched the attendant wheel his wife inside. He cranked up the Model T and motored over rough dirt roads to an excellent Port Chester inn where he and Flavia had dined in better days. After an hour spent with a fine meal and wine he drove up King Street, the dividing line between the states of New York and Connecticut. The area was hilly, rural, abundantly green.

On the Connecticut side of the road he drove down a lane and parked in front of a well-kept two-story farm house, between a sporty buggy and a large yellow Reo. A handsome woman in a tasteful black dress admitted him with a cheerful "How've you been, Harry?"

"Just fine, thanks, Belle." He laid his bowler and walking stick on a marble-topped table. Mrs. Belle Steckel was the daughter of a fine old Greenwich family. Early on, she had, as they said, gone wrong. She rebounded and some years later established this refined house that was never bothered by the county authorities. When Harry had first become a customer, he felt himself to be the worst sort of cheat and deceiver. He talked it over with Mrs. Steckel, who was intelligent and quite sensible about such matters. She reminded him that he was not an anchorite. An occasional visit would harm no one, certainly not Flavia. "And I'll bet if she knew, she'd understand."

"Martha is free and expecting you," Mrs. Steckel said. Harry thanked her again, paid her, and climbed the stairs. While he was approaching Martha's door, Mrs. Steckel started a piano roll in the parlor. "The Cherry Blossom Man from Little Old Japan," his latest song. Harry smiled and knocked.

"Hello, Martha," he said almost shyly.

"Hello, Harry, it's swell to see you again." Her robe fell open on her nakedness as she stood. She gave his cheek a platonic peck. Martha was short, on the dumpy side, with little education. But she had soft, round arms, and she understood why he needed to visit. To be with her for an hour enabled him to carry on with his life without regret or self-pity. He had only one deep and shameful secret. Sometimes, at the height of passion with Martha, he pretended she was Fritzi Crown.

He stayed the night at the home in Port Chester that he'd shared with Flavia. It was a dreary, ghostly place now. Sheets covered all but a few pieces of furniture. A smell of dust pervaded the rooms. He suspected he wouldn't sleep because of the Ziegfeld appointment, and he didn't. After rolling back and forth most of the night, he jumped out of bed an hour before dawn, drank half a pot of coffee, lit the Model T headlamps, and set out for Manhattan on the wretched roads. The trip of about twenty miles took nearly three hours.

Harry still worked independently, from his office in the Muldoon Building on West Twenty-eighth, the center of New York's music business. At one time or another all the giants of the industry had been located in the drab and ordinary buildings along Twenty-eighth. From offices on all floors of Harry's building came music, though Harry always thought of it as noise, because a dozen performances going at once, different keys, different tempos, different voices, amounted to cacophony. Or, as the anonymous wit who'd named the district had it, like tin pans clanging.

Because he spent so much time in town, Harry kept two rooms at the Hotel Mandrake on West Forty-fifth. There he shaved and dressed in a fresh suit, shirt, and cravat. Powdered and sprinkled with scented tonic, he turned up at the office of Florenz Ziegfeld twenty minutes before his ten o'clock appointment.

Ziegfeld kept him waiting until half past ten. "Glad to see you," the producer said when Harry was finally admitted to his office. Ziegfeld was an impressive man, forty or more, tall and rakish and stylishly dressed. Some said his dark good looks and slanting brows gave him a Mephistophelian air. At the moment he was married to the famous soubrette from Warsaw and Paris, Anna Held, but that didn't curtail his activity as a philanderer of renown. He consumed women like pretzels; single or married, it made no difference. Morals aside, he was known as a man who demanded and paid for the best in the shows he produced. He never shortchanged his audiences or his talent.

Ziegfeld noticed Harry eyeing a faded poster among many decorating the walls. The poster advertised an attraction called the Dancing Ducks of Denmark. A smile more like a smirk crossed Ziegfeld's face.

"Would you believe I was only twenty-two when I produced that show back in Chicago?" He offered a cigar humidor; Harry shook his head. Ziegfeld lit up. "God damn SPCA closed me down. Said I had stage hands lighting matches under the ducks' feet to make them perform." A solemn wink. "I suppose it was possible." Harry was too tense to do more than force a smile.

"You know what I'd like from you, kid?"

"I hope it's a song for your new show."

"No flies on you. What I've heard of your stuff I like. Time's a little short, though. The next edition of the *Follies* starts rehearsal at the Jardin de Paris in four weeks." The Jardin was a glass-domed venue on top of a theater building at Forty-fourth and Broadway, hell-hot in summer and leaky when it rained; patrons were urged to bring umbrellas.

"What I need is a jungle number. I picture forty or fifty girls" — Ziegfeld pranced around the desk — "a little palm frond hiding these treasures, another hiding this one, you get the idea. We'll wind up with them dancing in the damnedest rainstorm ever seen on a stage. But I don't have a song."

"I'll try to write something in a couple of days."

"Can I count on it?"

"I'll have something," Harry promised. "If it isn't right, I'll work until it's what you want."

"You sound like a professional. I like professionals. I hate bullshit artists who promise and don't deliver. I never hire one of those more than once. Then I make sure the whole street knows, so they don't hire him either."

His brow popping with little dots of perspiration and his voice cracking with excitement, Harry said, "I won't let you down, Mr. Ziegfeld."

The producer put a comradely arm over Harry's shoulders as he escorted him to the door. "Flo," he said. "Flo to my friends and fellow artists."

In the anteroom, two song pluggers of Harry's acquaintance looked at him with virulent envy. Both strained forward in anticipation of a few seconds of Ziegfeld's time.

"Go peddle your papers, boys. I'm auditioning chorus girls in ten minutes." Ziegfeld aimed his index finger at Harry. "Make it good." He went back in his office and slammed the door.

Harry was elated. He fairly danced through the noontime crowds. America, the land of opportunity! How right he'd been to dedicate himself to reaching these shores, there to work tirelessly at a profession he loved.

Harry's songs came out of his head through his fingers, but the music was in the city. He heard syncopated melodies all around him as he strode down Broadway devouring a hot roasted sweet potato bought from a vendor. He heard boats tooting on the river, feet trampling the pavement. He heard elevateds clattering and trolleys clanging and autos honking, a mouth organ growling and a black ragamuffin with thumb tacks in his shoes tap-dancing on the curbstone while an older black boy played a banjo. The song was "The Cherry Blossom Man." Harry gave them each a dollar.

He was perspiring and short of breath, filled with excitement. This was the year, this was the moment, he felt it. Getting a song included in *Girls Galore* had been the first step, but a Ziegfeld production would put him on top, especially if the song was a hit. Once he was in demand on Broadway, asked to write complete scores, he'd soon reach his other goal, his own publishing company.

Harry hated all the sordid things in the music business: composers who stole melodies, performers who demanded payoffs to perform a number, publishers who doctored royalty reports in their favor. But he forgot all the negatives when he dreamed of his own company. He had a wonderful name for it. Homeland Music. Its symbol, inevitably, would be a waving stars and stripes. Harry had never considered anything else.

"Wilbur, watch out for the gentleman."

The mother's cry roused him from his walking reverie. A lad of six or seven ran into Harry while examining a toy.

"Madam, my fault entirely," Harry said with a gallant tip of his bowler. Never mind that the little boy looked mean and ugly as a toad; Harry was willing to forgive almost any sin on this day of glorious opportunity. Suddenly his gaze became fixed on the toy in the lad's grimy fingers. A small elephant cut from tin and painted gray with white tusks. Although Harry was nominally a Jew, he was familiar with Christian literature, including St. Paul's vision on the Damascus road. Hardly daring to breathe, he said:

"Madam, may I buy this toy for a dollar?"

Startled, the woman said, "Why, it isn't worth a fifth of —"

"I insist." Greedy little Wilbur eagerly took the money. Harry clutched the tin elephant and fairly raced to his office, weaving in and out of the pedestrian mob like a football runner. He flung his bowler on the floor and slammed the keyboard open. By five o'clock he'd written "The Elephant Rag." He even forgot Fritzi while he did it.

> "Oh, the trunk will wag
> Like a jungle flag
> When the pachyderm does
> The elephant rag.
> All join in and (*stomp foot*)
> Do the elephant rag."

Flo Ziegfeld was wild for the number. Something about the combination of silly lyrics and catchy tune made the *Follies* audience jump up as one, screaming with joy, when forty-four girls hoofing in the artificial rainstorm all came down at one time with a thunderous *stomp*. An eight-foot-high elephant operated by two men inside danced in the final chorus.

Sales of "The Elephant Rag" curved up like a Fourth of July rocket trail, with deals made for the song in England and throughout Europe. Singing the song and stomping became a craze. Young and old stomped in schoolyards, on streetcars, in feed lots, even in church halls when the choirmaster wasn't looking. Proper Englishmen and stolid Germans stomped. Volatile Frenchmen and passionate Spaniards stomped. Eventually reports drifted out of Africa about Zulus stomping.

Every paper from the *Herald* to the *Police Gazette* sent reporters to the Hotel Mandrake for interviews with the man who had set the world stomping. A colleague expressed his admiration simply:

"Harry, you're a goddam genius."

41. Sammy

Across the ocean in London the sun rose unseen behind sheets of rain. Paul tramped from Leicester Square to St. Martin's Lane, poorly protected by his black umbrella. He turned into dark and narrow Cecil Court, where several film companies, including Pathé Frères and American Luxograph, kept offices.

He dodged a torrent of water coursing off the roof slates above the building entrance, shook himself like a wet spaniel, and dashed up the stairs. He'd stayed home with Julie an extra half hour to get the children started with their nanny, and to sit at Julie's bedside, holding her hand and worrying. Childbearing had never been easy for her. She was huge now, nearly full term, confined to bed most of the day. She insisted she was fine, able to handle all of her family duties, but her pale and haggard face told a different story.

Climbing the stairs with water dripping from his wet shoes and fedora, Paul hoped the long spell of bad weather didn't persist through the autumn; he was scheduled to photograph German army maneuvers in Bavaria. He'd been invited because his name, and his book, had drawn him to the attention of the German general staff. They valued publicity and cultivated those who could provide it. Kaiser Wilhelm II, ever eager to play soldier, always took part in the annual maneuvers.

To Englishmen the kaiser was the living symbol of "the German menace." He continually professed to be a great friend of England — was not his grandmother the late Queen Victoria, and King George V his first cousin (like the Russian tsar, Nicholas)? Michael Radcliffe sneered at these family connections. "A rotten club of inbred hemophiliacs and paranoid war lovers pretending to be the dearest of friends while awaiting the perfect opportunity to stab each other in the back."

Michael was right to be suspicious of the European monarchs. Vicious animosity lurked behind their friendly pronouncements. Kaiser Wilhelm II had mourned at his uncle's funeral but on other occasions had called the dead king "Satan," and "the worst intriguer in Europe." And Germany's aggressive naval program seemed directed against Britain. Admiral Tirpitz was building two dreadnoughts a year. The kaiser insisted this was solely for defense against unnamed enemies, but a large segment of the British population, including many Whitehall diplomats, felt sure the fleet would be used to attack their country. The penny papers were full of fanciful scare stories with titles such as "The War Inevitable" and "How the Germans Took London."

"Hello, Miss Epsom," he said as he let himself into the anteroom and shook off again. Miss Epsom, a spinster of fifty, greeted him with a polite nod and, when his back was turned, brushed droplets of water from her cheek. "Has he arrived?"

"Twenty minutes ago, sir."

Paul hung up his hat and umbrella and set a course for the inner door. "Will you bring us tea?"

"Certainly, at once. I will say the young man doesn't strike me as a proper tea drinker."

Persistent back trouble, and Julie's gentle persuasion, had finally convinced Paul that he should hire a helper. The applicant waiting in his office was the seventeenth person to answer the advertisement; he'd rejected the first sixteen. Two were outright dunces, several were hungry but not really interested in the picture business, several more were liars and pretenders quickly unmasked with technical questions. The rest were pleasant but for various reasons hopeless.

"Good morning, sorry I'm late." Paul's cluttered office seemed perfectly matched to his bent collar points, crooked cravat, bulging pockets, and generally careless style.

The young man jiggling from foot to foot, cap in hand, was swarthy and thin as a stick. A large wen sat on his chin like a raisin. His hair was black and shiny. Paul noticed grime under his fingernails.

"I have your name here somewhere." Paul searched through the hopeless mess of film cans, production schedules, bills, memoranda from his employer, Lord Yorke, cablegrams from the New Jersey office, trade papers, London papers, international papers, and the other miscellany of his trade.

"Silverstone, gov. Samuel G, for Garfunkel, Silverstone. I go by Sammy."

"Please sit down, Sammy." The young man's jittering made him nervous. Miraculously, he found a pencil, then a file card that hadn't been scribbled on. "How old are you?"

"Twenty-two."

"Do you have references?"

Sammy plucked a crumpled letter from inside a woolen coat that looked like it belonged to someone smaller. "This here's from Mr. Crutchfield, my boss at the Soho Strand."

"That's a picture theater, isn't it?"

"Yes, sir, and a fine one. It's in Deane Street."

"Any others?"

For a moment Sammy's bright dark eyes had a queer, speculative light in them. "Well, gov, no, not unless you'd want to ask the warden at Brixton."

Paul sat back in his squeaky swivel chair. "Are you saying you were locked up?"

"Right, sir. Petty theft. My sister Belle didn't have nothing to eat." He pronounced it *nuffing;* even Henry Higgins would be mightily challenged to correct the formidable accent. Paul presumed it came from the East End or some similar district.

"I only stole a couple of loaves for Belle," Sammy explained. "But I got pinched. I figured if you hire me, you'll find out about it one day, so I might as well tell you straight off and save time."

"Very thoughtful," Paul muttered, wondering what this rather sly-looking young man was all about. "When were you incarcerated?"

"If that means locked up" — Miss Epsom

tapped on the door and walked in with a tea tray — "I did me time fourteen months ago. I grew up in the docklands, on the streets, mostly." Paul felt an affinity for that; he'd been a street boy in Berlin.

"After I left the nick I swore I'd never go back to that hole, or any like it. I'd get honest work. Always liked the pictures when I could afford the tariff, so when I saw this card outside the Soho Strand saying assistant operator wanted, I popped right in. There was one bloke ahead of me, but while we was waiting he had a little accident."

"A little accident," Paul murmured. "Imagine that." He poured hot Earl Grey from the pot. To his surprise Sammy Silverstone asked for a cup, with milk and sugar.

"Fell down and busted his ankle, poor lad. Had to go home. Guess he tripped on something. Never did see what exactly." Paul tried not to smile. "Mr. Crutchfield hired me. I told him about the nick. I been at the Strand ever since. I patch up bad splices and torn sprocket holes, post bills out in front, mop up, run the projector when the reg'lar man's off — hard work, but I like it."

"Why would you want to leave?"

" 'Cause this here situation is a step up. Helper to somebody who actually makes pictures. A bloke who's written a book."

"You've read it?"

Sammy rolled his tongue beneath his upper lip, unable to hide his consideration of a lie. After a moment he replied:

"Can't say as I have. Frankly I don't read much. Mr. Crutchfield's got a copy, though. Says it's good, you go a lot of interesting places. I'd like that."

Samuel Garfunkel Silverstone had a kind of cheeky candor that Paul liked. "I'm leaving in less than a month to film army maneuvers in Germany. When could you be ready to go?"

With a grin Sammy said, "Right now soon enough, gov?"

Paul took a long breath, pitched the card in the overflowing basket in the desk well.

"All right, let's discuss salary."

Sammy lit up brighter than one of the electrical displays at Piccadilly Circus. "You won't be sorry. I can carry twice my weight, I'm a regular pack mule."

"You'll have a lot of chances to prove it."

42. Signs of Success

With some chagrin Fritzi found herself looking forward to each picture, and regretting it if there wasn't one immediately coming up. It wasn't the artistry of the one-reelers she enjoyed, because there wasn't any. It was the companionship. She liked Eddie, his wife, Rita, and their two children. She liked Nell Spooner despite white society's opinion that she oughtn't, and, on Griffith's advice, she befriended the cameraman, solid, reflective Jock Ferguson. Sometimes, together, they accidentally made a scene that was almost respectable.

Even so, she regarded the work as temporary, a source of income until she found the right stage role. Her integrity as an actress was preserved by the continuing anonymity of picture players. A few directors such as Griffith were identified in titles and trade advertising, and an actress named Florence Lawrence was being billed as "The Biograph Girl," but that was the extent of it.

Hobart saw a third-run showing of *The Lone Indian's Battle* in Logansport, Indiana ("civilization at rock bottom"), and wrote to praise her acting. As soon as his contract ran out and he escaped "this damned play — Moriarty is hissed and threatened by the audience at every curtain call," he wanted to visit Pal and study this new form of entertainment firsthand. That helped ease her mind. If Hobart thought pictures were acceptable, so could she.

Fritzi began to notice certain signs of change at Pal Pictures. B.B. started passing out fifty-cent cigars to favored visitors. Over Kelly's objection, the company moved to its own suite of rooms on Fourteenth, just down the way from Biograph. It suggested to her that she might improve her own living situation now that she had funds. She said a tearful goodbye to Mrs. Perella and relocated to two airy rooms on West Twenty-second Street, near the river.

B.B. proposed *The Lone Indian's Baby*, declaring that people loved babies almost as much as they loved money. This epic, which Eddie wrote under orders, put Owen in the role of temporary father of an infant left in a basket outside his tepee (an act never explained by the plot or title cards). Owen grew more conceited with each appearance as the heroic red man. He renewed his invitation to Fritzi at least once a month, hinting that she was passing up a chance to dine with one of the screen's new luminaries. She cheerfully declined.

They risked filming the new Lone Indian picture in the vicinity of Fort Lee. In preparation Eddie bought a .32-caliber Smith & Wesson double-action revolver with a short barrel. "Damn thing scares me, I'm not a violent person. But I won't go back to Jersey without a gun." He practiced shooting at bottles in a vacant lot in the evening. He said his wife was horrified. Jock Ferguson hired an armed guard to accompany them and stand by the camera at all times.

After their first morning's work they motored back to Rambo's Hotel. Two other cars and a wagon painted with the name of the Biograph were lined up in front. The Pal company trooped around to the rear of the hotel, where fifteen or twenty people were eating stew at plank tables set end to end under a grape arbor that must have measured a hundred feet long. She saw Billy Bitzer, and Mary Pickford, and Griffith. The director waved and smiled. He looked decidedly odd in a straw hat with the top missing.

Bitzer rushed over, Mary right behind. Mary's curls shone like gold leaf in the spring sunshine. Bitzer pumped Fritzi's hand. "By golly, you're doing well. What do you hear from Paul?"

"Very little," she admitted. "He's traipsing around Europe, I think. He and Julie are expecting a new baby."

When she asked about Griffith's hat, Bitzer laughed. "You know actors. Vain as hell. He thinks sunlight will keep him from losing his hair."

He went back to his meal, but Mary lingered. She checked over her shoulder, turned her head away from Owen, who was regaling a Biograph actress with anecdotes about himself. "I caught the Indian picture, the one where you fall off the horse and cross your eyes."

Fritzi frowned. "I thought it was a little degrading."

"Come on. You were hilarious."

"It isn't my ambition to be hilarious," she said with a sniff.

Again Mary observed Owen, then whispered, "What's degrading — what you should worry about — is appearing opposite that wooden Indian. You can practically smell his conceit. Talk to your director. Demand a different leading man. One who plays to you, not the camera."

"I doubt they'd replace Owen —" Fritzi began.

"Then maybe you should find a new studio. You've got experience. Think about it." Fritzi had in fact entertained the idea once but dismissed it.

Mary squeezed her hand. "I wish we saw more of each other."

"So do I." Despite Mary's youth, her sweet face, her ability to project an angelic disposition, she was tough and wise, a friend to value. Fritzi watched her hurry back to her company, her curls dancing and bobbing over the collar of her pinafore.

Two weeks after the release of *The Lone Indian's Baby*, B.B. Pelzer summoned Fritzi to his new office. It was a sultry afternoon, unusually warm and airless for spring. B.B. didn't improve the atmosphere with his smelly green cigars. A closed box of them sat in the center of his blotter.

"Fritzi, have a chair, I got something great to show you." He looked ruddier, and happier, than usual. Always the gentleman, he was buttoned up in a stiff collar and white linen suit and vest. Fraise sat forward, hands on knees, expectant.

"You like working for Pal?" he asked.

"It certainly is interesting and challenging, Mr. Pelzer."

"Well, I'm telling you today, you got a great future with us. Magnificent. Here." He shoved the floridly decorated cigar box to her side of the desk.

"Mr. Pelzer, I don't smoke."

He waved. "No cigars in there. Take a look."

She lifted the lid, decorated with some kind of goddess with a mighty bosom, a shield, and a spear. Puzzled, she peered at two stacks of letters and postal cards banded with red elastics. The letters on top were addressed crudely, one in pencil.

"You don't need to read 'em, I'll tell you what's in 'em. We got the first ones last fall. These people are crazy about the Lone Indian pictures, especially our latest. My wife was right, people are nuts about babies." With a twinkle he added, "Those letters are asking about the identity of our talent."

"I'm not surprised. Owen is a very attractive leading man."

"Forget Owen! Nobody asked about Owen!" He tapped his fingertips on his paunch and grinned like an uncle about to bestow a lavish gift on a favorite niece. "They're asking who's the funny one who fights the bad men, falls off the horse, rocks the cradle at the end of the new picture."

Fritzi caught her breath. Was this some kind of negotiating ploy?

B.B. whacked his palm on his desk; a small cased photograph of ex-president Roosevelt fell over. "Don't you get what I'm saying? They're asking, Who's the gel?"

She laughed, a short, nervous laugh of surprise and disbelief.

"Seriously?"

"B. B. Pelzer don't lie. I'm telling you, Fritzi, they all want to know one thing — *who's the gel?* I said to Eddie this morning, next picture we raise you to six dollars a day. Heck, make it six-fifty. Kelly wants to fight about it, I'm ready to go fifteen rounds."

Home at half past nine, she finished washing her hair and was drawing a bath when the tenant of the first-floor flat pounded on the door to call her to the communal telephone. Her wet hair was dripping, dark and stringy as seaweed. She wrapped a towel around it and ran downstairs.

"Hello? Is this Fritzi Crown?"

"It is. Who's this?"

"Harry Poland. Your cousin's friend, remember?"

"I couldn't forget. You're the man who's got half the country stomping."

"I finally found you," Harry said in an odd, bubbly voice.

"You've been looking?"

"Well, ah, what I mean is, I saw one of your pictures. The Pal office told me where to locate you. May I treat you to supper tomorrow evening?"

Fritzi hesitated. "But, Mr. Poland, aren't you married?"

"I am, oh yes. I'm not trying to be forward, Miss Crown. I only want to renew acquaintances, express my friendship. My admiration for your talent. What do you say?"

"Well, Mr. Poland —"

"Harry, please."

"Harry. Since you're straightforward about it, and you're also the composer of my favorite song, I'll say yes."

They met at Rector's. He could afford the best restaurants now. Arriving ahead of her, he leaped to his feet and waved from the rail of the second level when she walked in. How grand she looked, smoothly gliding up the staircase behind the maître d'. Her frock and hat were smart and new. He was intoxicated all over again by her blond ringlets, her brown eyes, her smile, her lively expression.

His hand trembled as he took her glove, pressing harder than he intended. Why did he feel such guilt over a simple courtesy? Because he was in love with her?

"You look wonderful," he said. "I assume your health's good?"

"Oh, yes, splendid."

"I saw you in a cowboy picture," he said after they sat down. "You were grand. Have you done many?"

"Quite a few more than I'd like," she said

with a rueful smile.

"Have you tried out for any plays? Any musicals?"

"Oh, I don't have a voice for musicals, Harry."

"Wrong. I remember our picnic. Perhaps your voice isn't operatic, but it's strong. You can put over a song."

Laughing, she opened her menu. "I'll keep that in mind if all else fails." She ordered oysters on the half shell, a salad of fresh asparagus, a veal cutlet, and a stein of Crown lager.

He lit a cigarette, straining for nonchalance. "How is Paul?"

"Busy, I expect. I don't hear from him often. He's quite the celebrity now that he's written a book."

"Oh, I read it. Just fine. I'm so proud to have him as a friend."

"He feels the same about you. So do we all. You're doing so well. I said you're the composer of my favorite song."

"Which one is that?"

" 'A Girl in Central Park.' "

"Yes, it's really caught on," he said, nervously flicking ash from the cigarette. Did she know or even suspect how important she was to its creation? Though aching to tell her, he simply couldn't. He tried instead to be elliptical. "I wrote it for someone special. Someone very close to me."

Fritzi's smile saddened a little. "Your wife. I know you've been with her a long time. How is her health?"

"Not good, I'm afraid."

"No improvement?"

He shook his head, then looked away quickly, sure that she'd discover his secret. Part of him desperately wanted her to discover it. He longed to take her hand, ask her to come with him to the Hotel Mandrake, and let him make love to her. He couldn't even hint of it. To do so would betray the poor muddled woman in the rest home in Rye.

A second stein of beer overcame some of his shyness. He told her about his plans for his own publishing company. She confided that she regarded picture making as temporary. Then she described some of her brother Carl's exploits as a team driver for the famous Barney Oldfield.

"He takes frightful risks, but it's his nature. I don't think he'll ever settle down."

"He must be very courageous," Harry said with a note of envy.

"Oh, yes, that's true."

Perspiring, his heart beating fast, Harry gazed at her in a dreamy way, conscious of the erection created merely by looking. Out of sight under the table he adjusted his napkin in his lap.

When they left the restaurant, Harry escorted her half a block, then stopped abruptly under the marquee of a darkened theater. He touched her arm.

"I want to say how much I enjoyed being with you. I don't know when I've enjoyed an evening more, Fritzi."

She moved slightly, away from his hand. "Yes, it was delightful, thank you. Now I'd better find a taxi —"

With a sudden move that startled her, he swept his arms around her there in the shadows, heedless of passing pedestrians who stared. For a few blissful seconds he tasted her warm mouth. Then she turned her head, pulled away, gasping.

"Harry, we can't do that."

"I couldn't help myself," he blurted. "You just don't know how much I —" Conscience choked off the rest.

She seemed more dismayed than angry. Giving him a curious searching look, she took three rapid steps to the curb and flagged a taxi. Harry handed her into the cab, red-faced but unable to take his gaze from her haunting face. He saw it even after the taxi disappeared southward in the blaze of headlamps and advertising signs.

Fritzi was still puzzling over Harry Poland's romantic advances as she climbed the stairs to her flat. Although his behavior wasn't proper for a married man, his interest was flattering and, in the few seconds his mouth touched hers, something had stirred within her. The memory was both pleasurable and slightly embarrassing.

She unlocked the door and stepped in without immediately understanding what her senses told her. A puff of air moved the old lace curtains at the front window overlooking Twenty-second Street. The window was open, bringing in night sounds. A couple arguing; an auto horn; a persistent rhythmic squeak, unfamiliar. Whenever she went out she closed that window and the one in the bedroom, against the possibility of rain or a sudden temperature drop.

She smelled barber's talc an instant before she saw the silhouetted head, torso, outstretched legs with heels resting on the table holding the talking machine. The hair on her neck stood up.

"Hello, Miss Fritz. Don't be scared. It's Pearly Purvis."

43. Threats

"I recognize your voice." Fritzi's calm reply qualified as the performance of the week.

"Shut the door. Let's have some lights." Purvis sounded affable. With a shaky hand she snapped the switch. The old ceiling fixture, frosted glass flowers cupping the bulbs, lit up an unexpected sight. On the table lay an autumn bouquet of asters, chrysanthemums, goldenrod.

Purvis stood. "Guess you're surprised to see me."

"*Surprised* is hardly the word. How did you open the door?"

He smiled. "You're asking a man who worked for Pinkerton's for fifteen years?" He pulled a ring of keys and lock picks from his coat, shook them in the air like a rattle meant to amuse a baby.

He was dressed up like a suitor. He'd shaved closely, and a small clotted cut showed under his ear. His thick silver hair was parted in the center. His suit was a single-breasted tan corduroy with leather elbow patches, his vest fancy maroon silk with a dark green stripe. His brown boots were buffed. The Masonic badge on his watch chain gleamed.

Agitated, she crossed in front of him, to the window overlooking Twenty-second Street. The maddening squeak turned out to be an old rag and bottle man trudging home with his two-wheel cart. She slammed the window so hard the glass hummed.

"Wasn't that hard to find you," Purvis went on. "All it takes is five bucks in the hands of the right casting agent. Took me a while to get around to see you, though, what with one thing and another."

Fritzi kept silent. Her legs felt wobbly, and she hoped she didn't swoon.

"Fact is, I'm never in any great rush to pay a visit to someone who's wronged me. Delay a while, it lets them think about it. Anticipate. It was a year and a half before I visited the man who drove me out of the Pinkertons."

She tried not to show dread in her voice. "What did you do to him?"

"His house burned down, with him and his wife inside."

"My God."

"Oh, don't take on, they escaped. Point is, I never forget. Elephant Pearly. Long memory." Again the brilliant smile. It chilled her.

"I've seen some of your pictures," he began. "We've got things to talk over."

"We have nothing to discuss. I'd like you to leave, Mr. Purvis."

"Call me Earl. Or Pearly. Either's fine."

"Did you hear what I said? You broke into my room, and I want you out. If you don't go, I'll scream my head off." She improvised. "In acting school they taught us to scream like banshees."

He frowned, as if he suspected mockery. He wasn't a bad-looking man, almost handsome when he smiled. But those pale eyes with the tiny nuggets of gold in the pupil were disturbing. "Look, I'm really not here to do you harm." He pushed back both sides of his coat — no gun harness. "I'd just like us to get acquainted."

Her legs kept shaking. Mercifully her skirt hid it. "Not I," she said. "Please leave."

"Hell, I even brought a peace offering. Those flowers will last forever, they're silk."

She had a wild impulse to laugh, but Purvis's eyes made her think again. "You may keep them, I don't want them."

"God, you're high-handed," he said, amused. He eased down into the chair. She sat on the sofa because she feared she'd fall over if she didn't.

"Maybe that's why I searched for you. I took a fancy to you in Coytesville. It's a queer thing, because you hurt me pretty bad. And that stunt that set me up" — he jabbed his index fingers toward her face — "listen, I've met a lot of tough females, whor— uh, ladies of easy virtue who look out for themselves with knives or hideout guns. But I never saw anything like that before. You did have an unfair advantage, surprise. It wouldn't happen a second time."

She unpinned her hat, lay hat and pin beside her. Her hands were clammy.

Purvis crossed his legs. "By rights I should hate you like rat poison. After that bastard Kelly flattened my tires and all of you vamoosed, I did. For about an hour. Then I cooled down and thought it over. You stood up to me. There's not a lot of men who would do that. You're a piece of work, Miss Fritzi."

Her skin crawled. She wondered whether he

was altogether right in the head.

"In case you don't understand yet" — a slightly harder edge in his voice now — "I want to be friends."

She pointed at the gold band on his fourth finger, right hand. "That's a wedding ring, isn't it?"

He touched it. "I keep it for sentiment. She's long gone. I caught her with another man, a milksop schoolteacher. Of geography, for Christ's sake, can you feature that?" Fritzi understood why his wife would crave a gentler man — any man besides Purvis.

"I divorced her after she got out of the hospital." He smiled again, rubbed his knuckles. He wanted her to know exactly what he was capable of. He was one of God's mistakes. She thought of *The Tempest.* He was Caliban with a tin badge.

"You aren't making this too easy, Miss Fritzi."

"I don't intend to. I want you to go."

"When I'm damn good and ready." He eased himself up, stepped toward the sofa. Her mouth dried. "Get this straight. The patents trust will nail your company, put it out of business. The only question is when. Be my pal and you'll make it easy on yourself when it happens, know what I'm saying?"

As he came near, she flung herself off the sofa, heading for the door. "I'm calling the police."

He was quick, agile for a man of his build. He stood against the door and grabbed her left arm. He forced the arm back so his knuckles gouged her breast. His warm breath smelled of cloves. *Like a suitor . . .* "Come on, be nice. I'm not so bad, am I?"

"You're a thug and a conceited pig."

He threw his left hand around her waist, pulled her hips forward against him. She wrenched away, toward the sofa. He held on. "You try that again, I'm liable to break your arm."

"Purvis, let go. Stop it."

"Sure, when you give me what I came for."

"Please don't," she moaned, praying she wasn't overacting. He pushed her backward; the sofa banged the backs of her legs. Uttering muted cries of fright, she groped behind her. He muffled her mouth with his left hand as he wedged his right knee between her legs, making a valley in her skirt. Finally she found the hat pin. With a vicious jab she drove it through corduroy into the side of his leg.

Purvis screeched in pain, and she gave him a shove. He tumbled on his back but sprang up in a second, fisting his hand to strike her. She dodged the blow aimed at her cheek, ran to the cooking alcove. Snatching up a water pitcher, she heaved it at the upper window light. The pane shattered and showered the pavement below.

She ran behind the table. His eyes looked yellow under his brows as he came at her. At the right moment she pushed the table into his left leg, bloodied now, a red wine color. He swore, visibly pale. She leaned out the window. "Police! Murder! Help, help!" She didn't need acting school to be convincing.

A gentleman with a leashed poodle dog was passing. "You got a problem, lady?"

"There's a man in here, trying to —"

"Bitch." Purvis hit the back of her head with his fist. She smacked her forehead on the window, an inch from a sharp piece of glass left in the frame.

He hit her again. Dizziness and darkness took her for a second. Then she screamed, stamping both feet on the floor, like a Spanish dancer. She heard people clamoring on the hall stairway.

Purvis heard them too and ran to the door. Gripping his bloody trouser leg, he gave her a hellish look that seemed to last forever. The yellow eyes promised terrible retribution.

He tore the door open and roared down the stairs, kicking and punching. A woman cried out — the wife of the first-floor tenant, she suspected. She watched him run out of the building. Angrily she hurled the silk flowers out the window after him. They fell into the gutter.

Purvis picked them up, then looked up. He clutched the bouquet against his coat and lunged into the street with a weird simian gait. A delivery truck came along, interfering with her view of him. When it passed, she saw a couple of gawkers on the opposite curb, but no Purvis.

Her sitting room filled with people. She couldn't understand their shouted questions. Delayed shock hit her. She started shuddering again, violently. She hid her face in her hands and sobbed.

44. Attack

Fritzi twisted a handkerchief in her hands. "I handled it badly. I was scared out of my wits. I got rid of him the only way I could think of, but I just made him angrier. He swore he'd get us, the whole company."

Al Kelly chewed a toothpick. His office was larger than B.B.'s, an expression of some continuing power struggle at Pal. On the drab wall to his left hung a gaudy chromo of the Virgin Mary with eyes raised to heaven. On the wall to his right, but hung crookedly, was a photo of a beaky woman with a mouth like a closed drawstring pouch, and two equally unappealing youngsters — the wife Kelly had divorced and the children he'd abandoned for the woman in an ornately framed photograph on his desk. This was Bernadette, an amply endowed ex-Floradora girl with whom Kelly lived, presumably in sin if he still practiced his faith.

"He can't hurt us if he can't find us," Kelly said, though his furrowed forehead didn't suggest confidence.

Eddie stood by the window, hands on his hips. "I'm absolutely against going back to New Jersey."

"The exchanges are yelling for another Indian picture," Kelly said. "You're overruled."

"But B.B. said he wants to bring his wife to the location."

"So we won't tell him what happened to Fritzi." Kelly grasped the edges of a large hand-drawn production calendar. He tapped an empty box. "Week from Monday. Put it on the schedule."

Fritzi and Eddie exchanged looks. The hanging judge had passed sentence, and there was no appeal. On the way out Eddie said to her, "I better catch up on my target practice."

Elaborate plans were laid for filming *The Lone Indian's Rescue*, a Hearn scenario in which Owen saved the local schoolmarm after villains cast her adrift in a flaming canoe. On Kelly's order, word went out along Fourteenth Street that Pal's newest western would film on the second Monday in October, near the Croton reservoir in northern Westchester County. On Thursday prior to the start of the picture, Bill Nix showed up, pleaded with Kelly for fifteen minutes, and was rehired.

The weekend before the appointed day, a pelting rain followed by a hard freeze accelerated the changing of the leaves. The start of the week promised to be clear and beautiful but sharply colder. On Sunday, Hobart telephoned to say he'd been given ten days off from the arduous tour, Moriarty to be played by an understudy while he was away. Fritzi promptly invited him to join her in New Jersey.

At five A.M. Monday morning, a wagon left the alley behind the Pal offices, carrying something bulky under bright Navaho blankets. Presumably there would be men trailing the wagon to Westchester; if the plan succeeded, they wouldn't discover they'd followed a decoy until noon or so. Other blanket companies used the same deceptive strategy.

Jock Ferguson had already ferried the camera across the Hudson in the closed wagon on Sunday night. He would proceed directly to Coytesville. No stops would be made in Fort Lee because of its population of Patents Company spies. No locals would be hired; extras were cast in the city.

Eddie had told the actors to dress drably, behave inconspicuously, and take the midtown ferry to Jersey City, where Bill Nix would pick them up in a property wagon. Though Hobart had listened to Fritzi's instructions about dressing, he disregarded them and turned up in a loud Inverness cape and deerstalker, fawn trousers and yellow spats, with a shiny, gnarled walking stick. His teeth chattered in the cold wind blowing over the ferry's prow.

"Damned lot of silliness, all this skulking about."

"You wouldn't think so if you met Purvis," she said.

Jock and Eddie had previously scouted a small remote lake in the woods beyond Coytesville. The lake was perhaps a half mile wide, deep blue in the morning light. The rain and cold had brought color to the surrounding trees — scarlet in the red oaks, a deeper reddish brown in the white oaks, brilliant reds and oranges in the maples, bright yellow in the birches. The company came together on the shore shortly after nine o'clock.

Eddie arrived driving the Stoddard-Dayton. He'd come over on the 129th Street ferry, Kelly sitting beside him muffled in an overcoat with a black velvet collar. B.B. and his wife were bundled under lap robes in the backseat. They rushed to greet Fritzi near a tepee Bill Nix and a helper were assembling from poles and ship's canvas. Nix wasn't complaining this time, but Fritzi noticed his nervousness. He spilled part of a can of paint he was using to daub crude arrows and bison and lightning bolts on the tent.

B.B. imprisoned Fritzi's hand between his. "I told Sophie, you got to meet this gel. Sophie, this is Fritzi. Fritzi, my wife."

"I'm delighted," Fritzi said to the small, button-nosed woman with cheerful brown eyes. She had to crouch to look at Mrs. Pelzer beneath the brim of an enormous hat adorned with three stuffed birds.

"Benny is so proud of you. I can't tell you how he raves," Sophie Pelzer said. Fritzi accepted the compliment with a modest smile and a murmur. Owen walked by, lower lip stuck out in a pout. He pretended not to see the Pelzers and Fritzi. He'd ignored Fritzi with greater consistency as her roles grew larger. After B.B. led his elfin wife away to camp chairs set up near the camera, Owen began loudly criticizing the tepee art.

Hobart sauntered over. He crossed his arms and slapped his sides. "Bloody cold out here. Is this all you do, stand around waiting?"

"Yes, there's a lot of that," she admitted, starting to run in place to drive the needles out of her toes. Nell Spooner had found a shawl for the schoolmarm, but it did little to ward off the chill. Fritzi's plain, faded dress was thin, more suitable to a prairie summer than a cold autumn in the Northeast.

Kelly stopped to inspect the tent. Stirring his paint while walking around from the other side, Bill Nix bumped him. Kelly jumped. "For Christ's sake, what's got into you? Look where you're going."

"Sorry, sorry," Nix said. "Just trying to do the job right." He hurried off, passing Fritzi. She smelled whiskey on him.

She put it out of mind as she took Hobart's hand and drew him forward. Kelly eyed the actor as though he might be a plague carrier.

"Mr. Kelly, you haven't met my guest, Mr. Hobart Manchester. Hobart, this is Alfred Kelly, one of the owners. Hobart's interested in the picture business."

"Swell." Kelly's handshake was swift and perfunctory.

"I appeared with Mr. Manchester in a Shakespearean play. He's a very well-known actor from the London stage."

Kelly plucked the cigar out of his mouth and looked the flamboyant actor up and down. "London, huh? Well, I'm Irish. Far as I'm concerned, they can write all that's good about Britain on the head of a pin. Try to stay out of the way, Manchester. We're on a tight schedule."

" 'Fit for the mountains and the barb'rous caves, where manners ne'er were preached,' " Hobart muttered as Kelly walked off. "*Twelfth Night*, act four."

"I know. Kelly's that way to everyone. I apologize."

"Not your fault, dear girl. The Irish are a quarrelsome lot. I've never been able to stand Bernard Shaw either."

The sun was higher, cooking steam out of the cold ground. Nix pushed a decorated canoe into the water and tied it to a stake. Eddie called, "Actors." Fritzi rearranged her shawl as she hurried to join two men in buckskins and false beards. Eddie consulted his copy of the scenario. "We'll do the fight scene first. Travis, you and Ollie start there, in the tepee, with Fritzi. You drag her out. She struggles, throws some punches, but they miss. You overcome her and carry her off that way, toward the canoe, camera left."

Eddie walked them through the action, working out the sequence of punches and falls so none of them would be hurt.

He certainly was taking hold of his job, Fritzi thought. He hardly resembled a staid Yale man any longer. Rita hadn't cut his hair in a while. A yellow cowboy scarf at his throat trailed down his shirt front. He wore a long tan duster over riding breeches; when the coat belled away from his hips his holstered Smith & Wesson showed.

"Everyone got it?"

They said they did.

"Okay, inside the tepee, let's rehearse."

Kelly shouted, "Why don't you just shoot it? You're wasting daylight."

"A rehearsal's cheaper than a second take," Eddie said.

"Let the boy alone, Al," B.B. called from his chair. "He learned his stuff from Griffith, and Griffith's a hot number." Silenced, Kelly chewed furiously on his cigar.

Travis and Ollie let her enter the tepee first. As she ducked her head, she saw Nix walk quickly to the wagon in which he'd delivered the actors, tent poles, canvas, and other properties. Eddie called action. The outlaws dragged her outside. Ollie Something mistimed one punch and almost clipped her jaw, but she avoided his flying knuckles, wrenching from side to side in simulated hysteria. They carried her out of the frame. Eddie was pleased.

"Let's take it. Ready, Jock?"

Ferguson whisked a speck from his lens with a blue bandanna, examined his footage counter, and nodded. Hobart nonchalantly unscrewed the cap of a leather-covered flask and nullified the cold with a hearty swig.

As Fritzi stamped her feet and blew out her breath, she noticed that Bill Nix was rummaging in the wagon. He looked anxious. B.B. and his wife watched like cheerful children as Eddie called places. Fritzi walked to the tepee; she and Travis and Ollie squeezed inside. "Everybody ready," Eddie shouted through his little megaphone. "Camera." Jock turned the crank, counting to himself. *"Action!"*

Fritzi was shoved into the sunshine. Out of the corner of her eye, she saw Nix pull something from the wagon. A long blue barrel glinted.

Eddie saw it too and smacked his megaphone against his leg. "Bill, what the hell are you doing?" Nix slammed the lever of the rifle down, up again, shouldered the weapon, and aimed.

Fritzi cried, "Jock." Possibly that saved his life. As he swung toward her, Nix's rifle drilled a round into the camera, toppling it on its tripod. A second shot tore open the case. Little gear wheels and pieces of metal flew out.

"Nix, you traitorous bastard! How much did they pay you?" Kelly screamed, a second before Nix shot at him. Kelly had presence of mind enough to drop on all fours and avoid the bullet. It struck the lake with a harmless plop. Time seemed to elongate, or perhaps that was only in her imagination. Nix turned in a slow and fluid way, searching for a new target. When he found her, he shouldered the rifle again. He squinted through the sight, dipping the muzzle so the bullet would take her in the knees. Eddie yelled like a madman and tackled her from behind.

Fritzi's chin slammed into the dirt. She swore later that she felt the bullet buzz through her hair as she fell. "Catch him, don't let him escape," Eddie shouted.

Nix dodged behind the wagon and started running toward the trees. Fritzi's heart beat frantically, her mind holding the terrifying image of the rifle muzzle. Nix had been sent to shoot and injure her, and she knew who'd sent him.

Spitting dirt and gasping, she saw B.B. hurl himself from his chair and churn forward to intercept Nix. Two steps behind, Sophie cried, "Benny, don't let him hurt you." Finally B.B. caught Nix's forearm.

"Here, you."

Nix tore away and reversed the rifle, intending to hit B.B. with the butt of the stock. Just as he swung, B.B. somehow stumbled and the flying rifle missed him, slamming Sophie above her right ear; the sound was sickening. The birds on Sophie's hat scattered feathers as she fell.

"*Sophie!*" B.B. knelt beside his wife. Eddie pulled his .32 and charged. Hobart was right behind him with his stick raised. Nix aimed at Eddie, pulled the trigger, but the rifle jammed. Skidding as he dodged out of the way, Eddie fired at Nix. He missed. Now the two were close. Nix lunged in, swung the rifle by the barrel, and connected with Eddie's knee. Bone cracked as Eddie windmilled backward and hit the ground.

Nix had just enough time to sprint to the trees and disappear. Kelly lobbed rocks and shouted useless oaths. Nix's crashing passage through the underbrush grew fainter. Then the sound died altogether, and the last disturbed branches settled in place.

Fritzi pushed straggles of blond hair out of her eyes. She looked around at the damage done to Pal Pictures in a matter of two or three minutes. Sophie Pelzer lay unconscious, her scalp bloody. Her husband held her in his arms, saying, "Sophie, Sophie," over and over.

Near the tepee Eddie lay on the ground, clutching his leg. Hobart vainly searched for someone to attack with his stick. Jock Ferguson picked at the bullet-riddled camera, sick as any father with an injured child. Kelly asked him about it. Ferguson shook his head. "Ruined."

And it's all my fault, Fritzi thought.

45. B.B. Decides

Travis and Ollie turned up in the woods. A doctor from Fort Lee splinted Eddie's broken leg. Sophie Pelzer was transported in an ambulance and taken to the city that night; a mild concussion was suspected.

Kelly and B.B. went to the New York police, who failed to find Nix at his last known address. When detectives questioned Pearly Purvis, who they found eating steak and eggs in the restaurant of the Hotel Astor, he laughed at them. He'd been in his office, conferring with associates — an iron-clad alibi. Fritzi and the rest were considerably demoralized.

Kelly called her to his office two days later, the first of November. It had been snowing since daybreak, a heavy, wet snow that horses and auto tires and the trampling feet of New Yorkers had already converted to dirty slush down on Fourteenth Street.

"Come in, Fritzi," Kelly said. He dominated the room from his desk chair. B.B. sat under the chromo of the Virgin Mary, holding his head.

Kelly shot his cuffs twice and cleared his throat. "Close the door. Please."

"Have they found Nix?" she asked.

Kelly shook his head. "My guess is, we never will. He was probably on his way to Alaska by the time the coppers got on the case."

Fritzi eased into the seat beside the desk. Kelly

nervously eyed his fingernails, then spoke in a near whisper. "I asked you to step in because we're talking to a few people. It's confidential."

She said, "I see," though she didn't.

"We can't stand no more of what happened in Jersey," B.B. said. "Sophie's out of danger, but that's just luck. She could be lying dead this minute."

As if they'd rehearsed, Kelly took his turn. "Cameras are expensive. Film is expensive."

B.B. said, "Eddie's still in traction."

"Yes, I'm going to visit him later today."

Kelly fiddled with a cigar butt in a heavy glass tray. "What we want to tell you is, we've decided to close this office for a while."

"I decided," B.B. said. "I don't want more trouble for the people who work for Pal. We're going to run away from it."

Kelly said, "California."

"Edison's a well-known cheapskate," B.B. said. "Maybe he won't buy railroad tickets for his thugs. Maybe Purvis will leave us alone."

"Yeah, and maybe trees will grow dollar bills," Kelly said.

"Doesn't matter," B.B. said. "We're going."

Fritzi interrupted for the first time. "Who is going?"

"The important folks," Kelly said.

"One of which is you," B.B. said.

Fritzi sat a moment, collecting herself. "Mr. Pelzer — Mr. Kelly — that's very kind, but I honestly don't want to work in California."

"Not even for the winter?" Kelly said.

"No, sir."

"Why not?" B.B. said. "How can you beat it when you got sunshine every day? Colonel Bill Selig from Chicago, he's there already, dodging the Patents crowd. Essanay, Lubin, Nestor, they all got location companies set up. Biograph's gone West the past couple of winters, and I hear they may move for good. Maybe they all will, including us."

From his waistcoat he fished a crumpled scrap of newsprint. "Listen to this. 'It is predicted by theatrical men that our city will be the moving-picture center of America next year.' " He thrust the scrap at Fritzi. *Los Angeles Times.*"

Fritzi stared at the newsprint, which seemed to blur appropriately to match her confusion. She started to shake her head. Kelly's voice took on a note of irascibility. "Don't be so quick to turn it down. You have a future with us."

"Right," B.B. exclaimed. "This business is growing like a rabbit farm. The trade papers say there's ten thousand moving-picture theaters in the U.S., and eight or ten new ones open up every day. Most of 'em do a daily change — a new bill seven times a week. Can't make pictures fast enough for that kind of market. Know something else? Youngsters are packing the theaters. Fact! Weekdays they play hooky; Saturday and Sunday they drag mom and pop. We're educating a whole new audience that's gone wild for pictures. The greenhorns pile off the boats from Hamburg and Cork, and before you know it they're lining up for tickets. In hick burgs in Ohio and Iowa they're ripping up the old opera house to make it a nickelodeon. In little dusty spots in Texas and Oklahoma, cowboys ride twenty miles on a Saturday night to see a picture show."

"Unless they're Baptist," Kelly muttered. "We still got a problem with the Baptists."

Eager as a child wanting to please, B.B. leaned forward. "We're riding the crest, Fritzi. California's only the start. We need you."

Snow from the bleak sky drifted past the window. She felt cold, and unhappy, because she hated to disappoint people she'd grown to like. B.B. was one.

"I appreciate it, I'm very grateful. But" — a deep breath — "I still want to make my career on the stage."

"Ah, hell, I told you." Kelly glowered at Fritzi. "So stay here. Just forget we were prepared to write a regular contract for your services. Hang around New York, sling hash, sell hankies. Who cares?"

"Now, now," B.B. said, running over to grasp Fritzi's hands. "Everybody calm down. Did you catch what Al said about a contract?"

"Yes, I —"

"What are you making now?"

"Six-fifty a day when I work."

"That's thirty-nine dollars if you work the regular six-day week. How does seventy a week sound? I mean, as a guaranteed salary. You draw it whether you're playing or sitting on your tushie."

A born salesman, B.B. brimmed with enthusiasm, chafing her hands and fairly dancing around her chair. "You're not signing up to live the rest of your life in California. We're just trying it for the winter. We'll throw in some nice extras. Take care of your rail fare and moving expenses. Pay your rent for a month or two while you get settled. Say, and how about this? Do you know how to drive a motor car?"

Taken aback, she said, "What?"

Kelly snatched the cigar out of his mouth. "A car? For Christ's sake, Benny, what is this? We didn't discuss a car."

"Al, you're overwrought," B.B. said. "Al takes the loss of equipment hard, Fritzi. What I'm talking about, Al, is a car available to be driven by all our important players, including this little gel. A Pal company car."

"Yeah? On whose money?"

"Ours, Al. And that's my final word, so do me a favor and shut up. If Fritzi goes to California, and I am down on my knees praying she does, she's going in style."

Kelly stomped to the window and glowered at the falling snow. B.B. lifted her from her chair, wrapped an arm around her waist, and guided her to the window.

"Look out there. Look at that mess. Oh, did you see that? That man there, he fell down in the slush, he's ruined a fine fifty-dollar overcoat. You don't have that in southern California. You enjoy beautiful weather. In your personal Pal auto. With the top lowered!"

He saw her hesitancy. "Isn't that good enough? What else can we offer to persuade you?"

"Nothing, sir. The salary's very attractive, and

the car too. But it's such a big step."

"You can't turn it down," Kelly said, practically threatening her.

Fritzi gazed at the snow. She'd endured New York's dark winters, chasing stage roles, and how many had she gotten? Of those few, how many had carried her to heights of success? Exactly none.

The steam pipes emitted strange whistles and pings. On the floor below someone banged their radiator, shouted for heat. Kelly sucked on his teeth, looked at her in a calculating way.

"Don't forget Purvis. You know he got to Nix. Hired him to shoot up the camera and you too. I saw Nix aim for your legs."

Pale, Fritzi could only nod and try to evade the memory. B.B. threw a protective arm around her shoulder. "Easy, Al. She's been through plenty."

"Then she ought to face facts. There's no guarantee we won't see Purvis in California, but it's a damn long way out there. You stay in this town, sister, you'll be dealing with him forever. He's got some kind of crazy hate for you, didn't you say so? Do you want to live with that?"

Fritzi started to shake. She fought it, kept her voice as level as she could. "I despise the idea of running, Mr. Kelly. I've always tried to be a strong person. Stand up to things."

"Sure, sure, we understand," B.B. said in a soothing way. "Nobody wants to be a coward, but we're not talking about that. There's no shame in taking care of yourself. This is no dime novel we're in the middle of, no sir. This is real. Nix was shooting real bullets. If not to do away with you, then to hurt and maybe cripple you. Don't take a swami to figure that out."

She was surprised at the faintness of her voice when she said, "When will the company be leaving?"

"Before Christmas," Kelly said.

"No, after," B.B. said. "Sophie and I got to celebrate Hanukkah too." Kelly's response was a bored shrug.

"I'll think about it, I really will. I'd like to discuss it with my friend Hobart, and with Eddie."

B.B. patted her shoulder. "Take your time. Take a whole day. Two if you need it. Come back and we'll ink the contract on the spot. You'll be happy, Fritzi, I promise."

Fritzi's long face expressed considerable doubt.

She visited Eddie at the New York Hospital on lower Broadway. Approaching in the avenue of leafless trees leading to the building, she met Rita Hearn on her way out. She asked Rita about her reaction to California.

"Oh, we're eager. I hate this climate. The children are excited about spending the winter where it's warm."

Eddie's bed was one of many in a dark, gloomy hall whose painted floor resounded with every footstep. The hall reeked of carbolic and bed pans. Eddie's leg was wrapped and elevated in a web of ropes and pulleys. It was the middle of the afternoon; many patients were asleep, but he was awake and alert. As she drew up the visitor's chair, he told her that the Rumanian gentleman on his right was suffering a rupture, while the unmoving lump on his left was a bank president who'd attempted suicide.

Fritzi quickly sketched her dilemma. Eddie nodded. "I know all about it. Pelzer's been here. He said you don't want to go."

"I realize it's an opportunity —"

"And we're only trying it for the winter, don't forget."

She scratched the back of her left hand. Her knuckles were red, her skin dry and cracked from the cold. In California you could forget about gloves, overcoats, overshoes, scarves, and similar burdens.

"I hate to give up serious acting."

"You're doing serious acting."

"We can debate that point till judgment day. Suppose I stayed with Pal a year or two. What could I look forward to? I don't want to be the queen of the prairies forever, and I'm sure that's what B.B. and Kelly intend."

"I'll make a deal. If you go, I'll do all I can to keep you from getting stuck playing the Lone Indian's girlfriend till you're ninety-five. We'll figure something out, I promise. Let's get away from Purvis and the Patents crowd first."

The ruptured Rumanian rolled over and cried, "Nurse. I need the pan. Hurry." A muscular woman in a starched uniform ran to his rescue.

Eddie reached out with his left hand, spilling trade newspapers on the floor as he grasped hers. She looked at him closely, saw the lines of a new maturity in his face. "I don't want to make a wrong decision, Eddie."

"Think of all you'd gain. A regular paycheck whether you work or not. Free rent for a while. That car B.B. offered. Don't you want to learn to motor?"

"Of course, it's the modern thing."

"Think of the ocean. The mountains. Orange juice. Good-looking men with suntans. What do you say, Fritzi?"

To her astonishment, Hobart's opinion was similar to Eddie's. He encouraged the move. Not on artistic grounds, certainly, but for the sake of personal safety.

"Consider it temporary. Until that vicious man finds another target."

She saw Purvis then — his strange yellow-specked eyes. *Elephant Pearly,* he said. *I never forget.*

"Perhaps you're right. There's no need for it to be permanent, is there?"

She wrote Eustacia Van Sant in England:

So it's California. Should I have said yes? Eustacia, I can't be sure. Do we ever recognize the right decision until long after we've made the wrong one?

46. A Toast to War

The Imperial German Army staged its autumn maneuvers in the mountains and valleys around Würzberg, a charming old city on the River Main where feudal princes of the region had once had summer homes. For four long, tiring days — fortunately free of rain — Paul and Sammy photographed entrenchments, cavalry charges, mock battles with live artillery shells lobbed dangerously near skirmishing troops. The fifty-one-year-old Kaiser took active part, directing the games by field telephone from his command position on the heights. Paul filmed the emperor striding back and forth under the eagle and iron cross banner that proclaimed GOTT MIT UNS. Wilhelm II was happy and enthusiastic as a boy, although no boy playing soldier had ever dressed in mirror-bright jackboots, a long military overcoat bedecked with medals and ropes of braid, the burnished silver eagle helmet of the cuirassier regiment to which he belonged. The Kaiser was a loud, often bellicose man with a showy mustache whose upturned points he kept elaborately waxed. His gloved left hand usually rested on his hip or his sword pommel; the arm was withered, a relic of a childhood injury. In one of his more famous outbursts against his grandmother's people, he once said the deformity was proof of English blood.

On the fourth night, the Kaiser, three of his six sons who were in the military, and almost three hundred officers gathered for a festive banquet. Rather than dining in the Residenz, one of the largest and loveliest Baroque palaces in Europe, the Kaiser ordered that the celebration be held in the great hall of Marienberg Fortress, a more warlike setting on the heights across the river. Two huge hearths lit the hall, along with some temporary electric lights on stands that cast a weird white glare and gave the celebrants a curious spectral appearance. The banquet featured boar, pheasant, and enough beer to explode the kidneys of a regiment.

Paul and Sammy circulated before dinner, Sammy wide eyed at so much gold braid and brass, so many plumes and decorations. The Kaiser admired members of the Prussian Junker class and collected them for his personal circle. A brigadier got down on hands and knees and imitated pigs and cows while the Kaiser's sons, Prince Joachim, Prince Frederick, and Crown Prince William, whinnied like jackasses to add to the merriment. The Kaiser held his sides and laughed mightily.

A sharp-faced blond officer drew Paul aside with a nod at Sammy, who was unaware of being scrutinized. One word came out of the man's slit-like mouth.

"*Jude?*"

"My helper? I don't know." It had never crossed Paul's mind to wonder whether Sammy was a Jew. "Is it important?"

"Be discreet with your dinner companions. They might not care for his company," the officer said, and walked off. Paul stared after him, stupefied. He knew that Europe was a seedbed of anti-Semitism, with no places worse than Germany and Austria. Sometimes, busy with things that made sense, he forgot.

Shortly, he saw the emperor and two aides bearing down. The Kaiser kept an enormous wardrobe of uniforms to acknowledge his membership in many regiments. Tonight he was splendidly turned out as a *Jäger zu Pferde* — mounted rifleman.

"Herr Crown, good evening. How goes it with you? Pictures satisfactory?"

Paul bowed. "Very satisfactory, Your Majesty."

"We are eager for the world to see the armor and mail of the fatherland. Your former president Theodore Roosevelt was quite impressed with the military review I put on for him in Potsdam this spring. Splendid man, Roosevelt. We share many opinions, including the absolute necessity to watch for incursions of the yellow peril from Asia." The Kaiser tended to speak in loud declarative sentences — pronouncements — allowing no room for disagreement or even comment.

"I have read your book," the Kaiser said. "The life of a journalist is most interesting."

"Hectic sometimes," Paul said, smiling.

"Are you a student of military affairs? If so, I commend to your attention a work which will be published next year. I've just reviewed an advance text. It was written by our own General Friedrich von Bernhardi. His topic is the coming war."

411

Paul's scalp prickled. "Will there be one, Majesty?"

"One hopes not," the Kaiser said with a dismissive shrug. "But many enemies surround the fatherland. Although I am a friend of England, the same can't be said of my subjects."

"What point is General Bernhardi making, may I ask?"

"He argues that war is a biological necessity, an inherent part of man's nature. Therefore a warrior state such as Germany not only has the right but the absolute duty to strike a first blow, to assure victory and continuity of its rule."

Now Paul's spine was crawling. He could think of nothing to say. Finally he summoned one word: "Remarkable."

"Yes, decidedly so. You must not fail to read it when it's published. *Germany and the Next War* is the title. By the way, will you see that we receive a copy of your films?"

"Through our Berlin exchange, depend on it."

"Good old German reliability. Fine. Good evening, then."

"Majesty," Paul said with another bow, his skin like ice and his belly knotted. Drenched in the *Gemütlichkeit* of the noisy party, he tended to forget the dark side of the German character, which the Kaiser exhibited all too freely.

At dinner, Paul and Sammy found themselves seated at one end of a trestle table dominated by Prussians, if Paul could judge from their accents: arrogant, preening asses. Not to be dismissed lightly, though. The German soldier was a top professional, war his lifetime study.

The stomach-stretching meal of breads and meats and side dishes was accompanied by loud conversation among the officers about tactics, the relative merits of different units, the low morals and stupidity of the French, the usefulness of females for sex and cooking. There were a couple of jokes about Jews and excrement. Paul was glad Sammy couldn't understand what was being said.

Then the toasts began — windy praise of the Kaiser, his wife, Kaiserin Augusta, his six manly sons, his daughter, Viktoria Louise, who held an honorary colonelcy in the Death's Head Hussars. Paul rose dutifully for each toast, dutifully drank from his tankard of beer.

A colonel at the head of Paul's table stood.

"Majesty — gentlemen. I give you a special toast appropriate to the events which have drawn us together. I give you the Day, when our armies will take revenge on all those who attempt to wall us in, threaten us and humiliate us, and restrict the rightful power of imperial Germany."

A hush had fallen; someone kicked a kitchen boy who was still turning a squeaky spit. In one of the hearths a log broke and fell, shooting up a geyser of sparks. The colonel lifted his tankard.

"Der Tag."

The Day. Paul had heard it for twenty years. The army was maniacal on the subject.

The Kaiser leaped up, and the several hundred fellow officers with him, shouting in unison, *"Der Tag."*

Casting a puzzled look at Paul, Sammy started to stand. Paul pulled him down. His heart was speeding, thumping in his ear. *Don't be an idiot.*

Heads turned, surprise swiftly changing to disbelief, then animosity. The colonel looked down the table at the two civilians still seated.

"You object to the toast, my friend?"

"With all due respect, Colonel, I don't celebrate killing. At least not the premeditated kind."

Far across the hall Paul could see the Kaiser's livid color. In the drafty stone hall the electric lights washed out faces so that all those staring at Paul and Sammy had the look of corpses.

The colonel's eyes flicked to one side, then the other. Aware that he was the focus of attention, he raised his voice.

"Then may I ask what you are doing here, presuming on our hospitality? That strikes me as grossly hypocritical."

Paul wadded his serviette and stood up. The beer and tiredness and disgust with this crowd had pushed him over a line he was usually too prudent to cross.

"Perhaps so."

"I suggest you raise your tankard or leave."

Paul swallowed, saw one of the Kaiser's sons with his sword half drawn. "Come on, Sammy. We've overstayed." He bowed. "Majesty."

The Kaiser didn't acknowledge it. His jaw was clenched, his blue eyes raging.

The moment they left the hall, a strange cry went up behind them — a roar of defiance and hate that reminded Paul of the baying of wild dogs. He forgot his bowler and overcoat as he dashed from the fortress into the courtyard and out the gate to the riverbank. Sammy scrambled to keep up.

They turned north, toward the central bridge over the Main. On the far bank the lights of the town glowed as pleasantly as miniature houses under a Christmas tree. "God, I lost my head. I shouldn't have let go," Paul growled.

"What the hell was that all about, gov?"

Paul explained the significance of *Der Tag*. "They live for it. Plan for it. Can't wait to see it come. Not all the German people are that way, but the ones closest to the Kaiser certainly are, and they'll drag the rest along with them."

Bending into the autumn wind, they crossed the river to their first-class hotel up by the Luitpold bridge. Paul asked the night porter for a railway schedule, found there was a train for Frankfurt at half past two in the morning.

"We'll take it," he told Sammy.

"Don't you want your hat and overcoat?"

"No. I wouldn't walk back into that viper's nest for ten overcoats. Let's pack."

On the way down to a taxi at a few minutes before two, Paul was hailed by the hall porter, who handed him a message with a cheery, "*Mein Herr!* Heartiest felicitations and congratulations." Paul translated the German in a second.

FRANCESCA CHARLOTTE BORN EIGHT TEN LONDON TIME ALL WELL YOUR WIFE EAGER FOR YOU TO SEE YOUR DAUGHTER FOLLETT

"Is it the baby?" Sammy asked, peering over his shoulder.

Paul looked at him with a strange, stricken expression.

"She's fine. Julie's fine."

But the world wasn't fine. It was dark and cold as the windy autumn night. Though proud in many respects to be German, Paul had no illusions about what it meant. Dark streams of poison ran in German blood. There was a fury in the German makeup stoked by national paranoia and heightened by arrogance born of exceptional past accomplishments in science and literature, music and education — the whole *Kultur* about which Germans could be so overbearing. The worst of German character was reflected in the high command, the Prussian Junkers. They wanted war and one way or another, he was convinced, they would bring it. This was the world his little newborn daughter had entered tonight.

47. In the Subway

With the decision made, Fritzi felt more at ease, though she found herself supremely careful whenever she was abroad on the crowded city streets. She scrutinized faces closely and looked behind her often, especially if something kept her out after dark.

Harry Poland telephoned three times, leaving messages. Twice she ignored them, but the third time, feeling sorry for him, she called the Hotel Mandrake. He asked for one more chance to see her, to make amends — prove that he could be a complete gentleman.

Fritzi hesitated. To go out with a married man a second time really wasn't proper. On the other hand, she'd enjoyed Harry's company until the moment of the illicit kiss, and even that had not been without its guilty pleasure. So long as she kept everything within bounds, would it hurt? Harry's wife was totally incapacitated, and he sounded overwhelmed with guilt.

"All right, yes — supper on Saturday. I'll tell you about my plans for the new year."

New York sparkled with colored lights as the stores decorated for the Christmas season. A warm wind from the south raised temperatures into the fifties. Harry called for her in a taxi, told the driver to take them to a restaurant called Bankers, on Liberty Street, just off lower Broadway a few blocks above Wall. As he helped her out of the cab, she saw headlights veer to the curb behind them on Broadway. Someone clambered out of another taxi and faded into the shadow of a darkened building. She felt an odd tingle of alarm.

Bankers was small, swanky, and expensive. Their dinner conversation was lively and polite, with no references to what had happened last time, though she did catch Harry gazing at her soulfully a couple of times. She told him about Pal's move to California for the winter.

"How grand for you, Fritzi — all that warm weather. One of these days I want to see the Pacific coast for myself. I'd be out there in a shot if you invited me."

"Harry," she said, raising her eyebrows.

"Sorry. You have that effect on me."

She smiled; she couldn't be angry. He was an attractive companion — charming, cultivated, yet still with a certain air of Old World innocence.

When they stepped outside, Fritzi reveled in the mild air, the sweep of stars above the skyscrapers of the financial district. Full of good food and wine, she'd quite forgotten her earlier anxiety. Harry asked if she'd like to walk a bit, and she readily agreed, taking his arm. They turned north on Broadway toward City Hall.

After two blocks he said, "Would you like to finish the evening in style?"

"What do you have in mind?"

"Riding the subway."

"The subway?" she repeated, astonished. "You enjoy that?"

"Immensely. The New York subway is one of the wonders of the age. I ride it whenever I have a chance. The financier August Belmont was behind it, you know. The original line to 145th Street opened in 1904. 'Fifteen minutes to Harlem,' that was the slogan. You see all kinds of people on the subway, socialites to shop girls. The cars are clean, the air underground is fresh and cool — all for a nickel! Shall we?"

"All right, why not?"

"There's a stop at Twenty-third Street," he said, rushing ahead toward a familiar structure of wrought iron and glass that was common to all IRT entrances. "Aren't the kiosks something to see? Did you know they're modeled after Turkish summer houses?"

Although it was nearly ten, there were still large numbers of people entering and leaving the station. At the ticket plaza Harry paid their fares and handed the pasteboard tickets to a uniformed guard who dropped them into a box. A rush of air and noise signaled the departure of a train.

"That was a local," Harry said, peering along the crowded platform. "There's an express every six minutes until midnight, with the locals between." Fritzi hadn't ridden the subway in a while. She'd forgotten how bright and attractive the stations were. There wasn't a straight line in the design of City Hall station, which was actually part of a loop on which trains traveled to reverse their direction. The edge of the platform formed a gentle curve. Terra-cotta arches inlaid with white and colored tiles created a pleasing, airy effect above it.

Fritzi heard another train on its way from the station to the north, Brooklyn Bridge. Harry said something, but Fritzi missed it because of the noise. Someone bumped her, pushing her near the edge. She caught her breath as Harry took her arm to steady her.

He glared at someone behind her. "You needn't stand so close, there's plenty of room."

Fritzi's eyes grew round. She heard strident breathing, watched as Harry turned with another annoyed look at the boorish passenger. *I know who it is. He's followed us . . .*

Urgently she gripped Harry's arm. "Harry, let's leave." With her head turned slightly, she saw him from the edge of her vision — the strange gold-flecked eyes, that damnable grin. A little cry of fear escaped her, unheard as the train came roaring along the tunnel.

Harry said something strong to the passenger, who grabbed him by the lapels and flung him aside. Pearly grabbed Fritzi's wrists, shoved her toward the edge as the train thundered closer. Fritzi never remembered reacting quickly, but she did. As one foot slipped off the platform she twisted her hand, savagely dug her nails into Pearly's wrist. He cursed and she pulled free, teetering.

Harry made a wild lunge to save her, shooting out his hand. She caught it and hung on; if she hadn't, she'd have fallen off. Pearly reached for his pistol under his jacket. People along the platform were yelling, screaming, retreating from the struggle.

Harry leaped at Pearly and shoved. Pearly swung the pistol to club him. The eight-car express hurtled from the tunnel, its poppy red paint reflecting the station lights. Fritzi grabbed Pearly's arm, yanked. He stumbled, flailed in the air as he fell over the tracks, and dropped.

A woman thrust her little girl against her and screamed like a banshee — or was that the howling and sparking of the braking train? If Pearly cried out when the first car crushed him, no one heard.

The train ground to a stop. Frightened passengers and the motorman stuck their heads out of open windows. The ticket guard was frantically ringing an alarm gong. In the gap between the platform and the door of the second car, Fritzi saw something grisly and red.

Harry pulled her against his chest. "Don't look. He didn't stand a chance. Some crazy man —"

"Trying to kill me. It wasn't chance, Harry. I know him."

"Good God," he said with a look of horror. He pulled her close again, enfolding her in his strong arms while she trembled with fright and shock. It didn't matter that he was married; she wanted his arms around her.

At police headquarters, Harry stayed with her while detectives questioned her. Fritzi identified the dead man for them. When she was told that he was all but unrecognizable, vomit rose in her throat.

Pulled out of bed, B.B. arrived wearing an

overcoat over his pajama bottoms. He quickly corroborated Fritzi's story of threats and harassment from the patents detective. She was released a little before one in the morning, without being charged.

B.B. drove her to her flat on Twenty-second with Harry riding along. "Poor defenseless gel," B.B. kept saying. "What quick thinking. You too, mister."

Harry saw her up to her door, gravely shook her hand, urged her to telephone if he could do anything at all. She knew he couldn't. She was responsible for a man's death. Her parents had taught her reverence for human life, even in its most despicable forms. The effects of what she'd done would be with her for days, years — maybe forever.

But she thanked him, then hurried inside, hoping she'd feel safer, calmer, in her own bedroom.

She didn't. She lay awake, arms crossed protectively on her breast, eyes wide, seeing those few seconds in the station again and again. An inch one way or another and she'd have been under the train instead of Pearly. He would never threaten her any longer. She felt different about California now. She urgently wanted to flee there, start anew, put the terrible night behind her —

As if she ever could.

48. Further Westward Ho

On her way to Chicago, Fritzi vowed to say nothing about her involvement with Earl Purvis, and the man's horrible end. Telling her parents would only confirm their fears about acting and the environment in which it was carried on. She really didn't want to speak about Purvis to anyone. He was gone, no longer a threat, but she would be a long time getting over the memory of him.

When she arrived, rather than hiring a taxi to deliver her to the Crown mansion, Fritzi checked in at the Sherman House. She felt sad about the decision but considered it prudent. She telephoned her mother the moment the bellhop deposited her luggage.

"Mama? I'm here overnight. I'm on my way to California to make more pictures."

"Why didn't you telegraph, for heaven's sake?"

"I didn't know how I'd be received."

"Oh, *liebchen.*" It carried a sad unspoken admission that she had reason for concern.

"I want to see you."

"I'll leave now, take a taxi," Ilsa said.

"You mean I can't come to the house? I'd like to talk to Papa."

"Not such a good idea. Of course, you're free to do as you please, but I wouldn't advise it. Your father, I am sorry to tell you, is still angry."

"With me?"

"With you, with me — the world."

"But I've actually had some success. He predicted I wouldn't."

"All the more reason he's angry. You proved him wrong."

After a moment of pained silence Fritzi said, "Call the taxi, Mama. I'll reserve a table in the dining room."

A strolling string player serenaded the candlelit room with romantic favorites. "A Girl in Central Park," usually a sure bet to dampen Fritzi's eyes, didn't touch her; she was still exercised.

"Mama, what in heaven's name is the trouble with my father? What reason does he have to be angry?"

"Shall I make a list? Number one, he's a man. He's growing old, can do nothing about it, and resents it bitterly. He's driven wild by the prohibition crowd. He's also, you know, a German. They are champion grudge holders, surely you remember."

"On Thursday, Mama, I had a birthday —"

"Oh, that's right. Congratulations. I sent a package to New York, did you get it?"

"Not yet. Never mind."

"Child, I'm a little forgetful. How old are you now? Twenty-nine?"

"Thirty, Mama. Thirty years old. Do you know what that means? It means I'm an old maid. But it also means I'm old enough to have my father respect what I choose to do with my life."

"Oh, *liebchen,* he does."

"That isn't true. You're just trying to make me feel good. But he will before I'm through." Fritzi pounded the table so hard the silver danced.

"I promised you, he will."

Ilsa fanned herself with a handkerchief and said in a bewildered way, "I must find out what became of your present."

Though the meal was sumptuous, and the meeting with her beloved mother comforting, Fritzi was emotionally devastated by the banishment which Ilsa thought necessary. She boarded the westbound train next morning in a mood of deep melancholy.

The steel-colored sky over the frozen Illinois prairie did nothing to relieve her gloom. Before the express reached the Mississippi at Alton, a blizzard struck. The engineer took the train across the river at three miles an hour, in howling wind that shook the trestles and terrified the passengers. On the Iowa side they waited out the storm for six hours, then chugged west behind a snowplow engine.

What am I doing here? Fritzi wondered. *Why can't I live a normal life? What's wrong with me?*

She pictured her silver-haired father's curled lip and scornful pointing finger.

"Du bist eine Schauspielerin."

"You're an actress."

It sounded like some debilitating chronic disease.

In western Iowa the snow disappeared, which wasn't entirely a benefit, since it might have prettied up the dismal scenery observed from the Pullman window — jerry-built towns beside the railway, hog pens and privies and, farther on, small creatures she took to be prairie dogs sitting up on their hind legs.

Unexpected warmth out of the south brought a winter thaw. The Pullman car stoves overheated as the landscape changed. Flat grasslands rolled by, here and there relieved by stunted trees or parched watercourses with a vein of yellow-brown sludge in the center. Forlorn cattle with their ribs showing posed for the passing travelers. Fritzi's spirits sank lower.

And then came a late winter afternoon a hundred miles or more into eastern Colorado. The Union Pacific engineer stopped to take on water from a great roadside tank in a forlorn little place called Agate.

Passengers fled the hell-hot coaches. The January air, if not quite balmy, was surprisingly pleasant. The evening light was the color of melted butter, shading to dark amber in the east. The desolate upland shone like a sheet of gold. A tiny black shape moved along the northern skyline. An auto, Fritzi realized; perhaps a Model T, though it was so far away she couldn't be sure. It dropped from sight under the horizon, leaving a vast yellow cyclorama lit by a single evening star. Fritzi shivered at the beauty, and something else. The primitive land wasn't primitive any longer. She was reminded of the dizzying changes in her craft, and of the amazing century in which she lived.

"Look there," said a frail gray-haired woman

at her elbow. "Are my eyes tricking me?"

Fritzi followed the pointing hand gloved in gray. Westward, running along the horizon like a saw blade, mountains thrust upward. A few peaks crested with snow gleamed in the fading daylight.

"No, I believe we've come to the Rockies. It's rather breathtaking, isn't it?"

Beyond the mountains lay a new life. What would she find on the exotic sunlit shores of California — "America's Mediterranean" as people called it? She couldn't imagine.

California might be a lot better than she expected. Perhaps — dared she hope? — she might even meet an intelligent, steady, handsome, and desirable man.

You don't have to stay forever, remember. Perhaps you'll like it. Even if you don't, make the best of it. You're a trouper, aren't you? You said you'd go, you've come this far, you've got to stick with it. If you didn't learn anything else in all the years since Mortmain's, surely you learned that much.

Long quiescent, Ellen Terry spoke.

I quite admire your spirit, my girl, if not your destination.

"Did you say something?" the frail woman asked.

With a smile and a toss of her blond curls Fritzi said, "I think we should get on board." She took the woman's arm to help her up the steps in the golden evening at Agate, Colorado.

PART FOUR

CALIFORNIA

How can an ex-huckster, ex-bellboy, ex-tailor, ex-advertising man, ex-bookmaker, know anything about picture quality? Hands that would be more properly employed with a pushcart on the lower East Side are responsible for directing stage plays and making pictures of them.
— MOVING PICTURE WORLD, 1910

There is nothing more absurd . . . nothing which destroys the art and beauty of the scene more than showing us greatly enlarged faces of the leading actors. . . . Many beautiful scenes are marred by showing these enlarged figures, with the head touching the very upper part of the frame, and the feet missing.
— MOVING PICTURE WORLD, 1911

The moving pictures may present figures greater than life size without loss of illusion. . . . Every change of expression is more clearly pictured than if they were truly before one, and one isn't embarrassed drinking the effect in.
— MOVING PICTURE WORLD, 1912

49. Welcome to Los Angeles

"Glendale. All out for Glendale."

The Southern Pacific conductor sounded as tired as she felt. She stared out the window not with wonder but despair. Torrential rain hammered the glass, gushed off the red-tiled roof of the Spanish–Moorish depot. She'd changed to the S.P. at Sacramento, ridden south through the sunbaked Central Valley, eager for her first views of the mountains surrounding Los Angeles. At Bakersfield clouds had closed in, bringing the deluge. Now she could barely see beyond the station sign.

"Conductor, what happened to the sunshine?"

"Rainy season. This way out."

She slipped and almost fell descending the metal steps. The wind would have torn her hat off but for the long pins. At the end of the platform four buggies and a muddy Pope-Toledo awaited the arriving passengers. She watched a young couple gratefully rush to the auto. Others from day coaches went to the buggies. Across a street that resembled a lake, two pathetic palm trees shook and rattled. The dispiriting scene was circumscribed by impenetrable gray murk. Where were the orange groves? Where were the suntanned natives?

"Excuse me," Fritzi said to a depot agent. "Someone from Los Angeles was supposed to meet me. Has anyone asked for a Miss Crown?"

"Nope. No one here except those rigs." Which were already rolling away through muddy waters. Fritzi huddled near the tan wall, to no avail; the wind assured her of a soaking. "Taxi man's yonder, by the far door," the agent said.

Fritzi picked up her valises and walked through the station. Each step squeezed water out of her shoes. Outside, a man leaned against a dented Ford flivver, holding an umbrella and chewing a toothpick. When he spied a potential customer he chewed faster.

She consulted a crumpled paper. "I'm to go to the Hollywood Hotel, at the corner of Hollywood Boulevard and Highland Avenue."

"I know where it is, lady. Way over on the other side of the hills. Never get there through the canyons in this weather. Got to head downtown, then out to Hollywood." The toothpick danced. "Four dollars."

"That sounds like robbery."

"Then take another taxi." The driver flicked his eyes at puddles on either side of his black auto.

Fritzi kicked one of her valises. "The least you can do is load those for me."

His day's profit made, the taxi driver grew friendly. "Why, yes, ma'am, and we'll be off in a jiffy."

According to publications she'd read for her journey, "the exotic jewel of Southern California" had grown to around three hundred fifty thousand people and was considered a boom town, friendly to free enterprise and hostile to trade unions. As the taxi lurched and banged toward the city, Fritzi saw only a very few signs of the exotic: a torn and faded billboard for the 1ST AMERICAN AVIATION MEET JAN 10–20 1910, another for the PASADENA TOURNAMENT OF ROSES, a New Year's parade she'd heard about. They passed through a neighborhood of cottages with oil derricks pumping away in side and back yards.

Frame and sandstone buildings three and four stories high clustered in the central business district. She saw a street sign for Broadway, but no spectacular theaters. Fences and blank walls were defaced by garish advertisements. LUMBER. DENTIST. STOVES, TIN & HARDWARE. BUILDING LOTS REDONDO BEACH — EXCEPTIONAL VALUE! A boxy black vehicle chugged by with a roof sign offering NEW CHEV. UTILITY COUPE $877. Los Angeles seemed little more than conventional office blocks and dry-goods emporiums, picture shows and barber shops like those found in cow towns on the prairie.

The usual urban clutter of wires crosshatched the sky above the streets. Large red trolleys ran on tracks in the center, clanging their bells, splattering mud, and intimidating persons or vehicles in their right of way. Fritzi saw the words PACIFIC ELECTRIC on several cars.

The driver detoured to the intersection of Hill and Third Streets to point out a civic showpiece, a tramway called Angel's Flight that carried people up and down a steep hillside. A block farther on, a steer with an enormous spread of horns bolted out of an alley, looked for a target, and charged the taxi. The desperate driver sounded his klaxon. Hardly fazed, the steer raked the side of the auto with the tip of a horn, uttered a baleful bellow, then lumbered on toward a woman in the middle of the street; she immediately fainted in her husband's arms. The steer trotted away as two men waving prods ran out of the alley in pursuit.

"Somebody forgot to shut a gate at the stockyards," the driver remarked.

"There's a stockyard here?"

"Oh, a big one. Place is kind of an overgrown farm town, y'know?"

She didn't know when she arrived, but she was learning fast.

The Hollywood Hotel, constructed in 1903, boasted a handsome cupola at its corner entrance. Atop the cupola an American flag waved bravely in the storm wind. The two-story hotel had a broad veranda and a comfortable, welcoming appearance. Its address was a misnomer, however. Hollywood "boulevard" was a dirt road full of mud holes. A trolley track ran down the center, and telephone poles marched away toward the city some four or five miles behind them. Hollywood the town looked empty, rural, and uncivilized — nothing but farmhouses, roadhouses, liveries, and small citrus groves with many desolate vacant lots in between.

"Is Hollywood a separate town, driver?"

"Was, but isn't anymore. The folks voted to annex to Los Angeles so they could hook up to the water. Engineer named Mulholland's bringing it down from the Owens Valley, two hundred fifty miles. Line should be finished in two, three years."

Fritzi gave the man a twenty-cent tip and handed her bags to a bellhop. In her modest but comfortable second-floor room she found a note of welcome from Sophie Pelzer, together with a bowl of golden California poppies and a small stack of flyers advertising houses and rooms to let. Sophie had marked these with arrows and underlines, and written a message on one. *All these areas are safe for young ladies, Mr. Pelzer made sure.*

She spent the rest of the day unpacking and listening to the rain and wondering about her future. After a quick supper in the hotel dining room she tumbled into bed with a distinct feeling of disappointment about California.

Next morning, while she was at breakfast, B.B. showed up. He operated her hand like a pump handle while apologizing for stranding her in Glendale. "I had this fella hired, he promised to be there. When I didn't hear from him by six last night, I ran over to the garage where he keeps his car. He said he wouldn't risk the car in the storm, so he didn't go to Glendale. By then I figured you'd either got here or hopped the next train back to New York, mad."

"The former," Fritzi said with a tolerant smile. "When may I start work?"

"Not until the weather's better and we finish

the outdoor stage. It's way behind schedule. I think the sunshine makes the locals lazy. I want you to see the lot we leased for a studio. It's in a little neighborhood called Edendale, ain't far from here. But there's no point in you swimming through mud to do it. Till the sun comes out you might as well look for a room. We'll pay taxis and carfare."

As if that was all it would take to relieve her feelings of gloom about this primitive and soggy place at the end of the continent.

The rain stopped. The sun came out. Steam rose from Hollywood's muddy roads, but not so much as to hide the hills framing the town to the north and northeast. West and south, the flat land ran to the ocean.

Flyers in hand, Fritzi set out to find a room. The weather allowed her to walk. Though she had to hike up her skirt to avoid puddles, it was a small price for a better view of the little residential community nestled in the largely empty countryside.

The homes she passed were conventional Victorian dwellings, usually two stories, mostly white with colorful shutters. They were widely scattered on the main and side streets, with two and three vacant lots between.

She marched up the walk to the veranda of a handsome clapboard residence on Selma, double-checked the number in the flyer, and knocked. She'd donned a pair of white gloves to attempt to look ladylike.

"I've come about the room," she said to the elderly man who answered the door. "Is it still available?"

"Yes, 'tis. Won't you step in?"

She followed him into a Victorian foyer properly cluttered with potted plants and bric-a-brac. A woman called from the kitchen, "Who is it, Herschel?"

"Young lady about the room." To Fritzi he said, "I'm Mr. Moore."

"Very pleased to know you, I'm Fritzi Crown."

"New in California, are you? This way," he said, heading for the staircase.

"I am. I've come out for a few months to make pictures."

She saw his back stiffen under his galluses. Rigid on the fourth step, he held the banister tightly for a moment before coming down to confront her.

"Do I understand you're a movie?"

"I'm afraid I don't know that word, Mr. Moore."

"Movie — someone who performs in pictures. The pictures move, they're movies. The actors move too, one room or hotel to the next, one step ahead of the sheriff or the credit man." He emphasized this with a wild swing of his arm that almost clipped her nose. "Never know whether they'll skip out in the night without paying what they owe. Folks in this town don't like movies. You should go back East where you came from, you're not wanted here."

Mr. Moore observed his wife in the hallway, wiping her floured hands on her apron. He coughed nervously and said to Fritzi, "Nothing personal, you understand."

"Oh, no, of course not. I'm sorry I troubled you."

Worse was in store the next afternoon, Sunday. Fritzi rode a Pacific Electric trolley to Santa Monica to look at a two-room flat. The ocean was two blocks away, breaking and crashing sonorously.

A lank woman with wrinkled gray skin opened the door. Sunlight through panels of stained glass luridly illuminated a stack of circulars on a table. CHRISTIAN CRUSADE FOR WHOLESOME ENTERTAINMENT. A subsidiary line identified its home as Pasadena.

"It is not my habit to do business on the Lord's day, young woman."

"Well, your ad didn't mention that. I have a feeling I should tell you I'm an actress in pictures."

The lank woman snatched a circular and thrust it at her. "Read this. You ungodly people should get down on your knees and beg the Lord's forgiveness. You're poisoning minds with your filth and vulgarity."

"Pardon me, I'm not out to poison anyone or anything. I'm only trying to rent —"

The woman interrupted, waving her arms and shouting. Fritzi heard "Christian values," "Satan's work," and "whore of Babylon" before she fled. She threw the pamphlet into the gutter, then felt guilty about littering and retrieved it. She fanned herself with the paper, thinking, If the crusade soldiers are all like her, I hope I never meet the general.

In seven more tries over the next three days, she found nothing except discouragement. At one house a placard had been tacked by the door to forestall conversation.

NO JEWS, NO PETS, NO ACTORS

She began to feel she'd die an old maid at the Hollywood Hotel. She had developed an active loathing for the narrow-minded citizens of Hollywood. In a town like this, the pictures — no, the *movies*, she must remember they were called that out here, along with the people who acted in them — in Hollywood the movies had no future. None.

As she ate lunch in the hotel dining room, she noticed a young woman watching her from another table. The girl was on the plump side, with a round, plain face enlivened by striking blue eyes and a lot of curly red hair that gleamed like a halo. She'd seen the young woman in the lobby the night before. Then as now she looked tired, as though she stayed up late. The girl walked over to Fritzi.

"I've seen you reading ads for days. Are you looking for a place to live?"

"Yes, and I'm having no luck. It seems all the landlords in this town hate picture people. Movies, they call them now."

The girl nodded. "I had to go all the way to Venice to find a spot. But I did, the whole second floor of a nice house near the beach. With its own inside privy," the girl said with a smile Fritzi found engaging. The girl extended her hand. "My name's Lily Madison."

"Fritzi Crown. It's really Frederica, but I hate that. Will you sit down?"

"For a minute. I'm moving today." Lily pulled up a chair. Her clothes weren't expensive, but they were well chosen for her coloring: a stylish shirtwaist of black lawn, embroidered with small green flowers; a pale green linen skirt; a racy dark gray cap; mannish oxfords with shiny patent leather tips. All very nobby, as Hobart would say.

"I assume you work for a picture company, then?" the girl asked.

"Pal Pictures. I believe their lot's in Edendale. I haven't seen it yet. Are you an actress?"

"Oh, no. I write stories. That is, I'm trying. I just sold one to Nestor, a silly little melodrama about a bank robbery. I got fifteen dollars for it."

"Congratulations. Is that your ambition, to write scenarios?"

"Yes. I like the life down here. The picture business is fun. The people are fun. And I like to make up stories. I'm think I'm pretty good at it, I've had lots of practice. When I was growing up and it was a gray day or something bad happened in school, I'd run off to my room and write a story on my chalk slate. Not very long, a slate's not that big, you know? But I always felt better afterward."

"I can understand that. Where's your home, Lily?"

She didn't answer for a moment. "Santa Rosa. Hick town north of San Francisco."

"Oh, yes," Fritzi said vaguely.

"Look, I don't mean to be forward, but I'm eager to find someone to share expenses."

"You mean your landlord would tolerate two movies under one roof?"

Lily laughed. "Yes, Mr. Hong will. Mr. Hong runs a little chop suey house near the Venice pier. His grandfather came to California from Canton in the Gold Rush, but Mr. Hong's still barred from all kinds of places in California. He understands having doors slammed in your face. He's a third-generation American, and he still has to sleep with a shotgun, he showed it to me."

Fritzi pondered. "Isn't Venice a long way from this part of town?"

"Not all that far by trolley. You take the Venice branch into the city, that's about a half hour. The cars run about every twenty minutes on weekdays. The cars are clean, and on a sunny day the ride's very pleasant. I guarantee you'd like Mr. Hong's house. There's a small room in front converted to a parlor, and two big bedrooms." Fritzi liked it sight unseen; Lily Madison's enthusiasm was infectious.

Lily jumped up. "Come look at it, won't you? If you don't like it, there's no obligation. Tell you what. I'll even pay the delivery man fifty cents to bring you back."

"Yes, why not?" Fritzi said, pleased.

Lily took her hand, and they started for the street like a couple of school chums. Maybe her search was over.

Venice, California, down on the tidal flats of Santa Monica Bay, was no Venice, Italy, though the developer, one Abbot Kinney, had hoped to duplicate the great city in miniature when he opened the tract in 1904. He built pretty canals, but now they were fouled by decomposing cabbages and orange peels and, Fritzi was horrified to see on her walk from the trolley, someone's four-legged friend floating in a state of rigor mortis.

The homes along the canals seemed well tended, though not opulent. To the west, where the sun glittered on the sea, a Ferris wheel revolved in silhouette and a calliope chirped "Ah, Sweet Mystery of Life." Fritzi said, "What's down there, an amusement park?"

"Yes, rides and booths along the boardwalk," Lily nodded. "That part of town's doing better than around here." Which was evident from two For Sale signs and several more saying To Let.

The neat and compact house of Mr. and Mrs. Hong backed up on one of the less odorous waterways. Lily let herself in with a key; the owners were already at their chop suey palace, as she called it. With a lively step she led Fritzi up the stairway in the center of the front hall. At the top, slightly to the left, was the precious private bathroom she'd mentioned. Floored in small white tiles, octagon-shaped, it was dominated by a throne-like water closet with a wooden wall tank and pull chain. The claw-footed tub looked strong as a small battleship.

Lily took her hand and drew her to the front

sitting room. Tall windows flooded the old but serviceable furniture with a golden patina. Mrs. Hong had placed several potted palms around the room to create a sense of being in a garden. Curtains of sun-yellowed lace fluttered and snapped. The smell of the salt sea blew on the afternoon breeze.

"So much light, it's wonderful," Fritzi exclaimed.

Lily grinned. "That's California. You'll get used to it."

Lily's spacious bedroom was on the left as you faced the front of the house. The other, on the right next to the stairs, was only half as large, but furnished with a good dresser, an upright wardrobe with a long mirror on the door, a side table and chair, a single bed, and three electric lamps. The Hongs clearly weren't cheapskates bent on gouging their tenants.

Sounding a little breathless, Lily said, "Do you like it?"

"Perfect. Oh, there's one thing. Are we allowed to cook?"

"There's no gas up here. Mrs. Hong lets me use the kitchen. She and her husband leave early and come home late, so they're hardly around. Can you cook?"

"No."

"I can, but I hate it. Actually, I hoped for a roomie whose father was a chef," Lily teased.

"I can fry bread in a skillet, and salt and pepper a boiled egg. We'll manage. How much is the rent?"

"Five dollars a week, or eighteen if Mrs.

Hong's paid by the month. She's a shrewd lady. Gets by on very few words. Your share would be ten dollars a month, or nine if we pay all at once."

"It's a bargain. I'll move in if you'll have me."

"Sure!" Lily squeezed her arm as they trooped down the stairs. "We're going to get along just fine. Let's have a beer. I know a place on the boardwalk that serves ladies. Game?"

Feeling good at last, Fritzi replied with an enthusiastic yes.

50. Wrong Turn

Carl drank from the double shot glass. The fiery whiskey slid down his throat as he set the glass aside. He watched the surface shimmer and grow still. The base of his skull ached. Whether it was nerves or the residual effect of his crash a few months ago, he didn't know. He'd picked up a ride in a Marmon, for a road race over the superb Savannah course built by chain gangs for the 1908 Grand Prize, an event sponsored by the American Automobile Club, the friendly enemy of the AAA. The course was crushed gravel, heavily oiled, winding through tidal wetlands, palmettos, and live oaks. He was running out in front by two car lengths when the tire blew. He never remembered striking a tree head first.

He stared at the double whiskey, his fourth of the night. The tavern tucked behind the sand dunes on the shore road in Ormond Beach was empty. The party had fallen apart when Barney went to the hospital.

Carl noticed the barkeep pouring liniment on a rag which he rubbed on his wrist. Carl said, "Were you in the fight?"

"Nah, this is from pulling corks. I never pulled so many corks in so many quarts so fast in all my life."

"When Barney Oldfield celebrates, he celebrates."

"If that's what you call it," the barkeep said

with a glance at the smashed chairs and tables. An elderly black man in plow shoes and a torn baseball jersey pushed a broom to clean up broken glass. Carl drank again. How could a day so fine end so badly?

It was Barney's temperament. Everywhere he went, he whored and gambled, drank and started fights.

That afternoon, in front of a roaring crowd that spilled over the dunes to watch, Barney had broken his own one-mile straightaway speed record of 132, set last year when he broke the 1906 record of 127.5 set by Fred Marriott. Under a cloudless Florida sky, with gentle white combers rolling in, carrying the smell of the salt sea, Barney drove his newest racer onto the hard-packed sand of Daytona, long a favorite place for challenging a record. Barney's 200-h.p. Benz was a chain-driven, bullet-shaped monster, white, with a gigantic four-cylinder engine cast in two blocks — the "Blitzen."

After he'd taken Bess for a practice run, he'd jammed fresh cotton plugs in his ears, crunched a cigar stub in his teeth, snapped on his goggles, and gave the thumbs-up sign. He drove up the beach, turned back, and accelerated to start his run. Carl was standing with the team manager, Will Pickens, watching through binoculars.

Smoke and flame gouted from the rear of the Blitzen. Pickens grabbed the binoculars. Carl's teeth clenched as the car howled back toward the timing stand. Pickens exclaimed, "Jesus Christ, he must be doing a hundred thirty-five at least.

His wheels are flying off the ground. If he blows a tire or hits anything —"

The Blitzen tore by with a sound like a bomb detonating. The crowd screamed. The car shrank into the south, then came back through the trailing smoke as the chief judge, nearly hysterical, shouted out the official new record — 133.4. An honest one this time.

Oil-spattered and grinning, Barney had signed autographs for nearly an hour. Then, as the sun dropped behind the western scrub land, he'd asked the location of the nearest saloon or roadhouse.

Two hours later Will Pickens had rushed him to a hospital with his scalp torn open and bleeding all over his face like a red waterfall. Carl stayed behind in the bar where the brawl had taken place, drinking.

Now it was dark. Carl's head buzzed. His mouth tasted sour. He watched a fly crawl over hard-boiled eggs spoiling on a plate on the bar while the black man's broom moved the pile of glass inches at a time. No hiding from the truth any longer. The dream Carl had chased to Indianapolis was a little dirty at the edges.

He heard the beach-side door open but didn't turn; he didn't care who came in.

The barkeep's surprised expression changed his mind. He swung around slowly, feeling heavy, tired. The moon was up, casting phosphorescent light on the sea visible through the door. A woman walked to the bar. He smelled her before he recognized her. The perfume she wore was something like lily of the valley; he remembered his mother using that. His eyes focused.

"Bess."

"I hoped you might still be here." Barney's wife avoided a direct look at Carl as she put her purse on the bar. Her white lace dress, crisp and pretty in the afternoon, was wrinkled and sweat-damp over her breasts. To the barkeep she said, "Give me a whiskey. Leave the bottle. Then leave us alone."

With a twitch that might have been a smirk, the barkeep served up a bottle and glass, then walked around the end of the bar into a back room. To the black man Bess said, "Lay off the goddamn broom and give us some air." The man grabbed a chair, caught a dangling cord that swung three connected heart-shaped palmetto fans on the ceiling. He sat down and worked the cord back and forth, moving the fans and stirring a little air.

Carl said, "How's Barney?"

"Took the doctor two hours to sew up the worst, and he wasn't finished when I left. He'll be all right. Barney's got a hard head. That's because there are no brains in it." This was the side of Bess the press and public never saw. When she hung on Barney's arm during interviews, she was lively, affectionate, always praising him. Bess was a sensually handsome woman with a big tolerance for suffering.

"He'll be good as new when the sun's up," she said, as though scornful of it. She swallowed her whiskey, poured another and swallowed that.

"I don't know how he does it," Carl said.

"You're right, he'll get up with a bandaged head and drive like a demon if that's what he decides to do. I can't drink that way."

"Looks like you're doing it tonight."

"Yeah, well, being around Barney sort of wears you out."

"Tell me something that's news."

She poured more whiskey. The fans squeaked. The Atlantic surf murmured like a seducer; the ocean sparkled with moonlight, all the way out to Europe. Carl pinched the inner corners of his eyes but couldn't clear his vision.

Bess's pale, soft hand lay on his sleeve. He hadn't seen or felt it descend.

"Carl. I don't owe Barney anything anymore. He's cheated on me a million times. If you come right down to it, he isn't very original either. Just another dumb hick who got rich too fast and doesn't know how to handle it. He's a fancy racecar, but they forgot the brakes. You, though. You're different." She licked her lip, checked to be sure the barkeep was still gone. Her fingers closed.

"Keep me company tonight."

Sweat drew the white dress down to a wet valley between her breasts. Carl's tongue felt thick as a piece of wood. Tempted, he gazed at her for a while before he said, "Don't think that's a good idea."

"The boss's wife? He'll never know."

"We would."

Anger made her sneer. "Little Lord Fauntleroy? I thought you were better than that." She slammed her glass on the bar. "You pay for the whiskey. I came all the way back here for nothing."

She walked out, silver as a ghost in the moonlight before she disappeared. Soon he heard the putter of an auto. He said to the old black man, "You can stop that."

"Yessir."

The barkeep walked out of the back room. Carl happened to be glancing at the floor. A large brown cockroach with twitching antennae stepped slowly, deliberately, over the toe of his boot.

"Party over?" the barkeep asked.

Carl shook his foot. The cockroach dropped off, and he stepped on it hard, breaking its horny brown back.

"It never started. How much for this whole bottle?"

Next day, about noon, having eaten nothing because he had the heaves most of the night, Carl sat at a wicker table on the porch of a Daytona rooming house where the team had put up. Barney was recuperating nicely at his hotel, though the suturing of his scalp had taken four hours. Under Carl's sleeve lay the *Florida Times Union* from Jacksonville, with triumphant front-page headlines.

BARNEY OLDFIELD UNDISPUTED SPEED KING OF THE UNIVERSE.

HUMAN THUNDERBOLT SETS NEW RECORD.

Kaiser Personally Telegraphs Champion —
"GREAT VICTORY IN GERMAN AUTO."

Carl licked the tip of a pencil, picked up a postcard showing an orange grove in sickly colors. He turned it over, wrote slowly.

Dear Tess, how are you? I am not so hot these days. Am starting to think I made a bad mistake joining up with "B"

He stopped there. Read the little he'd written. What did it really mean? Should he leave the team? It would be a lot to give up. There wasn't much to like about Barney Oldfield, but there was plenty to admire. The man had no nerves, and almost unlimited courage.

Or maybe he was just unhinged, which amounted to the same thing.

Carl loved driving. He loved the scream of wind past his goggles, the rising roar as he flamed down the stretch toward a packed grandstand. He loved wrestling the great cars he thought of as wild animals made of iron and wire and tubing with gas coursing through instead of blood.

He loved the rush of young girls to Barney's garage after a fairgrounds appearance. There were always plenty, and if Bess was nearby Barney couldn't touch any of them, not right then. Any single man could find a partner for the night unless he was deaf, dumb, and stupid.

All of the giddy girls left a hollow feeling, though. None was Tess. He could never care for any of them as he still cared for her.

He grimaced at the card, threw the pencil over a startled chameleon straddling the porch rail. He tore the card in pieces and stuffed them in his shirt pocket. She didn't want to hear his troubles. Christ, by now she might be married to that fool Wayne, or someone else.

He sat on the porch as the wet heat ripened and drenched him in his own sweat. The sun broiled his eyes; finally he had to raise his hand and shield them. The base of his skull hurt again. He wondered where this dangerous drift was carrying him.

51. Liberty Rising

Fritzi left the big red car at Sunset and Alessandro, in the district called Edendale. Following B.B.'s directions, she walked north in the morning sunshine, avoiding puddles in the road that hadn't completely dried. Even in damp winter a hint of sweet roses and oranges pleased the air.

Edendale was rural, mostly stables, one or two ramshackle stores, some cottages and shanties. After nearly a mile she saw Pal's stout owner waving a hanky from the front of a weedy lot.

"You found it. Sorry for the walk. You won't have to ride shank's mare too much longer. I'll shop for the car soon." B.B. worked her hand while she cast a suspicious eye at what appeared to be distinctly rundown real estate.

"Well, what do you think of it?"

Fritzi shaded her eyes with her palm. "It's very — large."

"Three point eight acres. We got a good lease, for the whole year, even though we'll head back to New York come spring." He urged her forward through yellowed weeds that left tiny burrs on her skirt. "Couldn't do it any other way. Fella who used to own it hacked up his wife and went to prison. Property's in the hands of a bank."

"That's heartwarming," Fritzi said under her breath.

They went up the rotted steps to the main

house, a weather-battered relic with peeling paint and shutters hanging by a single hinge. Somewhere out back hammers rang. She thought she heard Eddie's voice.

"Offices will be in here and upstairs," B.B. said as she dodged a cobweb in the entrance. "Al's already set up in the dining room. He's staying in a hotel downtown, like me. There's a study or den we'll fix up for a projection room. Hello, Al." B.B. waved at his partner. Kelly was seated behind a massive dining room table littered with bills, trade papers, and account books.

Kelly greeted them with a grunt, handed Fritzi a blue-covered document. "Your contract. Look it over and sign before you go."

"We start a new Lone Indian picture in two days," B.B. said. "Till they finish the stage we'll shoot outdoors, place that Eddie found called Daisy Dell." Fritzi examined the document, a stupefying blur of therefores and whereases. Something in the first paragraph caught her eye.

"This contract's with something called Liberty Pictures."

"We got a new partner," Kelly said.

"That's right. He's bringing in a lot of working capital," B.B. said.

"Who is he?"

Kelly answered. "Name's Ham Hayman. One of Benny's Hebraic kinsmen. From up in Frisco. Started as a furrier but switched to moving pictures."

"Al, how many times I got to tell you? People are calling them motion pictures now. *Motion.*"

Explaining to Fritzi: "Lots of bad reaction to pictures moving all the time. Moving, jittering — it makes people nervous. Motion sounds classier. I read it in the *World*."

Kelly said, "Hayman runs one theater, but he isn't primarily an exhibitor, he's an exchange man. Owns a string of 'em all the way through Nevada to Colorado and down to Arizona. Independent," Kelly added, as though he smelled bad cheese. "I told B.B. it's a mistake to throw in with independent exchanges. We should join the trust and distribute through Kennedy's General Filmco."

"We bought the new camera, that's enough." B.B. soothed Fritzi: "Don't you worry, the independents are doing just fine. Getting stronger and stronger. Day before yesterday I heard Gaumont of Paris is about to pull out of the trust, and Eastman's about to start selling raw stock to everybody, not just trust companies. Carl Laemmle at IMP has a slogan — 'Bust the trust' — well, it's happening."

Fritzi said, "That's all very fine, but I don't understand the name change."

"For his capital Hayman gets some leverage," Kelly told her. "Hayman says a horse bit him when he was nine. The pony had to go."

"We already have a swell new symbol picked out," B.B. said.

"Let me guess. The Statue of Liberty?"

"Give the girl a prize," Kelly said. "Sign the contract today, Fritzi." He bent his head over a ledger, as if she and B.B. didn't exist.

Pleased as a father with a new infant, B.B. took

her out through the dusty kitchen to a barn that would store scenery and house the company's property and paint shops. "Dressing rooms over here." Fritzi was dismayed. He was pointing at horse stalls that smelled of manure. "Don't worry, don't worry, we'll hang up blankets."

The center of activity seemed to be the rear of the lot, specifically a primitive construction B.B. proudly referred to as their stage. She saw carpenters on ladders, and two familiar faces — Eddie and Jock Ferguson, who was tinkering with an unfamiliar camera. Was this the new one B.B. had referred to?

"Right, it's a Bianchi," he said. "Named after the Eyetalian who used to work for Edison. Jock says it's lousy. Breaks down all the time. The image shakes and shimmies like Little Egypt. But it don't violate any patents. We'll shoot with old faithful but keep this one for display. If detectives show up, it should keep them scratching their heads, huh?"

He chuckled, but the beautiful sunshine had a touch of chill suddenly. She saw Pearly again, the moment he fell under the train at City Hall station. She often had nightmares about it.

Jock kissed her cheek to welcome her. Eddie escorted her onto the stage, a large rectangular platform with a bare wooden floor. "We can shoot at least two interiors at the same time," he said. "Three if we crowd them together. B.B. and Kelly want to step up production to three reels a week — one comedy, one drama, one western or Indian picture. That's the standard for successful independents."

B.B. planted himself in front of Fritzi, cheerful as a cherub. "Well, my gel, what's your opinion now?"

Somewhat bewildered, she smiled. "There's certainly a lot happening."

"And you're part of it. A big part."

Eddie put his arm around her. "The new Indian scenario's ready if you want to read it."

She said, "Of course."

Fritzi's bewilderment became amazement. The winds of change were certainly blowing. A new partner was already putting his mark on the company, which had a new name. A new camera was operating on a new site called a lot. In this strange new business both the product and the people were "movies."

She'd never admit it to Hobart, or any of her Broadway chums, but she was suddenly eager to go to work.

Ham Hayman made his first appearance in late January, having moved from the Bay Area to Los Angeles to work more directly in production. He was a small, fastidious man with pale hands, curly hair, and foxy eyes.

Eddie said Hayman not only provided much needed production capital, but paid a ten percent premium into the partnership for every finished and delivered negative. For this he had exclusive distribution rights to all Liberty pictures within the territory covered by his exchanges.

Hayman showed up regularly on the lot,

bringing with him strong opinions which he shared with actors, crew — anyone within earshot. One of them led to a certain person being hired.

"How can we speed up production without more scripts? We need a regular story department," Hayman complained within Fritzi's hearing. She didn't forget the remark. At an opportune moment she politely asked B.B. to talk to a young woman of her acquaintance who had sold one or two scenarios. Fritzi slipped a reference to Hayman into the conversation. B.B. cheerfully agreed.

That night Lily dithered with excitement while Fritzi counseled her about the meeting two days hence. "Take the stories you've sold, and anything you're working on. You want to impress him that you're literary."

"Hell, that's the last thing I am, literary," Lily said, with a lift of one shoulder that pushed her breast forward inside her blouse, which was thin and quite revealing. The moment seemed to speak eloquently of what Lily was and was not.

"Haven't you read any novels or poetry?"

"I like Poe, his scary stuff. And Dickens, I've read a few of his. Big words but interesting characters."

"Can you quote anything from either one?"

"Come on, Fritzi. I could hardly wait to get out the school door when I was legal age to leave."

Fritzi sat beside her on the bed in the larger bedroom, pondering. "Then we need to work up something that might charm Mr. Pelzer. Something worthy but not too obscure." She thought of a dozen poems she'd committed to memory in school. "Tennyson. He's just right. Listen to this."

On her feet, she put her palm on her bosom and declaimed:

"Break, break, break,
On thy cold gray stones, O sea!
And I would that my tongue could utter
The thoughts that arise in me."

Lily lifted her flounced skirt and scratched her thigh. "I don't get it."

"That isn't important so long as you sound like you do. It can mean whatever you want — the thoughts that arise can be all the stories spilling out of your head so fast you can hardly write them down."

Dubious, Lily stared at her. "If you say so."

Riding the red cars on the appointed morning, Fritzi was as nervous as her friend. She'd begged Lily to put only a faint dab of rouge on each cheek, not overdoing it as she did when she went out at night. Lily wore her most demure dress. Outside the main house, Fritzi squeezed Lily's hand. "Don't let him scare you. He's a very nice man. Good luck."

She could barely concentrate on her work with Eddie for the next hour. About half past nine, she finished a take, paused to dab her perspiring forehead with a hanky, and saw Lily dashing past the barn toward the stage, waving. Fritzi ran to meet her.

"What happened?"

"I'm hired. I'm the story department — a whole twenty dollars a week until you go back to New York."

"Lily, that's wonderful." They danced each other around in an improvised polka that amused Jock Ferguson and Eddie.

"There's more. Mr. Pelzer said that if I work out, I can have the job when the company comes back next winter. I owe it all to you. He *loves* Tennyson."

Another one of Hayman's great ideas led to someone being fired.

While Fritzi changed clothes in a smelly horse stall, she overheard the partners arguing outside the barn.

Hayman: "Kalem's putting out a list of the actors with every release."

B.B.: "I dunno, Ham, it's the brand name sells the picture. In the *World* one exhibitor said he advertises 'A new Biograph every day.' "

Hayman: "Phooey. You get letters asking about the actors, don't you?"

B.B.: "A few for Owen, lots more for Fritzi. But —"

Hayman: "Tell the names. *Sell* the names. They did it with Florence Lawrence pictures."

Kelly: "*After* she left Biograph. Biograph doesn't pump up anybody else."

Hayman: "They're nuts. They got the most valuable actors in America. Mary Pickford's getting a big build-up since she and her hubby left them for Laemmle's IMP outfit."

Kelly: "I'm warning you. Publicize personalities, they'll want more money."

Hayman: "So what? If we have stars people know and want to see, we'll make more money. Change, Al — change! It's like the ocean. It's always there, you can't fight it, but it'll carry you to fabulous new places if you let it."

B.B.: "I like this man's thinking."

Fritzi listened to a heavy tread she presumed to be Al Kelly stomping away from the discussion, outvoted.

For her next picture, *The Lone Indian's Escape*, they returned to the rugged and isolated area of North Highland known as Daisy Dell. About noon on the first day, B.B. arrived in a taxi and hiked down a rough trail to the spot where the company had set up Owen's tepee. Excited, he showed a picture postal card bearing a photograph of a stout hook-nosed man in cowboy clothes.

"Found this yesterday, selling for a nickel at a theater. Ain't it a swell idea?" Fritzi studied the legend with the photo.

ESSANAY LEADING MAN "BRONCO BILLY" ANDERSON

"Like it, Owen? Like to have your name and your mug on one of these?"

"Anything you say, B.B." Owen folded his grease-painted arms and gave Fritzi a smug look. B.B. rushed around the crude camp table where cast and crew had been consuming sandwiches and tepid tea.

"How about you, Fritzi?"

Surprised, she could only point at herself. Before she could add, "Me?" Owen jumped up with all the feathers of his great war bonnet quivering.

"Wait a minute, who's the star of these pictures, may I ask?"

B.B.'s brow wrinkled in a studious way. "Why, Owen, based on the numbers of letters she gets and you get, I'd have to tell you" — he laid his arm over the sun-dappled shoulders of Fritzi's pioneer dress — "it's this little gel."

Owen turned a distinctly darker shade of reddish-brown. "Oh, yes? Well, Mr. Pelzer, I'm not happy to hear that. I'm not happy at all. Her parts get bigger while mine stay the same. I tell you I don't like it."

To show how much he didn't like it, he tore off his war bonnet and threw it down and kicked it.

"We're having a talk about this, Mr. Pelzer."

"Sure, sure, drop in tomorrow and —"

"Right now."

B.B. sighed. "Okay." He and Owen hiked back up the trail. Owen's little talk lasted forty-five minutes, putting them behind schedule and seriously irking Eddie. The talk resumed in the studio office when the company returned at sunset. It was never clear whether Pelzer, the gentlest of men, fired Owen, or he simply quit. Fritzi didn't learn the news until she reported next morning.

"I want to know how we finish the damn picture," Kelly said.

"We find another Big Chief Hot Air," B.B.

said. "I finally had to tell Owen nobody's really watching him." He captured Fritzi's hand. "This is the one we got to take care of, Al. This little gel is the star."

The *star?* No one had ever used the word in reference to Fritzi. She knew she should be thrilled. In a certain way she was. Mostly she was terrified. She imagined herself on a raft being pulled irretrievably into a dark whirlpool, the movies, while distantly on the shore, Broadway lights twinkled and Ellen Terry waved a sad but resigned farewell.

52. Fritzi and Carl

"Sit down, woman."

"But that driver in the yellow car is my brother."

"D'you hear me? Sit." The man in the row behind gave her sleeve a rude yank. Fritzi turned and hit him with her handbag, a light glancing blow.

"Stand up if you can't see, you bully."

The scruffy man saw the fire in her eyes and stood on his seat rather than argue.

The three cars, Barney Oldfield's white one, a green one, and Carl's yellow racer took the starting flag and roared off for the second heat. Fritzi jumped up and down along with hundreds of others packed into the wooden amphitheater. "Come on, Carl. Beat him, beat him."

Fritzi had never seen a racetrack like this one at Playa del Rey, within sight and sound of the Pacific. Basically a saucer surrounded by a high grandstand, the racing surface was Oregon fir overlaid with crushed shells for traction. The board track was banked all the way around, and from the top of the grandstand there was a fine view eastward to the mountains, west to the sunlit ocean.

This Sunday, the last day of April, Fritzi had no illusions about Carl beating Oldfield. He'd written to explain the rigged exhibition races. Even so, natural excitement and sisterly affection drove her to cheer wildly when Carl won the second heat by a length.

Gas and oil fumes mingled in the exhaust smoke rising off the track. In the final heat, two laps from the finish, Oldfield suddenly cut in front of Carl, clipping his left front fender as he passed. The impact sent Carl toward the grandstand wall, then into a spin when he corrected. Oldfield shot ahead. The third driver veered to the inner rail and scraped along it, narrowly avoiding Carl, who spun to a stop and killed his engine. Fritzi kept her knuckles pressed against her teeth until Carl restarted his motor and chugged out of the way of Oldfield, who was coming around again without slowing.

Carl finished a bad last, leaving the track while Oldfield took a victory lap. She couldn't help feeling let down and angry. Oldfield had been reckless, almost involving her brother in an accident.

She fought her way down the stairs through the crowd afterward. The track garage was packed with hangers-on, heavy with smoke, everyone joking and shouting. Fritzi spied Carl off by himself, climbing out of an oil-stained coverall. She caught her breath when she saw a nasty purplish bruise on his left cheek, just above a smear of grease.

"Carl?" She waved and pushed toward him. He turned, and she got another shock. His right eye was barely visible in the slit between swollen and discolored eyelids.

"Sis, my Lord, how are you?" He flung his arms around her, bending over with an enthusi-

465

astic hug. She drew back in his arms, gently touched his bruised and grimy face. "What on earth is all this?"

"The eye? A little fracas last night. On the way to town we stopped for a few beers at a roadhouse in Ventura and — never mind, it isn't serious."

"Could you see to drive?"

"Just enough. I'm through for the day. Want to meet the great man before we go?"

"Of course," she said hesitantly, puzzled by the curious note of reluctance when he asked.

Carl turned his shoulder and thrust through the crowd like a Princeton lineman. She said, "How long will you be in town?"

"Till the end of the week."

"That's grand. We can see the sights. Mr. Pelzer, who runs Liberty pictures, said I could have time off to be with you. My director even rearranged the shooting schedule."

They found the Speed King in the midst of a group of admirers. His oily race goggles were pushed up on his unruly hair. An attractive dark-haired woman hung on his arm. She gave Carl an unfriendly look as they approached. Fritzi was shocked by Oldfield's sallow skin, the pouches under his red, watering eyes. Though a relatively young man, he looked old and dissipated.

"Barney, I'd like you to meet my sister, Fritzi. Sis, Barney and Bess Oldfield." Mrs. Oldfield stared at her, plainly hostile.

"Pleased to meet you," Barney said. "Your kid brother, huh?" Fritzi nodded. "He's a good wheel man. Sometimes too good. Hope you enjoyed the show. Come on, sweet." He pushed his wife and they walked off.

Fritzi pinned her hat as she left the noisy garage. "Carl, is something going on? Your boss seemed sore."

"The king lost his throne last Sunday," Carl said as they followed people toward the Pacific Electric stop. "In Daytona a young kid named Wild Bob Burman broke Barney's land speed record. To make it worse, he drove one of Barney's old cars. Barney's been on a tear all week. Last night at the roadhouse there was an altercation. With people he didn't know."

"Who started it?"

"Barney, after half a quart of whiskey. Three of us pulled him off, which he didn't appreciate. He socked me a couple of times."

"Oh, that's terrible. Why do you work for him?"

"I've been wondering that myself," Carl said. "Give me five minutes to clean up, and we'll get out of here."

When he rejoined her, his face was washed, his hands too. He'd put on a loose jacket and wrapped a dashing red silk scarf around his neck.

Back in Venice, they crossed Lion Canal on an arched footbridge as the spring daylight faded. She showed him where she lived. They strolled on several of the residential islands, then returned to the boardwalk. Within sight of the new and noisy Cloud Race roller coaster, they found a small German restaurant for supper. Carl rammed through the door like the spirited little

467

boy she remembered. He didn't simply sit in his chair, he dropped, making the chair creak and the waiter gasp.

Over platters of pork chops, cabbage, roast potatoes, and Crown's beer, they caught up on things. The easiest topic to start on was their parents.

"What's Pop going to do if the drys win and we have national prohibition?" Carl asked her.

"I can't speak with any authority. I don't see Papa or hear from him."

"Same old problem, huh? Too bad."

Fritzi looked away, wanting to avoid the subject. "I suppose Crown's and all the other breweries will have to close. Or manufacture something else that's legal."

"That'd kill Pop."

She sighed to agree.

Gradually Carl lost some of his tense, tired air. He talked with enthusiasm of his new interest in learning to fly aeroplanes. For dessert he ate two slabs of mince pie with ice cream.

Describing a driving exhibition in Denver, he mentioned a girl named Sissie. Fritzi said, "I also recall a Margaret, and one of your letters talked about someone in El Paso. Forgive me for being a nosy sister, but are you ever going to marry one of them?"

Carl's face grew grave. "Not likely. There was one I really cared about, up in Detroit. Her name was Tess. Her father and his pals were a pretty snotty bunch, but she was different. She was a wonderful lady. I thought hard about staying, trying to make it work out, but — I don't know. Something pushed me on. Something always does."

With a puzzled smile he added, "Sometimes I wonder if it's Pop. Maybe I'm scared he'll drag me back to Chicago somehow, and I'll have to deal with him every day for the rest of my life. I love him, but he's a tyrant. Hell, who knows?" He grabbed his coffee mug, almost spilling it. Still clumsy as a puppy, she thought, touched. She was aware of him changing the subject:

"How about your life, sis? Any men in it?"

"Not presently, no."

"What about the actors in pictures? Aren't some of them pretty handsome?"

"Yes, but they all seem to fall into three categories. Married and happy. Married and cheating. Or madly in love with themselves."

He laughed. "You care about settling down sometime, don't you?"

"Well, I have my career to think about. When we're back in New York this summer, I'm going to try the theater again. I've always said picture making's temporary."

"Sis, answer the question."

"Of course I care about settling down. I have feelings. I'm not a female eunuch." She tilted her head. "Are there female eunuchs?"

"I doubt it. Keep looking for your man. You'll find him."

To escape the subject she opened her handbag and drew out a picture postcard. "Here, I've been meaning to show you."

When he saw the photo, he exclaimed, "Hey, it's you." Indeed it was Fritzi, posed rather coyly in a frilly dress and picture hat, with printing beneath.

FRITZI CROWN
A Liberty Pictures Favorite

"Two of our other actors have cards. Theaters sell the cards for a nickel. My boss's idea. You'll meet him when I show you the lot."

At the end of three days Carl's bruises didn't look much better, but he seemed in better spirits, having been separated from his employer for a while. In an ice cream parlor, they sat on wire chairs beside a plate-glass window, eating chocolate cones. It was her last day with him. Saturday the Oldfield troupe headed for San Diego; tomorrow, and the rest of the week, she'd be working.

She brought up the subject she'd so far held in reserve. "You didn't tell me Barney Oldfield opened a saloon on Spring Street."

"He and a partner, some joe who used to work for a railroad." Carl licked a gob of ice cream about to fall off the cone. "Barney let the other guy do most of the setup. The saloon's one of the reasons we came to Los Angeles. I didn't mention it because I can't take you there."

"Why not?"

"It's a men's hangout. If it's anything like Barney himself, it'll be a rough place." He hesitated but went on. "Everywhere we travel, seems like there's a fight. Barney usually starts them. He plays nasty practical jokes on strangers."

"You really don't like working for him, do you?"

"Not anymore. Before I signed on, I couldn't think of anything better. I've gotten a belly full. Barney's great when he's sober. But the rest of the time, which is most of the time, he treats his help like dirt. All the money and fame did something to him, and it's a hell of a lot worse since Burman broke his speed record. You saw what happened at the oval."

"Did he hit your car deliberately?"

"I don't think so. He doesn't think straight, is the problem. He's in a rage all the time."

"Will you quit?"

"I think about it a lot."

"If you quit, what would you do?"

Carl couldn't meet her gaze. "There's the question. For which I don't have an answer. Maybe I never will. Maybe I'll never figure out what the hell I'm supposed to do with my life. Sometimes in the middle of the night, that scares me."

She took his hand and squeezed hard. Sometimes in the middle of the night, the same unanswered question scared her too.

"What about that girl, Carl, the special one in Detroit?"

She was startled by the stark, almost anguished look that came on his face; she hadn't realized the depth of his attachment.

"Tess? What about her?"

"Could you go back to Detroit and find her?"

"She's probably married by now."

"But you don't know that."

Carl's dark eyes seemed to show both pain and uncertainty. "Maybe I don't want to know, sis."

Fritzi had no answer for that.

53. Mickey Finn

Carl sat with a plate of the pickled sausages, a pencil and a postcard colorfully illustrating last year's air show at Dominguez Field. It was five o'clock, a day after his final outing with Fritzi.

He munched a sausage, licked the tip of his pencil, and wrote slowly. He hadn't mailed a card to Tess in months, had no idea whether she'd receive this one. Deep feelings compelled him to send something to show he was alive and was thinking of her. He thought of her more than he would admit in the scrawled words that reflected his lifelong losing war with penmanship.

About a dozen customers lined the long mahogany bar, all men, most from the local newspaper and sporting community. They argued boxing and baseball while cleaning off the free-lunch plates of sliced turkey and ham and cheese. A day after seeing the place for the first time, Barney decided "saloon" wasn't appropriate for a joint with his name on it. He ordered the exterior sign repainted to read OLDFIELD-KIPPER TAVERN. He told his partner, Jack Kipper, that the word *tavern* sounded more "high-class English."

Tavern or saloon, it made no difference to the six gray ladies from the WCTU marching in a circle on the sidewalk, holding high their righteous chins and their placards denouncing alcohol and those who served it. Patrons sober and otherwise entering the saloon tipped their derbies and joshed with the ladies, who glowered and admonished them with Bible verses. In noisy South Spring Street autos honked, wagons creaked, horses neighed and left huge pods of manure where pedestrians crossed.

Carl wrote a line about his interest in aeroplanes. At twenty past five the rear door opened and Barney swaggered in, chewing on a cigar. He spotted Carl.

"Greetings, kid. How are you?" The altercation in Ventura might never have happened. *Probably doesn't even remember it.*

"Doing all right, Barney, how about you?"

"Soon as I get a snootful I'll be better." He hovered by the table, a big canvas driving cap cocked on his head, a linen duster unbuttoned to show his dark purple suit, a sapphire tie pin big as a headlight. On the duster Carl noticed brown streaks — blood, he suspected.

"Have a good visit with your sister?"

"Fine, thanks. She'll be heading back to New York by the end of May."

"We're getting some movie actors in here. I met one named Arbuckle last night, hell of a card. Come on up to the bar, I'll buy a drink."

"I just had a beer, I don't think —"

"The boss wants to buy you a drink," Barney cut in. Carl could tell he'd already downed a few. Reluctantly he slipped pencil and postcard in the outside pocket of his shabby corduroy coat.

"Sure, I'll have one with you."

Customers greeted Barney as he and Carl stepped up to the rail. Above the cut-glass decanters on the back bar hung a huge and heroic painting of Jim Jeffries in boxing tights, fists raised for combat. Barney waved his cold cigar.

"Milo, give Carl a slug of that special stock we keep for friends."

"Beer's fine with me."

"I want you to try this stuff." At these words Carl's neck suddenly itched. He felt something unpleasant building. "Make it doubles all around, Milo."

Barney leaned back, elbows on the bar as he surveyed his establishment. Without looking at Carl he said, "My wife told me something I didn't like to hear, kid."

"What's that?"

"You talk about me behind my back. She says it ain't complimentary. That true?"

Carl was surprised. "No. I don't know why she'd make up such a story."

Milo served two oversized glasses. The dark whiskey shimmered and reflected the ceiling lights, fluted trumpets of frosted glass. With a twitchy little smile Barney said, "You wouldn't be calling Bess a liar, would you, kid?"

Hell's fire. Ever since he'd rebuffed Bess, she'd had it in for him, even though she slept with other men she met on the exhibition circuit. Barney couldn't be so stupid or besotted as not to suspect. Bess had singled Carl out for special punishment. Maybe men didn't often refuse her.

"No, Barney, I'm not saying a word against your wife. I'm only saying I don't talk behind your back."

"Well, we got two different stories here, don't we? Kind of hard to know which to believe. Got to think it over. Drink up."

A few minutes ago Carl had been sated from downing a stein of Budweiser. Now he was fiercely thirsty, liking neither the drift of the conversation nor the calculating look in Barney's eyes. He took a big drink of the strong, faintly bitter whiskey. Barney finished his double in two gulps.

"We got to sort this out, Carl. I can't have a driver going around behind my back saying rotten things about the champ. Those fuckers in Daytona let Bob Burman take my record, but I'm still the champ, got me?"

"Barney, let's talk about this some other —"

"Now." Barney shoved three stiffened fingers into Carl's chest. "We'll talk about it now."

Carl's ears erupted in buzzing. He saw two tie pins, not one, on Barney's cravat. Something sour and sick churned in his throat.

Barney smiled. " 'Less you aren't feeling so good. You look a little green, kid."

So that was it. Nauseated and woozy, he crossed his arms over his heaving belly. Barney loved pranks, one of his favorites being knockout drops in a drink offered in friendship. Carl swung around, yelled at Milo. "God damn it, did you slip me a Mickey Finn?"

Milo dried a glass with a towel and didn't look up. Jim Jeffries danced in his gilt frame. The electric ceiling lights began to fly around like comets. Barney was mightily amused.

"Fact is, you look like shit. Don't need a man

476

on my team who can't hold his liquor." Barney shoved his empty glass down the bar. "Hey, Milo, another double. None for this lily."

Swaying, Carl said, "You came in here to set me up."

"Yeah, I been meaning to settle accounts for weeks. Bess says you're a bum. A dirty lecher."

"Let me tell you" — Carl grabbed the bar as his knees went rubber on him — "about your sweet, innocent wife." Barney picked up the re-filled glass and threw the liquor in Carl's face.

"You say one word about her, I'll kill you, you son of a bitch."

Carl cocked his fist, stepped away from the bar. He wound up to hit Barney, but before he could swing, the room tilted and he felt himself going down. The back of his head slammed the floor. One flying hand upset a bar spittoon, dumping foul brown water all over his sleeve. His other arm stretched out toward the door. Barney stomped on it.

"You bum. You miserable, lying bum. Call my wife a liar, will you?" Barney kicked Carl's ribs. "You're through. You're fired." He pulled out a silver money clip in the shape of a dollar sign and contemptuously dropped a couple of bills on Carl's shirt.

Conversation in the saloon had stopped. All Carl heard was a vast rushing in his ears. His eyesight dimmed despite his resolve to stay awake. He rolled his head from side to side, picking up sawdust. He hoped he wouldn't puke all over himself.

"Couple of you boys throw this bum in the alley," Barney said. "Then it's time to celebrate. The old exterminator just got rid of some vermin. Barney Oldfield buys the next round."

Rough hands seized Carl's wrists, wrenched his arms over his head, dragged him across the floor. That was all he remembered.

He left his seedy downtown hotel that night, all his worldly possessions packed in one leather grip with a broken clasp. Barney had paid him a whole three dollars to call it quits. Carl had four dollars of his own. He didn't need to waste money on Pacific Electric carfare. Besides, he didn't have a destination in mind.

He thought of his sister. Could she find him a spare bed for the night? Pride canceled that thought almost at once. He'd sleep out in the country somewhere, free.

He turned up the collar of his coat and trudged out of the central city. His head hurt. His mouth tasted like sewage, and he wondered if he could ever again put so much as a crust of bread in his aching gut. That bastard Barney. Couldn't deal with him man to man, had to trick him and get the upper hand before he threw him out.

He lugged his grip through residential neighborhoods where parlor lights shone. No one had left a lamp burning for him.

He heard oil derricks chugging in back yards. A steam car full of revelers ran him off the road. A train wailed its whistle in the night. He wondered where the road would carry him now. He wondered if there'd ever be an end to that road. Around midnight, still hurting and retching occasionally, he lay down in the heady sweetness of an orange grove and slept.

Dusty and sweaty, Carl raised his arm in front of his eyes to hide the red sun. What he'd glimpsed from far down the road, distorted by wavy heat devils, took on clarity and detail.

The machine sat on its tail and two oversized, solid wheels, next to a red barn with a limp wind sock on its roof peak. The biplane's yellow wings were patched in many places. The pilot's seat was small, directly in front of the pusher motor. In front of the seat was a control rod with a wheel. Carl had read enough to know the plane resembled those built and flown by Glenn Curtiss, especially the "Golden Flyer" that had won an upset victory at the 1909 Rheims air show. Early Wright planes had skids and no seat; the pilot lay on his stomach on the lower wing to — what was the word? Aviate.

A sign on the barn advertised

RIVERSIDE SCHOOL OF AERONAUTICS
— *Professional Instruction* —
A. R. (RIP) RYAN, OWNER-AERONAUT

From inside the barn came the sound of hammering. Carl walked to the doors, tested them; a chain rattled when he tried to pull them apart. Around the corner he discovered a regular door, open. He walked in, saw a man on his knees with a hammer. The hammer struck a spark from a big nail head, glanced off. The nail was bent into a curved L; the man swore. He was trying to drive the nail with a misshapen hand. His fingers were gnarled as old roots.

Too hungry to be deterred by the man's anger, Carl stepped into a shaft of daylight falling through a crack in the barn siding. "Hello," he said. "Got any work here?"

Rip Ryan of Riverside was bent as a hilltop sapling tormented by the wind. Time had carved gullies in his sun-browned cheek; worry had dug them across his forehead. Not more than forty, he had a full head of white hair. He laid his hammer down and took a good ten seconds to rise to a standing position.

"There might be some work," he said after Carl introduced himself. "I know there's some coffee. Leave your grip and come on."

Carl followed him to a tiny cottage near the barn. It was slow going, for the small, wiry man listed to the left at every other step. Crooked fingers clutched the knob of a polished stick. "Arthritis," he said when he caught Carl staring. "Curse of my life."

Ryan poured coffee from a blue enamel pot. They sat on opposite sides of a scarred table. To start conversation Carl said, "Are you a native, Mr. Ryan?"

Ryan snorted. "Hell, do I look like some Spaniard with a land grant? Born and raised in Brooklyn, New York. Big city. Hated it. The smoke, the noise, the crowding. Lived in a tenement with bad air, no windows, a toilet pail in the corner. My old man swamped out the horsecar barns. Irishman, no education. Died of too much whiskey. My sainted mother followed him

480

two years later. I was seventeen."

He drank from his tin cup with a noisy sucking sound. Carl didn't say anything more; listen to someone attentively, they thought well of you.

"Put myself through business college," Ryan went on. "Read all the promotional books about southern California peddled by the railroads. Beautiful scenery. Clear skies. Healthful air. Soon as I could, I came out here. Went to work over in Redlands. Been there?"

"No, only heard of it."

"Kept books for the biggest feed and grain dealer in the county. Hated that too. Office no bigger than a two-hole privy. Didn't see all these blue skies they brag about, except on Sunday. Married a local girl, name of Marie Morrison. Wanted to have children but somehow we couldn't. One Sunday when Marie was visiting her parents in Bakersfield, I blew two dollars on a ten-minute airplane ride at a fair. God A'mighty" — his whole demeanor changed, the air of sour complaint gone — "it was like ascending to heaven. It was like having a woman the first time."

Ryan's beatific look faded quickly. He picked up his tin cup, barely able to fit his fingers around the handle. They were like hooks bending in different directions.

"Knew then and there I couldn't stay in Redlands. Couldn't tell Marie, though, she depended on me. Agonized for three months. Sleepless nights. Stomach in knots, bowels tied up for days. Finally one Monday morning I just quit. When I came home and broke the news,

Marie cursed me and locked herself in the bedroom. I knew that was the end, though she didn't leave for good until two months later."

He tilted his head to a streaked and grimy window where Carl saw the tips of the biplane's doped wings. "I had some savings. I put the Eagle together from drawings in magazines. That's what I christened her, the Eagle. Took me a year and three months to finish. I sorted oranges for the growers' cooperative, picked lettuce and sugar beets, God damn miserable stoop labor, to pay for it. But I was happy."

"Who taught you to fly?"

"Pilot who knew Glenn Curtiss back East. You know who Curtiss is?"

Carl nodded. Like the Wright brothers, young Curtiss had owned a bicycle shop, in upstate New York. Before he built and raced his own planes in competition with the Wrights, Curtiss was a familiar name in motorcycle racing — a chaser of land speed records, like Barney. One of his early patrons was the inventor Alexander Graham Bell. Curtiss adapted his compact and well-regarded motorcycle engine for airplanes and tried to sell it to Wilbur and Orville Wright. They dismissed him. So he went into business to compete with them. He was most famous for winning the *Coupe Internationale*, Gordon Bennett's trophy for the fastest twenty kilometers around the pylons at the international air meet in Rheims, France, two years ago.

"The Curtiss method," Ryan mused. "It's peculiar, but it works. I soared like an angel. I was a new man. Forty-four years old and I felt life was just starting. Had a terrible accident one after-noon, flying near here. A freak lightning storm hit the *Eagle*. I crashed into telephone wires, an aviator's worst nightmare. The wires stopped the fall, and I walked off with a few scratches. I thought I had a charmed life. Then" — a twist of his mouth as he held up his malformed hands — "this. I'd felt it coming on for a while. My old man suffered from it, one reason he drank. It hit me bad. I barely managed to rebuild the Eagle by myself. I can't fly her anymore, but I can teach others. The Curtiss method. I never touch the plane. You have any desire to fly?"

"I do, definitely."

"Then I can teach you. No cost, but you'd have to help me build an addition to the barn. Been waiting for someone to come along who could do it."

"I'm your man," Carl said.

"Thought you might be when you walked in," Ryan said.

54. No Laughing Matter

After B.B. hired her, Lily jumped into her new duties with enthusiasm. She worked late with her bedroom door shut and Fritzi admonished to stay out. Lily's boudoir table, once cluttered with perfumes and cosmetic jars, overflowed with books and newspapers she combed for ideas.

Her first story before the camera, one reel, was *Madolyn's March*. Lily had picked up on Sophie Pelzer's passion for the suffrage cause when she met B.B.'s wife. Kelly complained that the subject was too controversial, but he was overruled.

The heroine of Lily's scenario was a small-town girl who went to a nickelodeon where she saw the famous, often jailed English suffragist Emmeline Pankhurst, on her 1909 visit to New York. Without actually showing a theater screen, Eddie cleverly cut in actuality footage of Mrs. Pankhurst coming down the gangplank of a White Star liner, to a tumultuous welcome, then parading in front of Carnegie Hall with her American sisters. Instantly converted, Madolyn staged a one-girl march in her town, represented by a Hollywood residential street. A nasty sheriff jailed Madolyn, but her lawyer fiancé, after a largely unmotivated epiphany, won her freedom and swore to love, honor, and support a suffrage amendment after they were married.

Lily's quixotic spelling of the heroine's name charmed B.B. Amused, she said to Fritzi, "Hell,

484

you think I know the right way to spell anything? I just wrote it down the way it sounded. I don't guess I'll ever tell him that!"

When Eddie finished *Madolyn's March*, with Madge Singleton, a New York actress who'd appeared in several Pal pictures, he cast Fritzi in *A Merry Mix-Up*, a silly comedy he concocted in an afternoon. Fritzi objected to another comedy part, to no avail. She played twin sisters, Tess and Bess. Each had a suitor, brothers. The actor hired as one of them was a pie-faced young man named Roscoe Arbuckle. He was sweet-natured and round as a tub. Like most actors he was sociable and garrulous. He told Fritzi he'd been a scene shifter in vaudeville, a black face monologist, and a tenor in musicals before he began working as a movie extra. He went by the name Fatty.

In the story, much confusion ensued because Fatty and the other suitor, Pete, couldn't tell the twins apart until the penultimate scene, in which a rowboat tipped, dumping Tess into Echo Park Lake, near downtown Los Angeles. Since Tess was the twin who couldn't swim, Fatty recognized his brother's sweetheart when he rescued her. This prepared everyone for the ending, a double wedding at the altar, shot double exposure, two Fritzis.

Because Fritzi made a mild fuss about the slapstick, Eddie hired a utility player to handle the fall from the rowboat. He was an odd little man named Windy White. About five feet five, he had a wrinkled brown face, a sunburned bald head, and legs like parentheses. He said hardly a word to anyone.

For the shot he donned bloomers, a dress, and a wig. He tumbled out of the rowboat on cue, using a lot of hammy gestures, the acting style inherited from nineteenth-century stage melodrama. A more restrained technique suitable to the camera was coming in, but not for this picture.

After a second take, Windy trudged out of the lake and doffed his dripping wig to Fritzi. She noticed he was trailing a cloud of whiskey fumes. His eyes didn't quite focus. He'd stood in for her drunk, she realized with a start. What a foolish, risky way to make five dollars.

For a close-up, Eddie placed her in the lake about six feet from the bank. A prop man dumped two buckets of water over her, then adorned her head with smelly strands of seaweed. After the shot the water continued to drip off her nose and chin and elbows. Her makeup melted and ran. Ellen Terry chose to keep quiet, which was a blessing.

Sometime before, B.B. had bought the promised automobile. Though he could have chosen a cheap and efficient Model T, Reo, or Brush that cost under $700, his nature impelled him to a long, sleek top-of-the-line Packard with bucket seats, large brass acetylene lamps, and a gleaming brass side horn. Sophie Pelzer chose the color, royal blue. Rumored price, $2,700. Kelly fumed.

B.B. garaged the Packard in the barn on the

lot. "It's beautiful," Fritzi said when he showed it to her. "I'm afraid it'll take me a year to learn to operate it."

"Your papa never taught you?"

"No, he said a girl would always have a husband or chauffeur."

B.B. rolled his eyes. He promised to find a good driving instructor.

"When there's time," she had said with a little sigh.

Suddenly an answer to her problem walked in. An actor with a monocle came to the lot looking for work. Though in his late twenties, he was already bald as an egg, with a severe, not to say malevolent face. Emigrating from Vienna, he'd worked in a few pictures in New York. His first name was Erich, his last Stroheim, and he had a large mouthful of names in between. B.B. called Fritzi to his office to introduce her.

"We got no parts right now, but I hired him to teach you to drive."

The man clicked his heels, bowed. His shoes were coming apart, Fritzi noticed.

"I am informed you are German." Erich's accent was heavy as a barrel of sauerkraut. "*Wunderschön*, we shall speak it together. Call me Von, if you please."

Fritzi managed to say, "Charmed." He snatched her hand and kissed it. Only his politeness and his smile redeemed him from an appearance of utter and heartless evil.

Von turned out to be a capable instructor and, in contradiction of his looks, a likeable and good-humored companion. He forgave her initial clumsy mistakes at the wheel. Within two weeks she was driving competently.

During one of their afternoon sessions, they were approaching the corner of Figueroa and Eighth, downtown, when she suddenly yanked the wheel and slewed the Packard to the curb. She braked so hard she almost banged her forehead on the glass. Her instructor in the passenger seat paled. *"Gott! Gib acht."* Be careful.

She stood up in the open car, a hand over her brow to block the sun. "Say, what's going on?" Von stood up too. In the center of the intersection, policemen in tall hats and frock coats ran every which way, chasing civilians and bashing them with billy clubs while dodging a parked wagon and an auto going round and round in a circle, apparently out of control. A black police sedan had run up over the sidewalk, inches from a store window; steam spouted from its hood. In all four arms of the intersection, wagon and auto traffic was backed up. Irate motorists shouted and sounded their horns and klaxons.

"The police are rioting," Fritzi exclaimed.

"Nein, nein," he said with a nonchalant wave. *"Licht-spiel. Film."*

" A movie?"

"Ja. Biograph, I think. See there? *Herr Direktor."*

Fritzi spotted him on a far corner; in the confusion she hadn't noticed him, or the camera. The moment the director called cut, she said, "I know him."

All action stopped, though one actor threw a last brick. It sailed high, arcing down toward the

Packard. Fritzi cried, "Duck."

"Nah. *Felz.*" The felt brick bounced harmlessly off the hood.

Fritzi stepped out, crossed the intersection. Men from the film crew stood with hands raised, blocking the traffic. The air was blue with oaths and threats, the blare of horns. Someone had lost a billy club, which Fritzi picked up. Stuffed cotton.

The director, a burly young Irishman she remembered from Fourteenth Street, shouted at his crew. "It looked okay except for the skid. Dump another barrel of liquid soap and we'll shoot it again. Hurry it up or we'll be in the hoosegow."

"Mr. Sinnott?"

"Hi." Then, swift recognition: "Miss Crown. Hello. Wait till we finish this."

Fritzi stepped behind the camera as five cops piled into the black sedan. The driver reversed, bounced off the curb, and headed west on Figueroa. One of the men charged with stopping traffic was wrestling with a matronly motorist who belabored his head with her furled parasol.

A prop man ran into the intersection with a wooden cask. Before he could uncork it and dump the soap, everyone heard the rising wail of a siren on South Eighth. "Hell, we can't do another take." Mike Sinnott waved frantically. "Everybody clear out."

Like robbers caught in a bank with the alarm ringing, crew and actors scattered. Men threw props and the camera into an open touring car with amazing speed. The car took off northward.

As Fritzi watched the real police car coming fast, Sinnott grabbed her arm. "This way."

They dashed into a tea shop, to the rearmost table. The police sedan screamed by in pursuit of the camera car.

"How are you, Miss Crown?" Sinnott said, unperturbed by the chaos he'd caused. "I didn't know you were in Los Angeles."

"Working for Liberty Pictures."

"I saw *A Merry Mix-up*. You're a riot."

Which was hardly what she wanted to hear, but she smiled politely. "And you're directing."

"I groused long enough, and Biograph finally let me make a couple of cop comedies."

"Did you get a permit to shoot in the street?"

He grinned. "Permit? What's that?"

She laughed. "You could get arrested."

"Not if we run faster."

Von marched in, searching for them. When Fritzi introduced him, Sinnott raised an eyebrow. "Your driving teacher?"

Von clicked his heels and popped his monocle out of his eye. "That is correct. Actually, I am a performer and director, but I am not yet established. Teaching *Fräulein* Fritzi the fine points of motoring is more pleasant than delivering furniture or selling flypaper in Woolworth's."

"Sit down, join us."

"Danke."

After they ordered, Fritzi said, "Mr. Griffith's here, isn't he?"

"Busy as a tick, but he's no happier than I am. He wants to make longer pictures, like the ones coming from Italy. The studio won't let him, even though four- and five-reel shows are getting to be the rule instead of the exception. Other companies are wooing him with promises of artistic control. He's got a bug about some Civil War opus he wants to shoot."

They chatted over their tea until Sinnott checked his watch and said he should catch up with his crew. "First place I check is the city jail." He put money on the table. "I'll look you up when I need a funny leading lady."

You may look, but you won't find me, she thought as he sauntered out the door.

Hindsight made Sinnott's last remark seem like a dire omen. With a combination of avuncular wheedling and parental firmness, B.B. got Fritzi into *Pearl's Piano*, a new slapstick farce.

Her character, a young and naive music teacher, desperately needed a piano. A crooked salesman played by Pete Porter, another refugee from the New York stage, had conveniently salvaged one from a train wreck (Eddie cut in some dramatic footage of a derailment originally filmed for a crime melodrama). The salesman patched up the piano, then offered gullible Pearl a stunningly low price if she'd buy it sight unseen.

Needing students to pay for her mother's hospitalization, Pearl announced a recital for some boys and girls and their snooty mothers who would pay for lessons. When she sat down to play the gleaming new instrument, pedals and keys began to fall off. The top of the case sprang open. Felt hammers and twisted wires shot out, followed by two white rabbits (no explanation of how they got there).

A mean little boy pulled a girl's pigtail; there was an immediate juvenile brawl that quickly involved the mothers. Draperies were torn down, picture frames smashed over heads, furniture broke, goldfish bowls full of water and goldfish sailed through the air — the chaos was stopped only by the appearance of a young deputy sheriff, with the salesman in handcuffs. Of course, the deputy had a sister with a fine piano she would dispose of cheaply if Pearl accompanied the deputy to a dance. Pearl batted her eyes coyly and sat down on the only article of furniture still intact, the piano stool. Which naturally collapsed. Fadeout.

Fritzi was heavy-hearted about the picture. Fortunately, the calendar called a halt to what she saw as a dangerous trend in her career. At the end of May, B.B. and Kelly declared the Liberty lot closed until next winter. Fritzi packed up to leave Los Angeles with the rest of the company.

Lily begged her to come back. "Promise me." Fritzi said she couldn't promise. Both of them cried and hugged at the Glendale station. Lily stayed on the platform, waving and gamely trying not to sob as the eastbound train pulled out.

55. Inferno

Back in New York, Fritzi rented a parlor and bedroom at the refurbished Bleecker House. Oh-Oh Merkle was gone, a bad memory, though some of the old staff remained. New owners had brought a new respectability; no longer were the beds turned on an hourly basis.

A young Russian immigrant, a dishwasher in the hotel restaurant, gushed over Fritzi's adventures with the Lone Indian. She'd learned to take such compliments with good humor, even a degree of pleasure, damping down her true feelings of frustration about a theater career.

In her first week in the city she enjoyed a reunion with Hobart at the café near the Hudson River piers, where he seemed to know many visiting sailors, for reasons she now understood. Hobart was about to launch a half-year stock-company tour of the Pacific Northwest and Canada, doing Falstaff in *The Merry Wives of Windsor*, a cross-gartered and decidedly overage Malvolio in *Twelfth Night*, and, for ladies' matinees, Nora's repugnant husband in *A Doll's House*.

"Can you imagine performing Ibsen and the Bard in some place called Medicine Hat?" he complained. *"Aestuat ingens imo in corde pudor."*

"You'll have to help me, I hated Latin." Fritzi reached for a raw oyster on the plate between them.

"It's Virgil's *Aeneid*. 'Deep in his heart boils overwhelming shame.' "

"Sometimes I think I'd rather be doing plays in the provinces than these silly little pictures."

"I thought you enjoyed the work."

"I enjoy the people. Anyway, I'm getting out soon."

Easier to say than do; Eddie kept her working steadily. The company motored off to Cuddebackville, New York, in the Orange Mountains, for ten days of outdoor shooting in beautiful wilderness country. The replacement for Owen had come East for a few weeks, so they shot two Lone Indian dramas in the gorges and woodlands of the Delaware Water Gap, retiring at night to a rustic hostelry called the Caudebac Inn; there the men played cards and the ladies worked picture puzzles and read fashion magazines. Fritzi wrote letters: To her mother. To Julie and Eustacia in England. To Lily, saying, with honesty, that she already missed California, especially the bracing air, so different from the sopping humidity of an Eastern summer.

When the company returned to the city, Fritzi took up her old routine of visiting producers and casting agencies, listing her availability as next January 1, when her one-year contract with Liberty expired. Ira Mehlman was the only agent to offer even slight encouragement. After remarking that he'd watched a number of her pictures and recognized her even when unbilled, he said, "Not bad. There's a winter revival of *Captain Jinks of the Horse Marines* on the books. I could recommend you for Madame Trentoni."

"Here in New York?" Fritzi said, thrilled. The role in the Clyde Fitch play had made a star of Ethel Barrymore in 1901. Mehlman shook his head.

"Then what city?"

"Cities. Tank towns. Does Wheeling, West Virginia, appeal to you?"

"Very little."

"Oil City, Pennsylvania?"

"Mr. Mehlman, I've toured places like that. Is there nothing better coming up, sooner?"

"Do I have a crystal ball? A lot of producers decide on a show and mount it in three weeks. I'll be frank, Fritzi. Recommending you for anything will be touchy. If I've seen you in flickers, so have others. Breaking through in this town's as hard as ever. Where you've been the past year or so makes it harder. Didn't anyone warn you?"

"Many times."

"But you went ahead."

Or let myself be dragged, willy-nilly.

"I don't mean to sound negative, Mr. Mehlman. I want to return to the stage very badly. I'll be eager to hear about anything, including the *Captain Jinks* tour. I'll be grateful."

"Sure, Fritzi. We'll be in touch."

The old refrain. Harry Poland should write a song, she thought as she left, trailing clouds of disappointment.

On a sweltering night in late July, Eddie took Fritzi into the second-floor projection room at the Liberty offices on Fourteenth Street. An editor, Daphne Roosa, joined them. Daphne was a stout young woman with plump but delicate hands and an almost fanatic obsession with the details of pasting a picture together.

The tiny space was hot, windowless. It smelled of chemicals and yesterday's cigars. Fritzi slumped in a hard chair, waving a damp handkerchief in front of her nose to stir the air.

Eddie said, "I want you to see this before we show it to Kelly. Something bothers me, but I can't quite peg what it is."

"I had a similar reaction," Daphne Roosa said. The one-reel picture had been no trouble to film, but those who'd trekked out to Greenwich, Connecticut, didn't seem to have much fun doing it.

Ostensibly a comedy, *Mixed Nuts* came from a scenario Al Kelly had bought from a friend and forced into production. The antics of three escaped lunatics, one of them Fritzi, made her uncomfortable, the same way she'd felt during production. When Eddie turned on the lights, she said, "I think I know what's wrong. The jokes are funny, but they're at the expense of people who are feeble-minded. Making the sick or crippled into objects of fun isn't my idea of humor. It's unkind."

Miss Roosa agreed. Eddie said, "Well, it's Al's idea of humor." He reflected a moment. "But maybe you've got it. Something about the picture smells."

Miss Roosa wrinkled her nose. "Something around here smells too." Fritzi had been marginally aware of it for a minute or so. With unexpected haste Eddie shoved a chair out of the way, ran into the hall.

"Smoke!"

He disappeared toward the rear of the building. Fritzi smelled it strongly now. She and Miss Roosa exchanged alarmed looks and raced each other to the hall. Down at the end Eddie was opening the door of a storeroom holding archive prints of Pal and Liberty pictures. Smoke poured out, coiling up to the ceiling. Eddie threw an arm across his face and jumped back from the glare.

He ran back to them, pushed them toward the front of the building. Flames from the storeroom licked out to the wall opposite; the wall began to smolder. The light in the corridor brightened like some hellish daybreak.

"I doubt this happened by accident," Eddie said. "Someone saw Bill Nix in the neighborhood day before yesterday." Anxiously he looked back. "There's a fire-escape window in the room where the costumes are stored." He ran toward the advancing wall of flame, the two frightened women a step behind.

The heat increased, and the glare. Daphne Roosa faltered, short of breath. Fritzi caught her hand to help her along. The fire had nearly reached the door of the temporary costume shop. Fritzi well knew the risk of having nitrate film stored in a building with wooden walls, but it had always been an abstract consideration. She'd never imagined there could be real danger. The watery sting of her eyes, the suffocating smoke, the heat, the crack of crumbling plaster and lath, the crash of burning debris falling through to the floor below, told her she'd been a fool.

"Eddie, can we make it?" The door they had to pass through was half engulfed.

"Have to, there's no other way. Follow me." He meant right through the flames. Fritzi grasped Daphne's hand more firmly. The smoke grew blinding, the heat scorching. Eddie threw his arms over his head and leaped with the agility of a deer, disappearing into the fire.

"Run, Daphne. Fast as you can," Fritzi shouted.

"Oh, I'm scared."

"So am I, but we'll die if we stay here. Come on!"

She fairly dragged the stout girl, one arm raised to shield her eyes. She leaped through a curtain of light, holding her breath so as not to suck in the poisonous smoke. She plunged into the stygian dark of the unlit room. All of a sudden her hand clutched empty air.

"Daphne?"

She saw Daphne lying on her side, next to a fallen dress form that must have tripped her. The doorway disappeared in flames. Daphne lay too close; her skirt caught and smoked. Out of sight behind the costumes racked on iron pipe, Eddie yelled:

"For God's sake, where are you?"

"Daphne's hurt." The stout young woman was thrashing about, moaning. Fritzi heard Eddie coming on the run. Daphne's skirt blazed suddenly, and she screamed.

Fritzi grabbed something from the nearest

rack — a king's velvet robe studded with imitation gems. She threw it on Daphne like a blanket, then flung herself on top, kicking and beating the flames to put them out. The smoke had grown so heavy she could see little but the glare behind it.

"Here, get up." Eddie tugged her arm. Daphne was momentarily safe, the fire on her clothing smothered. Fritzi grabbed Eddie's arm like a lifeline. The three of them stumbled between the racks to the raised window. Down on the street, the bell in a corner fire box clanged the alarm. Voices clamored.

"Go through," Eddie yelled, pushing Daphne Roosa out to the iron fire escape, then Fritzi. He climbed outside as Daphne started down the metal stairs. Fritzi clutched the hand rail and followed.

Somehow she misstepped. She fell toward the landing where the last flight of stairs began. The floor of the landing, an iron grating, came up to meet her, slamming her face. She felt a cruel spike of pain in her ankle. Then it was all gone, the fire, the strident bell, Eddie, Daphne — gone into a black maw of nothing.

56. Carl Mows the Grass

Carl slept in Ryan's hayloft, warm and secure with blankets to cover him and straw to cushion him. The food was good; Rip Ryan loved to eat, huge meals of steak and eggs and local fruit and vegetables, though he was slow at the stove because of his arthritis.

Ryan had long ago done drawings of the barn addition. It went up fairly rapidly, thanks to Carl's strength and mobility. Once each week a local physician and a male science teacher drove out in their flivvers at different times for a flying lesson. To his amazement, Carl saw that Ryan was true to his word: he never touched the plane, just sat on a barrel by the landing strip, observing and instructing. At three-thirty on a Tuesday, Carl took his first lesson.

"She's easier to pilot than a Wright plane," Ryan said as Carl climbed up on the small, hard seat in front of the motor. "Take the wheel in your hands. That's right. Push her forward, the plane will nose down. Pull back, she'll come up. To bank left, turn the wheel left and lean that way. See? No harder than driving one of Mr. Ford's motor cars."

Not quite true, Carl discovered. Ryan first had him get the feel of the controls by sitting in the plane with the motor off. Carl slipped into the shoulder harness connected to short ailerons mounted between the ends of the upper and lower wings. When the aviator leaned left or right, it moved the ailerons via the harness. He'd have to practice to get the hang of looking over his shoulder at the engine without jerking the plane into a sudden precipitous bank when he was aloft.

His driving experience did help him learn fairly quickly. In a matter of days, Ryan fired up the engine and stood back while Carl taxied on the half-mile grass strip behind the barn. Ryan had wired the throttle so the plane couldn't lift off by accident. Carl bumped up and down the field, exhilarated by the motor roar, the wind in his face, the flare of sunlight on his old driving goggles. This exercise of beating back and forth Ryan called "mowing the grass." It was a staple of the Curtiss method.

When Ryan was satisfied with Carl's progress in mowing, he guided Carl through the installation of a special practice propeller that allowed the *Eagle* to race down the field and lift six or eight feet off the ground. Carl's first flight of about thirty-five feet, up and then gently down with a bump, set the blood to singing in his ears and made him feel like a conqueror of gravity. His second flight carried him fifty feet, ten feet above the field. The third time he made an error, pushed the control wheel too far, and slammed downward suddenly, fortunately only from a height of four feet; there was no smash-up. Ryan had built a strong plane.

In Riverside one Saturday, Carl called Los Angeles from the telephone office. He was eager to tell Fritzi that he might have found something he could do happily for the rest of his life. Of course, he'd felt the same way about driving, and look how that had worked out. Amid pings and whistles from the other end of the wire, Mr. Hong reported that Fritzi had left for New York.

The following Tuesday, they mounted the regular flight propeller. With his belly knotted so badly it surely must resemble one of Ryan's hands, Carl opened the throttle as he sped down the field. He drew the wheel back. With his hair flying out behind, his mouth open in a soundless jubilation, he felt the lift beneath the wings. *Eagle* left the ground.

He leaned to the right in the shoulder harness, climbed above the barn with its wind sock, flew over the newly roofed addition, painted with white primer the day before. He climbed slowly to two hundred feet, watching the world expand to an incredible panorama of orange groves and country lanes, meandering buggies and busy workers spread beneath him in sunlit glory. For fifteen minutes he practiced long, slow turns, climbs into the eye of the sun, gliding descents. Finally he saw Ryan signal him by waving his arms like semaphore flags. Carl landed with a feathery thump and a long roll, killing the motor six feet from his mentor.

Ryan hobbled over to the *Eagle* and leaned against the lower wing. "You've got the touch. You'll make a good aviator."

Carl shucked out of the harness, jumped down from the hard seat. He and Ryan looked at each other with perfect and slightly melancholy understanding. Ryan voiced it:

"A few more practice flights, the bird'll be ready to leave the nest. Got to hurry up and caulk everything and finish painting so we can call it quits."

On a lazy June afternoon with bees making noise in the flower beds Ryan cultivated near the cottage, they examined the new Dutch door in the addition. Ryan slammed it several times, then took a penknife to scrape flecks of paint from the windowpane. He declared the addition completed.

"So what now?" he said as they returned to the cottage. Carl followed a step behind as usual, to give Ryan time for each crabbed step.

"I'd like to get a job flying an aeroplane. Are there any jobs like that?"

With one of his rare smiles Ryan said, "Sure, if you don't mind risking your life once or twice a day."

"I've done it before," Carl said. "What are you talking about?"

In the kitchen a beef brisket simmered fragrantly in an iron pot. Ryan told him to sit down while he fetched something. He returned with a smudged business card with bent corners.

"This boyo passed through Redlands with his show last fall. Exhibition flyers. He told me that pilots quit on him all the time because the stunts are dangerous."

RENE LE MAYE
"Circus of the Air"
— *Rates Upon Request* —

The card bore a one-line address: General Delivery, El Paso, Texas.

"Frenchman?"

"Right. Lot of them interested in planes. Blériot, Paulhan — he was at the Los Angeles air meet last year. Americans are behind compared to the froggies. This Rene told me the bartenders at the Sheldon Hotel in El Paso always know where he's appearing."

"I'll look him up."

"Have you got money for a rail ticket?"

"I don't need a ticket. I jump on freights."

"Isn't that dangerous?"

"No more dangerous than flying." Or working for Barney. "Got to dodge the railroad bulls, that's all. They'll break your legs faster than a bad jump from a moving train."

"Well, you may be just the kind of crazy damn fool the Frenchman wants."

He shuffled and bobbed his way to the stove. They tore into the hearty meal of roast, boiled potatoes, California snap beans, and homemade sourdough bread washed down with some bourbon whiskey Ryan kept for special occasions. Ryan said, "I've liked your company. I'll hate to see you go."

"I appreciate what you taught me."

"Send a new aeronaut out into the world, it's like sending yourself. Well, almost." He saluted Carl with the whiskey, then knocked it back in swift gulps.

"Marie didn't like this flying business, or any of the new things, the new inventions. She didn't understand the thrill of going up. Looking at the cloud castles, the toy towns, the little people. It takes your problems and squeezes them way down, till they don't seem so important anymore." Ryan ran his hand along the polished stick lying on the empty chair between them.

"Till they don't hurt so much."

"You're right," Carl agreed. "I felt that the very first time I left the ground."

Maybe a new chapter was beginning for him. He wondered what Tess would have said about it.

57. Decision

Fritzi recuperated in the same New York Hospital where she'd visited Eddie. A doctor named Lilyveldt attended her, a handsome and austere man with a silver beard. He was aware of the circumstances of her fall and let her know immediately that he came of an old New York family that disapproved of actors. During his examinations he offered unsubtle advice about leaving the profession as soon as possible.

Apparently she'd wrenched her left ankle badly as she started to tumble down the last rungs of the fire escape. She remembered the spike of hot pain before she passed out, but nothing beyond that — not the impact that turned her forehead purple as eggplant, or the bloody gashing of her scalp that required six stitches. They'd shaved away her unruly blond hair to sew up the wound. When the dressing was changed, she saw herself in a hand mirror. She looked like a woman whose large bald spot had slipped to the right side of her head. It made her giggle.

Eddie's wife, Rita, volunteered to pick up her mail and bring it to the hospital. The first batch contained a yellow envelope — a cable from Paul. He would be in the States shortly to confer with his American publisher, then undertake a month-long lecture tour in the Midwest and South, filming as he went. She couldn't wait to hear news of Julie and the children, especially the new baby girl, Francesca Carlotta, whom they called Lottie.

B.B. brought candy, white roses in tissue paper, and apologies. "It's my fault you're hurt this way."

"I don't hold anyone responsible, except the man who set the fire."

"Nix," B.B. said emphatically. "Police picked up a tip. The bum was standing around swilling beer and bragging in a Third Avenue saloon. For a criminal, that fellow has the brains of an ant. They sweated him at the precinct house, and he broke down right away. He's going to the pen."

He pulled a chair close, chafed her hand while he said, "Liberty's talent is too valuable to risk this way. Sophie and I talked it over for hours. Here's what I decided. End of summer, I'm closing down production in New York. Not much left of the office anyway, the fire gutted most of the building. It's back to California."

A lump formed in her throat. "For good?"

"Right." The way he chafed her hand told of his anxiety. "We want you to go with us, you know that. I'm offering you a raise to ninety-five dollars a week. A hundred if I can squeeze Al. How do you feel about that?"

Fritzi lay back on the rough pillow, her mind in a whirl. "Honestly, I don't know."

"Well, please decide soon, that's all I ask. Just yesterday I telegraphed Lily to tell her she's on the payroll starting in September." B.B. patted her again, then put his chair back where it belonged. He twiddled his hat brim nervously.

"Please consider what Liberty Pictures is offering you, Fritzi. You got a great future."

She thought of the scornful Dr. Lilyveldt. "Thank you. I promise I'll think about it."

He waddled away down the aisle, tipping his hat to matrons and patients. Fritzi sighed. To throw her lot entirely with Liberty in California not only seemed cowardly, but a commitment to mediocrity. Yet that was a step better than not eating, wasn't it?

Harry Poland sent a huge floral basket and an elaborately phrased letter explaining that he'd heard of the fire and her hospitalization. He wished her a swift recovery, and apologized (two paragraphs) for failing to pay a visit to her bedside. He was wrapped up in rehearsals for the first Broadway show for which he'd written all the songs; something called *Pink Ladies*. The rehearsals were fraught with personnel and technical problems, he said. Each time he planned to break away during visiting hours, some crisis intervened. If she would accept his apology, he would make amends when things settled down.

The curiously intense, almost boyish tone of the letter brought a smile. She felt warmly toward Harry, not so much because of his slightly scandalous attentions but because of the quick and decisive way he'd acted when Pearly stalked her in the subway. She was pleased for his success, of course; she recognized and admired his talent.

Eddie and Rita visited together, sharing their enthusiasm about a permanent move to Los Angeles. "For me there's no choice," Eddie said. "Pictures are the future. Someday they may even be art."

After four days Dr. Lilyveldt released her, sternly warning her to favor her sprained ankle for at least two weeks. He insisted she wrap the ankle in elastic bandage, and he wanted her to walk with a cane, something her vanity would never allow. She hobbled into her two-room suite at the Bleecker House and sat down in the glow of a summer twilight, staring at her hands, still unsure of everything except her eagerness to see Paul, whose ship would dock next week.

Paul brought snapshots in quantity: Julie, the two older children, little Lottie in her fancy toddler's dress, standing with her tiny hand on a velvet pedestal and a fixed, glazed look on her round face. "The photographer put a clamp on the back of her head so she'd stay upright," Paul laughed. "Talk about medieval torture! Right after he got this shot, Lottie started bawling and that was the end. She's a sweet child, but I think she's headstrong."

The photos were spread on the starched white cloth of their table on the stern deck of the dinner boat. The boat was docked at West Houston Street, scheduled to leave at seven P.M. for a cruise around the harbor. Harry was due to join them but hadn't shown up yet.

The tables under the striped awning were rapidly filling. Middle-aged waiters wearing long white aprons glided among the guests, refilling champagne and wine glasses. A hot orange sky glared in the west; they were in the midst of a heat wave. Fritzi's ankle bandage itched unmercifully. With the toe of her other shoe she scratched it under the table while Paul showed a photo of a dark-haired young man with a cheeky grin.

"Sammy Silverstone, my right hand. An absolute gem. Why I resisted help for so long, I'll never know. Sammy saves my back, and I like his company too."

"But you didn't bring him over from England."

Paul shook his head, fanned himself with his straw boater; it looked new, but there was a ragged half-moon torn out of the brim, as though a dog had chewed it. "I couldn't justify the expense. I'm working for Lord Yorke only part of the time on this trip." He jumped up. "Let's move a bit, it's stuffy here."

He slipped the photos into a pocket of his summer jacket of tan linen, already badly wrinkled from the heat and grime of Manhattan. His round collar bore an ink smudge, and there was a blot on his striped necktie suspiciously like a catsup stain.

They walked to the stern rail, where the ensign of the cruise line drooped on its staff. In the harbor to the south, the great torch held aloft in Liberty's hand shone brightly against the deepening blue of the sky. The harbor itself had a rich green patina, like dark jade rippled with red highlights from the western sky.

Fritzi folded her hands and leaned on the rail. "There's something I haven't told you."

"You mean about California — whether you'll go or stay here?"

"No, it's something bad that happened to me when I was with Harry."

"He didn't mention it."

As quickly as she could, she described the horrible experience at City Hall station. "I killed him, Paul. I killed another human being. I think it'll haunt me forever. Even now it's hard to talk about it."

She started to shudder uncontrollably. He put his arm around her. "I understand. I've seen men die. No matter who they are, there's something profound and mysterious about it." He held her until the shuddering worked itself out.

Someone hailed them from the pier. "Harry," Paul exclaimed as the composer bounded up the gangplank. Harry embraced Paul, kissed Fritzi's hand. His face had a sallow, fatigued look not typical of him. Long hours rehearsing, she supposed; success took its toll.

In contrast to her cousin, Harry was sartorial perfection. His three-button suit was pale gray linen, single-breasted, with rakishly slanted flap pockets. A blue and white polka-dot tie matched the hanky flowing from his breast pocket. Every crease was sharp; there wasn't a single wrinkle, smudge, or stain to be seen.

"Sorry to be late. Problems with orchestrations."

The engines started, crewmen lifted mooring lines off bollards, and with a toot of its whistle and clang of its bell, the dinner boat put out into the Hudson. Fritzi remembered her manners:

"How is your wife, Harry?"

"Thank you for asking. I'm afraid she no longer recognizes me. A stroke victim who doesn't recover strongly often experiences a decline, I'm told. Every organ weakens from disuse until the most important organ of all, the heart — I'm sorry, I'm being far too grim. Waiter? Some wine here."

A three-piece band on the upper observation deck struck up "Alexander's Ragtime Band," the hit of the hour. Harry perked up. "Isn't that a swell song? Berlin's a friend of mine. He used to be Izzy Baline; he changed his name the same way I did. I told him that if he never wrote another note, 'Alexander' would guarantee him immortality."

"I'd second that." Paul nodded. "They play and sing it all over London."

Fritzi noticed their waiter hovering. He was a tall man with silver hair and imperial good looks. He set the soup course before each of them, hesitated, then addressed Fritzi in a rush:

"May I be so bold as to speak to you, miss? Zoltan Cizmaryk is my name. I am a great admirer of yours."

"Of mine? We've never met."

"Oh but we have, many times. I have seen you in every picture about the Lone Indian, and several others too. My wife and I are from Budapest, ten years now." So that was the source of the juicy accent. "Might I beg you to sign a menu for my wife before the cruise is over?"

"Of course," Fritzi said, pleased by the recognition but amazed again that silly little pictures could produce such a reaction in strangers.

A tail-coated captain snapped his fingers at Zoltan, who bowed and rushed off to his duties. "Quite the star you're becoming," Paul said with a smile.

"Yes, it's wonderful," Harry agreed. "I think it's only the beginning."

Basking in the flattery, Fritzi turned her attention to the excellent dinner served by Zoltan Cizmaryk and his colleagues. The dinner boat chugged slowly down past Battery Park, over to the East River, and north for a view of the Brooklyn Bridge. Then it backed around and chugged in the direction of the Statue of Liberty and the vast ocean beyond. Stars speckled the deep blue sky. The lifted torch blazed its message of hope and welcome, but Fritzi noticed that Paul's attention was fixed on lighted buildings on an island to their right.

"That's where Harry and I arrived after a hellish trip in steerage," he said in a hushed voice.

Harry said, "When my mother was turned back for eye disease and we were forced to go back to Europe, I knew I would see Ellis Island a second time or die in the attempt." His tone was light, casual, belying the emotion Fritzi saw in his eyes.

A few minutes later, finished with the meal, they strolled up to the observation deck, where couples and families gazed at the panorama of the harbor by night. Slowly, grandly, the copper-sheathed statue on its mighty pedestal passed on their right. Fritzi felt a lump in her throat. The statue hadn't been there when her father had come to New York in the 1850s, but, like Harry and Paul, the General revered everything she symbolized.

"Bartholdi was a genius," Harry murmured. "She says so much, that great lady. She says, 'Welcome, whoever you are. You needn't be rich, or renowned, there is a place for you anyway.' To me especially, she says, 'This is the land where you can realize your wildest dream if you work hard. So go forward, for that's where the future lies' " — Harry pointed — " 'ahead of you. You will never find it by going back.' "

Conscious of Fritzi's silence, Paul's thoughtful puffing of a cigar whose fiery end glowed bright, Harry laughed self-consciously. "I don't mean to dampen the evening with philosophy. Forgive me."

Impulsively, she put her hand on top of his on the starboard rail. "What you said was beautiful." Paul uttered a terse agreement; Fritzi thought there was a sudden, misty shine in his eyes.

The dinner boat described a long arc to port, ready to return slowly to the pier. Full darkness had fallen. Voices were softer, accented by the throb of the engines. New York City rose up glittering ahead of them. Fritzi heard the men discussing something, but she was far away, in a private place where she listened to Harry's voice.

Go forward, for that's where the future lies. Ahead of you. You will never find it by going back.

West Twenty-second Street was dark and empty. Their shadows moved on the pavement as they approached and passed under street lamps. A plodding horse hitched to a hansom came along, clop-clopping; the driver alternately dozed and started as the cab went by. A fire siren wailed across town. The air was cooler.

On the stoop of her building, Fritzi hugged her cousin. Paul stepped back, fanned himself with his boater with the bite out of the brim.

"You love this town, don't you?"

"Parts of it," she said, with a fleeting memory of Pearly.

"So what about California?"

"I haven't made up my mind."

"I expect Harry hopes you'll stay here. I don't think you have a bigger admirer in the whole world." Fritzi laughed, to brush it aside. "But you're the one who must decide. I was impressed when that waiter recognized you. You've made a mark in the movies. Is there anything for you here that's just as good?"

She was ready to give him a pat answer about the Broadway theater until she realized he was exactly right: in pictures she'd achieved something she'd never achieved in months and years of frustrating auditions, menial jobs, poverty — all for the sake of an occasional appearance in a flop.

She felt a cooler wind blowing over the Hudson from the west. Her head came up, and she seemed to hear a ghostly sound, like a key turning to unlock a door.

"No, Paul, nothing. Absolutely nothing. I won't be in New York when you catch your ship. I'm going back to California."

PART FIVE

NIGHTMARE

During that last July of the old order only the most sophisticated students of European affairs had any inkling of the rancors and hatreds and murderous lusts fermenting behind those picturesque facades. . . . The summer months of 1914 saw the prosperous European order turn into all the abominations of the Apocalypse.
  — JOHN DOS PASSOS, *Mr. Wilson's War*

If the iron dice roll, may God help us.
  — THEOBALD BETHMANN-HOLLWEG,
  Chancellor of Germany,
  August 1, 1914

The lamps are going out all over Europe; we shall not see them lit again in our lifetime.
  — BRITISH FOREIGN SECRETARY
  SIR EDWARD GREY, August 3, 1914

58. Loyal

A few days back in Los Angeles reminded Fritzi of all the things she'd missed: the smell of wet sage, the sunburst color of poppies on the hillsides, the clean and fragrant air, so different from the befouled skies of Manhattan.

Now and again she daydreamed of Harry Poland, his charm, his adoring looks — which ought to be reserved for his wife, she thought, bringing herself up short whenever she recalled him too fondly. She understood Harry's situation, but she also understood that it made him unavailable.

Then, in April 1912, something happened to banish memories of Paul's friend and fill her with happiness. It started, ironically enough, on a day when the papers were full of tragedy: the great White Star liner *Titanic*, termed unsinkable by her builders, had struck an iceberg on her maiden crossing to New York and carried almost 1,600 people to their deaths.

Fritzi and Owen's replacements were filming *The Lone Indian's Squaw* at Daisy Dell, the remote glen off North Highland. During the first hour Eddie found it difficult to get cast and crew to concentrate; nearly all of them, including Fritzi, had their noses in copies of the *Times*.

Jock Ferguson's assistant craned over Fritzi's shoulder. "How many'd they save?"

"Seven hundred and forty-five. That's not very —"

"Let's go, let's go," Eddie stormed, clapping his hands. Sighing, Fritzi folded her paper. He was beginning to sound a bit like Kelly.

For the first time she noticed the two extra players hired to play outlaws in the picture. One was short, bowlegged, and forgettable, but the other caught her eye. He was tall, thin as a stick, with a mahogany sunburn, gaunt cheeks, and a bold nose. Veins in his forehead stood out, giving him an air of suppressed tension even when he smiled. Whether facing the light or turned away from it, he squinted, as though he'd stared into a thousand burning prairie suns.

His weathered jeans and shirt and blue bandanna fit him naturally and comfortably. Long brown hair hung down to his collar. A six-inch scar disfigured the back of his wrist and left hand. He struck Fritzi as dangerous, a strange, inexplicable reaction that mingled delicious excitement and puritan guilt.

Eddie introduced him as Loy — a strange name. She asked where he was from. "Texas," he said, touching his hat brim. That was that. The man was polite, did what he was told, but didn't socialize. She kept darting glances at him when he wasn't looking. When she did, she breathed a little faster.

The company returned to Alessandro Street to finish a final day of shooting on the stage, in front of flats representing the interior of a trading post. Several buckets of rye flour stood in for a dirt floor. A white muslin canopy operated by ropes and pulleys was pulled across to filter the warm sunshine and rid the scene of sharp shadows.

Eddie's scenario included a switch on a scene already a western cliché: the bad men firing pistols to make the hapless tenderfoot dance. This time the victim was Fritzi, wearing a fringed and beaded Indian dress presented to her earlier in the story by the hero.

Loy and his partner shot blanks at Fritzi's feet. She fought back with an improvised dance that kicked dirt in their faces, then disarmed the bad men, ready to hand them over to the Lone Indian as he burst in. Eddie rehearsed the scene and filmed it in one take.

Since Kelly was nowhere to be seen, he asked to do it again, urging Fritzi to "let herself go." She retreated behind the flat, collected her thoughts, returned, and said, "All right." Eddie called camera and action.

This time her dance for the stupefied outlaws lasted a full twenty seconds, a wild combination of whatever she could remember from ballet, soft shoe, clog, one-step, with a French cancan finish — ideal for kicking the tall Texan in the stomach. Jock Ferguson laughed so hard he had to signal his assistant to grab the crank. When Eddie called cut, Fritzi rushed to the Texan, putting her hands on his arms without a thought. Under the rough cloth of his shirt she felt thick muscle.

"I hope I didn't hurt you."

"No, ma'am, not a bit."

Owen's replacement chuckled and said, "That's the only squaw I ever saw who came from vaudeville."

Eddie laughed. "Wasn't it swell?"

Loy beat his high-crowned Texas hat on his leg to knock off flour. "Sure was. This lady's mighty funny."

Eddie said, "We've known that for a long time. I'm trying to think up a comedy character for her."

"Oh, please," Fritzi said. "Let me be a serious actress for a few pictures."

Eddie shrugged. "If that's what you want. B.B. told me to keep you happy."

"That's a good thought," Loy said with a pleasant nod. He jumped down from the stage, walked off to make a cigarette by tapping tobacco from a small cloth pouch into a paper he rolled with one hand. Fritzi wanted to follow and talk to him. Unfortunately, Eddie said they were done. The extra players strolled away toward the main house for their pay. Neither of them looked back or said goodbye. Fritzi watched the Texan's long legs and tall hat until the men were out of sight.

She asked Eddie about the man's odd name. "Short for Loyal, that's all I know." He didn't notice her degree of interest. He was busy marking up the assembly sheet, a list of scenes Daphne Roosa would use to cut the picture together.

Loyal. The name rang in her thoughts all day.

Probably she'd never see him again.

Cowboys were drawn to Los Angeles because the standard weekly output of almost every picture company consisted of a comedy, a drama, and a Western or Indian story. The cowboys came from Arizona and Idaho and Texas — all over the West. People said a lot of them were hard cases on the run.

They hung out at Cahuenga and Hollywood Boulevard, a dusty, sparsely built corner already christened the Waterhole. Studios sent autos or trucks to the Waterhole to pick up extra players for the day.

At the end of the week of filming *The Lone Indian's Squaw*, Eddie didn't need her, so Fritzi took the Packard for a solo drive. It was a beautiful afternoon — one of the clear and pristine California days when the whole Los Angeles basin smelled of orange blossoms.

Von had taught her well; she drove expertly and with confidence. But she knew nothing about the internal workings of autos, so she was alarmed when the Packard coughed and began to balk. She pulled to the curb alongside a horse trough. After one more loud gasp, the Packard quit. She looked around to see where fate had stranded her.

She recognized a drugstore and, on the corner opposite, a new nickelodeon whose raw pine siding was still unpainted. The Waterhole. Though it was too late in the day for hiring, a few cowboys were still loitering. Two sat on a trolley-line bench playing cards. Some others lounged against the wall of the drugstore, chewing matches and gabbing.

Not wanting to look simple, she jumped out and started to unfasten the leather strap holding the hood shut. A shadow fell across the shiny blue metal.

"Having some trouble, little lady?"

From the unctuous tone she knew she wouldn't like the speaker even before she sized him up. He was a plump young man, wearing new jeans, a quilled and beaded vest, a big white sombrero, and a flowing purple neckerchief. With a smarmy smile he took hold of her arm.

"You just sit yourself back in the car, and I'll see to this tin horse."

"No, thank you," she said, flinging his hand off a little harder than necessary.

He grabbed her wrist. "Listen, lady, when someone tries to help and be nice, you ought —"

"Thad, what say you leave off there?"

The gaudy cowboy spun around. "What the devil you butting in for, Windy?"

Fritzi recognized the bowlegged man who'd taken a dunk the year before in Echo Park Lake. He was hatless, his sunburned pate showing. Even at six feet she could smell beer.

"Well, you're pestering a young lady who don't seem to want it. I'm acquainted with her. I'll take over."

Thad stomped over to Windy with his jaw stuck out. "Hell you will. You damn cowboys think you own this corner."

"And you damn city boys strut around pretendin' to be the real article. If you're a cowboy, son, I'm a cow pie."

"You got that right, you old bastard." Thad gave Windy a hard shove.

Not sober, Windy found his feet tangling and his arms windmilling as he fell backward. He sat hard, banging his head on the building's cornerstone. He let out a yell, momentarily cross-eyed.

Alerted by the shouts, someone walked around the corner; his long shadow fell in the street. The bold nose was familiar, and the crow lines around his squinted eyes. The sinking sun washed his face with red.

"You hurt, Windy?"

Still supine, Windy said, "Well, my hind end smarts some, and my noggin. Otherwise it ain't too serious, thanks anyway, Loy."

The Texan walked over to Thad, thumbs in his wide belt. The silver buckle ornament was a sculpted steer's head with horns. As Thad wiped his mouth with his bandanna, the Texan planted his old, dusty boots and stared.

"Pardner, Windy's not much bigger than a stump. But you'n me are a fair match. Why don't we see about it?" He nodded toward an alley in the middle of the block.

Thad shook his head, stammering, "No."

Loy laughed. "Didn't think you would. So why don't you light out of here and leave this lady be?" With a dismissive turn of his back, he strolled over to the Packard, where Fritzi stood wide-eyed. Behind the Texan, Thad swelled up and reddened. Windy yelled, "Hey," as Thad ran at the Texan and slammed a fist into the back of his head.

Loy fell forward, catching himself on the Packard fender. Slowly he pushed back and examined his palms; the left showed a small cut from the fender's edge. He wiped it on his worn jeans.

Thad regretted his sneak attack even before

Loy turned to give him a look. Two quick strides, the Texan had a wad of Thad's shirt in his fist. With his other hand he punched Thad's gut.

Thad staggered sideways. His hat fell off. His eyes bulged. As Windy got up unsteadily, the Texan boomed a left under Thad's chin. Thad spun away, and the Texan hit him with a flashing right that dumped him in the horse trough.

Water splashed over the sidewalk, on Windy's pants, the cursing card players on the bench, the boots of a couple of loafing cowboys watching the altercation with big smiles.

Thad came up flailing and spitting. Loy grabbed his sopping shirt, held him with his left hand, and hit him. The Texan's teeth clenched. His face was red and so were his knuckles.

Thad took the punch hard, holding his middle and gagging. Windy said, "Hey, Loy, that's plenty." The Texan squinted at Windy, then at Thad snorting and blowing red mucus out of his nose. He released Thad, and Windy stepped away.

"Don't let me catch you on this corner again."

The battered victim climbed out of the trough, sopping. With one trembling look backward, he picked up his crushed and soaked sombrero and limped around the corner.

Loy came over to Fritzi. "Some of these town dudes figure that if they dress the part, that's all it takes. Thad's pa is a banker downtown. You can round up all the blood-sucking bankers in the world and hang 'em, and it would suit me."

As if that explained anything. She was appalled at his burst of violence, yet sinfully excited by it too.

Then Loy seemed to relax, his shoulders losing tension as he stepped over to the Packard. "Let's see the problem here. Can't get your machine to run?"

"No, I don't know what went wrong."

He touched her arm — " 'Scuse me" — walked to the rear of the car and unscrewed the lid of the round fuel tank. He put his eye near the opening. "Dry as the Rio Grande in a drought."

"Oh, dear. I never thought to check before I started out."

"There's a store just up the way sells gas. I'll be right back." He walked off west on Hollywood Boulevard.

The bowlegged man approached Fritzi as though treading the rolling deck of a ship. If not reeling drunk, he'd had plenty. He smelled of it, and of leather and sweat.

"We met before, ma'am."

"In Echo Lake Park."

"Windy White's the name."

"Windy, that's right, how are you?" She offered her hand.

He stuck his out, missed, and sheepishly tried again. "Think I'll rest a bit, you don't mind." He sat on the end of the trolley bench, head on his arms. The annoyed card players had gone.

Soon the tall man loped back with a tin of gas. He poured it into the tank with a steady hand, spilling only a couple of drops. "That should take you home."

"I'm very grateful to you and your friend. May

I know your full name?"

"Loyal Hardin. Most call me Loy."

"I'm Fritzi Crown."

"Sure, I remember. Liberty."

"I must pay you for the gas, and your trouble."

"Oh, no, ma'am. Glad we could help." He had a deep voice, an easy manner now that rage no longer controlled him. She drank in details: his cracked boots, his worn leather vest. At the open neck of his blue work shirt some curling hairs caught the sun like glowing filaments. The sun in the west lit him from behind. Just the sight of him made her hot and dizzy.

"Best we mosey along, Windy." The small man grunted but didn't raise his head.

Heart racing, Fritzi spoke in a rush. "Mr. Hardin, if you're looking for more picture work, I know we have another western starting in three weeks." She knew no such thing. She'd beg Eddie to write one, she decided. If that didn't work, she'd plead with Lily. She was deflated when he scratched his chin and shook his head.

"Three weeks? Afraid I won't be here."

"Oh, you're leaving?" Lord, did he hear the silly schoolgirl terror in her voice? If he did, he spared her embarrassment. He leaned back against an old iron hitching post, crossed one leg over the other, boot toe on the sidewalk.

"Catching a steamer for Alaska. Snow'll be melting up there soon. Never seen that part of the world. Stay too long in one place, the place gets mighty stale and so do I."

"Will you come back to Los Angeles?"

"I expect so. I like picture work. It's not

steady, but it's easy. Doesn't wring out your brains too much. Appears to me you movie folk will be grinding out westerns till kingdom come."

"I think so. Perhaps we'll meet again."

"Sure, that'd be nice." She didn't know whether he meant it would be nice, affording some romantic opportunities, or it would be nice like eating a dish of ice cream on a hot day and then going about your business. She couldn't believe she was vaporing this way.

"I don't have many pals in town besides Windy," he added.

Pals? Was that all he wanted, another campfire crony? She had other things in mind.

Their eyes held for a second. He touched the brim of his hat, the way he had when they'd met on the lot. "Adios, Miss Crown. Let's go, Windy." He helped his friend off the trolley bench, bracing him up when he started to sag. The men went around the corner and on up Cahuenga.

A woman with a stormy countenance came out of a bakery down the block. "You going to park there all day? We like that spot for customers."

"Oh, sorry, I'm going," Fritzi said in a vague way. She was shaken by meeting Loy Hardin, attracted and frightened of him at the same time. She yearned to see him again, find out what lay behind those black eyes, that fearsome squint.

To celebrate May Day, Fritzi and others from Liberty went to a gala party opening the Beverly

Hills Hotel. Al Kelly soaked up free champagne and sneered behind his hand. "Who's going to stay at a hotel in the middle of some bean fields? Nobody."

Another summer heat wave killed the frail and the elderly in the East. Fritzi made *The Lone Indian's Peril* and *The Lone Indian's Christmas*. With Eddie pushing and cajoling, she devised some funny touches in them: a comic walk in wet shoes, a face accidentally dusted with flour as she worked in the kitchen. In the Christmas story she repeated her fall from the horse, this time with a rucksack full of presents. Each picture was a success for Liberty, generating good revenue, mail for Fritzi, and even an article planted in *Motion Picture Story Magazine*. Lily wrote most of it.

Tired of a one-note career, Fritzi went to B.B. and voiced her frustration. He responded with one of his soulful sighs.

"Listen, I understand perfectly, but I got to tell you, Fritzi, Hayman and Al are in bed on this, you'll excuse me for being crude. You're a money maker. Money, money, money — the word comes out of them like they were a pair of Victrolas. Is the talent happy? Who cares? I fight them tooth and nail. Sure, I can order Al to do what I say, but whenever I do, the whole operation goes to hell until he decides to stop sulking. Al's a genius with the books, I need him. It's frustrating. Sometimes I get as mad as you and want to go back to the optical shop. I'll find you something better, I promise."

True to his word, he loaned her to a new company, Adolph Zukor's Famous Players. In Zukor's *Stick 'Em Up* Fritzi played a brave female bank teller who foiled a robbery. Not exactly *A Doll's House*, but at least she kissed a leading man, the bank president's son, instead of a horse. She also saw a good deal of Mary Pickford for a week. She and Little Mary lunched in Mary's dressing room with the door latched. This permitted Mary to puff away on cigarettes; on the screen she didn't dare.

"They still have me playing twelve and fourteen because I can get away with it," Mary complained. Though only in her twenties, she was rumored to be making five hundred dollars a week. The studio called her America's Sweetheart. There was an open conspiracy to keep secret from the public her marriage to Owen Moore, a handsome leading man from Biograph who had the misfortune to be a drunk.

"The sweet little virgin, that's me." Mary rolled her eyes. "Get a load of this." She opened a smart leather case trimmed in brass. The case held rows of artificial yellow curls nesting in velvet. "A makeup whiz named George Westmore made it. I can sprout a whole head of curls in five minutes."

In turn, Fritzi told Mary about her frustration over her roles. Mary was incensed. "They'll chain you up forever if you let them. The moment I think I can press my bosses to the wall, I'll demand control, with my own production company. You should do the same."

"Oh, I'll never have the power. I'll never be a big star like you."

"Yes, you will, darling." Mary patted her hand. "Till then, keep a little sign in your head that says 'My Own Company.' "

At that moment America's Sweetheart had the steely eyes of a robber baron.

Fritzi dreamed often of the man from Texas. On a free day she drove to the Waterhole, parked, and waited. No sign of him. A fortnight later she went back and this time found bow-legged Windy White, half sober and hobbling on a crutch.

"Mr. White, do you remember me?"

" 'Course I do. Miss Crown, ain't it?"

"That's right. I'm sorry to see you had an accident."

"Wal, wasn't as if I didn't know ahead of time the shot was chancy. I jumped off a locomotive on a trestle and fell in a crick. The crick was a mite shallow. I'll mend in a week or so."

Fritzi shuddered thinking of it. "Do you do this kind of thing often?"

"Often as they want to pay me, yes'm. Windy White'll take a dive from an auto, a trolley, a balloon, a cayuse, a runaway wagon — anything that's movin' fast."

"That's dangerous work." She wondered how he dared risk it if he were constantly befogged by whiskey. "By the way, have you seen Mr. Hardin, or heard from him?"

"Loy? Nary a word since he left. Loy ain't the sort to write letters, though. Any special reason you're asking?"

"Um, the studio wants him for a small part."

"That so?" He sliced a wad of tobacco off a plug and slipped it into his mouth. He didn't embarrass her over the transparent question: what studio would send an actress searching for a bit player?

"Wish I could help you. I sure-God don't know what's happened to him. I hope some grizzly didn't catch holt of him. Anything on two legs Loy can handle."

He tipped his stained sugarloaf hat and hobbled off to join some cowboys playing euchre on the trolley bench. Fritzi crossed Hollywood Boulevard, in front of a wagon loaded with five-gallon bottles of mineral water, fighting back tears of frustration.

59. Flying Circus

Carl rode the boxcars to El Paso, and asked for Rene LeMaye at the gents' bar of the Sheldon Hotel. He was told that LeMaye's aerial exhibition team was making an eight-week circuit of Arkansas and Oklahoma. Carl washed dishes in a restaurant for two months. At the end of that time, as predicted, LeMaye returned to his base. He interviewed Carl in the bar of the Sheldon.

Rene LeMaye was a small, squinty man of forty, prematurely bald, and almost never without a cigarette. He'd learned to fly in France, at the school run by the Farmans, Maurice and Henry. In 1910 he'd come to the U.S. as a mechanic for the celebrated French flyer Louis Paulhan, and stayed when Paulhan's exhibition tour ended. Rene's remarks to Carl in fractured English were candid, not to say blunt:

"I will try you out tomorrow on our oldest plane. If you don't crash it to pieces, I'll hire you. Our troupe is different from many touring your country. We are not demonstrating machines in order to sell them. We have nothing to sell but *frisson*. The fluttering heart. The leaping stomach. Death-defying aerial stunts by daredevils who — always the faint unspoken hope, eh? — might fail to defy it this time. For the flyers too it is exciting — like drinking fine brandy, or having a new woman. Can you deal with all that, *mon ami?*"

"I can, and I'd like it," Carl said, with more hope than certainty.

After a successful tryout, Rene hired him. In the weeks that followed, Carl discovered that the little man had spoken truthfully. The yells and cheers rising from a packed grandstand after a dangerous stunt were heady wine. Once, he thought he should spend his life with racecars. Traveling from fairground to fairground with Rene's troupe, he realized he'd been wrong. He really belonged aloft, with the wind and clouds and air currents, challenged by a fragile machine that could carry him to spectacular heights, or fail and kill him in an instant.

After Rene, the most important man in the troupe was Tom Long, their mechanic. Tom was a huge, tall, full-blooded Cherokee with black braids, fierce dark eyes, and a passionate loyalty to the school that had prepared him for the world, the Carlisle Indian Academy in Pennsylvania. Jim Thorpe's school.

The third pilot, Chauncey Crampton, was a big, bluff Englishman with a perpetually red face and peculiar green eyes. He'd been hired in a San Antonio saloon as a desperation replacement for a likable young man named Alfie Burns. One day when the aerial circus was flying to another engagement, Alfie wandered off course, ran into a cloud of grasshoppers five miles wide, and crashed. He had the misfortune to be piloting the troupe's Curtiss biplane. Its pusher engine tore loose on impact, hurtled forward, and broke his spinal cord. He lived less than twenty-four hours.

Carl learned that Alfie Burns's replacement carried the nickname Harvard because his titled father had sent him to that school. Temperamentally a bully, Crampton had fared badly at the university. In his sophomore year he had knocked another student out the second-floor window of a dormitory during a drunken fight. The student hit the ground at a bad angle, crushed his skull, and died. Harvard was not only expelled; his father punished him for his scandalous behavior by banishing him from England. Like many another remittance man, Harvard lived on a stipend too small to satisfy large appetites for food, drink, and women. He never hid any of this — seemed to revel in telling it, rather.

Carl disliked Harvard from their first meeting, and it was returned. The Englishman provoked petty disputes. Who had the only chair in the shade. Who took the wrench the other wanted. Harvard packed a gigantic Colt revolver in a holster decorated with silver ornaments. He seemed eager to use it to settle their petty differences. Carl refused to take the bait.

Carl and Harvard had their first serious trouble in the summer. The troupe was back in El Paso for a week, readying their machines for a series of exhibitions in New Mexico. On their last night in town Carl entertained himself in a whorehouse Rene recommended.

The madam, Señora Guzman, had decorated the place with religious plaques and statues, and scores of altar candles burning in little cups of red or green glass. The Señora apparently saw no conflict between her deeply held faith and a lusty appreciation of the flesh.

Carl relaxed in a side parlor off the main hall, in his undershirt, his galluses down and his side-arm still strapped to his hip. He'd bought the gun, a Model 1911 Colt .45, on Rene's advice. The Southwest still had many of the rough aspects of the frontier; the aviators had been involved in a couple of scraps with small-town hooligans in West Texas and Arizona, and Rene deemed a pistol for each man to be a wise deterrent. So far Carl had never fired the Colt in anger or self-defense, but if he had to, it would deliver a wallop. The merchant who sold it said it could knock a man over even if the bullet hit him in the arm.

Though Carl was just thirty-two, he was developing the stomach of a man somewhat older. Harvard liked to rag people about such things. "Hey, mucker," he would say, poking Carl in the middle. "Carrying a little bun in the oven, are we? Won't be able to fit in your dress." Wearing an ankle-length dress, a gray wig, and wire glasses, Carl did a stunt in which he stole a plane warming up in front of the grandstand, then made zooming passes over the thrilled crowd with a second plane in pursuit. At the end of the stunt he landed in the infield, ripped off the wig, and took a bow.

On a low table next to Carl's chair was a brown bottle of *sotol*, the wickedest liquor he'd ever tasted. On his lap sat a plump girl in her twenties, full-skirted but naked from the waist up. Her breasts, big brown melons, were barely covered by a fringed purple rebozo. She teased Carl's nose, his eyebrows, his forehead, with a languorous hand. There was no hurry; he had engaged her for the night.

The girl gently licked his upper lip and whispered that she could feel his control stick beneath her, did all aviators have such big ones? Before he could answer he heard heavy boots. Harvard appeared with his long Colt strapped to his leg. Anxiously, Señora Guzman hovered behind him.

"I tell you, sir, Yolande's busy with this gentleman," she said in Spanish. Like the rest of the troupe, Carl had learned enough of it to make life tolerable.

It was a hot night; Harvard's face looked as if it had been cooked in a lobster pot. He grabbed the madam's arm, shoved her to one side, leaving finger marks on her flesh. "But I decided I want Yolande again tonight, granny," he said in English.

Carl waved. "Forget it, Harvard. No reserving the ladies in this house. Pick one of the others, they're all pretty."

Harvard clenched his teeth, the nearest thing to a smile he could manage. "She's with me, you mucker." He loved that word, used it often to incite someone to fight, or to humiliate them if they wouldn't.

Carl wouldn't. "No," he said.

Harvard growled, "Yes. Come on, we'll settle it."

Carl sighed. "Jesus, you're determined to ruin

the evening, aren't you?" He eased Yolande off his lap, wet his lips with a sip of the fiery liquor, slipped his galluses up over his shoulders. He unbuckled his holster and laid it on the chair. He had no intention of exchanging shots with the bullying Britisher.

"There's a yard in back where we can discuss this. We don't want to break any of Señora Guzman's furniture."

Harvard took off his holster and shoved it into the hand of the madam without looking at her. Carl flipped a casual finger at Harvard's soiled khaki shirt.

"The hideout gun too, if you don't mind."

It didn't seem possible that Harvard could turn redder, but he did. From under his shirt he produced a .32 knuckle duster charmingly christened "My Friend" by the manufacturer. It was an ugly little weapon, with no barrels; it fired directly from the revolving chamber.

Carl watched Harvard's eyes, wondering if the man was so angry that he might shoot without thinking. Yolande stood behind him, arms locked around his waist to drag him away from what would be, at best, an exchange of brutal punches lasting until one man dropped.

It didn't go that far. Rene strolled in, whistling "Alexander's Ragtime Band."

With one look he sensed the standoff, the animosity. He was a head shorter than Harvard but stepped in front of him and pushed his chest with both hands.

"We are all on the same side, gentlemen. We do not fight one another, whatever the pretext."

"Get your ruddy hands off me, Frenchie."
Harvard showed a fist. An eight-inch knife
seemed to leap into Rene's hand from nowhere.
He touched the point to Harvard's throat without drawing blood.

"I want grown men working for me, not quarrelsome children. If that's too hard for you, *mon
ami,* pack your kit. Go live on the pittance you
get from dear papa."

Harvard's eyes bulged as he strained to see the
shiny blade under his chin. He backed up slowly.
Raised his hands.

Rene said, "Very good, that's intelligent."

He withdrew the knife, snapped it shut. Harvard grabbed his gun belt from Señora Guzman.
As the Englishman stepped into the hall, he
looked at Carl with those odd green eyes.

"Another time, mucker."

"Any time," Carl said.

The Englishman stomped out of sight. Rene
sighed. "I am not always a perfect judge of character. I hired the wrong man. Go on upstairs
with your lady. He's my worry." He rolled a cigarette and attached it to his lip with spit.

Carl slipped an arm around Yolande's waist.
"No," he said, "we've all got to worry about that
one."

60. Viva Villa!

In the spring of 1913, Paul and Sammy Silverstone stepped off a steamer at Galveston. They transferred to the Gulf & Colorado for the long, bumpy ride to El Paso, sometime capital-in-exile of the Mexican revolutionists campaigning to bring down the central government.

Sammy complained that he couldn't understand who was who in the struggle, let alone pronounce the names. Paul said that no matter how complicated or confusing it was, what concerned the two of them was one basic truth. "There's bloody fighting going on, and bloody fighting is a staple of our trade."

Three months before, General Victoriano Huerta had overthrown the regime of Madero, the "apostle of democracy," placed him in custody, and soon sent him to a government prison for "personal protection." In Mexico City's midnight streets, assassins ambushed the caravan of heavily guarded autos. In a hail of bullets Madero was removed as a possible threat to the new leader, who promised the usual "thorough investigation." America's newly inaugurated president, Woodrow Wilson, deplored the killing and strengthened the U.S. military presence on the border.

Under the leadership of the First Chief of the Constitutionalists, Venustiano Carranza, two guerilla field generals had emerged to press the revolution, Emiliano Zapata in the south and, closer to Texas, Pancho Villa, *El Tigre del Norte*.

Rebel generals and bureaucrats had been back and forth across the Rio Grande many times, holding court, hunting funds, and buying weapons at El Paso's Sheldon Hotel, where Paul and Sammy took rooms. El Paso was a noisy, crowded warren of gamblers, whores, cattle rustlers, land speculators, cowhands, Indians, U.S. doughboys, journalists — a bubbling stew heated by war and seasoned with a sprinkling of arms merchants and aviators selling their goods or services to any buyer with cash.

Southwest of town, near a stinking copper smelter, they crossed the Rio Grande on a swaying footbridge of rope and boards. Camera and film cases were hidden under filthy blankets in their creaky mule cart. They carried tins of jerky and hardtack and three canteens, two with water, one filled with whiskey. Serapes and straw hats, old pants and rope sandals, helped deflect questions. Paul had folded his passport and hidden it, along with a letter of credit from his employer, in a cloth pouch tied around his neck with a thong. He knew a good deal of Spanish, and the Federal soldiers on the Mexican side waved them on immediately.

Below Juarez lay an arid region of sand hills studded with manzanita trees blooming pink and white, greasewood, prickly pear and yucca, spiny ocotillo with vivid red flowers at the end of each branch. On their right hand, curving around to form a barrier in the south, the Sierra Madres presented themselves as hazy blue ramparts of rock with vegetation on the lower slopes. General Villa, an idol of the poor, had brought the war to this northern state, overrunning the great *ranchos,* looting the haciendas, investing towns and villages to drive out *Federalistas.* He then recruited men for his Division of the North, promising a triumphant march on the capital, where Huerta and his followers clung to their power and privilege and, not incidentally, the goodwill of American oil and mining interests that helped fund their side of the war.

The chaparral gave way to raw and brutal desert. The mountains seemed to recede continually ahead of them. Thirst and heat and sand fleas tortured them waking or sleeping. Twice they saw black smoke columns on the horizon from burning *ranchos.* At nightfall on the fourth day, they came within sight of a town a few miles west of the National Railroad line connecting Juarez with Torreón in the state of Durango, two hundred fifty miles south. Through field glasses Paul saw Federal flags flying above the town.

He and Sammy bedded down in the open, in the lee of their cart. In the distance a wild animal howled. Paul felt lost in the vast moonlit landscape. From his gear he took a small hinged case, opened it, tilted it to catch the brilliant light from above.

The left side of the case held a photograph of his four children, taken at New Year's in an hour-long ordeal of squirming and fussing. Seven-year-old Betsy, pretty in her pinafore, sat on an ottoman with two-year-old Lottie beside her. Betsy held the baby, Theodore Roosevelt

Crown, eight months. Like the man for whom he was named, Teddy was a sickly child. Little could be seen of him in his infant's dress, just a pudgy, round face with shoe-button eyes. Shad, twelve now and visibly miserable in a stiff collar, stood behind the three, one hand on Betsy's shoulder, one stuck into his coat Napoleon fashion.

The other oval held a portrait of his beloved Julie. The keepsake was no substitute for home, but a few moments spent with the sepia images relieved his loneliness. He settled down to sleep.

Twelve hours later, Villa's army of horsemen, infantry, and female camp followers swept out of the desert and attacked the town.

A dozen horsemen stormed out of a cloud of tan dust. Orange fire streaked from Mauser rifles. A Gatling gun belonging to the Federals chattered in reply. The Gatling's revolving barrels projected from the doorway of a church at the head of the street where Paul and Sammy crouched; the gun carriage was hidden in the vestibule. The senior officer commanding the gun had stepped out a while ago during a lull, sweeping the square and surrounding roofs with field glasses. His uniform reminded Paul of those worn by Prussian officers. His helmet was the familiar *pickelhaube,* polished metal with an upright spike. There was a strong German presence in Mexico.

The rebel horsemen charged along the street toward the gun emplacement. The horses kicked dust into Paul's eyes as he and Sammy flattened against a yellow wall, beneath a bullet-torn slogan painted on it. VIVA VILLA! VIVA REVOLUCION! The rebels were advancing block by block, square by square; those at the rear were already celebrating the victory of the people by robbing and raping their fellow Mexicans.

Paul jammed the tripod into the dirt and started cranking, to catch the horsemen silhouetted against the sunlit square. The Gatling returned fire, slugs tearing a long trench in the yellow wall. Sammy put his arms over his head. "Gawd, I hope the old lady didn't miss the last payment on the insurance."

"I'm going forward. You stay back, out of the line of fire."

"Not bloody likely," Sammy growled. He was a loyal helper, brave and resourceful, one reason Paul had grown attached to him.

They crept forward. In the square raked by the Gatling, the rebels reined their horses and fired into the church. Paul tilted the tripod over his shoulder and ran through the dusky street to the glaring sunlight. At the edge of the square he passed a gut-shot rebel sitting against the wall with a bewildered look on his face and intestines peeping between his fingers. The Gatling stuttered, mowing down one of the horses. Spewing blackish blood, the horse collapsed under its rider. The Gatling killed the rider as he went down. His riddled corpse flopped against the dead animal.

Horses neighed and reared as the Gatling kept up its *rat-tat*. Paul darted beneath the awning of a *cantina*. He flung a table out of his way, saw that he still had one hundred seventy feet on the meter. Again he began to crank.

A rebel soldier on a frightened horse crashed into the poles supporting the awning. As the canvas came down and the horse bellowed, the soldier jumped off. Gatling rounds chopped into his face, blowing out an eye, ripping his cheek, blasting teeth from his jaw. Blood splashed on Paul's hair, in his eyes, on his serape, his hands, and the camera. In spite of it he kept cranking.

A portly soldier dismounted and led three other men in a rush up the steps of the church. One of the men carried a bayonet as a sword. The rebels charged both sides of the gun, vanishing in the vestibule. Paul heard a scream, then gunfire. A moment later the senior officer was hurled out the door, the bayonet jutting from his belly. He tumbled to the foot of the steps. His *pickelhaube* clattered on the stones. His hair was blond.

More pistol fire in the church signaled the end of the Gatling detachment. Two bodies were thrown out the door; then the smoking gun was carefully rolled into the sunlight and maneuvered down the steps. As the four yelled and celebrated, Paul's footage meter ran down to zero.

The soldiers reclaimed their horses and galloped off, leaving the Gatling gun to be claimed later. Paul surveyed the empty square, left his camera, and ran to the dead officer, who was beginning to smell. Holding his breath, he searched the officer's blouse for identification, found none. He did discover a small book in German.

Just then three armed men in sandals and ragged clothes, laden with bandoliers, came from the street he'd quitted earlier. In Spanish the leader shouted, "Here's the other gringo." A fourth man dragged Sammy from the dark street at gunpoint.

Paul started to reach for the holstered revolver hidden under his serape, but he checked himself when the three guerillas leveled their rifles. They walked toward him with eyes fixed on him over the rifle sights.

"Under arrest," said the man in front.

Paul slowly raised his hands.

Dirty, bloody, and tired, Paul felt a numb sense of failure. The soldiers searched him, stripped off his gun belt and holster but returned the little book after a quick examination. Paul shoved it in his pocket and fell in beside Sammy. One of the soldiers picked up the camera and laid the tripod over his shoulder. Paul wanted to tell him not to handle the camera roughly, but that would show that he spoke Spanish; he'd hold that card facedown for a while. The soldier was careful with the camera, which surprised Paul — and puzzled him a little.

Over the roofs of the adobe buildings, columns of smoke stained the sky. Gunfire banged in other streets, but less steadily than before. The procession left the square, ascended a sloping street, reached another square, and crossed to an undamaged *cantina* occupied by a dozen soldiers made cheerful by the capture of the town. Or maybe they were cheerful all the time;

Paul remembered that Villa's men were volunteers, in the fight because they believed in his program of land reform and education. The *Federalistas* who fought and died in the front lines were mostly conscripts.

Well away from the men, a voluptuous *soldadera* sat with a Winchester across her knees. Though she was grimy, she was also attractive in a rough way. Nipples big as cherries stood out black in her blouse. Using a rag, she slowly removed specks from the metal. In her eyes Paul saw the passion that gave Villa his strength and his advantage.

The general was centrally seated on a stool with a respectful space around him. He was a stocky man, in his mid-thirties perhaps. His dark, flat face suggested Indian ancestry. His full mustache resembled a black shaving brush. On the shaded table beside him rested a bottle of clear liquid. Paul saw the worm in the tequila.

Unlike his foot soldiers, the general wore a plain khaki uniform, dusty boots, military cap. His eyes, so dark brown they looked black, never seemed to blink.

"Speak Spanish, my friend?" he asked Paul in that language.

Paul replied in English, "I don't understand."

The general snapped his fingers. A wizened fellow with crooked teeth jumped forward. Spanish again: "Julio will translate. Do you know who I am, Yankee?"

"Know who he is — *el comandante?*" said Julio in barely understandable English.

"General Villa. I have seen his pictures."

When Julio translated, Villa beamed. "Bring a stool for the gentleman."

Sammy was shoved to a nearby table, the muzzle of a Mauser near his ear. Villa ticked his stubby brown fingers against the bottle. "Tequila?"

"Tell the general no, thank you, but could I have a cigar?" He patted his serape, stiff with drying blood.

A jabber of Spanish, then the translation: "The general says don't reach for your gun."

"I don't have a gun, you took it. I said I want a smoke." He pantomimed puffing. "Cigar."

"Ah. *Cigarro. Puro.*" Julio conveyed this, listened to the reply. "The general says, okay, smoke, but if you try anything we show you the adobe wall." Paul had heard the expression before; it meant the firing squad.

"Another time," he muttered, pulling out a cigar. The backs of his hands were colored by a wash of blood. He could feel it caked in his hair and eyebrows. He patted his pants for his matchbox, but somehow he'd lost it. Villa tossed him a sulfur match which Paul struck on the table. The general fired a question which Julio translated.

"He wishes to know who you are."

"My name is Paul Crown. I'm an American. I make news pictures for theaters."

Julio squinted, momentarily thrown. "I think he said he wears a crown, General. Also he paints pictures." Good God, the man didn't understand English at all. This could be disaster. Paul clamped the cigar in his teeth, found the soldier with the camera, pointed, then pantomimed cranking and said in Spanish, *"Cines noticias."* News pictures. Villa rocked back on his stool, laughed.

"Well, well. There are two of us playing tricks. I speak the language of you Yankees. I have been in the United States many times." He waved a hand. "Julio, sit down, you're an idiot."

Shamed, the ratty man disappeared in the *cantina*. Villa swigged from the bottle and continued, "I do a lot of good business in Texas and New Mexico. For instance, I take the cattle of the whoresons who rob the people of their land and birthright. My boys run the herds up to Columbus, New Mexico, by night. An accommodating merchant sells them, thereby sanctifying them in God's eyes before they go to the slaughter pen. You will understand that I can't reveal the name of the gentleman who helps me fatten the revolutionary treasury, since you and I are not well acquainted. You look trustworthy, but that can be said of many a spy."

He drank again. Villa might be an illiterate peasant, but he struck Paul as shrewd, and certainly he possessed innate military skills.

"You take the moving pictures?" Villa asked. Paul nodded. "I like the pictures. I have seen them in El Paso many times, five *centavos*."

"That's why I came down here, General. To make pictures of your war. I have credentials to prove who I am." He took hold of the thong that would pull out his passport pouch.

"Doesn't matter, I don't need to see them. I like you. On the other hand, you don't look stupid. Surely you know you are breaking the law.

President Huerta ordered all Americans out of Mexico. What you are doing is against the law, very dangerous."

Paul tensed. He struggled to keep his face composed as he said, "I know, but it's my job. I don't quite understand your concern. You're fighting Huerta and his regime. Why would you enforce his edicts?"

Villa scowled. "Too many Yankees have bled this country dry. How do I know you're not secretly in their pay?"

"General, I'm not, but I have no proof except my word. So tell me. Are we under arrest or free to conduct our business?"

Responding with a thoughtful smile, Villa said, "Let us say you are in my custody until we see how our talk comes out." He regarded Paul silently for several moments. Then his eyes showed mirth again. "I have been playing with you. Taking your measure. I heard someone was in town making pictures, my scouts reported it. I sent men to find you and capture you without harm." Villa scratched his chin. "So, what do you think of the people's revolution?"

"From what I've read, I'd say its goals are worthy. Mexico has a history of allowing all the land to fall in the hands of a few. Many are not your countrymen. Do you know the name William Randolph Hearst?"

"Yes. Very famous. He owns newspapers."

"Hearst also has huge holdings in your country. For obvious reasons he doesn't want land reform, or education for your people. So what you're doing is laudable in that respect. But there's a lot of blood being spilled. I don't like killing. I don't like war for any cause."

Villa tilted the bottle to his mouth. Some of the liquid ran down his chin. His shrewd eyes stayed on Paul, focused through the flawed bottle.

"I might get a lot of money for you and your friend," he said.

Paul shook his head. "It's been tried. Last year my partner and I were in Serbia. Bandits caught us and demanded two thousand pounds sterling or they were going to hang us."

"I see no rope marks."

"We escaped. You see, our employer's in London. He's a rich man but no fool. We knew he wouldn't pay. It wouldn't work if you tried it either."

Again Villa subjected him to a long, searching look. Then he waved. "Truly, I was not speaking seriously. I admire a man like you. Brave. Big balls." He stroked his mustache. "Let us talk about the pictures you make. Pictures are modern. They reach many educated people."

"All over the civilized world," Paul agreed.

"How would you like to make fine pictures of my army?"

"With your cooperation? I would indeed, General."

"I'm speaking of pictures which no one else would be permitted to make."

"Even better." *What the hell's going on?*

Villa set the bottle on his knee, a small punctuation mark.

"Very well. Pay me twenty-five thousand dollars, and you will be permitted to accompany the army, photograph all my battles, and no one else will be granted the privilege."

"You want money for being news coverage?" Paul said, to be sure he'd heard correctly.

"The revolution needs money badly." Like an old rug merchant the general leaned forward to wheedle the prospect. "I will accommodate your every wish. If we attack an objective, for instance, Juarez or Ojinaga or some other border garrison, I will agree not to engage the enemy until you are ready and say conditions are favorable."

Paul felt he'd fallen down Alice's rabbit hole. He took a deep puff of his cigar.

"General, you may not understand what I'm going to say, but please try. Pictures have to tell the truth because there's enough trickery and ignorance and other bullshit in the world without adding more. If you stage a battle according to some timetable we work out, that isn't the truth."

Villa understood well enough; his bland smile changed to a frown. "Is this your answer? Or the answer of the man who employs you?"

"I don't know how he'd answer, he's back in England. I'll tell him what I said when I see him. If he doesn't like it, he'll discharge me."

"And that is your answer?"

"Yes."

Villa's brow darkened, and he spat between his boots. He tilted the bottle and emptied it, then waved the bottle in Paul's direction. "I was wrong about you, gringo. When they brought you here I thought, ah, here's one with the look of a sensible man. I was deceived." He threw the empty bottle away, and it broke noisily on the tiles.

"Let me tell you something. I know other picture men come to El Paso. One of them will hear of my offer and accept."

"Probably," Paul said, nodding.

"I will do business with that wise man."

"I don't doubt it."

Villa jumped up, startling Paul and setting his heart to hammering again.

"You will leave this town and the state of Chihuahua. I will permit you to keep your camera so you will have a few pictures of our revolution, to make you wish you hadn't been so stupid. If you cross the border again, you and your helper, and we catch you, we will show you an adobe wall. There will be no conversation first. Take them away."

61. English Edgar

Fritzi and Lily rode the big red trolleys to Edendale six, sometimes seven days a week. Often Fritzi wasn't needed on Sunday, but Lily usually worked in her closet-sized office, or in her bedroom, turning out scenarios. "The Chinese Torture." "Mad for Love." "Smoking Pistols." She was facile, quick; she had a gift for telling stories. Pelzer liked her work, and he liked her personally. He raised her to sixty dollars a week.

Gaining confidence, Lily studied each finished picture, the rights and wrongs of it. If she disliked something, she said so. She had a running argument with Eddie:

"It's nuts to put the dialogue title at the beginning of the scene. It should be inserted right where the dialogue occurs."

Though an experimenter in some things, Eddie stuck to the conventional wisdom here:

"Everybody does it the other way."

"Do you care about everybody, for God's sake? The best people making pictures don't. Griffith doesn't. Try it, Eddie. Just try it once."

About the fifth time she hammered at him, he tried it, in a two-reel tear-jerker called *Where's Father?* He was big enough to admit it worked. He praised Lily for sticking to her convictions, promised he'd adopt the technique when it was appropriate. "The hell with what Al says."

B.B. and Sophie left for two months, sailing

from New York to England to set up a London exchange, then to cross the Channel to peddle Liberty's wares in Berlin and Paris. At the end of the trip, at Fritzi's insistence, the Pelzers had dinner with Paul and Julie at Café Royal in London. Julie later wrote that B.B. fought for the bill and won.

The Edendale neighborhood was growing busy. Fritzi's old acquaintance Michael Sinnott, rechristened Mack Sennett, took up residence on a lot not far up the street. Mack's company was called Keystone, after the logo of the Pennsylvania Railroad, which he freely appropriated. Mack had brought his diminutive girlfriend, a brunette named Mabel Normand, out west with him, along with some dependable actors. He continued to produce the kind of zany police comedies Griffith had dismissed as silly.

The wife of the affable and talented actor who'd replaced Owen as the Lone Indian, Geoffrey Germann, worked as a freelance costumer for picture companies. In the late summer of 1913, Maybelle was employed for several weeks at Mack Sennett's lot up the street. Geoff invited Fritzi to join them for an evening showing of a new picture, to be followed by a picnic of the kind B.B. often threw when Liberty closed up production on a picture.

Sennett's lot at 1712 Alessandro resembled Liberty's, though it had a more imposing entrance, a wooden arch with a large sign reading

MACK SENNETT
Keystone Comedies

Elaborate construction was underway just inside. Framing was complete for a new building with the skeleton of a tower at one corner. A man securing a tool chest for the night noticed Fritzi's interest in the tower. "His office goes up there. Steam room, private bath — got to hire a crane to lift the tub. I hear it's big as a swimming pool."

Sennett greeted her warmly by the picnic tables where actors, crew people, and guests filled their plates with slices of ham and turkey, potato salad and beans and biscuits. Fritzi congratulated him on his success. "It's wonderful, Mike — I mean Mack, I'm not used to that name yet. You're a tycoon. Your very own studio, with a lot of creature comforts in that tower of yours."

"We'll have a gym in the new administration building. Man's got to be fit and comfortable to do his best work." His smile faded as a new thought came into his mind. "But it isn't as grand as it looks. For the first time I'm responsible for a payroll. And a pile of debt." Despite his disclaimers he looked very successful in his fine three-piece suit of summer linen with a glittering cravat stickpin.

"Mr. Griffith's moved here permanently, hasn't he?"

"Yes, and most of the old Biograph gang came too. Billy Bitzer, Lionel Barrymore, Hank Walthall, the Gish girls. Little Mary left him for Zukor's Famous Players."

"I know, I saw her there."

"Hey, there's my leading lady. Over here, Mabel."

He introduced Fritzi to a voluptuous five-foot brunette with snapping dark eyes. Fritzi and Mabel Normand hit it off and in five minutes were chatting like old friends. Mabel cracked and ate peanuts while she told a lengthy dirty joke. As Fritzi listened with a smile, she was aware of the attention she was getting from a funny little chap with wavy dark hair and bold eyes.

Another old friend turned up in the milling crowd. Roscoe Arbuckle — Fatty, with whom she'd worked in *A Merry Mix-Up*. They hugged. "Here's someone new in the outfit," Fatty said, crooking a finger at whoever was standing behind her. It turned out to be the little fellow who'd been staring at her. Fatty introduced him as Charles Chaplin. "Our nickname for him's English Edgar."

"Charmed," said English Edgar, alias Chaplin, in an accent that would have identified him anywhere in the world. He kissed Fritzi's hand and batted his eyes. Then he tipped his derby and let it tumble brim over crown straight down his arm to his waiting hand. A show-off, but an amusing one.

Chaplin sat beside her on the grass during the showing of *Fatty's Fabulous Feast*. Fatty, a pastry cook, was pursued by Sennett's comic policemen, who mistook him for a jewel thief. Afterward, in the soft summer dark where fireflies winked, Chaplin tipped his hat once more, this time as a gesture of politeness.

"Very enjoyable meeting you, Miss Crown. I hope I have the pleasure again."

Something made her put her index finger under her chin, curtsey, and bat her eyes. "Charmed."

Chaplin laughed. "You're poaching in my territory, lass."

"Sorry. It isn't my forte."

"I'm not so sure," he said as they parted.

Their paths were soon to cross again. One Saturday night in September, Fritzi felt lonely and said yes to Lily's invitation to go to Poodles in Venice, where a colored jazz band played loud, peppy music. Not being welcome in established social circles, picture people entertained themselves with their own movable party. Every Thursday night the Hollywood Hotel rolled up its lobby rugs for dancing. Friday there was a picnic and dancing way out at Inceville, the ranch where Bison director Thomas Ince filmed his westerns. Saturdays, the party moved to Poodles, or the Ship's Café in Hollywood. Lily was a regular on the circuit. She'd disappear with some new Lothario, then sneak him into the house in the middle of the night. The man would be gone by the time Fritzi's alarm clock rang.

The night out lifted Fritzi's spirits. A large glass of Crown lager furthered the process. She refused the invitation of a man with thick glasses who wanted to dance. He asked Lily, who had no such reservations.

About nine o'clock Mack walked in with Mabel, Fatty Arbuckle, Fatty's wife, Minta, and Chaplin. As Mabel sat down and reached for the peanut bowl, Fatty saw Fritzi and waved. Chaplin came over, affecting a comic waddle that reminded Fritzi of penguins. He let his hat tumble down his sleeve, bowed.

"Dear lady. How grand to see you again. Care to step around the floor with me?"

"Yes, but please tell me what should I call you. Edgar or Charles?"

He led her by the hand. "Charlie, please."

The tune was "Oh, Gee," a Harry Poland foxtrot. Charlie was expert on his feet, whirling and turning Fritzi until she began to feel giddy.

"Another lager?" he asked when the music stopped. "Or would you prefer a stroll on the pier? It's a lovely night."

"Yes, let's go out."

The music of the colored band faded, overlapped by "Come Josephine in My Flying Machine" pumped out of the Ferris wheel calliope. Strung with colored lights, the wheel revolved prettily against the night sky. Rifles banged in a shooting gallery. Screams trailed out behind the hurtling cars of the Cloud Race roller coaster. On the long fishing pier, from which Mack's comedians had already driven a cop car more than once, a balmy breeze warmed Fritzi and induced a pleasant languor. The moonlit Pacific murmured. Charlie took her hand.

"Allow me to pay you a compliment. Fatty showed me *A Merry Mix-Up* the other night. Very funny."

"The leading men are funny, especially Fatty. The twin girls are just foils."

"Granted, but you're the one I watched. You have crisp moves. Fine timing. You deserve better comic material, something that's well thought out."

"What, and get hit in the face with blueberry pies all my life?" Fritzi mugged. "I keep trying to be a serious actress."

"Nothing more serious than comedy, love. It requires precise planning and flawless execution. Ruthless concentration to achieve both of those ends." When he saw her reaction he shrugged. "You've the wrong attitude, dear one. On the screen your face shines like a diamond. One can't help watching."

"That's silly. I'm not pretty."

"Pretty is common. Worth a penny or two. What you have, a kind of brightness — that's a thousand-dollar bill."

They reached the end of the pier and leaned on the railing. The full moon, huge and yellow-white, scattered needles of light on the sea. The effect was trite as a stage drop, but beautiful.

Charlie took her hand in his and gave her a soulful look. "May I tell you something?" His lips tickled her ear as he whispered. "I find you damnably attractive. Would you come back to my hotel room?"

Her heart raced. She was flattered — sorely tempted. He couldn't know how the proposition lifted her spirits. A respectable man found her worth looking at. Now if only Loyal Hardin would . . .

Stroking her hand, he whispered, "My dear?"

"Charlie, I like you a lot, truly. But not enough to — well, you understand. I hope you don't think I'm a terrible prude."

"If I thought that, I wouldn't have spoken in the first place. Is there someone else, may I ask?"

Fritzi gazed at the ocean. "I hope so."

"That's a damned odd answer."

"I know. I'm sorry. I hope we can still be friends."

"Well, my pride is damaged. I shall just have to take it in stride. God knows I've learned how. My brother Sid and I grew up in the foulest parts of London. We went back and forth between foundling homes so fast and so often we felt like a game of lawn tennis. That kind of upbringing teaches that one can't possibly hope for all the rewards of the world, only a few. A lesson I learned again just now. Of course we'll be friends. I not only like you, I confess that I admire your character, though I'd much prefer to admire you in my bed."

He smiled and batted his eyes. She laughed again. She liked this brash little fellow.

"Shall we go back?" he said. She took his arm as they walked up the pier in the moonlight. The calliope played "Over the Waves." The pretty colored lights of the wheel revolved in the night. The Cloud Race rattled and dived.

"How pleasant it is to be out here," she said, tasting the salty air. "I won't forget this evening."

"Oh, I expect most of it will slip away," Charlie said. "We're in a hectic business. Just don't forget what I said about being funny."

62. Inceville

In March 1914, Pathé premiered the first episode of a chapter play called *The Perils of Pauline*. Overnight, an actress named Pearl White became a star, and the serial form became the rage of Hollywood. B.B. and Hayman sniffed out other serials being rushed into production. *The Exploits of Elaine. The Hazards of Helen. Dollie of the Dailies.* Working together against a Kelly deadline, Eddie and Lily wrote scenarios for twelve episodes of *The Adventures of Alice* by April 1. Fritzi was dragooned for the title role, a spunky heiress whom a villainous relative sought to do out of her inheritance by doing her in.

She was tied to a moving buzz-saw belt, chained to a post next to a boiler soon to explode, thrown from a runaway freight train (a dummy substituted), dropped from a biplane (same), and subjected to other indignities on a shooting schedule that ran into early summer. When she remarked that all of the villain's henchmen were Latins, Chinese, or actors in black face (and shouldn't they balance things a little more with some white scoundrels?), Kelly put her down flatly:

"Forget it. This is a white man's country. The audience expects a nigger or a greaser or a slope head to be the villain." After a short but futile argument, Fritzi resigned herself, and even derived some pleasure from playing Alice, who was certainly an active and aggressive "New Woman" as opposed to a meek housebound frump.

The first episodes of the chapter play, released in June, were instant hits. B.B. held out a fresh carrot, $125 a week, and then gently beat Fritzi with a stick: one more picture with a Western background? This time with some comedy for her, Eddie's request?

"I had a flash, gave him a swell premise, he loved it. Please?"

"Oh, no. Oh, *no.* B.B., you promised me strong parts, not just silly ones."

B.B.'s mouth turned down at the corners. "All right, gel, I won't press you. Not when you're so negative to those who want to promote you. And we won't worry about all our folks whose wives and little kiddies depend on the success of this company. No, we won't. That's it. Finis. Kaput. The end." Ye gods. Now she had two disapproving fathers.

On a golden summer Saturday, Fritzi met her new friend Charlie for lunch at a general store across the road from Mack's studio. They bought bologna sandwiches and sodas and retired to a trestle table in a sunny grape arbor next to the store. A tramp lay asleep in weeds nearby. A wagon loaded with broken furniture and plumbing fixtures arrived at the store. The junk dealer went inside. Charlie sniffed.

"Not exactly Mayfair or the Ritz, this neighborhood."

Fritzi told him about refusing B.B. His reply was a terse "Good. You deserve better. Don't surrender."

Charlie's costume of the day consisted of over-sized shoes, baggy pants, a too-tight coat, a too-small derby, and a cane hooked over his arm. Fritzi commented on it, since she hadn't seen it before.

"Then you've missed my latest pictures, dear one. One morning a while back, Sennett discovered a hole in the schedule. He gave me thirty minutes to come up with a character. I grabbed any wardrobe pieces I could find and added the mustache as a last touch." It resembled a black toothbrush bristle. "The picture I'm working on is my third as the little tramp."

"Have the others done well?"

"Smashingly. The average number of prints for a Keystone comedy is twenty. Thirty's exceptional. On the second tramp picture they struck fifty, and it wasn't enough. The exchanges are clamoring for more. I'm very pleased."

Fritzi didn't tell him that Liberty routinely struck at least sixty prints for a Lone Indian picture. Instead she remained mum as Charlie took a delicate bite out of his sandwich. Just then an amber butterfly settled on his sleeve. He held still, not disturbing it. He gazed at the butterfly in a wistful way.

"Is something wrong?" Fritzi asked. "Have you lost your appetite?"

He shook his head; the butterfly flew off.

"I believe Sennett's going to fire me."

"For heaven's sake, why? You must be making money for him."

"Bales of it. And he's paying me a hundred and fifty dollars a week." More than B.B. had offered, but then Charlie was something of a comic genius, fat ego or no. He jarred her when he added, "I'm worth a thousand." As she stared at him, he frowned. "Money isn't the only issue with Sennett. He has a narrow philosophy. Shoot everything in a hurry. More is better. He said I take far too long to work out a gag. I told him that's because I want to do more imaginative things than slip on banana peels and tumble off ladders. Furthermore, I want to direct. When I informed him of that, he blanched and handed me over to his girlfriend, Mabel. Now *she's* directing me." He was shaking his head. "Never mind, it'll sort out. My success has not gone unnoticed elsewhere," he said with a wiggle of his eyebrows. "Say, tell me something. What is a barbecue?"

"A sort of picnic. The main course is meat roasted on a spit and slathered with sauce. Pig, usually. Why?"

"I'm invited to one tomorrow. A special party for some actor Tom Ince has engaged. They roomed together in New York when they were both on stage. Care to go? I'd welcome the company."

Fritzi had laundry and mending waiting, and unread newspapers, and a letter to write to her mother. "Thanks, but I don't think I should. Where is it?"

"Rather a long way. The Inceville ranch."
Cowboys?
"I'll go. What time?"

Charlie hired a buggy. The June afternoon was

glorious. The drive to the northern reaches of Santa Monica took an hour. They went up the old king's highway with the sunlit ocean on one side, and on the other dun-colored hills cut by canyon roads and brightened by poppies and purple heather.

Tom Ince had quickly become one of the town's premier directors. The Miller Brothers 101 Ranch Real Wild West Show wintered in California, and Ince had struck a deal to use Miller men and equipment in the off season. He filmed his big-scale westerns on eighteen thousand acres once part of a Spanish *rancho.*

They passed through an elaborate ranch gate and climbed a steep road. Grape vines splashed the hillsides pale green. Unpainted barracks with log porches sat like a row of shoe boxes on a bluff overlooking the Pacific. "Cutting and dressing rooms," Charlie explained. "They use them for exteriors sometimes. A fort, a trading post, that sort of thing."

"You know a lot about this place. Been here before?"

"Frequently. For their Friday night dances. Girls." He gave an exaggerated sigh and patted his heart.

Fragrant mesquite smoke from a barbecue drifted over them as Charlie parked among similar buggies and a few shiny autos. A large crowd, perhaps two hundred, were socializing around long food tables. Paper lanterns decorated an open-air stage where a few couples were dancing to music provided by a fiddle and a squeeze box.

Charlie introduced Fritzi to Ince, a portly, genial man with dark hair and lively eyes. He in turn introduced them to his new player, a hawk-featured man named Bill Hart. "Bill's a classy fellow," Ince said. "Done a lot of Shakespeare."

As shadows began to show on the eastern slopes of the surrounding hills, Fritzi and Charlie filled their plates with shredded pork, slaw and beans and German potato salad. Cattle and oxen lowed in the ranch barn. Restless mustangs trotted around a big horse corral. Near the corral stood an old stagecoach, much marked by time and weather. Behind it was a Conestoga with its hooped white top in place. They climbed up on the wagon seat with their plates.

The ranch fascinated Fritzi. Tough-looking men in cowboy clothes, men with a touch of swagger, outnumbered women two or three to one. Quite a few of the men packed pistols in holsters that looked more than ornamental.

A steady *thump*-thump, *thump*-thump began. "What's that?" she said.

"Sioux village. Tepees are beyond that hill. The Indians live here but keep to themselves."

Finished eating, they strolled to the bluff and spent a while watching the sun descend to the Pacific. Behind them the colored lanterns glowed in the purple dusk. More couples danced, even a few of the cowboys together, a holdover from lonely days on the range without women. Talk was lively, with occasional shouts and much laughter. On their way back to the picnic tables Fritzi froze in place.

"Charlie."

"Who are you looking at? That bowlegged runt? Migawd, is he the one you're sweet on?"

"No, no, it's his friend." She waved. "Mr. White. Windy!"

After a blink or two, recognition was followed by a bleary smile. Windy toddled over to them. "Why, hello again, Miss Fritzi." He almost knocked her over with whiskey breath as they shook hands. He'd brightened up his old cowboy clothes with a yellow bandanna. "Down at the Waterhole last time, weren't that it?"

"Your memory's very good. This is Mr. Chaplin. Are you working here?"

"Yep. Horse wrangler on a new picture."

"Mr. White stands in for actors, Charlie. He jumps off roofs, trolley cars, moving trains —"

"Damned dangerous," Charlie observed.

"Yessir, and there's no camera tricks to fake it. I'm proud to say I've carved out a nice reputation in this town. I knew I was making it the fourth time I went to the hospital with a bone broke. All the nurses recognized me an' called me by my first name."

Fritzi laughed, but her attention kept shifting to the crowd.

"Lookin' for Loyal by any chance? He's back."

"Is he here?"

"Yep. We're both workin' the Ince picture. I dunno where he's at just now, mebbe over to the Sioux camp. Loy talks the Indian sign pretty good."

"I'd very much like to say hello."

"I'll keep my eye peeled an' bring him 'round. 'Scuse me now, I feel a strong thirst prevailin' again." He almost tripped over the long tongue of the Conestoga as he left.

When Charlie excused himself as well, to look for feminine diversion, Fritzi walked to the outdoor stage, taking an empty plate and silver so as to blend in. She sat on a nail keg, nervously tapping one foot, then the other. A half hour passed.

She'd chosen the spot by the stage so she couldn't be missed. She wasn't. Windy came weaving out of the dark with the tall cowboy in tow.

"Lady's hankerin' to say howdy again. Fritzi, you 'member Loy Hardin."

"Oh, yes, yes I do," she stammered. Standing to shake hands, she was so flustered, she dropped the empty plate and silver in the grass. He laughed and gallantly retrieved everything.

Fritzi was alternately hot and cold. Thirty-three years old, and she felt twelve. Her legs wobbled. Her drawers were embarrassingly damp from excitement. Her mouth dried up and so did her words.

Windy rescued her. "Miss Fritzi came on down to the Waterhole one day, lookin' for you. Some part they had."

"Well, it was kind of you to think of me." He was bareheaded, his long, dark hair shiny where it curled over his collar. Windy belched softly, said he'd see them later. Fritzi couldn't settle her nerves. Did her hair look stringy? Were her lips red? She nibbled them while Loy waved to Windy as he left.

"You, ah, you've been away a long time, Mr. Hardin."

"Longer than I expected, that's true. After I poked around Alaska for six months, I drifted down here again. Went to Mexico for a month, but they're shooting gringos on sight, so I got out. Sailed from Corpus Christi on an empty cattle boat to Havana, caught another to the Argentine, worked with those gaucho cowboys till I hankered to hear English again." He leaned against the wagon, smiling. "You here with anyone, Miss Crown?"

"Please, it's Fritzi. I came with Mr. Chaplin over there. He's an actor at Keystone." Charlie had gathered three amply endowed young ladies and was mugging and cavorting for them. "I understand you're working for Mr. Ince at the moment?"

"Right, I'm an extra player in the new picture with that scissor-bill, Hart."

"Scissor-bill?"

"Old Texas expression. Means somebody who can't throw a loop or do anything else the right way. A tenderfoot — or some dude pretending to be a real cowboy." His scorn was gentle, but it was real.

"That's right, you're from Texas —"

"Yes'm, up toward Oklahoma. Little spot in the road called Muleshoe. You go to Lubbock, then you ask for a map."

He rested a boot heel on the spoke of a wagon wheel and smiled that melting smile. She couldn't get enough of him, the strong, lean look of his throat, his vivid dark eyes, his long hair dancing a little in the night wind. He smelled pleasantly of bay rum or some other tonic. She was nearly delirious.

"Do you have family in Texas?"

His smile remained, but it seemed a little hollow. "One sister, that's all."

"Do you go back to visit?"

"Haven't lately. Right now I've got to pick up another stake. Money's pretty easy to make in this business. I can steal a job from a scissor-bill every time."

The squeeze box and fiddle swung into the waltz from *The Merry Widow*. Loy said, "Care to walk around the ranch?"

"Why don't we dance?"

"Well, now." He made a soft sucking sound with his teeth. "I must admit I don't know how to do that. Just never learned."

"You can learn, it isn't hard." She picked up his hand and led him to the crowded floor. "Right hand goes around my waist, left hand up here in the air. That's the idea. Here we go, Mr. Hardin. *One*-two-three, *one*-two-three — that's the idea."

A few seconds passed without mishap; he seemed to be getting the hang of it. Then suddenly his boot crushed down on her left toe. Her leg nearly buckled. "Oh, my Lord, I'm sorry."

"It's nothing, I hardly felt it!" she cried, smiling to hide the pain. His grip on her waist strengthened. His hand held hers more firmly. He swung her. He danced. The terror in his face turned to amazement, then to pleasure. They waltzed under the colored lanterns and the California stars. It was absurdly old-fashioned and deliriously romantic. Fritzi forgot her aching toe. She thought that if her bliss became any more intense, she would perish on the spot.

For the next hour she and Loy Hardin walked and talked. That is, she let him talk. He soon dropped into an easy, conversational familiarity, friend to friend. He talked about all the cowboys pouring into Hollywood, most of whom he dismissed as scissor-bills, most especially Bronco Billy Anderson ("I don't care if he is big-time famous; he's just a stage johnny with a pot belly"). He mentioned one cowboy friend, Tom Mix of Oklahoma, whom he respected as the genuine article. He respected Windy too. Windy was an honest-to-God cowhand from Idaho.

"Drinks way too much, though."

"Yet he does dangerous work, diving off bridges and such."

"Says it's easy to do those things when he's lit. No fear. I can't talk him out of it. Wish I could. I'd hate to lose him."

Charlie came over with his arm around one of the girls, whom he introduced as Princess Laughing Water. She responded with a loony giggle.

"We should start back to town, dear heart," Charlie said to Fritzi.

She hesitated, wishing Loy would draw her aside, ask to see her again. Did she dare ask him? Somehow she couldn't do it.

"I hope we'll see each other again, Loyal."

"That'd be fun." Oh Lord, *fun?* Was that all?

"Might work in one of your pictures, you never know," he added.

Oblivious to Charlie's stare, she plunged

ahead. "It would be pleasant to meet sometime before that."

"Well, sure, let's see about that." *When? Where?* she cried silently. He shook her hand but didn't follow up. Charlie cleared his throat.

Slowly, reluctantly, Fritzi took her hand from the Texan's. Charlie saw the effect Loy had on her, grasped her elbow to steady her as they walked away. She'd have turned around and walked backward for a last glimpse of him if it wouldn't have made her look like an idiot.

On the drive back along the moonlit Pacific shore, Charlie said, "Is that cowboy the person you referred to when you told me there was someone else?" Fritzi nodded, seeing Loy's face in the white circle of the moon. "You fancy him, eh?"

"I do. I can't quite explain why."

"Who can explain *amour?* And why bother? Just enjoy it. What do you know about the fellow?"

"He's from Texas. He's footloose. That's about all."

"I'm not sure he's the marrying kind. Could be more the hotel-room kind. I'm an expert on that breed, being one myself."

She laughed and gigged him with her elbow. "Don't I know it."

63. Mercenaries

Back in December 1913, Rene had decided he didn't like the meager income the air show produced; he wanted to make more. He'd therefore listened to overtures from two gentlemen who approached him in Presidio, Texas. The gentlemen wore white linen suits and panama hats in lieu of army uniforms.

They offered Rene an attractive proposition and, the troupe being a dictatorship rather than a democracy, he accepted. He gave his men the option of coming along to fly for the Federals in the war zone. To Carl's regret, all of them, including Harvard, agreed. The officers in mufti left for California to buy a $5,000 biplane from the Martin company, to be modified and equipped like *Sonora*, the bomber flown by rebel mercenaries in northwestern Mexico.

Two weeks later, Rene and Tom Long piled into a pair of trucks carrying the crated pieces of the Martin. They bribed officials at the border and crossed without difficulty. To Carl and Harvard fell the job of taking the Curtiss and the Blériot across. They flew at night, a short trip but a dangerous one. Rene and Tom lit flares in the desert to mark their landing field. A down draft almost hurled Carl and the Blériot into the ground on the first approach. He sliced off the top of a towering candelabra cactus with his left wing, roared upward at full throttle, came around again, and landed safely, his throat tight and dry with fear.

At a Federal-held town in Sonora they assembled and tested the Martin. From there, working south in short hops, they reached their base in central Mexico by late January. As mercenaries they were well treated, given the honorary title of *Capitan* and a base wage of $300 a month, plus $50 for every scouting or messenger flight. The government was always late with pay envelopes, they soon discovered.

They traveled on a special train which always seemed to be retreating southward. Three flatcars carried the planes, along with portable loading ramps. Two Benz touring cars used by staff officers rode on a fourth one. A converted boxcar served as a machine shop, another as a magazine for storing aerial bombs. The train was a copy of one that Villa ran on the line farther north.

The three pilots and Tom were billeted in a private rail car bought or stolen from some Texas cattle baron. It had Pullman berths, red plush swivel chairs anchored to the floor, a mahogany dining table and chairs, and a separate galley with an icebox for which there was no ice. A spectacular set of steer horns decorated a bulkhead.

They were cared for by a ragged and skinny servant, a brown Indian boy of fourteen or so whose unpronounceable name had been abandoned in favor of Bert. Bert had run away from home in the Yucatán after his father fell a hundred feet from a chicle tree he was slashing to get the sap that was boiled to make chewing gum.

"It is terrible work," Bert said to Carl with a mournful shake of his shaggy head. "Way up high, just a rope holding you, and you got to swing the machete hard to gash the tree. My father, he cut the rope instead of the tree. He died. My mother wanted me to take his place, I said no, she beat me, so I ran away. Very much happier now. You like my cooking, *Capitan* Carl?"

"The bread you bake's always black and your scrambled eggs chew like rubber, but your personality makes up for it."

"That Harvard, he don' like me or my cooking."

"Don't take it to heart. He doesn't like anybody."

Bert slept under the railway car in good weather, or in the vestibule if they were traveling or it was raining. He had a pet, a three-foot hog nose snake with a snout like a small shovel. Bert called it Anselmo. He kept it in a box and let it out occasionally to burrow for toads, its favorite food.

"Anselmo good at catching rats too. Won't hurt you. Scared of people. Sees you, he just hiss and play dead."

He flew at five hundred feet above the dusty foothills of the Sierra Madre Oriental in Mexico. At the insistence of Major Ruiz, the army liaison officer attached to their unit, he'd stuffed an old geologic map in the pocket of his duck jacket. For aerial navigation it was useless; he followed the main railway line snaking northward to the town of Zacatecas, now in rebel hands. The plane was a Blériot, one of many built on the plan of the Model XI that Louis Blériot flew across the Channel in 1909, when he became the first to accomplish that feat.

Carl sat in the open above the wing of the small monoplane, his hair tossing, his red silk scarf snapping, his goggles flashing with reflections of distant lightning. Far away on his left, the mountains ran across the sky in ragged silhouette.

The dangers of this kind of flying weren't exaggerated. A hostile enemy was only one of them. There were no air fields, no ground crews, not even qualified auto mechanics here in the central provinces. The aviation gas supplied by the government was of poor quality, sometimes causing unexpected stalls or complete shutdown. On a scouting trip over Gómez Palacio before the rebels captured it, Rene had lost power and fought his plane to a near crash landing on a dirt road. Beleaguered *Federalistas* managed to find enough gas for him to take off again, but it was a close call.

Carl pulled back on the small wheel at the top of the control stick. The plane climbed, but not fast enough to miss the dark gray raincloud that quickly soaked his clothes and streaked his goggles. Just as suddenly he was through it, into a cloud-dappled blue sky. Great cathedral shafts of light fell on the land. He saw a farmer trudging behind a wooden plow and ox team. The man took off his straw hat and gazed up at Carl, whether in awe or dread, he couldn't tell.

He passed over fields where beans and maize grew. He passed over *casitas*, little huts with walls of wattle and gabled roofs covered with reeds. He flew above a town market, low enough to see the piles of gourds and pumpkins, the strings of chilies, the baskets of red and yellow tomatoes. Buzzards strutted in the dirt lanes between the stalls. Vendors and women shopping shielded their eyes to look at the plane, but one child, a little girl, waved at him. When a plane came from the south, it must be a government plane.

Twenty or thirty kilometers back, he'd dropped the last cigarettes and oranges brought along in a gunny sack tied to his seat. Most of the oranges went to some children yelling and waving beside a well in the village of Ojocaliente. Since the Indians and mestizos of the countryside were basically in sympathy with the revolution, throwing treats from a spy plane was good insurance in case the engine quit or the plane was shot down. His only protection now was the holstered revolver on his hip.

On across the town he flew, passing above its central square, whose finest building was a Baroque church painted red with yellow trim. The country people loved their churches bright. Carl liked the effect. In fact, he liked Mexico, and the Mexicans, so industrious despite their lives of grueling toil, so friendly and warm provided you were on the right side. Not even the Germans washed their clothes as often as a Mexican housewife did.

Far ahead, a white eye opened. A locomotive

rounding a bend with its headlight burning. A military train. Closer than expected.

He watched the headlight grow and blaze. This was what he had been sent to discover: how far the Tiger of the North had come in his steady march to the capital. All through the spring of 1914 the *Federalistas* had retreated while one town after another fell — Gómez Palacio, the rail junction at Torreón, Tampico on the coast. The rebels took Zacatecas on June 24, four days before the assassination of someone named Archduke Ferdinand in the faraway Balkans.

Despite the rebel successes, General Villa had lately fallen out with his titular commander, Carranza. Villa had disappeared in the north, ostensibly negotiating for coal and supplies. His subordinates were presently in charge, probing south but with less vigor than before. Sometimes the rebels advanced fifty kilometers, then withdrew their horsemen and their war trains half the distance, only to probe again a few days later. The Federals had to remain watchful. Pilots like Carl were their eyes.

He wiped his goggles. The stick-and-rudder Blériot flew easily one-handed. Forward and backward motion of the stick controlled descent and climb. To the left or right, the stick operated the wing warp and elevators. Foot pedals worked the rudder.

He moved his shoulders to get rid of stiffness, descended to five hundred feet again. With a small pair of field glasses he sighted on various natural landmarks, memorizing them for his report. A plume of wood smoke rose behind the approaching engine, mingling with blacker stuff trailing from charcoal pots. On the roofs of box-cars in the slow-moving train, soldiers, women, and children were preparing food. Some were taking a late siesta under umbrellas, or in shelters made of blankets and sections of crates. Small villages lived on top of these trains. The horses, deemed more valuable, always rode down below.

A sudden blast of the whistle stopped the cooking and roused the sleepers. The engineer had spotted Carl in the slanting light of late afternoon. His scalp prickled as it always did in moments of approaching danger.

Men raised their rifles, steadied themselves on the swaying boxcars. A moment later the old wood-burning locomotive shot beneath his wing. The engineer tooted the whistle, short blasts that smacked of mockery. Carl banked left and began his climb, away from the train. Dozens of Villistas fired, and he swore at himself for not pulling up sooner. The sight of the long war trains always fascinated him.

The Villistas shook their fists and shouted oaths he couldn't hear. A bullet spanged off one of the wheel mounts. Another pierced the skin of his left wing, but that wasn't serious.

He took the Blériot into a long banking turn toward the south. A few rifles continued to bang away, unable to reach him. His nerves unwound. He'd gotten the information he was sent to get, and earned another fifty dollars for the mission. Carl had enlisted in the centuries-old legions of nameless men who would fight — or in his case, fly — for whoever paid them.

As soon as he landed and reported the position of the oncoming train, the commanders issued orders. In the twilight artillery crews hitched up mule teams to move field guns farther south. Platoons of bedraggled conscripts retreated in the same direction in the midst of sunlit dust clouds. Steam was up in their locomotive, the planes and autos loaded and lashed down.

Carl sat polishing his Colt. From the galley came the scrape-scrape of a piece of scrap metal Bert used to clean grease from the black stove. For supper he'd fried some pork to the consistency of leather.

Rene came into the car with a Mexico City newspaper which he tossed in Carl's lap.

"More about Sarajevo. Things are very bad over there."

"I don't really understand it."

"Who understands the Balkans? It's trouble, that's all. Dynamite waiting to explode. This may be the lighted fuse."

Rene explained that the victim, Archduke Francis Ferdinand, was the nephew of Emperor Francis Joseph of Austria-Hungary, and heir to the throne of something called the dual empire. In the province the archduke had visited, Bosnia-Herzegovina, Slavic citizens hated the Austrians who governed them.

"Ferdinand, a noble fool, made his state visit even though there were widespread rumors of plots to kill him. In Sarajevo there wasn't any security. A bomb went off on the motorcade route. The archduke insisted on proceeding. His driver took a wrong turn. While he backed up, this young madman, Princip, stepped off the curb and fired at close range. The duchess took the next bullet, but she survived. The Austrians are enraged. War will come."

"You really think so?"

"No question. The Germans are allied with Austria, and they have planned it for years. Aviators will be wanted in my country. The French army officially organized an aeronautic corps some time ago. I may consider the opportunity. I fear we are on the losing side in this war." It was a conviction that had been growing in Carl too.

"How was I to know?" Rene said with a shrug. He pulled out his pocket watch, squinted through smoke from the cigarette dangling from his lip. "The Englishman is nearly an hour behind schedule." Harvard had gone up the line with the Martin bomber fully loaded.

Ten minutes later, Tom Long shouted through an open window. "He's coming in."

They ran outside to watch Harvard's approach over a stretch of level ground studded with small boulders. In the low-slanting light of evening, large rips in the biplane's wing fabric were evident. Harvard had been shot at and shot up. But the bomb rack located in a grid of wires below and slightly behind the pilot's seat was empty. He'd dropped all eight of the eighteen-inch iron pipe bombs loaded with dynamite and rivets. Detonator rods in the nose caps exploded the bombs when they hit.

Harvard came to earth with a succession of kangaroo bounces, then a final bump and roll, narrowly missing two large rocks. Tom Long ran out to meet him. Harvard jumped down from the seat; there was no such thing as a safety strap or harness to restrain a pilot. The mechanic fired questions, but Harvard ignored him, went straight to Rene.

"Success, *mon ami?*"

"Knocked bloody hell out of one of their box-cars. Killed some horses and maybe a couple of greaser sluts fixing stew on the roof." Harvard blew a gob of spit on the ground. "What bloody difference does it make? A bomb here, a bomb there, it's like sticking your willie in a dike to stop a flood. Where's that mucker Ruiz? I hope he passed out the pay envelopes."

"Not today," Carl said.

"Shit. Nothing for three weeks now."

"In any event, where would you spend it?" Rene asked with a philosophic shrug.

"It's the principle of the thing, Frenchie." Harvard slapped his hand into his palm. "The principle. You have to do something about these bastards."

"What can I do? Point a gun at them and order them to print money in the headquarters tent?"

"I don't give a damn so long as we're paid. My contract says I get an extra two hundred and fifty dollars for every run with bombs, and I've made two this week. I won't be fucked by ignorant greasers."

"I'm sure there is ample silver in the national treasury to pay us what we're owed. It's just the distribution that's a trifle slow. Take life as it comes, *mon ami*."

"Thanks, I'll have the wages instead." Harvard used a dirty handkerchief to wipe his nose. His green eyes gleamed in his dust-caked face like some nocturnal creature's.

"Let me tell you something. If this side won't pay me, I'll wager I know who will. I've heard stories."

So had they all: as much as $15,000 offered for any aircraft flown over to the Villistas. Rene bristled at the remark. "How dare you even think of betraying your comrades in this operation?"

"I take care of myself, Frenchie."

Carl said, "Major Ruiz hears about it, he's liable to invite you to see that adobe wall Villa's made famous."

Harvard dabbed his nose and stuffed the hanky in his riding breeches. "Fuck him, and fuck you too, chums. Anyone who gets in my way, or speaks to the major, I'll blow his fucking brains to China."

He disappeared into the railway car, screaming at Bert to serve him food *immediatamente*. They heard the sound of Harvard's hand smacking bare flesh, then a yelp of pain.

Three nights later, at sunset, Tom Long again reported Harvard overdue with the bomber. Carl played solitaire and drank a warm *cerveza* and watched the shadows of the giant columnar cactus beside the railway grow longer, then fade into darkness. About half past eight Rene snapped his pocket watch open, considered the time, snapped it shut.

"He has made good on his threat. We will not see him again. That is to say, not flying for our side."

Bert had been lounging by the galley. He grinned and whistled between his teeth. Rene shot him a look and threw his cigarette out a window.

"To me falls the thrilling duty of informing the major," he muttered as he went out.

64. The Day Things Slipped

Eddie scheduled filming of *The Cowgirl and the Flivver* for the following Tuesday through Friday. As usual before starting a new picture, Fritzi slept poorly. She jumped out of bed at five o'clock, dressed, and without breakfast caught the first car to the city. By the time she reached Edendale the sun was lighting the eastern mountains and carpenters were carrying their tools onto the lot. Liberty was undergoing a rapid and dramatic expansion.

Yellow pine framing for an addition to the main house was already standing. A new division of the company had been organized after much discussion between B.B., Kelly, and Hayman. Its product would consist exclusively of features — pictures of three to five or six reels.

More of these longer pictures were being produced all the time, despite constant complaint from exhibitors who didn't like them because they cost more to rent, twenty to twenty-five cents a foot, while split and single reels still cost a dime. Features also slowed down audience turnover, hence reduced profits further. So myopic and stubborn was the resistance, many exchanges still refused to release features in one piece, sending them out instead at the rate of a reel a week.

Studios believed short pictures would never go out of style, but features had a developing audience, created in part by a wave of lavish costume epics from Italy that proved immensely popular. *The Fall of Troy* and *Quo Vadis?* had played to packed houses. So did Griffith's American-made *Judith of Bethulia*. Major stage personalities such as Mrs. Fiske and Beerbohm Tree had muted their scorn and signed lucrative contracts for films.

At the back of the lot, workmen were digging the foundation of what would be Liberty's pride, a new shooting stage, walled and roofed with sliding panels of glass. Vitagraph, Edison, Pathé, Lubin were building similar stages, or had them already.

In a new, smaller building devoted to costumes and makeup, Fritzi found her cowgirl outfit on a rack. She carried it to a dressing room and proceeded to change, finding herself mostly thumbs, and shaky thumbs at that. One of the pins holding her padding inside her one-piece combination brassiere and bloomers was open. She closed it hurriedly, fidgeting and jittering because Eddie had hired Windy and Loy for the picture. He said he couldn't hold them past Friday:

"They're working on Griffith's big Civil War opus out in the Valley. Sounds like he's hired every horseman from here to Tijuana. He's cleaned out all the local saloons and flophouses too. Two dollars a day and a box lunch for wearing the blue or the gray. It must be some picture."

The morning's first shot took them to a stable a little way up Alessandro Street. Eddie now had an assistant, a beanpole named Morris Isenhour, or Mo. Mo had been smitten with pictures while in high school in Los Angeles. He quit after his junior year to hunt for a job. At twenty he was a two-year veteran, efficient and unflappable.

Mo arrived driving the secondhand Model T bought and repainted for the picture. He parked it by the fenced stable yard. Eddie checked the background with Jock Ferguson. Jock said, "I don't like those weeds behind the car." Eddie told Mo to find a scythe and whack down the tallest.

The three extras, Loy, Windy, and a man named Luther, arrived on schedule, dressed exactly like the ranch hands they were to impersonate. Loy strolled over to Fritzi, tipped his tall sugarloaf hat. "How've you been, ma'am?"

"Oh, fine, just fine, Loyal," she exclaimed too enthusiastically; she thought her voice was too high.

"Looking forward to this. Hear it's a comedy." With that he walked off. Let down, she watched the way his old holster and highly realistic revolver rode on his right leg. The man excited her beyond belief.

Then don't dither. Collect yourself and go after him.

The picture involved a modern-minded rancher who gave his daughter a Ford for her twenty-first birthday. (*There's a stretch,* Fritzi thought in reference to her own rapidly advancing age.) The daughter resisted the idea of giving up her favorite mount, Old Paint, for the auto, which her father said she must drive to keep track of their large range land while he was laid up with a broken leg.

The girl struggled through various attempts to master the car the same way she'd break a horse, convinced it was a useless contraption until the end of the story. Then she drove it to chase and catch one of the hands who had turned cattle rustler. Loy played that role.

In the first scene Fritzi had to try to mount the Model T like a horse. Throw her leg up, miss the running board, fall on her rear twice, then gain the seat on the third attempt. Eddie called, "Camera." Mo Isenhour sprang in front of Fritzi with the slate on which he'd chalked the number and title of the picture, and the number of the scene. "Action."

She approached the car, nervously aware of the three cowboys standing out of the frame, watching. About to raise her left foot as though to a stirrup, she saw a flicker of motion under the Model T. She heard the rattle before she saw the source.

Instinct told her not to move. Eddie said, "What's wrong? Go ahead and — oh, my God."

The snake must have crawled out of the disturbed weeds on the other side of the car. It was four feet long, yellow-brown, with irregular yellow cross bands speckled black. The diamond-shaped head was scaly, the eyes glittery as black ice.

"Nobody move," Eddie said. "Fritzi, can you back away?"

Terrified, she whispered, "I don't know." The rattler's head came up, fangs dripping. Her legs quivered like willow wands. Behind her, Loy said:

"Don't try it. Stand still."

She heard the click of a hammer cocking. He raised and extended his gun hand; she saw it at the edge of her vision. He fired one shot, then, rapidly, three more. The snake was blown in half. Loy ran past her and stamped hard on the rattler's head.

She collapsed in Eddie's arms. Everyone shouted questions at her. She said, "Yes, I'm all right, just shaky. I've never seen a rattler before."

"He was a real grandpa," Loy said. "Look at the length of his rattles. Back home we call 'em Texas rattlers, but they're all over the West."

He holstered his revolver. Despite her scare, the sight of the long blue barrel sliding into the leather sheath excited her. Jock Ferguson said, "Do you always carry live ammunition?"

Loy tugged his hat lower over his eyes. "Why would I carry any other kind?" He sounded hostile, but his expression gentled as he walked over to Fritzi. "Sure you're all right?"

"Yes. I do admit to being terrified for a few seconds. I've coped with mashers and hooligans, what I call hat-pin situations, but this was a lot worse. You were quick with that pistol. You're no scissor-bill." He liked that and laughed.

"I'll have to think of some way to repay you."

"Not really necessary, ma'am."

Go after him.

591

"Oh, I insist. Let's talk about it later this week."

Eddie broke in. "We'll get this shot, then move up the road and do the scene where the Ford dies and you cover it with a horse blanket to keep it warm, same as you do when Old Paint feels poorly."

Fritzi rolled her eyes.

In the afternoon they returned to the lot. B.B. brought Sophie out to watch them shoot on the outdoor stage in front of flats simulating a log cabin porch. The scene involved an exchange with Fritzi's troublesome ranch hand, Loy. When he got fresh, she fended him off with a wrench and a motor oil can filled with chocolate syrup. At the end of the slapstick tussle he churlishly dumped the "motor oil" on her head and walked away chortling.

After they shot the scene, Jock Ferguson moved in for a close-up of Fritzi peering through a mask of syrup, then one of Loy reacting with an evil leer that confirmed his base character. Close-ups had once been damned as faddish and grotesque, but David Griffith's artful use of them had made them respectable and even commonplace.

During Loy's close-up Fritzi stood near the Pelzers, wiping syrup off her face with a makeup towel. Sophie elbowed her husband. "That cowboy's a handsome fella. Very manly, don't you think so, Benny?"

B.B. looked cross about hearing his name in public. "Didn't notice."

"Well, notice, notice. Ought to have a better part, that fella."

I have one in mind, Fritzi thought with a delicious shiver of anticipation.

Ordinarily Eddie didn't welcome visitors on his set. He made an exception when Fritzi's friend Charlie showed up unannounced on Thursday morning. Charlie looked debonair in a smart new suit with a fine Malacca cane hung over his arm. She expressed surprise that he wasn't working.

"But I am. For a new studio. Essanay."

"Good heavens, since when?"

"Since Bronco Billy Anderson and his partners offered me a lot more dough than Mr. Cheapskate Sennett. I leave for San Francisco the end of the week. I'm a little worried about accommodations. They won't be able to match what I have now." Charlie had lately moved downtown to the Los Angeles Athletic Club, a sign of the success of his tramp comedies.

"What happens here?" he asked with a nod at the set, flats representing the rear and side walls of a ranch house parlor doubling as an office.

"The rustler's driven my cattle off. He's robbing the safe before he escapes. The Model T gets me back in time to stop him. I drive it through that wall, jump out, and foil him."

"Fascinating. Why not something simple, like walking in the door?"

"Because he's put some kind of cactus paste in the gas tank. It makes the car loco."

This time Charlie rolled his eyes.

Fritzi was hot and uncomfortable. The muslin diffusers hung above the stage softened the summer sun a little, but even so the heat was brutal. She tugged the front of her dress. The padding seemed loose. That damned pin again. Did she have time to run behind the stage and fix it? No; Eddie's voice boomed through his megaphone:

"Everyone ready? Mo, start the car."

Mo obeyed on the run. A few seconds later she heard the Model T puttering on a ramp behind the flat at stage left. Kelly had appeared from somewhere, folding his arms over his vest and planting himself next to the camera. He scowled like a man eating bad oysters.

"Get it right the first time, Hearn. I'm not rebuilding this set."

Loy pulled his bandanna high on his nose to conceal his face, crouched down behind a black iron safe that stood open. Fritzi smoothed her faded gingham blouse and climbed into the Model T. Eddie called camera and action. She gritted her teeth and accelerated up the ramp, smashing through painted wall boards rigged to break away easily. She braked in a cloud of plaster dust thrown by a stage hand out of camera range.

On his knees at the safe, Loy reacted as Fritzi jumped out of the car. "Caught you, Roy. This means jail." Eddie insisted on appropriate dialogue rather than improvisations such as "Stop hamming" or "What time's lunch?"

She started a dash across the room, but someone had set a footstool in the wrong place, a foot to the right of the tape marking its correct position. Seeing it too late, she fell over it and broke it. She saved herself by shooting her hands out and turning a somersault. Jock Ferguson called, "Cut?"

"No, no, keep rolling, that was funny."

"Wait a damn minute," Kelly protested. Eddie outshouted him:

"Jock, keep cranking."

By now Fritzi had bounded up, only to discover that her gay deceivers had betrayed her — come unpinned on one side and slipped down at a forty-five-degree angle, so that she had one lump more or less in the middle of her chest, the other near her hip. It struck her as hilarious in a macabre way.

Impulsively she turned her back to the camera. Reached under her collar and brassiere and with exaggerated wiggles of hips and shoulders, worked the padding upward to its right place. She turned around and smiled at the camera. Both bosoms promptly slid down to her waist.

She mugged, gave the padding a ferocious sideways wrench; the scene was beyond saving anyway. She popped her eyes at Loy, stuck out her index finger as a pistol, cried, "Hands up." Caught between surprise and mirth, he raised both hands. Fritzi grabbed them and began to waltz.

Not watching too carefully, she waltzed him into a chair. He bumped it, reeled away, fell against a cuckoo clock on the wall. The cuckoo sprang out, twittered, then flopped at the end of its wire, dead. Fritzi was breaking up, laughing and unable to stop.

Trying to help him stand, she lost her balance. Grabbing the shelf of a china cabinet to catch herself, she spilled and shattered plates, saucers, and cups. Playing along, Loy charged her but misjudged his position and went headfirst through an open window painted on the canvas flat. His legs stuck into the room, thrashing.

Caught up in the madness, Fritzi marched toward the camera. She wriggled her padding upward again, slapping her dress as though that might stick the gay deceivers in place. She looked down; the padding slowly sank to her navel. The effect was something like watching a pair of burrowing moles.

With a rueful smile and a shrug she gave up. She crossed her eyes, did a little curtsey, kicked up the hem of her skirt, and tripped out of the frame.

Kelly screamed. "*Cut.* Cut, Ferguson, or I'll break your goddamn arm."

Jock Ferguson let go of the crank. Everyone but Kelly was laughing. Mo Isenhour sat on the ground holding his sides. Eddie wiped his eyes with a red bandanna. Windy staggered around like a drunken man, not a difficult impersonation.

Charlie cocked his head and applauded. When Kelly glared, Charlie looked at him defiantly and cried, "Bravo, bravo."

Fritzi rushed to Loy, who'd extricated himself from the torn flat. "I'm sorry, I'm really sorry," she panted.

He managed to stop laughing. "You didn't hurt me, don't worry about it. You're a sketch, you know that? I've never seen anything like it."

"By God, I haven't either," Kelly said. "Will somebody tell me what's going on? Hearn, why didn't you cut?"

"Because she's hilarious."

"You think George Eastman's running a charity? You think he's giving the goddamn raw stock away?"

"Oh, see here," Charlie said with a flourish of his cane. "I suppose you're one of the studio muckety-mucks, but carrying on like that, you're a sap."

"What did you say?"

"Sap, spelled s-a-p. As in idiot. You're all idiots if you don't put Fritzi in a picture doing exactly what she just did, only without the cowboy claptrap."

"We don't need advice from a goddamn limey," Kelly shouted.

"Al, wait a minute," Eddie said. "Maybe Mr. Chaplin's got something. Maybe this is what we've been looking for. A character."

"Character, what character? I don't see any character. I see hundreds of goddamn dollars of lumber and props shot to hell."

"A character for Fritzi. A lovable imp who bangs up everything and everybody — breaks down doors, destroys houses, ruins fancy parties, never meaning to — and every time *it makes the story come out right.* I'm going to show this footage to B.B. and Hayman."

"This is some kind of conspiracy. I won't stand for it."

"Sure you will, Al," Eddie said with a cheery

smile. "You want to make money. B.B. and Ham want to make money. We all want to make money."

He walked up on the littered stage, slipped his arm around Fritzi. Plaster dust blanched her face. Her gay deceivers hung crookedly inside her dress; the lumps of padding at her waist gave her a total of four bosoms, all unsatisfactory.

And now Loy knows I wear padding. Oh, God.

Eddie squeezed her shoulder like an accordion. "Money, Al, you keep telling us that's what it's all about. Well, take a look. You want to strike it rich, I'm standing next to the mother lode."

Every carpenter on the lot was dragooned to rebuild the set. It was repainted, refurnished, and ready by noon Friday. Fritzi crashed the Model T through the wall again and this time finished the scene as planned. Eddie made the last shot at half past four. He was thanking everyone when his wife arrived with the children and three hampers containing a picnic supper.

Fritzi helped Rita arrange the food on a trestle next to the stage. Rita said Eddie had worked most of the night writing a scenario for a new comedy inspired by yesterday's mishaps. He called it *Knockabout Nell*. He intended to present it to B.B. and Hayman on Saturday, along with the unusable footage.

Eddie sidled up. "Fritzi, do I dare ask what slipped in your — that is, inside —"

Rita poked him. "No, you don't dare. Be a gentleman and eat this sandwich. It's liver-wurst, your favorite."

B.B. came stumping out from the main building. He approached Loy, who was chatting with Windy and the other extra.

"Hardin, my wife saw you work this week. She likes your looks. Very manly, she said."

Loy smiled and dipped his head in polite acknowledgment. B.B. snatched his hand and wrung it. "Sophie knows talent. Why don't we shoot a little test, hey?"

"Mighty kind of you, Mr. Pelzer. But I've got to say no, thanks."

"You wouldn't like a real part? Maybe a chance at a steady salary?"

"Don't think I'm ungrateful. I like what I'm doing now."

B.B.'s mouth dropped open. He ran over to Fritzi. "I offered him a part and he turned it down. Can you feature that? I never heard of anybody turning down an offer to star in pictures."

Fritzi murmured that it was certainly strange, but before she could say more, Loy set his high-crowned hat on his head and started his good-byes. "Excuse me," she exclaimed, nearly knocking B.B. down as she dashed around him. "Loy, I still owe you for saving me from that snake. May I treat you to supper. Say tomorrow evening?"

He was surprised and amused by her brashness. "Why, sure, that'd be fun. Tell you what. If you can get free, come on out to the Universal ranch in the afternoon. Watch the big battle scene Griffith's shooting. Then we'll find some grub."

Fritzi almost leaped into the air. "I'll be there."

"Don't dress fancy."

"Oh, no. No!"

"See you then. Look forward to it."

As he might say he looked forward to a good night's rest. Fritzi was disappointed again by his casual ways. She screwed up her determination. She'd make him fall for her, no matter what it took.

65. Crash Landing

The consequences of Harvard's desertion were more inconvenient than serious, or so it seemed at first. The senior staff tongue-lashed Rene but could not really hold him responsible. The one who suffered was Major Ruiz, the army's liaison to the flyers. He was ordered to ride along on each flight armed with a five-shot bolt-action Mauser rifle for use not only against the enemy but a pilot who might take it on himself to defect.

To accommodate a second passenger a new seat was installed on the Curtiss. The major fitted himself into it with all the composure of a frightened baby. In the wind fanning over his face as they flew, he sweated profusely. A strap had been rigged around the Mauser stock so it wouldn't fall and be lost. Twice on one flight the major's damp hand let the rifle slip. Only the strap saved it.

Carl shouted at Ruiz repeatedly, ordering him to sit still, shut up, stop badgering him with questions. The major took the reversal of authority without protest, he was that scared.

Some ten days after Harvard left, Carl climbed into the shoulder yoke that operated the ailerons on the Curtiss, and he and his passenger went up the line for the third time. Rain had fallen for forty-eight hours, flooding fields and waterways. A dark and cloudy afternoon had given way to a livid sky, copper colored, with

601

more thunderheads piling up in the north.

They flew over a railroad trestle spanning a stream overflowing with rushing water. Beyond it lay a scattering of *casitas* surrounded by the queer structures for storing maize that abounded in the region — columns of concrete or adobe brick held up egg-shaped bins covered over with thatch. Carl tossed down two oranges to a pair of boys feeding chickens. They waved, and as Carl waved back, Major Ruiz nearly yanked his arm off.

"For Christ's sake, what — ?" Carl began, shouting over the snarl of the pusher engine. He saw the fright on Ruiz's face, then the cause of it, sweeping at them from the northeast quadrant of the sky. The Martin bomber.

It climbed abruptly, passing over twenty feet above them. Carl saw the full bomb rack, recognized the red-faced pilot despite goggles and a canvas helmet. Major Ruiz motioned frantically toward the south, wanting no quarrel with the renegade Englishman.

"For once I agree," Carl said. He turned the rudder wheel and leaned to the right, his body in the shoulder yoke working the ailerons in tandem with the vertical rudder. The plane banked right to retreat.

In response the Martin executed its own turn and came back at them from the right, hurtling toward them on what appeared to be a collision course. Harvard was coming on so fast, Carl could see his teeth clenched in a spiteful smile. "Pull up, pull away," Major Ruiz screamed as Harvard drew his Colt revolver and started shooting. One bullet tore the wing fabric.

Harvard zoomed above the Curtiss at the last moment. Flying one-handed, Carl pulled his revolver. Maybe the encounter was accidental. Maybe Harvard had lain in wait. It didn't matter. They had a fight on their hands.

Against the stormy Mexican sky the two planes buzzed around one another like crazed moths. Harvard made a second pass at right angles to the Curtiss, this time flying below it so he could fire upward while Carl's line of fire was blocked by the wings. Major Ruiz crossed himself again and again. Three shots blasted from below. One nicked the propeller, and Carl shuddered.

He dipped low, a hundred feet above the ground, then fifty, zooming toward the trestle where the water rushed and foamed. The Martin caught the Curtiss, flying level on the left, where Major Ruiz sat with a dark stain at the crotch of his breeches. Harvard gave Carl a chipper salute, the barrel of his Colt touching his canvas helmet. Then he extended his arm and fired. Carl pushed the control stick forward, dove, leveled out, chopping the tops off columnar cactus with his landing gear. The Martin climbed, flying above them and to the left. Harvard smiled his toothy smile and pointed down with an exaggerated gesture.

The bomb rack. The son of a bitch meant to drop a bomb on them. The Martin veered to the right, directly overhead. Carl operated the rudder wheel and yoke to bank left. Harvard was a good pilot, and he followed. Major Ruiz wailed,

"He's going to bomb us, he will kill us." He grabbed the wheel at the top of the control stick, shoved it forward. The Curtiss abruptly dropped toward the ground.

Enraged, Carl shouted, "Let go. There isn't a chance in a million that he can hit us."

The major had his hands on Carl's, digging in with his nails to pry Carl from the stick. Carl rammed him in the head with his elbow. Major Ruiz bleated; the Mauser dropped between his legs and tumbled over the wing's forward edge, dangling by the strap, banging and tearing the fabric underneath.

Something sailed past the left wing. Carl watched the pipe bomb spinning earthward, then lost it behind them. After a loud detonation came a shock wave that rocked the plane as it sped toward the trestle. The engine began to run roughly. *What now?*

With a series of coughs and a spurt of smoke the pusher quit. Bad gas again? Whatever the cause, they were hurtling into a long glide; if they were unlucky it would drop them on the narrow trestle or hurl them against the wall of the cut, cracking them apart either way. He yanked the stick back, lifted the plane, praying they'd glide far enough to overshoot the trestle and land on solid ground.

He counted the seconds as the Curtiss lost altitude. Five. Six. Seven —

The trestle flashed beneath them. He banked slightly to the right, heading for a cart path between tilled fields. Ruiz was gibbering like a man deranged. Somehow he'd lost his glasses.

The Curtiss dropped to earth. Carl felt the landing gear crunch, bounce them high, then crack and collapse as they came down again. The plane nosed over, throwing its tail assembly in the air. The major somehow hung onto the wing. Carl's shoulder harness broke; he was hurled forward, tossed high, and dropped in the field with a sudden sharp pain in his left leg. It streaked upward to his hip like wildfire.

Blinking, dazed, he listened to the buzz of the Martin as it circled leisurely away from them, climbing to a thousand feet, then turning back. He pushed at the ground with both hands, dragged his right knee up, gained his feet only to fall. He couldn't stand on his left leg. Something was broken or torn.

Major Ruiz sat spraddle-legged in front of the crumpled plane, the Mauser in his lap, hair hanging in his eyes, tears streaking his olive cheeks. The Martin was returning, and they were perfect targets.

"Shoot at him," Carl shouted. Ruiz fumbled the Mauser to his shoulder as the Martin flew over. A pipe bomb dropped from the undercarriage rack, tumbled slowly downward.

Harvard's timing was faulty, though. The bomb landed fifty yards behind the Curtiss, shaking the earth with its boom and tossing up a cloud of dirt. As the Martin went over, Major Ruiz tried to fire but for some reason could not. He fumbled with the bolt like a bewildered child. Carl fisted his hands, began to crawl, using his right knee to push. His left was useless.

"Give me the rifle," he yelled as he crawled.

The Martin buzzed out of range, made another slow turn, and came back for a second attempt. Carl dug his arms into the rough ground, ripping the elbows out of his shirt, bloodying his skin, dirtying the red silk scarf. He jammed his right knee into the ground, pushed, jammed it in again, pushed. His left leg sent pain streaking through his body.

"I want the rifle," he yelled. The major stared at him blankly. "Do you hear me? Help me up. Brace me against the plane, then give me the goddamn rifle."

Grabbing the vertical wing behind him, Major Ruiz put his fist through the fabric, found a strut, and used it to pull himself to his feet. He stared at the approaching bomber, then at Carl.

"Damn you, you yellow bastard" — Carl was nearly incoherent with pain and rage — "help me!" Pop-eyed, Ruiz threw the rifle at him and ran.

Lying on his side, Carl stretched his hand out, caught the Mauser's barrel, dragged the rifle to his chest. The Martin's drone grew steadily louder. Carl shoved the rifle butt in the dirt, used it to raise himself to a sitting position by climbing the barrel hand over hand. Dizzy with pain, he got the rifle to his shoulder. The Martin approached from behind. If the bomb got him before he shot, well, that was that.

Shadows of wings flickered over the bare ground. The Martin appeared overhead. Carl fired upward seconds before the bomb detonated behind the Curtiss. A torrent of earth fell on Carl, blinding him.

He spat out dirt, rubbed it out of his eyes. The Martin was descending rapidly, veering into a steep right-hand bank. Harvard slumped like a rag doll, hanging onto his seat with both hands. Carl's round had hit him, a lucky shot. Harvard had to be fighting to stay conscious because he clearly couldn't control the plane. It nosed downward, straight to the ground. Carl watched with horror and fascination as the impact broke the engine loose. It flew forward like an iron guillotine. Harvard's head was sliced from his shoulders and sent spinning into the sky like a bloody medicine ball.

The engine buried itself in the ground. The Martin telescoped with a crackling and snapping of struts. One or more of the bombs detonated in a flash of fire and noise. Seconds later there was nothing left except wreckage and smoke ascending toward the storm clouds. Carl flung the hot metal of the rifle out of his hand, rolled over in pain, and threw up.

A mestizo found him. The man had a reticent air but the shrewd eyes of someone who saw an advantage. Yes, he had a mule. He would trade it for the rifle and Carl's Colt. Lying on the dirt floor of the man's hut, with a fiery jolt of pulque partially dulling his pain, Carl shook his head. He held the rifle in the air while clutching the pistol to his chest.

"You have this. I keep this."

After some argument the bargain was struck. The man found a rope and tied him on the mule's back. Carl guessed he was twenty-five or thirty kilometers from the Federal position. He set out at first light with more of the milky pulque in him and his gun hand resting on his thigh. The mestizo pointed him in the direction of the railway line.

At half past noon, with the sun frying his skull and his tongue a piece of dry wood, he spied something coming toward him through the heat devils above the glittering rails. He halted the mule and waited. Out of the haze came a hand car pumped by sweating *Federalistas*. Carl grinned an insane grin of relief, released his knee hold on his mount, and fell sideways to the ground in a faint.

The army doctor who examined Carl's leg said no bones were broken, though he'd surely torn or sprained something and should rest the leg until he could walk without severe pain. Carl followed orders by staying in a berth in the private car, where Rene brought news.

"The major was caught wandering around nude in a bean field. Why he removed his clothes no one knows. Since I had already relayed your account of his behavior, he was shown no leniency. He was shown the wall instead."

Carl took no satisfaction from it. He sipped tepid water from an old canteen Bert filled for him.

"By the way, *mon ami*. There is still no pay from our employers. That's two months and more we've gone begging. I'm out of patience. Besides, the rebels are winning. General Obregón's Division of the Northwest has taken

Guadalajara. Huerta stepped down day before yesterday, went into exile aboard a German naval cruiser. A man named Francisco Carvajal, former chief of the Supreme Court, is trying to hold the Constitutionalist government together. If we're to fight for these people, there should be some profit in it, if not some honor, or hope of victory."

Carl meditated on Rene's words for a moment. "Are they at war in Europe?"

"Not yet." Rene showed his thumb and index finger with a half inch between. "This close. Everyone is mobilizing. By August they will be fighting. I expect my country to be more reliable about pay for aviators." Rene was about to lick a cigarette paper. "Shall we find out?"

"What about our contract with this crowd?" Carl said.

"I suggest abrogating it in the middle of the night. Certainly I would give them no opportunity to punish us. We could strike for the gulf coast and work our passage on a freighter. To New Orleans, perhaps. We owe these people nothing, Carl. They have not dealt fairly with us. What do you say?"

Carl saw flashes of the terrifying aerial duel with Harvard.

"I'll let you know."

With a resigned shrug Rene went out.

Carl sat on a rock, by himself, well away from the train. Lying across his knees was Tess's red silk scarf. The scarf had seen hard use. Both ends were fraying, and the crash had marked the

609

fabric with dark brown spots of his blood. He'd already washed the scarf to remove dirt, and sewn up a three-inch rip. Now he worked with a cloth and pan of water, scrubbing the spots.

Fly in France, in another war? Well, why not? Recovering after the crash, he'd experienced a familiar pride and exhilaration from the simple fact of survival. He remembered similar feelings after brushes with disaster in fast cars. Maybe survival in dangerous situations would be the sole accomplishment of his life. Anyway, if he refused Rene's offer, what would he do? Limp back to Chicago and tell the General he was ready to go into the brewery? Even if he could stomach that, the papers said the U.S. was going dry; breweries might go out of business.

Carl stared at the spots. The water didn't remove them, only faded them a little. He tossed the cloth into the pan, hung the wet scarf around his neck, and went to find Rene, to tell him yes. He'd miss Bert, the Indian boy, and the legendary awfulness of Bert's cooking. But he would miss nothing else about this place.

66. Fritzi and Loy

"Don't dress fancy," he'd said. She wouldn't think of it. Saturday morning she spent a mere two hours trying on outfits in front of her mirror.

Dissatisfied with every one, she ran out of time and desperately chose the least objectionable — a tailored white shirt with a dark blue silk scarf, a full skirt with vertical blue and white awning stripes, a smart panama hat with a blue band, white stockings, and white buck shoes with brown accents.

She rode the cars to Edendale, where B.B. garaged the studio Packard. She'd arranged for its use by telephone last night. She drove over the rough, winding road through Laurel Canyon to the forty-acre Universal ranch in the San Fernando Valley; there Mr. Griffith was filming his version of *The Clansman.*

Despite Eddie's advance comments about the size of the production, Fritzi was still agog at the reality. Five or six hundred men had been marshaled, in authentic Civil War uniforms. Trenches had been dug, batteries of artillery put in place. The ranch was heavily treed and dotted with hills; she saw cameras on several summits for simultaneous filming.

The company was taking a late lunch on blankets and sheets spread in the sere grass. She assumed Loy was with the horsemen scattered across the location. Most were dismounted and resting. She'd find him at the end of the day, or he'd spot her. That was one advantage of her costume. She looked like a yacht flag.

Wandering in the crowd, she said hello to Henry Walthall from Biograph, the star of the picture. Then she fell into conversation with an affable young assistant cameraman who introduced himself as Karl Brown. She asked about the ammunition they were using.

"Live rounds in the cannon," he said blandly. "And firework bombs tossed by men out of camera range. What we shot this morning looked mighty real."

Members of the crew finished eating and drifted back to work. Most were stripped to the waist and pouring sweat. At the number one camera she saw Billy Bitzer conferring with Mr. Griffith. Bitzer looked ready to melt in his long sleeves, tight collar, and necktie. Griffith by contrast looked cool in a buttoned-up summer suit and straw hat with the top cut out to let the sun bathe his scalp. She remembered someone saying he believed sunlight prevented baldness. Griffith saw her, smiled, and tipped his hat.

The battle staged that afternoon was spectacular and noisy. Griffith had worked out an elaborate signal system using assistant directors with semaphore flags and mirrors to cue masses of men on the battlefield. Soldiers in rebel gray ran at breastworks defended by soldiers in Union blue. Cavalry charged and counter-charged. Playing a Confederate colonel, Henry Walthall led his men to the enemy lines and personally spiked a Union gun. In the dust and confusion it was impossible to find Loy in the galloping troops of cavalry.

The cannon pounded; the firework bombs burst and spread smoke that burned her eyes and made them water. For a few thrilling and eerie moments Fritzi felt she'd been shot backward through time fifty years. She had a taste of what her father must have experienced when he fought for the North.

Mid-afternoon, an actor fell off a horse and was carried away on a stretcher. That was the only injury. It testified to Griffith's careful planning. Late in the day the sun's angle changed and a perceptible haze weakened the light. Griffith polled his various camera positions, found all the operators satisfied with what they'd gotten, and called a halt.

She wanted to speak to Griffith, but he was busy, constantly moving, and she couldn't catch him. She camped in the shade of a hilltop eucalyptus grove as the extras collected their pay and dispersed to autos or the trolley stop. The crew loaded equipment into trucks. In about fifteen minutes Loy came tramping up the hillside, boots dusty, blue work shirt open halfway down his sweaty chest. Remembering his manners, he buttoned it hastily, then stepped up to her with a tip of his sugarloaf hat.

"I thought you might not find me," Fritzi said.

"Spotted you an hour ago. Can't miss those stripes." When he touched her arm to help her stand, the sensation was like a charge of electricity. "Hungry? There's a roadhouse that serves food close by. Or we can catch a red car and go somewhere."

"I have the studio automobile. We can go anywhere you'd like."

"Well, aren't you something?" He kept his hand on her elbow, steadying her in a gentlemanly way as they walked over the broken ground toward the access road. "I know a little *cantina* in south Los Angeles, if that isn't too far a piece."

"Oh, no." She'd drive to the North Pole if he was with her.

It took them about an hour to travel to the city, Loy relaxing in the passenger seat while she maneuvered through the traffic, horse-drawn and horseless, that seemed to grow heavier every week. She felt wonderful. Her driving veil trailed out jauntily behind the open car. Loy chatted amiably, his hat tilted over his eyes and one arm draped over the Packard's door. He had a puppy-like friendliness, the other side of that violent streak she'd seen in him.

The *cantina* was a dim, quiet place, without electricity. Candles lit the rough-hewn tables. Sawdust covered the floor. Loy ordered for them — flour tortillas with a hot beef and bean filling and a wicker-covered jug of red wine.

"When did you come to California, Loy?"

"Let's see. 'Bout four years ago now. Family had a ranch in Bailey County, right up against the New Mexico border. After our uncle died I got restless, and my sister — well, she couldn't handle the work anymore." Something unhappy clouded his eyes. "We sold out."

"You seem to be doing well in pictures."

"I reckon. Work's slowing down some. Week before I did the job at Liberty, the one where you got everyone laughing fit to bust, I was hired by Ince for another Western. He had to shut it down after the first day."

"Why?"

"Not enough horses. Griffith's corralled a lot of them. European buyers are picking up the rest."

"What on earth for?"

"Cavalry and artillery. They say everybody's setting up for a war over there."

Fritzi shivered. The mention of war upset her. She wanted nothing to spoil the delicious feeling she got from the wine and his nearness.

"I hope to heaven there's no war," she said.

He shrugged. "Can't see that it would bother us if it happened. You mind if I smoke?"

"Oh, no! Please!"

Her enthusiasm amused him. He lit a curved pipe packed with tobacco that smelled of rum.

"Is this your first day working for Mr. Griffith?"

"No. Last weekend he took a passel of men down to Whittier, outfitted us all in Ku Klux robes for what he called the big Klan ride to the rescue. I didn't much care for it. You see, Sis and I lost our folks early. We were raised by our Uncle Nate. He rode for the Confederacy in the war, Seventh Texas Volunteer Cavalry. But he didn't have much heart for the slave cause, he was like Bob Lee that way. After the war he said he was American again, and would obey American laws, including the ones saying nigras were free citizens, entitled to the same rights as white folks. Some around Uncle Nate's spread in Bailey County didn't like that. They burned him out twice. Men with hoods. Strikes me this Mr. Griffith's just a high-class copy. No hood, but the same old hate. You can see it in his picture."

Made bold by the wine, she said, "Do you think you'll settle down sometime?"

He took his pipe from his mouth and leaned back in his chair, as if retreating. Fritzi was alarmed.

"Doubt it. It's in my blood to drift."

A fat man in an embroidered shirt climbed on a stool with his guitar, began to play "Cielito Lindo."

"Will you go back to Texas?"

His mouth set. "Never."

"Not even to visit your sister?"

"Isn't much point. Likely she wouldn't recognize me. She lives in a state hospital. Always will." He tapped a fingernail on the bowl of his pipe. "Poor thing's not right in the head."

"Oh, Loy, I'm sorry. Has she always — ?"

He shook his head. "Something bad happened to her right before I left Bailey County. Just as soon not talk about it, you don't mind."

The moment of warmth and intimacy was ruined, as though a whole bank of arc lights had blazed on to illuminate the dark and grimy corners of the *cantina*, the cracks in the whitewashed walls, the stains on the waiter's apron. Loy pushed his plate away, emptied his wine glass, reached in his jeans for money. Fritzi

616

touched his wrist.

"I'll pay. I promised I would."

He didn't argue.

She dropped him at a corner in downtown Los Angeles at half past nine. He walked around to her side of the auto, helped her out for a stretch on the curb.

"You be all right driving home?"

"Just fine. The city's perfectly safe. In an emergency I always have this." She tapped the pearl head of her long hat pin.

"Well, then" — he extended his hand — "thanks so much. For the meal and the good time."

"Can we do it again? I'd like that."

He studied her, as if trying to figure her intent. "Why not? I don't have many friends, because I never stay put for long. I'd like to count you a friend. I don't have a telephone where I live, but the gents at the Waterhole will always get a message to me."

"Fine." Fritzi leaned forward suddenly, kissed his cheek. "Good night."

He smiled, gave her a long, warm look that melted her down to her toes. " 'Night." He tipped his hat, turned, and sauntered off in the glare of electric signs.

She walked around the gleaming hood of the Packard, slid under the wheel. Loy reached the corner and disappeared. She put her hands on the steering wheel, rested her forehead against them.

I'd like to count you a friend.

Oh, no, not good enough. Not nearly good enough for someone hopelessly in love.

67. That Sunday

Early on Monday B.B. called Fritzi to his office, a large room in the main house crowded with secondhand furniture and quirky wall decorations. These included a stuffed moose head adorned with a Scots tam, a color lithograph of Teddy Roosevelt in Rough Rider uniform, an eye chart topped by a giant E, a photo of a wrinkled woman with a peasant face, signed *To sonny love mama*.

"How are you this morning, my gel? Have a chair, make yourself comfortable. I'll be with you in one second." He ran out to confer with his secretary. Fritzi noticed a colorful steamship brochure on his desk. The cover bore a painting of a Cunard liner and a drawing of the British lion standing upright and balancing the globe on its forepaws.

B.B. returned and noticed her studying the brochure. "Pretty swank, ain't it? Next trip we make to Europe, Sophie wants a luxury suite."

Fritzi waited. B.B. cleared his throat, rearranged some articles on the desk, blurted:

"Hayman's wild for Eddie's comedy idea. When he saw the footage he nearly fell out of his socks. Al yapped about the waste of film, but that lasted about half a minute. He wants you in the picture too."

"I see."

"You're disappointed."

"Am I only good for pratfalls, B.B.?"

"Now, now. Eddie feels this is a big opportunity. The picture's sure to click."

"He would."

"Please go along with this. I'm pleading, Fritzi. Don't upset the apple cart when we're in high cotton and the Liberty boat's riding the crest." He saw she was not persuaded. "Listen, I'm not a slave driver. You really hate the idea, I'll tear up your contract. You want to go back to Broadway? Nobody will stand in your way."

Innocent as a Buddha, he sat with folded hands, waiting. The old trickster, she thought. Someone had told him about Loy. He knew she wouldn't walk off. She liked B.B. far too much to be angry.

"All right. One more comedy." She stood. "Then I want a dramatic part."

"That's my gel. That's my Knockabout Nell," he cried.

She wandered to the rear of the lot, where glaziers were setting panels of glass in metal frames. Two walls of the new stage were complete. They reflected the sun and clouds like polished facets of a diamond.

Fritzi walked on, brushing overgrown weeds with her fingertips. In her reverie she saw the star-struck girl who had stood before Sargent's portrait of Ellen Terry at the great Chicago fair. That child, that innocent, had been so full of dreams. What had happened to them?

Experience had taught her answers to that question. Unfulfilled dreams disappeared, tucked away in some ghostly bureau drawer of the heart like last year's unwearable style —

mementoes of what might or should have been.

Sometimes dreams changed. Hers had changed, the way her face in the looking glass was changing slowly, the first crow's feet at the eye corners, the first roughening of the cheek scarcely noticed until, one shocking day, they showed in the glass and couldn't be denied. For as long as she could remember, she had wanted to be an actress. She had broken with her father to be an actress. And she *was* an actress. But what kind? One who got letters praising her for falling off horses. She convulsed Eddie and Charlie with low comedy antics. Her dream had come true in a way she couldn't have imagined a few years ago. She wasn't Lady Macbeth; she wasn't even one of the Bard's clowns.

Her reflections created an image of a river in flood. A roaring river like that bore you along relentlessly. You could go with it, struggling to stay afloat, or you could give up and drown. Fritzi had no intention of drowning. She would always choose survival.

What of her other dream, though — the one pressing her heart so fiercely? Her dream of Loy as a lover and life's companion — would that change too?

Or disappear?

Fritzi heeded Griffith's advice about giving two hundred percent and hurled herself into the new picture. Eddie's two-reel scenario cast her as likable but clumsy Nell, employed as a temporary domestic at a posh mansion. The thin plot called for Nell to accidentally unmask a man pretending to be a European nobleman; he was in fact a yegg bent on lifting all the jewelry at a dress ball.

They shot exteriors at Chateau Holly, an overblown Gothic mansion on Franklin. The hillside property commanded a view of more modest real estate scattered along Hollywood and Sunset Boulevards. A banker named Lane had built the house in 1906. Lane's wife hovered near during the filming, no doubt fearful of desecration of her property by ill-mannered movies.

They returned to the studio the next day. One slapstick stunt followed another. A lot of pies were tossed. Nearly a whole crate of cheap china was broken. The climax called for Fritzi to swing on a prop chandelier rigged from the rafters of the outdoor stage. While extras in rented formal wear hammed it up, gasping and cringing, the chandelier fell, bringing Fritzi down along with a storm of debris. The floor was padded with two mattresses below the frame, but she still hit hard. They pulled the mattresses, and Jock Ferguson shot a close-up of her face at impact. She didn't have to fake the look of pain.

A message left with Windy at the Waterhole reached Loy when he returned from Catalina Island, where he'd gone to play a pirate in a sea picture. He picked her up one evening in a borrowed Ford. They drove north to Ventura and a ramshackle beach restaurant, set on stilts, that served wonderful clams and sand dabs.

A three-piece band came in at half past seven. On an open porch overlooking the ocean, Fritzi did her best to teach Loy the Castle Walk and Grizzly Bear. He really didn't take to dancing, but they managed, relying on laughter to smooth over the stumbles.

Near midnight, back on the porch in Venice, he told her he'd be off next week with Ince, doing a picture in Death Valley.

"I'll miss you." She wanted him to have no doubt about her feelings.

"No more'n I'll miss you. You're a real pal."

"A pal? That's all?"

Loy's face turned deadly serious. "Hell, I'm not in any position to offer a girl anything else. Never have been."

"You mean you're not inclined. You don't want attachments."

He slapped his cowboy hat lightly against his leg. "You see right through me." He laid the hat on the porch rail, gently took hold of her shoulders. "I'd like to keep things the way they are now, Fritzi."

Trying to be flip, she said, "Well, you know what they say about half a loaf. I'll settle for that tomorrow. But tonight —" She threw her arms around his neck, kissed him with more fervor than decorum permitted. Startled, he was awkward a moment. Then he slid his arms around her waist and hugged her, prolonging the kiss.

"Whew," he said when they broke apart. "Any more of that, I'll be in a real stew." He picked up his hat. "See you when I get back."

"I hope that's a promise." Her heart was beating fast. The embrace had loosened strands of her blond hair, and they straggled down both sides of her face. She must look a sight. She didn't care. He overwhelmed her.

"Sure," he said in a flat, almost reserved way. He strode down the walk, cranked up the Ford, and drove off. She leaned against a porch post, remembering the feel of his arms long after the red spot of a taillight disappeared in the dark.

An unexpected and initially alarming letter arrived from Terre Haute, Indiana. Hobart had been playing there in a tour of *Julius Caesar* when a heat wave struck the Midwest.

The temperature was so infernal, I am sure I lost several pounds each time the curtain rose. On the night to which I refer, both my knees and my sensibilities gave way at the same instant. The doctors say it was not simple heat prostration but a heart attack, which I was fortunate to survive. I shall be recuperating in this vale of rustic Philistines for at least three weeks. The cure may prove more dire than the illness!

Fritzi immediately telegraphed a Terre Haute florist to arrange for a large floral basket, along with a note urging the old actor to stay calm, get well, and consider coming to Hollywood at his earliest opportunity.

Liberty previewed Fritzi's picture at another theater on South Broadway, the Arcade. Alexander Pantages, operator of a big vaudeville circuit, had built it and put his name in wrought iron letters on the facade above the marquee. In 1910 the theater became the Arcade and converted to showing pictures. Inside, it still resembled an English music hall, with boxes flanking the stage and footlight sconces in place.

The two-reeler followed a showing of an Ince Western, *Desert Gold.* Loy appeared as one of a hard-riding outlaw gang, though only in long shots, unrecognizable. He had to identify himself to Fritzi. She sat on his right, Eddie and Rita on her other side. Loy was starched and neat, his long hair trimmed and a high polish on his boots.

The audience loved the Western's thrilling action and gave it a strong hand at the fade-out. Fritzi's stomach knotted when the projector flashed the next title.

LIBERTY
Pictures International

presents

"KNOCKABOUT
NELL"

Directed by EDW. B. HEARN

Her hand flew over to clutch Loy's right arm. "I'm scared."

"Hush, it'll be fine." He put his left hand on top of hers, squeezing gently. Her eyes stayed on the flickering screen.

She knew every scene by heart. She winced at some of her mugging, but the audience laughed at appropriate moments. Eddie kept up a whispered commentary. "Too fast." "I like that." "Should have shot that over." A burst of laughter greeted Nell's fall with the chandelier, and a cheer went up when she threw a flatiron over her shoulder, accidentally felling the would-be thief. At the end, the camera irised down for a circular close-up of Nell delirious with happiness after receiving a kiss from the handsome young scion of the household. The audience applauded the picture, though one old grump in the aisle said, "Chaplin's funnier."

They bumped into Kelly and Bernadette in the lobby. Kelly said, "It'll make money." From him that amounted to paragraphs of praise.

She held tightly to Loy's arm, elated by the picture's good reception. Surprisingly, she didn't hate herself as a comedienne. She was respectable, even more than that in a couple of places. Eddie was excited too, chattering to Rita like a schoolboy. He had to telephone B.B., who was in bed with a summer cold.

The summer evening was dry and warm. South Broadway was crowded; the people passing under the street lamps seemed carefree, unworried by news of a Russian army mobilization in response to Austria's declaration of war against Serbia earlier in the week. Russia stood with France and Britain in the Triple Entente, ostensibly allied against Germany and Austria, the aggressor in the Balkans.

As the four of them turned into a spaghetti house, Loy said to her, "We should celebrate the picture in style. I know a mighty fine place for a picnic, on the coast above Inceville. Want to go up there tomorrow?"

"Do you need to ask?"

He grinned. "Didn't expect so. Uncle Nate taught me it's the polite thing. I'll borrow the Ford."

"Mighty fine fried chicken," he said. "Pretty near the best I ever tasted."

"Thank you. I wish I could take credit."

Fritzi sat with her legs tucked under her and her skirt wrapped tightly to keep it from blowing and revealing too much leg, the way she'd learned as a girl. The sun beat on her face with a sensual warmth. The ocean wind tossed and tangled her blond hair.

"You didn't fix this?"

"Sorry, no. Levy's Boardwalk Delicatessen. Closed on Saturday but open Sundays. My mother's a wonderful cook. She tried to teach me the domestic arts, but I was a grave disappointment to her. I can't even make a neat bed."

"Well, why should you? Another year or two, mail coming in like it is, you'll be able to hire twenty maids." She laughed.

Far below the hilltop where they'd spread their blue and white tablecloth, the cobalt sea rolled in from Asia, breaking into fans of foam on shoreline rocks. A bright red touring car flashed sunshine from its fenders as it passed on the coast road. Like an image from a moving picture, it made no sound; the wind and surf saw to that.

Loy closed the slaw carton, placed it back in the wicker hamper. He held up their bottle of Buena Vista wine, checking the level against the sun.

"There's some of this wine left."

"I don't need another drop. This place is so beautiful, it would make a cold-water prohibitionist tipsy."

He smiled, stretched his legs out. He was wearing tan whipcord pants, a dark blue shirt and red bandanna — a workingman's outfit. To Fritzi he was as radiant as some Eastern mogul in silks and jewels.

He packed his pipe, cupped his hard brown hands around the match. Smoke trailing from the bowl and stem vanished in the wind. He ground the match head on his boot sole and carefully laid it on the checked cloth.

"Want to start back?"

"I want to stay here forever. I'm a hopeless romantic. Or haven't you noticed?"

"Fact is, I have. Never met anyone like you in Texas. Not anyone even half like you."

"I shouldn't imagine. Actresses are crazy."

"Oh, not you." In the sunshine his strong profile glowed like a bronze sculpture. Heat radiated through her legs and breasts. Why didn't he lean over and kiss her? They were completely alone.

A gull wheeled over, dove, and swooped by, checking for leftover morsels. Loy eased back on his elbows, squinting at the sea with his pipe in his teeth. She wanted him so badly she ached. She hadn't pinned in her padding that morning, hoping. She realized the initiative had to be hers.

"Loy."

"Mmm?"

"Thank you for bringing me here." She rose on her knees, rested her right hand on his shoulder. He laid his pipe on a flat rock. She kissed him, opening her lips a little to touch him with her tongue. "Thank you for today."

He threw one arm around her, pulled her to him for a harder kiss. Fritzi shivered, eyes shut, feeling her hair flying around her ears, brushing his face. He smelled of the salt air and his tobacco. She wanted to pull him down on her, take him in, show him how much she loved him. . . .

He broke the embrace. Patted the small of her back, giving her a swift, almost apologetic look. He took his pipe from the rock, bit down on the stem, and lit another match. The gull returned and left, disappointed.

Fritzi touched him again. "You know how I feel about you, don't you?"

"I've a mighty good idea."

She pushed hair away from her cheeks. "I suppose it's obvious. I've done everything except hire a man to walk around advertising it with sandwich boards. You probably think I'm a cheap hussy."

"I think you're a jewel, Fritzi. A little more modern than I'm used to, but a special woman. I knew it when I met you. I'm strong for you too. I'd like you to be my friend forever."

"Friend. It's always that kind of word."

He was silent a moment. "Can't be anything else."

"Why not? Because you're restless, roving every few months? I don't care. You can go to the South Pole, the Great Wall of China, anyplace. You can stay a year if you'll just come back to me."

He gazed seaward again, his eyes melancholy. "There's more to it than an itch to go yondering. I can't settle down, not even if I want to. I've been looking for the right time to tell you."

Cold, she leaned back on her haunches. Her hands shook.

"I left Texas because I had to, Fritzi. I don't sleep easy, here or anywhere. In the Bailey County jail — all the jails in Texas, I reckon — there's a dodger, a wanted poster, with my picture. I killed a man."

It had the effect of an earthquake. "Oh, dear God. How did it happen? Who was it?"

"You don't need the details. That way, anybody ever shows up asking questions, you don't know a thing."

She jumped up, ran away from him. He scrambled to his feet, hurried after her with loping strides. His face seemed to smear, as though he stood on the other side of a rain-drenched window. *Please, God, don't let me bawl.*

In the changing light the Pacific looked purplish, a poisonous color. The onshore wind blew cold. She dashed a hand across her eyes.

"You won't tell me?"

"Maybe someday."

"I think we should pack up."

"Sure. Can I still see you? I won't force it, but I'd like that."

Bitterly: "You just want me to be convenient, is that it? A *pal* — available whenever you decide to drop from the sky?" She hammered her fist on her skirt. "That's a lot to ask."

"But a while ago you said —"

"I know what I said. I said it before you told me about Texas. I'd have to grow old wondering every time you left whether I'd see or hear from you again, unless it was from some jail cell. Or maybe I'd never hear at all. What would they do if they — if — ?"

"Hang me. The man was a Texas Ranger."

"Oh, my God." She fought to steady herself. "Let's go back to town."

He didn't argue.

The ride to the picnic site had been magical, electric with excitement, expectation, the possibility that he might make love to her. The return trip was hellishly long. Neither said a word. She'd never known such turmoil, disappointment and, yes, anger.

On a corner on Sunset they saw a vendor hawking papers. Unusual for this late on Sunday. A few blocks on, Loy said, "There's another one. What's he yelling?"

"I can't hear."

The newsie had drawn a small crowd. One by one they paid for papers, scanned the headlines without visible concern. The newsie began to shout again.

"Must be an extra edition. I'll get one."

He swung the Ford to the curb in front of a closed barber shop. He strode to the corner,

630

bought the paper, looked at the front page, then walked rapidly back to the runabout.

"It's what they've been jawing about for weeks. Kaiser Bill declared war on Russia yesterday."

A new war involving Germany — she wondered about her father's reaction. Loy stepped on the running board, gave her the *Times* as he took his seat.

FOUR POWERS AT WAR, FRANCE IS MOBILIZING

First Shots Exchanged In Russo-German War

ORDER FOR FRENCH MOBILIZATION CAUSES THE WILDEST ENTHUSIASM

German Kaiser Unafraid, His Back Against the Wall

Still numb from Loy's revelation, Fritzi laid the paper in her lap. The thought of a widespread war shattering decades of peace and tranquility in Europe was disturbing. The General had long ago made his children understand that war, though it might at times be necessary, was most certainly not some high crusade carried out in radiant sunlight, but a dirty, nightmarish business that wrecked lives, destroyed dreams, and left its mark like a satanic cloven hoofprint even on those who survived.

Loy's eye followed an open-air bus full of

sightseers, then went beyond, to the Santa Monicas tinted by the dying light, and beyond that to some faraway place she couldn't reach. The weakness of her voice distressed her:

"I hope it has nothing to do with us."

"Don't see how it could," he said as he engaged the gears to drive on.

In Venice, Fritzi saw a paper fan flicker on the dark front porch — the Hongs taking the air. Loy started to slide out to open her door.

"I'll go in by myself."

"All right. Maybe I'll see you when I get back."

"Where are you going?"

"Arizona. For a month, maybe more. Ince hired me for a chapter play that doesn't use many horses."

"Good luck."

He reached for her arm. "Fritzi —" She opened the door and ran up the walk.

The Ford puttered off into the night.

Mrs. Hong's rocker creaked. Mr. Hong said, "Very bad day. You heard news?"

"Yes. Terrible," Fritzi said, though she meant something entirely different.

PART SIX

BATTLEFIELDS

The United States is today exactly in the position Harvard would be if she had about one good football player weighing one hundred pounds and another substitute perhaps turning the scales at one hundred twenty pounds, but rather poorly trained, the first representing the Army and the second the Militia. They know they have got a game ahead with a first-class team trained to the hour and with at least five men for every position. No one knows when the game is coming off, but we know it is coming someday, and what is worse, we know we are not getting ready for it. . . . All of us should do everything possible to wake up the sleeping public, for I assure you that the position is one whose gravity cannot be overestimated.

— GENERAL LEONARD WOOD,
UNITED STATES ARMY, 1915

There is no room in this country for hyphenated Americanism.

— THEODORE ROOSEVELT, 1915

68. In Belgium

Hot morning sunshine dappled the trees. Yellow dust hazed the air. Paul sneezed as he drove the milk cart into a copse where it wouldn't be seen from the road. The old farm nag pulling the cart tossed its head and snorted, as if glad to rest.

Sammy locked the Moy camera onto the tripod; Paul checked the magazine. Both men showed a week's growth of beard and smelled to heaven. Both wore berets and blue smocks. To the wooden shoes common in the countryside Paul had said, "Absolutely not."

They'd slept in a barn near a village a few kilometers east. As Sammy settled down for the night, he said, "That bit of fluff who owns the farm's a looker." Paul grunted. He'd hardly noticed; he missed Julie.

At daylight the sound of a motorcar woke him. He ran into the farmyard to find a magnificent tan Bugatti, the chauffeur bargaining for bread and milk with the aforesaid bit of fluff. Paul peered in the open window, discovered an elderly manservant in silver-button livery riding beside his employer. He tapped on the glass. The servant cranked the window down. Speaking French, Paul asked for news of Liège.

"Surrendered last night. All the impregnable forts fell. Thousands are coming behind us. Please step back, you're disturbing the countess."

Now, in the copse, Paul heard the sounds of

those refugees. Axles creaked, horses whinnied, chickens cackled, over the steady susurrus of trudging feet and the occasional spit and snarl of a fast car bumping along the shoulder to get around, get ahead, get away.

"You can stay here if you want," Paul said to Sammy.

"Not on your life, gov. Not every day a chap's in a war big as this 'un."

Paul hoisted the tripod to his shoulder. "Let's go, then."

It was Monday of the third week in August. The war was three weeks old.

After August 1, the day the Kaiser went to war against the Czar, the dominoes fell over one after another. On August 3 Germany declared war against France. Next day Britain retaliated with a declaration of war against Germany, and a special tactical force of the German Second Army breached the Belgian border, violating her status of neutrality.

The Germans invested Liège and bombarded the iron and concrete defense forts protecting it. Once Liège fell, the main armies could advance to the capital and on to Paris. It was General Schlieffen's war plan of 1895, executed at last.

Paul kissed Julie and the children goodbye on August 6, Thursday. That day the transatlantic cables carried the text of Washington's official proclamation on the European war. The United States would maintain strict neutrality. Its citizens could not enlist in the army of any belligerent. It would not aid in outfitting and arming vessels to serve either side. Paul assumed neutrality would please his Uncle Joe. The General still had strong emotional ties to the fatherland. Paul didn't.

He and Sammy crossed the Channel to Ostend and traveled on to Brussels with no difficulty. On the way they saw elements of King Albert's Belgian army mobilizing. The Belgians were brave but poorly equipped. Paul filmed a company of machine gunners drilling; the guns were pulled by large dogs. He shot fifty feet and then a Belgian officer threatened to smash the camera unless he moved on.

In Brussels, the American ambassador, Whitlock, arranged for a *laissez-passer*, an official document allowing unrestricted travel. That and their passports insured Paul and Sammy's safety. Supposedly.

In a café in the Boulevard Waterloo, Paul ran into an old colleague, Richard Harding Davis, on the scene with many other correspondents. Paul said he intended to film the German advance.

"I don't know how they'll take to it," Dick Davis said. "Show a camera to any army officer in the world, and he thinks one thing. Spy." Paul nodded, remembering the machine gun company. Davis pulled a pencil from the breast pocket of his smart linen coat.

"For once I'm happy to be an old-fashioned reporter." He waggled the pencil. "You be careful, my friend."

Tall poplars lined both sides of the road, like

green, leafy banks of a river. In the riverbed flowed an unending tide of human misery. Refugees by the hundreds, stretching to the horizon in both directions.

Paul set up his camera facing the oncoming throngs. A few people stared, but no one asked a question or called a greeting. Fear showed on every face. Paul started to crank. Sammy said, "Gor, what a sight."

Truly it was; the river carried men, women, and children on foot, riding bicycles with backpacks, driving old market wagons piled high. A grandmother dragged a dog cart without a dog to pull it. The cart held a small mountain of clothes, cook pots — the residue of a shattered life.

A black Daimler crept by, trunks and suitcases swaying on its roof. Anxious white faces peered out. A young girl passed with a flour sack that clanked with the family silver. A farm couple struggled with wooden cages of quacking ducklings and squealing piglets. A sweaty aristocrat in an Alfa Romeo nearly ran down a mother with two infants in her arms. He screamed oaths as he drove past.

An old man with the look of a scholar appeared, half a dozen books secured by a strap slung over his shoulder. Paul shouted, "How many Germans in Liège?"

"Von Bülow's whole Second Army. Stealing everything from paintings to postcards, the bastards."

The river of terror flowed on for several hours, then thinned, then dried up altogether. Paul suspected that the German advance was close behind. He filmed intermittently, but the stricken faces, the pathetic bundles of goods, grew repetitive. He and Sammy were sweating and filthy with dust. Two emotions mingled in him — sadness and anger.

He rested in the shade of a poplar, smoking a cigar. Sammy relieved himself against a bush. In surrounding fields bundles of grain lay waiting for harvesters who would never come. A silver shape floated into sight.

"Zeppelin," Paul cried, jumping up. Away to his left a massive dust cloud roiled in the sky. "Here they come."

Paul drove the old cart horse as fast as he dared toward the village. Twenty minutes after they arrived, the first Germans marched in, making a fearsome noise as their iron-shod boots hit the cobbles in cadence. They goose-stepped, young boys in neat gray-green uniforms, smiling and confident. Only the villagers were sullen. Paul and Sammy stood among them in the square, stared at but not disturbed. Paul had hidden the camera, fearing confiscation.

A caravan of motor transports passed through, then a detachment of Uhlans riding matched horses. Pennons fluttered on their lances. A woman ran out to greet them, offering yellow flowers. From the crowd someone threw a rock. The smile of the Uhlan officer became a glare.

Infantry with supporting units of cavalry and artillery passed through for over an hour. Occasionally an open staff car drove alongside the column, honking its way through the square before roaring on. Paul's legs and back ached, the effect of sleeping badly and standing for hours, nerves screwed tight. He felt his thirty-six years; he was no longer young.

Another staff car pulled into the square. This one stopped. A colonel stepped down, dusty but otherwise perfectly attired. His pink face shone as he took off his cap. He had red hair, neatly barbered. He shouted for the burgomaster, first in German, then bad French.

"Here, your honor." A plump man scuttled forward, seized the colonel's hand. For a moment Paul thought he was going to kiss the officer's signet ring. People muttered.

The officer began to snap orders at the burgomaster, gesturing, commandeering billets and food. A roughly dressed boy of ten or so ran from the crowd. The boy had a gun carved out of wood. Before his mother could snatch him back, he aimed at the officer and made shooting noises.

The startled officer frowned. In German he said to his aide, "We'll have none of that. They must show respect. Get rid of him."

"At once, Colonel."

The aide strode toward the boy, unlimbering his service pistol. The boy turned the wooden gun on him, banging away. The boy's mother ran toward him, arms stretched out, screaming. She was still five or six steps away when the aide calmly shot the boy through the head.

Blood and brains splattered the cobbles. The

boy twisted and went down like a cloth doll that had lost its stuffing. The aide blew into the muzzle, put his piece away, and gave his superior a smart little salute. The officer nodded crisply. The burgomaster's trousers showed a wet stain. Paul could hardly breathe. Sammy whispered in a trembling voice, "Jesus fucking Christ."

The mother dropped to her knees beside the boy. Flies were settling in the spilled blood. A few villagers with sticks and rocks edged forward, but a wave of the colonel's hand brought out the pistols of three other men in the staff car. Swaying back and forth, the mother keened, *"Dieu, Dieu. Fusillé par les Allemands."* God, God. Shot by the Germans.

The Germans advanced through the village until the light of the long summer evening faded. Paul was staggered by their numbers, the splendid state of their equipment, all the support units: horse-drawn kitchen wagons with smoking chimneys, hospital wagons, an open truck in which cobblers hammered away resoling boots, even a motorized post office. As the night came down they encamped, singing drinking songs and *"Die Wacht am Rhein"* in lusty voices. Paul approached a youthful infantry corporal writing a postcard and asked him how long the war would last.

"We'll be in Paris by Christmas. Home right after the New Year."

Paul and Sammy left the village in the middle of the night, driving the milk cart with the camera and film magazines still hidden.

Smoke clouds stained the horizons of Belgium. Where the Germans found resistance, they burned houses in retaliation.

Paul and Sammy drove through fields torn up by the iron wheels of caissons. They saw blue cottages with red-tiled roofs, all the windows smashed, doors ripped off the hinges. They saw trampled gardens of hollyhocks, others in which a few red cabbages lay like crushed human heads. Paul filmed where he could, but the wooden Moy was bulky, easily spotted. They stayed off main roads to avoid confrontations in which their papers might be examined, questioned, even taken away.

Near another village they came upon soldiers working with horses and chains to drag tree trunks from a road. Fallen trees weren't the only roadblocks put up by the Belgians. A little farther on, flames licked around the gutted frame of an auto lying on its side.

Paul and Sammy hid the cart and approached the village on foot. Paul carried the camera, sans tripod, wrapped in a blanket under his arm. Sammy had an extra magazine.

As they passed a barn and started to cross a fallow field at the edge of the village, Sammy jerked Paul's arm. "Got to hide, gov." They ran into the barn and breathlessly climbed to the hayloft. From there Paul watched a squad of soldiers march three men and three women of varying ages into the sunlit field. A young captain strutted in front of the civilians, all of whom had their wrists tied behind them.

"Ladies and gentlemen," the captain said in a loud voice, "you have placed obstacles in the path of General von Kluck's First Army. I refer to the fallen trees, the burned Panhard auto." He spoke excellent French.

"That kind of resistance can't be tolerated, I trust you appreciate that. We have our orders. Do you have anything to say before we carry them out?"

One man spat on the ground. A young woman fell to her knees, weeping. "Spare me the theatrics," the captain said. "You can at least take your medicine bravely."

Paul shoved the camera forward into the hayloft opening, checked the exposure, lined up to be sure his frame included both Germans and Belgians. He cranked, wincing at the racheting noise. Could they hear it in the silence? There was nothing else but the twitter of birds and motors revving on a distant road.

The captain tapped a cigarette on a metal case. "Sergeant, execute them."

The sergeant snapped orders. The soldiers raised their rifles. "No, no, not like that," the captain said. "We want a stronger lesson. Bayonets."

The kneeling woman fell over in a faint. A middle-aged farmer in boots and smock put his arm around his wife. The soldiers looked at one another, hesitant. *Schnell, schnell,* the irritated captain cried, waving his cigarette.

The sergeant cleared his throat. "Fix bayonets."

Paul kept cranking as the soldiers marched

forward and rammed their steel into the civilians. They pulled the bayonets out and kept stabbing until each Belgian was certifiably dead.

"Leave them," the captain said when all of them had fallen. His cigarette was down to a stub. As he started to toss it away, he happened to glance at the barn. There must have been a flare off the lens; the officer pointed.

"Up there. I saw something. Surround the barn."

"Come on, gov." Sammy dove for the ladder.

"Give me the other magazine."

"Gov, there's no time —"

"The other magazine, God damn it."

Round-eyed with fright, Sammy obeyed. Hurrying, Paul removed the magazine with the exposed footage, locked the other magazine on. He had no time to open the camera and thread the leader. He buried the exposed magazine under straw just as soldiers kicked the barn doors open.

"You keep quiet, not a word," he whispered to Sammy. "Whatever you do, don't show that British passport."

Rifle bolts rattled down below. Paul shouted in German, "Don't fire, we're Americans. American citizens."

"Climb down, hands in the air." That was the captain.

Paul went first. The captain couldn't have been more than twenty-five. He had a soft baby face, mild blue eyes. A map was neatly folded over his belt. An electric torch stuck from a pocket of his blouse. All the German officers carried a map with roads and key locations marked, plus a torch for night duty.

The officer clicked his heels. "Captain Herman Kinder. You speak German."

"I emigrated from Berlin as a boy."

"Ah, *ein Landsmann.* Have you papers?"

"Yes." Paul pulled them from under his smock. The captain unfolded the oversized parchment signed by Secretary of State Bryan and inscribed with pertinent details of Paul's age, build, approximate weight, eye and hair color, all filled in by some scribe with a beautiful hand. The captain turned the passport this way and that, studying it for an agonizing length of time.

Finally he handed it back. He next examined Paul's *laissez-passer.* "For your information the Belgians no longer control this country. Brussels fell on Friday. This document is worthless." He tore it in half and threw the pieces on the ground. He eyed the ladder. Sammy had stopped halfway down, one arm hooked over a rung. His face was pale, tense.

"What do you have up there? I saw a reflection, sunlight on a spyglass or similar."

"I have a news camera up there," Paul said. "I take pictures for theaters."

"*Kino.*" The captain smiled briefly. "Bring it down," he said to Sammy.

Sammy didn't understand the German. Paul repeated the order in English. Sammy started to speak. Paul stared at him. Sammy gulped and scuttled up the ladder.

He lowered the camera to a soldier, then

climbed down. Captain Kinder walked around the camera resting on the ground.

"You have pictures of what transpired in the field?" Paul nodded. To one of his men, Kinder said, "Destroy it." A soldier bore the camera out of the barn, and out of sight. Paul winced at the sound of the wooden case splintering.

"Since Germany and the United States are not belligerents, I am obliged to treat you courteously. But I advise you to leave the district at once. In the hands of a less conscientious officer you might be subject to execution without a hearing."

"I understand."

"If you're seen around here again, you will be summarily shot."

"Yes, right, we'll go." Paul dug his nails into his palms. They were almost free, almost out of the trap.

Remembering the film hidden in the loft, he signaled Sammy with a look. The two of them walked to the sunlit doorway and out. Sammy looked ready to burst with anger. Carefully, Paul laid a finger across his lips, keeping his back to the barn. He walked quickly, without running. Any moment he expected a bullet in the back. At the edge of his vision he saw black birds with leathery wings feeding on the red flesh of the dead.

When they reached the far edge of the field, Paul risked a glance over his shoulder. Captain Kinder and his men were marching away toward the village.

He pressed on, toward a low fence of stones

some farmer had built. There, quietly he said, "It's all right, Sammy, they're gone."

He'd never seen Sammy's face so ugly. Sammy kicked the stone wall. "Fucking bloody bastards. Fucking *savages*."

"Huns. That's the name I heard in the village." Sammy's expression was blank. "Like Attila's hordes." It still didn't register. He gave up, rested both hands on the stone fence and bent his head, sickened by the killings.

"It's lucky they didn't hear you say anything or I imagine we'd be dead."

"I'm one who follows orders, ain't I?" Sammy snarled, still visibly upset.

"You are, Sammy. You're that and much, much more. God bless you. Let's sit down and rest."

Sammy sat next to him, fanning himself with his beret. "Where next, gov?"

"We'll make a run for Ostend and the Channel. I'll pay some fisherman to carry us across." They sat silent until Paul said, "I think it's safe now. We can go back for the film."

"You stay here, I'll fetch it. Got to make sure those pictures get home, so people know what kind of fucking bloody monsters we're fighting."

Paul was about to argue, but the ferocity in Sammy's eyes kept him quiet.

69. Troubled House

Old age had carried off the well-remembered Nicky Speers, chauffeur to the Crowns for so many years. According to Ilsa's letters, the General said no one could ever equal Nicky for efficiency and good humor, so he'd chosen not to replace him. Fritzi was met at the Chicago depot by the close-mouthed Bavarian steward, Leopold, who was waiting on the platform.

"Welcome home, *fraülein.*"

"Thank you, Leopold, I'm glad to be here."

"Your mother and father will be happy to see you." In speaking ten words, Leopold was being loquacious. Plus, Fritzi suspected only half of his remark was true.

The sky above the noisy street was yellow and smoky. A rampart of black clouds in the west threatened rain. It was Thursday, October 1, three days before "Peace Sunday" proclaimed by the president as a national day of prayer to end the war.

With special dispensation from B.B., she had come halfway across the country at her mother's urging. On her journey she'd listened to fellow passengers with strong opinions about the war: The U.S. must follow Wilson's lead and remain completely neutral. The Germans were barbarians guilty of raping nuns, burning priests alive, amputating the hands of Belgian babies. Never mind, the whole thing would be over by Christmas. Fritzi had no strong opinions of her own at this point, and the war had nothing to do with her return to Chicago. She was here to celebrate her parents' forty-fifth wedding anniversary at a lavish party at the Palmer House. Guests at the annual affair included many of the General's senior employees, business associates, and friends from their years in German-American society in Chicago. After some hesitation, Fritzi had decided to venture home, hoping that the festive atmosphere would help her heal the rift with her father.

The family's maroon Benz touring car delivered her to the mansion at dusk. The servants were all new, unfamiliar. Her mother was still at a church committee meeting, she learned, and the General was away in St. Louis. He'd gone there to straighten out a problem at his distribution agency and would return late tomorrow.

Her old room on the second floor had a stale, disused air despite clean, starched sheets and a vase of flowers. Unpacking, she turned suddenly, sensing someone in the doorway.

"Joey!"

"Hello, sis." He limped across the carpet; they hugged. Joe Junior tossed his old cloth cap on a chair. Approaching forty, he was pasty and smelled strongly of whiskey. His waist was much thicker than she remembered. Joey hung on to his job despite his socialist disdain for capitalism. Mama said sadly that he traded his principles for drinking money.

"Nice California tan you've got, sis."

"Thank you, kind sir. You could use a little

sunshine yourself."

"Ah, who'd notice? I saw your new flicker, the one where you break everything. Funny."

"I'm glad you liked it. Tell me, how are you?"

"How should I be? I'm the same. Go to the brewery six days a week, work at party headquarters on Sunday."

Fritzi didn't like the tone of self-pity, but she didn't say anything. She sat on the bed. "Has the war had any impact in Chicago? Out West people hardly know it's happening."

"German people are pretty worked up about it. Pop's hung a big map of Belgium and France in his office downstairs, with colored pins for the two sides. Any day I expect to see him bring home a portrait of the Kaiser. He may be getting a little soft." Joe Junior tapped his head. "After all, he'll be seventy-two in March."

"What's your opinion of the war?"

"In one word? Criminal."

"Which side do you mean?"

"Both sides. The way international socialism looks at it, all governments are by nature corrupt, and wars are nothing more than policy extensions of that corruption. Common people don't start a war, sis. War is inflicted on them by the exploiters."

She smiled. "Papa would call that red talk, wouldn't he?"

"Sure, but it's the truth. I'll wash up now. Glad you're home." He turned to go, dragging his crippled foot. "Say, did anyone tell you? Carl's coming on a midnight train from Texas. He's on his way to France, can you feature it?

Guess you'll be glad to see him, anyway."

Joey's tone implied that she wasn't glad to see him. How sad he was, how lost. She doubted that anyone could redeem him from what he'd become.

Carl boomed into the house at half past four in the morning, his train delayed several hours. He came bounding up the staircase with a worn-out Gladstone in hand and a bedraggled red scarf draped around his neck. In her night clothes, Ilsa alternately hugged her younger son and urged him to be quiet — most forcefully when he bumped the newel post so hard it shuddered violently.

Fritzi yawned and waved at Carl from the door of her bedroom, promising to see him first thing in the morning. Joey hadn't bothered to get up.

Every year when the Crowns celebrated by hosting their party, the General adamantly refused presents from his guests, though he didn't object to receiving them from his children. Fritzi still had to buy hers. She asked Carl to go with her. He'd already wrapped up the best gift he could afford — a cheaply framed photo of himself, posed against a rickety airplane on whose wing panels bullet holes were clearly visible.

In the Loop they saw evidences that Chicago's large German-American population was far from neutral about the war. A State Street vendor stridently hawked tin replicas of the Iron Cross. The window of a music shop displayed Columbia gramophone records of German patriotic songs.

"Pop won't like it when I fly for the other side," Carl predicted somberly.

After shopping for an hour, with Carl complaining that he needed another cup of java to wake up, Fritzi finally bought a handsome clock. The lacquered cabinet was twenty-five inches high, encrusted with knobs and scrollwork and little balconies — very German. She wasn't sure her father would like it but her mother would use it. Ilsa maintained her orderly household with at least one clock in every room.

About to pay, she remembered something. Ilsa was in her late sixties, and her eyesight had deteriorated badly. "I've changed my mind. That one." It was identical except for larger hands and dial.

"Cost you two dollars more," the clerk said.

"Fine, wrap it up."

In the Fort Dearborn Coffee Shoppe on Wabash Avenue, Fritzi ordered tea and a biscuit, Carl a double-sized coffee. He unbuttoned his coat, let the red scarf hang loosely over his shirt. The disreputable thing was at least a yard long, with frayed ends and all sorts of stains. Finally her curiosity prodded her to ask, "Where did you get that old thing?"

"From Tess, the girl in Detroit. I told you about her."

She recognized something deep and serious in his words. "You cared for her, didn't you?"

"I still do."

"But you left her."

He nodded, saying nothing.

Fritzi brushed her hands together to rid them

of crumbs. "Do you know what that does to a woman?"

"How would I?"

"Of course you wouldn't. I'll tell you, because I'm in love with a man who's just about as footloose as you are." With great intensity, and a surprising sense of relief, she described Loy Hardin, her feelings for him, and the way he retreated each time she seemed to be drawing him closer.

"That kind of thing tears a person apart, Carl. It wrecks their sleep, their work —" She'd gotten a little angry, thinking there were now two men in her life, Loy and her brother, who refused any commitments to others, without thought of the consequence. Some of the anger came through as she took another tack:

"When you were a little boy, do you remember how you'd bang around the house and sometimes break something valuable? I remember a clock once. And a chair, and the marble top of a washstand — you were too little to know how to fix them properly. Maybe then it was all right to walk away and let Papa or one of the servants repair the damage. But you can't clumsily damage a human being and walk away without taking responsibility. Do you know where to find your Tess?"

"Far as I know, she's still in Detroit."

"Go see her, Carl. Do it before you're off to a place as dangerous as France. She deserves that much — one visit. I know. I've been on the other end."

The seconds ticked by. The waitress laid their check between them. Fritzi picked it up. Carl examined the frayed end of the scarf. Then he looked up, into her eyes, saying nothing.

The evening meal was called punctually with a bell at seven forty-five; nothing ever changed. Working up nerve at each step, she walked to the dining room with her chin high and a stiff smile on her face. In the archway she broke step, dismayed to see Joey and Carl and her mother, but not the General, though she'd been informed by one of the servants that he was home.

"Your father is in his office," Ilsa said in answer to her question. "I've sent Leopold to tell him we're sitting down." Ilsa clutched a lace hanky in her left hand, and Fritzi noticed that her knuckles were white.

Ilsa took her usual place at the end of the long, heavy dining table. Fritzi sat on one side, Joe Junior and Carl on the other. Carl talked animatedly with his mother while Joey slouched on his spine, looking like he was ready to punch the first person who annoyed him. Fritzi sat facing her brothers and the mammoth sideboard with the Bierstadt painting of Yosemite above it. The room was exactly as she remembered: old-fashioned walnut paneling, massive furniture, an elaborate electric chandelier long ago converted from gas.

She heard brisk steps, stood up without a second thought. Her palms were moist, her pulse beating fast in her wrists and throat. The General came in, slim and correct in his posture, though she was dismayed to see how frail he'd grown. His mustache and imperial were neat as ever, but his white hair was so thin she could see his scalp. His cheeks had an unhealthy choleric redness.

"Good evening, Fritzi," he said with a slight bow. It was civil but cold. Quite without thinking about it, she curtseyed as Ilsa had taught her when she was small.

"Papa, I'm so glad to see you."

A flick of his eyes acknowledged the remark. He marched down the other side of the table, behind Carl and Joey, and sat in his tall, throne-like chair. No kiss of greeting for her — not even a touch to demonstrate paternal affection.

Two girls in black dresses and white aprons came in to serve the meal. Ilsa said, "Isn't it wonderful to have Fritzi here for the party, Joe?"

"Very nice," he said, rearranging his silverware by moving each piece a millimeter or two. "I hope you are in good health, Fritzi."

Good health? Was that all he could think of to say? His meager concern infuriated her, but she managed to hide it.

Still with a false brightness, Ilsa said, "Doesn't she look fine, Joe? She is so busy in California —"

"Making those pictures." Satisfied with the silverware, he glanced at his daughter. The disapproval she felt was dismaying. "I have not seen any of them."

Reddening, Fritzi muttered, "It's all right, papa, they're not exactly great drama."

"I disapprove of a woman displaying herself to strangers. Paul's pictures, now — they reflect

655

important events. They have value." Carl was frowning. The General went on, "I cannot go to see my own daughter make herself look foolish. I'm only grateful that very few people in Chicago know what you are doing."

Joey laughed. "Pop, they know. Her new picture's a terrific hit."

"No one has mentioned it at the brewery."

"Hell, they're not dumb. Your opinions about Fritzi's career aren't exactly secret."

Ilsa said, "Joey, I wish you wouldn't use bad language."

"He doesn't know any other kind, unless it's his communist cant," the General said.

Defiantly, Joe Junior said, "Lots of people at Crown's know what Sis is doing, and they think she's swell. Lev Dunn in the bottling house told me he saw Fritzi in *Knockabout Nell* and almost split his sides."

"Lev Dunn," the General repeated. Fritzi feared the poor man was in for it. The emotional temperature of the room was rising.

The serving girls brought platters and silver-domed dishes to the table. The supper entree was sauerbraten, with thick, rich gravy and red cabbage. Everyone concentrated on filling their plates; Fritzi filled hers, though she'd lost her appetite. The German devotion to the ritual of eating was something else she remembered from this room.

Ilsa's false cheer persisted. "After supper we all want to hear Fritzi tell us about California. It's such a fascinating, faraway place. I long to see it someday."

"Southern California's lovely," Fritzi agreed. "The climate is supposed to be as mild and sunny as the Mediterranean coast."

The General put his napkin down. "I don't believe I have time for a travelogue. Two gentlemen are coming here for a meeting."

"Here to this house?" Ilsa said. "You didn't mention it, Joe."

"We'll meet in my office. We won't trouble you." It was a curt dismissal.

Infuriated for the sake of his mother and sister, Carl threw his napkin on the table. "What about me, Pop? Are you too busy to hear about my plans? I'm going across to join the French air corps."

"As a mercenary," the General snorted. "Your mother informed me. Needless to say, I consider the idea barbarous and, in view of this country's official posture, unpatriotic."

"Oh, Christ," Joey groaned, holding his head.

The target of hurt and angry looks, the General drew himself up with unconscious haughtiness. "I am trying to behave as a responsible citizen. The two gentlemen who will be here are business colleagues — brewers of good, wholesome beer." He reached for his stein of Crown lager, a constant at every meal. "We are planning a newspaper campaign to show the fallacy of what the President calls neutrality. In reality his policy means favoring Great Britain over Germany. If Wilson's neutrality meant selling food and medicine and arms to both countries, in an even-handed way, I could accept it. But that isn't the case. The whole Eastern establishment — the newspapers, college presidents, the free-love intellectuals, the arms dealers — they all worship the Allies and condemn the fatherland."

"Maybe it's with good reason," Carl began. "My friend Rene said —"

The General slammed the stein on the table. "Don't irritate me further, young man. I am grossly ashamed of what you are doing."

Fritzi could take no more. "Carl ought to do what he wants, Papa. He's a grown man."

The General's glance withered her. "Of course you'd say that, living the kind of willful, selfish life that you do. Defying the wishes of your —"

"Joe." Ilsa's whisper was strident. "No more, for pity's sake."

"I'm sorry, my dear" — he wasn't — "I have German blood and so do you, though you show signs of forgetting it." Ilsa sat very still. The General took a sip of beer, dabbed his mustache with his napkin, and stood. "You'll excuse me. The visitors will be here shortly and I have some work."

He marched out. Ilsa's voice faltered as she said to Fritzi, "Please, *liebchen,* eat something more. We don't want it to go to waste."

The words fell into a gloomy silence. Fritzi stared at her lap. Carl scowled at his plate. Joe Junior lit a cigarette, a sour smirk on his sallow and haggard face.

70. Taking Sides

Every year Joe Crown hired the same large ball-room at the Palmer House, the same musicians from the Chicago Symphony to serenade guests before dinner, then play for dancing. The guest list was composed of men and women who represented the spectrum of the Crowns' life in Chicago: not only brewery employees and half a dozen competitors, but local pols, including Mayor Carter Harrison. There were parishioners from St. Paul's Lutheran Church and members of the General's clubs — the Union League, Germanic, and Swabian. Ilsa invited women she knew through her volunteer work at Hull House. Its founder, Jane Addams, a spinster, came alone. In all, there were some two hundred fifty guests, speaking as much *Deutsch* as English.

The party grew noisier as the drink flowed: not only pitchers of Crown beer, light and dark, but champagne, *liebfraumilch*, Riesling, and Franconian red wine. Even modern cocktails were available, though the General disapproved of them.

Ilsa looked handsome in an evening gown of rich yellow satin with an elaborate lace bertha. Though long out of style, the gown was a favorite of the General's. Fritzi had bought her expensive dress in Los Angeles. The bodice of beaded black chiffon flattered her slender torso. The attached skirt was emerald green velvet, short enough to display her silver slippers.

The General's tails fit him smartly, but the same couldn't be said for Joe Junior and his brother. Their rented suits were baggy, reminding Fritzi of low comedians in a slapstick two-reeler.

She didn't know many of the guests. She needn't have worried; people recognized her. They introduced themselves and congratulated her on her success. One woman gushed, "How lucky you are, my dear. Moving-picture actors are America's new royalty." A startling thought she would not mention to her father.

They dined at round tables for ten. Fritzi sat with a rival brewer, Mingeldorf, and his wife, the mayor and his wife, two couples from church, and the Crown brew master, a widower. Ilsa had worked with the hotel catering department to present a certifiably German menu. The main dishes were *Kalb, Himmel,* and *Rind* — veal, mutton, beef — accompanied by sweetbreads, six vegetables, dumplings, roast potatoes, hard and soft rolls, Westphalian black bread and pumpernickel, all followed by sumptuous desserts, then coffee with bowls of fluffy white *Schlag* on the side.

Toasts to the celebrating couple followed. The General rose last.

"Ladies and gentlemen, dear friends. Each of you is special to my wife and myself" — Fritzi looked down at her hands — "though I would speak now only of one, if you will permit me." He raised his glass. "To you, Ilsa. Many years ago I found a flower that became a treasure. I am the luckiest of men."

Everyone rose to applaud. Ilsa dabbed her eyes. Carl clapped lustily; Joey whistled through his teeth. The musicians struck up "The Emperor Waltz." Joe led Ilsa to the floor amid more applause.

Joey disappeared, probably for the rest of the night. Fritzi saw Carl knock back another flute of champagne and immediately signal the waiter to fill his glass with dark beer. A bit later, she was chatting with Jane Addams when she heard Carl speaking loudly. She was alarmed to see him weaving on his feet in conversation with stout Otto Mingeldorf.

"You will defy the stated wishes of your own president?" the offended brewer said. Evidently Carl had revealed his plans. Mingeldorf shook a finger. " 'My fellow countrymen, we must be impartial in thought as well as action.' Those were Wilson's exact words."

"Sure, Otto," Carl boomed. "But what if he's wrong?"

The General stopped dancing. Crowd noise diminished as people responded to Carl's loud voice. Mingeldorf's wife tried to pull him away. He wanted to argue:

"Outrageous of you to say that! There is principle involved here. Principle!" He pounded a fist into his palm. "Germany and her allies are wronged by falsehoods, unfounded accusations —"

"You mean all the atrocity stories coming out of Belgium?"

"Lies! Where do you think they originate? The

661

propaganda ministries in London and Paris. I have read equally ghastly accounts of Allied war crimes. Cholera germs put in wells in occupied France. French priests giving German soldiers coffee laced with strychnine."

"Where do those come from, Berlin?"

The General strode over to his son. "Carl, kindly do not badger our guests."

"Sorry, Pop. Just wanted to tell him how things are."

In a low voice, almost a growl, the General said, "I believe you've had too much to drink. Kindly desist."

Anxiously, Fritzi watched her brother's face change, become almost truculent. "When I'm good and ready, Pop. Anyway, Mingeldorf, I fly mostly for the thrill of it. The thrill, and the pay."

The General grabbed Carl's shoulder, intending to pull him away. Carl said, "Hey," and started to push back. The General stepped to one side, and Carl was suddenly off balance. His feet slid from under him; he fell clumsily. His forehead smacked the polished floor. Everyone gasped.

Livid, the General said, "On your feet. *I said, get up.*"

Carl's head lifted a few inches. Fritzi was alarmed at the glazed look of his eyes. She ran forward to help him. Her father's voice cracked like a shot:

"Leave him alone. He deserves no help."

Almost in tears, Ilsa rushed to plead with her husband. "Joe, I beg you —" He turned his back.

The guests watched in varying states of shock.

Fritzi and her father stood four feet apart, with Carl the apex of the triangle they formed. The General's face had a purplish tinge. He and Fritzi stared at one another. Carl raised his head briefly, then passed out. Fritzi moved closer.

"Fritzi, don't touch him."

"We can't just let him lie here, Papa."

"I'll call the janitors. They pick up trash. I order you not to help him."

She was already kneeling by her fallen brother.

Dreary rain fell on Sunday morning, "Peace Sunday." Carl had vanished from the house before daylight, without saying goodbye to anyone. Fritzi's train for California left at eleven forty-five. Leopold came for her valises at half past ten. She followed him downstairs, where the General and Ilsa met them in their church finery.

The General's expression was severe. He and Fritzi had had no further conversation since she had defied him at the party. He said, "I am one of the lay persons speaking at the eleven o'clock service. We are unable to see you off. Leopold will drive you to the station."

"It isn't necessary, I can call a taxi."

"Must you quarrel with everything I say, Fritzi? Leopold will go with you!"

His anger beat on her like a tangible force. She drew a deep breath. "Fine, sir, thank you."

She embraced Ilsa, who was tearful again. The General stood apart, stiff as some petrified tree when she kissed his cheek.

"I'm sorry if my visit upset you, Papa. About last night —"

"We won't speak of that."

But we'll remember it, won't we? she thought bitterly.

"If you ever choose to see one of my pictures, please write and tell me what you think."

"It won't be possible. I'm extremely busy these days. Goodbye, Fritzi."

She hated the damnable war suddenly, the hardening of attitudes it caused. She'd come home to heal the breach with her father and only made it worse. She left the house in despair.

71. "Truth or Nothing"

The screen went blank, glaring white. Lord Yorke snapped his fingers. Recessed lights came on in the ceiling of the paneled projection room, part of the proprietor's suite of offices on the top floor of the building.

Paul and his employer had watched the bayoneting twice. Paul buried his cigar in the one of the brass sand urns placed between leather armchairs. Gray ash dusted his vest. His throat was dry. He was edgy, because of an earlier conversation with Michael Radcliffe.

"Remarkable," said his lordship. "Harrowing stuff. Tell me, who else has seen the film?"

"Other than lab people who processed it, no one." He carefully did not refer to labs in the plural.

"You can be proud of work like that, my boy."

"Thank you, sir. I'll take it back to the editing department for the weekly reel."

Lord Yorke eased himself from his armchair. "That won't be necessary."

"I'm afraid I don't understand."

"The pictures can't be shown in Britain. The government feels that material of such a negative and graphic nature will adversely affect civilian morale and reduce enlistments. Until further notice the war office will not permit reporters, still photographers, and cinematograph opera-

665

tors to visit the war zone or travel with our tommies."

"Michael warned me about new rules. What if
someone chooses to ignore them?"

"The penalty is severe. Death before a firing
squad."

"Good God. That I didn't know."

Velvet drapes shrouded the windows, but the
sounds of Fleet Street still came up: horns hooting, cab horses clop-clopping, vendors shouting
the latest headlines. "Your lordship, with respect — how can you go along with such a policy? The words people see when they walk into
this building stand for something." The motto of
the Hartstein publishing empire was chiseled in
foot-high letters over great bronze doors on the
ground floor. VERITAS, AUT NIHIL. Truth, or
nothing.

Lord Yorke blinked his frog's eyes and stuck
his thumbs in the arm holes of his vest. "In wartime we must all compromise."

"Most especially *not* in wartime, sir. Sounds to
me as though most of the so-called patriots in
Whitehall are principally dedicated to protecting
their rear ends."

"You talk like my son-in-law."

"Blame it on my teachers. The man who first
showed me how to use a still camera, an old
Irishman named Rooney, hammered one lesson
into me. Pictures can lie, but they must not."

"In this matter there is no question of lying or
not lying," his lordship said, growing testy. "The
pictures will simply vanish, as if they never existed."

"I risked my life and Sammy's to get them."

"My boy, let's not quarrel. The disgusting truths of this war will surface soon enough. It will not be over by Christmas, or for many months thereafter. The minister of war said as much privately when I dined with him last night."

Paul yanked a new cigar from an inside pocket, bit off the end, raked a match on his shoe sole. "Is that your final word?"

"Yes, Paul, it is. Don't be angry."

"I am. I want my film."

"I'm afraid that won't be possible." He turned his dumpy little body to draw Paul's eye to the slot window of the projection booth. The light had been turned off. "The reel is on its way down to the vault. The negative will be sent for and similarly stored."

"You have no right —"

"Kindly don't raise your voice to me, sir. The film is my property. Your employment contract is explicit about that."

"I don't give a damn, I want it."

"That is not in the best interests of the government and the war effort. I am a citizen of this country before I am a businessman. I might not have said that when I was poor and hungry, but now I can afford to be a patriot. A patriot criminal, to put a fine point on it. At least once a day I must condone deception — conceal the truth. Down in the streets our vendors are braying that the Central Powers have fallen back at the Marne. The temporary victory cost our side a quarter of a million dead and wounded."

"That many." Paul shuddered. "I had no idea."

"Nor will the public. Paul, you are a talented man and a brave one. I value you highly. You have been through an ordeal. That takes a toll. I urge you to rest for a week. Take your wife and kiddies to the country. With a clearer head you'll see we are doing what we must. You'll have to excuse me now. The editorial board of the *Light* meets in ten minutes."

He rolled toward the leather-padded door with his listing gait. Paul took the cigar from his teeth.

"Sir?"

"Yes?"

"I resign. Effective immediately."

Slowly his lordship came away from the door. His pudgy little fingers played with thick gold links of the watch chain strung across his paunch.

"No quixotic gestures, I beg you."

"Either put that footage on the weekly reel for theaters —"

"So we can all be arrested?"

"You've taken unpopular stands in the past. Stood up to Whitehall."

"This time I will not. There is a dagger poised at the heart of England." A melodramatic way of saying it, though Paul didn't doubt the man's passion or conviction. The whole country was in a state of nerves, fearful of a German invasion.

"Then it's my duty to get the truth out some other way."

"My boy, it isn't useful to posture and —"

"Posture?" The word exploded. "Did you really look at that film? Six innocent people were put to death, and not cleanly. They were butchered. The goddamn German officer in charge *enjoyed* it. That's the enemy we're fighting. That must be told."

"Not by this organization. I'm afraid you try my patience. You will follow orders, or you will call at the payroll office in the morning for your final settlement."

"I'll be there first thing."

Lord Yorke flung the door open. "Your family will suffer unnecessary hardship, you realize that."

"We've discussed it. Julie stands by me."

"You fail to understand the power of the men you're opposing. They'll grind you up for bangers and serve you for breakfast."

"Maybe not. They're only men. Cowards too, apparently. Afraid of the truth."

"You poor fool," he sighed, turning away. "I thought you were made of better stuff."

Lord Yorke's raised heels carried him down a marble hall, click-clack. Paul's hand shook as he lit another match for his cigar. He followed a labyrinthine corridor to a public reception hall three times the size of his living room. Sammy scrambled up from a bench, tossed aside a copy of the *Light*. He saw Paul's expression.

"Gov, what'n hell happened in there?" Briefly, Paul told him. Sammy was stunned, then furious. "Jesus, that's a bleeding crime."

"Apparently it's a worse crime to show pictures like ours."

"Going to do anything about it?"

"I already did. I quit."

Sammy's eyes popped. "Wham, like that?"

"Like that. I'll have to clean out my office in Cecil Court. His lordship will hire someone else, so Miss Epsom will be all right. You too."

"The hell. I'm givin' notice too."

"You can't afford it, Sammy. Let me take the responsibility."

"But it's wrong, gov. Start to finish, it's wrong."

Paul responded with a weary shrug. "We live in an imperfect world."

He rang a bell that jangled and echoed down the lift shaft. A filigreed cage piloted by an elderly attendant rose into sight. "The street, sir?"

"Fourth floor." To Sammy he said, "Michael's waiting to join us for a pint."

They stepped from the lift into a vast, harshly lit room filled with desks and the clatter of black iron typewriters. Copy boys snatched foolscap pages from the reporters and ran with the speed of smash-and-grab thieves to a central horseshoe station. There editors slashed at the copy with thick lead pencils. They threw the marked manuscripts into wire baskets that rode a web of trolleys to openings in the wall where they disappeared en route to the composing room. Over all hung the smell of cuspidors and a blue fog of tobacco smoke.

Paul strode down an aisle to Michael Radcliffe's desk. Most of the *Light*'s reporters affected a bohemian style of dress out of financial necessity. Not Michael. His white piqué waistcoat was buttoned over a starched shirt and brown four-in-hand cravat. The jacket of his handsome tan walking suit hung over his chair. Under a tin-shaded electric light, he typed with two fingers, a cigarette screwed in one corner of his mouth.

"Michael, I've been sacked."

"Oh, Christ. The Belgian pictures?"

"Yes."

"And you took it?"

"Actually, I quit before he could do the deed."

Michael squinted through rising smoke. "I don't know whether to give you a medal for valor or a kick in the bum for stupidity." He typed another couple of words, ripped the paper from the platen. "Boy!" He was already strolling up the aisle with Paul when the breathless runner arrived at his desk.

Outside, the three men discovered fog, regular Sherlock Holmes pea soup. It softened the ugliness and grime of urban London. Paul didn't turn around to look at the motto above the doors. If he did he might choke.

They walked west. Michael tapped the pavement with his stick, a jaunty rhythm. On the corner one of the paper's captive news vendors hawked the evening *Light* with a kind of guttural chirp no one understood. The man relied on his handwritten notice board to attract customers.

HUNS HURLED BACK AT MARNE

Paris Taxis Rush Troops to Forward Areas

ENORMOUS LOSSES STUN ENEMY

Marshal Joffre
"Savior of France"

Two blocks along, they stepped inside a smoky pub called Hare and Hounds. The place was packed with men laughing and slugging down pints and congratulating one another on the German withdrawal. As though they had something to do with it. A dwarf played "Pack Up Your Troubles in Your Old Kit Bag" on a concertina.

They found a table near the bar. Michael flashed three fingers at the publican. Paul scooted his chair around so he didn't have to look at the big poster on the greasy wall. Lord Kitchener, hero of the Sudan and South Africa, and newly appointed war minister, pointed a blunt finger at the viewer and silently cried BRITONS! JOIN YOUR COUNTRY'S ARMY! GOD SAVE THE KING.

Michael peeled off his smart gloves. "I am ready for the précis of the drama."

"He confiscated the film. I had no choice but to quit."

"He's the one should be shot," Sammy growled.

"Samuel," Michael said with a sigh, "you cannot imagine how many times I've had that very thought." To Paul: "How do you feel about this? Rattled?"

"Damn right. Martyrdom may be attractive in

some high-minded way, but it isn't restful or comforting."

"The old boy should have stood with you. Fought. Unfortunately, we're dealing with stupidity at the highest levels. The balmy bunch running things can't see the obvious."

"Which is?"

Sammy said, "They drive us straight to the arms of the bloody Hun."

"Quite correct," Michael agreed. "The German high command welcomes reporters." Looking around for eavesdroppers, he lowered his voice. "Two days ago I bought a forged Italian passport in Deane Street. I'll get to the front if I have to wear twenty Iron Crosses." He drank some stout. "You'll handle this setback, won't you?"

"No question," Paul said. "One of the other companies will hire me eventually. Until then I'll shoot film freelance and peddle it the same way."

"I'm goin' with him," Sammy declared. "He don't want me to do it, but my mind's made up." He saluted the smoky air with his empty pint. "Up your arse, your lordship."

Sammy was adamant about quitting. After making a strong effort to dissuade him, Paul was secretly grateful; the pains in his lower back had eased up considerably since he'd hired Sammy.

A few minutes later they said good night. Michael hailed a taxi cruising slowly through the murk. Sammy turned in the direction of St. Paul's, whistling. Paul felt better. There was something he hadn't told either of his friends.

He walked west, up the Strand and on to Piccadilly Circus, where the fog gentled the garish electric signs to pleasant pastels, almost pretty. LIPTON'S. BOVRIL. J. LYONS. He bought a dozen blue and white China asters from an old woman with a bent back and no teeth. "Bless you, sir."

It was a long hike to Cheyne Walk, Chelsea, but the autumn night was warm despite the dampness. Michael's slashing cynicism inspired him. He could travel through the German lines to the front on his American passport. He could use Michael's source to buy Sammy a forged one. He didn't have to like the Huns to photograph them.

He reached the flat overlooking the Thames about half past nine. He let himself in, tossed his straw skimmer on the rack, calling into the silence: "Hallo? I'm home."

Betsy, nine, bounded down the stairs from the first floor, the hem of her nightdress flying. She had her mother's dark eyes, and the promise of beauty once she blossomed out of girlhood. She flung herself into her father's arms. Her hair smelled sweetly of soap.

He hugged her and whirled her around with her bare feet six inches off the floor. Betsy still admired her father, obeyed him without question. Shad, thirteen, had reached the stage at which all parents were miraculously transformed to imbeciles, condemned to that status until the offspring stumbled back to sanity somewhere around age twenty.

Betsy eyed the flowers wrapped in tissue paper. "Are those for me, Papa?"

"Don't tease, you know they're for your mother. Where's everyone?"

"Lottie and Teddy are in bed. Shad's grinding away at Latin. I heard him cursing something awful."

"No tattling, miss. Good night." Hugging her again, he saw his pale and lovely wife appear on the stair landing. He followed Betsy up to her. As the little girl went on, he swept his arms around Julie for an ardent kiss, sorely needed. Betsy giggled and disappeared.

He presented the asters. "Piccadilly special, ma'am. Straight out of the fog."

"They've lovely. My sweet Dutch." She caressed his cheek. Then she felt his lapel. "You're all damp."

"I walked home."

"From Fleet Street? You must be exhausted. Have you eaten? Cook's gone, but she left steak and kidney pie."

"Let's have some." He jerked at his necktie and stuffed it in his pocket. They went down to the ground-floor kitchen. Julie served the supper, which he washed down with another mug of Guinness. He wished Crown's would distribute in England, but Uncle Joe said the U.S. made him all the money he needed.

Stabbing his fork in the flaky crust, he said, "I'm sorry to tell you it worked out pretty much as we feared. I had to resign. It was that or cave in. Sammy's going with me. Does it upset you?"

"Yes, darling, simply for all the pressure it

puts on you. As for the rest, don't worry. We'll manage."

"I'll shoot as much film as I can. Get it seen as widely as I can. If not here, then in America."

"I admire your determination. I always have."

He grinned. "Kraut stubbornness. Besides, I've gotten used to taking risks. I admit this is a big one. I really had no choice, Julie. The government is hiding the truth about the war. His lordship confiscated the Belgian film."

"I do wish I'd seen it first."

He laid his fork down. Under the hanging electric fixture that shed a cone of brightness on the table, he smiled.

"You will see it. The first day I got back from Belgium, I rang up Michael and he gave me an inkling of what might happen. So without telling anyone, before I turned the film in to the company laboratory, I visited another lab by myself. Lord Yorke thinks he's locked up one positive print and the only negative. It's a duplicate negative. I have the original, safe in my study. I can make and show all the prints I want."

72. Fritzi and Her Three Men

Shortly after Fritzi's return to Los Angeles, Mrs. Hong knocked on her door. "There's a gentleman asking for you."

Could it be Loy, back from Arizona? She'd been missing him terribly. She tore downstairs to the front parlor.

"Hobart!"

"Marry, it is I," he said with a sweeping bow. "Holes in my shoes, railway soot in my hair, hope in my heart."

After they embraced, she inspected him. His appearance dismayed her. His cheap green suit bagged at the knees. Shaggy gray hair straggled over his collar. Illness had pared at least twenty pounds off his portly frame and left him with a pallor. Both latches of his scarred valise were gone; he'd tied the grip with twine.

"Despite what I said in my note, I really didn't expect to see you in California."

"Reversal of fortune, dear heart. I have come humbly, to seek employment in pictures."

"Good Lord. Let me get a shawl, and we'll go for a walk while I digest this."

They strolled to the Venice fishing pier. It was Sunday and crowded. The Ferris wheel calliope pumped out "Moonlight Bay." She found that Hobart was perfectly serious, indeed, desperate.

She asked about his heart attack.

"The only word for it is *epiphany*. Convalescing amid drooling rustics and charity cases in that flyblown metropolis, Terre Haute — which, quite understandably, the author Theodore Dreiser, a native, fled from while still in possession of his sanity — lying there, might I say, I examined my life situation with a new clarity. It is ridiculous to imagine that the king of England will ever confer knighthood on an old poofter such as myself. What is left as a goal? To live in comfort. Which requires money. In London my personal reputation follows me like a mongrel dog. Vehicles suited to my talent are scarce in New York. The road is an unmitigated disaster, and producing is nothing but gambling against staggering odds. Why not, then, take a flyer in something popular? 'Twas your very sweet note with the posies that put me on to it. You know I've always found the flickers amusing — what is there to lose? May I buy you a bag of peanuts? I've twenty cents left."

They sat on a bench on the pier, cracking the shells. She loved the vain old actor, who could be so silly and pretentious, yet innocent and vulnerable as a child. Munching a peanut, she thought aloud:

"Photoplays of Shakespeare have done well for some producers. Mr. Pelzer might be persuaded to try one, he's high on culture. I'll speak to him first thing tomorrow."

"Ever the angel of mercy."

Inevitably the conversation turned to the war. Hobart said, "My dear, I know your German background, so kindly don't take it amiss when I express my opinion. I am an Englishman, with an inbred distaste for the German people. I believe they love war. They are certainly controlled by the military clique, men who trample anything in their path, no matter how fragile or defenseless. They must be stopped. Had I my youth, and the price of a steamship ticket, I'd sail home and enlist. Alas, I have neither. I shall find some other way to help my country. Young fellows like that Charlie Chaplin, though, had better hie over and do their duty."

Fritzi pleaded eloquently. B.B. signed Hobart to play the title role in a two-reel version of *Macbeth*. Kelly didn't like hiring an English actor but curbed his hostility when he computed the picture's relatively modest cost (all costumes to be rented at a discount, Birnam Wood coming to Dunsinane to be kept off screen). Hobart was no longer a top-rank tragedian, but he still had a certain cachet. B.B. insisted his name would add luster to Liberty's roster of players. When Hobart brought up the curse of the play, B.B. scoffed:

"Who believes that old stuff? You said yourself, it's superstition in the theater. This is movies! New, modern. Anybody comes around trying to hoodoo your picture, Hobie, B.B. Pelzer personally will fix his wagon." Eager to work, Hobart acquiesced without further protest.

The director in charge of the picture was new at Liberty. He was a stubby Viennese named Polo Werfels. Past careers to which he would admit included motorcycle racer, fireworks salesman, and circus knife thrower. He wore a black eye patch, called everyone "dollink," and smoked more cigars than cousin Paul. He flogged his actors and crew mercilessly, always with the same charge: "Shake your ass, dollink, you're costing us money."

Kelly loved him.

Eddie took Fritzi into his office and presented a typed scenario for *Paper Hanger Nell*, to start filming the following Monday. Eddie beamed like a proud papa while Fritzi glanced over the two pages.

She tossed the scenario back to him. "So this time I'll step in buckets of paste and wrap myself in sticky paper like a mummy. Swell."

"Hey, Fritz, what is this? You're not yourself."

"Oh, Eddie, I don't know. Everything's going wrong."

The day took another sudden and unexpected turn when B.B.'s typewriter, Miss Levy, tapped on Eddie's door. "There's a gent out front asking for you, Fritzi. Real slick fella," Miss Levy added with an envious roll of her eyes.

Fritzi's brief rush of excitement didn't last; *slick* was not a word people would apply to Loy. Feeling grumpy and put upon, she trudged to the front porch. At the doorway she saw a shiny red Reo parked in front but no visitor. Not until she stepped outside did she see him, peering toward the back of the lot from the end of the porch.

"Harry? Is that you?"

"Yes, indeed. How are you, Fritzi?"

"What brings you to Los Angeles?" As if she had no inkling.

"Sightseeing. I've been to San Francisco and along the wild coast of Big Sur. Now I'd like to see your town, and how these pictures are made. I have one more day before I must go back."

Fritzi wasn't sure *slick* was the right word to describe Harry's appearance either. *Smart* would be better — smart and rich. His three-piece suit of subtly striped gray wool was cut in the latest English style, buttoning high in front. His trousers had sharp center creases. His patent leather shoes shone, and a splashy yellow hanky bloomed in his breast pocket like an exotic flower. His hat was a trilby, appropriately rakish.

"It's grand to see you," she said with forced enthusiasm; no man but one could hold her interest just now. "I'll be glad to give you a tour around —"

She stopped, stunned. Harry had been standing in a way that presented his left side but hid his right. As he turned toward her, she saw a wide band of black crape.

"Oh, no. Your wife?" she said instantly. Gravely, Harry nodded.

"It was inevitable, but no easier for that. Flavia passed in her sleep five weeks ago. I'm just now settling her affairs."

"I'm so sorry to hear about it, Harry."

"Thank you. I couldn't bury Flavia in a Catholic grave, as she would have wished. We were married in a civil ceremony, and because I'm a Jew, she was automatically excommunicated. In

681

the eyes of her church she lived scandalously, in mortal sin. Any God who imposes that kind of stigma on a woman as fine as Flavia is not a God for sane and compassionate people."

He sighed. "Forgive me, I do get angry. Flavia's faith meant a great deal to her, but she was denied its comforts. We did find a priest who felt that was wrong. Father Pius was something of a renegade — willing to hear Flavia's confession secretly."

After a pause he went on, "In many ways the last few weeks have been trying. My doctor suggested a change of scene, so I'm doing what I said I would — seeing the Pacific for the first time." He tilted his head toward her, the emotion in his eyes unmistakable.

"Also seeing you again."

"Harry — um, let's go this way for our tour."

"Grand. Will you have supper? Perhaps show me the sights tomorrow?"

"Of course." She would feel too guilty if she said no.

She introduced him to people on the lot, many of whom greeted him enthusiastically, if not worshipfully; they knew his songs. Harry laughed and charmed them. But standing off to one side, Fritzi saw clearly that his eyes were marked by fatigue, and his step was less lively than she remembered.

He seemed to brighten at supper. They chatted about Paul's book and his growing family, Harry's newfound success writing scores for Broadway, the war. When he drove her home in the little rented Reo, he escorted her to the front door. There he remained a perfect gentleman, making no move to touch her, though she sensed that he wanted that. She'd vowed not to mention Loy; it would only hurt him.

"Tomorrow morning, then?"

"Yes, I've asked for the day off."

"I can't tell you what a tonic you are, Fritzi. I feel better than I have for months."

On tiptoe, she kissed him quickly on the cheek. "I'm glad. Rest well."

It was a whirlwind day: they rode the 10¢ Trackless Trolley to the heights in Laurel Canyon for a sunlit panorama of the distant downtown and the expanding residential suburbs, the gardens and citrus groves running all the way to the shining ocean.

At the Los Angeles central market they wandered among the stalls and produce wagons, bought juicy oranges, cut them open and laughed when the juice squirted them. They sipped sodas in an ice cream parlor and visited the great hall of the Chamber of Commerce building, whose most famous agricultural exhibit was a tusked elephant nine feet high, made entirely of California walnuts.

At the end of the day they repaired to another fine restaurant. There Fritzi asked a question that had occurred to her earlier:

"Do you wear that armband all the time?"

"Father Pius said it was appropriate. I'm determined to mourn Flavia properly."

"For how long?"

Harry's blue eyes locked with hers. "One year. Afterward I'll be a completely free man."

Tell him about Loy!

She knew she should, to save him false hope and, later, disappointment. Somehow it seemed cruel in light of his loss.

Light rain was whispering down when he returned her to Venice. "I do give you my condolences," she said as they sheltered on the porch. Lily's lively swearing drifted from the dormer window above them; no doubt she was in the throes of composition again. "You've become a dear friend, Harry."

"Is that all?"

"For the present, yes. Yes, I'm afraid it is."

The light falling through the screen door from the hall showed the disappointment lurking behind his smile. He was a wonderful man in many ways; he just wasn't Loy. She felt intensely guilty about sending him away with a rebuff.

That was why she went up on tiptoe, pressed his face between her hands, and kissed the corner of his mouth. He started to throw his arm around her — his right arm, with the mourning band. He didn't do it.

"Take care of yourself, Harry, please."

"I shall. Goodbye until we meet again." He settled the trilby on his head at a dashing angle, turned, and rushed down the steps as the rain fell harder.

The skies continued to pour. Rainy season's early, she thought as she wearily dragged herself out of Eddie's auto the following night. They'd spent a long and trouble-plagued day shooting the new Nell picture. Aware of her low spirits,

Eddie insisted on going out of his way to drive her home. She was grateful.

He urged her to take a sleeping powder and not worry about the new picture. Fritzi squeezed his hand, said good night. Mrs. Hong told her Lily had dressed and gone out about six o'clock. "I leave now," Mrs. Hong said. "Noodles on the stove. Eat some. Good for you."

Fritzi thanked her and wandered into the parlor. She sprawled on the horsehair love seat, too weary to drag upstairs and change clothes right away. In her reticule she had a copy of the *Times*. She rubbed her eyes to clear them, tried to catch up on the news.

It was more of the same: Belgians starving, the German general Hindenburg taking command on the Russian front, a ten-million-dollar war loan approved for France. Secretary of State Bryan, the peace apostle, insisted the U.S. must supply all warring powers equally. She knew she should care about all of it, but at the moment she didn't. She sat low on her spine, legs spread like a tomboy, trying to think nothing, feel nothing. She sat that way for twenty minutes while the rain hammered the roof and darkness fell.

Her head came up suddenly. She'd dozed. She noticed an auto parked outside, acetylene headlamps lighting the silvery raindrops. Its arrival must have wakened her.

Was it the police? Had something happened to Lily? She ran to the front door, stood inside the screen, trying to see. The rain blew onto the porch, flowed off the eaves, flooded across the walk.

The car door opened and shut. The driver splashed through mud, passed through the beams of the headlights, lit from the waist down. Then she saw his sugarloaf hat. *"Oh, my God. Loy?"*

She threw the door open, dashed to the edge of the porch. He bounded up the steps. She clasped his hand. "It's really you, where've you been?"

"Working. Ince's chapter play took longer than anybody expected."

Overwhelmed with emotion, and too tired to dissemble, she flung her arms around his neck. With her head tilted back she gazed at him. "I thought you were never coming back." She kissed him lightly. He smelled of tobacco and faintly of whiskey.

She leaned back, reluctant to let go of him. The wind blew rain onto the porch and over the two of them. "We should go inside."

She felt his arm slip around her waist, pulling her gently. He laughed, a soft laugh deep in his throat, almost a cat's purr. "Sure. But that was a real fine welcome to a weary traveler. Wouldn't mind repeating it."

Fritzi almost swooned. She locked her hands at the nape of his neck and kissed him hard while her heart pounded.

His other arm circled her waist. He held her close and she felt him harden against her leg. She tugged his hand, drawing him to the front door, where less rain reached them. Their clothes were already drenched, their faces dripping. Westward over the ocean, thunder pealed. Loy turned his head, looking into the house.

"Who's at home?"

"No one."

He kissed her throat, the lobe of her ear. "I sure did miss your company. Can we go upstairs?"

"Yes. Oh, yes. And no strings, Loy, I promise," she cried, carried away by the feel of him, his hands, his mouth, the stormy darkness, all her months of yearning. She kissed him ardently, her lips open, sliding on his. When she broke away to open the screen door, she was trembling. Loy shook water from his hat and set it on his head.

"I read this in a book once," he said, stepping forward. "Got to do it right." She let herself go limp, surrendering without fear or regret as he picked her up in his arms and plunged into the darkened house.

73. Revelations

What she felt with him first was anxiety, but that soon melted and fused into urgency. A rising passion blanked her mind to everything but raw sensation and did away with her fears of inadequacy. The passion set her brain and hands on fire, her mouth and her skin and her clasping legs. It lifted and shook her with a sweet fury that surpassed anything she'd experienced before.

Afterward, in the hot and rumpled bed, Fritzi caressed him, smoothing down the long, damp hair at the nape of his neck. Rain fell past the window, shining like golden beads. She studied it a moment, then exclaimed, "You forgot the headlights."

He rolled toward the window. "Damn if I didn't. Got carried away. Too late now." He bent over to kiss the corner of her mouth.

"How did you know when I'd be home?"

"Didn't. Windy told me you'd come around lookin' for me, so I came by once before. Talked to your friend Lily then."

"Did you speak to Mrs. Hong?"

"Never saw her." He touched her bare breast. His palm had a hard, callused feel, but he was gentle. "Didn't plan for this to happen, you have to believe that."

"Well, I wasn't exactly uncooperative," she said with a nervous little laugh.

He laughed too. He kissed the warm curve of

her neck. "Going to cause you any problems with the landlady, us being up here like this?"

"The Hongs won't be back until very late. They clean up after the restaurant closes. If Lily comes home, it won't faze her. If I let her, she'd stand in the doorway and applaud. She thinks I'm sort of a stick."

"I don't remember you that way anytime in the last half hour." It was true; she'd felt the joy and release of giving herself wholly without expecting anything of him beyond the moment. Still, she fretted:

"Was it really all right?"

"Perfect. Couldn't be better."

Rain hit the windows in stormy gusts. Fritzi pulled the starched sheet over them, shivering as her body cooled.

"You're sure? I worry that my mouth's too thin and my hips too big. Up here" — she brought his hand to her breast — "it's nothing to boast about either."

"Listen, do I have to go to some courthouse and swear on a Bible? You're just fine."

He slid his hand under his head to reflect. "Can't say as I know anybody who's altogether happy with themselves. Take me. I hate the name my mama handed me. Loyal, what kind of name's that? It was her grandpa's name. To me it sounds sissy."

"It's a fine name. Strong."

"I don't know. I wish they'd named me something common like Jim or Bill. Loyal got me into plenty of fights when I was a youngster, I'll tell you."

He was quiet a while before going on. "I don't know how to say this exactly right, but I want you to know I didn't come into bed with you just for sport. I like you, a lot. But I wouldn't want you to expect —"

She pressed her fingers to his mouth. "You don't need to say any more. I tried to tell you, there are no strings on this. I understand how you feel about settling down."

He leaned his cheek on her shoulder. "Wandering's in my blood, I guess. But there's more to it. My sister Clara."

"In the institution."

"Yep. You're entitled to know the story."

"Loy, I'm not asking —"

"I want to tell you. Remember when Mr. Pelzer offered me a part and I said no? I turned him down because of Sis in that godawful state hospital. I pay for better care than she'd get as a charity patient. Those people are locked away in a wing that's a hellhole. Bedrooms like cells. Food no better than hog slops. For a certain amount every month, Sis gets a window. Better food. Her hair washed once in a while." His voice went low, hoarse with pain.

"I wouldn't want my face on picture screens in Texas. If somebody should recognize me, the authorities would know where to track me down. If I'm locked up, I can't send any more money for Sis's care. Her poor mind just crumbled away after a man took advantage of her by force, him and two friends. They had her I don't know how many times, three or four hours of it. The man I killed was the one talked them into it."

Fritzi held his hand tightly. After a longer silence he went on.

"For about a year after they found Clara in her cottage with her dress in rags and her legs all bloody, she lived off in some dream world. I had to sign papers to put her away. Every time I visited the hospital, I asked her who did the deed — I thought there was only one. She wouldn't say anything, just stared through me like I was a windowpane. As she got a little better, spoke a few words once in a while, I kept begging for the name. I figured she'd tell me in her own good time, and she did. She told me there were three. Told me how they kept at it, having her different ways. I can't say to you all that they did. Afterward she told me she felt bad. Said she could have revealed the name long before, but she was afraid I'd do something and it would be foolish; the ringleader couldn't be touched, he was above the law. He *was* the law."

"A Texas Ranger, you said."

"Member of the state police force, sworn to uphold the law, protect innocent people. His name was Captain Mercer Page. Sis was right, he couldn't be touched, not by me anyway. Didn't matter, I went to see him."

The rain drummed. Fritzi held her breath. "Merce lived by himself, little cabin out in the country. I told him I knew he was the one who egged his friends into raping Clara when they came on her picking strawberries one afternoon when I was off in Waco. Captain Merce Page, the son of a bitch, didn't deny it. Brazen as you please, he said he and his pards had a jug of popskull that fired them up, and when they came on Clara — well, he took pleasure in telling me some of the things they did. He said he went first so he could have her more than once."

"Oh, Loy, that's terrible."

"He laughed pretty hard over it. Merce was one rotten apple. He said he didn't mind telling me 'cause he'd never liked me much and what could I do about it since Clara had gone crazy and wouldn't be a credible witness in court? If it ever got to court. Merce had friends all the way to Austin, brother officers to lie for him, alibi him. About then I lost my head, went loco. I remember yelling I didn't need a warrant or evidence or a trial judge. I pulled my pistol, and before he could grab his off the table, I killed him. He deserved killing, but it doesn't change the fact I committed murder. That was my last day in Bailey County. I rode my dapple gray half the night and most of the next day. Near rode him to death before I hopped a freight train in Lubbock. I'd already sold the ranch and was living in town, so that wasn't any problem. I went to New Mexico and hid out. I swung up north to Idaho a while, then drifted down to California. Like I told you, I expect there's a wanted circular tacked up in every two-bit jail from Muleshoe to the Rio Grande. If they found me, they'd lock me up or hang me, depending on the jury. Dead or in jail, I couldn't earn any more money, and they'd put Sis back in that hellhole section that smells like vomit and pig shit and fifty other things to turn your stomach."

He leaned on his elbows, brought his hand up

to cradle her chin. "That's why I stay just so long in one place. It'll always be that way. I don't want you to think it could ever be different."

She pressed her mouth to his. "Even having you a little while is wonderful."

The rain fell, softer now, almost like a sigh. She heard but didn't see it; his headlights had gone out, the acetylene gas exhausted.

"I wasn't sure I had the nerve to tell you. I thought on it quite a while. I figured we were friends and you might understand. I haven't told many. Windy knows, and a foreman I trusted up in Idaho. Not many."

She squeezed his hand, rubbed her forearms and felt gooseflesh. "I think I'd better put some clothes on."

After they dressed she saw him down to the door. She turned on lights in the parlor so the Hongs would think everything was normal when they returned. The rain was over. Water dripped. A sedan went by, four people, laughing and hooting. One of them threw a bottle. It landed in a puddle with a splash.

On the porch he hugged her, kissed her quickly, and went down the walk whistling. No formal goodbye. No promise of another meeting, nor even a mention of one. It wasn't even half a loaf, it was a crumb, and if he ever snatched it away from her — well, she couldn't stand to think of that.

At the curb he raised his tall hat and waved. She blew a kiss. She sat in the porch swing until his car chugged away, without lights. She feared for his safety. He couldn't see what was ahead.

As the car vanished in the dark, she realized she couldn't either.

74. Detroit Again

"Single room, sir?"

"The best you have. I'm only here for a couple of nights."

The haughty clerk scrutinized Carl's watch cap, cheap pea coat, the tattered scarf around his neck, his worn Gladstone waiting by the bell stand. "We prefer to settle the room charges in advance."

Carl shoved paper money across the marble counter and signed the register. There was satisfaction in returning to the Wayne Hotel as a paying guest, though it was an extravagance, perhaps the only one he'd be able to afford on his journey.

The Detroit weather was gray and dismal, with occasional rain. The boat horns on the foggy river seemed to mourn the coming of winter. After a hot bath and a breakfast of half a dozen eggs, fried potatoes, and a sirloin steak, Carl wrapped the scarf around his neck and set out for Highland Park.

He was overwhelmed by the size of the Ford plant that had been building when he left the city. It was an incredible structure, four stories high, seemingly a mile from end to end, though that was probably an illusion. What overwhelmed him was not only the size, but the vast number of windows. In a Chamber of Commerce pamphlet picked up downtown, the plant was called "Detroit's Own Crystal Palace."

Mr. Ford's architect, Albert Kahn, had designed the unique building, and in it Ford had refined and implemented the idea of creating the world's first moving assembly line. Carl heard it clanking and clanging its song through all of the windows, which stood open despite the rain and wintry air.

A guard wearing a Ford employee's badge on his slicker and swinging a billy sauntered through the gate.

"They aren't hiring."

"I'm not looking for a job. How many work here now?"

"Why do you want to know?"

"I worked here once myself. Well, not here, Piquette Avenue."

That softened the man slightly. "About twelve thousand five hundred on the payroll. Last year we rolled out better'n three hundred thousand automobiles. Should do a lot better this year, demand keeps growing."

"Mr. Ford's some kind of genius. I hear people are talking of him for senator."

"Or president. What did you say your name was?"

"Carl Crown. Mr. Ford wouldn't remember."

"I expect that's right, he's a real bigwig now. Captain of industry."

Carl nodded, smiled, walked away with feelings of awe, and a certain nostalgia, as the rain turned to sleet.

A black family lived in Jesse Shiner's cottage

on Columbia. The woman, scrawny and stoop-shouldered with an infant in her arms, told him she didn't know where Jesse lived now, but he worked at Sport's, on the east side.

"That's a barber shop. For the colored," the woman added, to be sure he understood. With the rain changing to sleet, Carl trudged away.

Sport's Tonsorial was a neat little establishment, four chairs. A stout, authoritative man, blue-black and bald, stepped away from a customer he was shaving in the first chair.

"I think you got the wrong shop, brother."

From the rear, the last chair, someone said, "No, Sport. I know him."

"Jesse!" Carl tromped to the rear, leaving a trail of water on the linoleum, which Sport eyed with disapproval. The shop was comfortingly warm, fragrant with talc and hair oil and pomades. Jesse was little changed, spare as ever, though some age spots marked his coffee-and-cream face now. When he hoisted himself out of his chair, he listed as he walked. It brought back that terrible night when the hoodlum had sunk the gaff hook in Jesse's leg.

"How are you, Jess?"

"Surviving. Used to joke about being in this trade, and look at me. Never expected you to show up again. Where you bound?"

Carl explained, then said, "I want to see Tess. Do you know anything about her?"

"Come on to the storeroom, let's talk."

Carl followed him to a crowded back room piled high with boxes of barber supplies. Jesse snapped on a hanging lightbulb, sat on a bench,

697

offered Carl a cigarette. Carl shook his head.

"Don't know much about her 'cept what I read now and then. Mrs. Sykes her name is."

Carl's face wrenched. "She married that son of a bitch?"

"Yeah, but he was killed a couple of years ago. Out joyriding with two roadhouse girls, all of 'em high. The car turned over. Broke his neck. The chippies were snoozing in back, they got out with scratches. Guess there's some justice after all."

"Anything more?"

"Don't think so. Oh, yeah — she and Sykes, they had a little boy. She's back in her pa's old house on Piety Hill. He's in some kind of old folks' home. Clymer car company's gone. Competition got too fierce." Jesse puffed his cigarette. "From all I can tell, that Tess is a fine woman. I 'spect you were a damn fool to leave her."

"At the time I couldn't do anything else. Can I buy you lunch?"

"Sport gives us a half hour. Not till twelve, though."

"I'll wait."

That night, with the sleet abating and a north wind howling out of Canada, Carl shivered in front of the Clymer mansion on Woodward Avenue. It was the same splendid house he remembered, three stories, ablaze with lights. He was surprised and a little hurt that Tess had married Wayne Sykes, the man he'd beaten half to death. But she'd always had pressure from her father, and he supposed the little bastard was a good catch. He couldn't have expected Tess to be loyal when she assumed he was never coming back to her.

He almost turned away from the iron gate, but he recalled the softness of Tess's embrace that long-lost day they made love, and the luster of her eyes, dark blue as he imagined the South Seas must be. He had to open the gate and take his chances.

A man in livery answered the bell, reacting to Carl's wet-dog appearance with predictable disdain.

"Tradesmen at the rear. We do not hand out —"

"I'm a friend of Mrs. Sykes's." The man's expression said that was highly doubtful. "Is she at home?"

"Mrs. Sykes is not receiving anyone this evening."

"That isn't what I asked, I asked if she's home. If she is, tell her Carl would like to see her."

"Your last name?"

"Just Carl."

He shut the door. The November wind brought a few snowflakes whirling past the street lamps. He shivered.

The door opened again. Tess stood there, stouter now, wearing reading spectacles. A great electric chandelier in the foyer put glinting lights in her blond hair. For a moment she seemed unsteady; he thought she might swoon.

"I never thought I'd see this moment, Carl."

Awkwardly: "Well, I didn't either. I'm passing

through. Catching a boat in Montreal, on my way to France."

"Dear Lord in heaven. Always the wanderer. You must be frozen. Please come in."

As she closed the door against the wind, he saw the large engagement diamond on her left hand, the slimmer wedding band. He said, "My friend Jesse told me you'd gotten married but lost your husband. I'm awfully sorry to hear that."

Tess drew a long breath. She was as pleasingly round as he remembered from those aching days of love and loss. "I never loved Wayne. I married him because Father always wanted it, and with you gone — well, no need to bring up the past, is there?"

From the back of the house, a small boy of five or six bounded through a swinging door. He raced up to Carl, looked him over, stuck out his hand. "Hello. You're the company. What's your name?"

"Carl," he said, amused. They shook hands. The boy was sturdily built, with short legs and wide shoulders. He had brown eyes like Carl's, but Carl saw mostly Tess in his face.

"Henry's my name," the boy said with great seriousness.

"My Prince Hal," Tess said, ruffling his hair affectionately. She patted his bottom. "Bedtime." Henry ran up the stairs, waving to Carl. "Henry is my father's middle name," Tess explained. She took his hand, gently tugged him toward a lighted parlor. "Tell me why you're off to Europe."

Tess rang for the manservant, who treated Carl with more deference as he served him a whiskey, and hot tea in a gold-rimmed cup for Tess. Her eyes were soft and warm as she indicated the scarf. "Still fighting the dragons and Saracens?"

"I guess you can say that. I'm going to fly in the French air corps. I've been piloting aeroplanes for a few years now."

"It's against the law for American citizens to involve themselves in the war, isn't it?"

Carl shrugged; the fine old bourbon whiskey thawed him a little. "I don't think Wilson will send detectives to arrest me, or anyone who helps the Allies. My friend Rene — he's the man who talked me into this — he convinced me we're wrong to stay neutral in this fight."

"But how can you join up when it's forbidden?"

"It isn't forbidden to join the French Foreign Legion. You sign up with them in Paris, they shuffle papers and reassign you to the air corps. Woodrow's content, thinking you're standing guard someplace in the desert." He gestured with the glass. "I had enough of that old fool when he threw me out of Princeton. Did I ever tell you about that?"

"How he lost his best football lineman? You did."

"Jesus, we talked a lot, didn't we?"

"In such a short time," Tess said with a searching look. "How I wish it could have gone on, and on —" There was a rush of color in her cheeks. She averted her eyes to her teacup.

They reminisced for an hour. Then Carl rose to leave. Tess slipped her arm through his; the touch of her round breast roused old desires, old conflicts, within him.

"You have a fine son," he said at the front door.

"Yes. I wish you could stay and get to know him."

"I promised to meet Rene in two days."

She sighed. "There are always more dragons."

"But not so many Saracens. The Huns killed them."

The feeble humor disturbed her. She pressed her cheek fiercely against his chest. "Don't joke. This war is terrible. We'll be in it no matter what Wilson says. Millions of boys are dying. Don't let one of them be you."

Tears brimmed in her lovely eyes. "Kiss me goodbye for old times' sake?"

He swept her into his arms. It was all he could do to break the embrace, touch her smooth, soft cheek one last time, and go out into the bitter night.

75. Million-Dollar Carpet

Fritzi worked on her new comedy with such energy that she was ready to swoon from exhaustion every night. Unexpectedly, she liked making *Paper Hanger Nell*. She added some little tricks of technique she'd learned by studying Charlie's tramp comedies. With a raised eyebrow, a sad smile, a lovelorn glance, Charles gave comedy an extra dimension of pathos that made it all the richer.

Fritzi's picture started with Nell's father, an impecunious paper hanger, breaking his leg on a sidewalk banana peel just before starting a big job. Nell took over to save the business. She blundered her way through mishaps with dripping paste brushes, leaky buckets, shaky scaffolds, and collapsing ladders. She fell in love with a building inspector but lost him to a shapely blonde. At the end of the second reel Nell was left alone with a big white glob of paste on her nose, like a sad clown. With a little shrug she scraped it off and flicked it out of the frame — into the eye of a passing policeman. Fade-out.

Hobart noticed Fritzi's manic energy. He had survived *Macbeth* without causing or being involved in a major accident. For the last day of shooting, on the lot, Hobart was costumed as the Thane of Cawdor in a blue velvet robe, crape hair beard, cardboard crown with paste jewels. He and Fritzi ate onion sandwiches and drank root beer in camp chairs in the sunshine.

"What has come over you, dear child?" Hobart said. "You're flushed. You chatter at everyone like a Maxim gun."

"I'm working hard, that's all."

"I might suspect a different cause. I am informed you have a friend, some kind of Wild West cowhand. I hear he's madly attractive."

She poked his stomach. "Stay away. He's mine."

Hobart laughed. "How splendid that you're happy. I'll have you know I too am in the same blissful state. Polo and I have become friends. Close friends, if you take my meaning."

"Love is in the air?"

"You're such a clever child," he sighed, adjusting his crown.

She saw Loy every day their schedules allowed, which wasn't often. He was working again, this time in a Western that substituted autos for hard-to-find horses. The picture starred a second-string actor named Brix, and was shooting on a ranch near Ojai. On a warm autumn Sunday they drove out there in the studio Packard, Fritzi at the wheel. In a secluded stable Loy showed her one of the animals from the picture, a quarter horse named Geronimo.

"See how small he is?" The horse nuzzled Loy's hand. "Barely fourteen hands. He's fast, agile on rough ground — a hell of a lot better than the big stable hacks they usually rent. We shot a chase today, Western Eighteen. That's eighteen frames a second. Projected at normal speed, the chase goes like lightning."

"What's the name of this epic?"

"Bud Brix in *Blazing Bullets*."

She giggled. "Will we actually see the bullets on fire?"

"I know it's stupid. I didn't think it up, I'm only a hired hand."

The stable was quiet, deserted. A convenient hayloft offered itself. Loy made no move to repeat the night of lovemaking, and though Fritzi longed for it, she was too embarrassed to be forward a second time. She sensed he'd pulled back. Once more she was just a pal.

Even so, she was happy. All day long, at unexpected moments she broke out in song. Lily knew she was wrapped up in thoughts of Loy. "You two could live together. Take a room in some hotel downtown. Hell, you can afford a flat, even a small house."

"He'd never do it."

"Why not?"

"He just won't. He's footloose. Every day I wake up and wonder if he might have left in the middle of the night."

Lily clucked her tongue. "Poor kid." She gave Fritzi a long and heartfelt hug.

In the picture colony people gossiped about Griffith's Civil War epic, *The Clansman*, scheduled to be shown for the first time early next year. Their envy was even more evident when they discussed Fritzi's friend Charlie. The whole country had come down with a case of "Chaplinitis." Dance orchestras were playing

"That Charlie Chaplin Walk." Department stores filled their shelves with Chaplin dolls for Christmas. Newspapers ran Chaplin cartoons and Chaplin interviews.

The autumn's big hit, *Tillie's Punctured Romance*, spread the epidemic. The six-reel feature, which took nearly that many weeks to film, was adapted from a popular stage comedy. Charlie had made the picture as one of his last for Mack Sennett. He currently earned a well-publicized $1,250 a week at Essanay. Fritzi's $150 a week which she'd been receiving since the first of the year was a pittance by comparison. A sense of injustice was beginning to gnaw on her.

Charlie returned unexpectedly from his exile in northern California. He'd suffered in the isolation of the Essanay studio at Niles. Rather than see him unhappy and risk losing him, Essanay leased a Fairview Avenue studio that had belonged to a defunct company called Majestic. Charlie would shoot his pictures there.

On his first weekend back in town, Charlie invited Fritzi and Loy for supper at the Ship's Café. He introduced them to Edna Purviance, a pretty young woman who was his new leading lady and girlfriend. When the café band struck up "Heart of My Heart," Charlie asked Fritzi to dance.

He was so polite, she remarked on it. "You don't sound like yourself anymore," she said as they stepped around the floor. "You sound like an Oxford professor."

"Elocution lessons. People think a Cockney accent's low-class. I like your Texas fellow, by the way. Quiet chap."

"Around strangers, yes. Edna's a dear."

Charlie mugged disappointment. "I couldn't have you, and I had to have someone. No, I'm teasing. I fell for Edna right off."

"You're happy now that they've moved you back to Los Angeles?"

"Yes, but you should have heard the Essanay fellows squeal about it. They're a bunch of cheapskates. They can't get away with it," he said with a sly smile. "I know my worth."

When supper was over, Loy shook Charlie's hand and Fritzi kissed him goodbye and wished him well. Charlie had a high regard for himself, but why not? He was already acknowledged to be the finest comedian in pictures, possibly in the world. Just as important, he knew how to capitalize on the value of his talent to others. That was where Fritzi fell short. She needed to give thought to correcting the situation, especially since *Paper Hanger Nell* showed signs of being a hit. While the picture was still being edited, B.B. reported orders for nearly one hundred twenty prints, and Eddie plunged into preparing *Firehouse Nell*.

The day that picture went before the camera on the new all-glass stage, B.B. made his usual appearance to wish everyone well. Fritzi took the opportunity to corner him. "I'd like to discuss something with you and Al," she said. "May we have lunch today?"

"I'm free. I'll check Al's schedule."

"Please tell him it's important."

That caught his attention. "Important, huh?

Well, we got to take care of our star," he said, patting her arm. "Matter of fact, we had plans to treat you to lunch someday soon, so this'll work nicely. Where do you want to eat?"

Fritzi had already decided. "The Palm Court at the Alexandria."

"Downtown? Will Eddie let you off that long?"

"I haven't asked him, but I'm sure he will."

B.B. cocked his head, gave her a knowing look. "Yeah, I got a notion he'll give you whatever you want. One o'clock, Al's office."

Eddie didn't quarrel when she asked for two hours off. Kelly's Mexican chauffeur drove Fritzi and the two men downtown to the Alexandria Hotel at Sixth and Spring. Kelly, looking natty in an ice cream suit, was unusually affable. "Ham Hayman phoned with an invitation for a big party Saturday night. Friends of his built a fabulous Oriental house up in the hills."

"I've seen it," Fritzi said. You couldn't miss the spectacular Japanese-style estate on its commanding hilltop above Hollywood Boulevard. B.B. said, "Thing is, Al's tied up and I can't go, because Sophie hates big, noisy parties. Ham wants somebody to represent the company. Who better than our Nellie?"

"I'll be glad to attend if I can take my friend Mr. Hardin."

"Say, I heard about you and that Texas galoot," B.B. said as the chauffeur parked in front of the hotel. "Sure wish he'd think about making a picture."

"He'll never do it. He's happy where he is."

"Nobody's happy where he is," Kelly said.

"He'll wake up one day."

Fritzi didn't comment.

Entering the lobby, she said, "Let's not go to the restaurant just yet. Let's sit down over here." Kelly and B.B. exchanged looks as she led them across the rich Oriental carpet. Tall oak chairs were scattered about the perimeter. Fritzi sat between the partners.

B.B. scratched his nose. "Fritzi, you're pretty shrewd. I have a feeling this conversation will cost me money."

"What are you talking about?" Kelly said.

"This." B.B. tapped his foot. "The million dollar carpet. They call it that because a lot of big deals are closed here. I got a hunch our little gel wants to discuss salary."

Kelly started to protest, but B.B. shushed him with a wave. A dewy perspiration clung to Fritzi's upper lip. Her pulse was fast.

"I know how many prints of *Paper Hanger Nell* the exchanges distributed," she began. "Exactly one hundred and twenty-four the first month. Plus, some sixties are still earning money." Sixties were prints in theaters for a second month. They rented for $20 or $25 instead of $30 to $50, the price range for the first thirty days.

"How do you know so much about this stuff?" Kelly asked.

"I make it a point to eat lunch with a bookkeeper once a week."

"Which bookkeeper?" Kelly asked sharply. Liberty employed three.

"Sorry," she replied with an angelic smile.

B.B. whipped out his silk pocket handkerchief

and mopped his face. "I get the drift. You don't think we're treating you right."

"Not treating her right!" Kelly exclaimed. "After we spent so much money for — ?" B.B. kicked his shin with the point of his two-tone shoe. Kelly folded his arms and glared.

"Three hundred fifty a week, how's that sound, little gel?"

Fritzi wanted to leap up, clap her hands, dance a jig. She'd planned to ask for $200. Kelly looked at B.B. as though his partner had lapsed into senility. Fritzi wondered whether B.B. had offered $350 because he expected her to demand more. With a vaguely suicidal feeling, she swallowed and said:

"I was thinking of four hundred."

"Four?" Kelly nearly choked on the word. "Jesus Christ, you think Liberty mints money?"

Sweetly Fritzi said, "No, but it seems the Nellie pictures do."

"Deal!" B.B. said, slapping his knees. "Yes, sir, and it's a bargain." Kelly flung one hand over his eyes to show his extreme pain. "We'd want to make it part of a new contract, though."

"Three years," Kelly said.

B.B. seized her hand and rubbed it frantically. "That all right with you, little gel?"

Fritzi was overwhelmed. The busy lobby seemed to tilt and blur. The chatter of guests, the rattle of an elevator cage, the pinging of a front-desk bell, fused into a cacophony. She couldn't think of a thing to say. From nowhere Little Mary's face leaped to mind. *"Remember. Your own company."*

"That is very decent of you, B.B. And of you, Al. But if we sign a new contract, I suppose I should have my own lawyer look it over, don't you think?"

Kelly waved it aside. "Not necessary. The company shyster will draw it up. It'll be very fair to all parties, don't you worry." Which was exactly why she did; he was much too glib.

B.B. jumped up. "Al, she can have her lawyer. That's enough palaver — we're here to celebrate. French champagne — the works."

The meal in the Palm Court was sumptuous and pleasant. Fritzi had never seen Kelly so cowed; he didn't say a word about the steep prices. She drank only one small glass of champagne because of the afternoon's schedule. They left the hotel at a quarter to three. Outside, a long, sleek Locomobile touring car, rich dark blue with wire-spoke wheels, was parked at the curb with the top down, unattended.

"I don't see your car," Fritzi said to Kelly.

"I sent it back."

"We'll take this one," B.B. said.

"Whose is it?" Fritzi asked.

With a distant sourness Kelly said, "Yours."

"A present for our big star," B.B. said expansively. "You made quite a deal today, little gel. We bought the car for you last week to show our appreciation. Now you got the car and a big bump in pay. Quite a little businesswoman, ain't she, Al?"

"Yeah, swell," Kelly muttered.

Fritzi was lucky not to faint on the spot.

76. End of the Party

Fritzi was still euphoric when she and Loy motored up North Sycamore to the Japanese palace on Saturday night. A line of expensive autos crawled up the hill behind them, Loziers and Cadillacs, Packards and Studebakers, with an occasional Maxwell or Briscoe, Oakland or Scripps, thrusting in like a poor relation. The lights of Hollywood and Los Angeles twinkled as a backdrop. The December air was crisp and sweet.

An attendant in a white shirt and duck trousers flagged them to a stop outside spectacular gates of wood decorated with iron studs. While the first attendant opened the passenger door for Fritzi, another ran forward to park the Locomobile. Loy snarled at him, "Be careful of the paint."

Fritzi wondered why he was so testy and grim. The unfamiliarity of a fancy party? She took his arm, hugged it to her side as a show of affection. He didn't react, or even appear to notice.

Fritzi looked smart in a new hobble skirt and fancy hat with white egret plumes. Loy had polished his boots and put on a regular four-in-hand with his suit. The noise of a large crowd, two or three hundred, drifted through the open gates. She and Loy passed through into a small forecourt, then entered the main house. Gilded rafters soared above them. They were surrounded by tall blue and white urns, Chinese lion dogs made of black iron, folding screens artfully inlaid with pearl. Every square foot of wall space displayed some form of Oriental art: Japanese tapestries, Chinese brush paintings, ferocious Balinese devil masks. Smoke from incense braziers hazed the air. Fritzi smelled whiskey, perfume, cigarettes, some with an unfamiliar grassy aroma.

Sliding wall panels of paper and bamboo opened on a huge inner court graced with small pagodas and arched foot bridges spanning ponds in which orange carp swam. In one corner a massive stone lantern dominated a Japanese garden with gnarled pine trees lining the banks of a miniature river made of smooth white stones. A dance orchestra played in a ballroom on the other side of the courtyard. Fritzi counted no less than five separate service bars where Orientals in white coats dispensed drinks with machine-like speed.

Ham Hayman spotted them in the crowd. Hayman wore a smart belted suit of brown tweed, an ascot, and a white-and-green-striped shirt. The ex-junk dealer had burst from his rusty cocoon to become an exotic butterfly of pictures, and he used his wardrobe to prove it.

"Some joint, huh?"

"It certainly is," Fritzi agreed.

"Two brothers named Bernheimer built it. Took five years. They came out from New York. Got rich running a big importing business, Chink and Jap goods. That's how they found all this stuff."

Hayman squeezed her arm. "You like your

new deal? Good. I personally okayed the terms. You want anything else, I'll take care of it, that's a promise. Just come see me. You're an important piece of property. Say, I haven't met your friend."

Principally because he hadn't stopped talking. She introduced the men, though Loy only muttered his hello. Hayman waved to someone, excused himself, and rushed off.

"So now you're a piece of property," Loy said, unsmiling.

"They're all crazy in this business. Don't take it seriously."

"Want a drink?"

"Beer if they have it. Oh, there's Mary. I'd like to say hello."

"Sure, go ahead," he said as he left.

As she pushed and squeezed her way toward Mary Pickford, she ran into a handsome suntanned actor carrying empty glasses. She remembered him from another party. His stage name was Fairbanks.

"Hello, Doug, how are you?"

"Fine, girlie, how's with you?" He flashed a big white grin but obviously didn't recognize her. One of the new gossip magazines said Little Mary and the actor were carrying on behind the backs of their spouses.

Though surrounded by adoring fans, when Mary spied Fritzi, she exclaimed and threw her arms around her friend. "Everybody, this is Fritzi Crown, my old pal from the Biograph in New York. Fritzi stars in those swell Liberty comedies about Nellie."

After accepting a flurry of compliments, Fritzi pulled away and Mary came over to speak privately. "How are you doing, kid?" she asked.

"Fine, I couldn't be better." Fritzi grinned. "In fact tonight Mr. Hayman, one of the owners, called me a valuable piece of property."

"Oh-oh. Got a good lawyer?"

"I've thought about it. Do you think I need one?"

Mary's sweet eyes grew hard as the steelies in Fritzi's childhood marble sack. Mary laid a comradely arm over her shoulder.

"Yesterday. Want a recommendation?"

Arm in arm, Hobart and Polo Werfels stood near the ballroom entrance, swaying to the music. Hobart wore a suit of black velvet accented with a flowing pink neckerchief held by a silver Navajo ring. He'd already drunk large quantities of champagne and spoke with a cheerful slur. "What's the name of that song, love?"

" 'Everybody's Doin' It Now,' " Polo said. "The little Yid who wrote it, Berlin, he says it's about fast dancing. I say bullshit, it's about copulating."

Hobart enviously eyed the couples gliding over the waxed floor. "Would we dare?"

"Are you cuckoo? Definitely not. This isn't a religious camp meeting, but we still got careers to think about. You can bet some harpies from the gossip rags sneaked in tonight."

"Shame. I fancied trying a few ballroom steps. I'd love to be Vernon Castle."

"Hey, dollink, I'm Vernon. You're Irene,

and don't you forget it."

Coming back to Loy after her talk with Mary, Fritzi said, "Did you see Hobart and Polo together? They're giggling and whispering like sweethearts."

"Maybe that's what they are."

"Back in Chicago, growing up, I didn't know about such things."

"Not in Texas either, though we had a school-teacher who hung himself. People said it was because the town found out he was strange."

"Well, if Hobart's happy, I'm glad for it."

Famous faces surrounded them at the party. Bill Hart was there, besieged with well-wishers; Ince had transformed him to a western star almost overnight. Fritzi said hello to Fatty and Minta Arbuckle, and to Mack Sennett, who was squiring Mabel. Mary and Doug Fairbanks seemed to be together.

She embraced her old driving instructor, Von. He was beginning to work regularly in villain roles, particularly those requiring the look of a foreign or Teutonic militarist. Von's bald head, the natural way he wore a monocle, and his superb talent for sneering could be counted on to trigger hatred in the most phlegmatic audience. He was, in person, a genteel and likable man of whom she was immensely fond.

She spotted some less attractive guests. Anonymous men with pinched faces and hard eyes. Young girls with heavy rouge, shrill voices, tight dresses that showed too much. In recent months Fritzi had noticed a change in Hollywood. The provincial town of Middle Western transplants she had discovered when she stepped off the train the first time was being invaded by a rough crowd. Loy said that on location in Ojai, he and the director of *Blazing Bullets* had run off two thuggish pimps offering girls from the back of a dilapidated truck.

Mr. Griffith appeared in the crowd. He greeted Fritzi warmly. She thought he looked more gaunt than usual — unwell. When she expressed her concern, he said he was getting little sleep, editing miles of film to get *The Clansman* ready for its premiere at Clune's Auditorium. "I'll save you two good seats."

Loy didn't mingle. For over an hour he stood by himself, nursing his whiskey and rebuffing strangers who tried to chat. Finally Fritzi suggested they leave. He agreed instantly, and she became concerned. If she asked, would he say what was troubling him?

They shook hands with one of the Bernheimers and thanked him. As they headed for the outer courtyard, they were accosted by a diminutive woman wearing a feathered hat three times as big as her head. She had a long nose and a squint.

"Fritzi Crown. Loretta Gash, *Screen Play*."

" 'Gazing at the Stars at Night,' " Fritzi said. She hoped her distaste for the trashy magazine wasn't too evident. Like gamblers and procurers and girls willing to sell their favors to help their careers, the publishers and writers of cheap gossip rags were proliferating.

"You're doing so well with your little comedies, dear," Loretta Gash said. "Is this your fella? I heard he's a performer. What's your name?"

Loy's answer was a stony stare.

Fritzi grabbed his arm. "Come on, we're leaving."

Loretta chased them to the gates. "Are you just friends, or do you have a cozy arrangement? How about a photo? I have a man standing by with a camera."

Loy spun around angrily. "No picture. Get away from us." His red face upset Fritzi. She'd seen the look just before he hit someone.

"Wait a minute, handsome, the public wants to know about —"

"All they need to know," Fritzi said sweetly, "they see on the screen. Dear." She tugged Loy's arm again, and out the gate they went.

Fritzi heard a snarl from Miss Gash: "Stuckup bitch."

The stars had a blurred look — dust stirred by the west wind, bringing the scent of rain off the ocean. Loy handed his auto check to the attendant. "I don't imagine that did you too much good."

"No, but it felt good. Loy, what's wrong tonight?"

He gazed at her with troubled eyes. "Been trying not to spoil the evening for you. Reckon I did, I'm sorry. Let's get away from here. There's something I need to show you."

When she heard that, the anxiety gnawing on her turned to dread.

Spatters of rain hit the windshield with increasing frequency. Street lamps spaced a block apart shone through the glass, making the droplets gleam. Fritzi turned her head slightly to study Loy's profile. His lips were tight together, his eyes carefully fixed on the road — no clue there to what had upset him.

"Thought we might have just a spit of rain," he said as it came down harder. "Reckon I'd better close up the top." He slid the long auto to the curb near a corner bungalow with lights shining in every window. He jumped out, pulled the canvas over, and fastened it. "Good enough light here, I guess." Seated again, he drew something out of his inside pocket, unfolded it, and angled it so the light fell on it.

"See that all right?"

"Yes," Fritzi said, puzzled over why he wanted to show her a studio photograph mounted on flimsy card stock. The rectangular image caught three men in chaps and tall hats riding hell for leather past the camera lens. The rider in front was bent low over his mount's neck. Wind had turned his hat brim up; Loy's face was unmistakable.

"Director lined up a second camera for that chase shot. Never knew about it or saw it till I rode past. When I saw *Blazing Bullets* cut together I couldn't believe it, but there I was, on the screen clear as day for three, maybe four seconds. Anybody down Texas way sees the picture, they'll be on me like a hound on a coon in hunting season."

Now she understood. "Did you ask the director to cut out the frames?"

"Sure I did. He's a high and mighty little pri—

toad. He kind of reared back and said did I know who I was talking to. I came close to knocking the hell out of him. But I didn't. I slipped a few dollars to the laboratory fellows to print out this frame. Seems they may be using it for one of the publicity stills."

"Don't worry about it. I'll speak to B.B. Maybe he can telephone someone and ask them to cut out —"

Loy's hand fell on her wrist quickly. Gentle but firm, the touch of his fingers frightened her somehow. "Never mind. Been thinking for a while that I should mosey on. This put the burr under the saddle blanket, that's all."

Fritzi leaned back against the seat cushion, holding her breath. In the quiet darkness a night bird trilled. One or two streets away an auto coughed along, then backfired and died.

"You're leaving town," she said.

He pushed stray locks of long hair off his forehead. "That's about the size of it."

"Because your face is on the screen accidentally for a few seconds."

"I told you about Clara," he began. "How she needs —"

"Is this just a convenient excuse, Loy? Because you think I'm trying to tie you down?"

Silence. In the corner bungalow someone started a piano roll. Fritzi recognized "A Girl in Central Park." She nearly wept.

Loy ran his tongue under his lower lip. He gripped the steering wheel with both hands and stared through the streaked windshield. The rain had let up again.

"I wonder that myself, a little."

Fritzi threw the picture in his lap. "I don't know what to make of you."

"I'm no storybook hero, if that's what you're looking for."

"I'm looking for someone to love me as much as I love him."

"I'm not that fella, Fritzi. Tried to tell you plenty of times."

"So what does this mean? Goodbye?"

"Reckon so."

"When?"

"Tonight. I plan to light out north in the morning. Buy me a ticket on the daylight express to Frisco. Figure I'll stay there a day or two, then go have a look at Hawaii, where the pineapples grow." He cleared his throat, almost like a minister starting a sermon. "No matter where I go, I'll never forget knowing you."

Bitterness spilled out: "What a comfort. What a consolation after being thrown aside like —"

"Listen here, I told you I could never —"

"Reckon I don't know that, mister?" she cried in a perfect imitation of his Texas speech. In the light from the corner she saw his face whiten as his hand flew up to strike her. She covered her face, but the blow didn't land. Lowering her hands to her lap, she watched him draw his fist down slowly, open his fingers.

"Yes, ma'am, you surely did, all right."

"Loy, I'm sorry. I didn't mean to mock you."

" 'Course you did. Did it damn well too. Forget it."

Though Fritzi's emotional control was shattered, she managed to say, "May we drive on before I bawl my head off?"

He started to reply, thought better of it. On the long drive to his squalid house behind a stable on Alessandro Street, she said nothing, digging her nails into her palms and hoping the sting would keep her from an outburst. When they arrived, he braked the car in the lane, stood outside with rain falling gently on his long hair. Fritzi pushed her door open and nearly fell on her face, she was so weak-kneed with grief and anger. She marched around the rear of the Locomobile. He stepped back respectfully, held the door as rain splashed into her eyes and mixed with tears.

"Are you steady enough to drive home?"

"What the hell difference does it make?" She flounced into the seat, blurry-eyed and barely able to find the wheel with her clammy hands.

Almost with a lover's tenderness he said, "Makes a big difference. There's millions of folks out there in the wide world who think you're special. They love you."

"The only one I care about doesn't."

"God damn it, Fritzi —"

"Take your hand off the car, Loy. Goodbye."

She wheeled the Locomobile around in the lane and jolted out to Alessandro Street. Though she tended to weave from side to side on empty roadways, and had one close call with a Pacific Electric car bound home to the barns, she made it safely to Venice.

Her darkened bedroom mutely witnessed an

emotional scene worthy of Duse or her idol, Miss Terry. Fritzi tore her party clothes off, trampled on them, and ground her heels to tear them. She rolled to and fro on the bed, stifling sobs with her pillow pressed to her face. Once she almost screamed aloud, but a pang of consideration for the Hongs and Lily forestalled it. Besides, at that point she'd been crying for two hours. Exhaustion set in.

She yanked at her ugly curly hair to make it hurt but quickly realized how ridiculous that was, and laughed, big, choking gulps of laughter without mirth. The suffering would last for years. Maybe it would never end. The loss of the boy she loved in long-ago Savannah was nothing compared to this. Loy had broken her heart beyond repair.

77. U-Boat

Thousands of miles east of Los Angeles, on the waters of *Jadbusen* — Jade Bay — in the German state of East Frisia, the sun was already up.

The new *Unterseeboot* bobbed gently on its mooring lines. Sammy unfolded the tripod on the U-boat's forward deck while Paul strode up and down, studying the light falling on the water, the iron conning tower, the slate roofs of Wilhelmshaven on shore. Paul and Sammy had come to Germany for more footage to fill out a planned lecture tour. Paul was paying his helper from his substantial book royalties. The execution film had been safely stored at a London bank.

The U-boat commander, *Kapitänleutnant* Waldmann, stood stiffly, observing them. Feet spread, hands locked behind his back, spine straight, the German officer personified military correctness. Several decorations including an Iron Cross hung on his starched tunic. The points of his thick brown mustache fluttered in a brisk wind churning up white water in the bay.

Kapitänleutnant Waldmann was only in his thirties, but devotion to duty had drawn deep lines in his wind-burned face. Paul liked the man. He lacked the swaggering arrogance of the Germans in Belgium; he was showing off his vessel to the visitors like a proud boy with a toy. He recited all of its fine points: diesel motors, advanced periscope optics, a powerful wireless transmitter, bow and stern torpedo tubes, remarkable cruising range — five thousand miles at eight knots without refueling. The U-boat was the latest addition to the navy's North Sea flotilla. Waldmann said Germany had made rapid progress with submarines since launching the first one in 1906, over objections of Admiral von Tirpitz, who thought undersea boats useless because of their limited range at the time.

Sammy locked down the camera and stepped back. "All ready, gov."

"Right you are." Paul straightened his cap and hunted for a cigar in a pocket filled with scraps of paper and flakes of Havana wrapper. Speaking German, he said to Waldmann, "I'd like to shoot your gun crew running a drill, is that possible?" Five of the U-boat's complement of thirty-five ratings stood at attention near the 150mm deck gun.

"Most certainly, Mr. Crown. Anything you wish."

"I appreciate your cooperation."

"We are eager to have our undersea craft seen by your countrymen. I am told you do not receive similar cooperation from the enemy." Fortunately, Sammy couldn't translate the last word; he looked belligerent enough without it.

"None. They've shut us out. Berlin, on the other hand, is very friendly to journalists and cameramen." Waldmann was right, the damn fools in Whitehall were still refusing to allow correspondents near their armies, their weapons, or even their training camps. Paul felt a certain guilt about moving freely and successfully in Germany; like Sammy, he believed she was the aggressor, and an increasingly pitiless and brutal one at that. But he needed footage.

"Where do you plan to take this vessel, if that isn't confidential?" he asked.

"Not at all. It is common knowledge that the high command in Berlin will shortly declare the waters around Great Britain to be a war zone. When that occurs, we shall most certainly be operating there, to prevent shipments of arms manufactured in your country from reaching English ports."

"Will you sink the ships?"

"I would hope they would strike their colors before that became necessary."

"We're talking of cargo vessels here?"

"Exactly so."

"In London I heard rumors that arms are being sent over secretly on passenger ships."

"Yes, we receive similar reports. It is said that some British liners carrying such contraband fly the flag of the United States to protect themselves. A cowardly deception, in my opinion."

"But even in a war zone, you wouldn't torpedo a ship flying a neutral flag, would you?"

"Oh, I am sure we shall never have to confront that unhappy question," the *Kapitänleutnant* said, evading. He stepped close to Paul so as not to be overheard by his men. "However, Mr. Crown, I would urge you to exercise caution if you plan any trip to your homeland in the near future."

"As a matter of fact I'll be going over for lecture engagements sometime next year. These pictures will be part of my program."

"Then I advise you to cross on an American vessel, not a liner operated by Cunard or White Star. While those may be passenger ships, they are not neutrals."

"I see. Thanks for the warning." Which he found appalling.

Gulls cried overhead, swooping above the whitecaps. The German ensign flapped and cracked on the conning tower flagstaff. Wilhelmshaven with its tidy streets and beach promenades had a quaint, peaceful look in the winter sunshine.

Paul reversed his cap and leaned into the camera. "Ready, here we go." *Kapitänleutnant* Waldmann snapped to attention and saluted the lens smartly. Sammy turned his back and spat over the side. Several of the crewmen saw him and muttered. Sammy gave them glares.

That evening on shore, Paul and Sammy dined comfortably at an inn decorated for Christmas with wreaths and candles and a crèche. A procession of children passed in the street singing *"Stille Nacht, Heilege Nacht"* in high, sweet voices.

Sammy asked for details of Paul's conversation with the *Kapitänleutnant* that morning. Paul obliged.

"When I pressed him about what would happen if he came on a passenger ship suspected of carrying munitions, he tried to leave the impression that neither he nor any other U-boat commander would open fire. He left room for doubt, though."

" 'Course he did, deceitful fucker." Sammy mopped up veal gravy with a chunk of black bread. "He'd torpedo a boatload of babies if some admiral ordered it — him an' all the rest of 'em in their fancy uniforms."

Paul believed there was reason for Sammy's pessimism. In this season of goodwill toward men, savage fighting that raged on the Western front threatened to spread seaward with the U-boat fleet. London repeatedly accused Berlin of scorning established rules of warfare, substituting a policy of *Schrecklichkeit* — terribleness.

Paul finished his glass of strong Christmas beer. "You may be right about that. I feel a duty to get back to the States and at least report what I see and hear. Millions of people are asleep over there."

"Fancy the Atlantic protects 'em, do they?" Sammy said.

"That's true. It's time America wakes up to what's really happening. Understands the threat. People have to be told the truth."

"It's noble of you to try, gov, but you can't do the whole job."

"I can make a start," Paul said.

78. Winter of Discontent

December settled early darkness on the mountains and the shore of California. Fritzi hated to see the sun set because it meant the hour of sleep was that much nearer, and sleep no longer brought her release, but instead frequent nightmares of loss, failure, pursuit, even death. In one dream that recurred she was Richard III, humpbacked and ugly, raging against fate. In another Loy rode away from her on a stallion with a flowing mane, always out of reach, and laughing.

She hated Christmas 1914 — found no joy in it, only burdens: shopping, wrapping, posting, giving, all empty and sad. Carols sounded discordant. Good wishes of the season voiced by friends and acquaintances sounded hypocritical, meaningless.

Of an evening she began to cook in Mrs. Hong's kitchen, for herself and sometimes Lily. She cooked simple fare that was hard to botch. Starchy, heavy dishes like spaghetti; if she was alone she would devour several plates of it, accompanied by beer. She brought home sacks of seeded rolls from a small bakery in Venice and ate two, three, four at a time. The eating was prompted in part by the comfort food provided, in part by a return of her lifelong conviction that she was scrawny, therefore undesirable.

She decided that too many bad memories lived under the bed in the room she rented. After talking it over with Lily and settling what she owed the Hongs, she leased a small house on a hilly side street off North Whitley, in Hollywood. California Mediterranean, it pleased the eye with its golden stucco and half-round red roof tiles. Or it would have pleased if there'd been room in her heart and mind for architectural niceties.

She moved in two days after New Year's. To commemorate the occasion and relieve the long, lonely silences of the night hours, she replaced her old talking machine with a new, fancier one, a Victor, with a painted flower-shaped horn that poured sad romantic music through the house.

On her first Sunday in her new home, her friends and coworkers surprised her with a housewarming, organized by Hobart and Polo. Those closest to her knew of Loy Hardin's abrupt departure, and the party was meant to cheer her up.

Eddie brought Rita, Jock Ferguson brought his Irma, B.B. brought Sophie. Al Kelly pleaded another obligation and sent a cheap vase of carnival glass. Charlie sent a telegram of good wishes.

Little Mary brought Fairbanks; their affair was an open secret in the picture community. The handsome actor's memory had undergone a marvelous rejuvenation. He bussed and hugged Fritzi as though they'd been chums since childhood.

Mr. Hong furnished the champagne, obtained at a cut price through a wholesaler he knew.

While Mrs. Hong beamed approvingly, Mr. Hong offered a toast to a happy house favored by the gods. No such luck there, Fritzi thought as she raised her glass. She had the solitude she craved, but no peace.

On Monday night, February 8, David Wark Griffith premiered *The Clansman* downtown at Clune's Auditorium. The picture had already been shown at surprise previews in remote locales such as Riverside, but Fritzi had heard little about it, except that a subtitle, *The Birth of a Nation*, had been added, and Negro groups had vainly attempted to block showings by going to court.

Tickets for the Los Angeles premiere cost two dollars. Despite the high price all twenty-five hundred seats sold out, and scalpers got as much as twenty dollars on the weekend before the showing. The gala event at "the Theater Beautiful" was somewhat disrupted by the presence of a dozen black people picketing under the Fifth Street marquee. Since the picture hadn't been shown locally, Fritzi assumed they were protesting on the assumption that it followed the racist story line of the Dixon novel. Placards identified the pickets as members of the National Association for the Advancement of Colored People, an organization less than ten years old.

Fritzi's escort for the evening was Hobart, who still managed to be a presence even though he was no taller than her shoulder. Edging toward seventy, Hobart refused to discuss age or birthdays. His heart trouble hadn't recurred, though

Fritzi from time to time cautioned him against overexertion.

Polo had friends in the tailoring trade, so Hobart's formal suit fit him well, minimizing to the extent possible his bow legs and his stomach, which of late resembled the front end of a Zeppelin. The old actor had long ago trimmed his shoulder-length Oscar Wilde hair, but time had removed it on the top of his head, and he insisted on covering his baldness with a ridiculous shiny chestnut wig that always seemed to sit a bit crookedly, one day listing to port, the next to starboard; in a brisk breeze it had a tendency to slip astern.

On the way into the theater, Fritzi nearly collided with Loretta Gash. The reporter's red satin cloak and turban shimmered under the electric lights. The look she gave Fritzi was hostile, the abruptness with which she turned away a calculated affront — if Fritzi had bothered to be offended.

A full symphony orchestra in the pit played the score for Griffith's film. From the first notes of the overture, a thrill of excitement swept the crowd. The tale of a Southern family before and after the Civil War enthralled the audience. Fritzi admired Mr. Griffith's ambition, and the genius displayed in composition and editing. The battle scenes, including the one whose filming she'd watched, were spectacular. Her heartbeat quickened when the Little Colonel, dapper Henry Walthall, charged the Union guns with a Confederate banner he spiked into the mouth of a cannon. After intermission, the Klan galloping to the rescue of the beleaguered family had undeniable power and excitement, intensified by the "Ride of the Valkyrie" thundering out of the pit. One of those hooded riders was Loy, she recalled sadly.

But stirred as Fritzi was by the technique of the film, she was at the same time repelled by the story. She remained a child of General Joe Crown, who had fought to make black people free and equal citizens, not buffoons of the kind Griffith depicted — ignoramuses in loud suits who gnawed chicken legs and tossed the bones on the floor of South Carolina's Reconstruction legislature. Griffith's Kentucky boyhood, his father's service as a Rebel officer, explained his sympathies, but she didn't see that it justified glamorizing night riders while turning blacks into satyrs and clowns. She was among the few who didn't stand during the final ovation. In the lobby she avoided the line of well-wishers waiting to congratulate the director.

Lily sauntered into the tent with a folded tabloid-size paper under her arm. The tent was white canvas, with a solid floor, set up behind the sun-bleached building that contained Liberty's regular, cramped dressing rooms. A small wooden sign hanging outside the tent said MISS CROWN.

"Say, Fritz, where the hell did this come from?"

Fritzi swung around on the stool in front of the makeup table. "The tent? It was here when I arrived this morning." Her studied shrug tried to minimize the significance, but Lily whistled any-way.

"A dressing tent of your own. You're coming up in the world."

She handed Fritzi the copy of *Screen Play*. "Go on, take a look. Page four."

One side of Lily's shirtwaist hung out, stained by something bright yellow, perhaps mustard. Index and middle fingers of her right hand were a darker yellow-brown. She lit a cigarette and leaned against the center pole while Fritzi turned pages. Lily had already missed two days of work this week. She was gaunt, with a gray pallor.

. . . Also seen at the premiere of Griffith's epic: Liberty's comedy star Fritzi Crown, on the arm of tragedian Hobart Manchester (NOT her usual escort, *Screen Play* can reveal for the first time). Miss C may be one of the new royalty of this town, but in private she's strictly declassé, playing "bunk-house" with a cowboy bit player with dirt under his nails and who-knows-what in his past. A lot of these Cactus Charlies who hang out at the Waterhole looking for day wages are reputed to be one step ahead of the law back home on the range. Careful, Fritzi!

"Oh, good God." She threw the paper down.

Lily exhaled cigarette smoke. "What'd you do to her?"

"Nothing. I saw her at a party in December. I wouldn't answer her cheap questions about Loy."

"He's gone."

"Obviously she doesn't know that."

Lily clucked and shook her head. "Lots of people read that bitch. Lots of them believe every word she writes."

"Oh, come on, trash like that can't hurt me."

Lily ground the wooden match under the toe of her red leather pump. "I sure hope not. Kelly's secretary said he saw it and didn't like it. Said it reflects badly on the studio. What a fucking hypocrite."

She got to meet Kelly face to face later that afternoon, in B.B.'s office.

"I called this meeting to discuss how we can speed up production of pictures starring this little gel," B.B. said. In front of him lay large sheets of pale green columnar paper inked with figures. Fritzi and Eddie sat in front of B.B's desk. Al Kelly hunched in a chair in the corner, regarding Fritzi with a bilious eye.

Eddie spoke first: "Do we want to do that? We might glut the market."

Kelly snorted. "We could finish a two-reel Nellie every third day and not glut the market. The exchanges are screaming for them."

"Even in England, where they got the war to think about," B.B. agreed. "Scandinavians and Dutchmen are standing in line. Froggies too. I'm heading over there in a few weeks to check the situation personally. Negotiate some better percentages. If they want Liberty product, they got to pay for it."

Fritzi said, "Is a trip like that a good idea with all those German submarines prowling? I read that they sank an American cargo ship, the *Wil-*

liam Frye, and it was just carrying wheat, not munitions."

"You're a sweet gel to worry, but we got an investment to protect, and I smell a rat in the woodpile. Some of those frogs and eyeties may be cooking the books and stealing us blind. Besides, there's a hundred ships crossing the Atlantic all the time, and only a few of those Hun subs. I got no worries. We're taking that fabulous Cunard boat, *Lusitania*."

The following Saturday, she worked a half day. In the afternoon Hobart and Polo arrived at the house with a noisy, lively present. A female dachshund puppy from a pet shop.

"You look so sad lately, dollink," the director said. "We thought a nice German weenie dog might make you feel better."

"You're sweet, both of you." Holding the wiggling puppy against her bosom, she kissed the men in turn. The wiener dog licked her chin.

After they watched the pup frolic for a while, Hobart said, "What will you christen her?"

That took only a moment's thought. "Schatze. It means treasure, or sweetheart." She picked up Schatze, who yipped and wriggled in the crook of her arm. Excited, the dog wet.

Fritzi held the pup at arm's length. "Girl, you need training. I know just the right paper to use. Hobart, be a dear and hand me that copy of *Screen Play* in the pantry."

Later, during the night Schatze barked and cried in the best style of a puppy thrust into a new, strange environment, namely the pantry where Fritzi had shut her up with a dish of ground-round steak rushed from the butcher shop at half past six. She'd also spread pages from Loretta Gash's publication over the pantry linoleum.

After an hour of listening to the poor dog's misery, Fritzi relented. Barefoot, she went to the pantry, opened the door.

"All right, Schatze, you win."

Excited again, the wiener dog leaped into the air and dampened the hem of Fritzi's cotton nightdress. She laughed, changed her gown, and sat with Schatze on her lap in the kitchen. Together they ate two bowls of warmed-up chili and twenty crackers. Fritzi, however, drank all the beer. At Lily's suggestion she'd checked her weight on a penny scale earlier in the week. Since Loy left she'd gained seven pounds. She'd never been able to eat and gain weight in times past. Was this another toll taken by age?

She went to bed with Schatze snuggled against her stomach as if she'd belonged there always. In a nightmare, she chased Loy across an endless dark void. As the pursuit grew more desperate, her failure more certain, terror gripped her — she'd never catch him. She woke shouting and thrashing, with the little wiener dog licking her sweaty face.

79. Air War

The new plane was fine, light and maneuverable. Nicknamed the Bébé, it was a smaller version of Nieuport's two-seat reconnaissance ship. Today was the second time he'd taken one up since three of them had been delivered to the N65 squadron operating in the skies over Nancy.

During his first months in the French flying corps, Carl had piloted a slow Farman, spending most of his hours aloft buzzing back and forth with field glasses, observing German entrenchments. Because he had a good deal of experience as a pilot, he was soon reassigned from the observation squadron to the N65, a true pursuit squadron devoted not to scouting but to chasing and downing enemy planes that menaced French-held territory. He'd left his friend Rene behind to shoot at German observation balloons, clumsy gas bags that could explode with deadly force. Pilots who ventured too near could be blown up along with the enemy balloonists.

Carl had rolled out of the French-style hangar of canvas and girders an hour ago. Though it was a warm day, he'd donned a fleece-lined coat bought in a Paris specialty shop that outfitted airmen. The flying corps had no uniforms. In the earliest days, his messmates told him, pilots wore nothing heavier than a driving duster, and consequently froze their asses in the slipstream at higher altitudes.

Tess's scarf was knotted around his throat and tucked safely inside the coat. The rest of his flight gear consisted of goggles and oil-stained motoring gauntlets. He wore no parachute. They were available, but far too bulky for a big man squeezed in a small cockpit.

New, hornlike streaks of white hair above Carl's ears testified to the strain of aerial duty. There were men in the squadron who had literally turned white in one night, usually after a harrowing air combat. Carl had been flying three and a half months and hadn't yet engaged an enemy plane, though he'd chased quite a few.

A casual observer would have said Carl looked rather seedy, but he fancied he looked rather romantic. That was an attitude common to aviators in this war. They felt they were stronger, smarter, braver than men fighting in the mud and filth of the trenches down below. Luckier too — they'd escaped the sordid horror of the ground war. Death was certainly no different in the air, but everything else was.

The Bébé clipped along at six thousand feet. The eighty-horsepower rotary motor droned smoothly. Three other pilots were aloft with Carl. German artillery below the horizon was hammering again, blanketing the land for miles with dust clouds in which shells burst like holiday sparklers. French artillery replied from positions behind him.

He bent to adjust the air and gas mix levers, and when he looked up again, he panicked. His three wing mates had vanished into a towering cloud. Suddenly, two thousand feet below, an

Aviatik two-seater with black wing crosses popped from under the same tall cloud, going the opposite way. An artillery spotter.

Quickly he planned his strategy: attack from underneath the Aviatik. A second German manning the rear-seat swivel gun made diving from above foolhardy.

A Fokker pursuit monoplane burst out of the cloud. The observer's escort. At once he changed his plan. Fokkers were deadly because their guns fired through the synchronized propeller. The race to develop a superior synchronizing mechanism was one of the great technical battles of the war. He must knock out the Fokker first.

At least he had more experience than many of the young Frenchmen sent to the front. Some had as little as five hours at flight school, and had never flown before that. Sending anyone out with training that meager was, in Carl's mind, tantamount to committing murder.

As he went higher, he turned. He thrust the nose over into a dive and felt a heavy vibration in the wings transferred to the fuselage. He streaked downward in spite of it, and in seconds he was on the Fokker, pressing the button to fire the big Lewis gun mounted above him on the upper wing.

His rounds missed. He dove past the Fokker, banked away underneath. The Fokker came after him.

Carl headed into the sun. The Fokker's fuselage-mounted machine guns chattered, and several rounds punched holes in the Bébé, a foot behind the cockpit. He yanked the stick back, and the plane climbed steeply in a *retournment*.

At the apex of the climb, he put the nose over and descended steeply again; again he felt the wings shaking horribly. But he'd gotten the Fokker off his tail.

Carl finished the evasive maneuver by flying in his original direction. He passed the German observation plane. The rear gunner tried to swivel to shoot but was too slow. When Carl was well in front of the Aviatik, the Fokker appeared behind it suddenly, dived beneath it, then zoomed up, closing fast on Carl's Nieuport.

He executed a *renversement*. He came out of it flying straight at the Fokker, his Lewis gun blazing. The Fokker returned fire. One round nicked Carl's propeller; a chip bloodied his face.

They were on a collision course, firing steadily. He could clearly see the enemy pilot's youthful face, blond hair, clenched teeth. Only Carl's hands and will controlled his plane; the rest of his body was running wild with fright. His bladder let go.

One of his incendiary rounds ignited the German's fuel tank. The explosion shook his plane, and the red fireball scorched his face as it rolled toward him, obliterating the sky. He dove like a madman, just clearing the lethal smoke and flame. The Nieuport vibrated hellishly. Small pieces of wing covering tore and blew off. Carl was hurtling nose first to a crash. He fought to bring the Nieuport out of the dive, thinking, *First and last kill in one day.*

A thousand feet above the earth, the plane responded. He flew with his eyes shut for a few seconds, feeling the wing vibration dampen and then disappear altogether. A glance overhead showed the Aviatik darting into clouds to hide.

His breeches dried before he landed, thank God. He turned the Nieuport 11 over to his flight mechanic and jogged toward an open staff car that would deliver him to the château where the squadron was billeted. Aviators rode and slept in style — dined that way too. In the evening mess, with a good whitefish and a fine bottle of Graves, Carl listened to his commanding officer, Major Despardieu:

"Fine work today. Your colleague Rossay was above you during the dogfight. He verified the kill."

The mess in the château's great hall was crowded and smoky. Of the sixteen pilots who flew regularly, twelve were present, playing the piano, laughing, tossing darts at postal cards tacked to a bulletin board. The cards, from a German company called Sanke, bore sepia photographs of German heroes of the air war, the most recognizable being Oswald Boelcke and Max Immelmann.

The major took the monocle out of his eye. "You do appreciate that the Bébé's wings tend to crumple and shear off if the machine is pushed too hard?"

"Yes, sir, I got that idea today. I didn't think about it long, I was pretty busy."

"Of course." Despardieu clinked his brandy snifter against Carl's. "Still, *mon ami,* you needn't worsen your chances."

No other words were needed; Carl understood perfectly. The men in the squadron talked a lot about the fact that the average life expectancy of a front-line aviator operating against the enemy was three weeks.

In an abstract way he was proud of his success today, but he felt none of the heady exhilaration familiar from his days of race driving and stunt flying. Maybe it was because the brief duel at six thousand feet had ended with another man's death. Probably a decent chap — some mother's boy just following orders.

He reached for the brandy decanter to calm a bad case of nerves. Next morning when he looked into his shaving mirror, the horn-like streaks of white hair were thicker.

80. Torpedoed

On the last night out, Captain Turner addressed hundreds of passengers in the grand lounge. Not all of them could crowd in; the ship affectionately nicknamed Lucy carried more than twelve hundred on this crossing.

William Turner was a veteran of the Cunard line, a solid, broadly built seaman who didn't mingle comfortably with his clientele. Which probably meant Bowler Bill was a damn fine sailor, B.B. decided. Bowler Bill's nickname came from his favorite off-duty hat.

Like all of the great ship's public rooms, the lounge was opulent. The period was late Georgian. Heavy furniture complemented rich tapestries on polished mahogany walls. The fine attire of the ladies and gentlemen was a perfect match for the surroundings.

Captain Turner took a wide-legged stance, hands behind his back. "Ladies and gentlemen. While I do not wish to alarm you unduly, it is my duty and responsibility as master of this vessel to inform you that we today received an Admiralty signal advising us of submarine activity in the area of Fastnet Rock."

The dire announcement brought a gasp from Sophie. She clutched the diamond choker glittering at her throat. B.B. nearly fell off the sofa arm where he sat holding her other hand. Others in the crowd reacted with degrees of concern ranging from mild to panicky.

"In response we have adjusted our speed downward and altered course so as to clear Fastnet by a margin of more than twenty miles. Further, in the morning you will see an armed Royal Navy cruiser alongside, our escort to Liverpool.

"Meanwhile, you will have noticed that we took certain precautionary measures immediately we had the message. All lifeboats were swung out on their davits, canvas covers removed and provisions checked. Stewards have already blacked out portholes of your cabins. We ask your indulgence in showing no unnecessary lights, particularly on the open decks.

"It is also my unpleasant task to recall that we conducted a lifeboat drill shortly after we left port, as required by maritime law. Although the drill is mandatory for all passengers, my officers who checked off names reported to me that half of our guests did not bother to attend. While I anticipate no need for emergency use of lifeboats, I urge you most strongly to find your station if you did not participate in the drill." B.B. had gone, but Sophie hadn't, preferring to sleep late.

A man raised his hand. "Captain? We hear Lucy was refitted with defensive cannon and ammunition lockers, down on F Deck where once there were cabins. Now you can't get down to F Deck because of steel doors." B.B. had picked up the same rumor: a dozen six-inch guns mounted on gun rings and concealed behind removable armor plate on both port and starboard sides. He hadn't told Sophie.

The captain looked as though he'd like to barbecue the questioner. "I cannot comment on that, sir. I must return to the bridge now. If you have other questions, kindly consult one of the officers. Thank you for your attention and cooperation. Please resume and enjoy your activities for the evening."

A few guests remembered themselves and applauded. Bowler Bill was already gone. B.B.'s dinner sat badly in his gut. He wasn't worried for himself, only Sophie, who looked pickle-faced with fear.

"Benny, are we in danger?"

"Definitely not. Hun subs are after merchant ships carrying ammunition and such stuff. Nobody attacks a floating hotel like this." His sweeping affirmative gesture nearly knocked aigrette plumes off the head of a passing grand dame.

"Suppose something did happen. Would we get off?"

"No question. I personally did an inspection hike around Boat Deck before dinner." Sophie worried a lot, so he'd memorized particulars. "This ship carries twenty-two regular wooden lifeboats and twenty-six collapsibles. Plenty for the passengers we got on board. Now, stop fretting. Want to go dancing or play cards?"

Sophie wanted to do neither. B.B. helped her to their royal suite, the ship's finest accommodation. It consisted of a drawing room, dining room, and two bedrooms; the unused one stored their twelve pieces of luggage. With Sophie settled in bed he returned to Promenade Deck, staring at the star-flecked sky over the Atlantic and enjoying the balmy May air.

B.B. said, "Say, Alf, what's that funny white line in the water?"

Alf Vanderbilt, the richest man on board, was one of B.B's new pals from first class. Vanderbilt peered at the bubbly streak lengthening under the surface as it sped toward the hull. The two gentlemen were taking the air on the starboard side of Promenade Deck. Sophie was resting.

It was a few minutes past two in the afternoon of May 7, Friday. The air was clear and warm. Stewards had opened portholes in the white and gold Louis XVI dining saloon, where B.B. and Vanderbilt had lunched on the balcony, exchanging anecdotes and arranging to meet for tea at the Ritz Hotel when they reached London.

An air of relief and anticipation had infused the ship during the morning. Although there was no sign of the promised cruiser, the Irish coast had been visible to starboard for some hours. B.B. fancied he could see a smudge representing the Old Head of Kinsale, a famous promontory. He did wonder why the captain wasn't taking evasive action, a zigzag course, in submarine waters. He supposed Bowler Bill knew what he was doing.

Vanderbilt craned over the rail as the white streak neared the ship just forward of midships. "That is very odd, Benny. My God, you don't suppose it's — ?"

The explosion shook the ship from bow to

stern. B.B. fell against the rail. Righting himself, he lunged past Vanderbilt to the nearest door. Alarms began to ring. People ran wildly and shouted questions. Someone at the rail pointed. "It's a huge hole. Water's pouring in."

The vessel listed to starboard. Deck chairs slid. A second, stronger explosion rocked the ship as B.B. lurched into the elevator lobby. All the electric power went off. An elevator pointer stopped between floors. People trapped in the cage started screaming.

Air ventilators in the wall suddenly gushed smoke. B.B. ran to the stairs. Alarms kept ringing, the seven short and one long that signaled disaster at sea. Another lurch to starboard hurled him against the wall of the stairwell. He gripped the hand rail and stumbled downward, then ran like a madman along the corridor because of a horrible certainty. *Lusitania* was already sinking.

A man from a neighboring cabin pulled his swooning wife into the corridor. The man was young, blond, British; B.B. had played whist with him. The tilt of the ship threw him against B.B., and he hit B.B. with his fist. "Out of the way, you fat kike." He dragged his wife on toward the stairs.

B.B. twisted the handle of the cabin door. Stuck. He kicked the door open with strength he didn't know he possessed. He bolted into the room as the liner listed more. The motion threw him face first onto the carpet. Sophie shrieked, then helped him up as drawers fell out of the sideboard. Glassware and a decorative vase toppled and broke.

"Sophie, we got to get to the boats."

"I'm ready." She'd dressed for shore, in a dark brown dolman wrap with mink collar bought especially for the trip. Her eyes were huge and dark under her black velvet hat with long willow plumes.

"Leave the hat, it'll only get in the way."

"Benny, I paid twenty dollars for —"

"Leave the hat." He didn't mean to yell, or grab her wrist so roughly, but his heart was pounding. Screams were multiplying in the corridors, the ship listed more steeply every few seconds. He flew into the corridor, pulling her with him. "Stay behind me."

He ignored a sharp pain in his chest and bowled toward the stairwell like a football lineman. He was overweight, out of shape, but he was determined. If they reached the boat deck they'd escape. Boat Deck, Station Two, port side, that was his goal.

Smoke and soot from ventilators blinded them on the stairs. Passengers shrieked and fought each other, but the strength of desperation kept B.B. moving forward. He gripped Sophie's hand as she stumbled upward a step at a time. With a feeling of elation he burst through the doors to Boat Deck.

Chaos! The port lifeboats, many of them half full, couldn't be lowered because the list to starboard swung them inward, over the rail. People scrambled into the collapsible boats anyway, though frantic deck officers shouted that the boats couldn't be raised and launched until the regular boats were in the water. All around him B.B. heard terror:

"Not enough life jackets."
"Where are they?"
"They're supposed to be stored here."
"The bow's going down!"

The slanting deck hurled everyone forward, tumbling them among loose deck chairs. A lifeboat cable snapped at the pulley. Lifeboat Two dropped, crushing the passengers in the collapsible boat beneath. B.B. saw blood, arms and legs broken like match wood. Violently, he pushed Sophie back to the doors. "We can't get off this side."

Soot-covered chefs and stewards and stokers milled in the elevator lobby while more came pouring up the stairs, as terrified as any passenger and just as frantic to escape. B.B. fought his way through to the starboard deck, saw a half-filled lifeboat to the left, dragged Sophie toward it. He forced her to climb the ship's rail. With a hand on her wide seat he boosted her into the boat. A few courageous officers struggled to free collapsibles from their deck chocks and raise their canvas sides. Smoke and soot kept spewing from the ventilators.

Lusitania listed again. The lifeboat swung outward from the ship as B.B. climbed up onto the rail. He teetered like a high-wire artist, windmilling his arms to keep his balance. Sophie stood against the lifeboat gunwale while other passengers screamed for her to sit down and the deck officer shouted, "Number two boat, lower away, lower away, goddamn it."

"Benny, jump," Sophie cried. B.B. jumped.

For a moment he seemed to float like an aerialist above the sunlit sea. Then he fell into the boat, nearly knocked out when his forehead struck one of the thwarts. Sophie caught him by the belt and dragged his legs in.

B.B.'s vision cleared. He saw Alf Vanderbilt still on the deck, smoking a cigar and watching the spectacle with unnatural calm. Perhaps six feet separated the lifeboat from the ship. B.B. waved his arms. "Alf, come on."

"Too far, Benny."

"Get a life belt."

"Aren't any."

"Then jump."

With a sad shrug Vanderbilt replied, "No use. Can't swim."

The ship took another huge lurch forward, burying its prow in the waves. The lifeboat tilted seaward at a sharp angle. Those not hanging on tumbled out at the bow. B.B. grasped a thwart with one hand and reached for Sophie with the other, but she flew past him and dropped from sight.

"Sophie!"

He tried to reach the bow through a tangle of arms, legs, pummeling fists, wild eyes, shrieking mouths. The lifeboat tilted again and a pulley gave way. B.B. cried, "Oh-oh," just as he fell out of the boat and dropped through space into the glinting green water.

Dazed, choking, he kicked and flailed to stay

afloat. Like an enormous steel fish, *Lusitania* was slowly diving bow first into the sea. Her stern rose high in the sunlight. Her hull stood nearly vertical. Passengers and crew continued to fall or jump, landing in the midst of furniture and wreckage.

An old man clinging to a sofa floated by. A little farther on, a ship's officer and a female passenger rested on top of a grand piano that had somehow escaped from the public rooms. In the wake of the vessel a whole fan of debris, chairs, tables, lamps, oars, smashed planks from lifeboats, bobbing heads, spread out in the sunshine. B.B. recognized a man wearing a *Lusitania* life belt, an opinionated pro-German from Pittsburgh.

"Hey, Rupert. Some hero you got, the kaiser. A murderer." Rupert drifted on, his eyes glassy.

The water was hellishly cold for spring. B.B. felt faint. He bit his lips till he tasted blood. He had to stay awake, find Sophie. Never a strong swimmer, he somehow found strength, dog-paddled and kicked while he shouted repeatedly, "Sophie? Sophie?"

He saw her, holding her head out of the water by grasping a dining table. The sunny sea resounded with a continuous grind and roar as the ship sank. She was already half submerged with her prow sunk in the sea bottom. Her aft section billowed black smoke. Unbelievably, some passengers still peered from cabin portholes. Others jumped, striking the water with an impact that surely broke their bones if it didn't kill them outright. B.B. saw Captain

Turner clinging to a life ring.

"Sophie, hang on, I'm coming." He nearly choked as a heavy wave threw nauseating salt water into his mouth. He spewed it out and swam hard, his soaked clothes dragging on him and slowing him. He was within ten yards of Sophie when she raised one hand to wave at him.

"Benny, hurry, I got awful cramps."

"Don't let go," he screamed, his throat raw. She kept her hand in the air, waving. B.B.'s strength was failing; he wasn't a young man. Somehow Sophie didn't understand that she needed to hold onto the table with both hands. Her gray hair hung over her eyes. Her twisted face bespoke agony.

"Oh, Benny, it hurts." She thrust both hands under water, to her middle. A wave washed over her. Gasping, she hunted for the table, but it floated out of reach. She fell back and sank while he was still six yards away.

"Sophie!"

With a final great roar and rush of water, *Lusitania*'s stern disappeared under the waves, leaving a foaming whirlpool and a sea of drowning passengers and crew. The ship sank eighteen minutes after the torpedo struck. Sophie Pelzer disappeared with her.

81. Marching

A flotilla of fishing boats and tugs from Queenstown rescued 761 people from the Irish Sea. Of 1,198 aboard *Lusitania* who died, 124 were American citizens, many of them notables: the theatrical producer Charles Frohman, Alfred Vanderbilt, and Mr. and Mrs. Elbert Hubbard.

Germany celebrated it as a great victory; the kaiser declared a national holiday. A wave of outrage swept the United States. *The Nation* condemned "a deed for which even a Hun must blush." Editorials called the embassy's warning advertisement "the death notice." Germany was guilty of "wanton murder," "a slap in the face of humanity," "the worst crime of a government since crucifixion of Christ." Some editorialists wanted an immediate declaration of war.

German-Americans nervously avoided public scrutiny. In some cities, bakeries, taverns, and sausage shops owned by first- and second-generation Germans had their windows smashed and defamatory slogans painted on their doors. At *Brauerei Crown* an unknown vandal set a small fire at night, destroying one delivery wagon and damaging a truck before the local fire brigade arrived.

Liberty rushed *Racetrack Nell* to the exchanges, but Fritzi was much too concerned for B.B. to worry about its fate. She wept for an hour when she heard the news of Sophie Pelzer's death.

Professional nurses hired by the studio brought B.B. home from England. He was too devastated to travel by himself. Doctors placed him in Haven Hill, a private hospital located on ten acres surrounded by the orange groves of Riverside. On the first Sunday after his arrival, Fritzi and Hobart drove out there with Schatze.

The dirt roads were washboards. As Fritzi steered around a gaping chuck hole, Hobart said, "Seems a rather long way from town. Surely there are other hospitals closer."

"Kelly chose the place. He said the important thing was the best care."

"Perhaps he was more interested in its distance from the studio," Hobart said dryly.

At the sanitarium Fritzi tied Schatze's leash to the gear lever. After a couple of plaintive yips the wiener dog settled down, and Fritzi and Hobart went into the main building. An attendant took them out a rear door, where they found B.B. sitting alone on a bench beneath a palm tree, blankly staring at four patients in bathrobes playing croquet. A hose sprinkler shot a fountain of water onto another section of the dry lawn. The croquet balls clicked in the silence.

B.B.'s curly gray hair had turned white. A light woolen blanket covered his legs. The front of his gown bore coffee spots and food stains. Fritzi was distraught to see him so listless and slovenly. "Hello, B.B.," she said gently. "How are you?"

"All right, how are you?" He noticed Hobart standing in the shade, nervously twisting his black beret. "And you," he added in a vacant way.

Fritzi took B.B.'s hand and pressed it between her palms, as he used to do. He didn't react. "Are you comfortable here?"

B.B. shrugged. "It's all right."

"We're all so terribly sorry about Sophie. She was a fine lady."

"Sophie." His eye drifted past the tan stucco buildings to the low hills covered with rows of orange trees. He pressed the fingers of his right hand to his brow, his classic worry pose. "Poor Sophie."

The conversation limped and lurched for another ten minutes. When Fritzi could stand no more she said, "Hobart, we must go." She patted B.B., kissed his pale, freckled forehead. "We'll come see you again."

His eye followed a croquet ball through a wicket. He said nothing. Fritzi fought tears as she took the old actor's hand and hurried them away.

Before they left Haven Hill, they met with the director, Dr. A. B. Gerstmeyer, an alienist. He was a small man with odd eyes. The irises were streaked with variegated color — green, dark blue, gray. One eye tended to wander distractingly every minute or so.

Gerstmeyer's office was cool and dark. Diplomas from Heidelberg and Harvard hung behind his desk. Venetian blinds painted slat patterns on the white wall.

"I am terribly concerned about Mr. Pelzer," Fritzi said to him. "I'm not sure he knows us."

"To the contrary, he recognizes all his visitors.

Mr. Kelly called on him yesterday, and afterward Mr. Pelzer identified him by name. It isn't a lack of memory or recognition. The patient is intensely focused somewhere else. He is a captive of those few moments in which his wife drowned. He goes over and over them, seeking ways in which he might have saved her. He can't leave the scene of the tragedy, at least not yet."

"He and Mrs. Pelzer never had children," Fritzi said. "Are there other relatives who might help him pull out of this?"

"I asked the same question. There are only two distant cousins whom he never sees. You must understand, Miss Crown, this kind of grief is common when one partner in a strong marriage passes away. Mr. Pelzer's sense of personal guilt only increases his need to inflict punishment on himself."

"By shutting out the world?"

"And reducing his life to nothing as penance."

"Will he recover? He's a brilliant man. Kind, decent — we all love and respect him. What's more, the studio needs him." She thought of Al Kelly, unusually solicitous of late. Why not? B.B.'s hospitalization made him sole operating head of Liberty. He could enforce every edict without fear of a veto, pinch every penny until it howled.

"Recovery is entirely possible, provided the call of Mr. Pelzer's work becomes sufficiently strong."

"Can you say how long it might be until that happens?" Hobart asked.

"No, sir. He might sit for a month or a year. Or

forever, if he is hurt badly enough. I can do nothing until and unless he wills it. No one can."

Despondent, Fritzi said, "Thank you, Doctor. May I leave my telephone number? Please call if there's an emergency, or any change at all. B.B. is very dear to me."

"He returns the feeling," Gerstmeyer said as she wrote the number on a pad. She reacted with surprise. "Oh, yes, he's mentioned you many times. I assure you, it isn't loss of memory immobilizing the patient. It's the world in which Mrs. Pelzer perished and he failed to save her. He wants no part of that world anymore."

Next morning Hobart began filming *Upper Crust,* a drama in which he played the well-heeled father of a society girl. The actress engaged for the role of his daughter was a short, dark-haired ingenue named Gloria Swanson. She was so outrageously good-looking, Fritzi was plunged back into a familiar funk of inadequacy. She recovered when Hobart invited her to lunch with Miss Swanson and she discovered that little Gloria was a humorless person fixated on her own appearance and career. She tried to compliment Fritzi, but it was plain she thought comedy contemptible, or at least far beneath a serious actress like herself.

Afterward, Hobart drew Fritzi aside. "You still feel strongly about the *Lusitania* matter, do you not?"

"Strongly doesn't begin to cover it." Sophie Pelzer's cruel death had driven her from a remote interest in the war to a passionate conviction that Germany must be defeated, very likely with U.S. intervention. She might be alienated from her father forever if she took that stand, but principle had to prevail. The General had run his life that way, and he had taught his daughter well.

"The local Preparedness League has organized a parade and rally downtown on Saturday afternoon," Hobart said. "I intend to march. Will you come along?"

"I certainly will if Eddie can release me."

"Splendid girl." Hobart swept her into his arms for a hug.

Three hundred marchers gathered in front of Morosco's Globe Theater on South Broadway. It was a mixed crowd of suffragettes, academics, scruffy bohemians, Socialists, students, and little old ladies from temperance societies. Hobart handed her a placard on a stick.

ARM NOW!

The HUN
Must Be
STOPPED!

Fritzi hoisted the placard and swung into line beside Hobart as a five-piece marching band led off, blaring "The Battle Cry of Freedom." She waved her placard in rhythm with the music.

Because the afternoon was cool and gray with a promise of rain, she'd put on a rather plain skirt and jacket of Scotch tweed, a white linen shirtwaist, and white ascot-style tie. She'd chosen her hat carefully: a large black silk sailor whose wide brim drooped all around, partially concealing her face. Though she wanted to march, she wasn't overly keen on attracting attention personally, and she thought the hat would help. She was naively wrong. The parade hadn't gone a block when a ragamuffin on the sidewalk pointed at her. "Look, it's Nellie from the pitchers." Soon a small crowd was following her.

Hobart saw her concern. "Nothing to be done, dear girl, you're famous. I should imagine they'll want you to say a few words at the square."

"Oh, I can't possibly —"

"Of course you can."

"I'm not prepared."

"Yes, you are. You're intelligent, you have strong feelings about recent events — if you have doubts, think of Pelzer." A shiver chased up Fritzi's spine. Without realizing it, she was on a path that had taken a sharp turn.

They paraded up Broadway to Second, west to Hill Street and south again toward the public square at Sixth. The band played "Onward, Christian Soldiers." Just below Fourth a crowd of rowdies outside a saloon called Wittke's Old Bavaria began to hoot and throw rocks and mud from the gutter. A white-haired professor two ranks ahead staggered when a rock grazed his forehead. A splat of mud soiled Fritzi's hat. More rowdies tumbled out of the saloon. One lobbed a bung starter at the marchers; the bass drummer knocked the flying stick away.

A man yelled at Fritzi, "Hey, you red slut, stick to your pictures."

He threw a piece of red brick. Hobart cried, " 'Ware!" jostling her aside. On the curb a man seized the brick thrower and punched him. The brick thrower knocked his assailant's hat off. Disgusted, Fritzi marched on as the opponents scuffled.

At the public square the marchers crowded together under the eyes of a few bemused bums and wine-heads. The president of the Preparedness League did indeed ask her to step up on the soapbox platform to say a few words. "Please," he said, holding her hand as she picked up her hem, "take off your hat so they can see you."

The sight of Fritzi's long face and frizzy blond locks touched off applause. She waved her muddy hat for silence.

"All right, you know who I am." The crowd laughed and she smiled. "But in marching with you today I'm just another American citizen. I'm here because I lost a dear friend on *Lusitania*. To attack a civilian ship was a crime, the act of a heartless government. I don't want to involve American boys in a foreign war, but we can't stand by and allow the Hun to destroy freedom and trample on everything that's right." The words came swiftly, up from the depths of her emotions.

"My heritage is German" — someone booed, someone else hissed — "but I have no sympathy for a country that callously takes the lives of innocents. By the last count, ninety-four children perished when *Lusitania* sank. Ninety-four babes and adolescents with no sense of the evil of which grown men are capable. Their lives were full of hope for a happy existence in the care of loving parents. What was their portion? Try to imagine it. Sheer terror as they were dropped into a cold and churning ocean with no warning, no sense of how to save themselves."

All her training, the many auditions and tank town performances, seemed to find a focus in this moment. Her voice built steadily. Under gray clouds with wind tossing her blond hair, she spoke with passion.

"Imagine them in that bitter sea, their minds on fire with fright as they sink once, then struggle, only to sink again. Their lungs burn. Vainly they search for their parents, but they see only strangers who are drowning as they are." The crowd listened in rapt silence.

"Ladies and gentlemen, we must stand fast against those who would consign children to that kind of hell. We must compel such men to end their slaughter and sue for peace. We must throw our moral strength behind the Allies, but the gesture will be meaningless if we do not at the same time demonstrate our strength. Not long ago I was too busy to pay attention to this war. Then, as events forced awareness on me, I decided we should take no part, spend no money, risk no American lives. I have changed my mind. I believe we must have funds for our military. We must have training for our men. We must recruit thousands to swell the ranks and prepare to show the Hun we are ready to intervene if those who kill children without mercy refuse to kneel at the altar of humanity and confess their crimes. If they will not come to that altar willingly, we must force them. And there is only one way we can accomplish that. We must prepare."

She flung her hand over her head, fingers spread like an exhorting preacher.

"Prepare. Arm ourselves. How many more innocents must die while we hesitate and argue? Sound the cry."

She clenched her hand into a fist.

"Preparedness. Preparedness *now*."

Shaken, she closed her eyes. What she said next — "Thank you" — was barely audible.

Flushed, she jumped off the soapbox. She hardly remembered half of what she'd improvised; it had all come in a rush. But it had stirred them. They whistled and cheered. Hobart hugged her:

"Marvelous, dear girl, simply marvelous. All those great ladies whom you worship would be at your feet if they heard it. You never gave a better performance."

"I meant every word."

"Of course you did," he said as the crowd broke up and they slipped away. "I do wonder how Kelly will take it. Being Irish, he would never help Britain."

"Perhaps he won't know I spoke. He took Bernadette to Yosemite."

"If someone else had made the speech, it's possible he would never hear of it. But you are Fritzi Crown. It might be wise to remember a word you used. Preparedness. Be ready for him."

82. Troubled Nation

Paul's ship, *Caronia*, crossed without incident, though with marked strain on her passengers because of *Lusitania*. He checked into the Hotel Astor on Times Square and telephoned his American publisher, the Century Company, arranging to meet his editor at the offices on Union Square the next day. While he was out shopping for a new shirt, a call from his lecture agent invited him to dinner.

Actually, the caller was his agent's widow. Bill Schwimmer, the energetic founder of American Platform Artists, had collapsed and died of heat prostration in the summer of 1914. Marguerite Schwimmer was a pale Nordic woman of German extraction, striving to be tougher than any male competitor. She slapped Paul on the back when she met him at Lüchow's. She wore black trousers and a boxy double-breasted black jacket with cravat. He had never seen Marguerite in anything frilly or pastel.

They drank beer under one of Lüchow's indoor trellises lit by colored lanterns. "How are you, kid?" Marguerite said. It amused him, since she was his age. She swore enthusiastically and smoked cigarettes constantly, to the dismay of head waiters and others in public. "Any second thoughts on the title of the lecture?" She'd cabled the same question to England. "The auditorium manager in Minneapolis wired yesterday.

He thinks 'Atrocities of War' is a terrible title, it will keep people away. Sure you won't change?"

Paul relit his stubby cigar. "I'm sure."

"Well, you may be in for rough sledding. The farther west you go, the more they like Germans."

"Then I should be a hit since I'm German."

"So am I, but I keep it quiet. I'd call myself Marguerite Smith if I hadn't printed so god-damn many letterheads and calling cards."

"Look, Marguerite, the truth's the truth. The kaiser and his gang are a bunch of maniacal militarists, and they're conducting this war like butchers. I can't understand why the German people follow them so devotedly, but they do. The whole lot of them have to be called to account."

"Dutch, I'm warning you, that kind of sentiment isn't popular or unanimous over here. Don't be fooled by the Eastern papers. There's still a big split in this country. Hell, some people are saying our State Department's to blame for *Lusitania* because they didn't warn people to stay off Cunard and White Star!"

"Therefore I'm supposed to tone down the lecture?"

"I've booked a fine tour, Dutch. First-class venues. If you want to revolt and alienate your audiences, it's up to you." She flashed a sour smile. "Of course, I have an interest. I'd like to keep APA in the black."

Paul slid his hand into the pocket of his un-pressed jacket, touched a medal Michael had given him in London. He damn well ought to show Marguerite Germany's cruel commemoration of the *Lusitania* disaster. On second thought it would just prolong an argument. The medal celebrated the "victory" with jingoistic slogans and grisly images of a grim reaper and a sinking ship.

"Let's talk about something nicer," she said. She licked her rouged lips with the tip of her tongue. "Would you like company at your hotel? I'm paying for this meal, but that's hardly a proper welcome for the weary traveler."

A schoolboy blush rose in Paul's face. "Marguerite, you flatter me. But I'm still married."

"God, you never change. I hate men with principles. So fucking superior." A passing waiter blanched and nearly dropped his tray.

In a tight two-inch Arrow collar with points, tight detachable cuffs, and a tight suit, Paul stood in the tight white circle of the carbon arc. His podium was set by the proscenium, stage right of the screen. Marguerite had booked him into the famous old Academy of Music on Fourteenth Street.

Only a few pale, oval faces were visible to him in the front rows and boxes. He spoke into darkness while images of the trenches flickered across the screen in tones of gray.

"I must warn you about the concluding footage. I filmed it in Belgium last summer. To prevent discovery by the Germans I hid in a hayloft with my camera."

The field appeared, the half dozen hostages and their executioners.

"If the pictures are too harrowing, please turn

away. I assure you this is real. This is the face of the enemy who threatens democracy wherever it exists."

As the first bayonet stabbed into the first victim, Paul heard gasps. Someone in the gallery cried, "No." A man in the third row dragged his wife to the aisle and left. Others stood in the orchestra, gathering their wraps.

And this was pro-British New York.

The scene ended. The projection lamp darkened. Paul was left alone in the arc light. Unnerved by the exodus, he started his brief closing remarks, an exhortation to the audience to look clearly at the question of U.S. intervention. He declared an urgent need for it, but he stumbled over the words from his note cards and finished weakly. The curtain came down to feeble applause.

In the wings the stage manager congratulated him in a halfhearted way and disappeared. Paul went to the dingy dressing room. Marguerite was supposed to be waiting. There was no sign of her; the doorkeeper said he hadn't seen her. After twenty minutes Paul trudged across Fourteenth Street to Lüchow's. The restaurant's noise and good cheer depressed him. He left his meal unfinished and walked back to the Astor in a drizzle that turned the pavement into a reflecting mirror splashed with bright colors. He was weighted by an inescapable feeling that he'd failed.

The next day, only a few reviews of his presentation appeared. The *Sun*'s commentary was typical:

Seldom has an hour and a half contained so much that is grim and unhappy, if not utterly repellent. Scenes of the German army at its daily duties, while authentic and picturesque, resemble almost any army anywhere, and add little to our understanding of the European conflict.

The final effect of the presentation is a pervading sense of ugliness. The concluding sequence showing the murder of six Belgians cannot be described in a newspaper which goes into the home.

Cinematographer Crown, unquestionably talented, courageous, and sincere in his purpose, has misjudged his American audience. "Atrocities of War" may fairly represent the reality of the current struggle, but it is not popular entertainment, and should not be presented as such in a country which is not involved as a belligerent.

At the box office on Saturday, over forty patrons showed up with tickets and insisted on refunds.

Paul started west by a southern route. Between lectures in Baltimore and Richmond he called at the White House with an extra print of the bayonet execution. He asked to see the president, thinking his credentials as a successful author would get him in. A staff man turned him away; the president had no room on his appointment calendar anytime soon.

Charleston, Atlanta, New Orleans, the dusty

cities of Texas — managers of the halls greeted him with little enthusiasm. Every night people walked out. Others groaned or booed. German-American societies sent demonstrators who heckled and tried to debate him as he spoke. In San Antonio someone threw a sack of rotten vegetables from the gallery. It fell short and two orchestra patrons threatened a lawsuit. In Houston someone stole every projector lamp, and the evening was delayed an hour and a half; by then he had twenty people in the audience.

Cities along his northerly return route, including Minneapolis and Des Moines, telegraphed cancellations, which Marguerite forwarded without comment. Paul grew testy and drank more beer than was good for him. He decided the problem wasn't so much that his listeners thought the Germans were saintly; it was the way he stubbornly hewed to what Wexford Rooney had taught him years ago in Wex's photography salon in Chicago. Wex said pictures must tell the truth unsparingly. Michael was right, in these divisive times there was such a thing as too much truth. He heard street-corner musicians playing a new hit song of the hour — "I Didn't Raise My Boy to Be a Soldier."

When Paul's train arrived in Los Angeles, he was met by a stout bowlegged Englishman, well up in years but wearing an atrociously youthful chestnut-colored wig. Paul knew about Fritzi's friend Hobart Manchester; he had spoken to his cousin over a rattling long-distance wire from Arizona.

"Fritzi is terribly sorry she couldn't come in person, dear boy," Hobart said as they walked to the baggage car for the film boxes. "They're shooting her circus picture on a merciless schedule. Success has its penalties as well as its rewards."

Paul asked a porter to arrange to send the film boxes directly to Clune's Auditorium. Hobart cleared his throat and looked uncomfortable. "If I may make a suggestion, why not send them to your hotel?" Before Paul could interject a question, he continued, "I am sorry to be the bearer of bad news, Paul. Your program has been canceled."

He felt like he'd taken a body blow. "I want to talk to the damn theater manager."

"We can certainly go there if you wish," Hobart said, nodding. "I have my automobile parked close by."

Rumpled and fatigued, Paul felt a consuming anger. Under the marquee of Clune's downtown, he took his cap off and scratched his head, noticeably gray now except on top. A bill poster was mixing water in his bucket.

One Night Only!

"ATROCITIES OF WAR"

Illustrated Lecture by
PAUL CROWN
News Camera-Man &
Author "I Witness History"

The bill poster's long brush slathered paste over the type in a way that was almost insulting. Up in the manager's office, Paul confronted a nervous secretary, and an inner door tightly closed.

"Mr. Semmel isn't in there, he's out."

Paul wanted to pick up a chair and smash the door down. He rubbed away ash on his vest and barked at the young woman instead. "Sure. Give him my regards."

She handed him a folded yellow sheet. "This came for you."

Another wire from Marguerite. It informed him that Chicago and Milwaukee had canceled in the wake of plunging ticket sales and complaints from managers where he'd already appeared. Marguerite ended her message by invoking the clause in the original agreement he'd signed with APA which said that either party could cancel at any time. The bureau no longer represented him. Marguerite would expect a commission on any remaining engagements he fulfilled, but he would fulfill them without her help.

He stormed down the stairs. *That's what comes of turning down an eager woman.* The cheap and bitter joke didn't lift his spirits one iota.

Fritzi rushed home from Liberty after working all day on *Big Top Nell* ("Until now I've never played a scene with a hundred-and-ten-pound chimpanzee in a clown suit, and I don't intend to repeat the experience, thank you very much").

"What will you do after the tour?" she asked at supper in her little Mediterranean house, which

Paul found charming. He, Fritzi, and Hobart sat on a small terrace, cool now that the sun was hiding behind the hills. Hobart refilled their wine glasses with an excellent Sonoma County red. It was half past eight, a fine summer evening.

After reflecting a moment, he said, "Why, I'll go home to Julie and the kids, then go back to the war zone, shoot more film, and try to find someone to buy it. That's all I know how to do."

"I'm sorry you've had hostile crowds," Fritzi said.

"They just don't understand. I'm hanged if I know why."

Hobart puffed his cigarette and watched a flight of birds in the amber sky. "The war still isn't real to most Americans. The furor over *Lusitania* seems to be dying down. The war is enriching America. Your countrymen want to profit from it, without any painful involvement."

After dark, in the small, cozy living room warmed by exposed wooden beams and bright Navaho rugs, Paul set up Fritzi's projector and ran his film. When the six Belgian men and women died in the field, Fritzi wept; Hobart cursed.

Paul switched off the machine, switched on the electric lights. Fritzi wiped her reddened eyes, sniffed, and tucked the hanky in her pocket.

"There's one person who must see the pictures, Pauli. Papa."

"Chicago's canceled. I'm not stopping there."

"Please reconsider. For me."

"You want me to set up a projector and force him to look at pictures that damn his beloved fatherland? You've already told me how he feels about the war."

"Yes, but you might change his mind. You can tell him you were reluctant but I insisted. I'll take all the blame. He can't despise me more than he does already."

Paul didn't reply. He sat low in a deep leather chair with his feet stuck out and his untied shoelaces dangling. The second button of his vest was fastened in the first buttonhole. His tie was loosened, his hair messy. He was very reluctant to compound the General's anger at Fritzi. Hobart sat sleepy-eyed, watching the interplay between the cousins.

"Are you just asking me because I took the pictures and I'm handy?"

"Oh, no, far from it. Papa doesn't respect me any longer, but he respects you. And you're family." She folded her hands in her lap. "So it's your duty. Papa's gone down the wrong road, Mama says so in every letter. You have to do it, Pauli — unless you no longer have a conscience or any kind of moral compass, which I know isn't true."

He winced at Hobart. "How do you like that? She lays a skillful trap, doesn't she?"

"There are expert instructors within our profession," Hobart murmured.

"Pauli, don't joke. This is a serious matter," Fritzi said.

"God, I know. Give me some more of that wine while I think about it. I could wind up with the General despising both of us forever."

83. Kelly Gives Orders

Fritzi took her head out of Roger's mouth. It was a monumental relief; Roger had terrible breath, possibly from all the steaks, chops, and ribs fed to him so he wouldn't be tempted to snack on the actors. Unlike Buster, the one-hundred-and-ten-pound chimpanzee, however, Roger was not inclined to tear her clothes off to satisfy his curiosity about the human form.

Roger was, in fact, a magnificent, if rather elderly, king of beasts. He weighed six hundred pounds and stood four feet high; his head was on a level with Fritzi's bosom. Roger badly needed to diet, though. His belly sagged.

Roger liked eye contact. He blinked his tawny eyes at Fritzi, nuzzled her chest, then opened his enormous jaws to yawn. Following this he lay down to snooze.

Eddie ran into the cage built on the original outdoor stage. Half the bars were rubber. Fritzi dropped her lion tamer's whip and wiped her perspiring face and neck with the hem of her striped tunic. "Lord, this getup's hot." She wore the tunic with pantaloons, oversized shoes, a fright wig, and clown makeup: huge lips, a red ball on the tip of her nose, a single teardrop outlined in black under her left eye.

"I know," Eddie sympathized. "The take looked swell, though. Could I have one more for insurance?"

"Oh, Eddie." Being professional, that was the extent of her complaint. "Will Roger cooperate?"

"His owner says the dope won't wear off for another hour."

"Let's pray he's right."

Roger flicked his tawny tail and made an unfriendly noise somewhere in his chest. Fritzi followed Eddie out of the cage and off the set. Behind the camera positioned to shoot through the bars, Jock chatted with Roger's owner. Farther back, Al Kelly was observing with his usual dyspeptic frown.

She plopped in a chair in the shade of a beach umbrella, and a makeup girl handed her a glass of lemonade. "Thanks, Mona." Stripped to his undershirt, Jock Ferguson said to Roger's owner, "How do you get him to open wide like that?"

"Lions are smart. They train well. Roger knows that when we're finished he'll go home to mama. African lions don't step around. They take one mate for life. If I told you any more, you'd be making thirty-five simoleons a day instead of me." Jock laughed.

In the cage Roger lurched to his feet. He made a lovelorn gargling sound and began to pace. A grip hastily padlocked a chain on the cage door — not much help if Roger discovered the rubber bars. Roger's owner reached through the bars and ruffled his mane. He spoke quietly to the lion. Roger tossed his head once, bared his few remaining teeth, flopped, and rolled over. Fritzi thought he looked cross, though. Performing for hours in the hot sun was no fun for any actor, two- or four-legged.

A man's shadow fell in front of her. Al Kelly stepped under the umbrella.

"Like to see you in my office, Fritzi."

Eddie overheard. "Boss, we need to get this shot before Roger gets testy."

"Last take looked fine to me. Don't waste money."

Kelly tilted his head to indicate that Fritzi should follow. It was hard to walk because her shoes measured twenty-five inches from heel to toe. In Eddie's improbable script, Knockabout Nell took over for the star circus clown, who'd eloped with an aerialist. She tamed a lion mistreated by a roustabout, foiled a firebug, prevented bank foreclosure on the circus, and, despite characteristic mishaps with buckets, hoses, trampolines, and tent ropes, once again saved everything and everybody while getting nothing for herself. Nell's secret love was the circus strongman. He preferred the cashier, who happened to be the owner's daughter. Nell was left at the fade-out sitting with her arm around Roger.

In his office Kelly wasted no time. "Fritzi, we pay you to perform at the studio. I hear you did an act downtown while I was up at Yosemite."

"I marched in the preparedness parade, if that's what you mean."

"Made a big speech. It went all over the country on the press wires in case you don't know it. I saw the *Times* write-up when I came back. I didn't like what I read."

She dabbed her melting makeup with a hanky. "I'm sorry. I think we disagree about the war. I spoke my mind."

"Take my advice. Don't get involved in causes. It steals your energy." He smiled with all the sincerity of a con man defrauding a widow. Being avuncular just wasn't in him.

Irked, she said, "There are more important things than being a picture star and signing autographs."

"Not in my cash book, sister. Everybody says Hollywood people are the new royalty, the only royalty this country's ever had. You're part of that. Look at all the press you get. The crowds you attract when you so much as break wind."

"Al, please."

He pressed on, a hard edge in his voice. "Take the wrong stand on a public issue like the war, your audience is liable to desert you. You can't afford that."

"I'll chance it."

"All right, Liberty can't afford it. I won't put up with it."

"Why, because you hate red ink?"

They sounded like a couple of children spatting, but there was nothing childish or funny about Kelly's snarl. "Stay out of those parades. Don't make any more speeches. That's it, that's the order. I run this studio."

"You don't run me, Al. Not outside the gates."

"Then you're making your last picture as Nell."

"*What?*"

"That lawyer you shoved down our throats — a real genius. He overlooked one thing. You signed a contract binding you to work for Liberty for three years. But you don't get any say in the kind of work — what pictures you're in. We have to pay you, but we don't have to use you."

"Have you lost your mind? The Nell comedies make money."

"Sure, but watch them go the other way if you keep opening your bazoo about the war. Half the people in this country want no part of it. Half, maybe more. Get this straight, Fritzi. Liberty created the Nell pictures, and Liberty owns the character. We can hire any actress for the part. We can send you back to playing Princess Laughing Rainwater in cowboy pictures. Do you get what I'm telling you? We can put you in blackface and make you play darky maids. Or the rear end of a horse."

"This is a bluff."

"Sure, all right. Play the hand out and see. Take a vacation, Fritzi. A good long one. After this Nell wraps up, go make as many goddamn speeches for England as you want. Oh, one more thing. Don't bother crawling to Hayman this time. Ham's with me all the way on this. He hates what the limey press says about studio owners. That a lot of 'em are German Jews and love the Kaiser."

He swiveled around in his chair and showed her his back. Fritzi reeled out of the office. Her funny shoes flapped and slapped. She felt like a novice drinker who'd gulped a quart of gin on an empty stomach.

A cool wind from the mountains dropped the nighttime temperature. She built a fire and put a new disc on the Victrola. Caruso singing *"Vesti la giubba"* filled the house. A song about a sad clown seemed appropriate.

She lay on the Navaho rug in front of the fire, toasting her bare feet. Her eyes misted as the music soared, and she thought of Loy. The mournful air ended; the needle scraped as the disk went round and round. She rewound the machine and started the record again.

The twists and turns and confusions of the world baffled and frustrated her as never before. All your life you dreamed of one man to love, and he turned out to be wrong. You started along one road where you thought success lay, but it didn't, so out of a combination of desperation and accident you took another road, less desirable, and lo and behold, there you found the rewards, the dreams fulfilled in a totally unexpected way — and then someone threatened what you'd achieved simply because you did what you believed right.

Were dreams always so thwarted, distorted, changed in ways you never anticipated? Was this what people meant by the riddle of life? If so, its solution was beyond her, though its pain and hurt were present and real.

What did it all mean? How could you understand? What could you do, beyond getting up next morning and going on? She fell asleep in front of the dying fire with the questions unanswered and the Victrola needle scraping in the center grooves of the record.

She hit on a scheme to take her out of Los Angeles for a while. She bought Schatze a pearl-studded collar, loaded her into a wicker traveling box, and boarded a train for Texas.

She rode the Pecos & Northern Texas Line, which ran from Lubbock to Farwell Junction on the New Mexico border. Yet she saw little of the countryside because of dust storms, yellow monsters that roared over the land, carrying off topsoil of the cotton fields.

At Muleshoe only two passengers left the train, Fritzi and an anvil salesman lugging a small sample. He disappeared in the dust, coughing. Fritzi looked around. A colored porter approached.

"Is there a hotel?"

"Yes'm. 'Cross the street."

"Thank you."

The clerk stared at her while she signed the ledger. Fritzi now understood that people stared at her the way they stared at Little Mary, or Charlie, but she still had moments when she stood away, remote from herself, a mystified observer who wondered how this could be. Dust blew past the grimy lobby windows as she asked, "Is there a local police department?"

"No, ma'am."

"Sheriff, then?"

"Yes'm, this is the county seat." He gave directions. People were extra helpful if they recognized you; that was one of the few advantages.

The sandstone courthouse matched the hue of

the dust clouds. The building smelled of spittoons and aging deed books. Sheriff Rob Roy Trigg's office was on the first floor. The sheriff was a big old buffalo of a man with a home haircut, handlebar mustaches, and neat citified clothes. She found him sorting through wanted flyers. Many more hung three and four deep on his bulletin board. She wondered if a flyer with Loy's likeness and description was among them.

Trigg nearly tangled his feet racing around the desk to hold the guest chair. "It's an honor, ma'am. My wife and myself, we enjoy you so much at the picture show."

"Thank you, Sheriff." No matter how often she had to listen to it, each person who said it fancied they were the first, so you couldn't be rude.

"I've come about a man I was acquainted with in Los Angeles. A resident of this town at one time. Loyal Hardin."

"Why, sure, I knew Loy." The words revealed nothing of his feelings. A fly walked across the sheriff's ink-stained blotter. He waved it off.

"Do you know his whereabouts?"

"No, ma'am, afraid I don't. No one's seen Loy in years. He killed a Texas Ranger, Captain Mercer Page, did you know that?"

"I had some hint of it. Loy and I worked in several pictures together. He handled horses, sometimes took small parts."

"Do tell. Didn't know." He brought a corncob out of his desk. "Will this bother you?" She shook her head. He packed the pipe. "Loy's sister, Clara, she's over in Lubbock in a home for the feeble-minded." Trigg's hand hovered over the old pipe with a lit match. He almost burned himself before he blew it out. "What happened about Merce Page was a real shame. Loy Hardin shot and killed him, then disappeared to hell and gone 'fore the whole story came out."

"What do you mean, the whole story?"

Trigg leaned back with both hands cupped around his pipe. "It got out that Loy shot Merce because he, ah, molested Loy's sister. After Loy ran off, women started coming forward. A young woman up in Lariat, that's in Parmer County. Another from Castro County, preacher's widow. Woman of sixty, can you imagine? Lord knows how many more kept silent. The man was an animal. Not fit to wear a Ranger's badge. Upshot was, the murder charge was sort of put aside. Only Loy never knew it."

The irony of it. When B.B. wanted him for a good role, Loy feared he might be recognized back home and be locked up, unable to care for Clara. Poor sweet man, if he'd said yes, he might be a picture star by now. Wherever he was, Loy was free. Probably he'd never know.

84. Heat of the Moment

In the midst of the fiercely hot summer, a season of mounting war passions, Joe Crown felt himself a man besieged.

The climate in which German-Americans found themselves steadily grew more stormy and hostile. Editorial cartoons portrayed all Germans as "cruel beasts" and "lying Huns." Newspapers ran wild scare stories about spy rings secretly financed by "hyphenates." It became sorrowfully evident to Joe that to be an American citizen of German origin was to be a pariah.

Though he didn't tell Ilsa, he worried endlessly about Carl, off there in France in a fragile aeroplane, risking his life. Carl never wrote letters, so he and Ilsa were left wondering about him, which only enhanced the anxiety.

He was beset by physical ailments. His eyesight continued to fail. A fall on the ice late in the winter had exacerbated arthritic pain in his hips. He tended to stoop, couldn't brace his shoulders back as he had for so many years, to reflect his pride at being a Union officer and then General of Volunteers in '98. He was no longer erect and military but old and bent.

Since his seventy-third birthday, observed on March 31, it seemed to him that things had slid downhill more rapidly. He and Ilsa had celebrated the birthday by themselves in the dining room of the Union League Club. Joe was aware of whispers, and some ugly looks, as they dined that night. Well, what else could be expected? His own friend Roosevelt was denouncing "hyphenates" in speeches.

Now, in the blaze of July, here was his nephew Paul fresh off the transcontinental train and eager to show him pictures.

"Why should I waste my time?" the General said after Ilsa had retired. He and his nephew sat with beer and cigars in the stuffy office on the first floor of the mansion. Wind shook doors and windows ahead of a storm blowing in from the prairies. Paul's train had come through downpours and a hailstorm.

"Why should I make myself miserable staring at unpalatable sights for an hour or more, tell me that."

"Because these pictures tell the truth about what's happening."

Joe Crown was old, tired, beset by aches and pains, prohibitionists, pseudo-patriots, and disloyal children. He wanted to rebuff his nephew in the harshest of terms. He drank the rest of his beer while Paul, whom he loved like his own child, sprawled in his chair, alert and hopeful.

"Why do you insist on this?" the General said finally.

"Because I respect your integrity, Uncle Joe. If you see the truth, I know you won't try to deny it. You're not that kind of man."

The General chewed his cigar. "You said you were last in Los Angeles?"

"Yes, I was there right as the tour went to hell."

"Did Fritzi have a hand in your coming here?"

Paul didn't avoid his uncle's eye, or even blink. "She wanted you to see the pictures, yes. But I take responsibility. I made the decision to stop in Chicago."

A lightning flash turned the windows white. Querulously, the General said, "All right. For you, not her."

Paul bounded out of his chair. "I brought a rental projector with me in the taxi."

After the more prosaic scenes of German soldiers behind the lines, and then the stark footage from the trenches, the Belgian field appeared. The captain tapped his cigarette on a metal case. The soldiers raised their rifles.

The captain demanded bayonets. The women kneeling fell over in a faint. The middle-aged farmer put his arm around his wife.

The impatient captain waved his cigarette. The soldiers fixed bayonets and lunged forward, ramming the steel into the six victims. When they fell in postures of agony the soldiers stabbed again, and again, many more times than necessary.

Joe Crown's cold cigar dropped to the floor. He held the arms of his chair as the screen went black. Rain spattered the window. He could only fall back on trite words. *"Mein Gott in Himmel."*

He staggered to his feet; Paul rushed to offer a supporting hand. "I need air."

"It's about to storm, Uncle Joe."

"Air. Come or stay as you want."

He blundered to the door like a gored animal.

Paul followed him through the darkened downstairs. The wind drove the front door inward with a crash.

The General went down the front steps unsteadily, buffeted by the wind hurling grit before it. An empty barrel blew along Michigan, whirling and bumping in a dust cloud. A pressure heavy as an iron anvil lay on Joe's chest suddenly. He leaned against an elm tree, struggling to breathe.

"Uncle, what is it?"

"A little pain. I have them occasionally. They pass."

This one took five minutes to pass.

"I'm all right now." The wind blew from behind him, making his white hair fly around his head. Paul's necktie snapped like a whip.

"Does Aunt Ilsa know about these pains?"

"No, she does not." He raised his fists in front of his nephew's face. "You must not tell her. I absolutely forbid you to say a word."

Profoundly shaken and disillusioned by Paul's pictures, Joe Crown slept badly the next few nights. His employees suffered sudden outbursts of anger, a sign of turmoil they recognized from occasional times of trouble in the past.

Businessmen of Joe's acquaintance approached him, asking him to let his name be used in an advertisement arguing for a negotiated peace with Germany and the Central Powers. Most of those already signed up were German-Americans. The visitors also asked for five hundred dollars to help pay for inserting the ad, in two languages, in the city's English and German newspapers.

"I'll sign, and I'll give you the money," he said. "But don't misconstrue my reason. I no longer have sympathy for the men running the war from Berlin. I want to see it over to stop the killing of innocents."

"By the Allies," said one of the callers.

"By both sides," he retorted.

The General's motives, of course, could not be deduced from the strident text of the polemical ad as it appeared. Reaction was instantaneous. One boiling hot night someone torched delivery trucks parked in a fenced compound at the brewery. Joe was summoned from bed at three A.M.

At noon next day, when he motored to the Union League Club for lunch, the temperature was already near a hundred degrees. The back of his suit of summer-weight wool was sweated through. On the club staircase he paused to mop his forehead, short of breath.

As he passed crowded tables on his way to his customary small one by a window, a man named Reginald Soames hailed him from a table where he sat with two other club members. Soames was British, attached to the consulate in Chicago. He and Joe had served on charity committees. Joe found him a self-centered blowhard. Soames had studied a year at Heidelberg and was always peppering his talk with German words and phrases, in a horrible accent. Still, courtesy dictated that the General acknowledge the greeting.

"Joe," said Soames when he approached the

table; he refused to use Joe's military title. "I saw the advertisement to which you subscribed." Soames's two friends stared at the General with ill-concealed repugnance. "I frankly think the sentiments expressed are beneath contempt."

"You're perfectly entitled to your opinion. And I needn't explain myself to you or anyone. Good day."

He felt the racing of his heart as he turned away. Sunlight glaring through the windows seemed to flash and blind him momentarily. His step was unsteady; one of the waiters rushed forward, but the General waved him off. Behind him, Soames said in a voice intended for his hearing, "Americans are the spiritual cousins of we English. Therefore to favor letting the Hun off lightly — how do you explain it? Not merely as misplaced loyalty, but something else. There's a good German word. *Gemeinheit.*"

Cowardliness.

It was not to be borne by a man who'd risked himself in the Civil War and again in Cuba. Purple in the face, the General whirled around and stormed back to Soames.

"I will not tolerate insults from the likes of —"

The sentence broke off. The General made a strange choking sound, clutched at his throat. *"Catch him!"* one of the others shouted as Joe toppled forward.

He flung his hands toward the table, caught the white cloth, and pulled it down with him. China and crystal smashed. Serving bowls spilled and shattered. A green wine bottle gurgled its contents on the club's expensive carpet.

The General lay half conscious, frightened and ashamed of showing weakness. The back of his head rested in a puddle of brown gravy. He tried to rise and couldn't. He saw anxious faces peering down, then nothing.

It must have been a hundred degrees in the room. And the smell! Liniment, perspiration-soaked sheets. Ilsa had forbidden electric lights, instead setting beside the bed, trimmed low, one of her treasured lamps from the days of coal oil — an expensive lamp, retrieved from the attic, carefully unwrapped, cleaned, filled, and lit. The globe and lower vase were milky glass, pale blue, hand-painted with American Beauty roses. The lamp had brightened the music room for many years. Fritzi well remembered how her mother loved it.

She knelt at the bedside, took her father's frail veined hand in hers. The General turned his head toward her on the bolster. His eyes looked small and queerly cold, like the eyes of a dead robin she'd found and held in her arms as a child.

White stubble covered his cheeks. He spoke from the right side of his mouth, the words thick, full of saliva. The left side of his face was stiff.
"Fritzchen."
"Papa. *Wie bist du?*"
"Besser."
He surely didn't look better. "I'm so sorry it happened, Papa."
"Danke." He tried to touch her hair, but he was too feeble. His smile was no more than a twitch of his lip.

"You'll get well, Papa, this will pass." Out in the hall, she and a surprisingly chastened Joey had heard the physician's verdict. Their father had survived the stroke and might walk again someday, but never unassisted.

"*Ja, wirklich.*" Sure enough.

"I came as fast as I could from Texas. I need to ask forgiveness for making you angry for so long. I had to go to New York, I couldn't have done otherwise, but I know the pain it caused you, and I'm sorry for it. No matter how we differ about things, I love you, always."

His papery fingers stirred ever so slightly in hers. "*Meine liebe Tochter.*" My dear daughter. And then, like a benediction, he uttered one more word. "*Vergeben.*"

Forgiven.

A foul odor rose from the bed. Full of despair, Fritzi searched the dark for the burly nurse. "He's soiled himself."

The General's eyes watered with shame. She touched his hand. "Rest, Papa. I'll look in again." A tear glistened in the candlelight as it ran down his cheek into the white stubble.

85. Bombs

Paul heard about the General's stroke the moment he stepped in the door at Cheyne Walk. Ilsa had cabled the news. He hoped he hadn't contributed to the seizure but had no way of knowing. At least his uncle was still alive.

Coming home restored Paul's spirits. This was true despite his son Shad's tendency to reply to any question or remark with what Americans called lip. Shad had grown into a tall and awkward boy. He attended a public school in the country. Betsy, eleven and budding into puberty, remained tractable and affectionate. How long that would last neither parent could guess.

Lottie was a trial, like most five-year-olds, but Teddy, three, had shifted overnight into one of those affectionate and docile stages beloved by harried mothers.

Their excellent cook, Phillipa, announced that she was leaving to work at a munitions factory, hand-cutting fuses for shells. Having chopped and diced with fine Sheffield knives for so many years, she was prized for her skill. Julia was sympathetic. Along with hundreds of other women, she spent long hours at a dingy warehouse in the East End, standing at a trestle table, packing soldiers' ration kits.

Paul and Sammy shot some yacht-racing and steeplechase footage on a freelance basis. Compilations of several picture subjects into a "news reel" were now in regular distribution in the U.S. He sold to the Pathé and Gaumont weeklies, and did assignments for a new one, Hearst-Selig News Pictorial. Even with occasional work, and no danger of starvation, he was unhappy, though. He carried the failure of his American tour like an invisible stigmata. Michael Radcliffe took pity on him. At least once a week they went out for fish and chips and beer, then a visit to a Leicester Square cinema. Not to be entertained, but to see the astonishing news film produced by the government.

A particularly stirring release depicted brave Tommies facing a bayonet charge by Hun infantry. The Huns were clearly savages, stabbing fallen enemies without mercy, as in Paul's Belgian footage. Surviving Tommies retreated across a stream and dug in. Artillery found the range to support them as the Huns mounted a second assault.

Shells landed in the stream, sending up huge water spouts. Shells exploded on the enemy-held side, and bodies of Huns flew through the air. Tommies with clenched teeth fired smoking machine guns until the last enemy dropped. Then the Tommies waved their helmets and cheered. The title card commended their GALLANT ACTION.

"I investigated this one," Michael said. He was sunk in his loge seat with a cigarette burning in his fingers. "Crock of shit, start to finish."

"Fake? I thought so." Paul had taken part in plenty of film fakery in his early days.

"I can guide you to the exact spot near Staines

where it was shot. The so-called Huns are some of our finest lads. There are protective buttons on the bayonets. A spring attachment on the rifle barrel retracts the bayonet when it strikes something. The shells exploding in the water are bladders filled with gunpowder, set off by electric wires. Ground bursts are buried powder cans. The flying bodies are dummies, obviously. It's all stage-managed by the high command. Another bloody triumph for integrity, what?"

Germany sent huge silver airships across the Channel to drop bombs and terrify the city. Several times Paul and Julie watched the spectacle from the roof at Cheyne Walk. The enemy airships coasted serenely at altitudes above seven thousand feet, untouched by the long guns on the ground. Bomb damage was generally light and spread over a wide area, but the psychological terror was enormous.

On a bright summer day, Paul arrived at the dark brown halls of the Reform Club, where Jules Verne's fictitious adventurer, Phileas Fogg, had wagered that he could circle the globe in eighty days. Paul was there in response to an unexpected luncheon invitation. Lord Yorke occupied his usual table, chatting up the first lord of the Admiralty, ruddy-faced Winston Churchill. Paul had met the egotistical politician in South Africa during the Boer War. Their greeting was mutually cordial. Churchill called him Dutchie and handed him a fine Havana cigar before he swaggered off.

"We had best get the nasty part out of the way

first," Lord Yorke said. Paul had accepted the invitation with a certain foreboding, which now seemed justified. "By appropriating and showing the Belgian footage — my property, I remind you, Paul — you violated my trust. I could have prosecuted."

"Why didn't you?"

"Because you have two qualities I admire. Talent, which is marketable, and integrity, which unfortunately often proves to have a negative cash value. Devil of a lot of good the pictures did you in the colonies. Walkouts, cancellations — not exactly a star turn, my boy. Setback for your career, I'd say. Punishment enough."

"Look, sir. If you invited me here to rake over the past, I'll leave right now."

"Oh, sit down, don't posture." His lordship waved flamboyantly. "What I wish to discuss with you is a reversal, or at least a modification, of certain official policies. Whitehall will shortly permit a limited number of civilian journalists and cameramen to travel with the army."

Paul almost laughed at the man's brass. "Are you offering me a job?"

"I am offering to consider your return to the fold, following negotiations."

"I walked out on you."

"Of course you did. I am prepared to overlook your headstrong, not to say unethical, behavior. I want to send you and your camera to the front. I desire, as always, to employ none but the best."

Paul was so excited, he almost shouted in agreement. He checked his enthusiasm: "Sounds like I'd be under government supervision."

"Indeed, yes. With rigid restrictions. Kits inspected so that no long-focus lenses are taken into forward areas. No filming within forty yards of an aircraft, that sort of rot. However, you would be working regularly."

"This is sudden. Let me think."

"Think over a scotch. I'll have one m'self. Waiter?"

Paul's head whirled. He couldn't deny his hunger to see the war firsthand, with proper credentials. It would require compromise. What would Michael do in his situation?

Wasp-tongued Michael always seized the main chance; he'd agree at once. Following a brief ritual of haggling, and an excellent plate of Dover sole and boiled potatoes, that was exactly what Paul did. His lordship was pleased. As they left the club, he stuffed a note into Paul's breast pocket.

"There's ten quid. Advance against salary. Take the wife out. A good dinner, a show, with my compliments." With a roguish roll of his eyes he added, "It was always my intent to lure you back. Be a good chap and ring the personnel director straightaway. Regards to the missus. Cheerio."

He leaped into his chauffeured Rolls limousine before Paul could hand back the ten-pound note.

The thought of an evening out pleased Julie. They'd lost Barbara, their maid, to another munitions factory in her native Scotland, so Julie arranged for Michael's wife, Cecily, to stay with

Betsy, Lottie, and Teddy. She and Paul took a taxi through darkened streets to the Waldorf Hotel in Aldwych, a fine old Edwardian establishment with an excellent carvery. They ate roast beef and Yorkshire pudding complemented with a good bottle of claret, then at half past seven hurried a few steps to the Vaudeville Theater in the Strand, where *Charlot's Revue* was playing. Paul had gotten a pair of tickets in the stalls, on an outside aisle.

About nine forty-five, in the midst of a comedy number performed by a tenor and the popular star Eustacia Van Sant, a rumbling explosion shook the auditorium. The quick-witted actress stepped to the footlights with a reassuring smile. "Ah, gun practice again." People who had risen in their seats resettled themselves. Paul stuffed his program in his side pocket and whispered:

"I doubt it. Do you want to stay here while I have a look?"

"Absolutely not."

He waited a minute, so it wouldn't appear that they were fleeing. They stepped into the curtained passageway that led up and out to the lobby. As they crossed the lobby, another explosion in the direction of Wellington Street lit up the night. Paul hurried that way, clasping Julie's hand.

Searchlights speared upward around the horizon, toward a point above the central city. Sirens wailed. Pedestrians fled past him in the dark. "Zeppelins. *Zeppelins!*" Looking up, he saw a long, tapered airship pinned by the intersecting beams.

Ground batteries in distant Green Park opened fire. Incendiary shells aimed at the silver leviathan traced blue-white trails upward but fell short. Two taxis with dim running lights, heading past each other, were caught by a second stupendous bomb burst in the Strand. The taxis disintegrated in a burst of fire.

Shop windows blew out. Pieces of glass sailed in all directions. Throwing his arms around Julie to protect her, Paul saw bodies hurled upward against flames spouting from a huge crater. Someone screamed, "Gas main!"

The ground guns kept up their barrage as the Zeppelin glided on above Cross Station. Another bomb landed somewhere. People poured out of nearby theaters, cafés, and pubs. "God, it's terrible," Julie said. "Shouldn't we get out of here?"

"I think so, let's — wait." Firelight showed him someone half buried under a pile of rubble in Wellington Street. An old woman, her white hair askew, one hand waving feebly.

A man equally elderly and frail turned a terrified face to Paul. "It's my wife, Liddy, can you help?"

Paul put Julie in the cover of a shop entrance, then dashed into the street to attack the rubble on his knees. The elderly man tried to assist, but he did little more than scratch at the broken stones. Grunting, Paul heaved them aside one by one. He uncovered a crushed gardenia corsage.

The old lady watched intently, hopefully, as he lifted a last block off her bloodied hose. The Zeppelin dropped another bomb as it cruised westward. Guests from a small hotel, some in sleep attire, milled around yelling questions no one answered. Traffic backed up in the Strand in both directions. As Paul lifted the old woman from the rubble, he felt her stiffen. Her head lolled over his arm.

Paul and the elderly man stared at each other in the flickering light. "Oh no, Liddy, please God, no," the old man said. "Please God, not Liddy. Tonight is our anniversary. Forty-nine years."

The searchlights swept the sky. Little monoplanes with flaming cowl exhausts rose in futile pursuit of the disappearing airship. In the crowd packing the north side of the Strand, he saw Julie waving her tightly rolled program. He wanted to wave back, but it was impossible with a dead woman in his arms.

Street wardens covered the dead woman and routed traffic into the narrow thoroughfares north of Aldwych and the Strand. Paul and Julie trudged west to the Haymarket, up to Piccadilly, and on to the vicinity of the Ritz before they found a cruising taxi. On Cheyne Walk, they sat with Cecily for an hour, recounting the horror of the raid, then found a cab for her.

Paul couldn't sleep. He held Julie in his arms while a screen in his head played an endless loop of film: the bright, moist eyes of the old lady as he lifted rubble off her crushed body. The sudden loll to the side when her eyes dimmed. He remembered again a night in Santiago, Cuba, at the end of another war, in another century. Michael had drunkenly shouted words from the Revelation of St. John the Divine:

There were lightnings, and thunderings, and an earthquake. And the cities of the nations fell. . . .

At the dinner table next evening, a stack of papers lay near Paul's hand, the *London Light* and *Daily Mail* among them. Paul picked up his cup of tea and looked steadily into his wife's beautiful dark eyes. With his other hand he tapped the *Light*'s front page.

"Zeppelins. Poison gas. U-boats. Good God, Julie, what kind of world have we dreamed up for our children?"

"Nothing like the old one," she sighed. "Let's hope we all survive it."

"Millions won't. What Michael calls the Great Meat Grinder is running full speed in France."

"But you'll go back."

"I have to go back. Sammy's willing. It's what we do, Julie."

"Of course," she said, holding his hand while tears welled in her eyes.

86. Casualties

In the late summer Carl shot down his second German plane. The kill wasn't any easier, or less scary, than the first, but it was different, less emotional. Downing the first one had entitled him to paint a black Maltese cross on the Nieuport's cowl. As he plied the little brush, he reflected that there was a mark on his heart too. One that would stay forever.

He was depressed by the news of Rene LeMaye's sudden death. Rene had gone once too often against a Drachen, the penile-shaped observation balloon called in jest *das Mädchens Traum* — the Maidens' Dream. Long lines of Drachens were strung along the German front, each moored at four thousand feet by a steel cable that carried a telephone line to the ground. Rene had closed in on a balloon as usual, to fire incendiary rounds and ignite the thousand cubic meters of hydrogen in the bag above the observation basket. Somehow his guns jammed, and he attempted to finish the job by slashing the balloon with his wing tip. A squadron mate said Rene accomplished that, only to disappear when some random spark set off the hydrogen, blowing up Rene, his airplane, and the spotter and his assistant in the dangling basket.

Carl lived with a mounting depression after he heard the story. The panache of combat flyers was just a veneer, he had discovered. Major

Despardieu had put it candidly: "There is relentless pressure on the mind and nerves. Four months is about all a man can take before he cracks. Assuming he remains alive, of course."

One beautiful October afternoon, about six miles into German-held territory, four planes from Carl's squadron encountered six triple-wing aircraft with red cowls. The Germans were soon swarming all over them.

One of the red Fokkers doggedly pursued Carl; no matter how he dodged and maneuvered, the German was always there. Maybe the pilot recognized him; aviators had ways of identifying a specific enemy. Carl didn't know the German, and didn't care to know him.

After an aerial fight that lasted nearly ten minutes, with no victor, Carl took a burst that damaged his engine. He peered over the side to check his position. Enemy anti-aircraft guns — Archie — guarding the moored balloons had swung around to bang away at the French planes. As black clouds bloomed and billowed, Carl signaled a wing mate, pointing at his damaged engine, then banked and headed west.

The Fokker was right behind but withheld fire. Carl's broken fuel line spewed aviation gas behind the Bébé. The balloons that spotted for the German artillery and watched for enemy advances were coming up ahead. Typically they were anchored three miles behind No-Man's-Land, which told him how far he had to fly to safety. He tilted the Bébé to slide between two of the Drachens; the assistant in the basket on his left fired three rounds from a rifle but missed.

Soon all his fuel was gone. The engine sputtered, coughed, died. He lost altitude. The thud
of Archie was fading. He snatched off his helmet,
looked back. The German was still there. Carl
expected to be shot down, perhaps not until he
was almost out of danger. That was the mission
of airmen, to down the other plane. But a certain
code of honor prevailed on both sides. If one was
feeling chivalrous, and the enemy plane had
been rendered useless, there was no absolute obligation to kill the airman too. Evidently the German pilot was in that mood. He swooped past
Carl on the right, saluting him with a smile of
self-congratulation and a cheery wave of a
leather gauntlet. Helmet and goggles concealed
all of the man except the smirk.

He peeled away and was gone. Carl held the
Bébé aloft until he saw the German trenches
and, beyond them in the distance, French balloons, Caquots, moored in a similar line. He
glided over the trenches at five hundred feet,
drawing some careless ground fire that did no
damage. He aimed the plane at a space between
shell craters in No-Man's-Land, well short of
the forward trenches on the French side. As
carefully as he could, he brought the plane
down, and down. . . .

The ground was rougher than it looked.
Something caught the undercarriage, standing
the plane on its nose and hurling Carl out of the
cockpit. He tumbled through the air and landed
violently on his left side. There was a red flash of
pain, then he blacked out.

He woke to feel excruciating pain in his arm.

Germans were firing at him from their trenches. He dragged himself the other way, smelling the filthy miasma of dirt and excrement that befouled the whole Western front. He felt no sensation in his left hand; his arm dangled like a broken twig. He crawled through loops of barbed wire, dragging himself with his right hand and pushing with his knees. The barbed wire raked the back of his neck; he bled on Tess's scarf again.

Nearly unconscious, he fell over the edge of a trench and croaked his name to a French *poilu* before he sank into comforting darkness.

"Look," they said, bringing him a small hand mirror in the hospital ward.

His hair was completely white.

"Your left arm is crippled," they said. "If it is only damage to nerves, you will perhaps recover the use of it one day. Or perhaps not. In any case, you can no longer fly. We are sending you home."

Carl was too weary and low to be relieved.

"This came for you, dropped in a canister by an enemy pilot," they said.

Carl translated the letter with no difficulty.

Reinhard Grotzman, the aviator whom you downed some weeks ago, was a friend and comrade. He came, as I did, from the infantry. Hearing of his death, I was determined to find the perpetrator and return the favor.

In the midst of our sky fight, I altered my course for this simple reason. Few aviators

803

have challenged me as you did, sir. It would be a pleasure to meet a second time, and not as adversaries. Perhaps you will one day visit the Fatherland under happier circumstances, and if so, I should like to shake hands with a man of your mettle. Headquarters will always know my whereabouts, as the Army is my career.

With every good wish for your well-being, I remain

Yr. Obdt.,
Capt. Hermann Goering

Carl threw the letter on the floor and turned his face to the wall.

The German officer was still acting out a pageant of bravery and courtesy — fighting a war that no longer existed. In Carl's squadron there were opinionated pilots who argued convincingly that air power shouldn't be restricted to strategic battlefield missions, but should be used tactically, against factories, railways, cities — and civilians — to destroy the industrial base, demoralize the population, hasten the surrender. *Hauptmann* Goering wouldn't understand such theories, though perhaps those who sent Zeppelins over London already did.

The German must be an old-fashioned, naive sort, Carl concluded as he lay with his good hand under his head, staring at nothing while others in the reeking ward raved and moaned. *Hauptmann* Goering was captivated by some kind of ideal that Carl had seen wither and die in the blood and suffering of a war that had become a slaughter.

"A telegraph message," they said, showing a folded and grimy flimsy. "Much delayed."

He read the first lines. "Oh, Jesus." Then he read more. The General had survived the stroke.

Carl smoothed the flimsy, placed it on the front of his coarse gown, and covered it with his hand. He stared at the ceiling. Someone screamed in agony. He closed his eyes, feeling useless and abandoned.

In Paris, on his way to the coast, he went to a cinema to see his sister. He felt better, though his left arm was still useless, devoid of all sensation but a feeble tingle now and then. He protected it in a black sling.

The war had almost completely shut down French picture studios; the theaters depended on American imports, none more popular than those featuring the character Knockabout Nell. The French called her Clumsy Nell. *"Nelle Gauche" à le Cirque* was the usual misadventure of the lovable hoyden who could do nothing right until the end. Nell knocked down a tent pole, and the entire tent. She lost the circus cash box down a well, then burned up the wet money trying to dry it on a stove. But when the lion got loose she saved the day, even with her foot jammed in a water bucket. Smiling and cooing, she tamed the beast; he lay down, rolled over, and licked her cheek.

Carl always felt strange watching Fritzi's pictures. She seemed remote from the older sister he'd lived with, teased, and forever adored.

She'd always wanted to be a great dramatic actress, but it was clowning that had made her famous. He knew Fritzi deserved her fame when he heard all the chuckling, the roars and whoops of the war-weary French people seated around him. He sat smiling while the silver shadows chased over his face.

When he went out, it was still raining. He sat in a hotel bar for two hours, thinking of Tess.

87. In the Trenches

"Must be the funniest damn war in history," Sammy said minutes before the bombardment. "Blokes just standin' still lookin' and shootin' at each other." Sammy and Paul had photographed Allied troops for a week, under close supervision, then followed a circuitous route, via occupied Brussels, for a return visit to the German front line. Film of the Tommies would go to Lord Yorke; the German footage was for Paul's own use.

The French howitzers fired their first rounds at four o'clock. Paul had given up filming much earlier, when the light of the winter afternoon was already failing. He and Sammy stood in a forward fire trench, peering over a wooden revetment improvised from pieces of a crate. The officer in charge of the sector, a Major Nagel, yelled into a field telephone while keeping one finger stuck in his ear.

Paul turned up his overcoat collar and chewed his cold cigar. Shells sent up geysers of earth in No-Man's-Land; dirt rained on them. The artillery barrage directed from observation balloons tore gaps in the barbed wire strung for miles in either direction. That was the purpose — to open the way for an infantry assault.

In No-Man's-Land a few shell-blasted trees stood like burned and amputated fingers, evidence that once there had been a pastoral landscape instead of mud and water-filled craters and the endless coils of wire. While he and Sammy watched, a tree trunk took a direct hit, bursting into flame and shooting off coruscating displays of sparks.

Major Nagel joined them. "We should see them come over the top in approximately one hour. The same pattern has prevailed all month. The French bastards call it nibbling us to death." Nagel was an overweight Bavarian, bewildered by this peculiar form of warfare and resentful of the conditions in which it placed his men.

Sammy and Paul jumped out of the way as two machine gunners ran into the fire trench from one of the saps, narrower trenches leading to forward gun nests. The men lugged their gun, tripod, and ammo chest. Other gunners appeared in similar fashion. Nagel shouted, *"Schnell, schnell,"* waving them to dark openings in the trench's forward wall. The gunners disappeared like rodents. "It's the equipment we're trying to protect, not the men," Nagel said sourly.

Major Nagel's position was in the sector stretching from Châlons-sur-Marne west to Epernay, in the department of the Marne. The major and his men faced units of Marshal Foch's Ninth Army approximately eighty-five miles northeast of Paris. On the way to the forward area, Paul and Sammy had filmed German soldiers doing laundry, enjoying mess, marching and singing, tending the mammoth Skoda howitzers and the Big Berthas from Krupp. Each scene was carefully arranged by senior officers to impress the outside world with German morale and materiel. Looking closely, however, Paul saw something else. The troops, even the newest and youngest reinforcements, appeared wan and frightened. Gone were the showy uniforms of last summer, replaced by camouflage colors and new-issue steel helmets.

The German entrenchments were defensive, built to hold last year's gains throughout the winter. Each trench was six feet deep, with three support trenches dug behind and parallel to the forward fire trench. Zigzag communications trenches ran at right angles, connecting them. It was all precise and fine except for the dirt, the smell of unwashed clothes, the reek of bodily waste overflowing the latrine trenches and churned into the mud by booted feet. Paul almost vomited the first time he smelled the trenches. He was told by the embittered Nagel that the whole Western front smelled bad.

As it grew dark, the bombardment continued. Nagel insisted Paul and Sammy go down into one of the dugouts. They huddled by a brazier made of an oil drum pierced with many holes. It gave off heat and a lot of smoke. You could suffocate breathing the smoke in the enclosed space. On the other hand, the smoke killed some of the stenches of soggy uniforms, unwashed armpits, excrement.

The earth above them shook as the French shells hit. Dirt fell in Paul's hair. He eyed the timber supports of the dugout. Sammy looked nervous. "Hell of a spot to be in, huh, gov?"

Under Paul's union suit a verminous visitor

was exploring. He dug beneath his muddy over-coat, vest, two shirts, and underwear to scratch. "I wouldn't want it for a permanent residence."

At the mouth of the dugout someone yelled, "They're coming." Paul heard rifle fire as the ar-tillery ceased. Major Nagel had sent sharp-shooters forward into the saps to enfilade the *poilus* charging across No-Man's-Land. Paul chewed his cigar to pieces as men began to wail and shriek aboveground.

Machine guns stuttered. Flashes of red and yellow reached the dugout — flares sent up to cast light on the attackers. The ground assault lasted forty minutes. The German position held; the lines remained unbroken. Finally the sounds of firing diminished. Quiet returned. Someone shouted down that it was all clear. Paul and Sammy climbed out of the dugout. As Paul came into the open, he saw a young corporal slumped over the lip of the trench. His jaw was shot away; his eyeballs stood out like boiled eggs. Paul gagged.

The *poilus* had gone back to their trenches. Under the cold, distant stars Nagel's men crept forward to drag bodies out of the saps and pile them in a heap several yards in front of the fire trench. Paul counted silently. Fifteen. Sammy sucked on a cigarette as they watched the activ-ity.

"How many dead in this whole war so far?" he asked.

"God only knows. A million Germans, a mil-lion Frenchmen, maybe just as many English. Is it any wonder the reds call war a conspiracy of kings and capitalists against the poor and power-less?"

Sammy darted looks right and left, said softly, "But we know which side's right, don't we, gov?"

"Yes. We do."

He slept half frozen in the dugout that night. At daybreak he loaded the camera, climbed out of the trench, and positioned himself to film the corpse heap. He remembered photographing the same kind of carnage after Colonel Roosevelt had taken San Juan Hill in '98.

The disk of a pale yellow sun shone through a thin morning fog. Sounds were muffled, but Paul could hear men moving in No-Man's-Land. He was just setting up when Major Nagel came tearing out of the fire trench to confront him.

"You can't do this, it isn't appropriate."

"Major, I have permission. I have papers signed by —"

"I don't care if they're signed by General Moltke. I don't care if the Blessed Virgin herself came down from heaven and signed them, it isn't appropriate," the distraught officer cried. "I lost good men last night. I lost my second, Captain Franz, a young officer of astonishing promise. What's left of him is scattered in little pieces. It isn't appropriate for you to photograph that, do you hear me?"

Suddenly ashen, he threw his hands over his face and sobbed. He swayed like a sapling in a storm. As a sergeant led him away, a lieutenant explained to Paul:

"You must understand about the major. He's a career man, the army's his life. Back home he has four children, girls. He adopted Franz like a son; he was bringing him along. This filthy war is destroying all of us. I must ask you to take cover again. This ground is watched by snipers, and the fog is clearing."

"All right," Paul grumbled. The winter cold and their uncomfortable surroundings had started his back aching again. Sammy trotted up and offered to take the camera. Paul gladly surrendered it.

"Keep low, please," the lieutenant said as he went ahead of them. Paul obliged, bending over despite the extra pain. Sammy evidently didn't hear the lieutenant. Talking around a cigarette in the corner of his mouth, he said he'd be thankful to retreat to some place where they could enjoy a bath and a hot meal.

"And women. How can a bloke get on without an occasional bit of — ?" A shot rang out, then two more. Paul watched the camera sail from Sammy's hand. Sammy pitched forward, his nose burying in the mud. The back of his skull was a red pit of gristle and blood.

Paul dropped to his knees, picked up Sammy's shoulders, shook him. "Sammy. Sammy!" The sight of his friend's vacant eyes, open mouth, shocked and sickened him as few things ever had before.

"I must ask you to leave him until dark," the lieutenant said, crouching near Paul. "I order it."

"Go to hell," Paul said, feeling tears on his

dirty cheeks. "You just go to hell. I'll bring him back when I'm ready."

The lieutenant retreated. Paul held Sammy against his overcoat, heedless of the blood and the sudden stench of the body. He cried. Sammy's death was the emblem of the nightmare that had enveloped Europe's golden summers of peace and confidence, turning them to winters of despair and ruin.

Under the pale sun, with the coils of wire growing visible again, he dragged Sammy's body to the fire trench. An hour later, he buried the remains in alien ground.

He examined his camera. It was broken beyond repair. He felt the same way. He held the camera in his arms like a dead child, wondering how long the carnage would last — how many millions more would perish with their dreams.

88. The Boy

They stood in the same finely appointed parlor where they'd visited before he left for France. Sunlight streamed in from Woodward Avenue. Melting icicles on the eaves dripped steadily. Carl looked bedraggled, underfed, in need of a barber. His lifeless left arm still hung in the black sling.

Using his other hand, he unwound the red scarf with its frayed ends and faded patches, its dark stains and clumsy stitching. Gravely, with ceremony, he placed it around Tess's neck, drew it down over her shoulders, straightened it.

"The dragons and Saracens are all dead, Tess. I've come home to stay. With you, if you'll have me."

Tess touched the scarf, holding back joyous tears. She smelled of sweet lilac water and yeast from the kitchen.

"I never wanted anything more. But what will you do? Work for your father? I'll live in Chicago, if that's what you want."

He shook his head. "Prohibition's coming, sure. Pop's recovering slowly, but the brewery may not exist in a year or two." He thought a moment. "I'd rather make automobiles than beer. Automobiles and airplanes."

"The Clymer company's gone."

"I know."

"But other manufacturers in Detroit are thriving. I know the right people. First, though —"

She drew him to a horsehair sofa, sat close to him. He reveled in her nearness and her warmth.

With her eye on a sunlit window she said, "You remember my saying when you left the first time that I'd never let making love turn into guilt — or a rope to tie you down? For that reason there's something I've held back, because I thought that telling you would be a kind of blackmail. I didn't want you here with me, and miserable, all your life."

He took her hands between his. "What is it, Tess?"

"You haven't suspected? It's the boy. I married Wayne so he'd have a name, but his name really isn't Sykes, it's Carl Henry Crown. I changed it legally after Wayne died. I've told him why."

"He's my son?" Carl said. "Oh, my God. All these years and I didn't — ?"

She kissed him quickly, ardently. "If there's any fault, it's mine."

"Does he know about me?"

"Yes, I explained. He's small but very quick. He didn't seem hurt, more curious. Principally about you. He asked a great many questions, then admitted he never felt strongly attached to Wayne. He said he always felt bad about it, but not after I explained. I called Hal on the speaking tube when they told me you'd arrived. He's waiting in the library."

She took his hand, tugged him toward the hall doors. "He's a fine boy, you'll like him."

They crossed the marble floor to an open doorway. In the library, the tips of his thumbs and index fingers touching in a way that suggested nervousness, the boy peered anxiously toward the sound of the footsteps. Carl saw the resemblance strongly now. He'd noticed it in the eyes before. His own eyes filled with tears.

"Hal, here's your father," Tess said with a loving smile. She stepped aside to let Carl pass. With excitement and a sudden strange sense of contentment, he realized he was stepping into a new world where, one of these days, all the broken dreams might be mended.

89. The Unfinished Song

"Yes, Mr. Folger, I have it written down. Outdoor rallies in Eureka, Santa Rosa, Napa, Oakland. Then the parade and auditorium program in San Francisco. No, I can't do any more after that. I've sublet my house. I've decided to return to New York. I'm tired of pictures, and the studio isn't using me. No, Mr. Folger, I'm not joking. Because of circumstances I can't explain; you'd die of boredom if I did. All right, thank you. Goodbye."

Fritzi hung the earpiece on the hook of the wall telephone. She lingered there, framed by a rectangle of sunlight. At the front of the hall a stack of empty brown cartons nagged her about packing. At the rear, in the kitchen, Schatze slurped water from her bowl.

The house had a still, dead feel. At two in the afternoon the December sun was already low, the light thin and lacking warmth. Fritzi pushed a strand of hair off her forehead and then lethargically moved away from the wall. She was scheduled to travel east in four days. She would visit her parents again, then continue on to New York and start over in the theater, shopworn and faded, and not a little jaded. Hmm, could Harry Poland write a ditty about that? Probably, but who'd care to buy it?

Schatze emerged from the kitchen to follow her. Halfway up the hall, by a wall mirror, something caught her eye. She put her nose near the glass, picked up a strand of hair behind her left ear. Gray. Ye gods — old age. What next?

She stomped into the front room, annoyed by the clutter — little ceramic knickknacks, playbills, scrapbooks of reviews of her films lying about, waiting to be wrapped and boxed. She kicked her way through empty cartons and cranked up the Victrola. She played "A Girl in Central Park" five times, loudly, then put on Caruso's *Vesti la giubba.* " She loved it nearly as much as Harry's song, though the clown's anguished tenor destroyed her every time she heard it. She knew why *il pagliaccio* cried.

Her status as a picture actress would open some doors on Broadway, but she suspected it would also restrict the parts she might be offered — loopy aunts and zany maids in farces, never Ophelia or Medea. She was typed. After a while, as she reached forty and the little roll of fat around her waist grew big as an inner tube and the gray locks multiplied like dandelions, what parts would be offered then? Any?

Leoncavallo's aria soared through the house. The hell with packing. She fell into the easy chair and lay back, gripped by lassitude. The loud music masked the arrival of a black and white taxi. She saw it through the window, over the Victrola horn. A man in an ill-fitting suit ran around to the curb side, opened the door to assist another passenger, feeble and white-haired.

B.B. Pelzer.

He clung to the arm of a man Fritzi recognized as an attendant from Haven Hill. B.B. came up the flagstone walk with short, tentative steps. He blinked like a nestling peeping at the world for the first time. Fritzi ran to the door.

"B.B. How wonderful to see you. How are you?"

"Who knows? My legs feel like toothpicks. You keep me standing here, they'll be broken toothpicks." B.B.'s smart chalk-stripe suit hung on him like a gunny sack. His round belly, and the rest of him, had shrunk drastically.

Fritzi helped him into the living room, settled him in the easy chair. "I'll wait in the cab," the attendant said, leaving.

B.B. blinked at the knickknacks and scrap-books, the packing boxes, the rolled-up Navaho rugs. "Eddie came to me. He told me. He said nobody could stop you but me. You ain't going to do this, are you?"

"Yes. Kelly's holding me to the contract, but he won't put me in a picture. He hates my speeches."

"Eddie told me." All at once B.B. bristled with energy. "That Irish bastard's out. He's out. I still got majority control. From here I'm driving straight to the studio to take care of it. Now, let's talk about you. You belong in pictures. Liberty Pictures exclusively. You don't want to work on Broadway again, all those drafty theaters, cold-water dressing rooms, cockroaches — pfui. Eddie has just the picture for you. He told me. Say, you got anything to drink? Some hot tea? I like English Breakfast."

Dr. Gerstmeyer had said B.B. could leave his mental dungeon if he wanted, but only when he wanted. She was touched that her situation had been the lever Eddie used to pry him out of self-imposed exile.

"I'm afraid all I have is Earl Grey."

"That's British, that'll do."

She heated a kettle and fixed a tray while Schatze sniffed B.B.'s cuffs. With a fearful look he patted her. "Nice doggy." Schatze growled and slunk off.

Fritzi brought the tea tray into the darkening parlor and served B.B. on a small lap tray.

"Ah, that's good." B.B. smacked his lips. "What I got to propose came from Izzy Sparks, he runs our Nashville exchange. You remember him."

"Oh, I do. He had two chorus girls with him each time he visited."

"That's Mr. Iz. A low-down cheater on his wonderful wife, but it don't seem to affect his brain power. He sent Eddie a bang-up idea. Iz loved you in the Lone Indian pictures. Never forgot you. So here it is, two in one. Eddie's writing it now, he's nuts for it." B.B. held his breath. You could hear trumpets.

"*Two Gun Nell.* Knocking them out in the Wild West! I know you had a terrible time, Fritzi. That cowboy vamoosing the way he did. Eddie told me. Work's good medicine, though. You want to work, we've got work."

Fritzi's eyes welled with tears. "Oh, B.B., I don't know if I can anymore."

"Sure, you can. You're a strong gel. You're professional, for heaven's sake. So what if you got a cold or the vapors? You do it anyway. That's acting. What do you say?"

Ellen Terry helped her out.

You say yes.

The first thing Fritzi noticed on Monday morning was Al Kelly's office, padlocked.

Her old friends welcomed her like a lost Queen of Sheba. Jock Ferguson hugged and kissed her lustily. Windy White, fittingly cast as a town drunk, offered her a snort from a flask, which she refused. No, he hadn't heard a word from Loy — probably never would.

Fritzi walked out of her makeup tent wobbling on high-heeled boots. Floppy sheepskin chaps over dungarees dragged in the dust. A blue and white gingham shirt fitted her new, plumper bustline nicely. She carried the huge sugarloaf sombrero they'd given her because as soon as she put it on, it slipped down over her ears to the tip of her nose.

On the glass stage, flats created a frontier saloon. Five extras from the Waterhole stood about. B.B. sat to one side of the camera in a canvas-backed chair.

Eddie approached with his little megaphone. His riding boots shone, his jodhpurs were spotless, his tan cap was tilted over his forehead. Eddie tended to strut these days, she'd noticed. Well, success entitled everyone to a little excess, didn't it?

"How do you feel, Fritzi?"

"I feel like an idiot in this getup." The truth was, she felt low. Little had changed; the same bleak questions persisted. Where was the laughter? There wasn't any. Just another performance. Oh, well. It was what she did, all she knew. Maybe she'd love it again someday.

Eddie said, "May we have a rehearsal? Time is money."

"We got another Kelly on our hands," B.B. said so everyone could hear.

"Fritzi?"

"I'm ready," she said in a weary voice.

"Jock, stand by. Fritzi, you know the moves. You dash forward, but you don't see the cuspidor. You trip, you fall on the poker table, the legs break away, the three card players tumble over backward in their chairs. Do you want padding in your shirt in case you land hard?"

Impatiently, she said, "No. Let's get on."

Eddie called, "Camera." Jock's assistant started cranking. Standing by the flimsy batwing doors mounted in a cutout, Fritzi poised herself for the take. Sunlight falling on the greenhouse stage dazzled her a moment. She saw a tall, broad-shouldered man hurrying toward the stage with a secretary pointing the way. Something about the man's build, his confident stride, reminded her of —

No, she was wrong. It wasn't Loy. It was Harry Poland.

"Action!"

Identifying him as she started her run threw her timing off. She missed the cuspidor, banged into an empty table, lost her balance, and reeled into a canvas flat head first. The canvas tore, and her head poked through. Eddie yelled to Jock to stop cranking. Six feet in front of her, on the other side of the glass — yes, it was Harry, waving yellow roses wrapped in green tissue paper.

"What in the name of hell's fire is going on here?" Eddie demanded. Fritzi pulled her head out of the flat, unhurt except for embarrassment. Harry stepped in through the hinged glass door and tipped his hat. Fritzi said:

"It's an old friend, Eddie. I saw him and it startled me."

"Harry Poland, ladies and gentlemen," he said. "I remember some of you from my previous visit. I traveled a great distance to see Miss Crown — I sincerely apologize if my presence disrupted your work."

Rosetta, the girl who kept track of the scenario for Eddie, clasped her notebook to her bosom. "Harry Poland the music maestro? 'The Elephant Rag' and all those? Oh, my God, Eddie, he's famous."

"Yes, and I have a picture to make," Eddie said, folding his arms to show how cranky he felt. "All right, Fritzi, speak to your friend." Eddie waved his megaphone at the others. "Take fifteen minutes. But I'm warning everyone, we'll have to work late to catch up."

Fritzi dropped the oversized sombrero on a table and tried to rake tangles out of her frizzy blond hair. She felt a perfect fool in her cowboy regalia, especially with Harry looking so smart, as always. His gold watch with a matching wristband gleamed almost as brightly as the tips of his shoes, where she saw reflections of herself. He tipped his hat a second time, presented the roses.

"Why, thank you, they're beautiful." She

looked around, as though for a vase, but of course there were no vases in a frontier saloon. Rosetta rushed forward to take the flowers, promising to put them in water right away.

Harry cleared his throat, reached into his coat. She saw folded papers in an inner pocket, but he left them there, turning to meet the inquisitive stares of the extras, the director, the cameramen, the carpenters and stage hands. He said in a stage whisper, "I wonder if we might go somewhere to talk?"

Fritzi pointed at the rear of the lot, still undeveloped and weedy. "There?"

"Fine, lead on."

They stepped outside. Harry spied an abandoned rusting wheelbarrow, sat down on one side of the broken wheel while Fritzi sat on the other.

"I'm so happy to see you, Harry. Do you have business in Los Angeles, or is this another vacation?"

"Neither." He looked at her intently. "A year has gone by."

"So it has." She hadn't forgotten.

"A bit more than a year, actually. I've been in London, rehearsing my new show. I brought a song for you. Not perfect, not yet finished, it came to me in a rush, on the crossing. Do you know that John Philip Sousa wrote 'The Stars and Stripes Forever' in similar fashion?"

"No, is that right?"

"He was coming home to America, severely depressed by the death of a friend, and the march wrote itself in a matter of minutes. I was not severely depressed — by no means! But I had the start of the lyric in a flash."

Out came the folded music paper glimpsed earlier. He cleared his throat and began to sing softly, in a pleasant if untrained baritone.

> "I keep insisting,
> You keep resisting,
> Saying you can't love
> As I love you.
> Dearest, until
> The day that you do,
> I have
> Love enough
> For two —"

Harry raised his head slowly, still flushed. "You see why it's imperfect, don't you? 'Love enough' — that's bad, difficult to articulate. Trouble is —" His Adam's apple bobbed wildly, and his blue eyes fixed on hers in a way that made the nape of her neck tingle.

"— trouble is, the words express the thought precisely."

"Harry, what are you trying to say?" She almost feared the answer.

"I'm saying I love you, and I'm doing a damn bad job of it."

She was stunned by his fervor, and flattered. She noticed blurred faces pressed to the glass of the stage. She turned her back on them, clasped her hands between her knees to steady herself.

"Now, Harry —"

"Please, Fritzi" — he spoke in a rush — "let

me say what I came thousands of miles to say. I dreamed of this country long before I saw it. I dreamed of all the possibilities in America, and when I got here I discovered the freedom a man needs to make dreams come true. I discovered new dreams as well. The very air of this land induces visions of what can be. All my dreams have come true but one, and it's the most important. You, Fritzi. Having you as my own. Being with you as long as I live. I've dreamed of it from the day we met in Central Park. I fell in love with you that day, but I couldn't do a thing about it. Except write a song. 'A Girl in Central Park.' Now I'm free. I want to know, I must know, if there's the slightest chance for me."

A bee buzzed near her face. She waved it off.

"Harry, I don't want to hurt you. You're a fine, decent man, a dear man. You deserve honesty. I like you very much. I admire you enormously. But I don't love you the way you want."

Instead of disappointment he showed enthusiasm. "It isn't necessary! You will in time, I'll make certain of it. Don't you see?" He held out the paper. "I wrote the song to say that."

Fritzi rocked back on the wheelbarrow, laughing in spite of herself.

"I must say, you're terribly confident."

"Yes, I am. In this country dreams come true."

She shook her head. "I don't understand it. I mean, your fascination with —"

He tossed the music paper in the weeds, held her hand in both of his.

"You're beautiful."

"Oh, Harry, that's not true."

"Beautiful — to me, from the very first."

Fritzi's blond hair tossed in the sunshine. "No one's ever said that to me."

"Then you are long overdue to hear it."

Looking at him with a new, wondering tenderness, she laughed again, deep in her throat. "You almost make me believe I might be, in another life, another century, perhaps."

"This life. This century." He drew her up from the rusted wheelbarrow. "Now."

"Harry, they're all watching —"

"I don't give a hang. I love you. You're beautiful. Believe it. I have love enough for two. Help me finish the song, Fritzi. Help me, and I'll make sure you never have a single regret," he said as he bent to kiss her.

AFTERWORD

I am happy to deliver at last the further adventures of the Crown family of Chicago. To the steady stream of mail from readers who liked *Homeland* there has been added e-mail, an average of a message every day or so (yesterday's came from a reader in Australia), asking about "the next book." That kind of inquiry is always heartening, but at the same time it creates a guilty conscience over delays.

I enjoyed writing *American Dreams* as much or more than I've enjoyed anything I've done, for two reasons. First, the period immediately preceding World War I is fascinating. An old order was dying, but few realized it. Barbara Tuchman in *The Proud Tower* used the word *sunset* to describe the process, and the moment. In little more than ten years, America, and the world, went from idyllic golden summers of peace to the bleak and bloody winter of war — war so apocalyptic, so destructive, it could hardly be imagined by most of those living at the time.

Second, with this book I happily engaged in writing a valentine to a group of people for whom I have boundless affection: all the men and women who pit themselves against the perils of the acting profession. Having started out with ambitions to be an actor, I shared Fritzi's struggle every step of the way. I also found her great company.

As always, the story's background and events are grounded in the historical record. In a few instances I have done a time shift with some real people, moving certain film actors and directors backward or forward by as much as a year for purposes of the story. In no case did I falsify what these people did, unless it's a case of an actor playing in an obviously fictional picture.

Fort Lee, New Jersey, was the movie industry's first "Wild West" location. Patents Company detectives did pursue and harass independent filmmakers, sometimes known as blanket companies, for the reason described. This continued until about 1915, when government action destroyed the trust forever.

D. W. Griffith's *Birth of a Nation* is rightly considered a masterpiece and, at the same time, virulently racist. When the great director adapted Thomas Dixon's novel, our country was only a half century removed from the war that tore us apart, redefined personal liberty, and set us on a new and better course. Passions still ran high among the defeated, one of whom was Griffith's father. Attitudes reflected in his epic film regrettably persist and trouble our land to this day.

Charlie Chaplin never served in the British military. Ultimately he was deemed too valuable as a morale builder. No films were more popular with the troops than Charlie's.

Fritzi's idol, Ellen Terry, stepped before the camera for the first time in 1916. She appeared in a British Ideal Film Company vehicle called *Her Greatest Performance*, playing a stage star who used her thespian skills to save a friend wrongly accused of murder. Dame Ellen went on to appear in other pictures before her career ended, and I suspect Fritzi would derive a certain satisfaction from this surrender to the medium.

Books by the British film historian Kevin Brownlow marvelously evoke and chronicle the era of silent films. Even better is the Thames Television production *Hollywood*, written and directed by Brownlow and his colleague David Gill. The thirteen hours, narrated by James Mason, were shown originally in the U.S. on PBS. *Hollywood* spans thirty years, covers every aspect, from stunts to sex scandals, and with rare footage vividly demonstrates why silent pictures became, in the last few years before *The Jazz Singer*, a high art form understood and loved around the world. You can find this splendid series in a boxed set in many video catalogs.

The descriptions of Ford Motor Company's Piquette Avenue plant are based on floor plans from the Henry Ford Museum. These were drawn from memory in 1953 by a man who worked at the plant.

New York subway trains still pass through the most beautiful of all the original stations, City Hall. But no trains have stopped there for some time, and the station is closed to the public.

Basic preparation for *American Dreams* was done at the Thomas Cooper Library, University of South Carolina, where I am privileged to be a Research Fellow in the Department of History. Dr. George Terry and the library's staff of professionals are unfailingly helpful.

Local librarians who must be thanked include Donna Errett, director of the Hilton Head Island Branch Library, and her staff; Jan Longest at the library of the University of South Carolina/Beaufort branch on Hilton Head; and the staff of the Greenwich, Connecticut, public library under the direction of Elizabeth Mainiero.

Others who provided specialized information include my friend and colleague Ken Follett; Carl and Denny Hattler; my son-in-law Bruce Kelm of Santa Rosa, and master brewer Tim O'Day; my friend and sometime writing partner, the composer Mel Marvin; my son-in-law Dr. Charles Schauer of Jacksonville; the ever reliable Dan Starer in New York City; my friend and neighbor Willis O. Shay, Esq.; my colleague in Western Writers of America, Dale L. Walker of El Paso; and Raymond Wemmlinger, librarian and curator of the Hampden-Booth Theater Library at The Players in New York. Special thanks also to the Panhandle-Plains Historical Museum of Canyon, Texas.

As always, I must state that no person or institution named should be held responsible for the final utilization of material. Sole responsibility for that is mine.

For special thanks I single out four people whose encouragement, enthusiasm, and editorial insights helped move the book along at various stages: In London, Barbara Boote of Little, Brown UK, and Andrew Nurnberg, my overseas literary agent; in New York, attorney Frank R.

Curtis, Esq., and Genevieve Young.

At my publisher, Dutton NAL, I am very much in debt to my editor, Danielle Perez, whose superb story sense and swift #3 pencil made completion of the manuscript a pleasure. I likewise thank Elaine Koster for her faith in this book.

I also thank Herman Gollob, who helped me conceive and shape the Crown family, edited *Homeland* and, before his retirement, contributed substantially to the planning of this novel. Julian Muller, Joe Fox, Herman Gollob: in the last fifteen years I have been fortunate to have been edited and coached by three of the great gents of publishing.

Last, as always, I thank my wife, Rachel, for her assistance, and her loving support and encouragement, which never falters.

— JOHN JAKES

Hilton Head Island, SC — St. John, USVI — Greenwich, CT
October 2, 1995 — September 25, 1997

www.johnjakes.com

PRONUNCIATION

The symbol ('), as in **moth·er** (muth'ər), **blue' dev'ils**, is used to mark primary stress; the syllable preceding it is pronounced with greater prominence than the other syllables in the word or phrase. The symbol ('), as in **grand·moth·er** (grand'muth'ər), **buzz' bomb'**, is used to mark secondary stress; a syllable marked for secondary stress is pronounced with less prominence than one marked (') but with more prominence than those bearing no stress mark at all.

a	act, bat, marry	**i**	if, big, mirror, furniture	**p**	pot, supper, stop		indicates the sound of
ā	aid, cape, way			**r**	read, hurry, near		a *in* alone
â(r)	air, dare, Mary	**ī**	ice, bite, pirate, deny				e *in* system
ä	alms, art, calm			**s**	see, passing, miss		i *in* easily
				sh	shoe, fashion, push		o *in* gallop
b	back, cabin, cab	**j**	just, badger, fudge				u *in* circus
ch	chief, butcher, beach	**k**	kept, token, make	**t**	ten, butter, bit		
				th	thin, ether, path	**ə**	occurs in unaccented syllables before **l** preceded by **t, d,** or **n,** or before **n** preceded by t or d to show syllabic quality, as in **cra·dle** (krād'ᵊl) **red·den** (red'ᵊn) **met·al** (met'ᵊl) **men·tal** (men't'ᵊl) and in accented syllables between **ī** and **r** to show diphthongal quality, as in **fire** (fī'ᵊr) **hire** (hī'ᵊr)
d	do, rudder, bed	**l**	low, mellow, all	**ᴡ̶th**	that, either, smooth		
		m	my, simmer, him	**u**	up, love		
e	ebb, set, merry			**û(r)**	urge, burn, cur		
ē	equal, seat, bee, mighty	**n**	now, sinner, on				
		ng	sing, Washington	**v**	voice, river, live		
ēr	ear, mere			**w**	west, away		
		o	ox, box, wasp				
f	fit, differ, puff	**ō**	over, boat, no	**y**	yes, lawyer		
		ô	ought, ball, raw	**z**	zeal, lazy, those		
g	give, trigger, beg	**oi**	oil, joint, joy	**zh**	vision, mirage		
h	hit, behave, hear	**o͝o**	book, poor				
hw	white, nowhere	**o͞o**	ooze, fool, too	**ə**	occurs only in unaccented syllables and		
		ou	out, loud, prow				

FOREIGN SOUNDS

A as in French **a·mi** (A mē') [a vowel intermediate in quality between the **a** of *cat* and the **ä** of *calm*, but closer to the former]

KH as in German **ach** (äKH) or **ich** (iKH); Scottish **loch** (lôKH) [a consonant made by bringing the tongue into the position for **k** as in *key, coo,* while pronouncing a strong, rasping h]

N as in French **bon** (bôN) [used to indicate that the preceding vowel is nasalized. Four such vowels are found in French: **un bon vin blanc** (ŒN bôN vaN bläN)]

Œ as in French **feu** (fŒ); German **schön** (shŒn) [a vowel made with the lips rounded in the position for **o** as in *over,* while trying to say **a** as in *able*]

R as in French **rouge** (R o͞o zh), German **rot** (Rōt), Italian **ma·re** (mä'Re), Spanish **pe·ro** (pe'Rô) [a symbol for any non-English **r,** including a trill or flap in Italian and Spanish and a sound in French and German similar to KH but pronounced with voice]

Y as in French **tu** (tY); German **ü·ber** (Y'bər) [a vowel made with the lips rounded in position for **o͞o** as in *ooze,* while trying to say **ē** as in *east*]

ᵊ as in French **Bas·togne** (bA stôn'yᵊ) [a faint prolongation of the preceding voiced consonant or glide]

THE RANDOM HOUSE

College Dictionary

RANDOM
HOUSE
DICTIONARIES

A widely acclaimed series of modern
authoritative dictionaries suitable for
many different needs and levels

Editorial Director: **Jess Stein**
Associate Director: **Leonore C. Hauck**
Senior Editor: **P.Y. Su**

THE RANDOM HOUSE

College Dictionary

Laurence Urdang
Editor in Chief

Stuart Berg Flexner
Managing Editor

Based on

The Random House Dictionary of the English Language
The Unabridged Edition

Jess Stein
Editor in Chief

Laurence Urdang
Managing Editor